the Ruins of Evermore

BOOK ONE

The TimeLight Awakenings

The Ruins of Evermore

BOOK ONE

The TimeLight Awakenings

A NOVEL BY

David J. Saccheri

A GOLDEN HOUR™ PUBLICATION

A GOLDEN HOUR™ PUBLICATION

First Edition

WWW.RUINSOFEVERMORE.COM

ISBN-13: 978-0615546162
ISBN-10: 0615546161

For the little girl I never had once.

And for the little boy I did.

Evermorian Schedule of Events

❧ Noble ❧

❦ Evermore ❦

BOOK ONE

The TimeLight Awakenings

Everything is what it isn't, isn't it?
- A wall plaque located somewhere in
The Bristol House Library

The Blue Pool of Moonlight

Was it the moon of blue-green gazing in through her open window that beckoned the girl forth from her restless submersion in sleep? Or was it the cool autumn breeze sweeping past the graceful swag of drapery that stirred the girl, brushing her cheek? Or perhaps it was a different visitor altogether, a celestial voice that murmured invitingly from the luminous stretch of moonlight cast upon the floor. Whatever the alluring source or sources, the youngster's long-lashed lids opened to the collective whisper of night. Throwing back the covers, she arose from the bed, and in her red-striped pajamas stepped into the gloom that quietly courted her.

Slowly the girl moved as if submerged, the breeze from the window causing her hair to gently rise and swirl. She bypassed a pillow that, having slipped off the bed, lay on end, a soft lump of violet with two pointy ears. Around her, sounds permeating the night seemed magnified and at the same time muffled, while the darkness felt alive and attentive, yet inexplicably aloof.

Heather.

The calling of the name rustled through the trees outside her window. It found voice in the low moan of the Bristol House plumbing and in the settling ache of the great structure's old wooden bones.

In a rush of wings, a large black-hooded bird landed on the sill, a rim of moon-glow framing its distinctive silhouette within the tall center window. Staring at the girl, the bird's luminous amber eyes were not altogether unfriendly and even held the glint of one playfully amused. Below its sturdy legs, sharp talons bit into the wood. One of the round eyes winked; Heather wondered.

Turning her attention down before her, she murmured, "A blue pool of moonlight."

Sinking to her knees, the girl leaned over the water. Fascinated, she smiled at the reflection of her face on the undulating carpet. It smiled back in vague and fluid distortions.

"The water, it's real."

Dipping a hand into the midst of her wavering image, Heather stirred the reflection, sending ripples across the surface: lap, gentle lap, gentle lap, lap, lap.

"And wet."

Withdrawing her fingers, she admired the dripping blue highlights. *Heather.*

Rising to her slender height, Heather turned to the bird. It surveyed her, its large eyes intent and profoundly knowing. They blinked. For no apparent reason, Heather's great grin rose mischievously.

"Dare me?" she challenged.

In a spirited twirl, Heather's attention swung back to the moonlit rectangle. Taking a swift step forward—splash!—her feet sliced the carpeted surface, plunging her legs and then torso into an embracing warm wetness, her willowy arms trailing overhead.

The girl sank. Then, as the wet world surrounding her became cold and murky, she began to kick, propelling herself upward towards a shimmering light-filled surface. When she broke the watery plane, a gentle rain sprinkled her face, all wetness and rivulets and sodden hair hiding eyes. Above, the heavily overcast sky seemed to gather and hoard the daylight, tainting the marshy land around her in colors both sullen and drab. Arms sweeping water, legs pumping, Heather flipped her hair aside with a jerk of the head. Maintaining buoyancy, she focused on the edge of the pond where pointed reeds were clumped and wild grasses emphasized a short climb of hill. But Heather's attention was drawn past the shoreline foliage and subsequent rise, to where large bushes huddled at the top. Without comprehension, the girl was being steered toward something hidden from her view, a dangerous something that lay beyond the crest.

Quietly swimming and then wading, she approached the shore. The growth in the shallow water brushed up and around her legs with long, slender fingers of slippery green, while large drops of rain began to drum down with heightened intensity.

"Where am I?" she whispered, pulling herself from the water.

The sopping girl cautiously maneuvered up the slight pitch of hill toward the denser bushes that offered cover. Once near, Heather slowed and crouched, her senses keenly alert. The air felt thick and the wind was rising in forceful gusts. Rain stung her face. Heather listened as words carried towards her, rhythmic incantations, sounds of an unknown language. Surprisingly, she understood their meaning.

"Yes, yes. Come. Come and tumble, rise at will, all bindings crumble, wrench, and spill, your wings on air, your purpose free, submit before the strength in me. Find to fall, oh, seep and crawl, make your way, your means our seal, and through the ageless Portals steal. Fill our sky, oh, fearless fly, the Realm bereft, in exile lie."

Ancient phrases took to the air, defying the wind, summoning the lurking invocations, the powerful enchantments, and the universal bonds of magic. Heather recoiled when she heard a grating of the heavens, and watched as the sky shuddered. Cautiously, the girl peered over the bush tops. She was stunned to see that a dark hole had opened among the clouds, a brooding vortex. Heather lowered her gaze. A short distance away, through the blur of a drowning landscape, she spied a tall woman standing upon a rocky knoll. Above her head, the striking figure's arms flowed sinuously, a conductor directing an unseen orchestra.

Unexpectedly from behind, a translucent object whizzed past Heather's head. Then came another followed by yet another still. In little time the sky was filled with a tumbling, morphing translucency, so full its forms distorted the shapes of trees and the clouds beyond. Furious hissing tore the air and winds whipped the trees ragged, while the ground below Heather's feet rumbled. Rain thrummed down fiercely.

The mysterious woman's features were lost to concentration. With robes billowing and slapping the air and jet-black hair blown behind her, she continued the recitations. Heather saw that her aura was throbbing a foul magenta on treacherous blue. Ignoring the battering rain, the enchantress pitched back her head, eyes piercing and ecstatic, lips mouthing the words that Heather could only just discern. The huge stones on which the sorceress stood began to tremble, yet she remained upright. The woman was screaming now, but Heather could no longer hear the words above the moaning of the earth and gasping of the sky. The enveloping sounds rose to a shattering pitch. Heather put her hands to her ears. The unseen objects, hurtling through the air, bounced off her back, arms, legs, and head—some pierced her body with icy cold and searing heat, racking the girl. She threw herself flat on the heaving grass-covered earth.

Whoosh! Converging on the whirling black hole that pierced the sky above, the supernatural forms accelerated, rushing by. Feeling as if her head were about to burst, Heather screamed, but her voice was lost, trampled beneath the greater din. Eyes and mouth clamped tight, she brought her arms up to bury her head. Pandemonium wailed about her ears, and the continuous impact of the fleeting shapes jarred her slight body. All at once, in crescendo, the heavens cast forth a thunderous groan, and then, with one enormous heave of suction, all stopped.

The silence rang out in all its emptiness. It was there, and it was gone, and what was left was not at all. Nothing. Just an invasive change at rest in a crystalline stillness.

Heather whimpered. Moments passed. Slowly, the girl dragged herself to her knees, her wet pajamas clinging and thoroughly muddied. The rain had stopped, and the leaden sky seemed drained, its spiraling hole sealed and no longer visible. Shakily, hanging on to the thin branches of the shrub before her, Heather climbed to her feet. Peering again above the height of bush, she observed the sorceress on her rock. Spent, the strange woman was torn down to her hands and knees, her head and neck sagging, her hair spilling soggily to the ground. Following a sobering shake of the head, the enchantress sat back on her haunches. She inhaled deeply, took a moment, and then swept her glistening hair behind her, water fanning from its ends. Rising unsteadily, she staggered, recovered, and then began to fumble, rearranging her garments. Fascinated, Heather watched, noting that the woman's aura had dimmed considerably, pulsing in diluted grays.

Mounting a flat, needle-like boulder that had fallen at an angle before her, the sorceress surveyed the land. She awaited something to reveal that the transformation had fully occurred, a confirmation of what she had wrought. And when the sky lightened and then the land, a smile spread to the woman's purplish lips.

At that moment, a twig snapped out sharply in Heather's hand. Quickly, she lowered her head.

The sorceress shot a blistering look in the girl's direction. "Ah, and what have we here?" Menace saturated the softly spoken words. "An inconspicuous observer?" She stepped toward the girl's cover, asking herself, "Who are you?"

Heather hunched down farther.

"How sweet." Another wickedly purplish smile. "You're shy."

Heather carefully released her grip on the branches, and they relaxed quietly into place. Meanwhile, the sorceress began to slowly descend the stony embankment, her feet finding their way among the broken rock without the guidance of her gaze—it remained focused on the hedge that hid the girl.

Heather quickly backed away, working through low-lying shrubs toward the nearby trees. Her heart racing, her head screaming, Hurry, hurry, hurry! she stumbled along the hillside.

With a sneer and an incantation, the sorceress cast a hand before her, long fingers sparking. In her fatigued state, the anemic red and yellow bolt that broke from her fingertips fell weakly before the hedge, tearing up a chunky layer of mud and grass. The woman tried again, compensating for her exhaustion. A second bolt of light flew faster and farther, and her intended target, the concealing bush, erupted into flame and began to burn.

"Who witnessed my most excellent banishment of magic from the Realm?" the enchantress said easily to herself, still walking. She casually threw another bolt, a lob in chance, beyond the hedge. It exploded not far behind Heather, the impact jolting her forward. She tumbled and then scrambled to her feet, dashing recklessly onward. Behind her, the thicket crackled and caught fire.

Run, run, run, run, *run*, Heather screamed to herself, dodging through the shrubbery.

The tips of branches poked, grabbed, and pulled at her sodden bed-clothes. She slipped and fell, and upon doing so, tore her pajamas and scraped a knee. Feverishly, the girl looked up. She saw before her that the brush and grass broke into an open glade before giving way to the trees and their promising maze of refuge. Pulling herself off the soggy ground, Heather made a limping sprint for it. Meanwhile her pursuer, topping the hill, robes flowing gracefully behind her, finally caught sight of the girl.

"Ah, well, a fleeing child. And look, she's limping," the sorceress said, her voice icy calm. Her eyes narrowed. "Shall I let you escape having observed this magical triumph of mine? No. No, I mustn't. A witness could prove most inconvenient."

Murmuring rapidly, drawing both hands up before her, she pushed into them with a grimace and a stride. A ferocious spear of light stabbed and crackled towards the racing Heather. It fell short and hit the ground, abruptly setting the grass ablaze. The bolt then ricocheted off a tree—splitting it—before careening to inflict a glancing blow to the girl's side. With the impact, she was twisted up off the ground, spilling end over end, seeing green over gray, gray over green, before a roiling fade to black.

Tumbling off her bed, the terrified child screamed out a muffled, "No!" as she landed face-first in a pillow, dragging the bedding to the floor. Chest heaving, eyes blinking back tears, Heather raised her head. She inspected her dry unsoiled pajamas, before affirming her presence within the familiar confines of her large turreted bedroom.

Through the open window, Heather saw the sun had not yet broken the horizon's plane, but that the sky had begun to lighten. Exhausted, she dropped her head, and grabbing another pillow within reach, mashed it over her face. Then she cried. Her dream had seemed so real, so frighteningly real. Heather lay motionless for a time on the floor, the fluffy envelopment of pillows offering seclusion and comfort. Afterwards, having finished her cry, she tossed them atop the bed.

"Ow!"

The act of throwing had drawn attention to her side. Perhaps she had hurt it when falling off the bed. She didn't know. Grimacing, Heather briefly rubbed her sore ribs.

Now walking across her room to the second-story windows, she stopped and pulled aside the drape that concealed the view east and south. At that moment, Heather noticed the sun poking its newborn light through the burning eyes of foliage. She threw open the window and looked down on intermittent lawns that meandered lazily about the Bristol House grounds. They would soon be covered with leaves shed by the garden's many trees.

Hands holding tightly to the sill, Heather leaned out into the cool morning air. She could see a raven perched on the rooftop's end, picking through dregs in the gutter. When the girl felt the rays of the rising sun warming her face, she closed her eyes, becoming motionless, relishing the sensation.

Roused from her preoccupation by noise from below, Heather moved past the center window and parted the drapes to her right. She looked down the terraced slope of Thimble Hill, across Whisper Creek, and observed the distant shape of Mr. Simpletripp at work doing something in his yard.

He was always doing *something*, thought Heather, wholly unamused at the sight.

Mr. Simpletripp made her uneasy, because even if he wasn't, he always seemed to be lurking.

Heather returned to the left window and the view across Afterglow Drive. She wondered if her best friend, Molly, was awake yet. She could see smoke billowing from the chimney of the Pringle's modest but attractive two-storied home, which meant her father was up and busily about. And that meant, in all probability, so was Mrs. Pringle.

Behind Molly's house, on a tree-lined hill above the Whisper Creek Bridge, yet well below the height of Heather's own Bristol House windows, stood Ms. Gardner's contemporary house. Along with a mixture of strange outcroppings, colorful metal sculptures, and outlandish garden knick-knacks, the building was enclosed by a run of modern metal fencing, all assembled and torched together in unrefined fashion by some famous contemporary sculptor. Heather brightened when she thought of the unusual habits and tastes of Ms. Gardner. She and Molly liked her, because their neighbor was so wonderfully different from most adults. And more importantly, she was fun to be around.

"Heather?" Heather heard the voice of Grandma Dawn calling up the stairs.

"Coming!" she said, and started towards the door. Then she stopped. Bewildered, Heather returned to the center window and its sill. Looking down, she inspected it, lightly brushing her fingers over the marred surface, tracing what looked like talon indentations in the wood. Heather's mouth puckered in contemplation. She looked out and saw the raven hopping atop the gutter, starting once again to sift through debris in search of insects and spiders to comprise its morning meal. Thoughtfully, Heather looked down again at the markings on the sill before her, then back at the raven.

"Heather?" It was Grandma Dawn, this time at her door. With one hand braced shoulder-high against the jamb, the tall dignified woman leaned in. "Breakfast?"

Following a shrug for the sill and its markings, Heather turned and faced the inquiring look of her grandmother.

"Yes, please," she said, her smile broadening, the girl finding comfort in the gaze returned. "Strawberry waffles?"

PART ONE
Noble

CHAPTER ONE

The Not So Simpletripp

"**N**ose?" Heather called out on a bounce, gaining momentum as she skittered down the steep tree-lined bank. Worn and dusty, the path below her hugged the northeast side of the Whisper Creek Bridge.

Her red shoes stopping just short of the water's edge, Heather headed under the old elevated structure. Dragging fingers along the rocky wall beside her, the blonde girl turned her attention upward to the span that reared overhead, its weathered timbers substantial and sturdy, the sunlight flaring between planks. She walked a short distance before drawing to a halt. To her right, the deep waters of Whisper Creek murmured and flowed with flat green placidity through the cool, retiring shadows of bridge and tree.

"Nose?" she said, too loudly.

Not waiting for a reply, Heather turned and retraced her steps, moving quickly downstream. She picked her way along the boggy bank, pushing past partially submerged boulders, avoiding bristly shrubs, and dodging trunks of trees, her arms raking aside their low growing leaves and branches.

Again Heather called out the word, "Nose?" and listened.

If Molly were hidden nearby, she would respond with the appropriate word *ring* to complete the phrase. If not, Heather would sequester herself in the vicinity and wait for her friend to arrive and call out the word to which Heather would then reply. All very covert, all very appealing to the girls.

Cut into the bouldered embankment close by, discreetly hidden behind brush, tree, and rock, was the narrow entrance to what Heather and Molly called Dead End Cave. Its interior dark and dank, Heather never hesitated to go inside when alone, whereas Molly would only enter when accompanied by her friend. The craggy opening was barely the height of the taller girl and the space inside more wide than long. Knee-deep waters swirled within, generously supplied by underground springs and surrounded by substantial boulders along the base of striated walls. At the cave's center, encircled by water, an enormous mass of stone pushed upward. Chunky and rounded, it was also conveniently flat on top for the pair of young explorers, who at Heather's urging, had once dared to wade through the dark waters to climb it. Arching overhead, the ceiling of Dead End Cave was four times Heather's height, which allowed her to stand just within the entrance on what little ground was dry. Concealed there, she awaited her friend.

Plop. On warm days, water collected on the ceiling and hung to eventually drip, hitting the pool below with a delicate, echoing splash. Plop. From outside, a sliver of light angled into the mouth of the cave, illuminating the water. Heather thought she heard Molly coming, tromping through the brush. The rustling gradually grew louder before it stopped a short distance away.

"Nose?" Molly called, knee deep in the yellowed grass of Indian summer.

Pressing herself to the wall in an effort to remain hidden, Heather heard her friend resume her approach through the scrub, brushing aside twigs and leaves. Chancing a glimpse, Heather saw that Molly had slowed, scanning the surrounding area while backing towards the cave. Heather withdrew to one side as her friend turned and faced the forbidding entrance. Indecisive, Molly lingered only steps away. She moved forward on the boggy grass and then stood directly outside, blocking the infiltrating light. Very slowly, very gradually, the girl leaned into the cave's mouth, into the darkness. Molly stopped and listened. She leaned in farther. Plop. Then she entered, attempting to sidestep the water that seeped from the cave. When the girl spoke, her voice was soft, tentative.

"Nose?"

"Hair!" Heather shouted, jumping with her arms stretched overhead, one shoe splashing water.

With a recoiling shudder Molly screamed sharply, and the girls broke out laughing.

"Oh, you! You scared me."

She retreated outside and Heather followed, her right foot still sloshing through water that, in due course, would find its way to Whisper Creek. Their eyes locked in merriment, the two giggled helplessly.

When Molly had sufficiently recovered, she asked, "Did you say 'hair,' like 'nose hair?' That *wasn't* the password." The girls shrieked some more, their shadows falling as one onto the embankment behind them and into the mouth of the cave.

Wiping tears from exotic green eyes, Heather was squinting into a harsh afternoon sun, her blonde hair flanking a fair-skinned face. Laughing with Molly, the girl's full lips framed a generous straight-toothed smile below a neatly pointed nose. Tall for her age, Heather Nighborne displayed a strong athleticism, and though in times past she endured growing spells of outright gawkiness, the girl had recently discovered—or rediscovered—her mastery of graceful movement. And despite the fact that she possessed a tomboyish inclination, Heather loved to wear dresses and bright red shoes—and currently one lay wet beneath the water. Yet, with the other still on dry land, she gave little consideration to either.

A precocious girl, Heather always seemed older than her twelve years. As might be imagined of someone both clever and advanced, she did very well in school, excelling in all subjects no matter how diverse. Some would even say that the youngster had *a knack*. Being outgoing and charismatic by nature, she had attracted various boys and mostly girls in her age range, but the friendships didn't last. And presently, she had only one close friend and confidante—from her age group, that is. That friend was Molly Pringle. Molly had witnessed Heather's unusual behavior and was never put off by it. As a matter of fact, Molly embraced the difference with relish, her world being what most would consider happily normal.

Impulsively, Heather pulled Molly back into the cave, making room for her friend along the narrow bank. In the meager bounce of light shimmering off the water, Molly saw Heather's features vaguely, swimmingly, their undersides tinted a watery green.

"It's cool in here," Molly said.

Plop.

"Yeah, I like it. Do you want to stay here, or would you rather go to Lower Bridge?"

"Lower Bridge, I think. We just need to make sure that my Dad doesn't see us."

Heather looked down. "Molly, I—"

"Come on." Molly pushed Heather lightly. "Forget it. After all, it's been over a month already. Dad will just have to get over it—at least that's what Mom told him when he went on about it." She giggled. "Anyway, he's going away on a business trip next week, a bankers' conference down in Orange Spoke. He'll be gone for five days. Then I can come and see you at the Bristol House. I just can't tell Mom where I'm going, or she'll have to tell me that I can't."

"Can't what?" Heather asked.

"Can't go, can't do things with you. I think Mom knows we still get together—honestly, it wouldn't surprise me if she knows we sneak out at night. And after—well, you know—what happened that day at school, when Dad said I couldn't spend time with you anymore, what you did, it-it didn't matter to Mom. She really likes you and stood up for you and even called you a dear. So, while she *thinks* she knows that we hang around together, I think she really doesn't want to know. Know what I mean?"

Heather laughed. "I think so."

"What I mean is, if Mom doesn't know for sure, then as far as she's concerned, I'm just doing things outside. I guess it's like a secret we agreed on without ever actually talking about it, because we're not sup-posed to be doing the secret thing to begin with—but only because Dad says so—even though Mom and I secretly think it's all right." Heather laughed, and it sounded strangely amplified in their surroundings. Plop. "Besides, it's not like I'm hanging out at the pool hall or in the bars on Whiskey Road. So, come on. Let's go. I don't have much time." Taking in the daunting interior of the cave with one final sweep, Molly said, "I'll race you to Lower Bridge." And with that, she darted outside.

Running into the sun, Molly's wavy brown hair bounced on her shoulders, and though the front of her blue and white striped blouse instantly lit up, her back remained in shadow.

Taking to her heels, Heather followed, screwing up her face to the sudden light. On long legs she charged forward, quickly overtaking her friend, yelling, "Come on!" as she passed. While Molly sought to keep up in Heather's wake, she alertly dodged the springy branches and bits of bush that the other had enthusiastically pushed aside.

Heather raced back along the bank. Just downstream from the Whis-per Creek Bridge, she came upon an oak that had toppled years ago during a fierce windstorm. Long since trimmed of its branches, the im-mense trunk spanned Whisper Creek, uniting both shores. Heather and Molly called it Lower Bridge. Currently, it was catching the late after-noon sun, while areas of the opposite bank lay soaked in shadows cast by the skyward reach of the massive Oak Triplets. Densely foliaged, they towered like shaggy sentinels above the creek, road, and bridge.

Skidding to a stop against Lower Bridge, Heather turned to look for Molly. When she didn't see her, the girl slid to a sitting position on the ground, the rough tree bark chewing at her back and bunching up her soiled blue and pink dress. Moments later, Molly arrived and carefully sat next to her, determined not to get her slacks and blouse any dirtier.

"I should have changed after school," said the winded girl, between gasps and a gulp, regarding her muddy shoes.

Heather didn't respond. Instead her attention was focused beyond the opposite bank in the direction of Mr. Simpletripp's house.

"Think he's home?" Heather asked.

"Might be. Why?"

"Just wondering." Heather sat lost in thought for a while. "I think he was digging on our property again, in the rough area. Grandma Dawn saw him out there with a metal detector when he must've thought she wasn't home. Later we found the holes."

"Digging for the treasure of Old Scarbones Bristol?"

"Yeah, that."

Heather grew quiet. Molly followed her lead. During the many times when Heather would retreat into herself, the normally resourceful Molly wouldn't know what to do or say. It wasn't that Molly felt uncomfortable. It was just that she wasn't sure she should be hanging around, like she was intruding and there was no need for her to be there. During such moments, Molly felt like an odd fixture in a room and at the same time locked outside its door. But then again, sometimes Heather seemed so sad inside, like she could use a good friend close by.

"Seen Aria?" Molly asked, intending to break the silence.

"Not lately." The girl paused. "Not ever." Heather laughed.

Molly smiled. "Well, you know what I mean."

"No," Heather said, "she hasn't come around." She went quiet again, picking up a small stone and carelessly tossing it towards the water. It didn't reach, landing on the bank before tumbling to a stop.

"You miss her, don't you?" When the girl didn't respond, Molly added, "It's been awhile."

"Yeah, it has. Two or three weeks now. I wonder where she goes." Another stone flew and this time found the water with a tiny splash. Plish.

"Don't worry, she'll come back." Molly was examining her friend's profile: the straight nose with a spattering of freckles, the rounded chin, the extraordinary eyes and long lashes.

Heather remained quiet.

"Hey, remember the summer issue of *Fashion Plate* that—?"

"Molly, shh-h-h," Heather said, her voice low and urgent. "Be still."

"What?" Molly shot, her whisper heated. "What is it?"

The blonde girl just shook her head and slowly placed an index finger to her lips.

Molly looked at her blank-faced.

Heather nodded downstream.

On the opposite bank, their neighbor Mr. Simpletripp had come to the water's edge. Unaware of the two girls, the large man lowered himself to the ground. He was dressed in a white sleeveless T-shirt and a utility kilt that sported many flaps and pockets. Situated on a small outcropping beneath a large tree, their unpleasant neighbor presented a view of mostly his back and side to the girls. From upstream, they could see his downturned head and partial profile, his intense concentration and hurried movements. Yet, with his body blocking their view, it was hard to tell what Mr. Simpletripp had removed from a large burlap sack. It now lay empty and rumpled behind him. From time to time, he would throw a furtive glance over his shoulder, in the direction of the Simpletripp house. If he had simply turned his head and looked upstream, the stealthy man would have seen Heather and Molly, fully exposed, their backs against Lower Bridge. In an instant, Mr. Simpletripp produced a knife from nowhere and deftly put it to work. The steel blade glinted sharply, occasionally catching and reflecting the dappled light, as it twisted and sliced. Starting at a source near his feet, the water began to bleed a rusty red.

"Oh, Heather..." Molly said, under her breath. She shrank against the log.

"Shh-h-h. Quiet now." Heather's words were barely audible. "Don't move."

After a time, Mr. Simpletripp stood. In flashes of something loose, moist, and red, his long arms flung what looked like entrails out to the middle of the creek. The heavier parts landed with a plunk and sank. The lighter ones fanned out and settled gently, where they were slowly dragged downstream on the current. Stringy, they clung momentarily to the surface before being absorbed into the watery green.

Glancing left and right, Mr. Simpletripp went back to a knee and rinsed the red from his knife and hands, a trail of blood washed away. The butcher rose up on his pale skinny legs with the thick black hair, of which the girls had often poked fun. Not now. He wiped the knife on his kilt and with a flick spun the blade into its filthy red handle. Mr. Simpletripp deposited the knife into one of his pockets with a swift palm and slide and then dried his hands on the front of his shirt.

The girls sat mesmerized. With their attention focused on the trail of innards, whatever this man had carved up escaped them, the remains having been returned to the sack.

Mr. Simpletripp grabbed the lumpy bag and turned to leave. When Molly saw the bulge in the burlap sack and the seeping spread of crimson, she gasped. Simpletripp stopped. For a moment he didn't move—as if a tumble of thoughts provoked by Molly's small cry caused his gears to momentarily disengage. Slowly his head rotated, scanning the creek. He stopped at the sight of the girls. Without the slightest movement, the parties contemplated one another. Then, with ominous gravity, Mr. Simpletripp turned his body and started upstream toward the girls.

Heather quickly stood. Keeping her attention fixed across the creek, her right hand frantically searched for Molly, who sat paralyzed below.

"Molly, come on," she said, finally finding her friend's shoulder. "Get up."

Simpletripp neared the opposite end of Lower Bridge, where he stopped. Mute, he continued to glare at the girls, his back to the sun. A brilliant round highlight burned on his sweaty shaved head, and a protruding stomach weighed down the front of his skinny but dangerous frame. Stretching before him, his shadow seemed to reach for the girls.

At Heather's prompting, Molly had climbed to her feet and backed around the tree trunk, ready to flee. Heather, her body electrified, held her ground. An odd vision flashed to mind at that moment: it was of seeing this man, Mr. Horace Simpletripp, at one time an accountant, walking to work dressed in a suit and tie.

She squinted. Was he smiling? It was hard to tell. Whatever the man's shaded face was doing, there wasn't anything friendly about it. Her eyes never leaving him, Heather reached for Lower Bridge on her left, patting its surface, getting her bearings should she need to jump the trunk and sprint upstream—and hopefully entice their neighbor to chase her and not Molly.

Mr. Simpletripp continued to stare. Heather couldn't get a read on his aura. With blinding sunlight reflecting off the water, she was having trouble seeing—seeing that his meaty mouth *was* twisted up at the corners. It made his face look heavy and contorted—sinister. Slowly nodding his head, as if he were memorizing this moment to draw upon, he wheeled and withdrew, stepping up the slight bank.

Heather and Molly watched as Mr. Simpletripp trudged away, the burlap sack still in his hand, one shoulder riding low. Head down in a hazy patch of light, his walk seemed ponderous, graceless, and ill defined. In silence, the pair continued to stare, as their neighbor grew smaller with the distance. He crossed into his yard. Near to where a metal sculpture of a scorpion was bolted to the wall, Mr. Simpletripp entered his house. The backdoor slammed.

CHAPTER TWO

At the Pringle's

"Wow!" Energized, Heather faced Molly. "He is one creepy guy!"

Molly was trembling.

"What do you think he was up to?" Heather asked.

Molly just shook her head. She managed a shrug.

"Come on," Heather said, patting the log next to her. "Let's sit for a minute. He won't come back. Besides, I don't think it's a good idea for you to go home right now."

Absently, Molly came around to sit on the trunk beside Heather. The two were silent for a while, with Heather tossing an occasional rock into the water from a handful she had gathered.

Molly finally spoke: "Do you think he's the Pet Stalker?"

"I was just thinking that same thing!" Heather said. She tossed another stone. Plish. "He could be."

The Pet Stalker had been haunting the small community of Noble for over a year. Skinned and disemboweled animals, mostly stray dogs and cats, had been found nailed to trees; draped across the tops of fences; dangling from posts and hydrants; spread across the windshields of parked cars; and left alongside the main roads. Some pets, having temporarily escaped their masters, had been caught and slaughtered by the Stalker, and then thrown into the owners' yards. Often in pieces.

"What should we do?" Molly asked. She crossed her arms. "Should we call the police?"

"I don't know. Let me think." Heather gazed toward the trees and in the general direction of the Simpletripp house. Finally, she spoke: "Well, first of all, who would believe us? And what did we see, anyway? Did you see what he put in that bag? I didn't. His big fat belly was in the way. Besides, if we tell anyone that we saw Mr. Simpletripp, then it might get back to your Dad that you and I were together, and we wouldn't want that to happen." The girl sighed. "I don't know, Molly. Maybe we should just ask Aria when she comes." Another rock found the water. She turned and regarded Molly. "Feeling better?"

"Yes. He's such a creep." Molly shivered. "Ew." Silence settled over the pair. Molly broke it. "Dad and Mom are going to the Farbel's for dinner tonight, a-a-n-n-n-nd..." while stretching out the last word, Molly glanced over her shoulder in the direction of her house, making certain that no one had come to the creek looking for her, "the babysitter should be here by now." She added, "Like I need one."

"Is she the one that just watches television and argues with her boyfriend on the phone all night?"

"That's her. And if I tell her I have a lot of homework and might need help studying for a big test, she'll be sure to stay away from my room. So I just shut the door. Sometimes I hang a little 'Do NOT Disturb' sign from the knob. That's why it's so easy to sneak out. Are we still on for tonight?"

"We're on," Heather said. "Same time?"

"Yes," said Molly, taking a deep breath and exhaling sharply. "Babysitters..." She rose. "See you later."

"Bye."

Drawing her legs atop Lower Bridge, Heather watched Molly go, heading under the old wooden overpass. Seeing her friend's distant figure emerge into the light on the far side of the bridge, Heather swung her attention downstream and encountered a surprise.

"Well, Heather," said a familiar voice, "did you miss me?"

Molly climbed the bank. Once over the rise, she saw the babysitter's dented car parked in the drive, with its peeling paint and missing hubcaps. Molly stopped to brush herself off, picking foxtails out of her socks and cuffs. She looked over her shoulder, an uncomfortable glance back the way she had come.

An only child, the brown-eyed Molly Pringle was average in height and weight for a girl her age. Although she possessed the coordination and skills to be a competent athlete, she chose instead to immerse herself in the world of words—of literature. If Heather was bright, Molly was brighter—brighter than any of her classmates when it came to books and studies. Concisely said, Molly loved school, occasionally wore unnecessary chic glasses, dressed conservatively but stylishly, and shared her fashion magazines with Heather.

Given her logical outlook, Molly had a way of balancing Heather's often curious and impetuous nature with her own practicality, although they both shared a strong sense of the humorous in most things that transpired. Heather, the inquisitive explorer, had a tendency to lead Molly, the cautious and oft times reluctant, on escapades Molly would never undertake herself. And where Heather was outwardly adventurous, Molly was inwardly so, unable to get enough of history, romance, and adventure novels. When wandering in the vast book-lined aisles of the Bristol House library, Molly loved to spend time looking through the old leather-bound volumes that filled the many shelves. And perusing such as this used to be done quite frequently and for hours at a time. But no more. Sadly, for the girls, the explorations in the Bristol House library had become infrequent, as had Molly's genial visits to the house.

Molly traversed the unkempt fields that led from the creek to her home and made her way through the wrought iron gate. She crossed the manicured lawn and then the drive, and was about to reach for the front door when it opened from within. Out stepped the babysitter in a state of agitation, her cell phone pasted to her ear.

"But I have to babysit. It's gas money and—" Here the babysitter rolled her eyes, shook her head, and offered Molly a scant smile as she brushed past.

Stepping aside, Molly said, "Hi, Megan."

Molly watched while the babysitter kept walking, head down, hand and phone clapped to her ear. Her back to Molly, she stopped in the driveway.

"Look, I have to. I need the money. Another time, okay?" She listened before stamping her foot in exasperation. Shaking her head with her mouth hanging open in disbelief, Megan stared above, as if expecting sky-written words of guidance. "So who's gonna pay for gas? You? You couldn't even buy me an ice cream on the square... No you didn't, I did... I did, too."

Molly's babysitter had black, shortly cropped hair that pressed in around her thin face. She was of medium height, possessed a spindly physique, and wore a thick black belt around her nonexistent waistline. Surprisingly held in place with so little hip were torn jeans below a wrinkled black T-shirt.

"Look, I have to go... No, really I do. They're leaving any minute ... No, they're waiting—what's that...? Really? No way... Oh, you're so funny. Are you sure...? Oh, yeah? When?"

Molly quietly closed the door. She half-ran down the hallway. Rounding the corner, the girl almost bumped into her quick moving mother, returning from the kitchen.

"Molly!" Mrs. Pringle said, her hands before her to cushion a possible collision.

"Sorry, Mom." Molly looked into her mother's face, and then impulsively grabbed her around the waist. She held onto her.

"What's this?" asked Mrs. Pringle, her arms momentarily held aloft, before lowering them around the girl.

"I don't know," Molly said into her mother's dress.

"Are you okay?"

"Yes." Molly pulled away. She didn't look at her mother, but past her. "What's for dinner?"

"Dad bought some Chinese food. It's in the fridge on the top shelf. Are you sure you're okay?"

Molly nodded.

Mrs. Pringle looked very pretty in a teal evening dress with an elaborate beaded necklace. She stepped away from her daughter and called up the stairs. "Ned? Coming? Honey, we're going to be late. Please hurry." She turned to Molly, "Where's Megan?" Without waiting for a reply, Mrs. Pringle inquired loudly, "Megan?" She glanced around and then cast notice up the stairs: "Ned? We have to hurry, honey. Please. You know how Mr. Farbel expects punctuality." She looked at Molly and whispered, "Your father's boss is such a pill." And then in her normal volume, "Okay, Molly, just heat the food when you're hungry, all right? Where's Megan?"

Upstairs there was a bustle followed by the rattle of the hall closet opening. A thud sounded.

"Ow! Lana, have you seen my black wingtips?"

Mrs. Pringle cocked an ear, the sounds of her husband's rummaging apparent.

"I put them in the bedroom closet, to make room for the new vacuum."

"Stubbed my toe..." drifted down the stairs. There arose a thumping hobble that decreased in volume as Mr. Pringle returned to the bedroom at the rear of the hall.

"Megan's outside on the phone, Mom. Don't worry, I'll eat dinner later."

Mrs. Pringle bent to kiss her daughter, her silver and turquoise earrings jiggling above her shoulders, saying, "You behave yourself tonight with the babysitter, okay?"

"Mom, do I really need one?"

With eyebrows raised for emphasis, Mrs. Pringle directed her gaze into her daughter's eyes. "Your Father's orders." Mrs. Pringle leaned in close for a quick peck on the cheek and then moved her mouth close to Molly's ear. "No, you don't need one, but for now you'll have one. Be safe, okay."

Molly backed away and slyly looked at her mother.

"What, dear?" Mrs. Pringle asked, surprise taking hold of her features.

Molly drew a smile. "Nothing."

Mrs. Pringle winked. "We've got to run. Remember, if the electricity goes out, there's a new flashlight under the kitchen sink." She wheeled to face up the stairs, "Ned, I'll wait for you in the car." Then to Molly: "Guess he can't get that black wingtip over his swollen toe. Bye, dear." Another kiss grazed the girl's cheek.

Molly half-heartedly raised her hand to the back of the rapidly departing Mrs. Pringle, the woman heading down the hall, small purse in hand. The girl watched as her mother laid it on the sofa table while she opened the closet door to remove her coat and scarf. Afterward, having retrieved her clutch, she headed for the front door. It didn't quite slam behind her.

"Bye," Molly said, in an undertone. The word bore a hint of melancholy.

Flashlight? There hasn't been any problem with the electricity. Molly reflected a moment longer and then beamed. She hastened a look up the stairs and decided to wait until her father left before retrieving the new flashlight for use later that night.

"Teacup?" Molly called out to her little white terrier. She saw the dog race by going from the kitchen to her bedroom at the back of the house. Molly went to retrieve her, when suddenly the little furry blur scampered around the corner, sliding on the polished hardwood.

"Come here, little one," Molly said, bending over to scoop her up.

The dog's tongue all over her face, Molly giggled and pulled away.

"Did you eat? Let's get you a little treat."

Walking to the kitchen, Molly recalled when, early in the school year, her dog Rufus had died unexpectedly, hit by a car. For weeks she had had trouble sleeping. Couldn't eat either. She just wasn't hungry. At the time, Molly had promised herself that she would never have another dog. And then her mother brought home Teacup.

"Oh," Molly remembered her saying, "it's not my intention to replace Rufus, dear. I just felt that the house needed a dog around."

At first, as adorable as Teacup was, Molly didn't want anything to do with the new pet. However, it wasn't long before she found the little white dog irresistible, and the girl was holding her near. One day, when Molly had mentioned that she hoped her mom didn't mind that she and Teacup spent so much time together, Mrs. Pringle only smiled and kissed her on the forehead.

Parents are so weird, thought Molly.

"It's good to see you, Heather." The familiar voice belonged to Aria.

"I'm so glad you finally came. There's so much to tell you. Wow! Just before you showed up, Molly and I were sitting right here, when Mr. Simpletripp came down to the creek. It was so creepy, Aria. By the time he left, Molly was so scared, she was shaking."

Heather related to Aria what had happened, how they saw Mr. Simpletripp down by the water, about the burlap sack and the guts, and how, after hearing Molly gasp, he turned and spied the two girls sitting against the log. Heather did most of the talking with Aria asking a question now and then.

When Heather mentioned that Grandma Dawn was probably making dinner and that she should start for home, Aria walked along with her. The two were immersed in conversation as they climbed the bank leading away from Whisper Creek.

"...and Grandma Dawn said she saw him using a metal detector," Heather said, "and the next day there were holes dug all over the Bristol House property. Some were pretty big."

"Your Mr. Simpletripp is trouble, I'm afraid, Heather," said Aria. "I don't know what we can do about it at the moment. Right now, let's keep a strict eye on him whenever possible. And," she added, "be careful."

"What do you think he does in his yard so late at night?" Heather asked.

"Who knows? What do you think he's doing?"

"He's a scary guy. It could be anything. I think Grandma Dawn might even be afraid of him. I know she doesn't want me to know, but ..."

"But you can tell."

"Yeah. It's her shine," said Heather. "It changes, getting really weird when she sees him. I'm not sure how to read it. I mean, it can't be what I think it is."

"But her reaction is pretty strong."

"Yeah, real strong."

Aria and Heather walked the path that wound alongside Afterglow Drive, eventually leading uphill to the Bristol House.

Slightly down the road and across the street, a motorized wrought iron gate was sliding open. Emerging out of the driveway was Mr. and Mrs. Pringle in their moderately priced luxury sedan. Like their house, it was gray in color.

Catching sight of the girl when they turned onto the road, Mr. Pringle said, "That Heather. Such a weird kid. And always talking to herself."

Driving by, Mrs. Pringle waved cheerily.

"Oh, Ned, I think you're being awfully hard on her. She's just a child—and a sweet one. And Heather Nighborne just happens to be your daughter's best friend."

"Not if I can help it."

Mrs. Pringle glared at her husband. Feeling the heat from her hostile eyes, Mr. Pringle continued to stare straight ahead. She noticed his mouth stiffen and that his soft banker's hands gripped the wheel ever tighter. The couple rode to town in silence.

Aria said, "There go Molly's parents. Is Mr. Pringle still not talking to you?"

Heather looked and waved. "Yeah, I don't get it." Downhearted, she stopped to watch them drive away before continuing up the hill. "I didn't do anything to him." A wave of blue descended over her.

"Look, don't let it bother you," Aria said. "He doesn't know or understand."

Heather chuckled and mustered a bit of spirit. "No one does. Except Molly and Grandma Dawn."

"And me."

Heather laughed. "And you."

Heather and Aria had just turned from walking near the road to climbing Thimble Hill, when Aria stood up straight, insisting, "Heather, I have to leave."

"Now? But you just got here. I-I wanted to tell you about my dream, and about the Pet Stalker and how Molly and I think it's probably Mr. Simpletripp…"

"It will have to wait. I'm sorry."

And like that, Heather found herself alone.

CHAPTER THREE

The Bristol House

The Bristol House stood proudly against the sky, a magnificent and spacious three-storied Victorian that crowned the steep rise of Thimble Hill. Perched high above neighboring houses and the adjacent road and creek, the dwelling could be found at the end of a long cobbled walk that wound up from Afterglow Drive through tiered, manicured gardens.

The prominent house attracted the admiration of many with its harmonious blend of orange stone in various shades and sizes, its decorative pattern of wooden slats that embellished the windows and supported the eaves, and its elaborate, spire-topped turrets. Beneath its numerous chimneys were tall, steeply pitched roofs with U-shaped shingles of orange-gray slate. Rising above the rooftops, toward the front of the house, a widow's walk faced a distant sea, whereas far below, at ground level, an expansive porch embraced the house on two sides. Recessed within was an elegant front door that warmly welcomed both guest and visitor.

With its strategic placement of hallways, multiple sets of staircases, and orderly arrangement of rooms, the layout of the Bristol House was practical and its soul a good one. Inside were over forty-six rooms at Heather's last count, all furnished in styles varying from Chippendale to Art Nouveau. Many housed vintage antiques, old fixtures, and accessories suited to the tastes and needs of previous owners and their curious guests.

Over the span of its many years, some remodeling had taken place, due to the practicality of technological advancements and the eccentric imaginings of the various Bristol House occupants. As a result, some of the rooms were not quite in keeping with the original design and décor, although they still retained most of the old furnishings.

Having explored on her own throughout the Bristol House, Heather had discovered that the number of rooms and their locations were never quite the same on subsequent visits. When she told this to Grandma Dawn, the woman responded with a knowing smile, saying that, personally, she often wondered how the rooms stayed so spotless and tidy, wherever they happened to appear that day. Heather rolled her eyes.

Grandma Dawn enjoyed doing much of the casual gardening herself: planting flowers in window boxes and beds; tending to bloom-livened greenery that cascaded from baskets along the perimeter of the porch; lending a practiced hand to the colorful border plants that wound alongside the paths; and keeping a knowledgeable watch on the herbage that spread low between the rough-hewn stepping-stones.

However, the bulk of the Bristol House gardening and maintenance, and most anything that required extensive labor, Heather's grandmother left to the full time gardener, Mr. Henry Branson—Hank, to friends. As a result, the Bristol House, stately, orange, tan, and ivied, rose up and out of its surrounding gardens like a dignified man of noble bearing, splendidly attired in terraced hillsides, neatly trimmed hedges, liberal stretches of lawn, and dapples of trees. Further enhancing the mantle of finery were blooming vines; plots of hollyhocks, penstemon, lilies, and foxglove; and rows and rows of roses in the shape of tree and bush alike.

Beyond the gardens, the remaining acreage became untamed and rugged, overrun by bush and grass. Oak, cherry, maple, and other trees—native or an offshoot from the garden's wide assortment—grew randomly across the untended property.

The Bristol House had been built in the early to mid 1800's by Terentius "Scarbones" Bristol, the infamous pirate captain turned respected diplomat. In the Bristol family for generations, Grandma Dawn inherited the house, along with a substantial sum of money, from its previous owner, the very great granddaughter of Scarbones, Allonia Bristol.

Miss Bristol was a spinster, an only child, and lacking close relatives of any kind, she gratefully took in Grandma Dawn—and later Heather—and treated them as the family she never had.

Following the untimely death of her husband, Alistair, Grandma Dawn had worked steadily in Miss Bristol's employment for well over twenty years. At first hired to do the occasional cleaning at the Bristol House, it wasn't long before the elder Allonia Bristol and middle-aged Dawn Thibble became good friends. Miss Bristol, quite the recluse in her later years, enjoyed the company of the somewhat reserved and intelligent conversationalist. Soon she had the conscientious, fastidious, and dependable Dawn working most every day at a variety of tasks, some of which were simply keeping the older woman company late into the evening on stormy winter nights.

During her third year of employment, Miss Bristol asked Grandma Dawn if she would care to reside permanently at the Bristol House. Enjoying the eccentricities of the extraordinary structure and the elderly Miss Bristol—herself a knowledgeable woman and world traveler, Grandma Dawn felt the time was right to move in. From then on, the community got to know Grandma Dawn as both a resident at the lovely house on the hill and as a respectful representative of Miss Bristol. And although Allonia Bristol had an accountant to handle her finances, a lawyer to take charge of her legal issues—scarce as they were—and a handyman to repair and maintain most everything else, Grandma Dawn attended to the more mundane tasks such as writing the occasional letter of complaint or compliance, shopping for groceries and hardware, cooking the meals, overseeing the expansion of the ever impressive garden, and of course, presiding over the more minor maintenance that the house required. After Allonia's death, the house that was well-built was well-maintained, and so provided little to siphon money from Grandma Dawn's pocketbook and a lot to stimulate and entertain Heather's active imagination. Suffice it to say, the old and unusual house and its environs were a trove of curiosities for young Heather, from its cluttered attic to its jumbled basement, from the top of Thimble Hill down to the banks of Whisper Creek.

Following Aria's hasty departure, Heather continued to climb the rugged hill leading to the fenced-in gardens of the Bristol House. Occasionally, she would glance up and admire the elaborate structure. Its attractive appearance gave her great pleasure, and she took special notice of her turreted room located high above the ground. Windows open, it inhaled the moist sea air that flowed inland from over the hills.

Heather was fast approaching a gate near the southwest corner, where the scrubland gave way to stone steps leading onto the well-tended grounds. Stepping through the gate, under a densely flowered archway, Heather ran up the cobblestone path that wound between tailored hedges, expansive beds of blossoms, and trees whose trunks were partially wrapped in an unrelenting growth of ivy. Cresting the hill and encountering the sweep of lawns, Heather applied more speed in a flurry of arms, knees, and shoes.

Bouncing up a short flight of steps and onto the covered porch, she found Grandma Dawn sitting in her large wicker rocking chair near the front door. In her hands she held an open newspaper, its leafy upper corner sagging on a crease. The woman was intently focused on the lower half of the page, her eyes pacing over the text. Next to her, on a small round table sat an empty coffee cup. Heather was sure her grandmother had been drinking some exotic blend, a product of her bright yellow coffee press, the one with the little black ball on top and matching black handle. Beside her cup, the remainder of the newspaper lay browsed over, folded, and piled neatly according to section. Grandma Dawn paid little heed to the Sporting Green, but set it aside knowing her granddaughter might take time to look it over.

Heather came to an exuberant halt in front of her grandmother, her thick blonde hair swaying before coming to rest.

Grandma Dawn muttered, in concentration, "Hi, there, young lady," her attention never leaving the page. Her reading glasses, half-mooned and stylish, sat partway down her nose. "I shall be with you momentarily."

Catching her breath, Heather waited, exuding a bountiful energy, and Grandma Dawn couldn't help but feel the young girl's presence before her.

Moments later, the woman removed her glasses and set them on the table next to her cup. She looked up, her handsome face a blend of many things: pleasantness, playfulness, a touch of light-heartedness, and all of it bound together beneath a layer of formal reserve. Heather loved when her grandmother looked at her that way, as if she were ready for a game. Grandma Dawn flashed her milk-white teeth—not all of them perfectly straight. Still, her smile was an attractive one. "Ready for dinner?"

"Yes!"

"Let's go, then," she said, folding and setting aside what remained of the paper before rising.

Grandma Dawn was a tall woman, slender and elegant—classy. In her mid-fifties, she had blue eyes and dark gray hair that swept above her head and was held in place with tortoise-shell combs. As was customary, she wore a high-collared blouse that framed her long neck and covered her slender arms. A blue lapis necklace matched her simple earrings.

Looking at her grandmother, Heather was amazed at how quickly this nicely dressed lady could throw on some old clothes and become the tough, hardworking woman taking on difficult tasks around the house. Even when she was working near Hank, the Bristol House gardener, he would sometimes ask her to relax a minute, so he could climb down from a ladder or tree to give her a hand with shovel, saw, or pickax. Yet, seldom would Grandma Dawn allow him to help when she was set on a particular task at hand.

"I started it, Hank," she would say with a smile, but rarely a pause in her actions. "I'll finish it, thank you."

And with her head bent in determination and long sleeves perhaps rolled once at the cuff, Hank would leave her to it, usually with a chuckle and a shake of his head at her surprising proficiency.

Heather reached the front door before her grandmother, and pausing, casually observed the antique doorknocker. The fixture was conspicuous to be sure, a large graceful mermaid supplied by none other than Terentius "Scarbones" Bristol himself. Some claimed it had come from the cabin of his ship, the *Ill Wind*. Directly below was a brass mail slot where the gentlemanly mailman, Wilson Talbott, delivered the daily post. On occasion, after a climb up the steep hill, he would refresh himself by having a cup of tea and a chat with Grandma Dawn.

Turning the bronze doorknob, Heather pushed inward, taking care not to place her free hand against the stained glass that embellished the upper half of the door. The same design also decorated the wide glass arch overhead and the stretch of flanking windows.

Inside, the Bristol House foyer was a welcoming open area with shiny walnut trimmings. Immediately on the right stood an antique coat rack on which hung a roomy, multi-pocketed purse of Italian design. On a small circular table to the left sat a generous bouquet of sweet-scented roses from the garden. Propped alongside was a framed photo of Heather, Grandma Dawn, and Allonia Bristol, a studio portrait taken by the town's oldest photographer, Deemis Bryson, now ninety-three.

Past the table and through a wide archway, two steps led down into the parlor. Within stood an antique piano on which Allonia had played, giving informal recitals for friends, and later in life, for just Heather and Grandma Dawn. The instrument of rich reddish wood dominated a portion of the cheery room, surrounded by wainscoting and an assortment of strategically placed chairs. Facing the foyer in the far left corner was a servant's door. If opened, it led down a flight of stairs and past the basement doors to their Bristol House quarters, long unoccupied.

Opposite the parlor, through yet another arch, the living room displayed its elegant furniture and rugs of patterned flowers beneath two large chandeliers. Against the farthest wall, a black slate fireplace with gold inlay served as an effective centerpiece, the room arranged advantageously around it. Heather noted Grandma Dawn's favorite chair by the fireside, her blanket folded neatly over one arm. Yet, Heather preferred the couch on which to lay and daydream, read, or sometimes nap. When she had once planned a slumber party and invited some of her classmates, it was her intention to host it in this room. That evening, however, Molly was the only one to show.

Heather momentarily locked eyes with the pirate Scarbones Bristol. He was the subject of a grand, life-sized portrait over the fireplace. On his face hung a cockeyed smile—neither friendly nor menacing, but his gaze held a mischievous hint of someone withholding an inside joke. His heavy blue coat with tarnished buttons partially concealed a red sash, his tricorn hat tilted low over the brow. Placed before him, large muscular hands rested upon a sword's twisted hilt, its scabbard agleam with golden highlights. The pirate's deliberate stance was assured, planting him firmly in the midst of his painted darkness. Overall, the effect of the portrait was highly eccentric and oddly compelling.

Heather loved the painting, loved to gaze at the pirate while lying on the couch. Yet the girl felt that Scarbones Bristol looked more at her than she did at him—even when Heather closed her eyes she could feel the intensity of his extraordinary gaze. And the girl loved the way that the pirate always seemed to have something a little different about him every time she walked by. Maybe his hat was slightly more askew or his head possessed a greater tilt—or maybe on that particular day he just needed a shave. Of course, if told, many would think these fanciful notions were simply the result of a young girl's overactive imagination. But Heather knew better.

Before the main hallway, a majestic staircase curved down from the second floor landing, spilling out over the inlaid flooring of the foyer below.

In the hall on the way to the kitchen, numerous archways and doorways led to many finely furnished rooms on the first floor of the grand old house, each more enchantingly peculiar than the last. Narrow tables and sideboards, repositories for Heather's found objects, hugged the walls and hosted lamps, vases, and decorative accessories. High overhead, pendant lamps lighted the long passage that led to the back of the house. Before the rear staircase, with two quick turns, Grandma Dawn and Heather entered the spacious old kitchen, where a comingling of aromas, at their most potent, greeted them.

"It sure smells good. What's for dinner?" Heather asked, although thinking she already knew. The girl looked up to glimpse the many ladles, pots, and pans that hung above the stove. She found herself forever fascinated by the dangling assortment.

Attached to the stucco wall on the left, between stove and refrigerator, were honey-colored shelves filled with crockery, pitchers, steins, and oversized bowls. It was here that Grandma Dawn removed two plates, laying them on the heavy mixing table. Above her, situated on the upper brick portion of the wall, three arched windows provided an abundance of light.

Having donned her apron, the energetic woman slipped her hands into fancy red oven mitts. Opening one of two black oven doors, she withdrew a small ham, much to Heather's satisfaction and delight.

Noticing that the round table near the wall was unset, Heather knew they would be eating in the small intimate dining room. Discreetly, her gaze wandered to the heavy wooden dutch door, located near the corner. On pleasant days, the door's upper half would often be open, looking onto the vegetable garden; at night, it was here that Heather made her stealthy escape to meet up with Molly in the treehouse timbers.

Wanting to assist her grandmother with the dinner preparations, Heather ran across the hall to be certain that the dining room table had been set for two. It had. A quick look told her that the fireplace had been stocked with wood and merely awaited a match and a chilly spell—or just an inclination. And although the interior of the Bristol House maintained a constant comfortable temperature throughout the year, a fire was something that she and Grandma Dawn enjoyed, with her grandmother claiming it 'countered the effects of inclement weather on the mind.' Heather just thought it was cozy.

The girl remembered how Miss Bristol had loved this room. Since her death, not much had changed. It was still decorated in warm green tones, with thick, velvety navy blue drapery that, between cascading panels, showcased the view from Thimble Hill. A few of Miss Bristol's favorite paintings were thoughtfully placed, and a majority of the room's mahogany furniture rested on an intricate Persian carpet. Heather took a last look at the elegant napkins, glasses, and utensils laid with good taste upon the stylish tablecloth, making certain that everything was in its proper place. As usual, it was.

Whether entertaining a large gathering or dining alone, Dawn Thibble was a creature of ritual, and her routines always reflected her fine taste in placement and detail. At times, when a spontaneous snack was thrown together while reading or working on an enormous jigsaw puzzle in the den, there was still a tasteful simplicity in the arrangement of place mats and utensils that sat atop the wooden eating trays—formally informal. Often, Heather and Grandma Dawn would eat their meals casually in the kitchen at the small round table, however lately it had been mostly a semi-formal affair for dinner.

By the time Heather had washed her hands, tidied up, and hurried back to the dining room to light the candles, Grandma Dawn entered carrying two plates. Once seated, their meals before them, Heather listened while her grandmother muttered a quick but heartfelt appreciation for the meal. Promptly upon its completion, Heather picked up her fork and knife and hungrily made inroads into the tender slab of ham, while Grandma Dawn inquired about her day.

"After school, I saw Molly down by the creek," said Heather, and then immediately wished back her words, fearing she would be asked about details.

"And what brought you two down there?"

"Oh, just playing around, I guess, before heading home to do our homework."

"Anyone else at the creek?"

Heather's fork, now heaped full of mashed potatoes and dripping gravy, stopped mid-flight to her awaiting circle of mouth. Slowly, she lowered it.

Heather wondered, Does she know we saw creepy Mr. Simpletripp? How could she?

Grandma Dawn stopped her eating and looked up, sensing a shift in mood. She waited.

"I saw Aria," Heather said, too brightly. "But she only stayed a little while."

"Oh," said Grandma Dawn, below her inquisitive eyes. "She's well?"

"I guess so. We really didn't talk a lot. I told her about Mr. Simpletripp, and how he dug holes all over our property."

"What did she think?" Grandma Dawn picked at her small salad, her fork merely rearranging the leaves, her concentration on the girl.

"She said that Molly and I should be careful and try to stay away from him." Heather poked another piece of ham into her mouth.

"I'd say that was good advice. Wouldn't you?"

"Yesh," Heather chewed, "rully guth." She swallowed.

Heather looked up and found her grandmother's eyes still nibbling at her, the tip of her salad fork at rest in her greens.

"What?" Heather asked, reaching for her glass of water.

Grandma Dawn shook her head. "Nothing."

Heather asked, "May I please be excused?" Her glass touched her lips momentarily and then pulled away. "I have homework to do." She sipped lightly.

"You've finished with dinner?" Grandma Dawn asked, surveying her granddaughter's plate. "You still have some salad and potatoes left."

Heather had devoured the ham.

"I'm full," she said, setting her glass to rest on the tablecloth. "May I go?"

Coolly appraising Heather, her grandmother nodded. Hurriedly, Heather rose and started to pick up her plate and utensils.

"Leave them. I'll take care of them."

"You sure?"

"Mm-hmm."

"Thanks, Grandma. Dinner was great."

Heather set the plate back down. They regarded one other: the child's face impassive, the grandmother's invitingly receptive. Heather looked away. She felt a tug of expectation, a sensation in the very air around her, and realized that there was a silent call for clarification—or confession.

The girl started to walk out of the room, trying not to hurry—although dying to break into a sprint. She turned to look at her grandmother who had just taken a sip of wine, while glancing out the windows. Heather knew she should tell her about Mr. Simpletripp, about what had happened at the creek, but was afraid she would be told not to go down there. If that happened, then where could she and Molly meet during the day when not at school? Her grandmother continued to wait.

Heather, struggling to keep the secret to herself, crossed the threshold to the hall. Once out of view, she increased her pace. With long strides, the girl mounted the stairs in twos and quickly entered her room. Closing the door behind her, she flopped onto the ample bed and kicked off her red shoes, one still damp from its earlier submersion in water. They hit the rug, each with a muffled clop. After a moment, Heather rolled to her side and propped her head on the softness of a pillow sham, tucking it this way and that for comfort. Finally, she settled. She fixed her attention across the sizable room, through the wide decorative arch that led into the turreted alcove with its comfy chairs, desk, and bookshelves, and then out at the late afternoon sky. With a glance at the clock, Heather realized the autumn darkness was falling ever earlier.

Rolling off the bed and onto to her feet, she walked and positioned herself before the windows, where she saw the babysitter's car in Molly's driveway. Heather hoped that her friend would be able to sneak out later and meet in the treehouse, their nighttime hideaway. The thought made her turn to the window on the right, where she looked down Thimble Hill at Whisper Creek, now mostly in shadow. Beyond its farthest bank, in among the oaks that bordered Afterglow Drive, the girl spied the treehouse perched high within the interlaced branches of the Oak Triplets. Heather could barely make out its crude but sturdy framework through the foliage. To the right and far below the treehouse stood the backside of the Simpletripp house, unappealing in its mundane construction and faded paint: light purple and deep green. Not seeing Mr. Simpletripp in his yard gave her pause. The imaginative Heather couldn't help but wonder where he was and what he was killing.

CHAPTER FOUR

To Meet in the Treehouse

er homework long since finished, Heather looked at the time on the shiny red alarm clock next to her bed. Black hands spinning over a maroon face declared 9:10. Heather was supposed to meet Molly in the treehouse in thirty minutes.

She set down her book titled *Two Girls and a Mystery* by May Hollis Barton, an absorbing old hardback that Molly had found some time ago in the Bristol House library. When she showed it to Heather, the blonde found its dust jacket intriguing. It depicted two girls cautiously entering a mysterious open door, making her want to read the book simply on the basis of the cover illustration. Also, Heather loved its title. And if that weren't reason enough, Molly had read and recommended it, adding that the book was a first edition published in 1928.

Heather surmised that by now Grandma Dawn was either reading in bed, or as an early riser had put out her light and was fast asleep. Her bedroom, located down the hall between Heather's room and the back stairs, made for trepidatious passage on treehouse nights, when Heather had to sneak past her door. It didn't help that the girl knew her grandmother to be a light sleeper. Luckily for Heather, Grandma Dawn had been keeping her door closed as of late. It hadn't always been the case and on occasion still wasn't.

Heather threw off her covers to reveal that she was completely dressed right down to her red tennis shoes. She had changed out of her pajamas after Grandma Dawn popped in briefly to say goodnight.

By the light of the old-fashioned floor lamp near her dresser, Heather hurriedly stuffed her pillows and shams under the covers to create a Heather-like lump, knowing that if her grandmother came in, she wouldn't be easily deceived. Yet, Heather figured it wouldn't hurt to go through the motions. Besides, she liked the idea of creating a 'sleeping

Heather look-alike.' Very cloak-and-dagger.

Reaching into the closet, Heather retrieved her wool coat. She slipped it on over her sweater and buttoned up. The girl made sure not to choose the jacket with the shiny fabric that let off a sort of squeak as it rubbed against itself. Having worn it one night when sneaking out, Heather remembered it had made all sorts of noise in the silence of the hallway. She had had to make an abrupt turnabout, returning to her room to change into the softer, quieter wool.

Heather picked up the two Nancy Drew books from the dresser, before adding *Two Girls and a Mystery*, and stuffed them into her small backpack before turning to shut off the light. With a twist of the antique lamp switch, the glow lingered before fading. Allowing a moment for her eyes to adjust to the darkness, she walked quietly to her bedroom door and opened it a crack, peering into the hallway. Heather listened and gradually opened the door wider. Cautiously, she peeked her head out, first scanning in the direction of Grandma Dawn's room and the back stairs, and then the opposite way towards the bathroom and the greater stretch of corridor leading to the front staircase.

In the nighttime stillness, wall sconces and the occasional lamp situated on a side table illuminated the lonely corridor while the mouths of doors and arches gaped at intervals along the lengthy passage. Until recently, Heather sneaked out by descending the front stairway to the foyer, then walking the long hallway to the kitchen, and from there exiting the dutch door. Yet, that was before she encountered what Heather described to Molly as the 'nightman on the stairs.'

Since then, she had decided to take her chances by creeping past her grandmother's bedroom, enjoying the challenge and thrill of trying to do so undetected. Heather thought it a good opportunity to hone her mastery of stealth, or what she called her spy skills.

Having slinked into the hallway, Heather quietly closed the bedroom door behind her. With a small lamp atop the sideboard providing an elongated fan of light onto the wall, she started in the direction of Grandma Dawn's room.

Careful to slowly and deliberately distribute her weight from footfall to footfall, lest the floorboards protest and wake her grandmother, Heather inched her way towards the back stairs. She passed a sitting room and afterwards a bedroom. Despite the delicate placement of her feet, the flooring periodically snapped out or found reason to groan. When this occurred, Heather would freeze—one hand lightly placed against the wall for balance, allowing the quiet to settle in before resuming. Creeping closer, one cautious step after another, Heather found—

much to her relief—that her grandmother's door was indeed closed. She saw, too, that her light was out and not shining as a thin strip of yellow beneath the door. It didn't change the girl's routine of a steady silent tread, however, as she bypassed the bedroom to reach the stairway that dropped before her, dusted in the depths of its shadows.

Heather lowered herself down, measured step by measured step. Every so often, the old stair treads would protest under the girl's weight, a sharp cry of discomfort or prolonged moan of agony.

Once in the dimly lit hall below, after a quick zig and zag, Heather entered the kitchen. At night, the room seemed unfriendly with a bluish light angling through the windows overhead, scarcely illuminating the common area and ignoring the blackness that clung to the corners, hollows, and undersides of tables.

Heather reached the dutch door that led to the garden. With a slow slide of its well-oiled deadbolt—she personally saw to the task, along with the hinges—she quietly opened the door and slipped out.

The slap from the fresh chill of air made the girl gasp and shiver-up. She closed the heavy door soundlessly behind her. Night blanketed the surrounding greenery and a full moon poured its ashen light between the trees, and by this emission Heather attentively picked her way through the vegetable garden. It wasn't long before she connected with the wide stone path leading down Thimble Hill. Stealing between tree, bush, and hedge, she eventually wound her way off the Bristol House grounds.

Following the dirt trail along Afterglow Drive, Heather approached the Whisper Creek Bridge. Though constantly on guard for oncoming headlights or pedestrians, she rarely stumbled, her night vision warily acute.

At opposite ends of the bridge, two streetlights spilled their illumination intensely onto the planks, discarding their excess light over the sides to mingle in obscurity below. Skirting the bridge, Heather followed the path from street-level down the bank towards the water. Once there, she slowed and advanced cautiously, the lamplight colluding with moonlight to sort out the tangle of brush, tree, rock, and water—but only vaguely.

Glancing to her left, through the deeper darkness that draped the underside of the bridge, she looked beyond to the deficiently illuminated bank upstream. It revealed no shape of the approaching Molly. At that, Heather headed in the opposite direction. With her hands helping to guide her through the growth along the water's edge, the girl eventually came upon Lower Bridge. She hoisted herself up and onto its cylindrical girth, aware of the forceful current that swept below, knowing that a misstep could prove disastrous. With her arms out for balance and her gaze locked before her, Heather's muted-red tennis shoes gripped the rough knuckled bark as she crossed.

Exhilarated, the girl reached the opposite side, and soundlessly lowered herself onto the bank of soft mud. Stepping away from the fallen tree, she stood still and listened. The creek gurgled and a gentle breeze rustled the leaves. Heather looked downstream to where, only hours earlier, the menacing Mr. Simpletripp had stood and glowered. She shivered.

Cold out tonight, she thought.

Heather hastened through the scrub under a diminishing light, remnants from an Afterglow Drive streetlamp. She soon reached the darker twining of the oak grove covering the narrow strip of land owned by Ms. Gardner. Abutting the Simpletripp property, Mr. and Mrs. Simpletripp had once offered to buy it, but Ms. Gardner had refused.

"Only more room to bury their secrets," Heather remembered her saying, the girl working her way through the underbrush. "Besides, I want as much real estate as possible between that man and me."

Heather understood.

Finding her way to one of the low growing branches belonging to the enormous Oak Triplets, Heather pulled herself up and onto its roundness. From there, she followed the elevated route as it twisted and started to climb, snaking in and out of concealing foliage. Mounting another thick limb and then a third, Heather placed her toe in a knothole and clambered to a higher bough still. Before her in the subdued light, hidden by a close network of branches, she found the new pieces of wood that she and Molly had nailed to the muscular trunk earlier that summer. Grabbing hold, one rung after the next, Heather climbed skyward into the leafy entanglement of limbs. Steadily ascending, she looked up to see the approaching rectangle of treehouse floor, dark against the random patches of starry sky.

As she neared the opening in the floor that led onto the decking, Heather softly called out the word, "Nose?"

She awaited Molly's coded reply. None came. Heather wriggled out of her backpack, first freeing the strap from her right arm, while her left hand firmly gripped the rung of wood. Switching hands, she shrugged off the bag and caught it easily, the backpack dangling momentarily before she swung it by its strap through the opening. The books hit the floor with a loud clump. Heather thought she could probably have cleared the rectangular hole while wearing her pack, but liked the idea of hanging suspended in the trees while removing it. Now, with her hands gripping the heavily reinforced planking, she pulled herself up and onto the treehouse floor.

Okay, thought Heather, so where's Molly? Usually, if she doesn't see me at Lower Bridge, she'll cross the upper one and wait for me here.

She checked her glowing watch. Five minutes to spare. Still time.

The girl crossed to the southeast corner of the treehouse, near the rope barrier. Through the leaves Heather saw Molly's home across the bridge and creek. On the bottom floor, an orange-yellow light shined steadily from the window. That wasn't unusual, however, because often Molly would leave the light burning when on her way. If she couldn't make their rendezvous, Molly would flick them on and off periodically over the course of the next half-hour or so, to be certain that her friend saw the signal.

Heather walked to the opposite corner of the floor. Here, she had to part the dense greenery to look down on the Simpletripp property. Not seeing any activity, she reached into the hollow of a nearby branch and felt around for her spyglass. Next to a bottle of water, some candy bars, sunscreen, and a pair of Molly's sunglasses, she found it. Protracting the antique piece, she placed it to her eye and concentrated on the house in the night. No lights, no life, nothing. Disappointed, she started to return the spyglass to its quarters, but thought better of it.

Lowering herself onto the decking, lying on her back, Heather propped the small pack beneath her head as a pillow. Again elongating the gilded scope, she sought out her favorite constellation, Orion, above the leafy treetops. From her vantage point, she was able to glimpse part of him, his unmistakable sword and belt. Heather thought it strange how, in the open air and depending on her mood, the starlight warrior was either soaring through the sky or falling from its reaches. Soon, the nocturnal focus of her spyglass began to wander to different pieces of the velvety heavens, attempting to identify other constellations. Meanwhile, she awaited her friend.

But Molly was trapped, unable to escape the confines of her room. To her ears, the voice in the background droned and waned like a persistent fly at the sill. And although restless, Molly sat unmoving on the bed, longing to fidget, to work at the wrinkles in her pants and the buttons on her blouse. Yet, she willed her hands into inactivity. Molly glanced at her bedside clock: 9:41. She was late.

On her desk sat a small pile of books. Nearby were two open others, the weightier volume pinning down the lesser. Molly's tortoise shell pen lay idle on a scribble-covered sheet of paper belonging to a spiral notebook.

"Can you believe he'd do that to me? Can you? And after all this time, too." Megan slammed her bony hand down on the desk. Molly and the books jumped. The babysitter continued to pace. "I'm just trying to earn some money so I can do stuff, you know."

Molly had gone quiet. She'd been listening to Megan's rant for over twenty minutes, wishing she'd go watch television. Her eyes sneaked to the clock.

"You know what he bought me for my birthday? Huh? Do you?"

Molly couldn't possibly have known. She stared glumly at nothing in particular.

"So, what do you think he got me?"

Molly shrugged.

"Close your eyes." Megan waited. "Go on. Close 'em."

Molly did.

"So, what do you see?"

Molly shrugged again.

"Nothin'?" Megan snapped, her eyes welling up. "Well, that's what he got me. I got nothin'."

Molly recognized the lines from a joke she had heard previously, when her dad had been teasing her about Christmas presents.

Please just go away, Molly thought, focusing on the floor. She felt Teacup, her little white terrier, brush up against her ankle as she peeked out from under the bed. The dog whimpered and retreated.

"I took *him* to play miniature golf and those stupid pinball machines," Megan continued. "I'm the one making money." She sniffled, dragging a forearm across her nose. The babysitter went quiet. It drew Molly's attention, and she saw tears running down Megan's cheeks.

Molly looked to the ceiling in exasperation. Oh, great, she thought. Here we go, a total meltdown.

She checked the clock again, then turned her attention towards the skinny babysitter: head down, she was crying in silence.

A wave of pity rolled through Molly. She got up from the bed and walked towards Megan, placing a hand gently on her arm.

"Maybe you should go out and call him," she said.

Jerking her shoulder free, Megan turned on the younger girl.

"I'm not calling that bonebrain! Do you know where he is tonight? Do you?"

Wincing, Molly took a long slow breath and sat down on the first available seat, her desk chair, inadvertently knocking to the floor a short stack of magazines she had intended to share with Heather. Leaning down, she gathered them, discreetly looking up to see that the babysitter was awaiting a response. Dark rivulets, a blend of mascara and eyeshadow, ran down her cheeks.

"Well, do you?"

Molly weakly shook her head, having paid little attention to the question.

"He's out with his buddies, that's where. While I'm babysitting, trying to make us some money to do stuff, he's out spending it. I think he's trying to punish me, that's what I think."

"Maybe some television would take your mind off him—"

"Off him? *Off him?* And why would I want to do *that?*"

Molly directed her gaze out the window.

Sitting up in the treehouse, Heather was waiting on Molly, waiting to see if her light would blink. It shone steadily.

Lying back down, not wanting to read by the glow of her small flashlight, the girl gazed at the stars instead. Scattered in their multitudes, they glittered with endless possibilities. After a while, she sighted a shooting star streaking overhead and thought it lucky. She named the star Lex and made a wish. Heather wished for Mr. Pringle to stop being mad and allow her and Molly to hang out like they used to—before that day at school.

She closed her eyes. Heather tried to dismiss the thoughts of her true-to-life nightmare. She had replayed the tiresome loop, wanting it to be rewritten—or better yet, to dissolve like confetti between the floorboards, to be carried off on the wind, never to have happened.

"Too bad Miss Lauren wasn't there," she muttered, now wishing that the strangeness of that day belonged to someone else far away and would never find her. Yet, the child knew that glimpses—painful reenactments—would always seek her out.

On that particular day, during the first week of school, their teacher, Miss Lauren, had been absent due to illness. The substitute, an old and shriveled, hatchet-faced woman named Mrs. Peck, had turned up, dressed in a sharply pressed checkered suit with her gray hair pulled back tightly in a restrictive bun. She had oversized ears that seemed to bloom on either side of her head, and wore black shiny pumps each sporting a big ugly buckle that Heather determined resembled the kind worn by Pilgrims.

In addition to her unpleasant appearance, she felt Mrs. Peck to be an awful person, unreasonably picking on the new kid in class. When Heather first found out that his name was Stilped, she was concerned.

"Stilped?" she had asked him. "Why in the world would your parents name you that? You know, it sounds a lot like *stupid*. I say, let's just call you Stil."

"Okay," came the little response.

Throughout the morning and into the afternoon as Mrs. Peck cruelly singled out the quiet boy on numerous occasions, Heather scrutinized her, locking in on various details, most of which she found disturbing. During lessons, the teacher's mouth was a twist of downturned lips that hung in a perpetual state of distaste—as though, Heather thought, she sucked on a permanent lemon. When Mrs. Peck spoke, she displayed lots of gum and glimpses of lengthy yellow teeth while her voice was cold, sharp, and biting.

As well, the girl observed that the elderly woman's shine, as Heather liked to call the auras she saw emanating from all living things, was an array of suffocating grays and acidic blues, though she would never use those words—or any words—to describe the phenomenon. To Heather, auras were simply a wash of feeling determined by the colors they gave off, and Mrs. Peck's unfriendly shine told Heather to steer clear.

At recess, Heather happened to notice Stilped sitting alone. She walked over to offer a bit of encouragement to the boy, only to realize he had been crying. Not wanting to embarrass him, she retreated. After lunch, near the end of the school day, when Stilped failed to respond to a geography question that probably only Mrs. Peck knew the answer to, she berated the boy.

When the teacher paused, Heather said, "Please stop picking on him, Mrs. Peck."

The upright woman wheeled and stalked towards Heather, a stack of papers in her hand.

"You!" she snarled, stabbing the air with her finger. "Stand up!"

Heather stood. Mrs. Peck emphasized every word with a hard poke in the chest. "You-will-not-tell-me-what-to-do-young-la-dy-do-you-hear?"

Shrinking a bit, Heather saw the teacher's shine emanating irate violet over sadistic blue. She said quietly while looking away, "Please don't, Mrs. Peck. That hurts."

"You will—" and here the churlish woman emphasized this next word with another poke in the chest, "—NOT tell me what to do!"

With the delivery of the hardest poke, Heather staggered backwards into her desk and chair. When she recovered and looked up at Mrs.

Peck, the girl set her jaw, rose, and stepped forward.

In a voice not quite her own, Heather said through clenched teeth with eyes turning amber, "I told you to please not poke me." Mrs. Peck was startled—and afraid—but she wasn't going to let on or back down in front of the children.

"Young lady, I told *you*—" and with a poke she attempted to once again set Heather back in her seat.

But Heather-cum-Aria quickly grabbed hold of Mrs. Peck's spindly index finger. She circled the woman at a run, dodging desks at the front of the class, spinning the teacher in clumsy pirouette. Then, with a sweep of her arm, Aria gave her a forceful sendoff, Mrs. Peck's papers sailing and scattering around her, the woman twirling in a blur. Slowing, staggering like a wobbling top, she lost her balance and, accompanied by a collective gasp from the class, toppled to the floor with what looked like a cushiony bounce. At that moment the bell rang, signaling that school was over for the day.

Aria turned to her classmates and slightly out of breath, but in a commanding voice, said, "All right, everyone. Class dismissed."

At first, as if in a trance, the students didn't move. Then with a start, they became animated, grabbing up their books and belongings. As they quickly filed out, a small number looked back over their shoulders, some with awe and others fear, a few perhaps noticing the girl's change in eye color and their momentary glow.

Molly stayed behind. She slowly rose, and pushing against the outflow of students, approached Aria and the downed teacher, only to stand by dazedly. Aria kneeled and slapped the pale instructor several times lightly across the face. Then she lowered her blond head and whispered in the old lady's oversized ear. Immediately, Mrs. Peck moaned and started to regain consciousness.

Aria said, "Mrs. Peck, here, let me help you sit up." She confidently slid one hand behind the teacher's upper back and eased her into a sitting position, then glanced at Molly, who continued to stand by idly in stunned disbelief, mouth ajar.

"Molly," Aria said, calmly, gathering the teacher's papers, "perhaps you should go to the drinking fountain and help yourself to some water."

Molly watched the amber drain from Aria's eyes, returning them to green.

Heather said kindly, "Molly, go." The blonde then noticed Stilped, standing alongside his desk, his books haphazardly under one arm, gratitude subtly lighting the quiet boy's face. Heather smiled. "You probably should go, too, Stil."

She turned her attention back to Mrs. Peck, who was moving her head slowly from side-to-side, her aura a garbled gray. The woman was sitting up like a rag doll, her pilgrim shoes pointing outward at the end of splayed legs. Opening her eyes, she looked at Heather with surprise, saying, "Oh, I must have fainted."

"Can you stand, Mrs. Peck? Here, hold my arm."

She helped to raise the old lady unsteadily to her feet.

"Oh, my! Where are your classmates?"

"They went home right after you fainted, Mrs. Peck. It was okay, though, because school had ended."

"Yes," Mrs. Peck said, distantly.

Sally Beegle, who didn't like Heather just because, had run to fetch Mr. Bennington, the principal. And when he and Sally arrived, Mr. Bennington found Mrs. Peck sitting at her desk with Heather alongside. Molly, returning from the fountain, waited just inside the doorway.

"Why, I must have fainted, Mr. Bennington."

"She didn't faint, Mr. Bennington," Sally said. "Heather made her dizzy, then pushed her down." She spied the girl near the door. "She did, didn't she, Molly? Heather pushed Mrs. Peck down."

The Principal's attention shifted to Molly.

Walking up, a broad grin spread across her face. "What?" Molly looked at Sally incredulously. "Sally, what an imagination you have. Are you okay, Mrs. Peck?"

"Did I faint? I must've fainted. My pills. I must've forgotten to take my pills."

"You didn't faint, Mrs. Peck," Sally insisted. "Heather pushed you down. I saw her do it."

"Now, Sally, don't you think Mrs. Peck would know if she fainted or not?" Molly said. There hung a bit of an awkward silence. "My Mom's waiting for me." She looked at Heather. "Coming?"

The Principal took over. "Here, Thelma, let me get the school nurse. I'd like her to take a look at you."

Undetected by Mr. Bennington, Molly and Heather exchanged nasty looks with Sally as they glided by on their way to the door. Sally surreptitiously stuck out her tongue.

Once outside and out of earshot, Heather excitedly turned to Molly.

"You were awesome, Molly!" Heather picked up the pace. "You should be an actress." She glanced over her shoulder to make certain Sally wasn't within earshot.

Blushing, Molly said, "You really think so?"

Heather reached into her backpack and pulled out a partially melted candy bar left over from lunch. It was missing one or two bites. "Here," she said, offering it to Molly. "Your first award, the chocolate Oscar."

"Oh, thanks," Molly giggled, then made a face as she took the candy and placed it in a pocket of her smart leather purse. "You and Aria were the ones who were awesome, Heather. Yikes! What came over you two?"

At first, Heather said nothing, her ebullience waning. Then she offered, "I don't know. I'm really sorry that Mrs. Peck fell."

Heather's voice suddenly hardened as her green eyes flicked golden. "She deserved it," said Aria, looking up slyly at Molly. "The cruel SnitterWik. What did she have against that poor boy anyway?"

Heather's eyes softened to green as she looked to the ground. "She's just a mean old woman, that's all. She probably can't help herself."

"Scutterdux. That woman deserved such treatment. She needed to be stopped. Have you so quickly forgotten how badly she was treating you and the boy? I'm glad I did it," Aria said. "Frankly, she's lucky that I only gave her a spin."

"Well, Aria, I would never think to do anything like that in a thousand years," Molly broke in.

Heather said, "Me, either."

The blonde girl slowed and grew quiet. Molly, keeping pace, watched her, waiting. Heather opened her mouth as if to speak, but no words emerged, the girl becoming lost to the sudden awareness of what had transpired and the possibility of further consequences.

"What, Heather?" Molly asked.

Her friend just shook her head, turned away, and broke into a run. She headed off towards the playground, her orange backpack jumping with each red footfall. Molly stopped walking and clutching her books tightly to her chest, watched her go.

Afterwards, though some of the parents talked among themselves, little ever came of the incident. A few simply didn't believe their children's stories and dismissed them as such. Others thought Heather strange, and told their children to simply stay away. Yet, ultimately, most parents in the small community of Noble saw no reason to get involved. A good many of Heather's classmates thought Mrs. Peck a bully and deserving of Heather's treatment. Of those, some kept their whispers among themselves. Still others didn't dare talk about the incident at all, afraid that Heather would somehow get wind of it and make them recipients of a similar unkind fate.

Receiving a number of phone calls over the course of the next few days, the Principal convinced the concerned parents that indeed Mrs. Peck had fainted by her own admission, and that children had a tendency to embellish such events.

Whatever the fallout elsewhere, the outcome was that Heather wasn't held directly accountable for her actions. The incident, along with Heather's reputation for strangeness, kept her classmates fearful and distant, except for Molly, who stood by her friend.

When Molly's father got wind of what had happened that day, he confronted his daughter. Molly told him the truth, omitting, of course, the appearance of Aria. Mr. Pringle, outraged, insisted on phoning the Principal, vowing to let him know what a threat he felt Heather posed to the upstanding people of their community—and to think that some of these people were his good customers! Mrs. Pringle tried to convince her husband not to overreact, to let the incident lie.

"After all," she said, "wasn't Mrs. Peck a mean woman and Heather such a dear? And didn't Heather bravely come to the aid of the shy Stilped Roarhowser? Why, that girl's a hero, Ned!"

Unfortunately, Mr. Pringle didn't see it that way. Disapproving of Heather's influence on his little girl, Molly's father reluctantly agreed not to phone, but only under the condition that Molly no longer spend time with Heather. To spare her friend, Molly grudgingly agreed, all the while keeping her fingers crossed behind her back. Standing nearby, Mrs. Pringle noticed. So was born the girls' secret relationship, which included clandestine meetings in the treehouse once belonging to Ms. Gardner's only son, Walter.

On the floor of the treehouse, Heather opened her eyes and focused on the nighttime sky, hoping to catch sight of another shooting star to reinforce her wish. Bringing her wrist before her face, she looked at her watch. Noting the time, with a sigh, she let her arm flop to the floorboards.

"Aria?" she asked of the night. "Are you here?"

Back at her house, Molly listened as the wall clock in the living room chimed ten times, and with each ring of the bell, the girl's hope to meet Heather diminished that much more. She was once again seated on her bed. Megan, her anger at her boyfriend having subsided, now channeled her energy in a new direction, extolling his many virtues.

"He did sing me a song on Valentine's Day, though," she said, reaching to grab a tissue from the box on Molly's desk. Upbeat, she licked it and began wiping her cheeks.

"Yeah, that's great," Molly said, as she collapsed backwards on the bed. "Just great."

At the sound of the heavy thump on the bedding overhead, a fearful Teacup made a sprint for the open bedroom door.

CHAPTER FIVE

When Sleep Comes

"**W**anna go watch TV?" Megan asked.

Lying back on the bed, arms flung overhead, Molly's eyes popped open. "You serious?" she asked, to the ceiling.

"Yeah, let's go. There're some old black and white movies on—one of those film festivals. You know, with the guy who's short, mean, and always has wet lips, especially when he's kissing what's her name."

"Eww. Megan!" Molly found herself laughing, relieved at the baby-sitter's change of mood, pleasantly surprised by the fact that, like with Heather, she and Megan shared an appreciation for old movies. She sat up and looked over the pile of homework on her desk. Her gaze flitted to the light switch that would signal Heather. "Yes, all right. But I can't watch for too long. I still have a ton of homework to do."

Molly did, but none of it due the next day. While trying to be polite and supportive, she wasn't all that inclined to spend the evening with Megan, but at this point there wasn't much else she could do. With her folks due home in the next hour or two, there was no longer time to venture out on a treehouse rendezvous.

"Coming?" Megan asked, leading the way.

Molly, purposely slow to rise, followed at some distance. Reaching the door and the switch, she turned off the lights—and then on and off once more—checking to see that Megan, her skinny frame moving quickly down the hall, hadn't noticed.

Heather also didn't notice the signal. Attempting to pull a sliver out in the darkness of the treehouse heights, she dug at her left hand with the short nails of her right.

"There," she said, when she succeeded in pulling it out of her palm. "You little rascal," she added, flicking it off her fingertips. She got up and parted the foliage once again, looking for some action in the direction of the Simpletripp house. No lights shone out, no movements stirred the night. She let the greenery spring back into place. Walking to the opposite side of the treehouse, she saw that Molly's bedroom light was off and assumed she wouldn't be coming.

Checking the time on her luminescent watch, she thought, I'll just stay a little while longer before heading home.

Turning to the sky, she awaited the sight of another shooting star. After all, that's where all the action seemed to be, what little of it there was. The moon was now in full view above the treetops. Heather felt a kinship in its presence, as if it were compassionately watching over her.

Once again on her back with the pack beneath her head, Heather reached for her spyglass. Its surface was cold to the touch.

She pointed the brass cylinder towards the heavens, careful to float the chilly lens above her eye. Heather studied the moon in its fullness, finding interest in its many surface patterns. Unexpectedly, a large bird flew through her field of sight, the circle of moonlight a contrasting backdrop to the winged silhouette. Heather pulled aside the spyglass and reflected on the vision a moment before returning the scope to her eye.

Without any further sightings of interest, the girl soon became bored. She shrank the spyglass as quietly as possible to its smallest form, and then set it down carefully with little sound. Heather suddenly and inexplicably felt that to make noise now would draw attention to herself, disturbing the night and all that was secretly going on around her. She found herself wanting to be a silent part of it, blending in like a rock or tree, aware of all that went on in her presence, though without her active participation. Heather also liked it here in the darkness, where everything felt unimportant, not needing to be regarded as either friendly or unfriendly. In the treehouse, there were no expectations of 'normalcy' placed on her, expectations that she felt she couldn't possibly fulfill; it was here that she could lose herself, in these shadows and to this world.

Unfortunately in moments like these, when the outer world settled in stillness around her, when she melded with the enjoyable buoyancy of nothingness, Heather's inner world awakened, and with tiny teeth gnawed at her consciousness.

It wasn't long before she asked herself, Who are you, Aria? And why are you a part of me? Yet, Heather didn't allow the words to escape her lips, not wanting Aria to hear. The question wasn't new, but it remained unanswered. Who am *I*? Am I Heather *and* am I Aria? And if she would just go away, I could be like everyone else. Normal. So happy and normal. Like Molly. Like the world! I could have friends, because no one would be afraid of me. And things like what happened that day at school wouldn't, because they couldn't, and I would be normal, just so normal.

Maybe someday I could even find my Mom and Dad. The image of her beautiful Grandma Dawn came to mind, and the shame of her disloyalty made the girl redden. Adopted since she could remember, Heather knew that her grandmother would always be there for her. She also knew that Grandma Dawn loved her. Heather took her hand out of her pocket and started to tap her fingers on the treehouse floor. Soon, they beat harder, and then when she turned her hand to employ a defiant knuckle, the striking became harder and louder yet.

I don't need a mother and father, she told herself. So, I'm different. So what? Who wants to be like everyone else anyway? And I love Aria. She's fun and she's my friend. Who cares what people think? Mr. Pringle's just a stuffy old banker, anyway, and Mrs. Peck's a creepy, mean old witch, and that tattletale Sally Beegle is just a wormy little snot, and that ugly creep Lloyd—stop it, stop it, *stop it!!!*

Heather moodily readjusted her backpack, and then plugged her hands forcefully into her pockets with a snort.

I'm not going to cry, the young girl commanded herself, feeling tears push at the rims of her closed lids. I'm not. I'm a rock. I'm a rock in the shadows, in this treehouse, up here in the nighttime sky. And I'm big and I'm strong and I'm not scared of anything. I'm that bird flying past the moon. She recalled with awe its wide graceful wingspan as the creature flew briefly in and out of her sight. Yes, I am; I'm that bird. Heather nodded her head and smiled, the tears escaping in two glossy trickles down past her temples and into her hair. And now I'm flying. She lifted her chin to the sky and inhaled the maverick night deeply, gloriously. Yes, I am, I'm flying. And I'm going so far away, so very far away.

In the distance, a dog, its voice a frail siren, broke the spell. Heather opened her eyes and blinked several times. Then she closed them to this world.

As Molly followed her babysitter down the hall, she stopped to shut the lights in the bathroom and pantry, knowing that her father would disapprove of the waste. Megan had forgotten to turn them off was Molly's guess—and it didn't matter. She found Megan in the kitchen.

"Should we make some popcorn?" the babysitter asked.

"I'm not really hungry," Molly said, not intending to spend a lot of time in front of the television. "You can, though."

"Nah, I don't want any if you don't. Come on."

Megan scooted out of the kitchen, and Molly followed only to return to switch off the light after making note to wash Megan's dishes before bed. They lay piled in the sink along with a water-filled pot that floated a large wooden spoon.

Off the hallway, Molly noticed the door to the garage was ajar and shut it, before hurrying to catch up to the lanky form in front of her. Last time Megan babysat, Mr. Pringle complained that they had come home to a house in disarray. Molly was going to do her best to see that that didn't happen again. Megan was difficult, Molly felt, but as far as babysitters go, she'd had worse. Much worse. And more importantly, Megan's self-involved activities usually allowed Molly the freedom to sneak out. For that reason, as long as Molly had to have a babysitter, it was important that Megan stay.

They reached the living room where the babysitter had cast cushions aside and pillows to the floor, undoubtedly while in heated conversation with her boyfriend. An elegant flowered throw hung off the arm of the sofa and gathered in folds at the floor. The television, left running, was bellowing conversation from a sitcom, the spatter of canned laughter trailing the lines. Molly grabbed the throw, spun it around her, and then sat, pulling up her feet. Megan, flopping down on the overstuffed chair, her bony legs thrown over the arm, grabbed the remote and flicked the television from its current channel. An old black and white movie filled the screen. Molly stifled a yawn as a gunfight broke out between mobsters.

"Isn't this great?" Megan asked.

"Yes," Molly managed as she concluded the yawn, her mouth hidden by the throw. It had been a long day.

"I've seen this movie, Molly. Check this next part out."

She did, and the high-speed chase was on. Molly saw old rounded automobiles speeding on rounded tires that screeched through rounded turns. Gunfire was noisily exchanged between vehicles. Molly lethargically followed the action.

Still up in the treehouse, Heather, her tears long dry, studied the stars overhead, connecting the dots, creating imagery. Occasionally a weak breeze would whisper through the boughs. The sound offered comfort like a distant wash of ocean waves breaking on the shore. Heather closed her eyes once again. This time she found herself drifting upon that breeze, aided by a large imaginary wingspan.

"Come on, honey, let's get you to bed." It was Mr. Pringle's voice, as he scooped the sleeping Molly up off the velvety sofa, pulling her from beneath the warm fortifications of her coverlet.

"Hi, Dad," Molly said from far away through a languid smile. She easily found sleep again on the bumpy ride to her room, though her eyes opened for a brief moment when Mr. Pringle laid his only child carefully on her bed.

He pulled the covers up, kissed her hair roughly—causing Molly to momentarily stir and roll—and when leaving doused the light.

In the living room, Mrs. Pringle was throwing cushions and pillows in place, though not with precision. The television, once blaring behind her, had also been put to bed.

Mr. Pringle paid the babysitter as Mrs. Pringle mounted the stairs to their room. A chill continued to grip the air between them, still festering from their conversation in the car earlier that day. Mr. Pringle glanced briefly at his withdrawing wife, and then dourly returned to pulling money out of his tight-lipped wallet to pay Megan. He saw the babysitter to the door and dutifully locked up behind her. Shutting off the lights, he paused at the bottom of the stairs, one hand resting on the banister. He inhaled deeply before climbing.

Heather awoke with a start.

Where am I? she thought in alarm.

In a moment the girl realized that she was in the treehouse and had fallen asleep. The night felt older and the stars above were unfamiliar from those she had observed earlier. The moon had moved on and was no longer visible directly above. Though her breath came in clouds, she still felt comfortably warm. She checked her watch: 1:52.

Yikes!

Heather scrambled to her feet. Grabbing a nearby rope with a clip on the end, she attached her backpack and lowered it through the hole in the floor. Satisfied with the length released, she knotted the remaining end to a branch. Afterwards, Heather began to descend through the rectangular opening, her feet feeling their way to the nearest rung.

On her way down, well below the floor's opening, Heather came upon the backpack swaying gently on the rope. She unclipped it and deftly maneuvered into the confines of its straps, then continued her careful but hurried descent. Upon nearing the ground, she jumped the remaining distance.

Heather made her way sure-footedly through the jumble of oaks, down to the creek's shoreline, across the span of Lower Bridge, and up the far bank. She was breathing heavily now, having pushed herself for speed along the way.

To save time, the girl veered from the path that ran alongside Afterglow Drive, cutting directly up the hill, angling toward the backside of the Bristol House, her feet stumbling over rock and shrub as she climbed. When the moon was lost to a strip of cloud cover, Heather took a moment to rest. Her breath came out rapidly, vaporously, and she looked through it at the veiled Bristol House. Its features rose above her, indistinct and withdrawn, conspiring with the night.

Resuming her trek, the flagging girl hastened her way up the infrequently used stone steps and through the gate at the northwest corner of the garden. To her left, spaced at regular intervals, was a row of Italian cypresses in groupings of four, on her right a waist-high hedge. Heather pressed on up the hill, the cobblestone path uneven beneath her sneakers. She slowed. The moon peeked out from behind the clouds to indistinctly light the way, only to quickly withdraw.

At the sound of something scraping, Heather froze. Silently stepping off the path, she positioned herself behind the conical column of the nearest cypress. The girl listened attentively, trying to determine what the noise might be and the distance between her and it. Concluding that the sound emanated from a source closer to the house, she edged slowly around the group of trees and back towards the path, hoping to get a look at who the noisemaker might be.

"Not that way."

Heather stopped at the whispered words.

"Aria?" she whispered in return. "How come?"

"If we go that way," Aria said, "I think he'll be watching for someone coming up or down the path."

"He?"

"Sounds like someone shoveling, most probably a man."

"I thought so, too," Heather said. "I bet it's Mr. Simpletripp. Don't you think if he's busy digging, though, he might not be looking at all?"

"Do you want to take that chance, that he's preoccupied—digging or whatever—and won't hear us approaching?"

Heather was at a loss. "Yeah, but if we go behind the trees, we'll be farther off the path. I'm not sure what's there; it's rough ground. In the dark, we might trip on a bush or a big rock or something. If we do, he'll hear us, and then we're really in trouble."

Aria said, "The side away from the path is the safest."

"It's not. So, come on."

Heather started on her way around the trees, when suddenly the muscles of her legs seized up. She couldn't take another step.

"What are you doing?" Heather shot in testy whisper. "Quit making my legs stop."

"We're not going that way. It's too dangerous. He'll see us."

"He will not."

"Heather, it's foolhardy that way. Come, let's go this way."

Aria started walking to the other side of the trees, away from the path, when her legs froze in place.

"We're not going that way, Aria. I know this garden better than you do, and I know my way is the best."

"No, it isn't."

"Aria, I was here first. Now come on, let's do what I say."

"Wait. Listen."

Stillness.

"If it's your Mr. Simpletripp digging," Aria said, "I think he's heard us."

The shoveling resumed.

Heather whispered, "Well, if it does turn out to be Mr. Simpletripp, then what?"

"We'll see what he's up to. I say let's have a look."

Heather smiled. "Yeah, that was my plan, too."

"So, come now, let's go my way," Aria said, trying to continue the route far from the path, on the other side of the trees. Heather wouldn't allow it, so they stayed in place, pushing and pulling in a tug of war. An observer would think that the girl's feet were cemented in place, and that she was trying to pull them free, heaving one way and then the other.

"Stop it."

"You stop."

"Darn—"

"Don't…"

They started to topple, and then regained their balance. Frustrated, Heather's voice began to rise in volume.

"Look, Aria, I stood by while you went after Mrs. Peck, and it got me in trouble. Not only that, now I don't have any friends, because what you did scared them away."

Aria's voice rose in response: "As far as I'm concerned, those aren't the kind of friends you want. Molly, that's your friend."

"Yeah, but now Molly can't even be my friend, because Mr. Pringle hates me. And it's all because of what you did to Mrs. Peck. You know that. He—everybody—thinks I'm crazy."

"Look, everyone thought you an odd snork long before that. And who can blame them? They've seen you countless times laughing in conversation with yourself—or what they perceived as conversation with yourself."

"You mean with you, don't you, Aria? They were conversations with *you*."

Heather couldn't see the mischievous gleam take hold in Aria's eyes. "Yes they were, and good ones too…"

With nothing else to say, Heather and Aria went silent. So had the shoveling.

From deep within the hollows and folds of her sleep, a thought tugged at Molly's consciousness. It shook, pleaded, and then pulled with all its weight at the furry lining of her slumberous cocoon. It had need to interrupt, demanding that its truth be known and known immediately. However, ignoring the disturbance that beckoned from the small corner of her sleep, Molly continued to doze. But the thought persisted, pressing on, pounding passionately on the outskirts of her dream, only to swell with rage at its impotence. The thought grew larger, and then larger still, until finally it burst.

Molly sat up in the dark.

"Teacup," she said.

Heather held up her hand.

"The digging," she whispered. "It stopped."

Aria nodded her head and brought her finger to her lips. The two listened.

Heather couldn't hear a thing. She looked up the path, and that's when she noticed the light spilling out from between two groups of trees.

"Look. I think it's a lantern."

Aria peered closely at the light.

"Could be. It's definitely not a candle."

Heather's features turned dumb. "You think?"

"Sh-h-h," Aria said, taking them forward.

The pair hugged the trees as they crept carefully closer. When they were two sets of tall cylindrical trees away from the light, it went out.

Molly turned on the nightstand lamp and draped herself over the side of her bed, her upside-down eyes on her upside-down face searching beneath. Her hair brushed the floor.

"Teacup?"

Slipping out of the covers and onto her feet, she walked down the hall. No Teacup. In the pantry, bathroom, kitchen, laundry room, and den, Molly called out, all for no Teacup.

"Honey?" It was Mrs. Pringle, in her nightgown, calling from the top of the stairs. "Anything the matter?"

Somewhat disheveled and still bleary-eyed, Molly asked, "Is Teacup there with you and Dad?"

"No, dear." Mrs. Pringle started her descent. "Where haven't you checked?"

"I've checked everywhere, under the sofa and behind chairs... She was under the bed earlier, and then ran out towards the kitchen."

"She's got to be here somewhere. The door to the garage was closed when we—" Mrs. Pringle stopped speaking when she saw the horror-stricken look on her daughter's face.

"Mom, earlier tonight I found the door open, so I closed it." Molly ran towards the garage. "I never checked to see if Teacup was hiding in there," trailed over her shoulder.

When Mrs. Pringle followed into the garage moments later, she found Molly looking under the car.

"Molly, I'm going to get dressed. When your father and I pulled in tonight, out of the corner of my eye, I thought I saw something white dash by." Mrs. Pringle glanced towards the large rectangle of the two-door garage. "It just didn't occur to me... Go get dressed, okay? Hurry."

Molly ran off towards her room.

Mrs. Pringle paused in her flight up the stairs, calling out, "We'll need that new flashlight!"

Up against the cypresses, neither Heather nor Aria said a word. They waited, and when Heather felt Aria's movement pull them forward, she relented. They moved towards the backside of the trees, away from the path—Aria's way. The duo inched forward, Aria barely breathing. She stopped and waited before placing her next footfall. Not far now. Just beyond the four cypresses directly in front of her was where the light had shown out and the digging sound had occurred. Aria moved forward stealthily. A sharp sound cracked out in the stillness before her, but to her wary amber eyes the night stood still.

"Teacup?" Molly called into the blackness.

She could see the distant halos of the streetlamps over Whisper Creek Bridge. Mrs. Pringle's voice, shouting for the dog, seemed as far away to Molly as the old wooden span itself, though her mother was only on the other side of the yard. Using the new flashlight from under the sink, Molly was sweeping it back and forth across the grass and through the distant gate. With horror, it struck her that the bars were spaced too far apart to confine her little dog.

"Teacup?" The deeper voice rang out from the front of the house and down the drive.

Molly recognized the voice of her father.

Another snap. Aria's amber eyes held a glow of one thrilled by the danger at hand. With her back still to the cypresses, she waited before quietly moving forward, approaching the source of the noise. Another step, the red tennis shoes silently flattening the grass before coming to rest. Aria paused and waited.

Slightly ahead, she told herself.

Heather, who had patiently set herself aside in giving way to Aria, wanted full control, or *possession*. Though she could see all that Aria was viewing, only with full possession would she have the power to see the shoveler's shine in the dark, and thus the person's location. Yet, she didn't know how to relay her want to Aria without whispering and giving away their presence—if it wasn't already known. So, at this exhilarating moment, she could only hope that Aria would willingly stand aside.

Aria placed another silent footstep and waited. She sensed someone breathing only steps away, behind the rounded tree. Just then, Heather started to surge for possession of her body.

For only a moment, she thought, just a moment.

Surprised, Aria went rigid and lost her balance as she fought Heather for control. However, had Aria not done so and fallen off stride, she might have received the full impact of the shovel that, wheeling in a deadly arc, hurtled at her head. The glancing blow sent her toppling into the tree and then face-first to the ground. Sprawled there, she didn't move.

"Any luck?" It was Mr. Pringle.

"No," Molly said. "Where's Mom?"

"The other side of the house."

Mr. Pringle started walking in that direction, his light sweeping and probing before him. Molly followed. They found Mrs. Pringle at the front of the house, her flashlight raking the bushes and small trees lining the drive. Periodically, she whistled for Teacup and called her name.

Without turning from her task, Mrs. Pringle asked of the two approaching, "Did anyone check down by the creek?"

"I did," Molly said.

"How about down by the road?"

"I checked along both sides," Mr. Pringle said. "I started down by the bridge and even went as far as checking in front of the Bristol House property, where it meets the street. I was tempted to go up the hill for a stretch, you know, up their path behind the hedges, but that ghastly house is even ghastlier at night."

With an irritated sigh, Molly turned away and started back towards the garage. Mrs. Pringle shook her head angrily at her husband before hurrying to catch up to Molly. She put her arm around her daughter.

Staring after them, Mr. Pringle shut down his old battered flashlight.

The heavy boots that approached and stood beside Aria's body were square-toed. Around the leather folds of the new boot's shank, at the ankle and resting high atop the left instep, a heavy gold chain bore a locket. A shovel tip bit into the earth and rested. When the square toe kicked at the lifeless form, it gave and fell back without an utterance. Briefly, the shovel picked at the backpack that had broken free, a cursory once-over. The boots turned away. The square toes stopped for a moment, their occupant perhaps surveying the night for a second young person. Apparently satisfied, they commenced their walk. Soon, the sound of shoveling could be heard once again, this time working on a much larger hole.

Mother and daughter were approaching the open garage door, its light normally a welcome beacon within the expanse of night. Neither noticed.

"It's not time to worry yet, Molly. I'll go out at first light and search some more," Mrs. Pringle said. "You can come if you want."

Molly wrapped both arms around her mother's waist, as they continued in an oddly balanced walk.

Mr. Pringle followed at a distance.

The shovel skidded easily on the upturned earth when cast aside. The larger hole had been dug, large enough to fit a tall child. Mashing down the newly turned dirt, the stiff boots strode around the Italian cypress, the breathing above them emphatic and labored. Reaching the spot where the girl had fallen, the boots stopped. So did the breathing—before it continued at a quicker rate. The shoes chewed into the earth as they rushed around the nearest trees only to return, their square toes pointing to the site where the child had once lain. She was gone. The right toe kicked into the backpack, vaulting it skyward before it hit and tumbled end over end. It came to rest against a large rock, its contents still contained.

Molly sat huddled on a corner of the couch. Mrs. Pringle, entering from the kitchen, carried two cups of hot chocolate.

"Are you sure you don't want anything?" Mrs. Pringle asked her husband. "Coffee?"

He barely shook his head.

"We'll find Teacup, Molly," her mother offered, along with the cocoa. "She can't have gone too far."

Her eyes moist, Molly said, "Yes, if she hasn't been—if she's all right."

Uncomfortable in the overstuffed chair, Mr. Pringle shifted his weight, his mind turning to home loans and interest rates.

Come on, Heather, stay with me, Aria thought, staggering forward. She was nauseous, her head screaming, throbbing with pain. Just a bit farther, Heather. Don't lose me. Come on, now, don't disconnect.

If Heather lost consciousness, Aria didn't know if she could carry them both. After all, she had never had to try. She might shut down completely herself.

Heather saw the landscape around her in a jumble, her vision blurred. Her sight was Aria's.

"What can I do?" Heather asked, her voice barely audible.

"Stay with me," Aria said. "Just stay with me."

Earlier, Aria had come to and had heard their assailant digging nearby, on the other side of the trees. Her head throbbing and on fire, she managed to crawl slowly to the next cluster of trees and around the large circumference, taking momentary rest to try to calm her emotions, organize her thoughts. Knowing the import of each passing second and that their attacker would most likely come searching for them, Aria staggered to her feet. In the fleeting absence of moonlight, she angled unsteadily back down the hill, crossing over the stone path and onto a brick walk. Hanging onto shreds of her consciousness, Aria climbed a short embankment, making certain not to leave tracks. Tottering, she traversed a series of stepping-stones through a rose bed and beneath an arbor, before stepping onto another brick walkway. On its far side was a short hedge, but she wasn't sure she could make it even that far, having become muddled in purpose and direction.

"Just a short distance now, Heather, and then we can rest." Aria felt Heather's presence, but knew her consciousness, like her own, was rapidly waning.

She managed to step over the hedge, and reeling, threw herself forward on long haphazard strides through a thick bed of ivy. Head heavy, Aria lurched out of the deep night and into a deeper shadow, halting under a tree, where she swayed and then fell recklessly up against the base of a hedge. She vomited. And then again.

Aria was breathing hard, sweat dripping and burning her amber eyes. Blood matted her hair. "Heather, we made it. We're safe…hidden."

But she felt Heather fading, and letting go, she followed, into a deeper shadow still.

CHAPTER SIX

A Turn for Daylight

ria opened her eyes. They searched the soft reclusive darkness, sorting out shapes, assessing potential danger. The smell of vomit filled her nostrils and her thick head ached, a dull throbbing beat. She became aware of blood that had previously run off her hair and drained diagonally across her face, some caking in the socket of her left eye. But Aria didn't move. She waited, partially hidden in the ivy, in search of any movement or sound that posed a threat. Aria had felt Heather stir, but refused to give up possession until she felt certain they were alone.

"Heather, how are you feeling?" she finally whispered.

"Okay, except for my head," came the softly spoken response.

That brought a smile from Aria.

"We need to get back to the house."

The rustle of the ivy sounded loud in Heather's ear as she gave a slight nod of agreement.

Aria continued in a whisper, her eyes still searching, "It won't be long until daybreak. Let's get ourselves inside before then."

Heather asked, "Who hit us?"

"I don't know, I didn't see his face."

"Mr. Simpletripp is my guess," Heather said, still in an undertone.

"You may very well be right." Aria began to rise. "We'll need to discuss this in more detail later, but right now—" Sitting up, her face suddenly contorted in pain; she brought one hand gently to the side of her head. "—we've got to get you home and cleaned up. If Grandma Dawn saw you like this, she'd faint."

Heather smiled weakly. "And she'd never let me play with you again." Feeling suddenly nauseous, the girl hung her head. "I think we're going to blow chunks. Again."

"No, let's not."

They sat motionless for a moment, their head spinning, eyes closed.

The feeling of nausea passed, and Aria unsteadily climbed to her feet in the seclusion of ivy and tree cover.

She set off towards the house. The night was much colder now, and the moon, reappearing from beneath its earlier veil of cloud, was low in the sky and spread an icy blue light over the land. Yet, it still failed to infiltrate and illuminate the densest foliage. And shielded within these leafy areas, moving at a heedful pace, Aria followed the hedge until it intersected with another. And then as quietly as possible, though not so gracefully, she scrambled over the barrier of neatly groomed shrubbery and headed uphill.

"I'll lead now," Heather whispered, familiar with the garden. Aria relinquished possession.

Heather scanned the immediate area to see if she could detect any glow of human auras. She couldn't and pressed on over the familiar wanderings of the garden.

When momentarily exposed by the moonlight, where her breath shown out as ghostly clouds, the girl immediately retreated and in stealth continued her trek towards the safety of the Bristol House. Stopping behind the large ivy-covered trunk of a pistachio tree, she waited. Looking up, she could see her turreted bedroom, its three windows dark and blank, yet seemingly aware.

"What are you waiting for?" Aria whispered.

"I'm not sure which way we should go in."

"Don't you always use the kitchen door towards the rear of the house?"

"Yeah."

"So, what's the problem?" Aria asked.

"When we get inside, if we go up the back staircase, we may run into Grandma Dawn coming down."

"And?"

"I think we'd be better off going up the front stairs."

"Yes. Great. Good idea," Aria said. "Is there a problem?"

"Maybe."

"Maybe?"

"Well, it's just that I haven't told you about the nightman on the stairs."

Mrs. Pringle gently disentangled the tilted mug from Molly's relaxed fingers; it still held cocoa. Distraught, the twelve year old had finally fallen asleep on the couch, where she lay on her side, her head framed in profile against a small orange pillow.

Mr. Pringle had gone back to bed, saying he had to get up for work in a couple of hours.

Mrs. Pringle pushed aside her creeping anxiety over Teacup and turned toward the kitchen to rinse the cups. Overtired, she knew she wouldn't be getting sleep any time soon.

"Who or what is the nightman on the stairs?"

"It's someone I saw one night when I was sneaking out to meet Molly. He was an old guy and he wore this hat and long jacket. I saw him on the front staircase, carrying a big old lantern. I don't think he was real—well, I mean, he might have been real, but I'm thinking he was a ghost."

Aria didn't say anything for a moment.

"Really," she finally whispered, emphasizing the word as if she'd stumbled onto something exquisite. "And what makes you think he was a ghost?"

"I could kinda see through him."

"Well," Aria said, "That sounds about right. Was he frightening?"

"No, he wasn't really scary—I mean, I didn't think so. But why take the chance he might suck the life out of me or invade my body or something? I thought it would be better if I just turned around and snuck past Grandma Dawn's room that night.

"Anyway, that was a while ago, and I haven't seen him since. But I haven't used those stairs at night, either. I wanted you to know about him just in case he's on the front stairs when we sneak up to my room."

"All right, your nightman is duly noted, Heather. Come, let's get inside before the sun comes up."

Mrs. Pringle decided to fix herself another cup of hot chocolate. Having done so, she returned into the living room, and sitting across from her daughter, watched her sleep.

Lost in her dream, Molly mumbled a few incoherent words and shifted slightly.

Mrs. Pringle frowned. She thought about how devastated Molly had been when Rufus died, how she had eaten little and moped about, her schoolwork suffering mightily. It was understandable, Mrs. Pringle surmised, after all, it was Molly's first pet and her first taste of loss. She had grown up with Rufus. And then when Ned wouldn't let her spend time with Heather, Molly was cut off from her best friend, someone who could lend comfort and support, distract her from the death of her beloved dog, and ease her through the painful transition.

She congratulated herself on having come up with the idea of getting a new pet for the house, rather than for Molly specifically. Believing her daughter would be reserved at first, Mrs. Pringle knew she would eventually warm to the newly acquired family member—especially if the little critter was cute. And Molly did, much sooner than expected. And now, if she were to lose Teacup, well, Mrs. Pringle just hated to think where it would take her daughter emotionally.

Heather will be there, though, she thought, even in her restricted capacity. And that's good. She just wished Heather could spend time openly with Molly. It would make things so much easier for everyone. And here Mrs. Pringle chuckled ironically. Except for Molly's dad.

Damn, Ned, anyway! Mrs. Pringle almost spat the words aloud. He makes life so difficult with his narrow views and iron-fisted ways. And at times, it's so tiresome to have to work around him and his ridiculous decisions, just to make things go smoothly and maintain harmony at home. That man is so good at his job, so good with numbers, and so good with the unfeeling, objective areas of life. But when it comes to the living, breathing interactions that involve feelings, he falls far short of the mark. And then all this becomes too much work.

Mrs. Pringle surveyed the room, the new curtains and carpeting.

It's just too much work.

Having grown up in the big city, Mrs. Lana Pringle, née Fleming, had met her future husband while they both attended college. After marrying and moving to Noble, she had a difficult time adjusting to the more constrictive aspects of her husband's hometown—he called them conservative; Mrs. Pringle, at times, called them suffocating.

Thank goodness I was young and flexible when we married. I'm not sure I would take on his provincial mindset now—or this town's. And thank heavens for Sis, too, because if I couldn't get away for a fix of big city life now and again, I know I'd blow a mental gasket.

Okay, she thought, enough, and willed her mind elsewhere.

She watched as her daughter turned onto her back, took a deep breath, and settled into a deeper slumber. Mrs. Pringle regretted having to wake Molly shortly to resume the search, but the night was getting old and morning would soon be arriving. She thought about its forthcoming aspects and possibilities. For starters, it would be a cold morning, and that's not such a hot note on which to begin the day, let alone a search for a missing pet. And after being up most the night, perhaps it would be best if she simply let Molly stay home from school. Why not? Mrs. Pringle looked down at her hands that cradled the cocoa mug, at the diamond-studded ring that sparkled—too many diamonds, she thought. But Ned had picked it out.

"Is this whole thing really worth it?" she muttered. She looked back at her daughter.

She brought the steaming cup of chocolate to her lips and drank of its warmth.

Having bolted the backdoor behind her, Heather stealthily made her way through the subdued light of the kitchen. Knowing she looked a horror, she peeked around the doorway to make certain that Grandma Dawn wasn't descending the back stairs. Seeing no sign of her, Heather set off down the hallway, quietly creeping towards the foyer. Once there, Heather stopped and listened, leaning against the side of the staircase that circled above.

A stair creaked. Then another.

Heather pinned herself to the wall. Feeling Aria push for possession, she held her off. The girl heard the tread of feet directly above as they descended the curl of stairs in a slow measured step. Enthralled, Heather watched as boots and an ankle-length overcoat came into view on the stair treads, with more of the apparition becoming exposed with every footfall. A lantern appeared next, swinging from the nightman's knobby left hand. Heather noticed its yellow-green glow, but the light dissipated quickly and did little to illuminate the surroundings.

Now almost entirely revealed, the ghost continued to wind down the staircase from the second floor landing. Heather could see that although short in height, the nightman was thickly built. Her eyes widening, she watched as the ghost's face slid into view. Though aged and somewhat stooped, he carried himself with menace, casting off an eerie glow.

Upon reaching the bottom stair, the nightman headed for the parlor, passing close to Heather. Feeling her presence, he stopped and turned towards the girl, holding the lantern aloft. In turn, Heather stepped away from the wall, giving herself room to maneuver. Unsure of how to fight a ghost, she was ready to bolt down the long hallway behind her, if necessary.

As the nightman appraised Heather, she appraised him, noting his wide-brimmed hat, pinched eyes, and flat hooked nose that almost touched his uppermost lip. His coat, heavy, worn, and bearing a thick collar, was unbuttoned and, hanging open, revealed the clothing beneath. Cutting diagonally across his barrel chest, Heather noticed a thick shoulder strap, and where it connected to his belt there hung a cutlass. Opposite the weapon, his right hand twitched and made ready to rapidly grab its haft for battle.

Heather shifted her gaze to his eyes. She could only see the empty slits. She also noticed a continuation of the room behind him, through the translucency of his face and body.

"Do you know Scarbones?" Heather asked in a hushed tone.

The nightman continued to stare.

"Do you?" she felt compelled to ask again.

Gradually, his face stretched to accommodate a lopsided smile above an insignificant chin. Instead of being afraid, Heather felt a protective kindness in his presence. However, she determined him to be far from handsome—a trait that the girl was more inclined to notice these days, as she approached her thirteenth year. But he was definitely someone who meant business, and Heather would hate to have him angry with her. Not only did the nightman look like he could handle himself in a fight, but he was also a ghost!

With his free hand, the nightman pointed towards the top of his head, and let out a low guttural sound.

"What?" the young girl asked, not understanding.

He pointed to his head again and then to hers.

"Oh," she whispered. Heather brought her hand up to her head and touched the thickness of her hair and the dried blood encrusted within it. She flinched. "You mean this, don't you?"

Slowly, he nodded.

"Yeah, it hurts."

The apparition stared at the girl, his facial expression suddenly melancholy, gloomy.

From a pocket, and connected to a long chain, the nightman produced a large watch. As big as it was, it became dwarfed in his oversized hand. He checked the time.

It wasn't Heather's imagination that he appeared to be getting more transparent. Through the living room windows, she could see the sky beginning to lighten. When Heather returned her gaze to the nightman, he had noiselessly crossed to the parlor. Walking past the piano, losing illuminative strength, he was headed for the entrance leading to the servant's quarters. Without bothering to open the door, the weakened image disappeared through it.

"Bye," Heather whispered, wistfully.

"Well," shot Aria, in an undertone, "You could have allowed me to have a word or two with our nightman."

"Aria, this was the first time he met us. I didn't want to scare him."

"Heather, he's a *ghost*. If I have this right, *we're* the ones who are supposed to be frightened." And then Aria added, riding upon her easy laugh, "Aside from that, have you given thought to the fact that, in our current condition, we look like something fresh from a graveyard?"

At the loud click of a switch behind them, the girls went mute. Heather didn't need to turn and look. She knew that, at the far end of the hall, the light above the rear stairway had just burst to life.

Grandma Dawn.

"Molly?" Mrs. Pringle was shaking her gently. "Molly, do you want to come and look for Teacup, or would you rather sleep?"

The young girl sat up, her face steeped in drowsiness. She looked at her mother from under heavy lids, her words thick. "I'm coming," she said.

Molly torpidly slid into her shoes and grabbed her coat, and soon mother and daughter were in the garden, checking around the perimeter of the house. Dawn was breaking, the new sun attempting to heat the lingering night air.

"Teacup!"

The word was shouted out and about the Pringle property.

Molly ventured down to the creek, afraid of what she might find, while Mrs. Pringle checked along the drive, walking towards the street. Unsuccessful, she worked back towards her daughter who was returning from the direction of the bridge.

Mrs. Pringle didn't have to ask Molly if she had had any luck finding Teacup. It was evident from a distance, in her carriage, in her arms that hung unoccupied.

"The street?" Mrs. Pringle asked.

Molly looked up. "Sure." The word was said without enthusiasm.

The couple walked to the gate. Unbeknownst to Molly, Mrs. Pringle had surveyed the small stretch of Afterglow Drive, looking for animals that may have been run down. She hadn't seen any.

The two walked on opposite sides of the street towards the bridge, Molly hoping to find Teacup, and in secret Mrs. Pringle holding out little hope: the night harbored too many dangerous creatures.

When Heather heard Grandma Dawn's distant footfalls on the rear staircase, she wasted little time in mounting the front stairs before her. With the upper half of her head slowly rising to peer above the top step and down the second floor's long hallway, Heather made certain that her grandmother was no longer visible and had descended into the kitchen to make her morning coffee. As quickly and silently as possible, the bloodied girl walked down the hall and to her room. Once there, she hung her jacket and shed her grubby clothes. Rolling them up, Heather stuffed them under the bed.

For now, she thought.

Heather then pulled the pillows from beneath the covers and mussed the bedding. Cautiously leaning out her door and glancing down the hall, with an armful of clean clothes, she eagerly raced to the bathroom two doors down, just past the linen closet.

Heather's slender fingers turned on and adjusted the hot and cold water taps. With that going, she decided to check her face in the mirror. She had put it off, afraid of possibly scaring herself. She confided as much to Aria.

"Afraid of scaring yourself?" Aria laughed. "I guess that would make you doubly fearful and very *very* frightened indeed."

"What do you mean?" Heather asked, as she positioned herself before the oval mirror.

"Never mind. And my, don't we look a mess." Heather watched as the amber eyes that held her gaze faded to light green.

"Yeah, but at least we're ready for Halloween."

Her grin cracked the dried blood and dirt on her face.

"Are we okay, do you think, Aria?"

"I think we are." Aria carefully touched the head wound. "And may I add, we're lucky to have escaped with our lives. When you tried to gain possession last night, you caught me by surprise. You know, if you hadn't tried to take over, I might have been able to allude that shovel completely."

"Well, I just wanted to see if I noticed anyone's shine in the dark, but I couldn't tell you that without having Mr. Simpletripp hear us."

"If it was Simpletripp. Come, let's take a shower, wash off this blood, clean ourselves up, and get down to breakfast."

"I'm not very hungry."

"Heather, you have to eat. And you want to do everything as you normally would. I don't think Grandma Dawn will notice the cut because it's under our hair. It bled a lot, but the wound itself feels small."

"Yeah, we sure hope she doesn't notice—Grandma Dawn notices a *lot*."

As Heather turned to step into the clawfoot tub, the shower drizzling noisily down within the enclosure of shower curtain, there came a knock on the bathroom door.

Grandma Dawn's cheerful voice asked, "How's Heather this morning?"

Heather noticed the door was unlocked. She grabbed a towel to throw over her head in case the knob started to turn—not that it would have done much good hiding the results of her encounter with the assailant. However, at the very least she could spare her grandmother the fright of seeing her current facial condition without first preparing her.

"Hi." Heather tried to sound casual and cheerful in return, her voice bouncing off the old patterned tiles.

"You're up awfully early. Are you all right?"

"See? I told you," Heather whispered to Aria. "She notices stuff." Then to her grandmother: "Yeah, I've got some homework due next week for Mr. Madigan's class. I thought I'd start it early." Heather wasn't lying about the homework.

"Are you going to want breakfast at the usual time?"

Heather wanted to bypass it and was about to say so.

"Yes," Aria hissed below the steam.

"Yes, please." And when Heather didn't hear Grandma Dawn respond, she added, "Thank you."

"Nothing?" Mrs. Pringle asked her daughter.

Downcast, Molly shook her head. They had searched for Teacup on both sides of the street and for a distance after they had crossed the bridge.

"Come on, Molly. Let's go check around the Bristol House. Teacup might have run inside the gate."

Mrs. Pringle started walking that way, and Molly soon caught up to her.

"Do you think Teacup's safe somewhere, Mom?"

Molly's mother looked down at her daughter, and with a lightly placed arm across her shoulders, drew Molly nearer. They continued walking.

"Honestly, I don't know." She felt Molly's shoulders sag ever so slightly. "Honey, we can only look for her. The other part is up to Teacup and fate, and that's the part we can't control." When Molly didn't say anything, Mrs. Pringle added, "Not very encouraging, am I? Look, let's do our best to find her. She might be lost or hiding somewhere on the Bristol House grounds, or maybe someone has discovered Teacup in their yard and will look at her collar tag and phone. There might even be a message waiting for us at home this very minute."

Molly looked up at her mother, her face pained. "Or maybe—maybe Teacup is..."

The girl couldn't bring herself to say the word.

Still not hungry, Heather was forcing down her breakfast, the pancakes tasteless and woolly in her mouth. They had awaited her, staying warm on a plate in the oven, until her arrival downstairs after showering.

"What's the occasion?" Grandma Dawn asked, her manner brisk, fresh, full of the morning.

She had just closed the dutch door behind her, having come in from fetching the morning paper at the gate. Cheerful, she hung up her coat on a hook near the door, and stretched the rubber band loose from around the newspaper. The willowy woman pulled out a chair and sat down at the circular table.

Heather looked up over her math book and from under the bill of her hat. Rarely did she bring homework to the breakfast or lunch table, and never to dinner. However, she thought it would be a diversion from the bright red baseball cap that sat loosely on her head.

"I'm sorry?" Heather asked, though she had heard and had an answer prepared: something about it being a 'baseball cap kind of day today.' And tomorrow, if she was still unsure of her appearance, she felt it could always become a 'baseball cap kind of week.'

She watched as her grandmother placed the wobbly O of red rubber band near her coffee cup and unfolded the paper. Grabbing the black handle of the yellow coffee press, Grandma Dawn poured a cupful.

Heather and Aria had agreed the baseball cap was the best way to initially disguise the injury, although Aria felt they didn't need it and that their hair was thick enough to hide the puncture wound. It had bled a bit after washing, but pressure with a towel eventually stemmed the flow. There was a lump, and it still throbbed, but Aria thought the symptoms perfectly normal for such an injury and that Heather shouldn't worry.

"How do you know?" Heather had asked, gazing at her thick head of hair in the mirror. "Are you some kind of doctor?"

"I just know," had been Aria's response, and Heather had been willing to let it go at that.

Grandma Dawn was scanning the front page. "The occasion for your baseball cap? I was just wondering—"

Hank the gardener rapidly knocked three times at the dutch door before letting himself into the kitchen. He exuded restrained energy, but still managed to churn up the serene morning air. He quickly wiped his boots on the mat.

"Dawn, do you mind? I'd like to use your phone."

Hank Branson stood before them under his weather-worn adventurer's hat with its fatigued brim, wearing his usual overalls and sun-faded shirt—all this on even the hottest days. He was normally a serious man who wasn't at all effusive with his words, although today he looked all the more serious. It wasn't lost on Grandma Dawn.

"Why, of course, Hank," she said, slowly with unease. Grandma Dawn rose. "It's right down the hall."

"What's up, Mr. Branson?" Heather asked, giving off an air of great unconcern.

"Morning, Heather," the gardener said, and absorbed, quickly entered the hall. Grandma Dawn stood looking after him.

Heather could hear him talking, but his words were unintelligible. Moments later, Hank was hustling through the kitchen. Grabbing the door handle, he said, "It's best you stay here. Sherriff's on his way."

"Hank, what is it?"

"Best stay here."

Branson closed the door firmly behind him. Heather watched as, engrossed in thought, her grandmother walked slowly back to the table. Before she sat, however, Grandma Dawn changed course and with increasing speed, walked to the coat hooks by the door. There, she slipped into her jacket and was soon hurrying out on the gardener's heels, but not before saying, "Heather, please finish your breakfast and get yourself ready for school."

As the back door slammed shut, Heather swallowed her mouthful of pancakes.

"Aria?" she said, rising.

Mrs. Pringle and Molly walked along Afterglow Drive in front of the Victorian fence that encompassed the Bristol House gardens. Rising above the sidewalk was a low retaining wall consisting of stonework with periodic pillars; between ran the wrought iron fencing: elegant, fancy, and painted glossy emerald green. Flowers pushed up through the ironwork, the groundcover flowing down over the stone.

Upon reaching the entry gate, between two pillars bearing lamps, Molly spun the cold metal clasp. The entryway was wide enough for two, and the arbor that arched overhead displayed late season blooms above a tangle of greenery. The wide path wound upwards, and once inside, Mrs. Pringle led the way.

"Teacup?" Molly called over the many hedges and beds that climbed the hill. She threw up her hands in exasperation. "Mom, if Teacup's here, she could be anywhere..."

"I know. It's a lot of ground to cover, honey. Let's split up and work our way around the garden. You go on the side facing the creek," and here Mrs. Pringle waved a hand in the general direction, "And I'll go on the other side towards the driveway."

"All right. I'll start here in front of the house," Molly said, "And you can search the back."

"Sounds good. And whoever finds Teacup or finishes their search, just call out and look for the other. And as much as possible, let's try not to disturb Heather and her grandmother."

"Sure." Molly looked at her mother with gratitude. "Thanks, Mom, for helping me look for Teacup."

"You're welcome. And don't give up hope, she could be just around the corner."

"Can you see them?" Aria asked, looking out the window.

The two were standing in the turreted part of Heather's room, gazing down Thimble Hill at the garden path that wound alongside the row of cypresses.

"Yeah, there they are. See them? Grandma Dawn is following behind Mr. Branson. They're on the way down to where we were bonged on the head, all right. What do you think is going on?"

"Don't know."

"It's hard to believe any of this happened. I mean, if this baseball cap wasn't hiding my sore head, last night would seem like a dream."

"More like a nightmare."

"Yeah."

"Heather, I'm thinking we need to revisit the scene of the crime."

"I'm thinking the same thing."

"Now that it's daylight, I'd like to have a better idea of what transpired."

"Yeah. What was Mr. Simpletripp up to anyway? And I just realized another reason we need to go back down to the scene of the crime."

"What's that?"

"My backpack is still there."

Hank saw the sheriff approaching. Following the gardener's earlier suggestion by phone, he had come up the northwest path.

"Harland."

Sheriff Harland Dane, black and lean, was covering ground quickly atop far-reaching strides. He nodded once, curtly, upon reaching the gardener. His face was boney above a long neck, his eyes blue beneath his sunglasses, and his mustache was trim below a broad nose. Dane had a great wide grin, though today few if any would experience the sight of it.

The Danes were old family in the town of Noble, where the sheriff's father and grandfather had run a barbershop in the now historic St. Symonds Hotel located on the town square. Harland Dane, breaking with tradition, had gone off to college and returned with a wife, a baby, and a degree in law enforcement.

Hank waited on the cobblestone walk and Sheriff Dane soon joined him.

"It's over here," Branson said. "I was checking on the watering system this morning, after noticing water running down the path. When

I got here, hoping to find what had busted, I found this instead." Hank stepped off the path and allowed the sheriff to pass. Dane walked between the trees and stopped.

When he came back, his face was grim.

"Okay, let's stay clear." The sheriff turned away, heading back to the site.

Hank spun when he heard the tread of shoes on the stony path above. He hurried to intercept the approaching woman.

"Dawn, sheriff says we're to stay away. I'm sure he's gonna need to talk to you in a minute here."

"Hank, what's going on?"

"Come on back a ways." Branson led Grandma Dawn gently by the elbow, walking with her a short distance before stopping.

"Hank, what is it? Why is the sheriff here?"

Heather and Aria came down the walkway leading from the house, and upon seeing the gardener and Grandma Dawn immersed in conversation below them, decided to veer away and walk on the opposite side of the conical trees. Quickly and carefully they stole from cypress to cypress, seeing to it that they remained undetected. In no time, they passed opposite Grandma Dawn and Branson on their way ever closer.

"Are you sure you want to look, Dawn?"

"Yes."

As the two walked down the path, the sheriff received them.

"Branson, let's have you wait here. The less disturbed the area, the better." Turning to Grandma Dawn, Dane asked, "Did he fill you in?"

"Yes."

"Let's have you take a look, then, Mrs. Thibble. Not too close, now." The sheriff guided her to a quick stop.

Grandma Dawn looked down and her mouth dropped in horror. She shook her head. "Oh, my word; oh, my word. Oh, my. The poor, poor soul."

Not far in front of her, completely buried except for his neck and head, was a boy. He was dead, and his eyes stared lifelessly before him.

Stuffed and protruding out of his mouth was the head of a green iguana and wrapped around his neck was a skinned cat. For a hat he wore the white fur and sweet face of the dead Teacup, the terrier's little head coming to rest atop the boy's forehead.

"Know him?" Dane asked Grandma Dawn.

"No," she said, her voice barely audible.

"Well, I've never seen him before," Dane said. "And Branson, here, has never seen him before. Someone around here must know who he is."

"I do," came the small voice from the other side of the tree.

Surprised eyes quickly found Heather.

"His name is Stilped. He's the quiet boy."

CHAPTER SEVEN

Life After Death

"Heather! Heather, look at me! *Look at me!*" Grandma Dawn said, her voice sharply snapping off like an electrified bolt. "Don't look down there. Look here. I want you looking at me."

"But that's Teacup, Molly's dog." The girl stood transfixed.

Grandma Dawn started to walk towards her grandchild. "Heather, I want you looking *here!*"

Heather ignored her.

"Heather!" Grandma Dawn tried to pass by the sheriff. Quickly, he stepped in front of her and clapped his hands loudly before the woman's face. She straightened up and stepped back. Heather looked over.

"Mrs. Thibble, I need you to stay right there." The sheriff half-turned to make sure Heather remained in place. "This is a murder scene, and I don't want anyone disturbing the site."

"But this is nothing a child should see."

Sheriff Dane turned, saying, "Heather, listen to me. I want you to carefully retrace each and every step, as exactly as possible, back to the path and wait for me there. I need you to do that now. I'll be having a word with you shortly. Mrs. Thibble, if you'd be so kind as to step back this way."

Looking past the sheriff, Grandma Dawn said, "Heather, I want to be able to see you when you reach the walkway above. Look for me. I want to see you."

Heather watched as Sheriff Dane escorted her grandmother with a gentle guiding hand placed at her lower back. Grandma Dawn walked distractedly, looking back over her shoulder, keeping a watch on Heather.

While escorting the woman, the sheriff unhooked the rectangular handheld radio that hung from his belt, its antenna tapering to a small black ball. Flexible, it wiggled slightly as the sheriff spoke, the radio's black glossy body pressed against the side of the sheriff's brown face, his darker beard-line evident.

"Millicent, radio Berle and Foley and have them join me immediately, will you? Bring the crime scene kit. And better wake Dawkins... That's right. Notify the coroner, too. What's that...? No, hold off. I'll talk to the paper myself. Do we still have the anthropologist here in town...?" Dane stopped walking, pointed Grandma Dawn firmly to the path, and furrowed his brow. "Oh, yeah? When did she leave...? Okay, let's get the vet out here then... Absolutely." The sheriff listened. "Good. Okay, contact Sal or Angelo and let's see if one of them can bring us two or three dogs... Right."

Heather returned her gaze to the dead boy. Quickly, Aria pushed to the fore, and the dazed Heather let go of possession. Seeing that the sheriff was occupied on the radio and with Grandma Dawn, Aria quickly surveyed the grounds, searching for the missing backpack. Unable to see it, she retreated, but not before whispering, "Heather, wake up!" to shake her.

Upon possession, Heather regained composure to a degree, and with one last look at Stilped, she started her retreat with the careful placement of her feet, hitting on her previous footfalls as much as possible in the flattened grass. Arriving at the cobblestone walk, she sat down, pulling up her knees to embrace her legs.

"Are you all right?" Aria looked down the hill to see the sheriff interviewing the gardener.

Grandma Dawn stood isolated farther below, where the woman sought out and found her granddaughter, her gaze lingering with concern.

"Stilped. I can't believe it," Heather said. "Aria, Mr. Simpletripp killed Stilped and was digging a hole for him last night."

"And by the look of the hole that was filled in next to him, he was probably digging one for us, too." Aria brought her hand up to touch the bill of her cap. "I'm glad we agreed to wear this. An extra layer of concealment."

Taking possession, Heather didn't speak. She picked up a rock and fired it sidearm at nothing in particular. She threw another. The second rock arced and bounced before disappearing into a bed of penstemon. As with the first, Heather didn't bother to follow its flight. From down the walk, her grandmother continued to observe the girl's actions while waiting to be questioned. Finally, Heather said, "Aria, Stilped was my friend. Mr. Simpletripp killed him."

"Well, we don't know that for certain—"

"I know for certain!" Heather's words were low but harsh. "And when Sheriff Dane talks to me, I'm going to tell him what Molly and I saw at the creek, how Mr. Simpletripp threw those guts in the water. And I'm going to tell the sheriff that Grandma Dawn saw Mr. Simpletripp digging holes all over the property. I might even tell him how Mr. Simpletripp hit us with a shovel."

Aria remained quiet for a moment, and then said, "Heather you may want to calm down a bit before—"

"I'm not calming down, Aria!" Heather's whisper sliced sharply. "Stilped was my friend! That creep killed him." Heather started to cry, but bitterly fought back her tears. "Stil was just a quiet boy," she said, wiping her teary beginnings roughly on her sleeve. "He was nice. He wouldn't have hurt a bug if it landed on his nose."

Aria waited. She could feel Heather's rage as it poured adrenaline throughout their system. Eventually she said, "Heather, I think you need to understand the implications of your emotional loss of control. If you go recklessly into the interview with your sheriff, you may reveal something in anger you could later regret. I'm not saying do or don't tell him about the Simpletripp encounters as of late, instead what I'm suggesting is that you have an idea of what you're going to say before you say it. And that implies knowing what you're not going to tell him."

Unable to find a rock to her liking, Heather pulled at the backend of a worm, stretching it out of its hole. She threw it. The worm didn't go far. It began to writhe and curl on the path, between the cobblestones.

"Heather, if your grandmother discovers that you've been sneaking out and were hit with a shovel and almost ended up like your poor unfortunate friend, Stilped, she'll curtail your activities—especially if she thinks there's a possibility that the killer may still be after you. Then, you can rest assured you won't be going down to the creek to see Molly during the day, let alone meeting in the treehouse at night. Furthermore, should Molly's father find out about your clandestine meetings, he would put a stop to everything. Everything. Not only now, but in the future, after the killer has been apprehended. So, you may just want to wait and see what happens before mentioning incidents involving Mr. Simpletripp and drawing attention to Molly and yourself."

"Aria, he killed Stilped!" Heather shot, her words still low, her moist eyes betraying her. "I liked him. And so did Molly. He was one of us."

Aria remained silent.

After awhile, feeling Heather's rush of emotion subsiding, Aria said, "Look, Heather, I truly don't care what you tell the sheriff or Grandma

Dawn. I care about you. Grandma Dawn will certainly tell Sheriff Dane about Simpletripp's digging on the grounds, and since he lives nearby, he'll definitely be considered suspect with his unusual behavior. You may not need to say a word about your own activities. That's why I say you should wait and see what happens before telling your sheriff about Simpletripp at the creek or about last night's episode. It will eventually give you more flexibility in your movements, even if not at first."

Heather considered Aria's words, pulling at another worm. This time she let it go beneath a bush. She thought about not being able to see Molly except at school, and the possibility rattled her. Then she reflected on how special it felt to be in the treehouse, alone with the mysterious night while the moon kept watch from above. Yes, she would certainly miss all that. Scratching up some loose soil, she covered the worm.

Heather thought about Stilped, about the grizzly sight so imprinted in her memory: of Molly's Teacup hanging over her lifeless friend's forehead, the trails of dog blood that had found their way over his brow and past his staring eyes, before dripping down his cheeks like wine-red tears. And the iguana head that looked as if it were a devil's tongue that had lived in Stilped's heart and crawled out of his throat. Then there was the collar of cat, its eyes like lifeless copper marbles in a cockeyed head. Heather joggled herself past the image. Instead, she focused on the shovel blow to her own head, and how she and Aria were fortunate not to have been buried next to Stilped. She shuddered.

"Aria," Heather said, waving briefly at her grandmother before looking in another direction, "I'm not sure what I'm going to tell Sheriff Dane. But we need to see if that backpack is still down there. If the sheriff finds it, then I won't have a choice. I'll *have* to tell him about last night. If I do, for sure he'll tell Grandma Dawn and Mrs. Pringle about the treehouse, and I definitely don't want that."

"All right, Heather. Let's see if we can make our way past the sheriff to be with Grandma Dawn, and then we can drift off farther down the path. I briefly scanned the area once but didn't see it, however I'd still like to look behind that tree where we were hit last night and took our fall. That's where we should find the backpack."

"On second thought, Aria, maybe we shouldn't."

"What—? Why?"

"The sheriff told us to wait for him here. Besides, I just thought of something: what do we do if we find the backpack? How are we going to get it up to the house without Sheriff Dane noticing?"

"Don't worry, we'll figure out something. You can leave that part to me. But the first step is to simply see if we can find it."

Heather shrugged. "Okay." The image of the quiet boy flashed through her head. "Poor Stilped! I still can't believe—"

"Heather, shake those thoughts loose. For now. I hate to sound callused, but you can grieve for your friend later. First we need to attend to your backpack."

With that, Aria rose. "Come now. We've work to do." She receded, and assuming possession, Heather started down the cobblestone walk, the flowers around her merrily displaying their colorful blooms like so many enchanted candies.

"Oh, Teacup," Mrs. Pringle said, stopping to place her hands on her hips, but only for a restful moment. Unsuccessful in tracking down the small terrier near the long pebbled drive that wound up from the street, she resumed her search, working her way north past the garage, storage sheds, and greenhouse, toward the backside of the Bristol House.

Molly, unable to find Teacup on the front slope of the property, eventually made her way around to the west side to search among the hedges and bedded flowers, amid the revealing retreat of the long morning shadows.

Sheriff Dane, continuing to ask questions of the gardener, had his back to the approaching Heather. As she neared, the sheriff addressed her over his shoulder, "I thought I asked you to wait for me up the path."

Heather pointed beyond him. "I want to be with my grandmother."

Grandma Dawn, who had been looking towards the creek with her arms folded in front of her, turned at Heather's words. Heather ran and hugged her, and the child felt her Grandmother's welcoming arms enfold her.

"Don't stray off this path. Understand?" Dane said.

Heather nodded, her head buried in her grandmother's jacket.

Turning back to Branson, the sheriff continued his inquiry before he finally concluded with the gardener. "Mrs. Thibble?"

Offering words of reassurance, Grandma Dawn disentangled herself from Heather. While Branson walked up the path towards the house, Dane started his questioning of Grandma Dawn, occasionally throwing a glance over the grandmother's shoulder to regard young Heather. Although preoccupied with his questioning, the sheriff watched as the red-hatted girl hovered briefly before nonchalantly easing down the hill. Curious, Dane gave her slack for the moment, keeping her under observation. Heather appeared to be looking for something, while talking to herself. Only when she showed signs of not finding what she sought did the sheriff reel her in.

"Heather! I'd like you to step back over here; I don't want to ask you a second time to stay put."

Heather wandered to the spot where the sheriff had indicated. There, she sat on a low stone curb, gazing down the hill and across the creek at the Simpletripp house. To Heather, the house seemed to float in the haze that the morning sun was burning off the creek.

What made someone want to commit such a horrible crime? Was the murderer Mr. Simpletripp?

Aria wasn't convinced, but Heather seemed certain. When the sheriff was ready to speak with her, Heather still wasn't sure what she was going to tell him.

Sheriff Dane's questioning of Grandma Dawn continued. Reaching her ears at a murmur, Heather barely heard his questions or her grandmother's responses. Yet, she could hear the gentle voice of the quiet Stilped on the playground, and still saw his face in flashes: on that day with Mrs. Peck when he had smiled at her, and just recently when Stilped walked to school with her and Molly. In his simple, easy way, he was their special friend. When her mind flickered to the image of Stilped that she had seen just this morning, Heather quietly called up Aria for a change of subject.

"So, where do you think the backpack is?" she asked. Heather waited. "Aria?"

"I'm here—just thinking. I'd say the obvious: that anyone who's been down this way since we were here last night could have taken it. What's in it, Heather?"

"Some books, a few magazines, papers from school, stuff like that."

"Things with your name on them."

"Yeah. Some of them, anyway. I know Molly's magazines have her name and address. Do you think someone will return my pack if they find it?"

"They might."

"Maybe Sheriff Dane has my backpack."

"He could. You'll probably find out when he questions you."

"I think if Mr. Branson had seen it this morning, he would have brought it up to the kitchen. Or he would have probably told Grandma Dawn he found it."

"Well, you better hope your sheriff or gardener has the backpack."

"Why?"

"Silly girl. If neither of them have it, then most likely the murderer does."

Searching among a circle of neatly trimmed juniper bushes, Molly's mother recognized the Bristol House gardener as he passed on his way towards the house. Although feeling somewhat foolish and guilty for prowling about the grounds without permission, Mrs. Pringle decided to inquire about Teacup. She headed in his direction.

Molly, around the corner on the far side of the house, carried on her search, becoming more and more dispirited with each empty eyeful. However, determined for her Teacup, she pushed on.

"Okay," Sheriff Dane said in preparation, looking down on Heather and her bright red baseball cap, the bill casting a diagonal shadow across her features. The man lowered himself so that he was face-to-face with the girl. "Heather, tell me about your quiet friend, Stilped, here."

Returning his gaze, the girl scrunched up her face to the morning sun. "What do you want to know?"

The sheriff's eyes roamed Heather's face. "Everything."

Two of Sheriff Dane's deputies arrived, coming up the northwest walk. With the shorter one carrying a large black and gray equipment bag, they strode purposefully towards Dane and Heather. Grandma Dawn stood nearby as the sheriff temporarily disengaged himself from the girl to consult and give orders to his men.

Foley, of medium height and build, rough-edged with thinning black hair and the makings of a second chin, started towards the house. Berle, older, shorter, and thickset, his mouth locked in a permanent scowl, began to cordon off the murder site with yellow tape. Arriving shortly after the two, Dawkins, tall, young, and muscular, his head full of blonde hair combed back, took to driving in stakes at intervals, his sunglasses bouncing down his nose between poundings and finger-pushes. His mouth worked nonstop on a wad of snapping gum, blowing the occasional bubble.

As the sheriff continued to quiz Heather, a perimeter was set up, and within, colored fishing line was strung between stakes to form a grid.

"So, where were you last night, Heather?" Sheriff Dane asked.

"Here."

Like a constricting rope, the sheriff's voice tightened: "Here? Right here?"

"I live here," Heather said.

"So, you were in the house?"

"My room is up there." Heather pointed at her bedroom window.

"You were in your room?"

"Last night?"

His lips taut, the sheriff nodded sternly.

"Yeah, I was in my room last night, Sheriff Dane."

"All night?"

Heather shook her head, causing it to hurt, but she managed not to show it.

"You *weren't* in your room all night?"

"No. When I ate dinner with my grandmother—that's her there," and when Heather pointed, Sheriff Dane drew a short, impatient breath, "we were in the dining room. And then when I went to the bathroom, I wasn't in my room. I went twice—no, three times—wait. Was it three? I think it was three. The last time to clean up and brush my teeth."

The sheriff's eyelids lowered, his eyes peering coldly through narrow slits. Heather noticed a shift in his shine from a composed light yellow to a menacing shade of blue and back again.

"And you didn't leave your room any other time for any reason?"

"I did." Heather's attention wandered to the two deputies working the gridlines for clues.

The sheriff waited. When Heather wasn't forthcoming, Dane said, "For?"

"Oh." Heather smiled sheepishly. "To go up to the library to see if I could find some books for Molly."

"Did you find them?"

"Yes."

"And you took them back to your room?"

Heather nodded.

"After you were back in your room, then what?"

"I read until bedtime. Grandma Dawn," Heather pointed, and the sheriff scowled, "came in and kissed me goodnight. I read for awhile, before I turned off the light."

"What I need to know, Heather, is whether you remember seeing or hearing anything unusual last night."

"I did."

"And?"

Heather didn't answer right away.

Dane's focused intensity seemed to make him grow. "Heather, what did you see?"

Heather hesitated.

"Heather?"

"Well, there was the ghost on the front stairs, Sheriff Dane."

Annoyed, the sheriff's eyes flicked away, but only for an instant.

Following Branson towards the house, Mrs. Pringle's attention was diverted to the unusual activity in the northwest corner of the grounds: yellow tape, men searching through a gridded area, and the sheriff talking to Heather with Dawn Thibble standing close by. Gripped with sudden anxiety, she turned from her pursuit of the gardener. As she approached the proceedings, her pace increased until she was half-running towards the dignified woman. Grandma Dawn hurried to meet her.

"Dawn, what the hell is going on here? And where's Molly?"

"Is there anything else you want to tell me, Heather?" Sheriff Dane asked. When the girl shook her head, he said, "It looked like you were searching for something down the hill," and here Dane pointed with a lift of his chin. "What was it?"

"Well," Heather hesitated, "I was just looking. You know." Heather wanted to squirm, but Aria held her firm. "I mean whoever did this, he might have dropped something or forgotten something or something. I was just curious to see if I could see it."

"So, you were going to find it for me, were you?"

"Maybe…"

"Uh-huh."

Heather took in Dane's shine once again, now a seemingly benign and almost friendly yellow, but the interspersion of a pulsing, cunning green made her uneasy. An image came to mind of white-gloved hands probing in darkness.

Heather returned Dane's stare through his deep orange-colored lenses. "Will you find him?"

"Him?" the sheriff asked.

"The man who killed Stil."

"What makes you think it was a man?"

Heather was about to say that men dig, men are strong like Hank Branson, and that normally girls don't dig, but then she thought of Grandma Dawn in the garden, and rather than bring suspicion to either, she held her tongue. Instead, Heather shrugged. The sheriff's intense gaze continued to work her face over, the girl never looking away. Finally, he stood up.

"Okay, I'm going to give you my card." Sheriff Dane reached inside his pocket. "Heather, if you happen to remember something—anything—I want you to give me a call. I know that sometimes our ability to remember can play games with us—it fools us—and our memory puts things on the shelf for a while. This is the mind helping us to get through a difficult time. And then later, we find ourselves remembering incidents that have happened to us, obvious things, things that can be important to a murder investigation, to finding who killed your friend, Stilped. So, here's my card. Keep it handy. And call me right away if you remember something you haven't told me. Okay?"

Heather nodded. She noted the sheriff's large brown hand, the long chapped fingers that squeezed the card when presenting it, the pink nails. Heather plucked it loose and looked it over, holding it in her light, smooth-skinned hand. After briefly regarding the printing alongside the insignia of a badge, the girl thought to put the card away for safekeeping. Instinctively, she reached down to grab hold of her backpack, thinking for a moment she had set it near her feet. Grasping at air, Heather looked at her shoe tops.

"Lose something?" the sheriff asked.

Mrs. Pringle was stunned. "I can't believe it," barely escaped her lips.

"I'm sorry, Lana," Grandma Dawn said, "I'm sorry for Molly and Teacup."

But Molly's mother was no longer listening. She was impatiently looking up the hill, searching for her daughter.

Grandma Dawn continued: "And I'm so *so* sorry for the girls' friend, Stilped, and his family. I understand he's—he was—fairly new here in town, but I—"

"I'm sorry, Dawn," Mrs. Pringle said, "But I've just got to find Molly. Excuse me, will you, please."

Mrs. Pringle detached from her neighbor and at a fast clip started up the steep walk.

"Whoa. Hey, there." Sheriff Dane's deep voice cut the morning air as he called out from near the cordoned area, "Mrs. Pringle is it?"

Mrs. Pringle whirled. "Me?"

"You. I'd like to ask you a few questions, if I could."

"But Sheriff, my daughter is somewhere on the grounds searching for her dog. What if the murderer is still nearby? I've got to find her. And I absolutely don't want her coming down here and seeing that ugly scene with the boy—"

"I've got one of my deputies searching and securing the grounds right now. He'll find your daughter—"

The sheriff's radio crackled to life. "Sheriff?"

The sheriff held up a finger to Mrs. Pringle, annoyance adding to her already impatient countenance. He took up his radio with the other hand. "Dane." The sheriff listened briefly, then said, "Bring her to me." He looked up and waved Mrs. Pringle to come join him. And she did, her back to the hill and the house, taking a last hopeful glance over her shoulder.

Having finished being questioned by the sheriff, Heather had hurried to her grandmother. When she reached her, she pushed snugly into the woman's comforting shape. After briefly inspecting her granddaughter for signs of shock or distress, Grandma Dawn's arm encircled the girl's shoulders.

Heather's grandmother placed a hand on Mrs. Pringle's upper arm as she passed, saying, "Lana, please stop by the kitchen after you've spoken with Sheriff Dane."

The word weighted, Mrs. Pringle said, "Okay," and continued towards the sheriff, who had completed his conversation on the radio. She asked, "What is it you need, Sheriff?"

The sheriff returned the radio to his belt. "Right now? A twisted murderer. Know one?"

"Heather! What's going on?" Breathless, it was Molly, deserting Deputy Foley's side as she broke into a run.

Caught off guard, he threw out a grasping hand. Molly eluded it and raced down the path. Foley, following a discreet signal from Dane, let her go.

Heather thought, Not good, not good!, quickly looking from Molly to Sheriff Dane and Mrs. Pringle—the couple engrossed in conversation—and then to the deputies busily engaged within the gruesome crime scene perimeter. The girl dashed up to meet her distraught companion, waving her hands before her. "Wait! Wait there!"

Molly tripped and stumbled, then righted herself before staggering to an awkward halt in front of her friend. Panting, she continued at a verbal gallop: "Heather, why did the deputy make me follow him? And what's the sheriff doing here—and why all his men? And what's with that yellow tape? Why is Sheriff Dane talking to Mom? Has something bad happened? Has it? *Well, has it?*"

Protective of the sensitive girl, Heather wasn't sure where to start and what to share.

"Molly," Grandma Dawn's voice broke in from behind Heather, as she rushed up to the two, "Come with us to the kitchen. You're mother will be joining us there shortly." Here, Dawn Thibble took a deep breath, as she tried to speak calmly. "She'll fill you in; in the meantime, you can keep us company. The sheriff may need to speak with you later."

"Why me?" Molly looked over at the sheriff. He was regarding her with a stony frown as he listened to Mrs. Pringle. "What's happened?"

"It's a long story," Grandma Dawn said, "And I think your mother can best explain it."

Molly looked at Heather. "It's about Teacup, isn't it?"

Heather's mouth opened but no words came out. Helplessly, she turned to her grandmother.

Gripped by her worst fear, Molly shouted past Heather. "Mom?"

Mrs. Pringle turned and looked up.

"Oh, no," played across her lips from a distance. She broke away from the sheriff and started to run up the pathway.

"Molly, don't go down there," Heather said. She tried to grab her friend's arm. "Molly, don't—"

The girl wrenched her arm free and took off, sprinting down the cobblestone path.

"Mom, what's happened? What's happened to Teacup?" Sensing doom, Molly's words spilled forth with her tears. "Is she dead? She's not dead, is she? *She's not dead!*"

Mrs. Pringle raced to intercept her. "Molly wait. Wait there, honey."

Sheriff Dane, Heather, and Grandma Dawn stood still as statues, while mother and daughter ran to each other. The three looked on while Mrs. Pringle tried to embrace her daughter, and watched as, frantic for answers, Molly pulled away. And they continued to look on while Mrs. Pringle explained to Molly that, sadly, her Teacup was gone. Then, after repeatedly shaking her head in denial, insisting that her mother was wrong, that she had to be, that Teacup was probably at home waiting for her this very minute, that it wasn't true, wasn't true, was *not true*, still rooted in place, everyone watched Molly crumble.

The sheriff indeed wanted to speak with Molly, but not that morning. After listening to the remainder of Lana Pringle's story, as she held her sobbing daughter, he put off the younger Pringle's interview. Instead, he and his men spent most of the day focused on the Bristol House grounds, investigating the crime scene, extracting what pieces of information they could from it, and trying to complete a coherent picture from an elusive puzzle. The coroner and the local veterinarian joined them. Carefully, they dug out the body of the dead Stilped, and afterwards excavated the hole nearby that the killer had presumably filled in. To their astonishment they found nothing. This the sheriff pondered. He pondered even more when Deputy Foley came upon the small puddle of Heather and Aria's blood in the vicinity of a nearby cypress tree. With the help of one of the many bloodhounds belonging to the Bartoli family, the sheriff followed the track and drippings across the grounds to the child-sized drop point at the hedge, and mulled over the disappearance of blood from that point on. Led by the long-eared droopy-faced dog, however, he continued his pursuit and traced the scent through the grounds to the kitchen door of the Bristol House. There the scent became confused, intermingled with the many that had come and gone before and since.

The boot prints were photographed alongside a yellow-tongued tape measure, and some impressions were taken in plaster. At one point, Dane, with lips pursed and squatting over a boot's indentation, ran a finger lightly over the rim of the depression. He looked up in the direction of the Bristol House, now soaking in the afternoon light.

The veterinarian supplied information on the animals that had decorated Stilped's head and neck, claiming that they were most probably pets, a fact that was in keeping with Mrs. Pringle's story. The coroner, though not a doctor, declared the obvious in a certificate claiming that Stilped was unmistakably dead. The boy had been initially stabbed and gutted elsewhere.

Another of the Bartoli bloodhounds brought to the Bristol House grounds traced the scent of the killer to the creek, only to lose it at the water's edge. Though the deputies utilized the dog's keen sense of smell for some distance along both banks of the wide creek, they were unable to rediscover the scent. They did, however, take more photographs and casts of similar imprints in the soft shoreline mud to compare with those previously taken near the body of the boy.

Of course, Heather didn't go to school that day. And neither did Molly. After breaking the news about the death of Stilped, Mrs. Pringle allowed Molly to spend time with her best friend. Yet, rather than run off and relish their time alone, the girls preferred sitting close to one another at the kitchen table, in the presence of the two adults. They didn't talk.

Periodically, Molly would begin to tremble and quietly weep. Initially, when Heather reached out to her, Molly shook her away—face buried in her hands, she refused to be consoled. In time, Heather gently took hold of Molly's wrist, pulling it free of her downturned face. The aching girl grudgingly allowed Heather to encompass her captive hand in both of hers, Molly's other falling away to rest limply on the tabletop. Weakly, she turned to Heather. The two looked at one another, neither speaking, tears silently rolling down Molly's face. When Molly unexpectedly gasped and noisily broke down, her friend reached out to hug her. And after Molly hesitantly returned the hug, that's when Heather cried too.

The two women, standing as they talked in hushed tones at the counter, let their conversation lapse while observing the girls. Grandma Dawn continued to look on, but Mrs. Pringle turned away and walked to the sink to wash out her empty teacup. Rather than set it in the rack, she took a long time to towel it dry, head bent with her back to the room, shoulders moving in conjunction with her unseen hands.

The late morning and early afternoon passed slowly for the four, the thought of food not at all comforting. Most of the time, Molly had her head resting glumly on the table, cradled in the crossing of her forearms. Heather felt that she, herself, should be doing something, but couldn't think of anything in particular that she wanted to do. And even if she had thought of something, she wasn't going to leave Molly to do it. In front of the girls, two neglected glasses of cool lemonade eventually warmed to room temperature.

Sheriff Dane stopped in for a short interview with a despondent Molly in the living room before the Pringles departed for home. He saw and heard from the girl what he had expected, including her wet words, sniffles, and tears.

By the time Molly's interview concluded, the day was worn and tired. Farewells were said between neighbors and friends, Grandma Dawn and Mrs. Pringle expressing a desire to talk *real* soon, with Heather and Molly hugging each other at the kitchen door. Mrs. Pringle took her turn to squeeze Heather in a hug, too, her cap smashing into the woman's chest, as Heather winced with pain. Watching from the hallway, the sheriff stepped forward and leaned against the kitchen doorjamb, his arms folded across his chest. He turned his gaze to the floor, a study in patience and contemplation.

When the dutch door closed on the Pringles, and Heather had returned to the table, Grandma Dawn asked, "Sheriff Dane, is there anything else I can do for you? Surely, you've had a long day. Would you care for something to eat? A cup of coffee or tea?"

"No, thanks, Mrs. Thibble. Though I might just sneak a smoke in the car on the way home. That'll be our secret, though, just in case you see the wife downtown. But right now I'd like to talk to Heather once more, if you don't mind. Alone."

Heather was taken by surprise, and she looked first at the sheriff and then Grandma Dawn.

"Heather?" Grandma Dawn said.

The girl slid out of her chair. "The living room?"

The sheriff nodded and started down the hallway. Heather obediently followed.

CHAPTER EIGHT

Under a Red Cap,
Within a Small Town

Heather sat across from the sheriff. She waited. The sheriff continued to scrutinize her.

"I'm sorry about your friend, Stilped," Dane started.

Heather shrugged and nodded, staring at the floor in front of her.

"You liked him a lot, didn't you?"

Heather nodded again.

"Did you go outside to meet him last night?"

Now contemplating her shoes, Heather was startled by the question. After missing a beat, she continued to lightly tap her sneakers together.

"Did you?"

Heather shook her head. She bit her lip, pinning it closed. Her heart pounded.

"That's a nice baseball cap," Sheriff Dane said. "I like the color red."

"Thank you," Heather mumbled. The living room walls seemed to be moving closer, and she began to feel hot.

"May I see it?"

"What?"

"Your cap. I think I'd like to buy one just like it for my daughter." Sheriff Dane put out his large hand, pink palm upward. "If you don't mind, just a quick look."

Heather reluctantly reached up to grab the cap's bill, flinching slightly when she peeled it off her head. She placed the hat in the sheriff's expectant hand, on loose fingers, where it swayed gently, a pendulum counting down time. When she looked at his face, the sheriff's eyes weren't on the cap; they were examining her hair.

"Still hurt?" Dane asked.

"What?"

"Your head."

"I'm sorry, Sheriff Dane, but I don't understand—"

"Stop it, Heather. I know."

She began a protest, but then shut down. Heather saw the sheriff's aura change to an aggressive red, though still muted in grays.

"What were you doing down there on the grounds last night?" the sheriff asked.

Heather's eyes met Sheriff Dane's. She looked at his smoky blue irises, his lashes, and roamed along his ample brow line, before she found his eyes once again. She said, "I was coming back from the treehouse."

"What time?"

"I fell asleep. I think it was about two."

"In the morning."

Though it wasn't a question, Heather responded with a, "Yes." The word was softly spoken, a capitulation.

The sheriff leaned forward, his brown fingers pinning the red cap stationary.

"Who hit you in the head?"

Heather shifted moodily. Again she shrugged, but remained quiet. Intrusive tears welled up, as her frayed emotions surged to the surface, battering her with a barrage of rapid-fire thoughts. Poor Stilped. Heather felt so sad for her friend, whom she couldn't rescue from the man who killed him so horribly. She thought of Molly, so hurt because Heather couldn't save the little dog she loved from dying. And then she thought of Grandma Dawn, and how her grandmother might have felt if Heather had been found dead alongside Stilped.

And now, sitting in front of Sheriff Dane, Heather felt trapped, and from this point forward the meetings with Molly that she kept so vitally secret would come crashing into the open. Earlier, Heather had thought it would be best to tell all, to finger Mr. Simpletripp, but now doubts swirled about her. She felt that she had no choice but to betray Molly, her only remaining Noble friend, and tell the sheriff about the treehouse and how she, Heather, had sneaked out to meet her. Heather was sure that he would tell Grandma Dawn and Mrs. Pringle, and then any chance she had of seeing Molly would end. And afterwards, no one would like her, not even Mrs. Pringle; and Grandma Dawn would be so disappointed that she would never trust her again. Devastation flooded her. Still, Heather fought back tears, concentrating once again on her tapping shoes.

While considering the laces, a crisscross of white on red, Heather felt aware of Sheriff Dane's stare as he probed her features. She felt exposed without her cap, imagining his eyes as they crawled up her temples, burrowed through her hair, and then focused on her encrusted, tell-all wound. Again Heather shifted, but still felt the eyes. They examined her dishonest mouth, waited on her sealed lips, and then took note of her fingers that wrestled openly in her lap. The girl squeezed them still. She hoped Aria stayed away with the sheriff so close at hand.

"Heather?"

Expectation continued to hang on the air. Aware of its demand, Heather looked toward the hallway, where, if she divulged, Grandma Dawn might unexpectedly walk in and overhear all. Yet, if nothing were held in confidence between her and Sheriff Dane, what would it matter?

Following her eyes, Dane took a deep breath and said, "Come on, Heather. It's been a long day." The sheriff rose. "Let's go out and sit on the porch, where we can get some fresh air." He looked down on the girl, and then held out the red baseball cap. He had never given it a second look. "Then you're going to tell me exactly what you know. And I mean all of it."

In a cellar, under a lone bulb, a man leaned over an old porcelain sink. Carefully, as if bathing a newborn, he washed dried mud off the square-toed boots, residue from a murder scene. From around the shaft of one boot, he had removed the locket and chain, but kept the token near him.

Not too much water.

He didn't dare. He didn't want to saturate the leather, the boots rarely worn, almost like new. The man checked his watch. Having been at the delicate task for some time, beginning with the undersides of the boots, he was now gingerly working the piece of cloth around the square-toes.

"Soon, you'll be as shiny as your sole." He ceased all movement. "Shiny as your sole," he repeated, laughing softly, the rag meticulously resuming its wipe. Then quietly, "Shiny as your soul."

Outside and seated on the porch, Sheriff Dane again found himself inspecting the young girl and again Heather could feel the prying steel of his astute blue eyes. Her cap was now back in place on her head, and

Heather returned Dane's gaze. His shine was still aggressively red, perhaps now even more so.

Heather shifted her attention. She looked over the stained glass designs on the closed front door—but only for a moment. Wandering, her vision slid over the bronze mermaid, down to the ornate door handle, and then to the mailbox, before skimming back up to find a bird's nest, long since empty, in the rafters above. Her restless gaze subsequently ventured past the sheriff's head and the porch railing to peruse the grounds, now spoiled somehow, dirtied by what had transpired in the night.

"How could someone do that here?" Heather found herself saying aloud.

Dane was amused. "You find it insulting, do you, that someone defiled your yard?"

Heather nodded, her anger rising. "Did Grandma Dawn tell you about Mr. Simpletripp, Sheriff Dane?"

"Heather, why don't *you* tell me about Mr. Simpletripp?"

And so she did. Dane listened intently as Heather disclosed all. She told him about Simpletripp at the creek and how Grandma Dawn saw him digging on the property. The sheriff heard about the previous night in the treehouse, how when Heather was coming home she saw a light and heard digging, how she was smacked in the head by what she thought was a shovel, afterwards how she managed to make her way home, about the lost backpack, and finally how Heather and Molly regularly snuck out to meet and why. Of course, she omitted any mention of Aria.

"You pushed down your teacher?" Dane asked.

Heather held her breath before asking, "You're not going to arrest me, are you?"

The sheriff shook his head.

Heather sighed. "Mrs. Peck was picking on Stilped, Sheriff Dane. She's a mean old lady. And she kept poking me. It really hurt. I didn't *mean* for her to fall—I just grabbed her finger—besides, someone had to help Stil."

The sheriff found himself smiling. "Go on."

"Well, I guess I got Mrs. Peck to think she fainted. Mr. Bennington, our principal, thinks so, too, because, well, that's what Mrs. Peck told him." Then after a moment's insight, Heather rushed, "You won't tell him I pushed her, will you? Or Grandma Dawn?"

The smile left the sheriff's lips. "No, I won't. But no more pushing down old ladies, okay, no matter how mean they are. They could end up busting a hip. And then I'll *have* to arrest you." The sheriff laughed, and

Heather saw his wonderfully generous grin. She loved its shape.

Heather appraised the sheriff in a new light: she found herself starting to like him.

"Sheriff Dane, are you going to tell Grandma Dawn about the treehouse?"

The sheriff thought. "No. Not unless I have to. But you have to make me a promise, Heather. And this is very important, because if you break this promise, you might just be the next victim whose ugly murder I'm investigating."

"I know what you're going to say. You don't want me sneaking out and going to the treehouse."

"Right. Molly either. Do you understand? Not until we catch this murderer. That could very easily have been you down there, planted next to Stilped."

Heather drew quiet. She called up the harsh vision and quickly pushed it from her mind, but not before a shiver passed through her. "I know. I've thought about that." Heather's gaze returned to the empty nest. "Are you going to arrest Mr. Simpletripp?"

"If he proves to be the killer."

"But I told you about all that stuff we saw. He's got to be the killer."

"You leave the investigation to me, okay? Sometimes things are different than they seem. I'll deal with Simpletripp. And everyone else. When the guilty party is found, I'll make an arrest. It's that simple."

"So you won't tell Grandma Dawn or Mrs. Pringle our secret?"

"Not if you stick to your promise."

"I will, Sheriff Dane. And I know Molly will too."

"Okay, then, we have a deal." Dane didn't tell Heather that both Grandma Dawn and Mrs. Pringle already knew the children had been sneaking out. "So, Heather, if I tell you something, will *you* promise not to tell?"

Surprised, Heather grinned, almost giddy with relief. "What?"

"Now this is our secret, okay? You can't ever tell a soul."

"I won't. I promise."

"Okay, Heather. Suppose I tell you that Mrs. Peck was my teacher in the fifth grade."

"Really?"

"Yeah. And she was mean back then, too."

"Did you ever push her down?"

Later that day and into the night, Sheriff Dane and his deputies interviewed the Bristol House neighbors. None in the neighborhood were overjoyed when fingerprints and buccal swabs were selectively taken for evidence, and before daylight gave way to night, farmer Overall Whittingham's crop-dusting plane could be heard buzzing overhead, used to obtain aerial photographs of the crime scene and its vicinity. Twenty-four hours later, in a follow-up, the Sheriffs Department interviewed everyone again, including Lana and Molly Pringle, Dawn Thibble, and Heather Nighborne.

Sheriff Dane found that Mr. Simpletripp had an alibi, claiming he was down on the town square in his little gallery, *The Clay Pigeon*, during the day and home all that evening and night. Mrs. Simpletripp—Vera, to the few in town that knew her beyond acquaintance—a nervous, bespectacled, squat and graying blonde with a face of downy white hairs—corroborated his story. Vera Simpletripp, who had married Simpletripp following the untimely death of his first wife, maintained that her husband had been in her presence and had never left it.

Word of the murder traveled fast in the little town of Noble, though where the spread of the grisly news had originated no one could say for certain. None of the neighbors interviewed by Dane and his men saw anything, except for Ms. Gardner, who lived on the other side of Afterglow Drive, across the road from the Simpletripps. She asserted to the deputy during his inquiry ("Oh, Deputy Dawkins, such a handsome young man! However, your mother should have taught you *not* to chew with your mouth open. It's unattractive. Is it gum? It is. And such a *large* piece, too…") that when she was walking her five dogs, all little yapping butterfly-eared Papillons, late that evening, she thought she saw a young boy Heather and Molly's age down by the creek. He seemed to be *dilly-dallying*, she said, as if he were waiting for someone. She alleged that when one of the dogs spotted the boy—she thought it was the littlest one, Magritte—he's very attentive, you know—between the railings of the bridge, that each and every one of the dogs created quite a stir, climbing all *over* each another in what she could only describe as a barking frenzy. She thought that with all the noise they had probably awakened the comatose down at the hospital on Alder Road. Nevertheless, that's when the boy quickly ran for the shadows near the bridge or into the oaks. It was hard to tell. That was between eight and nine, though she couldn't be sure of the time. And since she was up on the bridge and the glow from the streetlights were so horribly poor when cast below, it was hard to say for certain just *who* that young man might have been. However, the more she thought about it, the more she felt that, most assuredly, he was the boy who met his horrific demise later that evening at the hands of a very sick, sick psychopathic killer indeed.

She also told Dawkins, on his follow-up with her, that Sheriff Dane (she knew his father and grandfather. Had she mentioned this before? All good people, they were. They used to cut her husband's hair, God rest his soul—and *all* their souls, for that matter) and his deputies should concentrate their efforts on her neighbor, Mr. Simpletripp. And didn't he, Deputy Dawkins, think that accountants that turn into artists have quite a bit of pent-up emotion locked away, festering for so many *many* years in what she could only describe as a backlog? And once those emotions were released—you know, nasty thoughts and all from having had to fill out *all* those disgustingly boring and regimented forms, form after form, year after year—well, wouldn't those emotions be hard to recapture once they got loose and found freedom, so to speak? And anyone who creates *that* kind of revoltingly kitschy art, you know, clay figurines of famous people with the big eyes and all, well, it only proves her point. They don't even look like the people they're supposed to—why, they all look like *him!* Doesn't that constitute *fraud?* It should. Why, he should be investigated, and even if he didn't commit the murder, he should still be locked away, for heaven's sake—and for the sake of *all* good art everywhere.

Deputy Dawkins took notes on his little pad in his clumsy hand, kindly bobbing his head and smiling, and when the interview had concluded, he thanked Ms. Gardner for her information and suggestions. He would certainly pass it all along to Sheriff Dane. And yes, he wouldn't forget to mention that she thought his father and grandfather were both good men and that, yes, yes, he would try not to snap his gum.

On the day of the macabre discovery of the dead Stilped, in the early afternoon, the schools in Noble began to empty long before their final bell, the children being released to concerned parents, and all social and sporting events were called off for the week, if not longer. School was canceled the following day.

Though few in town seemed to know, or know of, Stilped Roarhowser, they knew his widowed aunt, a longtime resident with whom he stayed. In a fine display of Noble convention, the town showered her with compassion and support in the form of visits that brought her cakes, pies, and cookies—along with the occasional self-help book from

The Dream & Fable Book Shoppe on the square.

The following day, Noble's only newspaper, the Daily Compass, ran a cover story on Stilped's death under the massive headlines: MURDER STRIKES NOBLE. It told vaguely about the boy's dead body on the Bristol House grounds, how the gardener had discovered him, and that the Sheriffs Department was working around the clock to bring his murderer to justice. There were quotes from Sheriff Dane, the coroner, and some of the neighbors, with Grandma Dawn and Mrs. Pringle, among others, declining to be interviewed. While no mention was made of the murder site's gruesome details, word leaked out nonetheless in a whisper among the Noble residents, with the sordid details eventually finding their way to nearby Willards Lamp. Fear seized the small communities, whereby few went out alone at night, small groups of armed men roamed the streets, vagrants found shelter, and all wanderers wisely left town.

Also featured on the front page of the Daily Compass that day was an accompanying article titled *The Roarhowser Misfortunes*. It was a story about the life of Stilped Roarhowser, aged thirteen, and how his father, Weston Stilped Roarhowser III, aged forty-four, had been a renowned history professor at a small college in the Pacific Northwest. His wife, Ellen Avondale-Roarhowser, aged forty-two, an accomplished vocalist in her own right, taught voice classes in the Performing Arts Department at that same college. Along with a class picture of Stilped taken the previous year, the article described in detail the once happy family of three, stating that the father and mother had traveled the world extensively, and that they were avid adventurers and explorers. They were also amateur archeologists, who first became acquainted while participating in an excavation in eastern Africa. The pair was married eight months later.

Tragically, the article described Stilped's parents as having met an untimely end when the cave they were exploring in Central America collapsed during an earthquake, sealing in the two Roarhowsers. Though Stilped's mother was able to dig her way out while hurt and initiate a rescue effort for her husband, she later died in hospital from her injuries. Stilped's father was lost and presumed dead when more of the tunnel gave way in a series of subsequent aftershocks.

The article went on to relate how Stilped, after being passed around among family members, eventually came to Noble to live with his only aunt, Muriel Stendant, sister to Stilped's mother. From there, Mrs. Stendant described Stilped's fascination with stamps, coins, and comic books, and how he had a small collection of each. She also described what a wonderful boy he was, although shy and given to few words, and how he maintained a tiny ant farm behind glass on his bedroom shelf. The article ended with the dates and times of his funeral and services.

Molly read the article and cried. Heather read it and became incensed.

CHAPTER NINE

In Search of Peace and Sleep

Heather lay in the darkness, fitful beneath the covers. Again, she rolled onto her back, staring into the emptiness that loomed above, enshrouding the ceiling. Her pillows felt hard and lumpy, and she readjusted the placement of her head. Before long, however, Heather found herself turning once more, this time onto her side. Keeping her mind active, she began to examine her bedroom, sifting the shadows, discerning the shapes. Heather didn't want to fall asleep, didn't want to dream with the possibility of Stilped's desecrated head appearing before her as it had so many times since she happened upon his murder scene.

Instead, the girl forced herself to envision the Stilped that she had observed earlier in the week at his viewing. When Grandma Dawn had suggested it would be a good idea for Heather to attend the wake and see her friend one last time, she was initially reluctant to do so. Yet, Heather was glad she had finally agreed, witnessing firsthand Stilped's face, calm and undefiled, in the open casket.

Recalling the funeral—the line of cars following the hearse to the gravesite, the gathering of mourners, the recitation of prayers, the uncomplicated truths spoken by the bereaved aunt, the generic overview of an unfamiliar Stilped by the town priest, the lowering of the unadorned casket into the earth, and the sprinkling of petals over it—the flashback of these incidents that reeled forth brought tears to Heather's eyes, causing the stains of night to run together. She didn't bother wiping the wetness aside, the thin streams seeping out and finding their way across her face to be absorbed into her pillow's downy thickness.

On that crisp autumn morning, as mourners stood by, Heather remembered walking up to Stilped's grave. Looking into the open mouth that would soon devour her lifeless friend, Heather cast upon the coffin the most beautiful rose she could find that morning in the Bristol House gardens. The girl believed it was not only from her and Grandma Dawn, but also a gift from the Bristol House itself. Somehow, Heather felt the Bristol House would have wanted her to do as she had, although she couldn't exactly explain why. Aria had suggested that perhaps the blood-red rose signified giving up the promise of a life in payment for that of Stilped's, the Bristol House offering in sacrifice one of its own. In response, Heather just shrugged and intoned that she didn't know.

Heather had forced herself to look up from the sunken coffin and the rose, turning instead to Stilped's aunt, Mrs. Stendant, and observing her glistening cheeks beneath the short black veil that hung before her face. Too, Heather noticed her desperately bleak aura. After bestowing the rose and withdrawing, Heather glanced at the somberly clad figure of Grandma Dawn. The girl remembered how the dignified, grave-faced woman discreetly nodded her head in approval, and how, when returning to stand in front of her grandmother, she placed her hands on Heather's shoulders during the culmination of the services.

When Jim Forrester, who owned and worked at one of the town's three cemeteries, began shoveling earth to fill the hole, burying Stilped and his life in Noble forever, Heather and Grandma Dawn turned away and started for the car. In front of her, Heather watched the beautifully dressed Molly, head down as she walked, one parent on either side.

Sadness all around, Heather focused on her alternating shoes in flashes of subdued red, clicking and scraping on the cement below the hem of her dress, here and gone, here and gone, and then felt Grandma Dawn's arm as it wound over her shoulders. That's when Heather leaned against her grandmother and again found comfort in the welcome softness of her velvety folds. Burdensome clouds in the sunless sky weighed heavy on her mind, so the girl shut her eyes and only occasionally opened them as she walked, letting her grandmother's movements guide her. Now pulling the covers over her head and shutting out the darkness of the real world, Heather recalled how the sun refused to show itself all that day and the next.

But try as she might, Heather's visions would not be turned away and followed her under the coverlet. Rather than think about the luncheon that followed the burial, and how she saw a stricken Molly only briefly when leaving, Heather threw aside her covers and stepped out into the cool darkness.

After an awkward shuffle, Heather's bare feet found her slippers, and slid comfortably into the snug lining of their furriness. Quietly, she walked across the floor and through the wide archway into the turreted alcove. Through the open drapes, Heather saw that the sky was starless, overcast. Resting her knees on the chair before the tall center window, the girl leaned her weight forward onto the upholstered upright and looked out over the grounds below. She saw little in the night, though Heather waited and watched to see if anything would draw her attention.

On the day of Stilped's death, Hank Branson told Grandma Dawn it might be a good idea if he slept on a small cot in the Bristol House kitchen for a while, in case the murderer returned. Heather's grandmother gratefully agreed. Though she believed that in all likelihood the killer would not come back, she felt it would make her and Heather feel safer and sleep easier when the Bristol House began its nightly round of creaky complaints and groaning objections. Thereafter, every evening before nightfall, the Bristol House gardener arrived in his green pickup truck to drag out the cot and take up his post in uneasy repose. Always within reach, his rifle gleamed the length of its barrel, narrow highlights of nighttime blue, reflections of the three arched windows overhead.

And for the first time ever, Grandma Dawn began locking the Bristol House doors after sundown.

Try as she might, Molly couldn't get used to sleeping in the guestroom. She simply didn't like it: it was too close, too stuffy, too *something*, and in general, just too *everything*.

On the night following Stilped's murder, her mother asked her if she wouldn't mind sleeping upstairs in the room that had once been her bedroom as a younger child. Mrs. Pringle promised it would only be for a while, and Molly had agreed, not wishing to sleep downstairs alone.

And now she lay awake for yet another night, sleep refusing to settle in and bring her rest—and much needed escape. Sometimes she would drift off only to wake and wonder, for a dreamy hopeful moment, if what she feared hadn't actually happened. Then when that crushing wave of reality would again wash over her, tumbling and submerging her in such overwhelming sorrow, she realized that Stilped and Teacup were truly dead after all, and horribly so. She had struggled with this every night since the deaths of her friend and pet, and it continued to wear her down. It didn't help that the security she had once felt within the safe and stable confines of her family circle was now in question, tenuously fragile and apt to collapse.

Molly recalled while at dinner the evening following the murder, her mother had informed her father that from now on she was going to pick up Molly and Heather every day after school. This she had arranged with Dawn Thibble.

A revelation to her, Molly had looked up, surprised and hopeful. Yet, the next moment, her optimism was quashed.

"Why should you pick up Molly *and* Heather?" Molly remembered her father saying. "Can't Dawn Thibble pick up her own grandchild? You know I really don't like Molly hanging around with that girl."

"I know you don't, Ned, but Heather is Molly's best friend. Also, I'll be taking Molly to Heather's house in the morning, and from there Dawn will be taking the girls to school."

Molly was again surprised, working hard to restrain a brimming excitement, yet also bracing herself, knowing her mother was more insistent than usual. This could only force an uncomfortable showdown with her iron-willed father.

"Lana, I don't like it. Not one bit." His tense lips stayed thinly parted around a breath, and he shook his head. "Not one bit." Refusing to look up, Ned Pringle could have been speaking to the dinnerware on the tabletop. He stabbed at his meal, but brought nothing to his mouth.

"Yes, yes, I know this, Ned." Molly noticed that her mother's voice remained calm and measured. "And I do understand how you're feeling. But I think it's important that Molly be able to spend time with Heather right now. I probably shouldn't have brought the subject up over dinner. This wasn't a good time. I'm sorry. If you like, we can discuss this more later."

But as she examined the memory of the kitchen scene there in the darkness of her bedroom, Molly felt that her mother *had* wanted to bring it up in front of her and over dinner, though she couldn't say why.

Molly remembered noticing at one point how her father just stared at her mother, his eyes deadly hot.

So angry, so angry, thought Molly. She squirmed farther beneath the covers, pulling them tight around her chin.

For some time, her father hadn't said anything. Then, very gently, he placed his fork and knife atop his partially eaten dinner. The utensils clinked lightly against each other and on the exposed rim of the plate. Sliding his chair away from the table, he stood and tossed his napkin carelessly onto the seat.

"It seems there's nothing more to discuss."

Not bothering to push in his chair, Molly watched her father stalk out of the kitchen, his dark hair closely cropped and his white neck skinny, while his narrow shoulders were wrought up tightly beneath a collared shirt. Molly and her mother listened as his footfalls faded, sharp clicks echoing down the hallway, until they heard the front door open, rasping slightly; the shoes registered a hollow clack on the metal threshold. The door closed, surprisingly, with just a faint metallic tick as the latch slid snugly into place. Outside, a car door slammed. Shortly thereafter, following multiple revs of the engine, her father's automobile gasped and clung to life. Then, with an abrupt bark, it accelerated and pulled away as if forever. Yet, Molly knew from experience her father and his car would calmly be returning later that night.

She remembered, too, how with elbows on the table's edge, her mother had lightly touched her fingertips together, bowed her head and closed her eyes. She listened. Finally, when the sound of the car grew distant and then faded altogether, Lana Pringle exhaled ever so softly.

"Finished?" her mom asked, rising.

Her voice sounded loud and sudden. Looking down at their plates, Molly saw that neither had eaten much.

The girl just nodded, and her dish was whisked away.

Heather looked down over the illuminated Whisper Creek Bridge, into the vague shape that was Ms. Gardner's house. There, a single bulb burned orangish in the mass of muddled black below what was now a star-filled sky. Turning to the Simpletripp property, all was left to darkness. With nothing to hold her, the girl's gaze wandered to the stark loneness of the bridge, and from there to the shadowy creek, before following the rise of hill onto the Bristol House grounds.

There it was again!

The eerie light crawled slowly up the hill. Several nights ago, when Heather saw the beacon for the first time, she was alarmed. It had made her quickly grab up her binoculars, heart racing.

And then just yesterday, while rummaging through the sideboard in the hall, Heather had overheard Sheriff Dane as he stopped by to speak with Grandma Dawn. At the time, the woman was in her office going over the Bristol House ledger, paying some bills. The girl listened as the sheriff apologized for the intrusion, claimed he needed only a moment of the woman's time, and kindly refused an invitation to lunch. Dane carried on by saying that Deputy Dawkins, who normally worked the night shift, had been periodically driving by, checking for anything out of the ordinary. On the previous night, Dawkins had reported seeing a light moving through the grounds near the northwest corner of the house, where the Roarhowser boy had been murdered. However, when the deputy stopped the car to investigate, he found that the light had vanished. Dane wondered if it might have been the gardener. If not, he thought it would be best to have Branson continue sleeping in the kitchen a while longer just in case. Grandma Dawn agreed. Departing, Sheriff Dane closed by saying that he would continue to have Dawkins drive by and keep an eye on the Bristol House, especially in that particular corner of the garden.

Heather watched the unearthly light as it steadily climbed the walkway towards the house. Picking up her binoculars from the small table, she focused once again on the ghostly figure of the nightman on the stairs, his lantern slowly swaying with each diligent step, his head peering into the night left and right. His presence, more than the gardener's, made Heather feel safe. When she told this to Aria, Aria said it was good that he made Heather feel secure. However, where was her nightman when the two of them were clobbered over the head, not to mention when her murdered friend, Stilped, was buried up to his neck? Heather said she thought the ghost was only working in the house at the time, and that since then, the nightman had begun to include the garden when he went on his rounds. That's when Heather found herself looking up at the ceiling, as Aria momentarily took possession to roll her eyes.

Molly was glad to be openly seeing Heather again, so glad that her mother and Mrs. Thibble were taking them to and from school. She also liked the fact that her mom was making frequent visits to the Bristol House, and spending time talking to Heather's grandmother on the porch, in the parlor, living room, or kitchen. This allowed the girls to venture off to Heather's room or up to the Bristol House library. Molly loved to sit in the rounded turret of Heather's room, looking out at the view from atop Thimble Hill, reading, sharing magazines and books, and talking about boys, music, and whatever else came to mind.

One subject they hadn't spoken much about was Stilped, and for that Molly was grateful. She found herself uneasy when thinking about him, especially when alone at night. She became queasy and easily drawn to tears. Should she tell Heather? How could she? Oh, how she hated to relive that time at all. If only Heather hadn't taken so long that morning. Or if she, Molly, had only taken longer.

It was the morning of Stilped's murder. Walking to school, Molly didn't wait for Heather in their prearranged spot when she saw Stilped ahead, crossing at the corner. The girl quickened her pace, and it wasn't long before she caught up with him.

Unsure of herself, Molly passed the boy, but didn't want him to know that she had sped up to do so. Once the girl was far enough ahead, she let her colorful scarf slip from her shoulders and gently float to the ground. Intentionally oblivious, Molly walked on.

"Molly?" came the soft, almost imperceptible voice behind her. "Hey, Molly?"

Molly stopped and turned, but only after losing something else: a knowing little smile. "Did you call me?"

Stilped was on one knee, picking up her fashionable scarf. The quiet boy looked up. "I think you dropped this."

"Oh, did I?" With her free hand, she felt up around her neck. "How funny." Molly's ensuing laugh felt forced, and to her ears rang metallic, as she walked back to retrieve the length of gauzy fabric that was held out to her. Accepting it, she searched for something to say. The handful of times when the three had walked together, Heather did most the talking, asking the questions and filling in the lapses in conversation with casual ease. However, Molly wasn't accustomed to talking to Stilped alone, and she found herself shy. "Thanks," was all that came to mind.

The two walked alongside one another, and for some time neither spoke. Molly was painfully conscious of the silence, and desperately sought for words to dispel it, only she couldn't think of any. The farther they walked, the more Molly became glaringly aware of their lack of conversation, and the louder the silence, the more she wished she possessed the magic to disappear.

As they began to descend the hill on Lone Oak Avenue, Stilped asked, "Is Heather sick today?"

"Oh," said Molly, and laughed, relieved and surprised that Stilped would be the one to initiate conversation. "I guess she's running a bit late. So, I thought I'd just—well, I better just, you know, hurry. To school."

"Oh."

There followed another pause, and then, "I see you're on time. I think. I mean, *we* are, aren't we? We're on time? Right?" Molly said, and found herself nodding her head. Perhaps a bit too much? She stopped.

Stilped seemed concerned with the sidewalk, its cracks, and all the weeds and grasses that grew and passed below his feet. "Yeah."

The two walked on.

After a long silence, Stilped asked, "Does your mom ever try to get you to do things you know you won't like?"

Molly thought. "Maybe sometimes. You mean like making your bed or taking out the garbage?"

"No, I mean like doing things that you should have fun doing—that *everyone* has fun doing—but you know you won't."

"Like what?" Molly asked.

"Well, like riding a horse, or bowling, or playing little league. Ever since I got here, Aunt Muriel has been trying to get me to do these things I don't like." After another silence, Stilped added, "I know why, though."

"Why?"

"She thinks I need to make friends." And here Molly saw Stilped blush, and even though he wasn't looking at her, she felt compelled to look away. He continued, "She thought I should join the school band this year, and so during the summer, she tried to get me to learn the clarinet." Stilped laughed.

"Did you like it?"

"No. It was horrible. I kept making it squeak."

"Did you look inside?" Molly asked. "Maybe there was a little mouse in there."

Both the youngsters laughed.

"You and Heather don't always walk together, do you?"

Now Molly blushed.

"My father won't let us."

"Really? Wow."

Molly knew that due to his shyness, Stilped would never ask why. And Molly would never tell him it was because Heather had stood up for him that day at school.

"So, now we just meet up in the treehouse at night."

Unexpectedly, Stilped shot her a look, and for the first time since she had known him, he became animated. "Really? Wow!"

"We have to sneak out, though. Sometimes we meet at the creek first, sometimes in the treehouse. It's up in the old Oak Triplets."

Stilped became excited. "What's it like up there at night? Is it scary?"

"Oh, no. It's beautiful! The stars are all around. And it's so high off the ground." Molly omitted how frightened she was when first climbing the wooden rungs and how she only did so with Heather's encouragement. "We can look down on the bridge, at my house, and even Ms. Gardner's house. People walk by and they don't even know we're up there." Molly giggled. "Sometimes we can hear what they're saying." Molly saw the impact she was having on the quiet boy, and so decided to share more. She liked the fact that Stilped was shy, and it was she who was drawing him out. And Molly secretly loved his soft-spoken ways, and how his words were directed just to her. "Want to know a secret? Sometimes we spy on Mr. Simpletripp when he's in his yard."

"No way!"

"We do."

"I've seen him in his gallery. That big fat guy gives me the creeps. His wife has a beard, too."

They shared the laugh.

She remembered saying, "You know, Stilped, tonight Heather and I are going to be up in the treehouse."

In the seclusion of her room, Molly started to cry. She lowered her head to hide her mouth beneath the covers, and wished back all the words that followed that morning. Why, oh, why did she have to say *those* words, the words that would burn in her memory for all time? Over and over she wrestled with them, trying to disperse them, wanting all those traitorous slippery words to vaporize. But they just came out; they just slid off her tongue so easily. Molly had been over the scene time and again, and she couldn't take them back and she couldn't change a thing. Molly knew they'd always be exactly those same words in exactly that same sequence. And yet it had been so easy, so electrifying, so *heady*, when she said to Stilped: "I'm sure Heather wouldn't mind if you came and joined us."

Molly remembered Stilped's face, how it lit up, and how he shyly said, "You mean it? Oh, Molly, that would be so much fun. I think I could sneak out, too, just like you and Heather. Where should I meet you?"

"How about down at the creek?"

"Yeah, okay. What time? After it gets dark, about eight or nine?"

"Sure, if you don't mind waiting. Heather and I just sneak out when we can. Wait for me near the bridge. From there, I can show you the way to the treehouse." Molly added, feigning casualness, "I mean, if you want me to."

"Yeah. I do. I really do."

She watched Stilped smile and was thrilled: it was for her.

With the school now visible in the near distance, Molly started to speed up. She didn't want any of the kids to see her walking alone with Stilped for too long. Word might get around, and she knew they would be relentless in their teasing. She couldn't have that, especially for Stilped. It might scare him off.

As Molly started to pull away, some may have noticed that her step was just a bit livelier.

"See you," she heard Stilped say.

Feeling self-conscious with so many students walking and loitering nearby, Molly didn't dare wave or verbally respond. Imagined or not, she felt the inquisitive stares of her peers and so increased her pace.

Back in her room, wanting the bed to swallow her whole, Molly wished now that she had turned to Stilped that morning and said goodbye. If only she had, oh, if only. With a wrenching ache, her tears spilling freely, the girl promised herself that one of two things she would never tell Heather—or the world—for as long as she lived, was that she once had a crush on the quiet boy. The other was that she had invited him to his death.

Turning onto her belly, Molly screamed silently into her pillow.

CHAPTER TEN

The First of Two Dreams

The rain beckoned, its crystalline fingernails tapping insistently on the turret room windows. Tck, tck; intermittent tck; intermittent tck, tck, tck; intermittent tck. Attracted, Heather looked up from her writing, her homework splayed before her in handwritten papers and books askew. It was late evening, and she found that in the declining light her desk lamp was necessary, spilling forth its yellowish glow in warm contrast to the pervasive chill of lonesome grays. Morose, the darker shadows slipped like stealthy cats into the tight spaces, coming to nestle between chairs and tables, climbing high atop the bookshelves, and stretching out languidly, though aloofly, along the rounded baseboards.

Tck, tck; intermittent tck. With a quick stroke of her pencil to mark her place in the school text, Heather was drawn away from the desk to take up a new post looking out the windows. There, she studied the soft obliterating grayness that hung in dense sheets of rain, watching it create a greater sense of distance between her, her neighbors, and the horizon.

In the small town of Noble, winter was drawing near, with the weather bringing rain or an overcast sky most every day. It had been a long slow six weeks since Stilped's death. Though no murderer had yet been apprehended, the town had relaxed from its collective state of panic, preferring instead its current, more unguarded mode of cautiously aware.

The investigation of young Stilped Roarhowser's murder was at present being conducted out of the public view, having gone underground weeks previous. Knowing their readers hungered for the latest information—any information—the Daily Compass ran short articles of little consequence, and for good measure they tagged on some incidental quotes. Sheriff Dane and his deputies remained steadfast in their pursuit of the murderer and in their duty to follow up on the various leads whenever they happened to trickle in. Publicly, Dane stated that a murder investigation takes time, and that all aspects of the case needed to be scrutinized, and all leads thoroughly explored. He asked that the public please continue to be patient. Privately, however, officials in the mayor's office knew that Dane was doing a tap dance in an effort to gain time. To date, he appeared to have no prime suspect, and every lead had turned out to be a snout-tail chase to nowhere.

Hank Branson, at Grandma Dawn's urging, had felt it safe enough to abandon his post as armed guardian of The Bristol House, leaving the cot and kitchen for the more comfortable accommodations of his own home. His wife, Gladys, and their two teenage boys, Tad and Derek, were glad for his safe return, and told the congregation so at church the following Sunday.

Tck; intermittent tck, tck, tck. The dreary evening light accentuated Heather's bleak reflection in the window. As she studied her image, Heather thought of Molly, of her tired eyes that always found cause to look away, and her too-infrequent smiles.

Though the girls still shared time together during Mrs. Pringle's visits and in weekday carpools to and from school, Heather sensed a growing distance between them. Aria remarked that she thought Molly looked haunted, and when Heather asked exactly what she meant, Aria only repeated her statement, adding that Molly seemed to be suffering. Heather considered this. Yet, try as she might to comfort her friend, Heather found Molly unreceptive and unable to talk about the death of Stilped. So, Heather simply let the subject go unexplored, hoping that at some point Molly would return to her playfully fun and occasionally silly self.

Tck, tck, tck; intermittent tck.

"Aria?" Heather waited, and then called again. Still no response.

She turned her attention to the drops of water that hit and clung, beaded to the slickness of the window's pane. Eventually, most lost their grip and slid downward, only to collect in safety on the horizontal muntin below. It seemed to her, however, that the more that gathered and found safe haven there, the more that were eventually pushed over the edge to make room for the new arrivals. Heather looked up when the sky darkened. The rain persisted, its spatter ceaseless against the glass.

Most nights Heather continued to find sound sleep difficult to attain, threading her way in and out of wakefulness. Often, she would wrestle with her pillows, finding uncomfortable and sleepless entanglements, before the yawning ache of morning climbed bleary-eyed through her windows. It was then that the sleep-deprived girl would try to freshen up, going into the bathroom to throw water on her exhausted face before descending the stairs, to buoyantly enter the kitchen for breakfast and her grandmother's perusal.

Heather felt the pretense necessary. She knew that her grandmother was worried about her, and noticed that Grandma Dawn was continually probing, asking Heather questions about how she felt, did she sleep all right, and were the nightmares of Stilped persisting? Heather told her that the dreams didn't happen as often, and when they did, they weren't as real or as scary. Though it wasn't totally true, it wasn't an outright lie, either. The dreams did seem real enough, yet Heather found herself unafraid. What she withheld from her grandmother, though, was that sometimes Stilped's damaged face would appear even during the daylight hours, and she would close her eyes and shake her head to make him go away.

The drops of rain continued to peck at the window, now with a greater frequency that Heather found comforting. She turned the wall sconces on, dimming them to a lower light that was just enough to chase the gloom. She thought about starting a fire in the bedroom's fireplace, having previously stacked kindling and firewood upon the grate. She chose not to, however, preferring to stay in the turreted room to complete her homework.

Deciding to take a rest—but only for a moment—Heather eased into the soft recess of an upholstered chair that sat nearby, below the center window. From within the turret's circle of light, she inspected her shadow-ladened room that spread out spaciously before her. Heather's gaze rested on the bed that hugged the far wall, its pillows and shams softly yielding, invitingly piled high atop the thick down comforter. Below, around the perimeter, the bed skirt flowed lazily in soothing rolls and gentle tucks. The paintings on the walls hung in blurry-edged frames, some being landscapes recomposed by the subdued light to look otherwordly, perhaps suggesting a new elsewhere, a place where Heather would find happiness and peace. In other paintings, people posed themselves casually, easily conversational, warm and friendly. Sluggishly, the girl dragged her eyes to the dresser, a piece of furniture that barely managed to stand out against the secure shelter of the dimly lit wall. Over the sea of carpet that forever stretched between the seated girl and her bed, Heather's heavy-lidded gaze slowly swam the distance, struggling, struggling, before succumbing, sinking into its plush depths and among its cozy denizens. As the soft drops of rain nibbled about her ears, the exhausted girl slid deeper into her chair, and she welcomed the permeating fog of a much-needed slumber.

Heather made her way through the mist, past swift-moving figures that seemed to reveal themselves abruptly before her. They hastily stepped forth to shed the encircling swirl of white, before being swallowed quickly and once again. All around, muffled conversations drifted to find her ears, and the clangs and cries of engaging metal to metal and latch to latch rang out, though their sharpness seemed greatly diminished. From somewhere, a bustling individual appeared and bumped into Heather—though hardly noticing or slowing—setting the girl back and knocking her small suitcase to the fog-covered ground, where she bent to fish it out. When slowly rising, she noticed the mist had begun to thin.

With her head thrown back, mesmerized, Heather found herself slowly turning, though to her it seemed the room was spinning instead. All around, the hazy envelopment was patiently disclosing itself. A huge multi-paned window stared with gleams of frosty light from one end of the dreary edifice, and large columns, connected by a multitude of arches, rose throughout, lending a sense of support to the vaulted and cavernous structure. Floating above, rows of elegant glass chandeliers, despite their combined efforts, shed a contemptibly weak light, doing little to ward off the invasive dimness. The impatient cry of the whistles and the huff of steam-and-chug filled Heather's ears from somewhere unseen and perhaps far off. Constantly in motion, the moil of travelers in assorted shapes and attire continued on their impetuous course.

Heather surveyed the steam locomotive the next track over. Black and dull, its aged spirit tarnished, it was her train to catch, though how she knew this to be so, she could not say. The fatigued engine, a collection of interlocking cylinders punctuated by smaller circular rivets, bided time until departure. As if releasing a withering ghost, a trickle of vapor escaped its stack.

But why must she be on that train? Certainly Heather knew she could wait for another. Couldn't she? After all, wasn't her mother to be here, somewhere, wandering among the milling crowd? And weren't the two to meet? After having waited her entire life to do so, Heather was certain she didn't want to leave without first having found her. But where could she be?

Hurriedly, Heather deposited her small suitcase alongside some large others near her train. She jostled her way—and in turn was jostled and knocked off-stride—running from person to person. But where was her mother? Hadn't she told Heather she'd come? And without knowing what she looked like, how was Heather to find her?

Rushing past in hustling blurs and fragments of intervening shapes, women in the station were swarming all around, fitted with long white trench coats strapped tightly at the waist. Below, their legs worked with piston-driven purpose, snugly fitted within the black-patterned nylons that slid neatly into glossy black heels of single-minded intent. Before long, from all corners, the women surged and bled into everywhere and everyone, their red gloves toting purses, bulky bags, and suitcases large and small. Upon their heads were black hats of various sizes and shapes. Frilled or austere, wide-brimmed or not, all derbies, cloches, and pill-boxes were curtained with black-laced veils, the facial features obscured and lost in vague retreat.

Heather had seen people dressed like this before, but couldn't remember when and where. Was it in old movies and photos? In books? Perhaps a time or two in Molly's fashion magazines?

Nearby, a whistle blew, a train no longer tolerant at being berthed. If Heather was going to find her mother, she knew she needed to hurry.

The girl found herself drawn to the taller women—as she herself stood tall. Upon engagement, Heather attempted to reach and pull aside their concealing veils. Always a red glove would dart to intercede, grabbing her wrist or forearm to rebuff her inquiring hand.

"Please, who are you? Are you my mother?" she would ask.

But the elusive figures would brush her aside and swiftly move on, silently and without comment, as if Heather's intrusions were an off-hand annoyance of little note. Heather rushed on to the next woman, and then the next, encountering indistinct face after indistinct face, and meeting rejection after rejection. Tears of frustration arose, flashing in narrow streams.

"Heather, here I am."

"Mom?" Heather spun. "Where are you?"

"Right here, Heather. I'm here."

Nearby, a whistle screeched mightily. Heather glanced in the direction of her train, only to notice that all the passengers had boarded. Frantic, Heather looked from covered face to covered face.

A porter called to her from near the passenger car. "Heather, this train is leaving. You must be on it."

The gathering mists were heavier now, as objects and bodies became confused in the haziness.

After helplessly glancing at the porter, Heather turned back towards the sea of black and white stippled with red, feverishly scanning the crowd. "Mom, I-I have to go," she said, backing towards the old loco-motive.

Heather wheeled. Her little suitcase sat alone on the quay. She ran for it.

The porter now stood withdrawn on the steps leading into the car. Like a charcoal sketch come to life, everything about him was dull and dark, save the gold buttons that gleamed on his collar and down the front of his coat, and his shoes that held a somber scuff of highlight.

"Hurry, young lady," his mustachioed mouth said, "give me your hand."

Her suitcase at her side, Heather took the porter's proffered hand, hopping onto the lowest stair below him.

"But Heather," the pleasing feminine voice called, "I'm here."

Heather glanced over her shoulder. A tall woman had pushed forward, separating herself from the throng behind her. A red rose stood out, pinned to one side of her curtained hat. She was waving and dashing towards Heather.

"Heather!"

"Mom?"

"My train is there, Heather," she said, slowing and pointing nearby to a sleeker, high-speed locomotive. Through the haze, it gleamed in royal blue modernity with a long yellow streak above the many windows that extended from its first car to its last. At the front, the engine resembled a bullet in its sleekness with a few small windows. "Come on! Join me! I'm leaving soon; you can ride along."

"Really? Can I?"

"Of course. It's a much nicer train. Do come, Heather," her mother shouted from the quay. "I know you'll like it so much more."

Heather glanced at the porter's face, perhaps searching for signs of permission. Though his features were slightly more delineated close up, they, like the rest of him, seemed shrouded and smeared. "Okay, I'm coming, Mom," and with that, Heather clumsily turned around with her suitcase in the confined space. As she stepped down to run to her mother, the porter's arm encircled her chest. Heather squirmed. His polished cuff link bounced and blinked in the dim light.

"Let me go!"

"You can't, Miss. This is your train, and you're meant to be a rider."

"Let me go. Please, you have to let me go," Heather said, her tears springing anew as she grappled with the porter's arm. "My mother's here. Can't you see her? Look, there she is; she's right there waiting for me. *You let me go!*"

Hurriedly, her mother drew closer to Heather's car, the red of rose still conspicuous in the mist.

"Mom!" Heather felt a jolt as the train lurched forward. Helplessly, she watched while through the mist the ground slowly began to glide past, the train gaining momentum.

"Heather, why are you leaving?"

The girl turned and achingly reached out her arm towards her mother. Heather cried out, "Mom!" the word echoing throughout the cavernous station, but the train continued to roll. Kicking and throwing elbows behind her, with blonde hair whirling about her head and tears spinning off her cheeks, the child ferociously battled with the shackling arm. "He won't let me go! Mom! Mom, wait! Wait for me!"

"Don't go, Heather." Her mother's pace slowed to a resigned walk. Her red-gloved hand was held high in a longing stationary wave. "I'll be waiting for you."

Shaking with convulsive gasps, Heather stopped struggling and felt the constraining arm relax its hold. She watched as the figure of her mother, isolated on the quay, became smaller.

"What do you look like?" Heather thought to shout.

She watched as her mother reached up, and within the billows of mist drifting across the track, pulled off her hat, her hair tumbling free. But Heather couldn't see her mother's face, couldn't see through her tears and the thickening fog. She wiped her eyes with a sleeve.

"What's your name?" Heather yelled, but the train had turned away, rounding a bend. Garnering her strength for a final effort, the girl tried to break free of the porter.

With a sharp twist of her upper body, Heather awakened with a start. She was breathing heavily. Tears from the railway station stained her cheeks and clung to her lashes. The vast emptiness within her child's heart lay exposed, trampled and sodden, its pain a burning pyre. She wept quietly.

After a time, Heather opened her eyes and stared at the ceiling, its murky but familiar presence somehow comforting. She took a deep breath and exhaled, before wiping away any trace of tears. Night was evident through the three windows, and Heather stood before them in the muted glow of the turret room sconces. The rain had stopped, and a starry sky could be seen through gaps in the cloud cover.

Across the room, the bedroom door opened. Light from the hallway filled the rectangular space behind the recognizable shape that entered.

"Heather?"

The girl turned. "I'm over here."

Grandma Dawn closed the door behind her. With a flick of the switch, the room's light shone like an unexpected sun.

"Looking out the window? Would you rather have the light off?"

Heather nodded, and the room plunged into darkness once again.

Her grandmother joined her in the turreted alcove, and as was usual, Heather pressed into her. They stood for a while, gazing out at the night.

"Bedtime," Grandma Dawn said, turning her attention to Heather. "I thought I'd tuck you in."

"You do every night." Heather paused, before adding, "But you really don't tuck me in anymore, do you? It's more like a bedtime visit."

Lost in the dimness, Grandma Dawn smiled. "I know. You're too old. When did that happen, anyway?"

Heather shrugged.

The two almost swayed together, each with an arm around the other. More stars were visible with the cloud's steady dispersal. Heather's head fell against her grandmother.

"The weatherman says the rain will be back tomorrow, lasting throughout your long weekend," Grandma Dawn said. She felt Heather nod her head in understanding. "Not much to do outside."

"That's okay. I'll find stuff to do inside."

Her grandmother's hand found Heather's shoulder, and she administered a quick squeeze. "Come on, let's get you to bed."

The two broke apart, and Heather went to change into her pajamas by the light of her bedside lamp. Meanwhile, Grandma Dawn, having turned off the turret room lights after pulling up the window's sash, joined her granddaughter as she was settling into bed. When Grandma Dawn leaned over her, Heather shut her eyes to the nearness, and felt a light peck on the forehead.

Hovering over Heather's lamp-lit features, Grandma Dawn said, "You sleep well."

"I will."

Grandma Dawn turned and doused the lamp.

"Grandma Dawn?" The softly spoken words split the fresh stain of blackness. The lamp burst to life.

"What, young lady?"

"Will I ever meet my mother?"

Grandma Dawn smiled, a bittersweet smile, and shook her head. "I don't know." It took a moment before she added, "But if the moon has its way with you, you might just be surprised."

Heather yawned. "What does that mean? You've told me that before." Lightly, she smacked her lips.

"It's an old saying from my childhood. It means the moon is your compass, a guide in the night. It also means you ask the same question a lot." Grandma Dawn started to say something more, but bit back on the words. Instead, she pulled the covers up around her granddaughter's shoulders, before stuffing in the loose corner. "There. I just had to tuck you in for old time's sake."

Grandma Dawn reached over and with a pull of the lamp's chain, pitched the room into darkness once again.

"Grandma Dawn?"

The light flicked back to life. "What?" Lighthearted irritation teased the word.

Heather looked her grandmother over and this inspired a half-smile from the girl. She shook her head and said, "Nothing."

The light snapped off. There was a laugh as the door opened and the amused grandmother withdrew, bathed in hallway light once again. When the door closed securely, Heather was left alone with the moonlit night.

CHAPTER ELEVEN

A Second Dream

Heather yawned and soon started to doze.

In her dream, she was a great bird of the night drifting across the gentle moonlit plains of sleep, the cool wind at her face like the rush of air that swirled beguilingly into her room.

On wing, the girl watched as the land's muted colors moved swiftly by below, becoming obscured beneath an advancing fog that had settled in over the hills. Angling on a stiff wind, Heather found herself diving through that fog, hugging the blur of terrain, the land eventually giving way to the incessant wash of shoreline: the mingling of sand, surf, and luminous spray amid tireless rumblings and oceanic sighs.

Outside Heather's bedroom window, in a starry clearing, the moon hung like a celestial jewel, its surface ravaged but still sparkling placidly. Its beam reached into the turreted alcove milky blue and lustrous, shimmering as an alluring pool upon the carpet. Nearby, following another breathy gust, papers on the girl's desk were swept up in a spirited whirl before gliding gracefully to the floor.

A low moan escaped Heather's lips, while above, her hair-draped brow lay tangled and knotted and tied to her dream. Rolling onto her side, she swept a pillow to the floor, the slight disturbance causing the rectangle of moonlit carpet to sway as liquid.

And still Heather dreamed.

She was flying inland now, an airborne witness to the slow rolling hills and abundance of trees. Steady on the breeze, Heather glided to a lower altitude, sailing above rock-strewn meadows and star-filled streams, chasing her moonlight shadow. And then lower still, her shadowy wingspan ever more distinct sliding over wall and rooftop, creek and bridge, speeding its way up the gumdrop hill toward the dormant eyes of the sleeping Bristol House.

Restless in her bed, sensing an approaching presence, Heather clawed her way from sleep. At the rustle of wings, she awakened to the darkness and raised her head. The girl spied the hooded night bird that had just landed upon the sill, its luminous gaze unwavering. Noticing the stretch of moon glow cast upon the floor, Heather slipped out of the jumbled bedding and, entranced, was drawn across the room.

Astille Lia. The hushed words permeated the air, quietly calling to her, murmured invitations to explore a dream.

With each unhurried step, the blue pool of moonlight rippled easily. Heather approached to stand along its edge, her reflection staring up in watery fluctuations.

Turning toward the sill, she saw the bird rear up unexpectedly and spread its wings. Then, much to Heather's astonishment, it leapt and soared off into the night. For a dream-filled moment, she thought about following to the window to look after the creature. However, the next instant the bird was streaking back in, wings tucked, and, like an angling dart, plunged into the depths of the luminescent pool.

With a protective hand to her face, Heather was left splashed and speckled with moon glow. Minding little, she peered into the water that sloshed at her feet and saw distorted clouds passing in the wetness, the earth far below. Without waiting for the liquid's disturbance to calm, Heather followed after the bird, jumping feet-first into the pool of day-time sky.

The girl felt herself descending in a freefall, hurtling out of the clouds. In a windy rush, her pajamas flapped and swelled, her blonde hair whipping above. Looking about, Heather tried to catch sight of the hooded bird, but it was nowhere to be seen.

As she continued to plummet, she stretched her arms out to her sides and found them to be long feathered wings, and so began to methodically beat the air. Now gliding, Heather looked at the earth that was quickly approaching, its features increasing in size.

Below, divisions in the land were distinct, a patchwork of greens and oranges, reds and browns, bordered by stone walls and cauliflower-shaped trees. The expanse of countryside that sprawled beneath Heather was carved up all the more by stretches of road and shimmering, snaking waterways.

Unsure of her destination, Heather allowed her knowing wings to guide her, and soon was skimming over a vast forest. Lying exposed in a clearing was a clutch of buildings, imposing and dramatic in their architecture. Heather circled and descended before alighting on the branch of a lofty tree. Nearby, windows framed in white, containing panes that were cracked, broken, or missing, stood out starkly against the building's brown brick and invasive green ivy.

Reflected in the glass before her, Heather saw a massive tree, its leaves sparse. Also mirrored, with large talons grasping hold of a branch, was the familiar, black-hooded night bird. Its eyes were brilliant, even in the fresh light of morning. Taken aback, Heather felt herself start at the sight of the image, and the bird in the window did the same. She shook her head in disbelief, and the bird followed suit. Heather spread her wings and began to alternate the weight on her legs, first hopping one way and then the other. The reflection of the bird emulated her movements.

Wow! That's *me*! Heather thought. I'm that strange bird that I keep seeing on my windowsill!

With a leap, she took to her wings, soaring over the gray-striped rooftops, the main building, largest of all, stretching out below.

What is this place?

She dove at a lengthy angle past the many windows. Landing on a marble handrail alongside a wide staircase, Heather saw a recessed entryway beneath a tall façade. Like the upper storied walls that she had observed only moments ago, it was overwhelmed by dense vines and unrestrained greenery. Within the vaulted entrance, Heather observed shattered windows above decrepit doors and brickwork that had fallen and lay scattered upon the white marble flooring. In various places, remnants of vagrant fires littered and scorched the enclosure.

What happened to this building? Heather wondered.

The bird turned to look at what might have once been well-tended lawns. Surrounded by broad broken walkways, they were weedy and overgrown.

She was then drawn to a large monument that graced the area opposite the main entrance. An elevated building in sparkling white was at its center with stairways on all four sides, each lined with statues of girls in robes. Some appeared to be approximately Heather's age while others seemed older, all with long braids of hair. Many were depicted reading, holding large open books before them, while others were writing with long quills over thick volumes, or conversing among themselves in twos and threes. Encircling the base were armored women of action carrying weapons and riding big furry beasts that resembled lions, only larger, with tufts of hair behind their legs, front and rear.

Spaced evenly around the perimeter of the building's roof were cowled persons made of red stone, nine of them, their heads downturned in solemn observation of those below. Beneath their hoods, each face was carved in white, but it was hard for Heather to tell if they were men or women. From what she was able to discern, the draped faces looked to be elderly.

Atop the peaked roof, centered within these nine hooded carvings, arose the tallest of figures, a statue of an elegant young woman balanced on four interlocking spheres. Her beautiful and dignified face was thrust back blissfully with her arms spread wide in a welcome embrace of the heavens. She wore a billowing robe, and her long marble braid twisted in an imaginary wind behind her. At her feet were books, some opened and others closed and stacked. Unlike the massive brick building nearby, the monument appeared to be well cared for, with the white of the women and girls still glistening, sparkling with flecks of gold. Heather marveled at the site.

Pushing off the handrail, Heather took to the air. She climbed and circled a nearby clock tower, its walls crowned with four spires and a steeply pitched roof. Curious for the time of day, with a glance Heather saw that each of the four clock faces were missing hands, one or both.

This place is so beautiful! thought Heather. But so rundown. What happened to it? And where are the people?

Beating her huge wings, the bird was soon rising, turning into the sun. She drifted before descending, following a meandering river. Ahead, a stone bridge spanned the water, three tunnels in its side. Heather pointed herself towards the center passageway, the largest of the three, and then hurtled into its gaping mouth.

The day's brightness that lit her way soon faded. Water dripped from rock walls, and the dank passage was unexpectedly long, the air getting progressively colder. Far in the distance, Heather spotted a light in the blackness and beat her wings to gather speed. As the exit neared, shrill winds whipped down the stone corridor, periodically cuffing and slowing the bird's progress. Heather pressed for more speed, and with a whoosh, she burst from the tunnel, rushing headfirst into the bitter face of a snowstorm. She was surprised at the sudden turn in the weather, surprised that in such a short span of time the sun could vanish and leave the land smothered with a dense covering of snow.

How did *that* happen?

Defiant in the face of battering winds, Heather rose up and away from the stone bridge. In a slow airborne pivot, she saw that the snow had begun to adhere to her wing feathers.

Fighting the winds amid poor visibility, the great bird found it difficult to navigate. And so she flew low, following an urge to retrace her path over the snow-covered bridge and above the frozen waterway. As the snowfall began to subside, allowing her visibility to increase, the bird ascended to locate the buildings she had seen previously, although only in sunlight. Circling, she spotted the clock tower rising cheerless against a colorless sky. Its green peaked roof and small surrounding spires were loaded with snow, as was the main building below. Icicles clung to the eaves.

Heather was surprised to see that the windows held a warm glow of light, as did lamps lining the walks and entryways. People were trundling through the snow, some with books, their thick garments protecting face and body, keeping them warm and dry.

Heather flew over the monument again, and although the surrounding land was covered in snow, the stone figures lay untouched by the inclement weather. People were actively ascending and descending the four staircases, entering and exiting the elaborate white building at the top. What so many were doing once inside the small structure Heather couldn't determine. And how could they all possibly fit in there? Moving on, the bird flew around the uppermost statue on the roof, that of the young robed woman. She still stood proudly, strong and beautiful, her face upturned to the dwindling snowfall that settled elsewhere, leaving her features unsullied.

Nearby, the main entrance to the larger building was engulfed in snow, but paths had been established and people still progressed to and from its doors. No longer overwhelmed with ivy, Heather saw a sign on the building's façade. With her keen bird eyesight, she was able to read:

MAIDENHALL
ACADEMY
OF THE
SHADOWSLIP WOOD
AUTUMNSLOE

MaidenHall Academy? thought Heather. Autumnsloe? Where's that?

The bird came to rest on a limb of the same tree she had visited previously. Nearby, through unbroken panes of glass, the window up and slightly ajar, Heather could see that a class was in session. Before the students, a distinguished man dressed in handsome robes paced back and forth as he lectured. Occupying heavy ornate desks were young girls slightly older than Heather, all appearing to be tall and slenderly built, and each possessing porcelain skin, a hint of red in the cheeks, light reddish-brown hair, and lips of orange. Heather thought the girls extraordinary in robes of differing colors, especially against their white skin. Through the areas of glass that were not frosted, her bird sight allowed her to observe the blue eyes of the girls as they followed their instructor, never distracted, never looking away. Heather continued to watch with curiosity as KnowledgeLamps, a small decorative lamp hovering at the corner of every student's desk, instantly lit up following a question. Always, the professor pointed to or called on one of the girls whose light gave off the brightest glow.

What are those little lamps? Heather wondered, The brighter the shine, does that mean the student is surer of knowing the answer?

Following another question, the professor, with raised chin and brow, looked down his nose for a student to call upon. He pointed, and a young girl, previously hidden from the bird, stood.

The fact that her lamp wasn't glowing in the least intrigued Heather. She thought the student looked troubled, her mind far away.

Nevertheless, the girl that rose was astonishingly beautiful, more striking than the others. And although her skin was also white, her hair was raven while her extraordinary green eyes shone with stark intensity. Her lips were not orange, but rather a glistening red. Heather was intrigued and wanted to see more, yet the windows, from the heat in the room, had glazed over to a point where she had difficulty peering through them. The bird blinked and waited, looking left and right, considering what to do.

As if on cue, the window opened to its fullest, six large panes sliding up.

"Is that better?" the instructor asked rhetorically of the class. "It is a bit stuffy in here." His voice trailed off as he adjusted his sash, turned away, and readdressed his pupils. "All right, now where were we?"

"The TimeLight Bridge, Iso Syrus." The extraordinary girl's voice floated out to Heather, soft but self-assured, respectful in her professor's presence. Yet she refused to look at him directly.

"Why, yes, correct. Thank you." The instructor paused for a moment, his eyes glued to the girl. He cleared his throat. "You may sit down." He tore his gaze from her. "Yes, the Age of the Archannites and the Time-Light Bridge that eventually led to the TransPorts …"

Dissatisfied with her vantage point, Heather carefully edged her way down the branch, alongside the window. Snow fell from the supple limb with the bird's every shuffle and hop, and that in turn caused more snow to spill on the branches below. Heather didn't dare get too close, not wanting to draw attention to herself.

Just then, the bells in the clock tower rang loudly, striking out four times.

"All right, Maidens, class has ended for the day. Permission to leave is granted. I'd like my two young assistants to stay behind, if they would. I've some work for each. The rest of you are to proceed to your Studies Interval before the next session."

The large bird, still unnoticed outside the window, watched as the stunning girls rose up from their seats, the KnowledgeLamps floating down to settle into resting places upon the desktops. Filing out, the Maidens carried themselves with regal bearing, their long auburn plaits swaying easily with every step and stop.

"Moderre, I need you to go to the bookshop for me. Would you be so kind as to do that today?" The older man in sweeping robes looked over his glasses at the girl.

"Yes, of course, Iso Syrus. I am honored by your request."

The door closed on the last of the departing students, leaving only the two assistants with the instructor, as he sat down at his large desk. From her spot in the tree, Heather observed the man as he took a long quill in hand and began to scrawl on a piece of paper.

The bird shifted her attention towards the black-haired girl, the one she thought so beautiful. In her winged guise, Heather was unable to read the Maiden's aura, however, she sensed her to be ill at ease—fidgety—as she crossed her arms before her and then an instant later let them drop.

The elderly gentleman finished with a flourish, and placed the quill back in its holder. "There!" He dabbed the paper with a dry cloth. "Have these to me by early tomorrow morning, my young Moderre, if you would, please. All should be available."

"Of course. I'll set about it first thing after classes. Thank you, Iso Syrus."

Departing, she turned and briefly acknowledged the other. The instructor followed Moderre to the door, closing it behind her and spinning the key in the lock. There he stood for a moment, unmoving.

"Your QuillCraft Writings from the Tomes were again unfinished," he said to the door. Head down, his back was to the girl, his hands still grasping the key and lock. "That is your ancient text, to be explored, reproduced, and committed to memory." The instructor turned. "And," he stressed the word, "that's the third time these past two weeks."

"Yes, Iso Syrus, I know. And I apologize—"

"*That's not good enough!*" He paused and collected himself. "Once again, I'll have to punish you."

"Please, Iso Syrus, don't." The words were barely audible.

"You must do as I say," the instructor said, tightening the circle, as he walked around the stationary girl. "It's a Maiden's duty to understand obedience; it is my duty to teach and enforce it."

"Please don't."

"Can you not see that it is my responsibility to insure that you finish your work?"

There was no answer from the girl.

"I asked you a question. I am an extremely reasonable man. And you are a rebellious young girl. I see that I'm going to have to take extreme measures to insure that you learn the meaning of obedience."

Again, no answer.

"Please fetch the switch."

The girl didn't look up. "Don't. Please, Iso Syrus. I haven't been able to concentrate. My mind is occupied elsewhere, and I've not been able to absorb my studies. I've tried. I'm sorry."

"You've not been able to concentrate?"

After a pause, the girl spoke, still barely a whisper. "Not since the last time—not since you—" the girl's white skin flushed, "not since then."

"*Then* is when you were the recipient of what you undoubtedly deserved. The switch, please."

"Please, Iso Syrus. My vows..."

"The switch."

Without another word, the girl went to the closet to grab a long and tapering rod. Obediently, she brought it to her professor, and going down to a knee, the girl laid it across his eager palms.

Syrus ran his hand up the length of the shaft, across its three tightly braided cords.

"The Switch," the professor announced, spinning it before his dazzled eyes, fondling it with admiration. "How it loves to bite the flesh and set the world to right. Yet, for you it is only the beginning. Sadly, the scars of your disobedience will disappear immediately following the application of this magic taper. So, there must be a greater lesson still, a lesson that you will carry for a lifetime."

"Iso Syrus, the Rite of Purification is to be soon. Please..." Heather watched, mesmerized, rooted in place, as the girl pleaded. "It's all I have worked for," the beautiful white face looked at the floor, her words now barely audible. "...to become a Maiden of Evermore is everything to me."

Outside the window, a snowflake floated before Heather to gently alight on her beak. More flakes followed, lazily drifting down and around the great perched bird.

Whack!

The sound lashed out, striking on the ears of the bird through the open window. Heather's gaze slowly roamed about her, watching the flakes that fell so simply and beautifully, so insignificantly. Large in their elegant crystalline design, they lightly touched down on feather, sill, and branch, to further encompass a world so serenely cast in white.

Whack!

Heather's rounded golden eyes followed the meandering paths of the snowfall, tracing the vagabond life of the flake, easily floating, drifting here, now there. Then settling.

Whack!

A gasp.

Flakes so effortless in their freefall, so painless, and trouble-free. So pure.

Whack!

So untaintedly white, like the smooth unblemished skin of a Maiden.

Whack!

Reluctantly, Heather found herself drawn to the open window once again, where the Maiden's watery gaze looked out to meet her own. And the bird saw how the beautiful young face held her sadness with a weight that Heather could never explain to another, a weight that rested so heavily in her own heart, or perhaps in that of the bird.

Whack!

The white face jerked with the impact. Her jaw set, the girl refused to flinch. Or cry out.

Heather took note of the desk, the robe, and the instructor's chair, and sensed that, even in surrender, the girl retained her Maiden dignity.

"Have we had enough?" The professor walked around to face the Maiden, his back to the window, the switch tapping the opposite palm. He lowered his head near her ear, his eyebrows raised, the words whispered too loudly: "Now do we understand the meaning of the word obedience?" The professor withdrew from her, the switch still tapping impatiently on his upturned palm. His face was flushed. Through his glasses, the graying man clearly leered, observing, observing. Once again, he dipped his head close to hers. "Do we, my young Maiden? Do we understand obedience?" He shook his head slowly. "I think not."

It's just a dream, Heather thought to remind herself, *only a dream.*

The white-skinned girl looked up at the man. She was shaking. Was it fear or anger? Heather couldn't say.

The snow was falling heavier now, making the bird's view through the window all the more difficult. Heather heard the professor's heavy footfalls.

"No, please, Iso Syrus …"

Heather willed away the softly spoken words. Profoundly disturbed, with a thrusting of her large wings, she took flight. The professor heard the snowy commotion outside the classroom window. He stopped to look briefly in its direction, but not for long.

Whack!

CHAPTER TWELVE

The Bristol House Begins to Play

The great bird flew at the storm, rage seizing hold of her heart, her mind churning. Wanting the tempestuous winds to assault her, cast her sideways, and bounce her about, Heather flew heedlessly away from the windows that had staged for her such a distressing scene.

No, no, no, no, *no!* her mind pounded out.

The snowfall began to increase, and with it the bird's visibility once again diminished. Heather didn't care. Impetuously, she followed a frozen waterway, and though the notion entered her mind that she could very well become lost in a blinding blizzard, Heather quickly dismissed it. She simply wanted to fly, craving to mindlessly keep moving.

When the familiar bridge and its three tunnels appeared before her through the confusion of white, Heather was neither relieved nor concerned at having found it; the structure was simply *there*. With little thought, she rose high enough to cross the span, before climbing steeply and banking sharply on the potent winds. Throwing herself into a slashing dive, she pierced the tunnel's snow-shrouded orifice, her momentum propelling her onward. Again allowing her knowing wings to guide her, Heather was retracing the course of her flight, heading back the way she came.

Into the stone corridor she shot, pushing herself to fly with the utmost speed, determined to lose this world of Autumnsloe and the MaidenHall Academy. Faster now, the dingy walls tore by as a blur, their details smeared, and though a variety of sounds rang out, they fell upon the deafest of ears.

Faster, Heather urged herself, faster.

And faster she hurtled, spurring herself on all the more recklessly. Now she was a streak propelled on furious wings. And still the bird pushed herself, faster and faster.

Ahead of her, she saw a distant stab of light striking out in the gloom. It grew quickly, and Heather drove towards the core. Upon bursting into its brilliance, the girl's eyes opened in a flutter and flood of sunlight, arms outstretched, her chin buried in pillows. Emerging from beneath the tousled covers, her upper body lay at an angle across the bed. She blinked and grimaced at the morning light. Her mind flashed on the disturbing dream, and she worked to quickly dispel the vision.

"It's only a dream. It's only a dream. It's only a dream."

Distracting herself further still, she asked, I wonder what's for breakfast? and then concentrated on the possibilities.

Heather arose, stretched, and found her slippers. Through the archway, the morning light extended into her room, picking its way over the furniture with a sweeping, radiant reach. Walking over to take up her favored post of looking out the turret room windows, she kneeled on a warm, sun-drenched chair. She saw the garden sloping down and away, basking in the new day's glow skimming low and from the east. Turning her gaze skyward, Heather noticed the soft violet-gray clouds that gathered fitfully above the horizon, their nimbus riders breaking loose and surging forth on the prevailing winds. They brought with them the skulking pall of haze.

Nonetheless, the impending stormy weather didn't dampen the girl's enthusiasm for the long weekend to come. In a spirited retreat from the alcove windows, pushing away the difficult conclusion of her dream, the pajama-clad girl hurried down to Grandma Dawn and breakfast.

With the cylindrical shaft of a long pole saw bouncing on one shoulder, and a smaller saw grasped in his thickly callused hand, the Bristol House gardener slogged through the mud and grass on the rough part of the estate's acreage. Occasionally, Hank Branson could feel his boots lose traction and slide, yet he was always able to catch himself and remain upright. Trudging along the little worn path leading down from Thimble Hill, he had long ago tired of the rain and was thus thankful for the sunlit morning and the smell of its freshly scented air.

Branson loved being out in the open and away from the confines of any room, alone with the Bristol House gardens and grounds. A rugged individual, his job suited his retiring nature, and he disliked occasions when he had to hire extra hands and supervise the more involved garden tasks, preferring instead to be away from human interaction for long stretches of time. Though his wife Gladys and the in-laws never under-stood—and he found himself unable to satisfactorily explain this need of his— over the span of their marriage the wife had come to accept his inclination for detachment, finding girlfriends with whom she could share her more intimate emotions and concerns. And when matters too private dictated that she couldn't confide in them, she sought refuge and consolation in the church.

Humming an old tune, Branson glanced at the sky, and thought, Maybe I can get a bit of work in before the rain starts up again.

Clumsily fighting his way through the dense underbrush, maneuver-ing the awkward pole around bushes and boughs, he came to a clearing and halted. Confounded and frozen in place, his humming died.

Heather climbed into her chair at the circular kitchen table, where, much to her delight, a plate of strawberry waffles was lowered before her.

"Lana Pringle phoned," her grandmother said. "She'll be bringing Molly by a bit later this morning."

"Great! When they get here, could you please send Molly upstairs? I'll either be in my room or the Bristol House library."

"You seem pretty excited. I hate to dampen your enthusiasm, but just so you know, although the sun is out now, it's probably going to rain today—like the forecast predicted. I hope you find plenty to do indoors to keep you occupied."

"I wrihl," Heather said, chewing on a mouthful. "Mohry, tuh."

"Good. Did you sleep well last night?"

"Mmm." Heather took a drink of her milk. She swallowed. "Pretty good, I guess. I had a strange dream, though."

"Did you, now?" Grandma Dawn said, sitting and sliding in towards the table, her cup of coffee and small bowl of berry-covered oatmeal before her. "Want to tell me about it?"

Heather nodded vigorously, milk and waffle being worked over in her mouth. "Well," she said, adding a few more chews before swallowing the soggy assortment, "I was a bird and I flew to an old school."

Grandma Dawn was unfolding the newspaper, her attention drawn to the splash of headline. "Uh-huh," she said, absently, her eyes grabbing at details in the finer print. "An old school?"

"Yeah. It was the MaidenHall Academy of the ShadowSlip Wood, in Autumnsloe."

Grandma Dawn's attention stayed fixed to the paper, but she was no longer reading. Heather noticed a change in her aura as its glow intensified, dancing in oranges, reds, and yellows. A stealthy gray tried to conceal the excitement of the brilliant colors, but was unable to do so. "It was, was it? The MaidenHall Academy?" Her tone was casual.

"Yeah, it said so on a sign—but not at first. There was a big white statue of a tall girl on top of a house, too. She was wearing a robe and her hair was braided and blowing behind her. It was really long." Heather hoisted her large glass of milk, before adding, "It wasn't really blowing, though. I mean, it couldn't have been, right, because it was made of stone. But it sure looked like it." She took a two-gulp swallow, before setting down her glass. A line of white accentuated her upper lip. "Anyway, same with her robe. It was speckled with gold, too. Know how I know? I had really good eyesight, because I was a bird."

Heather was proud of her summation, but had left the disturbing finale of her dream untouched, not wanting to revisit it. She wiped her mouth on a napkin.

Grandma Dawn scrutinized her granddaughter. "Interesting name, Autumnsloe."

"Mmm-hmmm," Heather said, working on a new mouthful. "In the ShadowSlip Wood. I remember—"

"Dawn?" Hank Branson had opened the door, sticking his head in. "Sorry to intrude. Can I see you a minute?"

"Of course," Grandma Dawn said, rising, reluctant to leave the conversation. "Heather, excuse me a moment." She saw the worried look on her gardener's face. "What's wrong? Oh, no, Hank. Not another—"

"Heaven's, no, Dawn! But I thought you'd like to know I've found more digging on the property. The holes are days or weeks old, probably. Any footprints that were left I'm sure have been washed away with all the rain we've had—except for mine, of course." Out of character, Branson let loose a horselaugh, despite what he saw as a serious situation. "I didn't know if you wanted to phone the sheriff, or not. The holes are on the rough part of the property, outside the grounds."

"Where outside the grounds?"

"Over the fence and back near the trees, far enough away that whoever was digging them probably knew they wouldn't be seen from the house. I only noticed the holes because I went to prune that old patch of diseased aspen."

Grandma Dawn sighed. "All right, let's put a call in to Sheriff Dane, Hank. I thought this stuff had all but gone away after the murder of the boy." She shook her head and emphasized the word, "Darn."

"If you don't mind calling, Dawn, you can just have the sheriff meet me on the grounds. I'll be near the garage, cutting back some of the juniper and creeper."

Branson glanced over his shoulder and screwed up his face to the now leaden sky, noting the accumulation of clouds. The wind was picking up in gusts and displacing his thick hair, normally combed straight back, leaving strands to flow in long, undisciplined locks. He ran a hand over his head, his fingers raking in the strays. "Looks like the makings of a downpour, and much sooner than I expected. Maybe I'll start relining those baskets instead. Dawn, okay if we have the sheriff meet me in the greenhouse or the shed?"

"Of course." Grandma Dawn thought a moment, before adding, "I'll phone the sheriff now and then send him your way when he arrives."

Branson withdrew and Grandma Dawn exited the kitchen for the telephone down the hall. Having finished the waffles, Heather rinsed her plate. When heading upstairs to change into her clothes, she could hear the murmur of her grandmother's voice as she spoke to the sheriff.

Heather felt the tingle of both danger and excitement at the thought that Mr. Simpletripp was digging again, searching for the treasure buried by Scarbones Bristol. And even in the rain! She hadn't told Molly yet, but at some point Heather intended to catch him at it. But how? The girl figured that her neighbor wasn't going to take a risk and return to dig anywhere near the house until Sheriff Dane and his deputies stopped patrolling. So, knowing there was little she could do at the moment, the girl was content to bide her time.

Back in her bedroom, Heather saw that a heavy downpour had begun to thrash the windows. The room was gloomy and she turned on the pendant fixtures overhead. In the warm glow, Heather thought about Autumnsloe as she dressed. The girl had decided earlier that morning that she would head up to the third floor and the Bristol House library to see whether there were any books on the subject.

Molly loved the way Dawn Thibble's entire face beamed when she looked at her.

"You'll find Heather upstairs, Molly," Grandma Dawn said, in anticipation of her question, "either in her room or the library."

"Thank you, Mrs. Thibble."

Grandma Dawn watched the girl depart and heard her sluggish tread on the stairs outside the kitchen door. Grandma Dawn was concerned about the disturbing change that had come over Molly. The child seemed worn down, her expression fatigued, and her overall bearing weighted in despair.

As if sensing her thoughts, Mrs. Pringle said, "She's not right, is she?" Eyes glassy, she held her tears.

Turning from the door, mug in hand, Grandma Dawn momentarily inspected her neighbor. She said, "Come on, Lana. Let me get you some tea."

Pitched by the wind, a spray of rain splattered the high kitchen windows. Limp green leaves slapped violently at the glass before a whip-like retreat.

Distractedly glancing up at the windows and their faltering light, Grandma Dawn said, "I'll start a fire here in the hearth, and then we can talk."

Surprised, but not totally, Heather held the heavy book in her slender hands. The tome was bound in rich brown leather, and elegant scrollwork framed the cover, back, and spine, embossed with subtle geometric design. Across its face, the gilded letters spelling ΛUTUMNSLOE were recessed and shone feebly in the somber surroundings. Heather ran her fingers over the inlaid jewels at the cover's corners. They winked and blinked weakly with the dull light filtering through the ceiling's frosted windows, the glass currently under a rainy onslaught.

"Heather?"

Heather heard Molly's voice float to her from one of the library's many rooms, each elaborately furnished with a differing decor.

Poised high atop a ladder, near an open glass panel, Heather shouted, "I'm in here, Molly!"

She heard Molly's voice, now louder as she neared: "Where are you?"

"You're getting warmer," Heather replied, the fun of the tease finding her. Hearing Molly giggle, Heather kept watch over the room that lay below, the aisles of bookshelves intersecting its long carpeted spine at intervals.

"These rooms are always in different places," Heather heard her friend call out, her voice muffled. "It mixes me up. I think I've passed through two library rooms I've never seen before..."

She saw Molly enter through the side doors to her left, located about halfway down the narrow room. The young brunette scanned the rows of carved walnut bookcases that rose from the floor and stopped partway to the ceiling. Coming up empty, she headed out through the opposite set of doors.

"Heather?"

Heather waited before playfully casting her voice towards the next room. "You're getting colder."

Moments later, Molly wandered back into the room. Tentatively, she stopped and turned down the center aisle, her back to Heather. Walking past row after row of bookcases, she peered down the side aisles, all the while moving towards the far entry doors. Heather whistled softly. Molly stopped.

"All right, where are you?"

Heather whistled again, and Molly turned her way. The brunette's gaze followed the lengthy aisle of plush green carpet, up the sides of the bookcases that lined it, and upon seeing a ladder rising against the far wall, climbed the rungs to its apex. Catching sight of her friend, Molly laughed, for Heather was holding the oversized brown book in front of her face. Slowly the girl lowered the weighty volume, her eyes revealing themselves over its top. They danced merrily.

"Look what I have."

The sky outside the arched ceiling brightened, and with it so did the room. Heather held out the book for her friend to see, its colorful jewels glistening in the cascading light.

"What is it?" Molly asked.

"A book."

"I know *that*." Molly's weary face broke into laughter. "But of what?"

Pulling the book in tight, and with countless volumes forming a vertically stroked backdrop, Heather began to descend the ladder, rung after rung, shelf after shelf.

"A place you've never heard of," Heather said.

"Try me," the knowledgeable Molly challenged, a spark of interest taking root in the dimness of her eyes.

"Autumnsloe."

"Where?"

"Autumnsloe. A place I just visited."

"Really? When did you go there?"

Heather reached the bottom of the ladder. "Last night."

"You went there last night?" Molly looked puzzled.

Heather nodded. "In a dream."

Elbows resting on the kitchen table, Mrs. Pringle was looking at Grandma Dawn over the top of her tea mug.

"Has he been reasonable?" Grandma Dawn asked.

"He thinks he's been. But of course, he doesn't bend much."

"How has Molly dealt with the friction between you two? Or has she even noticed?"

"Oh, she's noticed, all right," Mrs. Pringle said. "As a matter of fact, she usually leaves the room when Ned instigates an argument. And of course, I'm tempted to follow on her heels."

Their laughter rang out and so did the doorbell, bonging melodically, one, two, three, four.

"Who can that be?" Grandma Dawn asked, setting down her coffee mug and rising, her chair squeaking with a slide. "Excuse me a moment, will you, please, Lana?"

Grandma Dawn walked briskly down the long hallway, past the front stairs, and into the foyer. Taking hold of the elegant doorknob, she gave it a twist. Upon seeing her visitor, Grandma Dawn managed to keep her smile stiffly in place. The caller was her neighbor, two houses down on Afterglow Drive, Mrs. Eloise Glutten.

Mrs. Glutten was a short stout woman with large breasts corralled in a drooping neckline, accented by a canyon of cleavage. Below a sag of double chin, she was attired in a dark blue dress with frilly pink trim and large colorful polka dots. Extending beyond each side of a generous waistline, Grandma Dawn saw the extremes of a very large pink bow. She was reminded of a nursery rhyme gone awry.

"Why, hello, Eloise. What a surprise." Grandma Dawn's words danced pleasantly off her tongue, despite her feelings.

"Hi, Dawn." Mrs. Glutten was breathing hard. In one hand was a creased piece of paper and in the other a furled umbrella with ruffled trim, tip down and dripping. She inhaled deeply. "Whew! Long walk up from that street of ours." She took another deep breath and gave a short laugh. "Used to have asthma, you know."

Grandma Dawn continued to smile politely, her arm gracefully extended, holding the open door. She was a bit surprised to notice that her neighbor wasn't wearing a coat.

"You're not cold?"

"Lot of walking."

"Mmm. What can I do for you, Eloise?"

Mrs. Glutton's small black eyes peered out over her chubby cheeks like two puncture wounds. Below her overly pert nose hung a frozen grin, like a lifeless painting. With her ample chest heaving as she gradually caught her breath, the air slipped between her parted teeth with a slight whistle. Grandma Dawn noticed the perspiration that perched in beads on the woman's brow and drained down her temples, in spite of the cold. Though she guessed that, in all probability, dark stains also encircled Mrs. Glutten's armpits, Grandma Dawn graciously refused to look.

"See this paper, Dawn?" Eloise Glutten thrust it before her, held out in her small pudgy hand. "It's a list."

Instinctively rearing back, Grandma Dawn said, "Oh?" and the paper was immediately retracted.

"We're on a scavenger hunt for the Last Gasp Charity, you know, the one out by the old church on 34th Street."

All the churches were old in Noble. With a look, Grandma Dawn encouraged her guest to continue.

"Well, Joan's down in the car—er, Joan Crendall-Lake. You know old Joan. She'd never make it up here to your porch without an escalator. She's a smoker, too, even though she says she's quit. But between you and me," and here Eloise Glutten lowered her voice and leaned forward in an attempt at confidence, "I think she's been sneaking them, because I can still smell smoke on her—unless she's not washing her clothes, which could very well be. But never mind.

"So, let's see, Dawn. Well, right now we want..." Mrs. Glutten brought the list to her face, "...canned goods, toilet paper, or paper towels. Got any?"

"Well," Grandma Dawn was taken by surprise. "I might—"

"It's for the poor."

"Mm-hmm. Let me check the pantry—"

"If you'd like, you can go shopping first and then we can come back and get them later."

Having begun her retreat across the foyer from the open door, Grandma Dawn paused in her tracks. She turned to face Mrs. Glutton. "That's very thoughtful of you, Eloise, but it's not necessary."

"Your neighbor, Ms. Gardner, gave us an antique bi-plane."

"For the poor? Is it on your list?"

"Oh, no, but she was *very* generous. We like that."

"I'm sure."

"Of course, we couldn't fit it in the car."

"Of course."

"We'll have to pick it up later at the airstrip."

"Mm-hmm."

"Still flies, though."

"Great."

"We'll take cash, too."

"Pardon?"

"Cash. We'll take cash. See, it's here on the list." Eloise Glutten was pointing, but the poised woman was unable to read it from where she stood. She simply nodded in acknowledgement.

Grandma Dawn continued across the foyer towards the hall, and glanced over her shoulder. "Eloise, why don't you come—" Without warning, the large Bristol House door slammed shut with a BANG! "—in."

As the bell rang again, Grandma Dawn hurriedly returned to the door. She opened it.

"Oh, I'm sorry, Eloise. It must have been a breeze."

Mrs. Glutten was standing on the porch smoldering, her squat body framed by the doorway, her bulbous breasts pushed up and out by her meaty arms that lay crossed beneath them. Her umbrella had fallen across her shoetops.

Slightly flustered, Grandma Dawn said, "Perhaps someone opened the kitchen door and let in a gust—although I must admit I don't know how that could possibly have had an effect over here on this side of the house."

"We'll take cash," Mrs. Glutten said.

"Pardon me?"

"Dawn, we'll just take cash. It's for the poor."

"Yes, you said that earlier, didn't you? Well, my purse is right here." Grandma Dawn pointed to her left and stepped away towards the coat rack. On the porch, Mrs. Glutten bent to pick up her umbrella. BANG! The door slammed shut once again.

"Oh, my," Grandma Dawn murmured, purse in hand, as she rushed to reopen it. She looked before her. And then down.

"Oh, Eloise. Are you all right?"

Mrs. Glutten was sitting on her ample bottom, right hand cupping her nose. The umbrella lay angled across her chunky thighs.

"Eloise, I'm so, so sorry. This has never happened before. Here, let me help you up." Grandma Dawn began to extend her hand in assistance.

"Nogh!" Mrs. Glutten vehemently shook her head. Before her, she held up her palm and fingers like a chubby little stop sign. Blood trickled down into her spacious cleavage, seeping past a hand that was clamped firmly to her face.

Grandma Dawn said, "You may want to tilt your head back—"

"Nogh! Cahsf. Wehl juhfst tahk cahsf," the downed woman said. Mrs. Glutten had struggled to her knees, and with her free hand she grabbed hold of the doorjamb, clambering to her feet. Her umbrella toppled back and to one side. "Ihtz ohn thagh lihtz."

"Here, let me get you a tissue—"

"Nogh! Juhfst cahsf, thahkz."

"Of course." Grandma Dawn quickly pulled her wallet out of her purse. "How much?"

"Aht lehst twehnty."

"Twenty."

Looking down and fingering the bills in her wallet, Grandma Dawn grimaced. "At the moment, I'm afraid all I can give you is a ten, Eloise. Anything else will leave me short. Will ten do?"

Mrs. Glutten's brow came down in a hard "V" over her coal-button eyes, her free hand balling in a fist at her side. "Twehnty! Igh whant twehnty! Ihtss fohr thagh pohr!" She turned, and kicked her umbrella away. It clattered awkwardly behind her, bouncing off a wicker chair. "Twehnty!"

Grandma Dawn retreated a step. "But all I can spare is a ten—"

The pinpoint gaze registered disgust. "Agh, juhfst fohrgeht iht."

"You don't want ten?" Grandma Dawn had produced the bill and was holding it up in her right hand. "Surely the poor can use it."

"Fohrgeht iht." Seeing Dawn Thibble's bewildered look, Mrs. Glutten felt the need to clarify: "Yugh askzt howh muhch Igh nehded, ahnd Igh sahd twehnty."

One hand still pasted in red outline to her nose, Mrs. Glutten bent and with scrabbling fingers searched blindly for the white crumpled list lying somewhere at her feet. Upon finding it, her plump digits gobbled it up into a wad, consuming it within the hollow of her palm. Straightening and turning indignantly, chin up, she stalked towards the rain-soaked edge of the porch, the piggy twist of hair that protruded off her bun bouncing with every step. On the way, she kicked the umbrella that once again lay across her path. It rattled and crashed to a standstill. Eloise Glutten clomped down the stairs and into the rain. Stepping onto the walk, the short woman slipped momentarily, before regaining her balance and her sanctimonious posture. Only then did she resume her march.

Thinking it the last of her, Grandma Dawn exhaled with relief. She tucked the bill neatly into her wallet.

Looking up, the woman was surprised to find her neighbor mounting the stairs once again. Dripping wet, one hand still pressed to her nose, Mrs. Glutten stooped to reclaim the umbrella from the recesses of the porch. The portly woman then turned to her neighbor, who was standing in the doorway, staring with wonder. Eloise Glutten held the pointy device before her, displaying it for Grandma Dawn to see.

"Ihtz ohn thagh lihtz."

"Oh," Grandma Dawn said, nodding, as if an age-old mystery had been solved.

Stepping out from beneath the overhang of the porch, Mrs. Glutten trudged into the soaking rain yet again. Stifling a laugh, the refined woman watched her neighbor go, her large pink bow drooping with wetness.

Turning to replace her purse on the coat rack, Grandma Dawn stopped, as the movement of the Bristol House door caught her attention. It swung slowly and easily, before gently closing shut and locking into place with a secure click.

The blonde girl brought the large volume over to a nearby table, Molly in tow. Excitedly, Heather set it down.

"Look," she said. "Isn't it beautiful?"

The book's chiseled inscriptions glinted.

"Yes. And look at the jewels!" Molly said. "Oh, Heather, they *are* beautiful!" Molly couldn't restrain herself as she timidly touched the largest one, then instantly pulled away. She giggled. "They're real."

"Of course, they're real, silly." Heather found herself laughing. She looked at Molly in anticipation. "Time to look inside."

Taking hold of the large cover, Heather swung it open. She began to turn the gilt-edged pages. She turned more. And more.

"I don't get it, Heather."

Heather was leafing through the many cream-colored sheets, encountering blank after blank.

"That's weird, huh?"

Molly nodded. "Wait! What's that?"

"What?"

"Go back a few pages. I think I saw some writing."

Heather revisited the pages recently passed. Nothing.

"Sorry, Heather, I could have sworn I saw something."

Heather shrugged, and leafed quickly through the remaining pages.

"Hey, Heather, what's this?"

Heather turned to see Molly crouching to retrieve a piece of parchment off the green rug.

"Let's see."

"Must've fallen out of the book…" Molly said, inspecting the document. "It's a poem." She handed it to Heather.

The parchment was old, its pages yellowed and imbued with swirling design. In a cursive hand, the gold words glowed on the page.

A burst of bloom

With fronds and leaves,

A wheel to spin,

The flow it weaves.

With heat and light,

Yes, bud and shoot,

Within its door

A clue takes root.

"A game!"

"What?"

"It's a game, Molly. Don't you see? It's the Bristol House," Heather looked about admiringly, speaking to the room. "It wants to play a game with us."

"A game of what? What are we supposed to do?"

Heather read the poem aloud. "Well, I think it wants us to go to this place." She handed the paper to Molly. "Only, we don't know where it is, so we have to figure it out."

"But what's there?"

"Molly, that's the *game*. We find out when we arrive."

"Oh." Molly giggled and put on a goofy face. "It sounds like the Bristol House garden," she said, rereading the lines.

The room darkened once again, and the rain commenced its patter on the library roof.

"Yeah, but I don't think the Bristol House would send us out into the rain," Heather said, glancing at the skylights.

"Well, is there a conservatory up here?"

"A conservatory?" Heather blushed.

Molly looked at her suspiciously. "You don't know what that is, do you?"

Heather laughed, her face now redder. "No. But I bet it has a burst of blooms and fronds and leaves."

It was Molly's turn to laugh. "It's like a greenhouse, where a bunch of plants are grown. I've read about people building them onto their houses. They usually have a lot of glass to let in the sunlight, and sometimes people put out furniture and sit in there."

"What for?"

"Beats me. I guess if it's indoors, then they don't have to worry about getting stung by bees or bitten by bugs."

"Or stepping barefoot on a snail." Heather shrugged. "Must be one of those things that only makes sense to adults. I like bees and lizards and stuff." She grew quiet, before popping up with, "Hey, I think I know where there might be a conservatory."

"Where?"

"Follow me."

CHAPTER THIRTEEN

Along Visiting Hours

"Mrs. Thibble?" The deep voice called out from the hallway. Grandma Dawn and Mrs. Pringle looked up from the table in the kitchen. Each had a partially filled mug in front of them. Flames cast red and warmth from the recessed mouth of the fireplace. The fire spit, with sparks snapping briefly in air before dying.

"Sheriff Dane?" Grandma Dawn called. She stood.

The sheriff walked into the kitchen. He had removed his boots, revealing thick wool socks of khaki green.

"Mrs. Thibble, your front door was wide open."

"Really?"

"I hope you don't mind my entering this way, but if it's any consolation, I left my raincoat and muddy boots on the porch. The wife would kill me otherwise. And I have a sneaking suspicion you would, too."

"Heavens, no, I don't mind you entering that way! Please do come in, Sheriff Dane. But I think it's time you started calling me Dawn. You remember Lana Pringle."

Dane acknowledged the woman.

"Coffee?" Grandma Dawn asked.

"I could use a cup, but I can't stay long."

The sheriff declined milk, sugar, and a seat, and took the steaming mug from Grandma Dawn. Leaning back against the counter, he blew on the hot liquid before taking a careful sip. His expression registered approval.

"Saw the holes," Dane offered on exhale.

Both women looked fixedly at him.

"What do you think?" Grandma Dawn asked.

The sheriff blew on his coffee once again. "Someone's digging on your property." He sipped and swallowed. Concentrating on his brown hands that cradled the mug, Dane asked, "Someone looking for the treasure?" He smiled ruefully.

"You know, Sheriff," Grandma Dawn said, "I don't know what they're looking for. That treasure rumor has been floating around for years—"

"The hidden treasure of Scarbones Bristol," the sheriff announced. "A fortune in plundered booty." He laughed softly and sardonically, showing off his white teeth. "I remember the legend from when I was a kid." He shook his head and took a mouthful of coffee. Eventually, he bunched his lips before saying, "Well, I couldn't get anything from the footprints due to the weather we've been having and the lateness of the discovery."

"Hank figured as much," Grandma Dawn said. "Have you checked in with my neighbor, Sheriff?"

"Simpletripp? Yeah." Dane watched the coffee swirl and slosh, spinning the remaining liquid in his mug. "I just paid him a visit before I came here. Doesn't know anything about any holes, he claims, or anyone digging them. Says if something has happened, you can rest assured he was busy working at his gallery, and will be when future events of a similar nature occur. Always. And of course, his wife will be there to confirm it." Dane looked up from his coffee. "Always."

"So," Grandma Dawn continued, "you don't think these holes have anything to do with the boy's murder?"

"Hard to say. No body." Following a conclusive swig, Dane set his mug on the counter with finality. "Well, ladies…" he said, and looked nearby for his hat. His face flashed with irritation when he remembered he'd left it on the porch, and furthermore, that it was soaked through.

Mrs. Pringle asked, "Sheriff Dane, so how's the investigation going?"

With the same rueful smile climbing to his lips, the sheriff rocked back towards the counter, his large hands gripping the edge behind him. His face dropped all expression, and he said rotely, "Well, ladies, I can't comment on an ongoing investigation, as you probably know. Let's just say we have our suspicions and we're continuing to investigate all leads."

"That's it? But with all due respect, Sheriff, I could've gotten that information from the Daily Compass—and have. It's been quite some time since the murder."

"I'm sorry, Mrs. Pringle, but that's the best I can do. Now, I've got to go."

"Here, Sheriff," Grandma Dawn said, "I'll walk you to the door."

The two moved in silence down the hallway, the sheriff keenly aware of Dawn Thibble's presence on his heels all the while, like a contemplative shadow. In the foyer, the woman drew alongside.

"This door has been giving me trouble all day," Grandma Dawn said, as she held it open for Sheriff Dane. "It slammed shut unexpectedly and knocked Eloise Glutten on her backside."

"Then I suggest you don't fix it."

The woman followed the sheriff onto the porch.

"Thank you, Dawn, for getting in touch with me. If the digging happens again, let me know. And thanks for the coffee."

"My pleasure, Sheriff Dane."

He reached down and grabbed his muddy boots. Maneuvering into a chair nearby, the sheriff sat to put them on.

Thoughtful moments passed. "Sheriff, mind if I ask you a question?"

"You just did, Dawn," Dane said, slipping into his second boot with a grunt. He began to lace and tie it. "Besides, if you're going to ask what I think you're going to ask, the answer is no." He shifted his attention to the first boot, and began to lace it.

"I was going to ask if you had any suspects in the Stilped murder investigation?"

"Confidentially, that's what I thought you were going to ask."

The thin man, bearing a rigid, hard-packed authority, rose, grabbing his raincoat and hat. He shook the latter and placed it on his head.

Sliding into his raincoat, the remaining water leaping off with a shrug, Dane said, "Dawn, all these holes? Be careful, okay? We still have a murderer to catch."

"Wow! I can't believe it!" Heather jumped with an exuberant spin, her arms stretched jubilantly overhead.

"Oh, Heather, this is…" Molly was at a loss for words, as she looked around the spacious, light-filled room. She finally settled on, "Breathtaking!"

"How did we find this room again?" Heather asked.

"I don't know. I just followed you."

The two walked farther up the trail of stepping-stones and away from the entrance. From somewhere yet undiscovered, the sound of trickling water met their ears. Butterflies floated by, bees flitted from colorful bloom to colorful bloom, and birds chirped, darting to and from limbs with a rustling of wings.

"Look, Molly," Heather pointed, "in the birdbath."

A golden-yellow bird with gray wings and an orange and black head splashed about and then bolted to a branch above, where it preened.

Surveying the lush environment, Heather said, "Now I know why adults like conservatories."

The girls laughed.

Molly took in a prolonged whiff of air and then exhaled, her weary face taking on a hint of bliss. "Oh, it smells so heavenly; so fresh and pure. Heather, this place is absolutely…divine."

On three sides, a series of elegant columns braced the walls, and through their uprights, against a backdrop of hazy light, the girls could see more trees and lush greenery in adjoining rooms. Colorful ground-cover hugged the earth and elsewhere, large rocks made their massive presence known. Not far from the path, ponds with brightly colored fish were visible through waist-high shrubs arrayed with blue and lavender blooms. Trees reached high, their boughs rising to soak up the sunless light filtering through the girder-framed windows far above.

The girls crossed over an arched bridge above a lily pond, before the sloping footpath began to wind among the fruit trees and towards a small stream. Heather increased her pace, and Molly began to skip. And whistle quietly. Yet, soon her whistled tune grew in volume, leaping happily on air. All at once, she stopped and pointed.

"Look, Heather, a waterwheel!"

Molly broke into a run. Heather followed and caught up, and the two raced towards the stone house whose large wheel alongside was driven by the water that rushed, splashed, and gurgled beneath it. Heather slowed to let Molly reach the bank of the stream first, watching as her friend kneeled and shoveled cool water onto her face. Afterwards, throwing her head back, Molly began to laugh. She dipped her head close to the stream and repeated the watery gesture, again finding pleasure in the simple act. Subsequently, she turned her face skywards and took in a deep, restorative breath.

When Heather knelt nearby at the water's edge, Molly sloshed water on her. In an instant, the two were splashing each other, having a playful water fight and laughing as they became wet.

"Stop!" Molly said. She put up her hands and sat back, giggling in spurts, catching her breath. "Heather we have to stop."

"Okay, okay." Heather's face grew serious.

"Now," Molly said, "We have to figure out what the clue meant—"

With her friend's guard down, Heather unexpectedly launched more water in her direction, and the girls were soon at it again, soaking one another.

Laughing uncontrollably, Molly stood, drenched from head to foot. *Look at me!* Molly gestured with her hands.

With her own rollicking laughter ringing out to join Molly's, Heather rose and stood alongside her. Yet, when their eyes met, Heather watched as the gaiety drained from her friend's face, to be replaced instead by overwhelming sadness. Molly was now crying hysterically. And at a loss, Heather's own merriment faded.

"What's wrong, Molly?"

Molly just shook her head as wrenching sobs racked her slender body. Placing a hand to her chest, Molly found herself too weak to stand upright, her head bowed, her brown hair pendulous. She wanted to scream out, but no sound came forth, just an agonized O of the mouth stretching slender rails of saliva.

"Molly, what?" Heather placed a hand on her friend's shoulder. She looked up under Molly's downturned head, trying to catch her eyes. Molly backed away.

"I don't know," she managed between sobs, her words slurred. "Heather, I don't know. I was just laughing…a moment ago…"

With a gentle hand on her arm, Heather guided Molly to a nearby boulder, where the two sat. Heather watched as her friend's aura broke loose in tormented violets and disconsolate shades of blue. Worried, she knew that the sorrowful Molly continued to be shaky and not at all herself. Heather and Aria, after many brief discussions, both attributed her behavior to the deaths of Teacup and Stilped. Aria thought that Molly felt a deep sense of guilt and loss, because Teacup had gotten loose that night while under her care, and along with Stilped, had been murdered so abhorrently. Heather only knew that Molly hadn't been the same since and still didn't want to talk about what had happened that day.

"It's okay, Molly. You're okay."

Molly nodded, attempting to restrain her tears.

"You're okay." Heather's hand reached out to soothingly rub her back. Molly inhaled deeply. Shortly, she began to mildly snuffle.

"You okay?" Heather asked.

Molly laughed slushily. "I thought you just said I was."

"Well, I always thought you were. Still do."

Molly's brown eyes sought Heather's green, and she began to cry again. Molly reached out and embraced her friend. She held tight. Heather's arms enfolded Molly in turn. She gently rocked her.

"You are, Molly," she whispered. "You're okay."

After a short while, Molly broke away, collecting herself, taking another deep breath.

"All right," she said, sniffing and wiping away tears with a wet sleeve. "'*The wheel to spin,*'" Molly remembered, "'*The flow it weaves.*'"

Heather looked up and noticed that the water did indeed weave, winding through the plantlife to disappear from view.

"Molly, where's the riddle?"

Fingers burrowing, Molly dug into her waterlogged pocket and retrieved the decorative parchment. She handed it to Heather, who unfolded the paper and again looked it over. Somehow, the parchment had remained dry.

"Well, since we found the wheel, I know we're in the right place." Molly agreed.

"Okay, so what are we looking for? '*A clue takes root.*' Another clue?"

"Yes, but where do we begin to look?" Molly stood, regarding the room. "The conservatory goes on in three directions."

"I wonder what it means, '*bud and shoot,*'" Heather said, "when they're all around us? Which buds and which shoots?"

"How about we follow the path for a while. Maybe we'll see something that stands out."

Heather stood and slapped dirt off her bottom. "It doesn't say anything about a path in the poem. What if we follow '*the flow it weaves*'?"

"You lead."

And Heather did. The girls followed the water's course for some distance, stepping over plants and bushes, maneuvering around trees, over boulders, and past ponds and fronds.

After a time, Molly said, "Heather, let's look at that poem again." They found another rock on which to rest. Molly read: "'*Within its door, a clue takes root.*' The door of what?"

"Of the conservatory, silly."

"No, I don't think so, Heather. Of '*bud and shoot*'?"

"Well, to answer your question: '*Yes, bud and shoot.*' Says so right there. See?" Heather pointed at the paper, looking over Molly's shoulder.

"'*Of bud and shoot, of bud and shoot…*' Oh, I don't know."

Molly gave the paper back to Heather.

"Come on, Molly. We'll find it. Hey, where're you going?"

"Sounds like a waterfall over here," Molly said, moving through some bushes.

Tucking the clue away in her pants pocket, Heather followed. Sure enough, water from the small stream was flowing over rocks, and after breaking up into many smaller falls, spilled into a large lake below. Molly just gazed in wonder.

"Wow, Heather. Who would believe us if we told them that the Bristol House had a lake on the third floor—? Heather?"

"I'm over here. Look, Molly. Some of the water is going down into this small cave."

Molly turned to see Heather leaning into the cave's mouth. All around her and covering the hillside were masses of tiny buds belonging to the prevailing foliage. They were denser around the cave opening.

"Hello, down there!" Heather shouted into the cave. Her voice echoed its return. "Dark in there," she said, withdrawing.

With a giggle, Molly just shook her head.

Unexpectedly, all the buds around the cave and upon the hillside unfurled into bloom: oranges, violets, yellows, blues, and reds; at their small circular centers, each appeared lit as if by a small light. Astonished, the two girls exchanged glances.

Molly said, "I think this means we're on the right track."

"Yep. We found the buds, all right. *Yes, bud and shoot.*' Molly, can a cave be a shoot?"

Knowingly, Molly's face lit up. "It sure can. A shoot can be an inclined channel for moving something. In this case, water moving through a cave. What are you doing?"

"Climbing into the shoot."

"Heather, what if—?"

"Come on! The water's not moving very fast."

Heather sat and the water rushed up against her bottom and lower back, before managing its way around her. The cave walls began to glow an eerie green. She edged slowly, carefully down into the cavern, drawing herself forward with her hands on the smooth glossy walls, and pulling against the shallow floor with the heels of her soggy red shoes. In an instant, she hit a slick spot, and with aid from the water's flow, Heather was off on a toboggan run of a ride. Hurtling down through the glassy-surfaced tunnel, she rode up a sleek wall around a bend, only to be bounced back down before careening up the other side, and then propelled forward in a streak on a long straightaway. Head bouncing, Heather was leaning back, hands on thighs, looking over her red shoes at the murky tube that unfolded with rapid twists and turns in front of her.

"Whoaaaa-a-a-a-ah!"

Carried by her momentum over a sudden rise, Heather was thrust high up the side of a curving wall, and her path temporarily ascended in a long arc before heading down, continually down, into the recesses of the earth. Streaming, pitching, snaking, plummeting, jetting, now skimming and skittering, in a rush Heather streaked her water-slicked course. With a slight rise and bump, she accelerated through the adjoining mouth of the cave, and out into a rocky landscape heading ever downward.

Facilitating her uncontrollable flight downstream, water from adjoining creeks flowed in over the walls of the polished half-chute that formed a trench beneath the sliding girl. Large boulders on either side flashed by, and the spray of water made it difficult to see clearly. Yet, Heather managed to look past her shoe tops and noticed the run coming to an abrupt end, the land falling off into a precipitous canyon below. There was no way she could slow down. Lying back, Heather tucked her arms, crossing them over her chest. She kept her eyes open.

"Whoaaaa-a-a-a-a-a-a-a-a-a-ah!"

The girl was cast gushing out of the chute, hurtling forward into midair. As she flew, her feet gradually lowered and her body became more vertical. Far below, the canyon opened up in a wide expanse of mountainous terrain, meadows, trees, and lakes, before the scene faded into an ever-blackening void. Moments passed in blackness until her feet slammed into a gauzy, forgiving surface that, stretching, slowed her momentum prior to giving way. Bursting into the light, Heather found herself toppling onto an extremely large bed with an extremely large bounce.

"Umph!"

There she came to rest.

"Wow!" Heather relished the rush of the past moments, exclaiming, "Wow! Wow! *Wow*! Now *that's* a shoot!"

Thus energized, she sprang off the bed and looked around her.

Heather found herself in a spacious room, opulently furnished. Near the bed with its plush brocade coverlet was a tall lamp whose shade was comprised of glass peacock feathers, multi-eyed in greens and blues. A lacquered davenport sat in one corner, matching in style the nightstands on each side of the oversized bed. To the left of the small desk were narrow bookcases rising to the colorful ceiling, where four small chandeliers hung, ready for use when the stained-glass windows that lined the opposite wall were insufficiently forthcoming with their light.

Heather looked down at her clothes and noted with surprise that they were completely dry. The girl then focused her attention on the wall behind her. Above the bed's tufted headboard was a large painting of enormous cliffs with a lengthy waterfall plunging steeply before landing in a meadow's blue lake, among a gathering of trees.

Heather walked over and lifted one corner of the painting's frame. Peering beneath, the curious girl checked to see if there existed a hinged door of some sort that she might have fallen through. Unable to find one, Heather rapped her knuckles on the wall a couple of times hoping to identify hollowness, but detected no such thing. She lowered the painting carefully back into place. Impulsively, Heather reached above the headboard and slid an index finger into the painted waterfall. When her forefinger emerged wet, she licked it.

"Mmm. Blueberry."

Heather's gaze wandered the room. Intrigued by the davenport in the corner, she began to walk towards it.

"Aghhhh-h-h-h-h-h-h!"

Heather started and whirled in time to see Molly come flying out of the painting, to be deposited on the cushiony bed, large bounce, bounce, bounce. Lying on her back, stupefied, Molly simply stared at the ceiling.

"Molly?" Heather said.

Molly rose up on her elbows, looked dazedly at Heather, and then dropped back down onto her back with yet another bounce, splaying her arms out wide.

"Wasn't that incredible?" Heather asked. "Wasn't that fun? Wow!"

Molly rose up again and faced Heather with the same stunned look, and then dropped back down.

"You know, Molly, with the Bristol House being magic like it is, a purple elephant might just come shooting out of that picture any second. It would probably crush you."

Molly giggled. She rolled to her stomach and then slid off the peacock-inspired coverlet and onto her feet. She regarded Heather, her eyes ablaze with exhilaration. After a moment or two of standing silent, summing up the wild experience, Molly said, "*That* was stupendous."

They laughed.

"Did we end up in the right place?" Molly asked.

"Who cares? I say let's go again."

"What room is this, anyway?"

"I think it's the Master Guestroom Suite. And look." Heather pointed.

"What?"

"On the desk. It's another clue."

Wilson Talbott didn't mind the walk up Thimble Hill to deliver the post. As a matter of fact, he relished the hike up through the Bristol House grounds, taking in the stunning display of greenery. It reminded him of some of the gardens from his childhood, so wonderfully designed and carefully tended. Often he wondered how Branson and Dawn Thibble managed by themselves with just occasional help from the townsfolk.

Dawn Thibble. Such a lovely lady, tall and reminiscent of women he had known back home in his youth. He figured it must be why he found himself so attracted to her.

He was glad that the Bristol House was on his carrier route. Not only did it allow him the opportunity to stop in and see Dawn, but some days it provided the chance to wander and get a closer view of the promise held by such a beautiful garden in sunlight.

In the kitchen, Mrs. Pringle pushed in her chair. "Dawn, thank you so much for listening to me blather. I hope I'm not a bother."

"You're not a bother, Lana, not at all." The women began to walk towards the dutch door. "I think you're going through a difficult patch right now and talking helps you sort yourself out. Sometimes, too, when we doubt ourselves, we need help reinforcing our positions and, ultimately, our decisions."

Concurring, Mrs. Pringle reached for the iron doorknob. She turned and pulled. The door wouldn't open.

"Is it locked?" Mrs. Pringle asked.

"The door? It shouldn't be."

Mrs. Pringle pulled again. "It's not budging."

"What is it with the doors today?" Grandma Dawn said, taking hold of the knob relinquished by Mrs. Pringle. "I guess the Bristol House doesn't want you to go home!"

The ladies laughed, and following a second tug from Grandma Dawn, the door grudgingly gave way.

"Whew," Mrs. Pringle said, retrieving her coat and umbrella. "I thought for a second I was going to have to spend the night."

More laughter.

"Good morning, ladies."

The pair turned and welcomed Wilson Talbott, the postman, as he approached the house. He handed Grandma Dawn a small package and some envelopes.

"Dawn, I thought if I dropped the package off at your back door, rather than leave it on your porch, that you might have me in for tea. However, it seems that you've had your allotted company for the day," and here Talbott good-humoredly inclined his head towards Mrs. Pringle, "so I shan't intrude further."

In his early fifties, Talbott was a tall man who possessed a kindly face and a posture that was ramrod straight. The gracious mail carrier took a sincere interest in his postal patrons, being unfailingly courteous to Grandma Dawn and the people along his route. He hadn't been in town all that long when timing and luck landed him a job as a mail carrier with the Noble post office. Having spent his youth in England, he once told Grandma Dawn that he had married an American woman when he was in his twenties. He didn't say what happened to the marriage or his wife, but Grandma Dawn, knowing Wilson Talbott to be a private man, never asked and thus was never told.

"Well, Wilson, I'd be happy to invite you in for a bit. I've had my share of coffee, but it's been a visitor's day, and I wouldn't mind the company for a short while."

"And I wouldn't mind getting inside where it's warm and dry. Lana," Talbott said, turning to Mrs. Pringle, "must you leave us?"

"I was just on my way out, Wilson, but I'll be back soon enough. I have some errands to run while there's a let up in the rain." Large drops began, and Mrs. Pringle put out her hand. "By the look of things, I'd better hurry." Then quickly, "I'm going. Bye."

Goodbyes were casually tossed in return, and as Mrs. Pringle walked briskly through the vegetable garden and towards her parked car in the drive, Talbott the postman followed Grandma Dawn into the kitchen for some hot tea and pleasantries.

A head with a twist,

One eye for its sight,

Its secrets are seen,

But only at night.

Standing alongside the writing desk, Heather looked at Molly. "What's it mean?"

"*'One eye for its sight.'* You wouldn't happen to have a Cyclops chained up somewhere in the Bristol House, would you?"

"Very funny. I don't think it's a *thing*. I think it's probably a clue to another room."

"Are there any rooms with only one window?" Molly asked.

"Not that I know of."

"Well, then, what room would be used only at night, so that people can see its secrets?"

"I don't know. Let's see. What happens at night? Sun goes down. We turn on our lights. Stars come—the stars come out! Molly! One eye: the telescope! A head that twists: the domed roof spins! The observatory!"

"Well, Dawn, I'm sorry to hear that the digging has resumed on your property," Wilson Talbott said. "Any idea who it could be?"

"Sure. I've seen him."

Talbott's rigid posture shot up even straighter. "You have?"

"Yes. It's my neighbor, Mr. Simpletripp. I've seen him on a few occasions, though I have to admit he was quite far away each time."

"He's a frightening fellow, isn't he? He makes me very uncomfortable when I deliver his post. He just stares. I can't simply hand his mail to him, because he refuses to take it. Instead he makes me walk past him to the box at his door, giving me the evil eye all the way there and back, until I'm finally on the sidewalk and off his property. Such an unpleasant man. Have you told Sheriff Dane?"

"Yes, but he's currently unable to do anything, because as the situation stands, it's my word against Simpletripp's. And, as I said, our digger was some distance away when I saw him out on the rough part of the property. Mind you, because he was bundled up in the wee hours of the morning, I couldn't be certain, beyond all doubt, that it was or wasn't my gregarious neighbor." Grandma Dawn's face creased with just an inkling of frivolity.

"At first, I thought it was harmless, the occasional holes on the property. Someone looking for Scarbone's treasure, it certainly wouldn't be the first time. However, after the boy's murder and burial on the grounds—"

"Yes, an unfortunate incident." Talbott's posture continued to ride straight up in agitation. "Unfortunate, indeed. That's a horrid wretchedness this good town must bear."

"So true, and I think we all do, everyone in their way. Did you know Stilped Roarhowser?"

Talbott looked angry, his hands jerkily unable to stay stationary on the tabletop. He pulled them off and lowered them onto his lap.

"It was a disgrace what happened to that boy! Dawn, I may have seen him or not, I don't know. I *do* know that he and his aunt didn't reside on my normal route, however there's a good possibility that I may have taken over another carrier's and delivered to his house for a day. But the point is, the children! We need to protect our children! We can't let this happen in Noble—or anywhere! And the sooner Sheriff Dane puts the perpetrator behind bars and justice is served, the better for all concerned." Talbott brought his mug down hard on the wooden table for emphasis.

Grandma Dawn was taken aback by Wilson Talbott's eruption. To her, it seemed unusual for the normally composed and gentlemanly mail carrier.

"More tea, Wilson?" she asked. Her words were gentle.

Talbott spoke to his hands, contrite. "Dawn, please excuse my outburst. As you can no doubt tell, I feel strongly that it's very important that our children be safe, and that no harm should ever come to them. And when something like the Roarhowser murder takes place, I find myself very, *very* reactive. Why, he was just a lad, for heaven sakes."

Grandma Dawn was pouring more tea into his cup. She continued to speak gently. "There's no need to excuse yourself, Wilson. Everyone in town shares your feelings." Grandma Dawn withdrew the teapot. "Except for maybe one."

When searching the room for another clue, Heather and Molly had finally caught their breaths. Previously, the two had rushed up a circular stairway, within a cylindrical tower of the Bristol House, and bounded into the observatory. There, unable to see a decorative piece of yellowed parchment in plain view, they mounted their hunt.

The space in which they found themselves was circular and fair-sized, with a domed metal canopy overhead. In groups of three, small square windows were periodically located around the perimeter, and curved shelves of astronomy books and writings lined an expansive area of wall. There were other shelves occupying other spaces and on them rested a variety of things, from less significant books and journals to small cabinets containing many smaller drawers. Near a larger window was a writing desk and chair with a wood-burning stove close at hand.

Throughout the room, solitary chairs had been scattered, and hanging on partitions and exposed areas of the wall were old photos and etchings of various celestial bodies. A small black clock on a shelf, its metallic pendulum rhythmically swinging to catch a wink of window, stood within view of anyone seated at the desk. It let loose with ten dainty bells.

Mounted on a cylindrical stand in the center of the room was a sizable telescope, and protruding from beneath its belly was a spoked brass wheel. Standing alongside was a frustrated Molly.

"All that's left are those books you're searching. Are you sure this is the right room, Heather?"

"Has to be, Molly." Heather had just finished looking through yet another row of books, flipping through the pages, hoping for the decorative parchment to stand out or fall to the floor.

Molly was gazing above her at the dome.

"That slit in the ceiling must open by turning those cranks." She shifted her focus. "And this, obviously, is the telescope. I dub thee Big Bertha," Molly said, standing at attention next to the cylindrical body and giving it a ceremonial pat on the flank. She then leaned down to peer through the lens. "Never looked through one of these before," she said, her mouth askew.

"I bet you never named one, either." When Molly didn't laugh or respond, Heather added, "You're not going to see much, except for maybe a close-up of the three hairs on the head of a fly up there. It's supposed to see far away into the night sky, you know—heavenly bodies and shooting stars, stuff like that."

"That's what you think."

Heather glanced up from sifting through a book. "What do you mean?"

"Come here and take a look."

Setting the thick volume down, Heather rose and joined her companion in the center of the room. She placed her eye to the lens. Immediately, she pulled away to look at Molly. Heather shook her head in amazement.

"It's the next clue."

When the clock in the observatory tapped out twelve bells, Heather and Molly were long gone. By then, they had searched and found clues leading to the study, lounge, and den, with each of the rooms having mysterious routes in and unexpected passageways out. Sometimes it wasn't the solving of the clue that took the time, but the finding of the room. On several occasions, when searching for a particular room, one of the girls would exclaim that the one they were currently passing through looked familiar. It would turn out that not only had they passed through the room previously, but had done so while in a different part of the house.

When taking a break from their game, the girls walked down the rear stairs on their way to lunch. Heather noticed Molly's annoyance.

"You're having fun, aren't you, Molly?"

"Yes. At times."

"At times? What do you mean? Molly, this game isn't about winning, you know. So, let's just have fun. It's not like we're on a time limit or something."

"But I am. Don't forget, I'll have to go home this afternoon."

"We can always pick up where we left off tomorrow."

"Only if Mom can convince Dad to let me come over, and hopefully without a huge argument. *And* if the Bristol House still wants to play."

Heather wasn't sure how to respond.

"Besides," Molly said, grumpily, "isn't it *interesting* how the Bristol House gets to make all the rules, mixing up rooms, telling us where to go and what to do?"

Heather stopped and turned, temporarily blocking Molly's path down the stairs. "And isn't *that* what makes this great fun? And it makes sense that the Bristol House makes the rules."

"Why?"

"Because it owns the game board. Molly, the Bristol House cares about us. I know it. The game will be here when you come and play again."

The two continued their descent in ruffled silence. Upon reaching the bottom of the stairs, outside the kitchen, Molly grasped her friend's arm.

"Heather, just now, I shouldn't have said what I said. I'm sorry," and here, Molly looked up, "and I apologize to the Bristol House, too. Really, I *was* having fun. I don't know why I said those things on the stairs. I know we don't need to win. Heck, we don't even know what we're doing, why we're going from room to room. But it is fun, isn't it?" Molly went quiet for a moment. "Maybe—well, maybe I'm just jealous that your house is so much fun and right now mine isn't like that. Not at all. Mom and Dad are fighting a lot, and—and I don't like being there."

For a moment, Molly's confession left Heather at a loss. But she rallied up: "Molly, then you'll just have to come over and have fun with *us.*" Heather cast her gaze above her. "And I'm sure the Bristol House agrees."

Molly produced a grateful smile. "Heather, what do you think we're hoping to find at the end, anyway? I mean, where does all this lead?"

"I have a feeling the Bristol House will tell us when it's ready. So, I say, Why worry about it?"

Molly agreed. "Well, whatever the Bristol House is planning for us, I bet it's going to be really, really great."

When the girls entered the kitchen for lunch, Grandma Dawn was amazed to see the change in Molly over such a short period of time. She seemed animated and talkative, a far cry from the Molly of just that morning. And though she still carried a worn persona, the observant woman could see renewed life in the child—like a replenished Bristol House flower after much needed rain.

"Hello, there, young ladies." Talbott beamed at their presence.

The girls greeted the mailman cheerily, but returned to talking between themselves.

"Your sandwiches are on the counter, girls," Grandma Dawn said. "Help yourselves to something to drink. There's lemonade in the fridge."

"Well, Dawn, I think it's time to get back to work on the mail trail. Thankfully, it's a light load today."

As the postman got to his feet, the dutch door opened and the gardener stuck his head in.

"Well, hello, Wilson," Branson said. "Dawn, I just wanted you to know that I'm done for the day. With the short break in the rain, I was able to clip back most of that holly. Weather permitting, I'll finish it up tomorrow, if that's all right with you." The gardener fought to keep hold of the door handle as a blustery gust of wind attempted to wrest it free.

"Thank you, Hank. Yes, it's fine. See you tomorrow."

The postman said, "Cheers, Hank."

"Wilson," Branson concluded, closing the door behind him.

"Right, then, young ladies, I'm off," said the mailman.

After looking up and offering brief goodbyes, the girls returned to conversing.

"It was good seeing you, Wilson. I'm glad you stopped by."

"Thank you, Dawn. We'll do it again and soon, I hope."

As the mailman reached for his raincoat, the dutch door burst open, the wind forcefully thrusting its way in. Light on his feet, Talbott was able to dance aside, the door swinging wildly just past his face. It crashed against the doorstop, causing Heather and Molly to jump and the cooking utensils to rattle. But it took only a moment before the girls were again lost to themselves and their discussion.

"Oh, I'm sorry, Wilson," Grandma Dawn said, grabbing hold of the unruly door. "Hank must not have closed it firmly when he left. I didn't think that having tea with me could be so explicitly dangerous."

"No harm done, Dawn. A carrier's job is fraught with such dangers. We're used to it," Talbott said with a wink, his mood still cheery. "Goodbye, and thank you again for your hospitality."

With that, the postman set out on his rounds once again. And this time, Grandma Dawn made certain that the door was closed securely behind him.

There's food and some drinking,

Yet, that's not why you're there,

To eat at this table,

Brings but grief and despair.

"That one's easy to figure out," Molly said.

Having finished their lunch, Heather was leading the two on their way back up to the third floor.

"No way. Why would someone have grief and despair after eating at *this* table, wherever *this* table is? The food?" Heather asked.

"Because it's not an eating table."

"What kind is it? A multiplication table?"

"Ha-ha. Funny. It's a pool table."

Heather lit up. "The billiard room. Come on. I know the way."

Molly giggled.

"What?" Heather asked.

"Sure, you know the way—if the room is still in the same place."

Heather's laughter trailed her bounce of blonde hair up the stairs.

Following a spirited couple of knocks, Mrs. Pringle let herself into the Bristol House kitchen, along with a wind-blown flurry of rain and leaves.

"Well, I'm back, Dawn. It seems this rain never gives up."

Grandma Dawn looked over from the sink, where she was rinsing out the girls' cups and dishes.

"Oh, hi, Lana. The kids came down for lunch, but they've gone back upstairs to further pursue their adventures. More tea?"

Mrs. Pringle was hanging up her wet coat and scarf and laying her umbrella next to the door.

"How about a large glass of water? I'd be happy to get it."

"Help yourself." Grandma Dawn was wiping dry a pan. "Get all your errands done?"

"Yes," she said, taking a glass off the shelf and joining her neighbor at the sink to fill it, "and Ned surprised me by coming home for lunch. He wanted to talk."

"And?"

"He seems to think that it's time for a weeklong vacation."

"Oh? Great! Get out of this gloom. Where does he want to take the three of you?"

"There's no 'three of you' about it."

Grandma Dawn looked perplexed.

"He's going by himself."

"I like this room. I've been here lots of times," Heather said.

The walls were of a rich and glossy two-toned burl, with a commanding fireplace to one side. Three lights hung from the ceiling, illuminating the pocketed table. Molly had an urge to brush her fingertips over the green felt and did.

"You've played billiards before, haven't you?"

Picking up the cue that was lying diagonally across the table, Heather responded, saying, "When I came in here and found the table, I had to give it a try. It took a little while to get the knack."

"Well, I'd try it, but I'd be afraid of tearing the felt."

"Don't worry, Molly. At first, I kept ripping it every time I tried to hit the ball hard, but the table always healed up." Leaning over the green, preparing a shot, Heather slid the stick back and forth easily on her planted hand. Only two balls were visible on the table. "See a clue anywhere?" Heather asked, without breaking one-eyed concentration.

As Molly's gaze roamed the room, Heather hit the white cue ball, knocking it into the red one, and depositing the latter neatly in the corner pocket.

The floorboards began to shake. Heather dropped the pool cue and the two girls retreated as the table sank below floor level.

"This is getting too easy," Molly said.

"Maybe the Bristol House knew you were on a time limit."

"You know, Heather," Molly paused, marveling, "It really wouldn't surprise me."

The two descended some steps, and Heather set out across the top of the table that was now a green felt floor. Reaching the far side, Heather turned and saw an anxious look cross Molly's face, as she began to delicately place her steps.

"Molly, you can't wreck it, remember? It heals. And it's probably self-cleaning, too."

At her friend's words, Molly adjusted to a more natural stride, though not completely, and finally skittered across the remaining surface after a small leap over the discarded cue stick. She joined Heather, who was walking into a lightless corridor. Behind them, the table rose to lock back into place, sealing any retreat to the previous room and throwing the girls into utter blackness.

"When does he plan on going?" Grandma Dawn asked.

"He didn't say." Mrs. Pringle sipped her water.

A melodic BONG, BONG, BONG, BONG momentarily interrupted the conversation.

"The door. Again. It's been a busy day. Can you hold that thought, Lana?"

"Eloise coming back to haunt you?"

"Don't scare me. She can certainly make someone think twice before answering their door. Excuse me, a second, if you would."

Once again Grandma Dawn walked the hallway to the foyer and opened the front door. Standing before her was a young boy and his father. The father, in a black raincoat, was of average height, in his mid-fifties, with an ill-fitting jet-black toupee over severe features.

The boy, standing before the father, was a year or two younger than Heather, with wet brown hair and darker brown eyes. Wearing a large open coat currently dripping with the day, he exhibited a glimpse of green sweater over a yellow button down shirt, all rumpled and a bit worn.

"Good day. I'm Gloster Elderberry and this is my boy Duncan. Duncan?"

The boy cleared his throat. "Ma'am, my name is Duncan Elderberry, um, like my father, here, said. On behalf of my sixth grade class, from C. Phillip Phaulphunnie Elementary School, we're trying to get enough money to visit our nation's capital in the spring. If there's anything you'd like to donate to our cause, my classmates and I would be very grateful."

"Would ten do?" Grandma Dawn asked.

"Dollars? Really?" He turned and looked up at his dad and then back again. "It sure would." The boy was still somewhat reserved, but his bridled excitement was evident to the woman who towered above him.

"Let me grab my wallet, it's right here."

Reaching into her purse, Grandma Dawn withdrew her billfold, and retraced her steps to the waiting boy.

"Here you go, Duncan." Grandma Dawn handed him some bills.

The boy thanked her, and the father nodded graciously, his wavy toupee inching farther down his forehead above acutely pointed brows.

Grandma Dawn shut the door and returned the wallet to her purse. As she pivoted to go back to the kitchen, there was a timid knocking on the door.

"Who now?"

Grandma Dawn hastened to answer it. Standing before her yet again was the boy.

"Ma'am, you gave me too much money, more than the ten." Duncan was holding out the extra bills.

"No, I certainly didn't. I'd like you to keep it." Grandma Dawn smiled her smile. "May you and your classmates have a splendid trip."

"Really? You don't want it back?"

"Thank you very much," the senior Elderberry spoke up, again standing behind the boy. "It's very generous of you."

"Goodbye, now," Grandma Dawn said, and closed the door.

Heather and Molly were feeling their way along pitch-black walls. Heather ran her fingers atop the bumpy surface as she led, one arm searching before her.

"Seems these walls are made of rock," Heather said, her voice sounding strange within the enclosed space.

"At least it's not sloping down, like that first tunnel."

"The cave?"

"Yes."

"Wouldn't it be great if it was and there were lights on the walls and we were rollerblading?"

"Heather, you can't see me right now, but I am *so* rolling my eyes."

Molly bumped into a stationary Heather.

"Hey!" Heather said.

"How come you stopped?"

"Because the wall ends here. I'd try to go through it, but I don't think it's possible."

"Ha. Ha."

"I think we've reached a dead end."

"Are you sure? Heather, we can't go back. That pool table closed us in."

"I know. Okay, Molly, let's feel along these walls for an opening of some sort. You take that wall behind me and I'll take this one in front."

"I can't see which way you're facing."

Heather reached out, and finding Molly's hand, placed it on a wall.

"That's your wall. Start where it ends here in the corner, and work your way back towards the billiard room."

The two began to probe in the darkness, Molly starting as high as she could reach and working tentatively downward, Heather feeling around on the wall marking the tunnel's end.

"Molly?"

"Where are you?"

"Back here, still on the short wall. I found a handle of some sort."

"Can you turn it?"

A rusty creak gave out as Heather twisted the handle. The floor below her began to move.

"Molly, hurry up! Get over here. The floor's rising under my feet!"

Molly ran towards Heather.

"Give me your hand!" Heather said.

Kneeling on the end of the escalating square of floor, she reached down and grabbed Molly's hand, dragging her up onto the ledge. Quickly on her feet, Heather felt the wall to her right as it slid by. She extended an arm above her into the emptiness.

"I can't feel a ceiling."

"Heather, there's a wall on every side now. It's like we're going up an elevator shaft."

They kept rising.

"I feel it now! There's a rock ceiling above us."

"I feel it, too."

"Molly, the ceiling isn't opening. It's not doing anything, just staying put."

The floor continued to ascend.

"We're going to get crushed!"

Mrs. Pringle chuckled. "And you gave him the rest of your cash?"

Grandma Dawn threw her head back and laughed. "Lana, I guess it's the difference between taking and giving. You know, Eloise came to my door expecting, and this boy came to my door asking." Grandma Dawn held her grin. "He allowed me to give."

"You realize, you were so generous, he might come back looking for an antique bi-plane."

"Then I guess I'd have to steer him towards the dragon's lair—better known as Eloise's doorstep." Grandma Dawn added, "But I doubt that boy is her type. Not yet, anyway. That mindset comes later, if at all.

"Now, may I ask you a serious question, Lana, as a confidant? Knowing that Molly is emotionally fragile right now, how do you think she's going to react, seeing her father go off on vacation alone?"

Lana Pringle pondered the question. "I don't know. In the past, when Ned has taken business trips, Molly and I would join him whenever possible just to get out of town. This time, I'm sure she'll suspect something is amiss, but," and here Mrs. Pringle shrugged, "Molly already knows there's a problem. Maybe she'll simply see it as a greater division that's developed between her father and me.

"I think what's interesting, Dawn, is that Ned wanted *me* to take the vacation when he originally breeched the subject, fully expecting me to leave Molly home with him. It was the weirdest thing—the way he acted when he proposed it, I mean."

"I can't see you allowing that to happen."

"That's because it never would," Mrs. Pringle lowered her voice, "especially in Molly's current state. I think Ned would know that. Makes me wonder…" She glanced guiltily at the door to be certain Molly wasn't within earshot. "And to think, you've known me for only a short while. Ned's known me our entire married life and longer—well, maybe 'known' is too strong a word. He just can't see past himself."

Grandma Dawn joined Mrs. Pringle at the table, refilled mug in hand. "Shall I go up and gather the girls?"

"No, let them play until they're ready to come down."

"Lana, are you sure? It may make you late getting home."

"I know. That's what I'm counting on."

"Molly, get on your knees. Quick!"

The girls dropped down. Anxious moments passed, the floor continuing its upward flight. And then, abruptly, the surface below them ground to a decisive standstill.

Scrambling to her feet, Heather said, "I can barely stand up." Leaning away, she felt the ceiling directly above her head.

"Heather, I'm feeling around, and there's a wall on every side but this one."

"It's another tunnel. Let's go."

Heather warily groped before her, leading Molly down the new passageway. They didn't go far before encountering another dead end.

"Stop," Heather said.

Molly ran into her.

"I said, 'stop,' you nut."

"Another wall?" Molly asked.

"Yeah, and another handle. Here we go again. Ready?"

Molly moved in close, and Heather cranked the handle. The floor began to drop.

"Oh," said Molly. "I thought for sure we'd be going up again."

Suddenly, the floor halted its descent.

Feeling about the walls, Molly asked, "What now?"

In the pitch of stationary darkness, she heard Heather say, "I don't know. We're trapped on all sides."

"Sure seems that way." Molly sighed heavily.

In an instant, the floor started moving again. This time it was rising.

"Very funny," Heather said.

"What?"

"I think the Bristol House thought it was clever, playing with us."

Molly said, "Whatever you do, just don't make it mad. Especially now."

The two continued their ascent, the walls sliding downward on all sides.

Above, the ceiling began to part down its center, a widening sliver of illumination. As they continued to climb, the anticipation on their upturned faces became more discernable in the gradual bloom of light.

Rising up and out of the floor, the two found themselves on a large stage draped with plush red curtains. Before them, wide carpeted steps led down to a dance floor of glossy inlaid woods, while above, three tiers of balconies with theatre boxes looked down on the ballroom and stage. As they glanced about, the girls were dazzled by the brilliance of the lavish gold ornamentation that embellished every surface. Beneath the balconies, they saw fancy chairs, where attendees could sit to watch plays, operas, symphonies, or simply one another. Frescoes covered the ceiling, their painted scenes depicting women in flowing dresses with long plaits of hair, though a few were represented without any hair whatsoever. To Heather, the women's overall appearance looked uncannily familiar.

"We're on stage," Molly said, looking out and confronting an unseen audience.

"It's the Bristol House Ballroom."

Heather was gazing at the backdrop behind them. On it was painted a lush garden with a waterfall of red and cream-colored roses cascading to the ground. Exotic birds were pictured throughout, perched on branches and gathered around a fountain. The fragrance of roses permeated the air.

"You know, Heather, after every room, I keep thinking that the Bristol House can't impress me any more. But it keeps doing it. This could be called a royal ballroom. I've seen them in books." Molly looked at her companion: "So, what next? Do we start by checking on every seat for the next clue?"

"I'm not."

"What, then?" asked Molly.

"I think we should dance."

"What?"

"Come on. Let's dance on stage." Heather began to go through her ballet steps that she had learned when taking lessons in nearby Stone Toad Junction, where her brusque instructor claimed to have once been a renowned prima ballerina from a famous dance troupe that toured Europe.

"Heather, I hate to sound mean," Molly said in a teasing tone, "but I'd have to say that right about now you seem in terrible need of a new brain."

Unable to stay consistently on point in her red tennis shoes, Heather traipsed away, occasionally dipping at the waist, arms elegantly reaching here, now there, leaping and tip-tapping in small steps across the stage.

Molly stood observing, hands on hips, unable to contain her laughter. "You know, you're really doing stupid stuff." Passing before her, Heather grabbed the unsuspecting Molly.

"Hey, what—?"

With Molly loosely hanging on for her life, Heather dragged her friend helplessly along as she danced a ridiculous imitation of a waltz, looping spasmodically around the stage. Laughing, Molly broke away.

"Enough! Now, let's find the clue."

"I already know where it is." Heather kept moving.

"Where?"

"It's—right—here," Heather said, each word punctuating the end of a revolution. She was now doing awkward pirouettes, her tennis shoes squeaking, as she whirled towards the back of the stage. The decorative parchment was hanging on a string in front of the fall of painted roses. She plucked it in passing.

Molly said, "You probably knew it was there all along."

Heather still spun, scattering petals that had previously fallen to the floor. "I did. I saw it when we first got here. It's just that I always wanted to perform on stage."

Molly clapped. "Bravo. If I had a bouquet of those painted roses, I'd throw them your way."

Dizzy, Heather stopped and bowed inelegantly, almost toppling. "Thank you."

"Did Molly seem to be enjoying herself today?" Mrs. Pringle asked.

"The kids have been upstairs most the day. She looked in good spirits when she and Heather came down for lunch. I haven't seen her that talkative in some time."

"She's been shaken to the core by all of this. I can't help but think that maybe Molly and I need a vacation after all."

"Well then, I believe the two of you have come to the right place."

"Are you sure this is where we should be going?" Molly asked.

"How else are we going to follow the clue?"

Huddled in the cramped space of a dumbwaiter, Heather and Molly slowly ascended, powered by the Bristol House.

"Here, see for yourself." Heather pressed the parchment into Molly's hand.

"Oh, sure, now you give it to me. How am I supposed to read it when we're stuffed in here?"

The platform beneath them slowed before stopping. Heather pulled up on the door, and it slid neatly behind the wall above.

The girls disentangled themselves, climbing out into a modest-sized kitchen. It was well stocked and orderly, containing wheeled carts for the transportation of food or the placement of tableware and related items. Built into one wall were a modest-sized oven, stove, and sink, while nearby stood a series of glass cabinets and drawers, each properly labeled. A slew of pots and pans hung from the ceiling, and ceramic jugs and little used dinnerware occupied the shelves high up.

Heather said, her excitement mounting, "We're almost there. It should be the next room over."

"Wait. I want to read the clue first to see if I can figure it out before we go in."

Heather paused and, trying to curb her impatience, craned her neck to look through the curtained doorway and into the next room.

"Molly, it's a pretty easy one."

She read:

An extra long table,

And so many chairs,

With candles and goblets,

And flavorful fares.

"The dining room?" Molly asked.

"Banquet room. Check this out."

Heather shepherded Molly before her. It wasn't long before the brunette stopped in her tracks.

"It's…" Molly took in the room's grandeur, and then added, "splendidly stellar!"

The lofty room was dominated by a massive banquet table situated off-center on a carpet of swirling design. Along its finely woven tablecloth, high-backed chairs were neatly tucked in vertical repetition. Enormous mirrors in richly enameled frames hung between drapes of thick velvet, their soft folds holding at bay a majority of the exterior light. Situated at either end of the room, sailing into the gloom above two gaping fireplaces, were towering paintings of clipper ships, one flying the Jolly Roger.

Yet, above all else, the room possessed three striking features that captured Molly's attention: "Heather, look at those chandeliers!"

Suspended from the high timbered ceiling were three monumental chandeliers, their intricately layered forms beginning in narrow circumference and expanding in girth to hang low and circular above the tabletop, like upside-down mushrooms comprised of a multitude of dangling crystals. In the muted light, the crystalline shapes glinted meekly.

Below, spread out before the girls, were two place settings accentuating the run of elaborate tablecloth. At each end, resting beside spoon and napkin were plates with domed silver covers.

Walking to the nearest one, Heather said, "This card has your name on it, Molly, so this must be your place, here."

"Then that must be yours way-y-y-y-y down there." Molly giggled.

Heather looked down the expanse of tabletop, past the silver candelabras and swan vases bearing fragrant and colorful floral arrangements, toward the gray light that strained in through the windows. "Must be."

"I wonder what's under the silver cover?" Molly asked.

"Take it off and see."

As Molly removed the cover, the chandeliers began to illuminate. The surge of yellowish light gradually increased, radiating from its many elegant globes and crystals, dispelling the somberness of the room. Flames sprang to life within the two fireplaces and upon the circular candelabras, while the wall sconces blushed with a soft restrained glow.

On Molly's plate sat an elegant goblet-shaped cup with a very long stem, its tiny jewels showing off their many sparkles.

"It's ice cream!"

"Wow! What kind?"

She picked up the spoon and took a small sample. "It's my favorite, peanut butter and chocolate."

"Well, my favorite is strawberry," Heather said, dashing to the far end, calling over her shoulder, "Want to bet that's what I have in my cup?"

"There's only one way to find out." Molly sat down, quickly unfolded her napkin, and placed it on her lap. Eagerly, she hoisted a spoonful to her mouth. "Mmmm."

"It *is* strawberry, it's fresh strawberry!" Heather called from the other end of the table.

Molly could barely see her past the table's décor. The girl leaned to one side.

"This is simply superb!" she said.

"What?" Heather asked, goofily cupping a hand to her ear.

"I said, 'This is simply superb!'"

Heather shook her head. "I can't hear you. You're too far away. Send the waiter with a message."

"Oh, brother!"

"Saw it once in an old movie."

Molly groaned and made a face.

Heather said, "Too bad your Dad didn't let you guys come to last year's Bristol House Christmas party. It was really great. So many people from town were here. There was Mr. Branson and his family, Old Sheriff Hickock and his, and even the mayor was here. Grandma Dawn hired a full staff. All of them, including Grandma Dawn, had been cooking for days."

"Boy, I wish I could have come. Really? The mayor was here? Come to think of it, I'm surprised that the guests were able to find this room."

"Well," Heather said, "knowing the Bristol House, I bet it loved showing off, so it was on its best behavior." She took a mouthful of ice cream and reflected. "No, I don't remember anything out of the ordinary happening." Then Heather held up her long-handled spoon like a wand and laughed. "But now that I think of it, you know Mr. Wyland who owns the hardware store down off the square? Well, ever since his wife died—she got sick and died on her seventy-fifth birthday—I guess he started drinking a lot, because she wasn't there to stop him. Anyway, when he didn't show up for work the next morning after the party, his oldest boy, Seth, came looking for him. They found him face down on a couch in the study."

The girls laughed.

"Mr. Wyland kept saying he tried to go home, but couldn't find his way to the stairs, and that all the rooms were in different places. His son thought he had been drinking way too much. Kinda makes you wonder…"

Molly giggled. "I'm not wondering."

"Anyway, after that, Seth told Grandma Dawn Mr. Wyland stopped drinking…"

All conversation ceased when the girls began to eat their ice cream in earnest, gazing here and there around the room as they enjoyed the many mouthfuls.

"Heather, have you noticed something?"

"That the ice cream never runs out?"

Molly giggled. "Yes. I can eat and eat and my cup keeps refilling itself."

Noticing an envelope that rested nearby on the table, Heather began tearing it open, saying, "That means we can eat all we want until we explode." She perused the contents. "Hey, Molly, do you have an envelope on your end, near your glass?"

Molly noted the beige envelope with green and gold edging. Her name was written in fancy script across its face. "What's in it?" Molly picked hers up and started to carefully unseal it.

"It's an invitation."

"To what?"

"A parade."

"I can see that now," Molly said, looking hers over, "and here's another clue." She read aloud:

> *"It's basting and joining,*
> *On needles and pins,*
> *Or hemming and hawing,*
> *When spooling in spins.*

"Needles, pins, hemming, basting—it sounds like it has to do with sewing. Does the Bristol House have a sewing room?" Molly asked.

"If it has a lake," Heather called from her end, "it probably has a sewing room." Heather looked at the face on a large grandfather clock situated against the wall nearest her. "Hey, it's getting late, Molly. Your mom is going to be here pretty soon to pick you up—or she might even be here already. We better get downstairs. I say let's search for the sewing room in the morning. It says on the invitation to be there at 10 o'clock sharp."

"But why the sewing room? For a parade?"

"Molly, it's the Bristol House," Heather said, as if that would explain away any and all questions. "Maybe we'll see the March of the Colorful Spools. They'll probably be playing little tiny instruments and wearing thimbles for hats."

"Funny."

"Just make sure you're here at nine in the morning, and then we'll start."

"Boy, Heather, I sure hope I'll be able to come."

"Tomorrow it's supposed to rain. Do you have any plans?"

"Mom or Dad might. I don't—except to be here at nine." Stuffed, Molly set her spoon down and slumped back in her chair. "Whew! Heather, hasn't this been just a glorious day?"

"Splendidly stellar."

"How exciting," Molly said, thinking about the parade, while admiring the sparkling luminescence of the chandeliers that cascaded down from the ceiling. "I just can't wait to see what the Bristol House has in store for us."

CHAPTER FOURTEEN

Musings of an Earthbound Maiden

"Even a rock gets worn with its seasons," Grandma Dawn whispered aloud, reciting a saying from so long ago. And *my seasons here are winding down,* she thought to add.

Her neighbors having departed, and with Heather upstairs taking a bath, Grandma Dawn found herself alone with her thoughts. She stoked the fire, and it reignited the consuming of logs in exchange for heat. The woman reached down beside the hearth, and taking more pieces of wood from the rack, tossed them on the blaze.

But Autumnsloe? Grandma Dawn thought. *Heather's been dreaming about* Autumnsloe?

It brought back such fond and vivid memories from her childhood. And difficult ones. She reached a hand to her graying hair and ran her fingertips slowly across the twisted coif, remembering how it used to be so long, so lustrous, and hanging down her back in a single braid.

The woman of many years returned to the large chair near the fire, its heat warming the normally temperate room to just the right degree, warming her legs. She looked up at the painting of Scarbones Bristol.

Oh, what you had to do to survive here, Terentius, Grandma Dawn thought. *But you made it respectable at the last, didn't you? You could have disgraced us, but in the end you chose not to. And your descendant, Allonia, who left me your Bristol House, heard only a faint utterance passed down through the generations, of what you—what we— were truly all about. Allonia couldn't have known that you and I—that she and I—were distantly related. How could she?*

The new logs blazed, their combustion feeding the flames.

And although the coming of the Reclamation was foretold, we never really knew for sure, did we? I know at times I wrestled with my doubts. Yet, here we are: Heather and Autumnsloe. What joy! What absolute joy! Imagine, the Evermore Portent coming to fruition during my life-time, becoming the impetus for what we always hoped would be our deliverance, our redemption. But of course, the child could still die, and the bloom of promise with her, if she's not carefully tended—especially if our enemies suspect she's the One. They will have no choice but to seek her out and kill her to retain their power, their control. And so many lives depend on her security and prosperity. Heather may very well be at the hub of the Reclamation, yet so much can go wrong; so much can be taken away with merely a shrug from the Universe. I know. I remember…

I've done my deed, made my sacrifice For the Four. It's taken a life-time out of me. Now this spark of new hope, this seed of change in the form of a child, must ultimately become bigger than I. And eventually, Heather will leave my Maiden Jurisdiction, and fate will continue to make its play. If she doesn't survive her rise to power, there will be yet another child at some future time. Then we must begin our wait anew.

But if we do, how many more in our Realm must die? And how many more must live miserably until that future time? Oh, Universe, in your machinations of all deeds on all worlds, must we wait a moment longer for an end to the pain and suffering of a Realm thrown into such chaos?

Around Grandma Dawn, the rain on the family room windows continued its tireless barrage. Yet, the woman hardly took notice. She watched with interest as the blazing fire continually ate up the wood that sustained it, as an Evermorian Staarfly eventually consumes its host, and time all life.

Alistair Thibble. Such a beautiful man; such a wonderful husband. You seem like a dream so long ago, much like the hazy youth I spent elsewhere. But you did bring the sweet bliss of rejuvenation into my life. Until that moment my stay had been so bleak in the mundane tasks of the everyday, grieving my great loss of child, and stoically awaiting another assignment. But isn't that what we Maidens do? We're loyal and obedient, like the greatest of bodyguards, only in service to a Realm, a spiritual practice, and a way of life. For the Four; For Evermore.

The words came to mind without rancor.

Alistair Thibble, isn't it surprising that, stranded alone on this distant planet, I ever found you? After all, I wasn't looking. I surely had no in-tention of romance, living out my days, awaiting the Word and with it the possibility of another child—the possibility. But you made me think differently: love, that earthly experience that so awakened my emotions that it caused my blindness to duty—caused me to stop awaiting the Word. To think that I actually neglected my Maidenhood, while becoming happily immersed in the ways of your people. Your love caused me to dream beyond Evermore, and it gave me reason to think I could disown my world to embrace yours. Such folly!

And yet, was anything promised to me in certainty from my Realm? No! I could have been left waiting, like so many other GuardianMaidens, for a second chance, for a child that might never come. And then my sacrifice would have seemed meaningless and my life an empty wash. So why not experience more fully this abbreviated lifetime away?

Grandma Dawn smiled her gentle smile, further wrinkling the skin born of her duration upon this planet. Though it would have been different had she remained in Evermore, where she could have had eternal youth, ageless after twenty-eight years—unless of course, she should die in defense of the Realm. But as a young dutiful Maiden assigned to Guardianship, she would never have thought of refusing to come to this new world, despite having had to embrace its Earthly ways and limitations, most notably the forsaking of magic and an acceptance of the aging process. As with all HumanKind here and in Evermore, growing old takes place so swiftly—particularly in the eyes of a Maiden.

She gazed into the flames, but only momentarily. Clasped and at rest on her lap were her still elegant but well-used hands, spotted from sun, veins pushing the surface in well-worn paths of blue-green. She ran a finger to trace one's course.

Grandma Dawn pondered: Aging is so frightening to many of us, because it forces us to continually breathe in the air of our own mortality, an air that permeates all we see, if we choose to look. When I accepted this position, the decay of age was only a distant eventuality. Now it's beginning to settle in my bones and burrow deep to line my thoughts in muted colors that once burned so vividly. And this I can accept, although, had I really felt I had a choice, I would have preferred to die a warrior in battle.

Grandma Dawn gave thought to those who had come through the TimeLight Bridge before her: one GuardianMaiden lost in the transgression of the second Great War, another in a fatal hit-and-run accident.

And my dear Catherine Ryan, oh, you lovely, lovely girl. You were the first Maiden child brought to me, the one previous to Heather Nighborne, previous to my meeting Alistair, who found me lost to such despair at your all too human and untimely death. I sincerely thought you might be the One, but then came the deadly virus, that unseen thing that the naked eye can only view through its manifestation. And ultimate destruction.

Catherine, you were gone so quickly at only eight years of age, vulnerable to the mortal liabilities of one belonging to this world. I understand it's all in the Universal plan, your sudden arrival and shocking departure. It did take its toll, didn't it? I was left reeling, lost for so long. I blamed myself for your demise. And I died a thousand deaths to go on living.

We just never know the fate of our emotional investments—who'll go first, who'll be left behind. Still, despite Catherine's early death and its devastating impact, I can't imagine my life never having been touched by that child. How empty those years would have been. And for the rest of this human stay of mine, gratefully that precious child will always be with me. How could she not? She altered my life and was the first to stir emotions buried far within my being, those emotions usually relegated to dormancy in the life of a Warrior Maiden. Ah, motherhood, such a difficult road for those who choose to invest in the journey. However, Catherine's brief presence did prepare me for the timely arrival of Alistair, and eventually that of the tiny adoptee, Heather Nighborne, that beautiful, beautiful green-eyed baby.

And for me, having agreed to take on the human aging process and all that life on this planet is predisposed to, I can only ask, now as a mortal being entering, perhaps, the final phase of her stay, what new world awaits me after this time is used up? Will it be so unlike this world or that of the Realm, beyond all concepts of HumanKind or that of MaidenHood? I suspect so. And if energy recreates itself, as I was taught, and if I should see them again, in what new form will Catherine and Alistair and Heather take shape? Will they even take shape at all? Will I? I can only dream and hope that it's not all dust for them and me.

Ultimately, by coming here have I sold out my birthright, my one chance at immortality? But knowing then what I know now, would I have done anything different? And would I have wanted to miss out on that wondrous HumanKind emotion, love, and the people in my life that have come to rouse it? Ah, the questions of the aged. As a young girl of MaidenHood, I never thought to question or refuse any direction proposed. Though, in the end, I have to think that all roads chosen are the right roads, if I'm to believe in such a thing as destiny. And the Portent.

Grandma Dawn rose out of her chair and threw another log on the fire, its flames swollen and dancing with their current potency. Yet, she knew that soon they would diminish and be more modest in strength, before settling into the less effective embers of that which once was. And then sometime afterward, they would lose that spark altogether. Ash and dust.

The wind outside the Bristol House had picked up, and Grandma Dawn could hear it wailing, carrying on with its lonesome howl, raging at immovable obstructions, and throwing itself passionately at the emptiness of space. Oddly, the sound only made her feel cozier near the fire.

Her mind wandered back to Heather.

Of all the MaidenAdoptees scattered throughout the universe, of all times and places, *my* Heather was chosen as the Maiden Portent. But can I be certain of this? Or should I continue to be reserved in my hope? Yet, why would Heather be introduced to Autumnsloe, even in dreams, if she weren't the One? I have to admit, however, that until today I never even considered it! After all, Heather is only half Maiden. Come to think of it, it's odd that she was even born at all. But *that* should have been my first clue. Never, in the past, would a MaidenStray like Heather's mother have been able to give birth. I couldn't. Yet, interestingly enough, the rare males of the Pool, like Terentius Scarbones Bristol, haven't an issue with fertility when they've partnered with a female of HumanKind, though their offspring are always mortal, as is Heather, I'm sure.

My young Heather. Should you truly be the One, you will carry such an immense burden, borne of the great hope of so many—and yet you're merely a child, a beautiful child. With all that's at stake, the Maiden-Hood must vigorously protect you, for word may get out, and the Bristol House could yet have TimeLight visitors bearing the deadliest of intentions. The great assassins of the Crown are forever traveling the TimeLight Bridge in search of Maidens hidden to be reared elsewhere, all possible heiresses to the Portent. Without conscience, they've found and taken the life of many to insure the future dominance of the powers that be. That won't bode well for your continued welfare, child. Or the future of the Realm. Clearly, we must be vigilant to insure your safety.

The fire sputtering before flaming anew, Grandma Dawn continued to bask snugly at its side.

Her mind was wandering with the rain and flame and pitch of wind. Now in a sleepy trance-like state, the woman was pleased at the thought that her life might yet have the fulfillment for which she had hoped, and not only for her, but for all those who had put their faith in her; who now patiently awaited the The Reclamation, the unification and rebirth long promised by the Evermore Portent. Following the horrifying Bloodlet Overthrow and all that resulted, she felt a renewed sense of spirit, of fight, of—dare she admit it?—exultation in the fact that The Reclamation was, at this very moment, a probability—and in her lifetime, at that.

Heather may be the One. Grandma Dawn's mind danced around the possibility before lapsing into the gentle comfort of pre-sleep.

The woman lay back peaceful in her chair. As she drifted deeper into her barely conscious state, she sighed contentedly.

Alistair Thibble, you were such a wonderful man, such a glorious detour from my true journey. But try as I might, my MaidenHood seems to have found me nevertheless.

Grandma Dawn reclaimed her gentle smile as she let go and embarked on yet another dream by the fireside.

CHAPTER FIFTEEN

A Voice Comes Calling

Heather was laughing, her white teeth framed in a flawless grin, gaiety ascending at the corners, like a curtain rising to reveal an inner happiness. At times like these, one couldn't help but think that her smile was too large for her face, though wonderfully so. The girl was soaking in her claw-foot tub, the water warm and sudsy in its envelopment, her knees protruding like segments of a hump-backed serpent among islands of lather.

"Aria, you should have seen poor Molly's face when she came shooting out of that painting and onto the bed. She looked so funny!"

"I'm sorry to have missed it, especially the ride in the cave."

"Yeah, that was really awesome. I think you would have liked the strawberry ice cream, too."

"If *you* did, chances are I would have, also. However, I probably would have refrained from consuming so much." Aria picked up of the bar of soap and ran it up and down her arms. After setting it down, she picked up the washcloth. "It seems that you were able to get us quite dirty." She began to scrub vigorously.

"Wet, too, but that didn't last long."

"So you said. All in a day's work." Aria was rolling water up her arms, rinsing off the excess soap. "I'm glad that The Bristol House provided some pleasure and entertainment."

"Me, too. It was great to have fun for a change." Heather slid down farther into the tub, the frothy waves lapping against her chin. She placed her finger in a bubbly mountain and stirred it around, creating a small whirlpool. "Aria, where do you go when you're not here with me?" The mountain dispersed.

Aria thought for a while. "Oh, places, Heather. Just places."

"You can't tell me more?"

"Sometime I will, you have my word. But now is not that time. Speaking of which, I'm due elsewhere and may already be late. I'm sorry I missed the fun today, but I'm glad I popped in. Please give Molly my regards when you see her. I'll try to make it to the parade, but I can't promise. All right? Until soon!"

"Aria, wait—! Aria?"

The last word hung. The bathroom suddenly seemed larger to Heather, bigger in its hollowness, greater in its capacity for emphasizing the emptiness. Rising, her soapy seascape drained away with a swash of intermingling water. Heather stepped out onto the mat that she had previously laid alongside the tub and grabbed a towel off the rack. Starting high with her blonde hair, Heather began working downward, toweling herself dry.

Child, are you there?

Heather froze, bent at the waist. With handfuls of towel stationary at her knees and draped about her feet, the girl listened attentively. When she didn't hear anything, she resumed her toweling.

You're there, aren't you, child? The voice was calm, melodious, sweet— a woman's voice.

Heather slowly stood upright. Blindly reaching to her left, she haphazardly placed the towel on the rack. Bunched at the bar, it hung at an angle, draped in defiance to the tidy vertical.

"Are you calling me?" Heather asked.

The voice laughed, a pleasant soothing chuckle. *Of course. You're the only one there, aren't you?*

"Yeah." Heather looked around, and caught sight of herself in the mirror. "I better be."

The voice laughed again. Heather suddenly became self-conscious and covered up.

"Who are you?"

I'm someone from long ago. I just wanted to see you again.

"Where are you?"

Right now, I'm downstairs. I was wondering if you have a moment to reintroduce yourself. Let's get to know one another.

Heather was slipping into her clean clothes. "I could—if Grandma Dawn doesn't mind."

Grandma Dawn? She's there too?

"Yeah—well, no, not here. Not now, I mean." Heather looked around. *Ah...*

"Isn't she there with you, downstairs?"

I can't see her at the moment. But come down. Let's reacquaint ourselves, shall we? The voice was gentle, dreamy, attractive.

Heather finished buttoning her blouse and looked in the mirror. "Can I comb my hair first?"

The soft laugh filled the air, not too loudly. *Of course. Don't you just love your hair? I love mine, so long and black. What color is yours?*

Heather stopped brushing. "How can you talk to me like this?"

Like what?

Her brush at work again, back and forth with a twist of the head, the girl said, "Like this. I don't see you—"

Well, you will. That's why I'm waiting for you downstairs. When you're done, I'll be here.

Heather set the brush down with a clink on the porcelain. She hurried out of the bathroom, walked quietly to the end of the hall, and stopped at the top of the front staircase. Placing one hand on the rail, Heather leaned over and peered down into the foyer, while she listened for the voice of the Bristol House guest.

As she began her tentative descent, Heather asked, "Where are you?"

Right here. The words were returned at almost a whisper. *Waiting.*

Heather stopped, hanging onto her latest breath. Again, she slowly scanned the entry below. Unable to see into either the living room or parlor, Heather descended a cautious step or two before pausing, only to continue. Upon reaching the bottom of the stairs, Heather heard the crackle of a fire. She edged her head around the corner to peek into the living room.

Asleep on her favorite chair was Grandma Dawn, a colorful quilt now covering her long body from chest to ankle. The fire burned low on the grate. Heather looked at the empty chairs nearby in puzzlement. She withdrew and walked over to the parlor. Leaning in ever so gradually, she was surprised to find that the visitor wasn't in that room either.

I'm still waiting, said the voice, pleasant, assured.

"I'm here. Where are you?" Heather asked, standing in the foyer, a bit annoyed.

Downstairs.

"Downstairs from downstairs? In the basement downstairs?" Heather asked. "What are you doing in the basement?"

I'm waiting for you. The voice laughed pleasantly. *I look forward to meeting you, child, and getting a good look at you after so long.*

"How did you get in?"

You have many visitors that come to see you, I'm sure. So, like all of them, I simply entered.

"I think I should wake Grandma Dawn and tell her that we have a visitor downstairs."

You don't want to do that, child.

Heather felt lightheaded. "I don't?"

No.

The girl looked in on her grandmother. "You're right. She's probably really tired."

Oh, she is. Let's not disturb her.

Heather agreed.

"When you said you wanted to get a good look at me after so long, how long ago is 'so long?'" Heather asked, her manner more cheerful.

Oh, it was a very long time ago, I should say. But I dreamed about you, and thought I'd pay you a long-overdue visit. The laugh, gentle, rounded, easy on the ears, sang on the air before softly fading.

"Really?" Heather thought of her own dreams. "Are you my mother?"

Your mother? Funny you should ask that. Ah, yes. Yes! That's why I've come to see you.

"Really?"

Heather was walking, now half-running, across the parlor towards the servant's door, leading to their quarters and the basement below.

Hustling down the stairs, Heather came to the heavy-planked basement doors of forest green. She grabbed one of the large metal rings and pushed the right side open. It swung easily inward revealing a dim lofty room, with a row of small arched windows shedding scant exterior light from high on a wall. The vagueness revealed layers of obscure shapes: cabinets, trunks, and other furniture of the ages, most of it draped in dusty sheets.

"You're somewhere nearby, aren't you?" Heather asked, taking in what she and Grandma Dawn called the Entry Room.

Never far away, child. Never at all. Keep going. I can't see you yet.

Carefully, Heather picked her way around the furniture, shrouded objects in very unfurniture-like shapes. Under cover, the girl thought some groupings looked like crouched animals ready to lunge, and some phantoms rising, while others wrestled among their entanglements.

Finding her way temporarily blocked, Heather looked for passage to one side of a large steamer trunk. The chest was upstanding, cracked open on the vertical, its drawers disgorging clothing and old shoes in a rumpled pile.

Weird, she thought. Heather didn't remember that particular trunk being open and emptied like that on her last visit through.

Shuffling to her left, she managed to squeeze between a sofa and an armoire to keep moving.

Heather's heart was racing at the possibility of meeting her mother. Yet something nagged at her, but the girl was unable to pinpoint why, her mind unable to find the logical bridge. Sensing her befuddlement, she tried to elicit caution in her every movement. Until the next moment, that is, when her sleeve caught hold on an old brass coat rack, its hooks curled like talons in waiting. Having grabbed onto the girl, it held fast, its prey turning and jerking heavily on the hook. It was then that the rack toppled noisily to the floor. Blushing, Heather looked around to be certain that her mother wasn't watching, embarrassed at what she felt to be her clumsiness. The girl bent to pick up the stand.

Are you all right, child?

"Yeah, I bumped into something—knocked over a coat rack." She laughed sheepishly. "It wouldn't let me go, but it's okay now. I just set it back up." Heather searched for the individual belonging to the voice. She didn't see a person or thing move. "It didn't have anything on it, though."

Ah.

"No coats."

The laugh, so pleasant and gentle. *I understand.*

"Are you in the next room?" Heather asked.

Maybe. I'm not sure, actually, since I didn't come in the way you've chosen. But I'm here and waiting.

"What makes you think you're my mother?"

We can better discuss this when I see you. Though, I think you'll notice our resemblance.

Heather momentarily stopped walking. "Really?"

The laugh. *Of course.*

Her excitement intensifying, Heather finally reached the doors on the other side of the Entry Room. Pushing them open, she found herself in the room Grandma Dawn called the Armory, filled with suits of armor, plumed helmets, shields, swords, and lances. There was an assortment of other weapons, too, weapons that could certainly end an opponent's life with a well-placed swing or thrust.

The space around Heather was neatly laid out, with rows displaying full suits of armor from various times and places. At attention, facing solemnly ahead, were intimidating metal warriors, lengthy halberds in hand. Others, their metallic faces long with alert slits for eyes, stood in poses with swords and shields at the ready. And others, still, sat proudly holding the reins belonging to shiny hollow stallions.

To Heather, the battle-ready figures appeared ominous. And possessed. As always, some of the heads turned and followed the girl as she passed. Having ventured through this room many times during previous explorations, this wasn't unusual, but it was unsettling just the same.

Turning as she exited, Heather waved, saying, "Fun seeing all of you again," but the cheery words did little to make her feel more at ease, a distant apprehension tugging at the periphery of her awareness.

Leaving the Armory didn't increase Heather's comfort level, either. Rather the opposite, as she was now in a murky room filled with marionettes, ventriloquist dummies, and hand puppets. Bunched on stages in small theatres were puppets bearing resemblances to people and animals: kings and jesters, queens and pirates, sea monsters, monkeys, and kangaroos, to name a few. Sitting straight up or on the incline, wooden dummies were strewn about, with their heads thrust back, resting on their chests, or gazing far off with dead eyes that stared and glared and longed to awaken.

From sources unseen, lights illuminated areas of the great room's walls, casting at angles the skewed images of shadow puppets shining in dramatic idleness. Among those on display were soft-edged images of deer running and girls flying, pirate ships and mermaids, dogs and cats, winged fairies and princesses, big-eared rabbits, along with mice, kites, and cowboys. As stationary images, they craved direction and manipulation, a reason for being, a theatrical life to lead. Like Heather's visitor, they, too, were waiting.

"Hello? Are you in this room?" Heather had stopped walking.

No, the voice sadly answered. *But I know you're near. I can sense your presence. Not far, child; you're almost here.* The words flitted and slipped about in whispers near the girl's ears.

"I don't mean to be rude," Heather said, "but can't you come towards me, while I walk towards you? That way, we can meet sooner."

But what if we miss? I might get lost, and then we'll have to try to find each other in all these rooms.

"Aren't we kind of doing that now?"

That laugh. Be patient, child. It won't be long now. I can't tell you how good it will be to see you. Yes. So good.

Heather looked at the many marionettes that hung obscurely from the ceiling, legs and arms bent motionless. Some faces were garishly distorted, others pinched and stern. Some wore hats and others oversized lips with wicked leers; soldiers bravely bore weapons and pink-cheeked girls their pigtails; some string puppets looked lost to leaping dance while others were simply monstrous in appearance, with enormous heads and jagged teeth. As in the previous room, eyes and heads followed Heather's passing.

The girl reached a wide door made of broad planks bound with straps of steel. She slid it sideways, where the panel rolled to a jerking halt. Revealed was a room Heather loved. Despite the continual addition and subtraction of mysterious doors leading to new places, she was thankful that rooms in the basement, unlike those on the third floor, were generally found in the same location. This allowed her to easily return again and again to the place where she could bring a particular fantasy to life.

Striding into her favored workshop and studio, Heather passed by the many sculptures: classical and contemporary, figurative and otherwise, all captive in their movement. A masterful panther stood poised on a limb; three ballerinas stood on point, each repeating the elegant pose of the other, but not quite; costumed gallants courted women in finery; life-sized, a turbaned man rode high atop a bejeweled elephant; five plump women cavorted in a circle, their faces uplifted, their arms interlaced; and a muscular man wrestled to loosen himself from the grip of an enormous octopus and its encompassing tentacles.

More sculptures, all in various stages of completion, lined shelves along the walls with tools of the trade scattered within their vicinity. Heather often wondered who worked here. Throughout her many visits, she had never met a soul.

There were also partially finished sculptures resting on platters that spun, making all parts easily accessible to artists at a turn. Heather's sculptural effort—her fantasy—stood on one of these stands, not far from the rough-hewn marble beginnings of a mother and child by an anonymous sculptor, the faces mere chiseled scrapes, their hands and limbs crudely rendered. Inspired by the unfinished piece nearby and the brand new tools and fresh clay mysteriously provided by the Bristol House, the girl's sculpture was a head of the mother she had yet to meet.

Heather had imagined her just so, and was determined to flesh her out. After many reconfigurations of the face—raising the eyes, making smaller the nose or fuller the lips—and none to her liking, Heather just let the work sit, the features undeveloped. At some point, she felt her mother would materialize, and then she would complete it. Perhaps the time had come.

"Am I closer?" Heather asked.

Almost there.

Heather exited to the next room through double doors of sky blue, each accommodating a circular window. Upon release, the doors flip-flapped to a standstill.

And here you are, said the voice.

Heather looked around. "But where are you? I can't see you?"

I'm here. Do come in.

The central area was large with many lesser rooms extending from it, most open and viewable from the door. At its heart was a laboratory surrounded by comfortable living spaces for lounging, dining, studying, or cooking. Previously, Heather had investigated some of the doors within these smaller rooms. Most led to more rooms of a similar style while untried others led to Heather knew not where.

Occupying the laboratory floor were multi-drawered tables. On top were vials, beakers, test tubes, open books, and burners. Cabinets, bookshelves, and antique desks lined the available walls. Four tremendous bell jars, larger than Heather herself, rested near one corner. Each was marked with a season of the year and contained various relevant specimens.

It wasn't the tidiest room that Heather had ever seen in the Bristol House, she determined, but it certainly looked lived in.

Child, I'm over here.

"Where?"

Why, here, of course. I'm over here.

Heather was drawn to the sound of the voice. It seemed to be emanating from a dimly lit corner of the lab, where a large grandfather clock stood close to a counter of microscopes, a sink, and what looked to be furniture draped in thick black cloth.

Heather approached. She heard breathing, the gentle intake of air and its release, prolonged and repeated, as if one were sleeping.

The voice spoke: *You're there, I can feel you.*

Heather spun, looking around her. She couldn't see an aura. "I don't feel *you*. I don't even see you."

I'm here.

"Where?"

Right under the black cloth in front of you.

Heather stepped back. After staring at the idle folds, waiting for them to move or do something, she asked, "Why are you in there?"

Because I'm waiting for you."

"Why?"

Because I want to see you, see my daughter that I haven't seen for ever so long.

"Can't you just come out—?"

No.

"—step out from behind there?"

No.

There was another silence, then the voice said, *Do you want to see me, see your mother?*

"Yes," Heather said, meekly. The abstract urges derived from 'danger' and 'flee' repeated themselves over and over, but lay lost behind clouds of diminished reasoning.

Well, I'm right here behind this cloth. Come, lift it, and let's have a look at you.

Heather stood motionless. Haltingly, she extended her arm to lift the cloth, but fought the desire. She dropped her hand.

What's wrong? Don't you trust your mother? The voice sounded fuller, more persuasive—with a tinge of eagerness.

"I don't know," Heather said. Her head felt thick, her eyelids heavy as she continued to stare at the black, unmoving material. She struggled to get out the words, "I don't know you."

Don't you? Well, lift the cloth then, and let's acquaint ourselves. Let me see your beautiful face.

"You said you had long black hair. I think I've dreamed about you, with your white skin. Is that you? Are you really my mother?"

There's only one way to find out, child. Lift the cloth.

The room felt colder there in the corner area. Perhaps it was a wintry draft, the chilled air making her shiver. Mesmerized, Heather reached above her, the slender fingers of her left hand grabbing hold of one corner of the drape—yet, her right hand was held at the ready, balled in a fist. Slowly she peeled back the fabric, a small bit, a little more, gazing behind it, trying to see into the blackness of what lay hidden. She dared to reveal a small amount more. More still. And then even more. Was it a floor-length mirror? From her angle, she could hardly see…

"Don't touch that!"

"Agh!" Instinctively throwing the cloth up and away from her—and back into place—the child whirled. "Who said that?" She continued to look every which way.

"I did," said a masculine voice.

Heather looked but didn't see anyone. "Where are you? Are you behind some other piece of cloth in here?"

"I'm right here, right in front of you."

"Are you a ghost?" Heather's heart was racing. She threw a glance behind her, back at the cloth. It hadn't moved.

A chuckle. "I'm hardly a ghost. As I said, I'm right in front of you. See my face? I'm blinking my eyes."

Drawn to the movement, Heather looked into the face of the large grandfather clock. Though numbers one through twelve ran around the rectangular perimeter, its slightly protruding face was real, an elderly man with bushy eyebrows and a bulbous nose, his beard hanging down to the glass cabinet below. And with the hour and minute hands at four and eight, his face wore a lopsided mustache. Within the upper portion of the chest cavity, a red light blinked with every swing of the pendulum.

"Oh! I'm surprised I didn't see you there—you know, with your—" Heather pointed, "your heart lighting up like that here in the dark."

"You were hypnotized by the Voice, young lady, the voice from the mirror. Your susceptibility is not at all unusual, especially when one is unfamiliar with its power. And the closer you get, the stronger its pull."

Heather became quiet. "I couldn't help myself. I knew better, but couldn't stop, even though I tried." She glanced uneasily at the drapery, and then backed away.

"I must be getting too old, falling asleep on the job like that," said the clock. "It's my fault. I should never have let you get close to that mirror."

"Why?"

"Why? Why, indeed! You don't know who's on the other side of that mirror staring back, that's why."

Sulkily, Heather said, "She said she was my mother."

"Do you think she was?"

Heather turned again to face the draped cloth. "I don't know."

"Was she calling you?"

"At first? Yeah. And she wasn't even in the room."

"But you were near a mirror and that's how she made the initial WhisperEye connection. Did she call your name?"

"No."

"Well, she didn't know it, then, or the Voice might have had an even greater influence over you."

"Why did she want me to remove the cloth?"

"So she could see you. Why would someone be searching for you, wanting to see your face?"

Suddenly uncomfortable, Heather shrugged.

"Anyway, that's how it works. And anytime that black cloth is removed, a TimeLight caller can see out through any mirror in the entire household."

"How can I tell when it's that kind of mirror?" Heather asked.

"A WhisperEye Mirror? Good question. I guess you can't, unless there happens to be a mirror nearby calling out to you." He chuckled. "I've heard that some people can feel a cold dra—"

"I did!"

The grandfather clock paused. "You did?"

"Yeah, the closer I got to it. A draft."

"Hmm."

"What?" Heather asked.

The clock just smiled, and seemed to appraise Heather in a new light.

Heather changed the subject. "Well, I'm glad, then, that I didn't remove the cloth."

"Lucky for you. So, because they couldn't look in when imprecisely trolling along vast expanse of the TimeLight Bridge, they couldn't discover your exact location."

"What? What's a TimeLight Bridge—?"

"It's a good idea never to look in any WhisperEye Mirrors. They have eyes. They were once part of a large labyrinth of mirrors connecting the kingdoms of Evermore to each other and the rest of the universe. But the network was overtaken by the Followers of the WhisperSign, those practiced in the Art of the Voice. Needless to say, the mirrors are no longer used with good intent and their operation has long been discouraged in the Realm."

"Where do they come from?" Heather asked.

"The Followers of the WhisperSign?" With a scoff, the grandfather clock said, "Who knows? Evermore somewhere. Some say they once made their home in the Lost Hills of Autumnsloe, others say the neglected Territories of Winterspire. I've even heard some say they come from the boiling wasteland of SummersBreath Still, the SkarrèdKretch, the desert within a desert. But who's mastered the Voice that you heard today is anyone's guess."

Autumnsloe again? Evermore? Winterspire? SummersBreath Still? TimeLight Bridge? Heather's mind was attempting to absorb it all, grasping, shuffling through the names.

Taking a softer tone, the grandfather clock asked the girl, "Was there anyone looking out of the mirror?"

"Well, it was dark in there, under the cloth. If there was someone looking out, I didn't see them," Heather said.

It was then that the deliciously soft feminine laugh rode the air. *But I saw you, child.* She laughed again. *I saw you.*

CHAPTER SIXTEEN

A Difference in Chairs

Heather glared at the black drape that covered the WhisperEye Mirror.

"I'd say there's someone very sinister on the other side of that glass," the grandfather clock said. "I would say—"

Heather held up her hand. "Don't say anything."

"Well, if that isn't rude..."

"She hears us."

Heather was walking over to a table a short distance away. She slid a chair out and carried it back to the corner and the presence of the draped mirror. The girl again felt the lingering cold that permeated the area.

"Who are you?" Heather demanded.

The voice continued its purring lilting words: *Well, it sounds to me like the child is angry. Tsk-tsk. It's not good to lose one's self control.*

"Who are you?"

Who do you think I am? The voice continued calmly. *I'd love to see more of you, of where you live, child. After all, you do look vaguely familiar. Would you like to share? All you need do is remove the cloth.*

Heather continued to stand before the mirror, her two hands gripping the chair. Her words were a whisper: "Who are you?"

The grandfather clock began, "I think—"

Heather held up a hand and instantly the old man went quiet.

"I'm going to ask you one more time." Heather's words seethed, low, harsh. "Who are you?"

The laugh. *Who am I, you ask? Who am I, you dare insist? Why, child, I told you. I'm your mother.* Yet again, the soothing voice laughed her laugh, its sweetness mocking. *I'm the mother you've never met, that you'll never meet, the mother that abandoned you long ago, because you weren't worthy of a name. Child, I'm the mother who will never love you, because you're simply not worth loving. I'm a mother that finds you repugnant and a disgrace, a child who's ugly and selfish, rude and undeserving, weak and trivial, a child that our world will soon possess and consume with a spark from my fingertips. That's who I am.*

Summoning all her might, Heather swung the chair. It slammed into the cloth—and the WhisperEye Mirror—shattering the glass. Heather swung the chair again and more glass splintered, the frame jerking behind the cloth.

"No, no, no, no, *no!* You take *that!*"

The chair landed once more, and then again and again, back and forth, back and forth, the cane chair arcing through the air repeatedly, its devastating impact causing the mirror's frame to buckle and diminishing the capacity of the Voice within.

"You are *not* my mother! My mother wouldn't say such cruel things to me. Ever!"

Crash!

"Never!"

Crash!

"You hear me?" The chair came down on the splintered frame and fabric one last time: "Never!"

Crash!

When she had finished, breathing hard, Heather just stared. She dropped the crippled chair.

"Never," she said, quietly, her chest still heaving.

From the fractured remnants behind the black fabric, the Whisper-Voice spoke, continuing in its soft fashion as it began to fade: *I know what you look like,* and the voice spit out the next word, *Child.* Then from far away, breaking up, it added, *We'll find you. And destroy you.*

Moments passed noiselessly.

Finally, the clock spoke up. "My, my, my. Remind me, young lady, never to insult you. Your strength is surprising for such a young girl. I think that chair did the trick the first time you applied it in such fashion."

Heather continued to gaze at the sagging drapery, suddenly aware of her surprising savagery.

"In the past, it has been my observation that HumanKind usually uses chairs for the purpose of sitting."

Shaking, Heather looked down at her hands.

"Sounds as if someone is searching for you, young lady."

Without acknowledgement, Heather walked away.

"I fear this is not for the best," the clock called out.

The blue doors swung behind the girl. Flip-flap, flip-flap.

After a brief and frenzied night chase through the Bristol House gardens, three raccoons eventually cornered a stray cat within the umbrella-like enclosure of a willow tree. Warily, they advanced and the calico hissed, her head low and back up, furry tail barely a-twitch.

The largest raccoon was first to lash out at the feline, darting to take hold of her fur, teeth attempting to sink in near the black sequined collar bearing its distinctive charm. The cat, a familiar sight in the vicinity of the Bristol House, rapidly cuffed the raccoon, and he retreated, but not before his two masked companions sprang at the stray. With lightning quick claws jabbing and scratching, furious hissing and growling, roiling glimpses of streaks, stripes, and patches, the calico cat was quickly at a disadvantage. She whirled and retreated, bleeding near one eye, a patch of fur torn loose on the leg. Bristling, her back hunched, she hissed, her small teeth bared. Still the raccoons pressed in, their bodies arched.

Yet before they could renew their attack, a sword sliced loudly through the cascading boughs of the weeping willow, and through the opening stepped a spectral figure. At the unexpected action, the creatures scattered, the stray bounding only a short distance before stopping. Turning, she saw the ghostly nightman on the stairs emerge from under the tree, watching to insure that the raccoons departed, their ringed tails disappearing into the night. Returning his sword to its scabbard, he held his lantern aloft, the lamp shedding its eerie yellow-green glow. The feline stared as the apparition silently trudged away towards the Bristol House, where in the windows of a turret room, a single light burned. A moment later, it went out.

Heather lay in bed, unable to sleep. The night was cloudy, though no rain coursed earthward.

Earlier that evening, all through dinner, Heather had been self-absorbed. Grandma Dawn asked innocuous questions about her day with Molly, but Heather felt neither talkative nor hungry. When she looked up to find the woman regarding her, Heather quickly averted her gaze. She wanted desperately to confide, but found herself unable to talk about her distressing encounter with the WhisperEye Mirror. When Grandma Dawn mentioned that she 'wasn't eating,' all Heather could think of for an answer was to shrug her shoulders. Her strawberry jubilee desert went untouched.

Now, to her night-filled bedroom, Heather asked, "Aria?" to no response.

She pushed aside the covers and sat up. The clouds outside her windows had parted, and the soft haze from the moon filtered in weakly. Seeking out the moonlight, as it was apt to comfort her, Heather walked through the large arch and into her rounded alcove to sit. She threw her long legs over the side of an upholstered chair, turned and repositioned herself, and then pulled her knees up under her chin, hugging them.

Was that truly my mother in the mirror? Would she really treat me so horribly? Why would she do that? My mother would love me, wouldn't she? Did she really just throw me away, because I wasn't lovable? Maybe she's right. Maybe I'm not.

Heather's gaze drifted over the ill-defined shapes in her room, trying to make out her favorite musical figurine on her nightstand, the one she'd had since she could remember. Grandma Dawn once said that Heather had arrived with it.

But how do I know if I'm lovable? she asked herself. *What am I supposed to do? Whatever it is, can someone please just tell me?*

And what did I ever do to the WhisperEye Mirror anyway? Why would my mother—if that really was my mother on the other side—want to destroy me? I can't be that *unlovable. Can I?*

And after dinner why did Grandma Dawn suddenly say she'd like to have a serious talk with me? About what? Just like the mirror, she's probably going to tell me everything that's wrong with me. Or maybe she found out I broke the mirror. Boy, if she did, Grandma Dawn has really got to be disappointed in me, especially if that grandfather clock told her how I lost my temper. Or if she doesn't know yet, maybe I should be the one to tell her I broke the mirror and why. But then would she believe that the mirror wanted to hurt me and maybe my mother was on the other side?

Heather sighed heavily. "My head hurts."

She closed her eyes. Images of the late afternoon's events played out before her. When Heather thought of how she had busted up the mirror, she cringed.

But I had to, didn't I? It hypnotized me; it was making me do things, and that was dangerous. Ew, that voice, she thought. *That laugh.*

A shiver rattled her body.

If the Voice didn't belong to my mother, who was that person, and who would want to kill me? And why?

The girl suddenly flashed on what she had forgotten in her preoccupation with the WhisperEye Mirror, what she had seen on her return upstairs. In one of several ground-floor windows that shed light into the basement's Entry Room, the room of covered furniture, Heather had glanced up to see someone peering in, their face at the glass, hands framing the eyes, the body dark against the waning evening light. Upon seeing Heather passing through, the watcher had immediately pulled away. Recalling the image, Heather hadn't been able to tell if it was a man or a woman. In her angry state and subsequent march up the stairs, she had forgotten completely about the incident. Until now.

"It had to be Mr. Simpletripp," Heather thought aloud. "It had to be." But then again, maybe it was the Voice sending someone to find and destroy me, like it said it would. I sure hope the Bristol House and the nightman on the stairs are protecting me. After all, the destroyers could be in the house this very minute.

Heather again scanned the room.

She made note to tell Aria about the Voice and the observer, and then turned her attention to the nighttime sky. The moon again hidden, patches of deep blue were still visible, the mist-covered stars hazily winking in the heavens. Tonight they brought little comfort. Heather tried to think about tomorrow's parade, but couldn't drum up any enthusiasm in her tired and agitated state. She returned to her bed, flopped down, and pulled the covers around her.

What a fun and creepy day, Heather reflected in summation.

She gave quick thought to Molly and all the rooms in which they had had fun. Heather then pondered the Voice, the clock, and the alarming words of the old timepiece when she was leaving the laboratory: *Sounds as if someone is searching for you, young lady.*

Boy, I hope not.

She heard the doorknob rattle and saw her bedroom door open slightly in a splinter of light, the strip of yellow reaching out and crawling over her bed at an angle. Heather closed her eyes, but balled her fists under the covers, making ready to fight for her life. Through her lashes she saw a tall person enter the room and loom over the foot of her bed. At first, Heather couldn't make out the image, as the hallway light was bright and the figure so dark in front of it. She felt her heart pounding in her chest.

Here we go! Heather thought to herself, her arms tensing, ready to throw off the covers and surprise her attacker. If it was someone sent to hurt or destroy her, Heather wasn't going to go down without a fight.

But then the girl relaxed.

Coming to the side of the bed, Grandma Dawn hovered. She leaned close, her head near Heather's ear.

She whispered, "Sleep well, my lovely child. For in my stay, I will do everything I can to see that no harm comes to you. From this world—" With her fingertips, Grandma Dawn gently swept the hair from Heather's forehead, and kissed her there, softly, "—or the other."

Still feigning sleep, Heather briefly wondered at the words, discreetly watching her grandmother, as she stood motionless above her for some time, gazing down. The familiar shape retreated before returning with Heather's desk chair.

Placing it near the bed, Grandma Dawn seated herself to keep vigil. In the stillness, it wasn't long before Heather's soft protracted breathing could be heard, belonging to a deep and restful sleep.

CHAPTER SEVENTEEN

Parade Day Begins

Heather awoke to a blaze of morning sunshine that spread a dusty warmth throughout her room. She recalled Grandma Dawn's unusual behavior from the night before, and looked to find the desk chair in its proper place and her grandmother nowhere to be seen. She yawned and set the incident aside.

The girl had slept well and was feeling excited about her day, and the sunlight buoyed her spirits.

Parade Day!

Heather was quick to dress and hurry downstairs to the Bristol House kitchen, where she was greeted with a pleasant morning countenance belonging to her grandmother.

"Sleep well?" Grandma Dawn asked.

"Yep!"

"Good." She rose to collect the makings for Heather's breakfast. "Orange juice?"

"Yes, please! In my small glass, the one with stars." One of Heather's favorite glasses had stars suspended in a blue liquid night, and every time she took a sip, they shifted, forming new constellations within the hollow sides.

"Mrs. Pringle phoned about fifteen minutes ago, and said that Molly would be here at nine."

Heather looked at the antique wall clock. Its hands claimed just past eight.

"Great!"

Cereal was served, and Heather enthusiastically started in on it. Grandma Dawn sat, returning to her oatmeal and coffee.

After a time, she asked, "So, what are you girls going to be doing today?" Heather hastily spooned down her meal, her unbounded energy entertaining the woman. Then, from below raised brows came reproval: "You may want to slow down devouring your breakfast, young lady. I'd like to think that you're tasting your food."

Heather nodded vigorously, having worked through another spoonful with a swallow. "Parade Day."

"Parade Day?" Grandma Dawn took a slow sip of coffee, and looked up at the blue sky outside the kitchen windows. It held a few fluffy, late autumn clouds. "It's a beautiful day for it. I don't recall any mention of a parade in the Daily Compass. Is it down on the courthouse square?"

"Oh, no. It's by invitation only." Spoon halting midair, Heather looked up from her meal to see if her Grandmother was impressed. Across the table, she only appeared more attentive. Heather hurried, "When we were having ice cream yesterday, the Bristol House invited Molly and me to a parade. But you know the Bristol House…" Heather laughed uncomfortably, and then cleared her throat. She hoped that she hadn't given away too much information, so that her grandmother would decide a Bristol House parade in an unknown location wasn't such a good idea.

She pushed away her bowl, an act declaring the meal's end. Running her tongue over her front teeth, Heather announced, "Teeth check." She flashed them straight and white, holding a fixed grin for her grandmother to inspect from across the table. "Clear?"

"Clear."

"We have to be in the sewing room at ten—at least we think it's the sewing room. Molly and I had to figure out a clue, and we're pretty sure that's the answer."

"Mm-hmm." Another sip, a concerned sip. Her features showing signs of fatigue, Grandma Dawn regarded Heather.

"We have a sewing room, right?" Heather asked. "I think I've seen it a few times."

"We do."

"Third floor?"

Her grandmother drew out the word, "Yes." It lay on the air, a gentle affirmative—slightly curious.

"Thought so. May I be excused, please?"

Grandma Dawn smiled, but the seriousness never left her eyes. She nodded. "Please be back by dinnertime, all right?"

"Okay." The child glanced at the clock. "Can you please send Molly up to my room when she gets here?"

"I will."

Heather pushed in her chair. She grabbed her bowl, spoon, and glass, and skillfully carried them to the sink in a precarious balance of table-ware. There she rinsed them before taking a moment to hold up the glass between her and the blue sky-filled windows overhead. The backlighting illuminated the translucent liquid and caused the stars to sparkle in contrast. Heather liked that.

Setting the glass to drain near her bowl and spoon, she headed towards the hall. On her way, the girl hurried by the thoughtful façade of Grandma Dawn.

Over her shoulder, her grandmother said, "Have fun!"

In a rush, Heather returned to kiss her grandmother on the tilted cheek that was offered. "Thank you! We will." She added an impromptu hug and darted off.

Grandma Dawn turned, her arm draping over the back of the chair. She watched Heather leave the kitchen, her footfalls soon beating out a rhythmic rise up the stairs.

"And be careful," she thought to call after her.

Heather didn't hear.

"I've been meaning to ask you, Heather," Molly said, "how did you know where to look for the Autumnsloe book in the library? The place is so huge, and with all those rooms, it could have been in any one of them."

The blonde girl looked at Molly, a twinkle to her eye. "It was in the first place I checked."

"No way."

"Way."

"Really?"

The two were climbing the stairs to the third floor. Though she hadn't commented, Heather noticed Molly had taken special care to dress stylishly today, something she hadn't done for some time—since the day of Stilped's funeral.

Heather continued: "I just thought, 'Where would I be if I were an Autumnsloe book?' And then I figured that the book had to be old, and would probably be found on a shelf in some protected section. So, I thought about all the library bookshelves that have glass covers over them, and that's where I started. When I climbed the ladder, there it was."

"But don't a lot of the library rooms have glass-covered shelves?" Molly managed between breaths on the stairway.

Heather halted and turned, Molly almost bumping into her. "You're right. And I bet if I had checked one of those other rooms first, I would have found the book there." Once again, she began to climb.

"What do you mean?"

"I mean the Bristol House wanted me to find that Autumnsloe book."

Molly stopped, her hand on the handrail. She watched as Heather continued her ascent. She hurried after her and met up with her friend on the landing, where Heather stood pondering, fingers lightly tapping her lips.

"Molly, I think I might have passed through the sewing room before."

"Really? Where was it?"

"Depends."

"Meaning?"

"I *mean* it depends on whether you're asking me where it was the first time I found it, or the second or third."

Grandma Dawn set aside the newspaper with a sigh and a toss, sitting up straight. Her mind had trouble absorbing the words assembled in vertical columns that marched as serifed characters across the page. She was glad that Lana hadn't been able to stay for a morning visit. After greeting mother and daughter briefly at the kitchen door, with a few words she sent Molly up the stairs to Heather's room. And following a few more words, Mrs. Pringle was off with errands to run and a hair appointment.

Grandma Dawn stifled a yawn. It had been a long night. Twice she had thought she heard sounds that might have been visitors—intruders—and gratefully, twice, her fears proved unfounded. As she sat warily in the night, with Heather asleep nearby, she had strained to hear the slightest sound. Her magic was rusty, she knew, and the woman was probably no match for the assassins, if they came. But she wasn't raised a Maiden to lie down easily in Heather's defense. She could still put up a fair bit of resistance, she figured. But would it be enough to save her granddaughter—to distract the intruders long enough so Heather would have time to flee? But to where?

I see we'll have to come up with a plan, she thought. Never suspecting Heather could be the One, the Intended, I didn't think it necessary.

Grandma Dawn was aware that the WhisperEye Mirror had been smashed. She hadn't used it in years, knowing the once safe network had been penetrated long ago. Too, she was aware that Heather had been behind its shattering, thus severing the only immediate connection to her superiors in the Realm—but not before the WhisperEye Mirror was compromised by a dangerous Bristol House infiltrator.

But who? she wondered. Someone capable of speaking in shades of the Voice, that's who. Not a good omen.

Grandma Dawn rubbed her eyes.

Followers of the WhisperSign? She wasn't so certain. They knew the network, to be sure, infiltrating it for their own personal knowledge, but had no interest in seeking out and disposing of the One, unless they were now hiring out as TimeLight mercenaries. Yet, that seems highly unlikely, she thought. Little was known of the group, and they had a tendency to keep to themselves, preferring separation from all involvement in the affairs of Crown and Realm.

So then who was the WhisperVoice? A frown twisted the woman's brow. I do hope that our friends who listen and keep watch along the WhisperEye Network heard the exchange between Heather and the Voice and will act accordingly. If only it were safe for me to directly contact those who need to know, but the risk is far too great. We could inadvertently reveal our location to dangerous others in the process.

The woman knew the alternative was to travel once again to the Realm of Evermore, but she no longer had the PassKey to that particular Portal. And she didn't know where one could immediately be found. Isolated this way, cut off from all contact with the Realm, it didn't bode well for her and the child.

Had someone sensed the extensive use of magic in this TimeLight Expanse and searched the area via WhisperEye? Apparently, she thought, because I sensed it also, the children interacting with the Bristol House and its magic. Yet, perhaps they had other ways of knowing of the child who may ultimately be the answer to the Portent.

So, Grandma Dawn asked herself, exactly how much information were they able to gather from their contact with Heather? How much did they see?

The woman rose and emptied her little-touched coffee in the sink. If she was to be sharp throughout the night, she needed rest—and a nap. Grandma Dawn turned her head briefly towards the ceiling, as if she could see clear to the third floor and Heather.

Oh, magical Bristol House, she thought, whatever you have planned, watch over my grandchild. Please. And Molly.

Grandma Dawn then thought of Stilped's gruesome death on the Bristol House grounds. She realized there was only so much protection that the magically imbued house could provide.

"Did you really bust that mirror?" Molly asked.

"Yeah, in a million pieces."

"So who do you think was in it? Was it really your mother?"

"Beats me. All I know is someone is trying to find me, and I don't think that's good."

"It sounds so creepy. Does your grandmother know?"

"I don't know, Molly. And I'm not sure I should tell her either."

"Why not?"

"Because she's worried enough about Stilped's murder and the investigation. She even wants to talk to me about it. She said so at dinner—at least I think that's what she wants to talk to me about. She seemed pretty serious. Molly, I think Grandma Dawn's so upset, so worried, she sat by my bed all last night."

"All night?"

"Yeah, I think so. I really can't say for sure, though."

"How come?"

"Because I was sleeping, silly."

"But Heather, what if something happens to you?"

"How can it? I broke the mirror."

"But the woman said she saw you."

"Maybe she did, or maybe she's just saying that to scare me. If she really did see me, why did she want me to take off more of the drape?"

Molly shook her head. "I don't know, Heather. It all sounds pretty scary to me."

"Well, I'm not scared. I think this is it, Molly."

The two girls stood before an unusual door, a door similar to that of the kitchen, which was dutch, but unlike the kitchen door, its frame rose in a graceful arc to terminate at a point above their heads. Recessed into its thick wood planks were sewing spools of various heights and sizes. Placed on end, they created a pleasing relief design overall. Heather turned the old brass knob and the door gave way.

It opened on a large room that, despite its size, felt both intimate and cozy. Near old sewing machines on black wrought-iron stands, aligned in three rows of four, were tables of honey-colored wood strewn with fabrics and patterns. Standing along the walls were open cabinets with bolts of multi-colored cloth stacked to fill their many shelves. In one corner was a freestanding full-length mirror near a changing room and some chairs.

Positioned near every table were assorted dress forms and mannequins, the majority headless and armless. Though the mannequins never
directly stared, the waxen faces discreetly followed the girls, until Heather or Molly looked their way.

Some of the dress forms and mannequins stood clothed while others
were fitted only in undergarments and hoop skirts, awaiting petticoats
and outer wear. On many of the dress forms were Victorian bodices
in beautiful satin fabrics, with a variety of rich texture combinations
and extravagant appliqué. Some sleeves were puffy and bunched, others
straight and three-quarter length; others, too, were full at the shoulders
and long to the wrist; and a great many were frilly with ribbons and lace.

Below the bodices were full-bodied skirts and dresses, ranging from
lavishly ruffled to uncomplicated, tucked effusively or gathered behind
at the hip to elegantly drape long and flowing to the floor.

Molly was at the side of one of the mannequins, her fingers caressing
the fabric of shining blue with stripes of charcoal gray. Matching tassels
embellished the wide, bell-shaped sleeves.

"This is so beautiful." She gazed up and into the glamorous face of the
model. "And so is she." The lady looked down on the girl benevolently
and smiled at the compliment before returning her head to its properly
held position. Molly retreated a step and looked around. "I love this
room. It's creative and—" Molly took a deep breath, "—gorgeous."

Heather laughed. "And splendidly stellar."

Molly ignored her.

Heather was quick to add, "You love this room because you love
fashion."

Enchanted, Molly was walking from one magnificently dressed mannequin to the next, past the chemises, corsets, and other tasteful undergarments. She stopped in front of a stunning Victorian gown of purple
velvet with swirling reds and lacy magenta trim. Molly ran her hand
lightly over the fabric.

Heather impatiently eyed a red enameled clock against the opposite
wall. "Molly, I think we're kinda in a hurry. So, as soon as you're done
petting those dresses, we need to find out where we're supposed to be."
Heather turned. "There's a door over there. Hopefully it leads to the
room we want."

"Heather, can you wait a second? I think the Bristol House wants me
to see and admire these dresses. And you know why we won't be late for
our ten o'clock appointment?"

"Because pretty soon I'll be dragging you into the next room?"

"No. We're not going to be late to our next appointment," Molly said, inspecting yet another mannequin, this one wearing a dress of reds and white, "because the Bristol House won't let us."

Heather thought for a moment, pondering Molly's logic. "Well, you're probably right," she said, walking towards the small door, "but we don't know that for sure and it's almost ten." Again the girl cast a glance at the grandfather clock. "But can't you go shopping later? I say let's find out where we're supposed to be. We only have a couple minutes."

"This gown must belong to a sorceress," Molly said aloud to herself. She held out one of the flared sleeves that hung almost to the floor. The sorceress mannequin stood tall above Molly, the eyes inanimate, opaque, and glossy. Yet they seemed to be studying the young girl from beneath a barbed headpiece that encircled the forehead.

"Darn!" Heather said, trying both the upper and lower halves of the dutch door. "It's locked." In appearance, it was much like the pointed outer door, only smaller. Frustrated, the girl looked around her. "Well, this *is* the sewing room—I mean, it *looks* like a sewing room."

"Heather, don't worry. We're in the right place," Molly said. Nonchalantly, she continued her perusal of the sorceress, examining the weighty bracelets and the long blue fingernails.

The fashionable grandfather clock whirred, clicked, and began to boomingly count out ten bells. BONG! BONG! BONG!

"It's ten o'clock!" Heather said, her voice crying out over the sound of the clock.

Helplessly, she looked around for a clue, some indication that they were where the Bristol House wanted them. BONG! BONG! BONG! As the bells of the clock continued their finite count, Heather became frantic. She began scrambling around to the tables, looking high and low for clues. BONG! BONG! BONG!

"Come on, Molly! Aren't you going to help?"

BONG! As the tenth bell rang out, Heather gave up her mad dash. She threw up her hands, crestfallen.

"I guess that's it, then. We've missed the parade."

Molly, however, continued browsing, nonplussed, inspecting the black and golden-toed shoes that ended in a point.

Hands on her hips, Heather heard a latch snap out. She looked over to the small door that had previously been locked. The top half of the Dutch door slowly and tantalizingly swung inward before stopping.

Momentarily looking up, Molly said, "There. See?" She resumed browsing.

Heather walked over and pushed on the upper door, causing it to open wider. With her stomach balanced on the lower door and her red shoes lifting off the floor, the girl leaned in to peer about.

"Molly." Her voice came across as distant, cast into the adjoining room.

"Heather, hold on a minute, all right?" Molly continued inspecting the dress of the sorceress. "The Bristol House won't mind," she said, distractedly, her fingertips now gently lifting the substantial and elaborate necklace from the upper chest of the mannequin. "This is really something, Heather. Look at these jewels."

"Molly, you need to get over here. If you think *that's* something, just wait till you see *these* outfits!"

Molly looked up. "Really?"

"Yeah. And I think they're ours."

Molly let the necklace drop back into place. "I'm not surprised," she said, her words filled with excitement. She scampered to join Heather, the mannequin staring after her, brow furrowed. Molly's companion stood just within the threshold of the next room, the lower door ajar. "I knew the Bristol House would get us to the right place in time." With an admiring glance back over the room behind her, she entered the adjoining one, coming to a standstill alongside her blonde companion.

"Oh, Heather," was all Molly could manage, awestruck.

Before the girls, on mannequins equal to their own size and height, were two lavish costumes, each bearing a full facial mask. On the taller figure was an ensemble in blues, with flourishes of violet and gold, and smaller touches of green and silver, all shades of the night. On the costume's mask, centered over the right eyebrow and rising above the forehead, was a large crescent moon, its subtle face in profile. The lacy metal moon was composed of graceful golden flourishes, bejeweled with turquoise and white cut stones. The mask itself was a blend of sparkling gold-violet and blue, the left half covered with a flowing gold sequined design, the other half less so. The painted lips were of rich glossy maroon. Tucked, draped, and swirling about the head before elegantly dropping to enfold the chin, were layers of night-blue fabric adorned with silver and gold stars and colorful planets amid white pearls and silver beads. Similar embellishments were repeated on various other parts of the elaborate costume below. Attached to the sides of the mask, long earrings dangled down, replete with glimmering jewels.

Not far from the moon-bedecked mannequin stood another, shorter in height, draped in colors of the garden, of flowers and the spring. Among white and a myriad of greens were strokes of red, yellow, blue, orange, and magenta. A large butterfly dominated the mask, its great wingspan spreading to cover each side of the face and beyond, the eye-slots becoming part of the wing's decorative pattern. Pearl chains elegantly swung from parts of the multicolored butterfly, connecting the wings to the body of the mask. Like Heather's, the flamboyant full-bodied costume consisted of a variety of textures, thick to sheer, sparkling to matte, simple to ornate, that swirled about to envelop the body. Attached here and there on Molly's costume were smaller butterflies, with jewels and beaded ornamentation, enhancing the highly decorative finery.

Shaking her head, Molly said, "I've never seen anything like it."

"Of course you've never seen anything like it!" said a fast-talking voice out of nowhere.

"Oh, no," Heather said. "Not another Voice." Extending a guiding arm, she backed Molly behind her and towards the door. Heather looked around, inspecting the mirrors in the smaller room.

Molly looked at Heather with incomprehension. "Who said that?"

"Why, I did, of course!" said the voice. "Who else?"

"Who are you?" Heather asked. "And *where* are you?"

"I'm right here in front of you, on your moon costume."

Leaning forward, Heather and Molly approached to spy a brooch in the shape of a crescent moon attached near the outfit's left breast. Unlike the moon on the mask above, which was flat in profile, this moon stood out in a three-dimensional, three-quarter view, and upon closer inspection by the two girls, it seemed to be alive. Heather thought it looked like a small blue and gold banana with a little face.

"Hey, *my* costume doesn't have a talking brooch," Molly said, comparing the two.

"That's because," said the moon, wiggling its eyebrows, "you don't happen to be as lucky as your companion here."

Heather and Molly momentarily locked eyes.

"That voice is going to drive me crazy," Heather stated, under her breath.

"I heard that! Don't be rude. I'm part of your costume."

Heather didn't know what to say.

"Apologize," the brooch said.

"What?"

"Apologize." With Heather struck mute, the voice added, "I'm waiting."

"I-I'm sorry," Heather said, sounding more thoughtful than apologetic.

"Hmm. Well, okay, it'll have to do." A clearing of the throat ensued. "The name is Fallasha," the moon went on at its quick pace. "Many of my friends say that I talk a great deal, but I can assure you, that's not necessarily the case. I was—"

"Excuse me," Heather cut in. "Why—?"

"Young lady, *I'm speaking!*"

"Oh."

"Apologize."

"What?"

"Apologize."

"I'm sorry."

"Okay, better."

"But why are you here?" Heather asked. "I mean, what are you supposed to be doing? I don't mean to be mean, but are you going to be with us all day?"

"Rude!" blared the moon. "Apologize."

"But you're a *brooch!*"

"Rude! Apologize."

Molly laughed as Heather rolled her eyes in exasperation. "Sorry."

"The last one was better. Anyway, as I was starting to say," and here the moon shot Heather an irritated look, "my purpose today is to accompany the two of you to the parade as your own personal tour guide. Be thankful."

The girls once again exchanged glances.

Heather said, "I think this is going to be a long day."

"Rude! Apol—"

"I'm sorry, I'm sorry!" Heather blurted. "Geez…"

"Good. All right, then." Fallasha hardly seemed mollified. "Mind your manners, Heather. That goes for you, too, Molly." And when the two girls simply stood dumbfounded before her, the moon added, "Well, come on. Snap, snap! The parade is starting. Don't just stand there. Let's get dressed!"

CHAPTER EIGHTEEN

Keys to a Portal

"How do I look?" Heather asked Molly.

"We look *sensational!*" Fallasha said, the brooch admiring her own reflection in the mirror. She flashed a large grin and liked it.

"Molly?" Heather asked, ignoring the brooch.

Molly was looking in the mirror, thrilled with the beautiful flower motifs on her supple leather boots that were cuffed below the knee and moderately curled at the toe. Tucking in the hems of her billowy pants, adjusting the various fabrics of her outfit, pulling here, gathering there, she looked at her friend and smiled beneath her mask. Heather noticed.

"Hey, Molly, are the lips of my mask moving, too?"

The girl laughed. "Yes. Fantastic, Heather! When we put on these masks, they become our actual faces. It's like an extra layer of skin, only with a bunch of jewelry attached."

"Molly, is my mask's nose all bunched up?" Heather made a face, pushing out her lips.

Molly giggled. "Yes."

"Okay, can you see my tongue?" Heather stuck out her purplish-red tongue.

"Yes."

The moon girl turned to the mirror, still holding out her tongue. She saw her mask break into a wide grin and then watched herself laugh. "These costumes are so great!"

"You really do look beautiful, Heather," Molly said, before adding, "And mysterious."

"Boy," Heather said, continuing to gaze upon her likeness in the mirror, "I wish Aria could see us. Wait until I tell her; she'll wish she'd been here."

Giving her mask a final adjustment, Molly turned and struck a spirited pose, presenting a full-length vision of herself. "What do you think?"

"Wow, Molly, with all those colors, you remind me of the Bristol House garden in spring. You look great."

"Don't we *all* look fantastic?" said the small brooch. "I think so. And would the Bristol House sewing room have it any other way? No, of course not. Now, come on, you two, let's grab the key to the Portal."

"Where is it?" Heather asked.

"On the key ring by the door," said the moon.

Heather looked to see hanging on a large metal loop a multitude of keys, all different in size and design, and all bunched and climbing around the ring that shackled them together. She walked over and, leaning against the wall, reached up to lift the ring off a large hook.

"Umph! Hey!" came the muffled voice of Fallasha. "You-you're squishing me!"

"Oh! Sorry," Heather said, backing away from the wall. She held up the cumbersome ring with all the keys, and shook it. "Which one is it?"

"Whichever one fits the Portal," the brooch said, making faces, wrinkling her nose. "That hurt."

"I'm not used to having you there."

"Where's the Portal?" Molly asked.

"It's behind you," Fallasha said, "in the alcove."

The two girls turned to face the corner niche, where there was a door of similar size and shape to the entry door. To its right were an elaborate bronze sculpture with clock, a narrow cabinet, and a rack of spools with multicolored threads near a single sewing machine. All this lay beyond the two mannequins that were currently draped with Heather and Molly's discarded clothes.

Heather said, "Wow. Look at that clock."

"Clock? It's more like a sculpture you'd see at a museum," said a fascinated Molly. "I didn't even notice it before. I must have been too busy looking at the costumes."

The pair walked towards the large bronze sculpture that sat on a carved marble pedestal. The sculpture was configured with three life-sized females in a triangular arrangement, two standing on each side of a sheer cliff and one positioned on top before a rippling bronze pool of water. Below the uppermost figure, centered on the cliff face was a large recessed clock, its numbers fluid in design, the hands pointing out the current time. On either side of the timepiece stood the two copper-colored women with lengthy plaits of hair, their long garments flowing about them. They were laughing, and while leaning away, each tugged playfully at the adjoining ends of fabric that stretched up to encircle many times the young girl above. Her head shaved bare, her hands were held up, as amused, she looked down at the swathing of her bundled body.

Heather softly mouthed the word, "Maidens," as if the sound itself were magic.

"Heather," Molly said, "the girl in the middle..."

Astonished, Heather stopped in her tracks. Molly moved nearer, and with wonder gazed upward.

"She does, doesn't she, Heather?" Molly continued. "She looks like you."

"I can see a resemblance," said the moon brooch, " but it's only happenstance, I'm sure."

"Maybe," said Molly. She turned to Heather, who continued to stare at the likeness of herself, before resuming her approach for a closer look.

"If we want to be certain," said the brooch, "we can always shave Heather's head and compare the two."

Ignoring the moon's comment, Heather said, "Wow, Molly, I think you're right."

Almost undetectable on the rocky surface, near the clock face, Molly pointed and said, "Hey, that looks like one of those old fashioned keyholes."

"Where?" Heather asked.

Fallasha said, "It's there, to the right of the clock. We need to figure out which key fits, so we can enter the Portal."

Surprised, the two girls looked at the moon, Heather awkwardly viewing the brooch beneath her tucked chin.

"The clock is the Portal, not that door?" Heather asked, pointing.

"It certainly is."

Heather held up the large ring before her, burdened with keys. "It'll take awhile to go through all these keys to see which one fits."

"Let's look more closely at them," Molly said. "They're all so different. There may be one that's more like the clock."

"What do you mean?"

Fallasha said, "She means that there may be a key more befitting the manner of the clock's style or theme, in how the key itself is shaped."

"Oh," said Heather, annoyed with what struck her as the know-it-all demeanor of the brooch.

In her layered but comfortable costume, she knelt easily in front of the clock, setting the key ring on the floor.

"You're right, Molly. They are all so different," Heather said, spreading and disentangling the assortment.

There were keys that were short without elaboration, some that were intricately designed, some with spiky adornments, others that featured crooked, thick, or narrow shafts, while some keys flaunted graceful clover-top designs. There were keys of spindly wood and shiny metal, gleaming gold, brass, copper, or silver. Intermingled were many in a tarnished state. Some keys were topped with a figurine, skull, horse, or other small sculpture, whereas some shone with the sparkle of inlaid jewels.

Heather asked, "Now, where do we start?"

"I think the key we need would probably be unusual looking," said Molly. "Not one of the simple ones." She was squatting next to her friend, inspecting the variety.

Thanks to Heather, the keys had been spaced around the circumference of the large ring, taking up most every circular degree.

"Pick some, Molly."

"Let me see… How about the two next to that wooden key that looks like a small flat tree, an-n-n-n-n-n-n-d…" she said, scanning the keys, "…that one there." She touched one with her finger. On its larger end was a bronze fish. "It goes with the pool of water."

Heather worked the keys around the large loop, opened the clasp, and removed them. One by one they were inserted into the clock. None fit correctly, until the last one. The fish.

"It fits," said Heather. The eyes within the two masks met in anticipation. "Ready?"

"Sure am. Have been," said Fallasha, though the question wasn't asked of her.

Heather turned her attention back to the key. She spun the pronged implement, and it moved in a short abbreviated turn before stopping. Heather tried again, pulling the fish key out, reinserting it, and giving it another spin. It wouldn't move any farther than it had previously.

Heather jiggled the key, working it. "I'm afraid it's not going to turn, you guys," she said, still wiggling it this way and that.

"It almost did," said Molly, sounding cheerful. "Let's look some more."

Gazing down at the countless keys spread below, Heather said, "Fallasha, how come you don't know which one is the right key? After all, you work here."

"Do you know how many locks there are in the Bristol House?" the moon brooch asked, "And that's not counting the rooms on the third floor that haven't arrived yet."

"Yeah, but the key we're looking for is supposed to fit the clock right here in the sewing room."

"So? I don't spend all my time here, you know. I've got other significant engagements that require my magnanimous presence."

"You're just a little moon brooch," Heather said a bit icily. "What other *engagements* could you have? Lunar Eclipse Night in the observatory?"

"Rude!"

"No, it's not," Heather said. "I've studied lunar eclipses—"

"Rude!"

"Come on, you two," Molly said. "Stop fighting. We need to find the key to the Portal."

"Apologize," said Fallasha.

Heather crossed her arms beneath the brooch. "No."

"Apologize."

"For what?"

"Apologize."

"But I didn't do anything."

"You did. You were rude. Apologize."

Heather said, "I don't believe this."

"Apologize."

There hung a stilted silence. The eyes within Molly's mask pleaded with Heather.

"Okay," the blonde girl said, looking away from her talking clasp. "Sorry," she mumbled, barely audible.

"Pardon me? Did you happen to say a little something, a little something that was perhaps both courteous and polite? If so, those sweetly scented sounds didn't quite reach the awaiting and welcome ingress of my ears," said the brooch, her air indignant, her nose up.

"Oh, please," Heather said, her disgusted expression displayed openly on the features of her glittering mask.

Heather looked at Molly and noticed her aura surging an irritated slushy brown.

"All right," Molly said. "We need to get on with this, you two." She turned, giving equal attention to the brooch. "The parade has probably started. So, can we please make up?"

Heather nodded at the floor and exhaled wearily. Irritated, and wrestling with her pride, she waited before forcing out a robotic, "Sorry, Fallasha."

"That's more like it," the moon said. "Now, watch your manners. It's not just *any* brooch you happen to be wearing."

"Yeah, I know; it's a stuck-up, little blue-faced banana that can't keep its moon-mouth shut."

"Rude!"

Exasperated, Molly stood up. "You two stop it!"

"Apologize," the moon said.

"You deserved it."

"Apologize."

"Can I take you off?" Heather asked. "Really, you're such a pain—"

"Rude!"

Molly put her hands on her hips and glared at the sparring pair. From inside her decorative, butterfly face, her forceful voice boomed out, "Look! We've got to find the key to the Portal. Time is wasting and you two keep bickering. We're going to miss the parade. So, I'm going to ask you both to behave yourselves and get along." She looked at Heather. "Isn't going to this parade important to you?"

Heather looked uncomfortably at her friend. She saw that Molly's shine was pulsing a sharp-edged, fiery red around her colorful costume. "Yeah." Then to the brooch, "I'm sorry, little moon. Really."

"Well..." Fallasha was caught off-guard by Heather's sudden sincerity. "Okay, then."

An awkward silence passed among the three. Finally, the moon brooch said brightly, "Any other key possibilities?"

"Well, there's the one that looks like a rock with three red jewels," Molly said. "It kind of matches the rocky surface of the clock."

Heather began moving the keys around, positioning the rock-and-jeweled key to be near the clasp, when she noticed a uniquely compelling key. On the large end was a red-cowled figure that tapered to become the tarnished shaft, ending in a small beast with four prongs that were its miniature legs. The hooded image had a white pearlescent face, its features resembling that of an old man or woman. It reminded Heather of the statues that she had seen in her dream, atop the small building outside the MaidenHall Academy.

"This is it," she said, displaying more of the key for the others to see.

"How do you know?" Molly asked.

"Because I saw statues that looked like it." Heather began to remove the key from the ring.

"Really?" Molly asked. "Where?"

"In a dream."

"A dream?" the brooch said. "Oh, bother *me!* What makes you think that any silly dream of yours has anything to do with a key to the Portal?"

"Rude!" Heather said, the features of her mask suddenly knotted in irritation.

"You two—" Molly began.

"Apologize," Heather said, looking up and to her left, addressing from her knees the reflection of the moon-brooch in a mirror positioned near the wall.

"But—"

"Apologize."

"I didn't say anything inappropriate—"

"Apologize."

Molly said, "Fallasha, can you please just apologize?"

"Oh, and now you, too? Well, okay, then. All right." In a huff, the moon burst out with her apology, a rambling discourse rationalizing why she would say such a thing to Heather, and how her intent was really a clarification of the matter at hand rather than a divisive and dismissive attempt at ridicule. She ended with, "So, if it makes you feel any better, I apologize on behalf of all brooches everywhere, on behalf of every costume that has ever slighted its wearer, on behalf of every ill-fitting or contemptible mask. Yes, young Heather, I offer you this humble apology, an apology befitting a queen. If I could, I would fall to a knee at your feet."

Silence ensued, before Heather said, "Geez, remind me never to ask you to apologize again. I was a year younger when you started that whole thing—"

"Heather, don't—"

"Rude!" the wounded brooch sounded out.

"Your apology took so long," Heather pressed on, "that now the parade is probably over and everyone has gone home."

Following a sharp intake of breath, Fallasha blurted, "Rude!"

"It's true, and I'm not going to apologize—"

"Rude!"

"Look, you little rotten, fruity, space banana—"

"*Exceptionally* rude! Well, all right, *that's it!*" the brooch shot. "What about *your* stupid dreams, eh? Oh, yes, sure, statues that remind you of PortalKeys! How can anyone be so, so, so—?"

"Really, really, *really* rude!" said Heather.

"—so, so, so—?"

"Apologize!"

"—so ridiculously *stupid?*"

"Apologize, I said!"

"Not while you have breath, *crater-hater.*"

"Eclipse-lips!"

"Moon loon!"

"Why you little—" Heather stuck the tip of her pinky finger in the tiny moon's mouth. "That ought to shut you up." Then: "Ow! You bit me, you,

you, *you…* " at a loss, Heather was searching for words, "you splendidly stellar piece of moon poop!" She pinched Fallasha's nose and held it.

"Agh!!! Stahp thaght! Apahllajize!"

"*You* apologize! You know, I used to like moons once…"

Molly took the key from Heather's distracted hand, as the two continued to argue, Fallasha currently spouting, "Ohw! Ohw! Ohw! Unhahnd me, bruhtish moohn!" When Molly placed the key in the black pit of the lock, it slid home with a click. She gave it a spin.

The butterfly girl stepped back as the clock statue began to shudder. A horizontal crack appeared at the base of the bronze cliff, and began to grow outward in an ever-increasing rectangular shape until a large ornate door had fully formed in the sculpture's center. Meanwhile, the uppermost figure sank into the sculpture's mutating façade, only to reappear positioned on her belly. She was now facing forward, her head extending out and peering down over the newly formed PortalDoor, her legs bent at the knees and feet kicked up playfully behind her. With one hand loosely set on the rocks below her face and the other easily at rest against her cheek, her amused expression reemerged still intact, though slightly altered, as if she were merrily watching all who entered and exited. On either side, the two Maidens had twisted and transformed into watchful, unflinching sentinels, replete with armor.

Heather and Fallasha stopped their squabbling. All three stared with fascination at the door that had materialized before them. The clock face was now small and circular above it.

"I knew it would do that," Fallasha said, recovering her composure after witnessing the magical transformation. "You know, I was *certain* that was the correct key the entire time."

Heather gave her brooch hardly a glance. The key still in the lock, she strode up, and grabbing hold of the door's handle, turned to Molly.

"Ready?" she asked.

The butterfly mask nodded.

"Fallasha?"

"Of course."

Heather turned the handle, and when she opened the door a crack, crowd sounds and up-tempo music poured into the smaller sewing room. Before continuing, however, Heather took a moment to take a half step behind her. Throwing her costumed-head back, she peered up at the bald likeness of herself that gazed upon her from above the door.

"So, what's so funny?" Heather asked of her bronze reproduction. The bald young Maiden continued to beam down charmingly on her guest. Heather could have sworn she winked. Turning to Molly, the moon girl said, "It's parade time, you guys. Come on, let's go!"

And with that, Heather pulled open the door, and the three stepped into a new world, with its cavalcade of brightly costumed people.

Grandma Dawn was slowly rocking in the wicker chair. She felt the morning to be chilly, but the breeze was light and fresh, and the woman couldn't see herself staying inside on this, the first blue sky day in quite some time. Sitting on the covered porch, she looked out at the sun-blanketed garden, the foliage lush after the recent heavy rains. Though hardly at rest, the soft shadows cast lazily over the plantlife seemed weightless, abstracted, and lost in a wistful drift. All around, the few remaining blooms within her view stood perky and attentive to the light and warmth, as if appreciative, knowing what the upcoming season held in store.

The tired woman felt the late autumn, felt it penetrate and occupy her aging bones. The shortened daylight hours were infused with a drowsy solemnity, and the garden echoed the mood with what would be the last days of life for some greenery and a long withdrawal into dormancy for others. And though the grounds lay tossed about, battered and lethargic, the weather hadn't been cold enough to commit the garden to its most profound journey, the barren and timeless road to rejuvenation. But Grandma Dawn felt it wouldn't be long now as she sensed the hastening approach of winter's icy tread beneath an ever-weakening sun.

What to do about the vulnerability of the Bristol House? she thought, setting down her book and then resuming her rocking.

She wanted to protect her granddaughter from TimeLight predators and executioners, but had concluded that the task was too much for any one person, and that what awaited Heather was not solely dependent on her grandmother's assistance. It simply relied on fate. If Heather were indeed the One, it came down to surviving because it was her destiny to do so. But that didn't mean lying down in battle. Surely and once again, if confrontation were called upon, it was with confrontation that an enemy would—by all means—be met. Of this Grandma Dawn had no fear, and she felt her warrior-sense deeply, just as surely as she felt the primeval permutations of the autumnal season.

But what could she do? Surely, it wouldn't hurt to take precautions, but there was no way in heaven or seasonal Evermore that she could guard or seal all the Portals in and out of the Bristol House. One reason she couldn't do so was that she had no idea where they were. And actually, she only knew of one, and for most of twelve years now it had remained keyless and inactive—but then again, she hadn't had any reason to seek out PortalDoors. And of course, from her experience as a young Maiden, she knew that not all of the magically infused Portals needed keys. She also knew that the Bristol House received occasional and undeclared visitors known only to itself.

And wasn't it time? she asked herself. Well, wasn't it? Most certainly.

Grandma Dawn felt—knew—that it was time Heather learned about her connection to Evermore and its history, becoming aware of her remarkable potential, and the consequences of being that chosen soul. And though she had previously made personal note and mentioned to the child that they needed to talk, Grandma Dawn had not yet initiated the discussion, allowing the Bristol House time to do its part. She also feared that to bring the words to life would make everything all too real, the risks and dangers at what the future would likely hold—and that the momentous knowledge would change her granddaughter into something other than the child she'd grown to know and love.

Here, Grandma Dawn laughed at herself, asking: But hadn't she just recently rejoiced that Heather was the answer to the Portent? Then why assume the worst?

It suddenly occurred to Grandma Dawn that she had been harboring a nagging sense of foreboding, and she realized now that it had been slyly infiltrating her thoughts, persistently looming, and never retreating too far afield. And though sensing it, she had refused to recognize it. Now, having at this moment done so, the woman confronted her feeling of impending disaster, willing it to dissipate, but the apprehension continued to linger.

Be strong for Heather, rather than afraid! the grandmother scolded herself. It's not wise to project your fears onto the child. She can apparently take care of herself. Didn't she rise up to disable the WhisperEye Mirror? The fact that she wasn't seduced completely by the WhisperVoice speaks of her power.

And there it was. In a flash of clarity, Grandma Dawn realized it was *she* who was afraid, afraid of losing Heather as Catherine Ryan had been lost, afraid of again living daily with the corrosive thought that she had somehow been negligent in her Maidenly duty, afraid of facing the staggering emptiness that she knew would follow Heather's death, an emptiness that would blight her remaining days. Feeling herself being pulled down emotionally, Grandma Dawn allowed it, letting her mind wander to the loss of her child Catherine Ryan, approaching that searing abscess of pain that would never heal, could never heal. Ever. And she didn't want it to.

Love, she thought, such a wicked contrivance. The woman chuckled, thinking not for the first time, Assuredly and without a doubt, the Universe must possess a perverted sense of humor.

With a shake of her head, as if clearing her mind of a murky and richly incessant smoke, Grandma Dawn let the thoughts waft away, bringing her awareness to the tangible reality of her time-gnawed surroundings. Then she watched, as suddenly, the garden's leafy shadows swam in a gust, like a school of darting, flickering fish. All about, leaves swirled to the ground. Others were swept away.

With renewed conviction, Heather's grandmother committed herself to the task of talking to her granddaughter and soon. Perhaps tonight after the parade or tomorrow morning.

But how much do I divulge? she asked herself. Too much information could be paralyzing, and not enough could leave my granddaughter dangerously ignorant. Again, I mustn't forget that Heather is only a child.

Her gaze wandered and held to a large bud just beyond the porch, where ablaze, it soaked up the morning light. The petals were beginning to unravel and emerge, aglow with the promise of something exquisite and exceptional.

"And there you are."

Her tired eyes glassy, Grandma Dawn, turned away, and chin down, stifled a yawn. Before her she knew would be another long sleepless night after tucking in her granddaughter. With one hand, she pulled at the quilt that wrapped her legs, drawing it higher, and then entangled her hands in the insulating folds that gathered on her lap. Leaning her head back and slightly to one side, she began her sleep-deprived slide. The rocking chair continued its course to and fro, to and fro, once, twice, and thrice—only to gradually slow, before it ceased all motion. Soon the gray haired Maiden-in-exile was dozing, at one with the hint of winter.

PART TWO

Evermore

CHAPTER NINETEEN

Welcome to Autumnsloe

"The PortalKey!"

"What?" Heather asked, tucking her chin to look at her brooch, though finding it difficult to pull her attention from the scene spread before her. "Did you say something?"

"The key," Fallasha said. "Don't forget the key to the Portal."

"Why do we need the key?" Heather asked, looking distractedly away.

"If we don't bring the key along," Fallasha said, "that means we'll have to leave the PortalDoor unlocked. It also means that in the time we're away, if anyone happens to walk through that door, they'll have direct access into the Bristol House sewing room. And they can lock us out."

"Molly, " Heather said, reluctant to turn from the view, "can you grab the PortalKey? We have to lock the door."

Molly reentered the sewing room, removed the key, and then closed and locked the door after her. From beneath the decorative overhang, she approached and handed the unusual key to Heather, who absent-mindedly placed it in one of her costume's many pockets.

"Oh, Heather, look!"

"I am, Molly, I am—*I have been*," the moon girl said, her masked features infused with the excitement of the day and the newness of all that encompassed her.

"Isn't it just, just… breathtaking. Oh, I love it!" Molly leaned over and hugged a suddenly bashful Heather. "Thank you for bringing me."

"Hey, give me some air!" Fallasha said. "Having only just met, I find you overly familiar: getting far too near, invading my space, rumpling my dignified bearing—my, my *brooch-couture.*"

"This is so exciting, Heather," Molly said, stepping back, her hand still resting on her friend's arm. "Don't you think?" She found herself wanting to bounce.

Heather just nodded, quick little nods of fervor.

The two girls stood looking down from a porch and over a colorful and expansive courtyard. It was situated amid unusual buildings of free flowing architecture, their vibrant façades commanding a view of this normally peaceful and sparsely occupied area. But not this day. Parade Day found the courtyard bustling with costumed activity. People all around, they were trailing through, over the checkered brickwork inlaid with spirals and curls. Rising up to dominate the entrance closest to the girls was a large tarnished statue of a distinguished man standing high atop a tapering pedestal.

The courtyard entrance opened onto a narrow, bustling lane that paralleled a small river as it twisted through the city. Across the teeming street, grassy bank, and gracefully designed footbridges, on the far side of the boat-strewn river, was yet another busy stretch of grass, and beyond that Heather and Molly saw a wide avenue swarming with more people, most all of them exquisitely costumed. They appeared to be spectators, looking on, cheering and clapping as down the center of the thoroughfare the parade advanced in regimented formations and brilliant attire. Distant music, along with the clamor of the crowds, swept up to reach the girls' ears, and excitement vibrated throughout the air.

All around, in contrast to the hard surfaces of the buildings, many trees showcased the glorious spectacle of their delicate leaves in a spectrum of hues: vivid yellows, radiant oranges, fiery reds, and blushing crimsons. Together, the architecture and its vivid surroundings provided a mesmerizing eyeful for the first-time visitors.

"Pardon me, girls," Fallasha asked, "but is there something wrong? Perhaps you're not feeling quite right, a little dizzy or disconcerted after your journey, or maybe you possess nervous, upset stomachs?" Her rapid-fire words yanked their attention from the breathtaking panorama that spread before them.

"What?" Heather asked.

"Is there something wrong?"

"No, not with me, Fallasha," Molly said. "Not at all. Why?"

"Because you're both so quiet," said the brooch. "I was wondering if possibly there was something wrong? A little PortalSickness? Headache? Nausea? I have to inquire. Remember, I'm your tour guide." The moon smiled broadly.

Shaking her head, and looking at Heather, Molly said, "Well, I was just looking around at the unbelievable beauty of this place. I'm, well, I'm—"

"Just wondering," said Fallasha, eclipsing into another self-satisfied smile.

"—astonished," Molly finished. "Just astonished."

"Why would there be something wrong?" asked Heather, thinking the place surrounding her was beyond anything that she could have possibly dreamt. Then again, knowing her dreams—especially as of late—she quickly reconsidered.

"Never mind. Forget I asked. Just go about your business. Pretend I'm not here." The moon started whistling.

"Well, Fallasha," said Heather, "you have to be the strangest brooch I've ever met. Or seen. Or worn. Of course, I haven't worn that many. Haven't met that many, either..."

"But everything's all right, girls? Hunky-dory? Fantastical? Outstanding? Superb? Remarkable?" Fallasha inquired again, the words speedily running along. "You're enjoying the sights?"

Laughing, Molly said, "Everything's great. Why wouldn't it be?" She held out her hand to the view. "Just look. It's like another world."

"Molly, it *is* another world," Heather said.

"Just being thorough," said the brooch, "making sure you're comfortable. That's my job." Another smug smile.

"So, Fallasha, that's it?"

"What do you mean, Heather?"

As she spoke, the girl's attention stayed fixed on her surroundings. "I mean, we just walked through a PortalDoor. Aren't we supposed to get all googly inside or materialize in a puff of smoke or something?"

"No, I'm afraid not. Used to be that way, though Portal travel has been refined over time, and now is extremely smooth in its transition from one location to another—seamless, we call it. There is only the worry of travel sickness, and it seems that was not an issue here today."

"Wow," said Heather, pointing, "will you look at that," her gaze wandering over the nearby structures.

"I've never seen buildings like those," Molly said, attempting to absorb it all. "Everything—well, everything just runs into everything else. It's-it's *extraordinary!*"

"Magic, I think, Molly," Heather said. "Has to be magic."

The unique Autumnslovian architecture that had caught the attention of the two costumed girls was comprised of varicolored brick and tile in rounded, flowing shapes. Nothing seemed square or rectangular save the corners of the building facades, and even those weren't all sharply angled. Some of the window frames were wide at the top and curved at the corners, or lay heavy at the bottom in exaggerated teardrop shapes. Stairways stepped up out of the earth; entry doors rose and merged with oversized circular windows that had living divisions of vine and plant holding in place their stained-glass panels. Balcony railings of sturdy branch and twig displayed their elegantly undulating designs, all in organic sweeps and swirls. Doors weren't just doors or windows windows, their only intention being practical and utilitarian; instead they were glass and wood sculptures with their sides fluidly bulging and receding, intertwined and arising out of the nature that surrounded them.

Some posts and pillars grew as trees out of the ground before magically transitioning into carvings of ornamental leaves and blooms that climbed to support balconies with a spread of architectural fan and curl. Other less decorative pillars were encircled with vine and blossom on their way up to meet and embellish the brow lines of the many buildings, their rooftops lavishly tiled in a variety of hues.

"Where are we?" Heather asked Fallasha.

"Well, I thought you'd never ask." Following a grand intake of air, the little moon cleared her throat and proudly trumpeted, "Ladies and gentlemen—well, ladies—ahem—*girls,* allow me to introduce to you the scenic capital city of Elderraine, located in the magnificent land of Autumnsloe, one of four kingdoms belonging to the wondrous Realm of Evermore." The brooch quickly added in a whispered aside, "So, what do you think?"

Molly looked at Heather. "Autumnsloe? The place you dreamed about really exists?"

"I guess so," Heather said, shaking her head, looking at the expanse of throbbing life around her. "Molly, this is so weird: my dreams, they're all becoming real."

"I think the places were already real, Heather."

"But what do you think of this beautiful architecture surrounding you," Fallasha asked, with a wiggle of her eyebrows, "its lovely flourishes, the winding river running serenely below, the colorful trees, and the populace before you, dressed in their sumptuously rich costumes on this most glorious Parade Day in Autumnsloe?"

"I think you're sounding like a commercial—"

"I think it's so absolutely beautiful, Fallasha," Molly quickly interposed.

"Yes, I thought you would." The little moon beamed.

Heather was antsy, bobbing on her feet. "I say let's go down to the street," she said. "I'd like to get closer to the parade."

"Yes, let's go," said Molly.

"Wait!" said Fallasha. "There are a few things you need to know as first time visitors. Currently, as you undoubtedly realize, you are in a world that is completely foreign to you. So, as your fully sanctioned tour guide, I suggest that you practice caution in all endeavors and interactions. Unfortunately, in the time allotted, I haven't been able to brief you on Autumnslovian culture and politics."

"So, what you're saying is that we shouldn't talk to people?" Heather asked.

"No, I mean just be aware of what you do and say."

"Is it all right that we're visiting," Molly asked, "and that we came through a magic Portal to get here?"

"It's all right," the brooch said, "but I wouldn't advertise it, if I were you. You never know whom you're talking to and what their affiliations are. Once again, be aware of yourselves and your actions. If you're not, there could be grave consequences. Remember that how people behave on your planet isn't necessarily how people behave in Autumnsloe. And also remember that you're representatives of the planet Earth, so behave accordingly."

"Okay. Are we done, Fallasha?" Heather asked, impatient to get moving.

"Not yet. If for some unlikely reason we become separated from one another, we'll meet here. Heather, you have the key. If Molly gets here first, you're to wait for Heather, only because, well, you don't have a choice." The moon brooch laughed at her own little joke. "And conversely, Heather, should you arrive here first without Molly, we'll wait before going through the door. So, Molly, we won't go in without you. Knowing this, if you don't see us, wait here, and nowhere else, because we're on our way."

Heather asked, "So, *now* are we done?"

Fallasha gave Heather a faux-mean look through constricted eyelids. "Yes."

"Come on, then, you guys. Let's go!"

As Grandma Dawn slept on the porch, an indigo-clad form peered furtively from behind a tree, on the far side of a hedge. Although knowing that to prowl about during daylight hours was risky and bold, the person thought it necessary when dealing with the urgent task at hand. Besides, the stealthy visitor found that the Bristol House grounds were spacious and full enough to conceal anyone at will, and so felt it easy to become lost within the random growth and among the orderly arrangement of tree, bush, and hedge.

Waiting and watching for nearly an hour now, the observer knew the gray-haired woman to be unmoving and most probably asleep. Warily, the shape drew closer to the house while keeping a vigilant watch on the dozing woman. From within a concealing wrap, the stranger's disciplined eyes examined the porch, the arrangement of furnishings, and their relative position to the front door. Then quietly, having committed all to memory, the figure receded to roam within the concealing greenery, moving slowly and with quiet deliberation towards the basement windows. These, the watcher knew, gave view into many of the Bristol House rooms that lay below ground, veiled in a mystery all their own.

Having descended the steps at a bounce, Molly, Heather, and Fallasha soon found themselves pulled along amid the flow of the noisy throng, jostled here, occasionally pushed there, but they made headway crossing the heavily populated greenbelt and bridge. After weaving across a second strip of greenery, the crowd thickened and their progress stalled near the wide Avenue displaying a long procession of Parade Day participants.

"Come on, Molly," said Heather, currently crushed up against a costume in front of her.

She turned, and with Molly riding her heels, fought to make a path away from the parade, back the way they had come. While drawn along in the flow of energetic movement one minute, the girls found themselves battling an oncoming current the next, until the pair finally reached the grassy rise beside the river.

"We're headed over there, Molly, towards those trees," Heather shouted, grabbing her friend's hand, while pointing out the foliage evident above the mass of costumed parade-goers. Molly allowed herself to be dragged along, rarely looking to see where her friend was taking her, captivated by the sights in vibrant moil around her.

With Molly in tow, Heather navigated past loungers and picnickers, street magicians and stilt-walkers, costumed onlookers and a few plain clothed curiosity-seekers. Streaming and dodging, the girls picked their way among square and oblong blankets that turned the expanse of green into a pulsing multicolored quilt.

Unexpectedly, Molly was knocked aside by three youths dressed in torn and ill-fitting shirts of black, aggressively pushing through the celebrants. Tied around their upper arms were swatches of purplish cloth. They weren't wearing masks.

"Hey, watch out!" said one, swinging an angry arm before him.

"Oh, sorry!" said Molly, as she was bumped again and, off-balance, toppled sideways onto a blanket, finding herself the center of attention in the midst of a family feast. An elderly man and middle-aged woman, their masks removed, helped Molly to her feet, and she began to brush herself off. "Sorry. I'm so sorry."

"Quite all right, my dear."

Heather stopped at her friend's words, and turning, glared at the departing rowdies, their auras a nasty and violent brown.

"Those RogueTag boys!" someone declared. "They're trouble brewing."

"Returning from their rally, I presume," said another.

"They're mean spirits, they are. They're to be watched. And avoided. Are you all right?" asked a costumed spectator, walking up, his mask talking. "Rude demons. I saw them push you down. I'll report them, don't you worry."

Nearby, someone mumbled, "Some good it will do."

"Yes, thank you, I'm fine," said Molly, adjusting her mask. She looked down at those still seated. "I'm sorry I disturbed your meal."

"Quite all right. Would you and your friend care to join us?" a man asked, his own mask still intact as he ate into what appeared to be a chicken leg. He dabbed his metallic lower face with a napkin, while others on the blanket stared after the RogueTags, some whispering among themselves.

"Do come! Do come!" said a little girl, her enthusiastic movement bouncing the small glittering wings of her costume. She spoke out of a sequin-lined mouth encircled with a smear of whipped cream.

"Yes, join us!" said three others, looking up from their sitting positions nearby.

"No, thank you," Heather said. "You're very kind, but we have to hurry." She pulled Molly after her and away from the small gathering. In the process, goodbyes were hurtled back and forth.

The moon girl was surprised how cool her costume stayed, the day being so sunny and warm. She glanced over her shoulder.

"Molly, are you hot in there?"

Molly laughed. "No, not at all. You'd think I would be under all these layers."

"Well, I'm not either. I think our costumes are magically air-conditioned."

Fallasha piped up, saying, "Of course they're designed to keep you comfortably cool. Don't forget where they came from."

"Heather," Molly spoke over the din, "where are we going?"

"Over there. See those large boulders near the trees?"

Heather and Molly plowed to a standstill, with pressure applied by the people behind inadvertently pushing them into those ahead.

"I'm suffocating down here," Heather heard her brooch say through layers of fabric, but the girl could only manage to move her upper torso a small degree to get Fallasha some air. Having done so, she was able to hear the little moon's words float up, "...and it upsets my brooch's astute sense of decorum." In the tight space, Fallasha puffed up haughtily.

Soon the throng began to move again, allowing Heather and Molly to break away from the streaming mass, zig-zagging between more picnickers, revelers and soldiers, to finally arrive at the base of a large grouping of boulders.

"This way," Heather said, and Molly followed.

"Wait! Heather!" Molly said, grabbing her friend's arm. "Look over there. A vendor."

"What's he selling?"

"It's hard to tell from here."

"Come on!" said the moon girl. "Let's go see."

Heather and Molly soon found themselves near the vendor's cart. On it was a sign advertising hot-dipped sporry curls, rainbow drukken rotators, and squashed dorsillen fizzers.

"Want one?" Heather asked.

"Yes. But what are we getting?"

"Heck if I know. Looks like something to eat. How about if you just pick a name off the menu and I'll choose something else?" Heather watched a young boy walk away eating something green, smoking hot, and wiggling. "I know I don't want *that*," she said, pointing discreetly.

"You might burn your tongue," Fallasha said. "But the sensation doesn't last long."

"And that's a treat?" Heather asked, watching as the boy emitted a spurt of green flame from his mouth and a toot of smoke from his ears.

"But you might *not* burn your tongue, and that is. You'll just have to purchase one to understand the game."

"Heather, it doesn't matter. We can't buy anything anyway," Molly said. "We don't have any Autumnsloe money."

"Sure we do," Fallasha said, her voice low. "Right pocket, Heather, at the waist. Compliments of the Bristol House. It would never send you to a parade without money for concessions."

Sure enough, reaching in, Heather pulled out a handful of gold and silver coins: Autumnsloe feallans.

Approaching the vendor, a fat man in a comedic mask below a conical hat, Heather asked, "Well, Molly, what do you want?"

Molly giggled. "I'll have a rainbow drukken rotator."

"Okay," Heather said, "and I'll have a squashed dorsillen fizzer."

Upon receiving the treats, Heather held out her free hand with some loose change scattered on her palm. The vendor took out what he needed and thanked the girls.

"This is weird," Molly said, inspecting her treat, as the two walked away. It was a craggy sphere with many holes sitting on a cone. Suddenly, the sphere twirled, and when it stopped, little critters intermittently popped their heads out of the various holes. As she held onto the cone, the spherical top spun another time, and the creatures once again popped their heads out of different holes at unexpected intervals, all the while making high-pitched, babbling noises.

"What am I supposed to do with this?" Molly said, laughing.

After making certain that she couldn't be heard by any passers by, Fallasha said, "When they pop their heads out, you're supposed to try to catch the little drukkens with your teeth."

"And eat them? No, way," Molly said. She watched, as the ball twirled again. Colorful heads began to peek and hide.

"Try it, Molly," said Heather, laughing. "I dare you."

Fallasha said, "Those little creatures aren't really alive. They're candy that's magically made to pop up like that. It's a candy toy."

"Oh," said Molly. "Really? All right." The girl sounded unconvinced. In preparation, she pushed the butterfly mask back on her head, exposing a great deal of her face. "Fallasha, all I can say is that you better be telling the truth about these drukkens being made of candy."

The ball rotated on her cone before coming to a standstill, and Molly, anticipating the sudden emergence of a creature, picked one of the holes, and positioned her open mouth over it. She waited and then bit down, only to come away empty.

Heather said, "Don't bite too hard, you might lose some teeth."

"It takes practice," Fallasha informed Molly. "And patience."

"I guess. So, what do you have to try and eat, Heather?"

Heather, leaving her moon mask in place, was looking her treat over, holding the strangely shaped drinking glass out before her. Suddenly, its contents began to fizz and bubble up, filling the glass to its brim with an orange liquid before receding once again towards the bottom. Heather was rotating her treat, inspecting it from all angles. "What's in here, Fallasha?"

"Well, it's a dorsillen that's been squashed, obviously—"

"Obviously," said Heather, continuing her examination of the glass.

"It's that green blobby thing at the bottom—it's putting out a fizz that rises up to the top of the treat glass. The fizz is of a different color every time the dorsillen erupts."

"Mmm. It really tastes good," Heather said, having taken a tentative sip through a straw that was attached to the side of the glass.

"Well, the game is that each fizz has a different taste that's delicious. All but one, that is, and you have to make a guess at what color you won't drink at first. But once you find out what color doesn't taste good by attempting to drink it, the dorsillen picks a new color to sour. And then the one that tasted so poorly will probably taste good, depending on the craftiness of your squashed dorsillen."

"Well, it sounds pretty complicated. Can I still drink it even if I'm not sure I totally understand how?" Heather tried a sip of the fizz that was currently brewing up. She perked up. "Purple is a good fizz, too." She took a much larger swig. "Mmm. The purple and orange fizzes are really good. And they each taste different."

"Gah' 'un," said Molly, the little blue drukken's body sticking out of her mouth at the neck. Its feet wiggling, the creature's tiny fists were pounding against Molly's front teeth.

"Suck it in!" said Fallasha.

Molly did, and chewed cautiously a few times before stopping. Her face broke out in a state of delight. "It's good!" She chewed some more and swallowed.

"How does a squirming little guy like that taste?" Heather asked.

Molly thought. "Like nothing I've ever had before. But it's sweet. And really good."

The two sat down on an empty patch of grass below the boulders and continued to eat and drink their Autumnslovian treats, looking around in wonder. Soon they switched desserts, each trying the others. Heather was very adept at catching the wiggly drukkens, and sometimes after sucking them in, she would let them run around in her mouth, claiming that it tickled. Molly laughed when she saw Heather's cheeks bulge with a drukken pounding to get out.

"Eww," Molly said, wrinkling her face in an unpleasant expression while smacking her lips. "I guess turquoise is the color I didn't want to try."

"But now it should be okay to drink when you see it again," Heather said.

"Maybe," said Fallasha. "Maybe not. You can always refuse to taste it and the dorsillen will produce another."

"Come on," Heather said. "If we want to see the parade, we'd better get to that place I saw on the rocks before it gets too crowded."

Molly and Heather set free the remaining drukkens along with the dorsillen before tossing the glass and cone in what looked to be a refuse bin. The girls didn't stop to notice that their discards magically disappeared.

"I thought you said they weren't real creatures, Fallasha," Molly said, placing a hand over her tummy.

"They're not," the little moon said.

"Then why are we setting them loose?"

"Why would you throw them away?" the brooch asked.

Molly, her mask now back in place, exchanged looks with Heather.

"Good question," Heather said. She watched as a black felynxx, a small cat-like creature, dropped out of a tree to stalk one of the freed yellow drukkens. "Come on, you guys, let's go."

The grass was now more crowded than it had been only a short while ago, when the two girls and their tour guide had stopped for treats. Yet the girls quickly made their way through the parade-goers to the backside of the boulders. After scrambling up a small hill, Heather led Molly along the shoulder of an immense rock partially buried in the slope. From there, the two maneuvered behind onlookers, before jumping onto an adjoining boulder of even larger proportions and then another afterwards. There they threaded their way to a clear area, positioning themselves between two groups of standing spectators in Parade Day's creative attire.

Turning to Molly, Heather said, "Now we can watch the parade without people getting in our way."

"Brilliant, Heather!" said Molly. "We can see everything from up here. And I'm glad we're out of that crowd."

"Me, too," said Fallasha. "I think I broke my nose back there."

"Let's see," said Heather, looking down on her little companion. "Your nose does look a little crooked." The girl brought her hand up, her slender fingers reaching for the brooch. "But I think I can fix it with one good tug."

"Don't you *dare!*" said the small moon, cringing.

Several people gathered nearby turned at Fallasha's words, their curious glances lasting overlong behind a variety of captivating masks. Immediately, the brooch had made her face an immobile mask of its own.

"Hi, there," Heather said, waving.

Molly gestured shyly.

Hands waved and hellos were returned, before the group of five costumed onlookers returned their attention to the parade. Heather saw
auras of pleasant oranges and reds, with one in discordant blues.

Someone is grumpy, she thought, gazing with interest.

His costume was very much a male's in its bold geometric pattern
and line, the mask simply painted, lacking jewelry and frill, with the
hat comprised of a series of short burnished points. Heather tried not to
stare at his pouty mouth and red star eyes, instead concentrating on the
thinly gloved hands protruding from his puffy sleeves. They were large
and bony, with one in black and the other in red.

Turning her attention back towards the parade, she saw from their
advantageous position high upon the rocks that large red umbrellas lined
the street at intervals, providing places where spectators might seek refuge from the sun. Scattered along the street were smaller parasols, moving and at rest, and throughout the crowds, Heather spotted costumed
children waving brilliant flags. The girl felt a thrill when she recognized
that all along the parade route Maiden statues, each in a unique pose,
rose skyward on elaborate pedestals above the crowd. Along the street,
lampposts were adorned with bunting and painted in swirls of color, and
bold banners waved their frilly ends to emphasize periodic gusts of the
Autumnslovian breeze.

The moon girl soon found herself drawn to the sight of a large troupe
of acrobats dressed in flamboyant costumes. As they progressed down
the parade's wide Avenue, the athletic group climbed upon each other, creating advancing pyramids and tall swaying poles of interlocking
limbs—that joined up with other tall swaying poles of interlocking
limbs—until they eventually disentangled, flipped, dived, and tumbled
their way along the procession's course.

"Wow! Molly, did you see that?" Heather leaned over to ask.

Captivated, Molly briefly acknowledged her friend, and then returned her gaze to the parade.

There were dancers that seemed to magically float and glide, sparks
swirling in their wake, ever-changing formations of military men rigid
in their finery, musicians toting and playing strange instruments, and
other participants in unusual and fantastic attire. Spaced between, there
came a large dragon float, a multi-sailed ship float, and Molly made sure
to tug on Heather's sleeve and point at the dazzling blossoms belonging
to the flowered garden float, where unfamiliar animals paced, lazed, and
preened among the blooms.

Heather became aware that Fallasha was giving a running commentary of the parade, but her voice was so low, that the girl was unable to

understand all that the small moon was saying.

"Fallasha, I can't hear you."

"Sh-h-h-h-h," said the brooch.

Heather lowered her voice. "What?"

Fallasha's lips were moving, and Heather, in an attempt to hear her better, angled her decorated face to give the brooch a more strategically-placed ear. After awhile, she shook her head, the earrings trailing back and forth.

"Fallasha, I still can't hear you."

The moon brooch glanced suspiciously about before saying with added volume, "You don't want those around us to know that you're magically aided."

Heather looked around. No one seemed to be listening, including Molly, their attention focused on the passing parade. "You could have told us that sooner," Heather whispered. "Why?"

"It's just not wise. You never know who might be interested."

"Then why are you talking, announcing the parade when no one can hear you?"

Fallasha looked at Heather with small surprised eyes. "Why, of course, because it's my job."

Heather considered this. "Oh."

The large rocks on which Heather and Molly viewed the parade were becoming more populated. Soon, the two girls and Fallasha found themselves squeezed alongside the five costumed youths to their left that they had previously waved to, with little space available to their right. Screeching out from that direction, the continuous cry of a long-suffering baby made Heather and Molly crowd the five more.

"Hello!"

Heather and Molly looked up into the face of a young lady, her sequin-covered mask rising to engulf her head in an explosion of frill and feathers. Below, her gold lips looked real, and moved as such, but as with all Evermorian masks, the girls could never be certain.

"Hi," said Heather. "Sorry we're getting so close, but that baby over there keeps crying."

The gold lips broke into a grin.

"I know," she said, "we were standing near them before you came. Their baby wouldn't sit still, crying all the while. It was driving us so to frenzy that we moved away." She looked the moon and the butterfly girls over. "You look enchanting, the two of you."

"Thank you," Molly said, speaking for both. "You look pretty enchanting yourself."

"Did you make your own costumes or get them at The Crown & Scepter?"

"No," said Heather. "They were made for us by a good friend of ours."

"Just lovely. My name is LoeSyra, by the way," said the gilded lips, her visage friendly, agreeable.

"I'm Heather, and this is Molly."

"And her brooch's name is Fallasha," Molly said, not wanting the small moon to take offense at not having been introduced properly, fearing she might just scream out *rude!*

"Pardon?" LoeSyra asked. She looked at Heather. "You named your brooch?"

"She means," Heather said quickly, remembering Fallasha didn't want anyone to know that the girls were 'magically aided,' as she put it, "that I was so in love with my little moon here, you know, when I first put on my costume, that I couldn't help but name it. So, I called her Fallasha."

"That's a lovely name."

Molly's masked face took on a look of surprise. She knew something was amiss when Fallasha didn't respond, preferring to stay stone still and act like a normal brooch.

On Heather's mask, a glimmer of tease lit the features, her lip at a slight curl. "Thank you," she said. "I still can't believe I made it up. Do you really think Fallasha is a good name?"

"Well," LoeSyra said, "I thought so, but I suppose—"

"You know, I tried to think of something better," Heather continued. "At first, I was saying to myself, 'Falla*sho,* Falla*shee,* Falla*shut-up'*—but could only come up with Falla*sha.* And then, to make matters worse," she laughed, "I didn't even know if this thing was a boy or girl."

"Heather, I think—" Molly began.

"And I didn't have much time, either. If I did, I'm sure I would have thought of something much, much better to name this here little moon," Heather said, patting Fallasha's pointy head a little too roughly with her finger, "you know, something a bit more, well, moon-like."

Molly, mortified, noticed Fallasha's face turning red, but to her credit, the moon didn't blink a tiny eye.

"Yeah," Heather continued, "I thought real hard, real *real* hard, trying to come up with a name, a good name, a name a moon could be proud of. I don't know. I think I failed. I mean Fallasha is okay, you know, but I'm thinking there has to be something way better. So, maybe at some point, I'll just rename her—well, I mean, *it*—something not so goofy."

"And look, it changes colors, too," LoeSyra said, admiring Fallasha's transformation to an anguished crimson.

"Yeah, it's an amazing brooch, my little—well, whatever I decide to name it," Heather said, looking down at the motionless clasp. "Loe-Syra, you wouldn't happen to know a better name for this little moon, would you?"

"Well, I don't know," she said. "I suppose I could—"

"Look at that!" Molly thought to say, pointing to the parade.

More dancers were strutting, and now their long legs leaping and spinning, while dresses ballooned full at their turning in a myriad of dizzying spirals. The ladies sprang up, flying high off the ground, and their partners, dynamic men in capes and hats, caught them one-handed as they floated to earth.

"My friends and I," and when LoeSyra gestured with her head towards her companions, the frills on her mask shook, the sequins winking with sun, "we come from GarthenShale, just north of here."

"Why is everyone wearing these costumes?" Heather thought to ask.

The girl laughed. "Why are *you* wearing yours?"

"Well, when we were invited to this amazing parade of yours, our friend, like I told you, made our costumes." Heather laughed. "I guess we forgot to ask why we were dressing up."

"That's silly," said LoeSyra's costumed companion, standing nearby. At first glance, Heather thought she looked like an electrocuted parrot, with curling bits of this and that springing off her blue-feathered head. "And they didn't tell you why?"

"This is Terrellena," said LocSyra. "And I may as well introduce the others. This is Avarra, LaoCuria, and Borray. We all attend the university here in Elderraine, except for Borray."

"He's my younger brother," Terrellena said, as if it explained all.

Heather noted that Borray's aura hadn't changed color, still being comprised of dissatisfied blues, but it had withdrawn a bit, ringing his body in tighter circumference.

"Hi, I'm Heather," the moon-girl said, "and—"

"I'm Molly."

While everyone offered greetings, Borray remained aloof, scrutinizing the moon and butterfly girls.

"Parade Day is a celebration of our beauty," said Avarra, "of our inner beauty, and we wear these exquisite costumes on our outer selves to symbolize this. So on this day, everyone has the opportunity to reveal and express the miracle inside of us: exalting that we think, feel, breathe, and that we love—appreciating that we've been given life on this planet, in this universe. That's what we're celebrating."

"Sounds a bit preachy to me," another protested at a grumble. It was the grumpy one. Heather didn't like his voice. It was distinctive, nasally, a dull wet rag of unhappiness. "Besides, that's not it. Well, not entirely. It's about our freedom—"

"Responsibility," said Terrellena.

"Yes, well, if you say so, Sister," he mumbled all the more, his aura turning a leaden and weighty blue.

"It's about freedom *and* responsibility—" Avarra chimed. "You can't have one without the other."

Disgusted, the young man scoffed. "The way you spout this, this *my-thology*, I can tell that all of you have wholeheartedly digested the teachings of the Maidens."

"Nauseating, isn't it?" said LaoCuria, with a laugh.

"Well, what's wrong with having done so?" Avarra said.

"There's a need for change," Borray said, "that's all."

But, to the hostile young man, that wasn't all. Inside, the sullen Borray raged. He wanted to scream at the top of his lungs for all to hear: How can the Maidens ever know what it's like to be HumanKind, to be imperfect? How can they? *How?* They'll never know what it's like to think like HumanKinders, to have the same fears and desires, suffer the same disappointments, feel the same pain. Maidens will never know what it's like to have a blemish, a scar, a compulsion, will never feel the ravages of old age and approaching death. *No, never!* So, how in Evermore's name can they be qualified to lead us?

But Borray said none of this. Instead, his sneering mouth only repeated, "There's a need for change."

"So you and your muscle-headed RogueTags seem to think," Terrellena said.

"We're not the only ones who think that way, *Sister*. There are others, many others all over Autumnsloe—all over Evermore—that believe the time of the Maidens has come and gone. HumanKind knows what HumanKind needs. We're tired of the tyranny and the suppression of the Maidens. So, we're coming together for a cause, a cause for change."

Terrellena laughed scornfully. "A defiant cause staged by unhappy boys who bully and destroy. It's obvious the tyranny is all inside your infantile heads. The Maidens lead us well. Evermore has had generations of peace and prosperity—"

"Their rule will end," Borray interrupted. "The myth must die."

Terrellena stared. "It must be humiliating for a skinny boy, who only yesterday was hanging onto his mother's skirt, to be further dominated by more women, more mommies. That's it, isn't it? It can't be easy for all you tough darlings."

"Argh!" Borray growled. "Change is coming, you'll see. And it's a change for the better. And the Portent will come true, and the Maidens cast aside, as they should be."

"Will they? And for how long, dear brother? It seems you believe in the teachings of the Maidens, and the Portent Prophesies, but only when it suits you."

Heather glimpsed his face when Borray lifted his mask in disgust. Wiping his heated brow, he looked away.

Avarra looked at Terrellena. "Is Borray still stewing over the fact that he couldn't go to the RogueTag rally?"

"Yes, Mother wouldn't let him."

The girls laughed. Heather saw Borray's aura flinch scarlet before lashing out in bursts of overheated orange. He lowered his mask into place.

"What do you followers of the Maidens know, anyway?" Borray spouted. "There's no doubt that HumanKind would be better off in so many ways without them; we'd be far more technologically advanced, far more industrious, and far superior as a race without our dependence on the Maidens and their magic to *lead* us. And from what I'm hearing, it's obvious that going to university hasn't made you any wiser. You're all just simple dumbed-up annendoles, stupidly grazing in the meadows of the Ancient Ones, swallowing without question their old and obsolete pasturage."

"And you and your RogueTag friends are all so rabid and full of hate!" Terrellena said. "You're the ones that are truly blind."

"The Maidens?" Heather piped up, looking for a change of subject and some information. "What are they like? I mean, what do they do?"

Eyebrows went up.

Unnoticed, Fallasha's features tightened with apprehension. Careful, Heather, she thought.

Avarra laughed. "You really don't know? They're our spiritual principals, our warriors, and our teachers," she said, gushing. "They're not our leaders, though—I mean, our elected officials."

"And speaking of which, below us, *are* our elected officials," LoeSyra pointed to the parade route. "The Royal Procession is passing at this very moment."

Everyone turned to the parade. Heather and Molly were able to see two majestic and lavishly appointed floats, each being drawn by eight to ten grenishens ornamented in silver and gold attire.

"Look at those weird animals, Heather," Molly said, pointing to the horse-like creatures with thick round legs, long barrel necks, and tapering snouts.

"Haven't you ever seen a shorthaired grenishen before?" Avarra asked. "They're found mostly in the milder climates of SummersBreath Still."

"Well, they're beautiful!" Molly said.

"Wow," remarked Heather. "Who's the guy with the staff and all the jewels?"

Surprised and curious glances were again discreetly exchanged among the small group. On Heather's lapel, quietly, the moon brooch let out a nervous sigh.

"The one on the raised platform in the float out front? That's Emperor Kratkuffe. His ancestors once ruled all of Evermore," said LaoCuria, politeness keeping her questions in check.

"Now we supposedly rule ourselves," countered the grumpy one, before sneering, "with the help of the Maidens and the Council of Overseers. At the moment, our HumanKind Emperor is just a figurehead. At the moment."

"Ignore him, girls," Terrellena said to her friends. "Next time he'll be staying at home with his mommy."

"Who else is on the float with the Emperor?" asked Molly, wanting to dispel the edginess of the conversation.

"That's the Royal Family," said LoeSyra. "And on the float behind are the Regents. Every kingdom has them. As CityState representatives, they act on behalf of the CityDwellers in government, and as ambassadors when negotiating necessary policy with tribes of the outlying regions and territories."

"Can you tell that LoeSyra is planning a career in government?" LaoCuria asked, laughing.

"Are there a lot of tribes in Evermore?" Heather asked.

"Yes, countless," LoeSyra said. "Perhaps you saw some. Many of them passed before us earlier in the parade, dressed in their traditional tribal garb."

"And they all possess such wonderfully distinct styles of clothing," Terrellena said. "Wouldn't you say so, LoeSyra?"

The girl agreed, her mask's adornment bobbing with the motion.

As Molly turned her attention to the adjustment of her gloves, Heather looked back at the parade and the Emperor's float in the lead position. She saw the Royal Family waving, all dressed in plush and tasteful costume, positioned below Emperor Kratkuffe on a much wider platform. Tiered farther below was the Royal Staff, servants indentured to the Crown. None waved, but stood solemnly at attention, heads high.

When Heather's gaze wandered, sliding to the front of the float, she was struck by a sight both disturbing and familiar. Alone amid the flourish of stately decorations, her long black hair taken up by the breeze, stood an imposing woman dressed in a ceremonial robe of deep purple with flame-like adornment. A barbed headpiece, similar in style to the one in the Bristol House sewing room, encircled her head. In her right hand she gripped a staff that twined up to terminate in the rearing of three serpent heads, their fanged mouths agape and red eyes aglow. The sight filled Heather with repugnance and anger, as she recognized the sorceress, her aura emanating a dull and menacing black.

The moon girl recalled the dream in which she had risen from a pond and climbed to the top of a hill to find the sorceress before her, casting spells. And how, when the evil woman had noticed her, she attacked with magic, causing Heather to run for her life. And when a blazing firebolt from the sorceress glanced off her side, the girl relived the sensation of tumbling through the air as clearly as if her dream were reality.

Unconsciously, through the many layers of costume fabric, her hand sought to gently rub her side. It again struck Heather that the woman below on the Parade Day float had wanted to kill her, the 'why?' haunting her.

Now, the moon-girl watched, as with turning head, the sorceress prowled the masses. Heather heard Fallasha gasp when the woman went still. They watched her straighten, her pale hand dropping from the railing. The sorceress leaned keen, as if sniffing a peculiar scent on air. Moments later, her gaze resumed its crawl, over and past the river, up along the grass, only to rest motionless at the boulder's face. Then her chin slowly rose, head tilting backward, her deep-set eyes creeping ever upward. Transfixed, she abruptly froze. Focused. Sharp. Intense. Heather noticed the frightening woman's aura burst forth in sparks of malevolent green curiosity. The sorceress held her glare in the direction of the girls. Heather, unflinching, stared back.

"Danger lurks, time to run," Fallasha said, barely audible even to Heather. Crossing her arms before her, Heather covered the moon brooch with her hand. It wasn't long before she could feel the itty-bitty teeth trying to bite her.

Heather whispered to her brooch, "We're not going anywhere yet."

She looked up to see that Borray was looking at her and Molly suspiciously.

"You've never heard of our Emperor? Or of Maidens?" he asked, his expression hostile.

Oh, burdledurk! Fallasha thought, gritting her teeth, wishing the RogueTag would let the girls alone.

"We're visiting," said Molly. "Only here for the Parade Day—"

An enormous roar suddenly went up from the multitudes assembled.

"Look!" Avarra shouted. "Here come the Maidens!"

Heather turned, electrified.

The float with the sorceress had passed, and leading the oncoming Maidens in a V formation were nine robed persons in red. They walked slowly, heads bowed, their cowls concealing all but a glimpse of their lower faces, white and aged.

Molly leaned closer to Heather, talking loudly over the crowd noise. "Just like the PortalKey," she said.

Heather agreed, her ravenous gaze never leaving the procession.

Following the Ancient Ones came the ranks of Maidens, their ivory skin in contrast to their striking ceremonial headpieces with narrow sheaths that, worn back or to the side, covered rich auburn braids. Each level and category of MaidenHood displayed their uniquely colored garb, a seemingly endless line of shimmering hues, all exhibiting red inner linings and ornamental collars. Other ranks wore helmets and armor reflecting glints of blinding sunlight; they carried weapons and decorated shields, long spears and belted swords. And then, to even louder acclaim, advanced an elite group of riders, poised in stately fashion atop beasts that resembled woolly lions. Heather remembered the creatures as white statues from her recent dream of the MaidenHall Academy.

She turned to LoeSyra. "What are the names of those animals they're riding? I think I've seen them before."

"They're called Archmounts. In Evermore, only Maidens ride them, and I'm sure that's because only they can tame them. They come originally from the frozen climes of Winterspire, where they mostly run wild in packs. When they're riled, they can be terrifying. Where have you seen them?"

"If I told you," said Heather, "you'd never believe me."

LoeSyra's golden lips climbed in amusement, her white teeth catching sun. "If you say so, probably not."

"Heather," Molly nudged her friend, "aren't the Maidens just so absolutely... *intoxicating?*"

Heather laughed and rolled her eyes.

"And look!" Molly pointed at another wave of Maidens clothed in unadorned dun-colored robes, their white heads shaved to the skin. "They look just like you did, when you were on top of the clock sculpture this morning!" Then she giggled. "Of course, you still have your hair," she patted Heather's voluminous headpiece, "somewhere under there."

Bringing up the rear of the spectacular parade came the youngest of Maidens. Some waved while others crouched to gather the many bouquets and flowers previously tossed by the adoring crowds. They placed them in baskets that they carried, slung to one side.

Heather noticed the way the tall Maidens walked: erect, elegant, and with noble bearing. In a flash, she was reminded of her grandmother, but dismissed the image. And though her youthful posture was very good already, the girl felt herself rising to stand even straighter, to her utmost height, within the bulk of her loose-fitting costume.

As the crowd continued to roar, they watched the tail end of the parade, the Maidens stretching far en route to their right.

"Amazing!" Molly said.

Exhilarated, Heather joined in the cheering, her eyes lapping up the last of the Maidens. "How come they disappear once they go through that arch?"

"It's because they're on their way to the next kingdom," LoeSyra said.

When spectators on all sides of them began to slowly disperse or focus their attention on personal gatherings and belongings, Borray turned a dour presence to listen, his three other companions locked in conversations of their own.

Molly looked at the green mask and gold lips. "The next kingdom?"

"Of course. They—"

"Where are you from, anyway?" Borray interrupted, confronting the girls. "You've so many strange questions, the two of you. Haven't you ever seen a Portal before?"

"Well, obviously we have. That's how Molly and I got here."

Borray glared at the moon girl. Fallasha kept her facial expression neutral, trying not to reveal the anxiety she was experiencing with the girls' inadvertent admissions to the hostile young man.

"What is the next kingdom and where is it?" Molly quickly asked LoeSyra.

Borray jumped in, "So, you aren't from this area or the Realm, are you?" When neither of the two visitors responded, he added, "I thought so."

The questioning made Molly uncomfortable, Heather more irritated.

LoeSyra patiently stood by, and when she was sure Borray had finished, said, "Well, this is Autumnsloe, so the next kingdom is Winterspire."

"And then Springshoot Green and Summersbreath Still." It was Avarra speaking, having concluded her conversation with the other two. "Seasonal Sequence."

"So your kingdoms are named after four seasons," said Molly.

"Yes. Set up by the Archannites long ago," said LoeSyra. "They were the ancient race of people that introduced TimeLight travel and the way of the TransPorts. They connected all four kingdoms, located on completely different planets, thinking that we would best be dependent on one another for our survival."

"I believe they thought that in time, all four worlds, if left unconnected, would perish without benefit of the resources belonging to the others," offered Terrellena. "So, through TimeLight Portals, they linked us."

Borray said, "You still haven't told us where you two reside."

"Yes, you're from where?" Avarra asked. Unlike the young man's, her voice was cheerful.

"You're TimeLight Travelers, aren't you?" Borray persisted, as if the two were guilty of something sinister.

Fallasha moaned under her breath.

"I suppose so," Molly said. "We've never—" she looked at Heather, "I guess we've never really thought about it." She forced a laugh. "We're just here to watch the Parade."

Glances were exchanged among the others.

"I mean, where we come from," Molly said, "we just call ourselves travelers or visitors. Nothing else."

"Maybe sightseers," said Heather.

Everyone laughed except the malcontent: "Or maybe Maiden infiltrators."

Addressing Heather and Molly, Avarra spoke up, "If you haven't guessed yet, it seems that our overzealous Borray wants to go into the Emperor's service as a Soldier of the Crown, perhaps a Royal Interrogator. But right now, he's more than content simply being a RogueTag." She turned on him: "Don't be stupid, Borray. Look at them. Do you really think that these two girls have come looking to dethrone our Emperor?"

"Yeah," said LaoCuria, "And destroy the Realm?"

The girls began to laugh with mocking merriment at their friend.

"Yes, maybe they're the ones who will set the Portent in motion, annihilating the majority of Maidens and scattering the remainder in the process."

"The mighty moon and the deadly butterfly!"

They were really laughing now.

"You shouldn't joke about such things," an indignant Borray mumbled. "It could happen, you know."

"Oh, sure it can," Avarra said, still laughing. "At any moment now."

"My brother, Borray, the annoying prophet of doom," said Terrellena, shaking her head. "How do we know *you* won't be the one to initiate the Portent's cycle?"

The girls laughed more, Heather and Molly finding themselves laughing with the others, though they were uncertain as to why.

"It's going to happen," Borray insisted, "It's written. You know that."

"If you believe the Chronicles."

"Why wouldn't you believe?" Borray said, unable to let it go. "They were written by the Mystics of the Ancient Archannites."

"If you believe that all the writings found were truly theirs," said Avarra, moving in for the kill. "And yet no one has established that for a fact."

"You're all wrong, all of you," the sneering mask said. "Watch. You'll see. And when it happens, recall that I, Borray, warned the bunch of you." A sulking Borray turned and stalked off, looking to join those that were steadily departing.

"Oh, come on, Borray," Avarra said.

"Yes, be a sport."

"We were only having our way with you."

"Do come back."

"Yes, do."

Under her breath, Heather heard Terrellena say to her friends, "I'm tempted to let him depart. I don't know what's happened to my brother. He certainly won't be asked to spend the day with us again. I'll see to that."

The young man, his head low, his back to the group, stopped. When he began to turn around, the girls once again began their coaxing.

"There you are, Borray, come on now."

"Yes, come."

"There's a good man."

Borray looked over. He tried to shed his sullen demeanor and failed, yet Heather saw his aura lighten, though not by much.

"So, from where do you come?" LoeSyra asked, moving forward genially, looking to keep the conversation light.

Don't tell them! Fallasha's brain screamed. *Don't!*

"Well," Molly said, searching for the right words, "we're actually a long way from home, I would say. We're from—"

"The Milky Way," Heather interrupted, thinking it prudent not to mention the name of their Earth, just in case the Ancient Archannites named it, too. Instinctively, she thought the girls safe, but beyond a doubt, Borray was not to be trusted. "We're from the Milky Way."

The moon brooch exhaled in relief. Pent up, she would have found herself fidgeting or pacing nervously, if she possessed the ability to do so.

"The Milky Way?"

"Such a lovely name."

"It's near?"

Heather and Molly looked at each other, with Molly catching onto her friend's desire not to give the name of their home planet.

Fallasha waited, hoping the girls would not disclose any damaging information. She admonished herself for not being thorough in conveying behavioral safety tips and procedures upon their arrival. But how could she have known the pair would become involved with a RogueTag partisan? The brooch held her breath.

"Oh, yes, it's near..." Molly shook her head, shrugged, and meekly pointed to Heather. "Go ahead. You tell them."

"Oh, it's over there. You know," Heather said, pointing vaguely overhead in the direction of some trees. "Near some nebula or other, and-and-and," bouncing the words, she nervously paused before continuing with, "some lunar eclipse somewhere. Forgot the name of it. Probably close to the, the, the—" Heather looked at Molly.

"The Blue Moon!" she said, looking at Heather's mask.

"— and the Bristol Constellation."

"Yes," Molly said, "that's it! By Haley's Comet."

"That's right. And the big dipper." The two were nodding in agreement with one another. "And the Moray Pantaloris."

Molly stifled a giggle.

There was a moment's pause.

"North Star!"

"Yeah," Heather said, "the North Star."

"That's the area, anyway," Molly said, in conclusion.

"The Milky Way," LoeSyra repeated the words. "And the others, such wonderful names, don't you think?" She was looking at her companions. "Wonderful."

"Welcome."

"Yes, welcome to Autumnsloe."

"To Evermore!"

Fallasha sighed with relief. Now, she thought, if I can just get these two home safely without further incident.

Four of the five hosts welcomed the two costumed visitors in a shower of kind words. Still brooding behind his unsmiling facade, however, Borray chose to remain silent, standing one step back, one step removed.

CHAPTER TWENTY

Visitors, Visitors

Heather and Molly, once again navigating carefully in their voluminous costumes, followed their new acquaintances over and off the boulders, keeping their distance from Borray. Standing on the grassy area below the small hill, the Autumnslovian students took turns hugging the young TimeLight travelers, with Borray aloof. He continued to observe the visitors warily, his lanky frame stooped at the neck.

"You girls are wonderful, and truly we hope you'll come back and visit Autumnsloe once again," LoeSyra said.

"Yes," LaoCuria joined in, adding, "It's been our pleasure to have met you."

"Thank you," said Molly.

"What are you going to do now that the parade has finished?" LoeSyra asked. "Some sightseeing?"

All but Borray laughed. Impatient, he focused his attention elsewhere.

"No, it's time to go home, I think," said Molly, with a glance at Heather.

"Yep, it's back to the Milky Way for us."

"Well, goodbye, then," Terrellena added. "Safe transport."

The groups separated, with Molly and Heather heading back towards the footbridges, storefronts, and the courtyard of colorful tile work.

"Wow, Molly, that was really something back there."

The departing throng had stalled, bottlenecked before the bridge.

"Yes. Wasn't that parade just, just *breathtaking?*"

"Yeah, and the Maidens! Wow! They're so *awesome!*" Heather's mind replayed the many Maidens that had passed before them on the parade route. "I want an Archmount," she announced, picturing herself perched atop the beast like a proud Maiden. The moon girl imagined riding it to school, where it would garner instant awe from her peers and respect from the townsfolk, people like Mr. Pringle.

"Yes, but what would you feed it?" Molly asked. "Dog food?"

"Mr. Simpletripp."

The two girls laughed.

"You'd poison your Archmount," Molly said.

They laughed some more.

The congestion eased, and soon the girls had crossed the bridge, stepping between picnickers on the grass and coming to the narrow street that ran before the shops.

"Hey, Molly, want to look in some of the shop windows?"

"Yes! And inside the shops, too. I wonder what kinds of clothes they have here."

Fallasha spoke up. "I don't advise it, girls. It's best that we get home quickly and not overstay our welcome. That Borray character is difficult indeed, and I suspect there are many more like him—in fact, I *know* there are—wanting to disrupt the festivities. They're trouble, and I strongly recommend that we return to the safety of the PortalDoor at once."

"Just a quick look, Fallasha? Come on, the windows are right over there."

"Please, Fallasha," Molly chimed in, "just a few shops and then we can go."

The small brooch pondered. "I advise against it. It's not on the schedule, you know, and I can get in plenty of trouble with my Bristol House superiors over this."

"Come on, Fallasha," Heather said. "Just a quick look, that's all."

"Please?" Molly asked.

Fallasha pondered before speaking. "You know, I can't blame the both of you. I suppose like any visitor inspired by the beauty of what you've witnessed here today, you'd like to see a bit more of what Autumnsloe has to offer."

The girls exchanged eager looks, sensing a breakthrough.

"Yeah!"

"Can we?"

Fallasha watched the spectators that filed by, still departing. She and the two girls were standing off by themselves, beneath a streetlamp, and not far from the heavily populated grass, where many parade-goers were spending the remainder of their sunlit hours. Others were wandering around, making a day of the festivities.

The brooch took a deep breath. "Well, I don't think it would hurt…"

The costumed girls broke into cheers, with Molly jumping up and down a few times. She stopped abruptly and self-consciously looked around.

Heather noticed Molly's sudden restraint and laughed, saying, "Come on, let's go."

"Wait!" the reluctant tour guide added. "All right, we'll go look at the shops, but please, girls, all I ask is that since this is not a part of the Parade Day schedule, please be extra careful and don't do anything that would get us—me—in trouble or that would draw excessive attention to yourselves."

"Fallasha," Heather said, "we're already dressed as a moon and butterfly. I don't know if you've noticed or not, but these costumes are so, so…" she looked at Molly.

"Spectacular? Remarkable? Prominent? Outstanding?"

"Yeah, all those, that everyone keeps looking at us. We're *already* drawing attention to ourselves." When the brooch didn't say anything, Heather added, "So, come on, then, let's go look at the shops." She stepped back into the flow of the masses on her way toward the stores.

Molly followed.

Fallasha frowned. "I'm not feeling good about this. Not at all," but her voice was small and lost among the sounds of the crowd.

In a spacious and windowless basement room of the Bristol House, a large fresco, one of many on a wall of large frescoes, rippled momentarily. The painting of an unearthly winged beast in a forested area began to spin in a blur. The panel commenced to contract in some areas and expand in others, until it took on the large rectangular proportions of a doorway. Having thus transformed, it sank deeply into the wall.

It was then that, within the newly formed doorway, a man dressed in black materialized in a wisp of transcendency, of rapid and ever-increasing opacity, a soundless *foosh:* a blink of the darkness. Once whole, he remained unmoving, blending with the basement's encompassing and lightless obscurity. At a glance, from beneath a thin mask, the visitor queried the newfound surroundings within his limited field of vision, sponging up the delicate and reticent shapes, the murky gaps and secretive corners. Ears keenly aware, two catch-alls awaiting sound, any sound, the slightest shred to be captured and amplified on the drum. Slowly the figure crouched and slid low to the floor, his body a fluid coil of muscle. Waiting, waiting, listening.

Where within the Bristol House am I?

Peering, intent, patient, in and among the shadows he crept, painfully slow, painfully wary, inspecting, slinking forward, forward; a surveying glance, one cautious step succeeded by yet another, past a large dresser and crate, by an aisle of old clothing displayed openly on racks and lumped sprawlingly upon open chests, navigating around a collection of antique dressers and bureaus, tall and wide, fat and lean, housing drawer and cabinet, passing beyond an old floor lamp. The stealthy visitor slipped along below a mirror, lost to vision, lost to unwanted reflection, onward, an outline painted black on the blackness. He stopped. Aware. Attentive. Now waiting. Then, soundlessly breathing, soundlessly advancing, soundlessly at one with the foreignness of his surroundings—inhaling, exhaling: a shallow almost imperceptible activity, a cautious necessity—moving, moving, the man stole to finally merge with the wall near a door.

Lost in the gloom, a wall clock continued to count out unceasingly and nevertheless: tick-tock, tick-tock, a monotonous and lifeless sound for all life's passage, the pendulum swinging to, swinging fro, never labored, never passionate, always steady, and ever on time. Loudly and abruptly, it chimed out the hour.

The mysterious visitor tensed at the unexpected sound, then relaxed. Stalled, he waited, as the pealing played out. Quiet, now, quiet. Unhurriedly, a gloved hand reached out to lightly take hold of the knob, becoming one with its ornamental recesses and protrusions, with its weight and with its turning, with its inner engagement. Slowly and smoothly the bolt slid out of the groove within the door's jamb. Now at one with the swivel of hinges, with the smooth and heavy planks, with their woody knots and vertical grooves, the door was soundlessly opened, but only a sliver: daylight.

The figure slowly peered into the crack, peered into the adjoining basement room, past the door. In the small amount of light supplied by the ground level windows, the cold stare inspected the vagueness. Effortlessly, indulgently, the silhouette made sense of the indistinct shapes, their locations and their sizes, their possibilities and their liabilities, easing the door open just wide enough, with just enough movement, and just enough effort. Then, akin to a night's shadow, the person stole inside, settling and fusing once again within the absence of light.

Daylight. The word sat in the mind of the now stationary visitor as dispassionately as a tick of the clock. Nightfall was the time. Tick-tock, tick-tock. The TimeLight Assassin withdrew further, seeking the temporary confines of a sheltering structure as, yes, nightfall was the time.

Bills, bills, I should be paying bills, Lana Pringle thought to herself. And the wash, I've got a ton of wash to do.

Her tears were running freely, and she laughed through them—at herself, at her crying.

I've been so numb, I didn't think I had anything left, she thought, sniffing, clumsily wiping her cheeks with her wrist and then knuckles. Her mouth entertained another loose, watery laugh, finding brief consolation in the photographed image before her.

Look at my Molly, so tiny and beautiful.

Her tears again made paths.

Who took that picture? Probably Sis. Must have been one of the few times we visited as a family, one of the few times that Ned allowed himself to leave his beloved town of Noble to vacation.

Lana Pringle looked at herself, a young naïve self, holding close the baby Molly. And next to her was Ned, so rigid, so incapable of relaxing even then. His thick square glasses reflected the brilliance of a flash, his smile was forced, a barbed-wire fence to his innermost feelings.

Unless he's talking business, Lana thought, there's so little to say. Numbers are safe; they don't bite, sting, or maim: harmless unemotional things in straight lines and curls. All so safe, so safe for Ned the inflexible, unchangeable banker.

Good Lord, what was I thinking then?

She laughed again through her tears.

So, Lana Pringle asked herself, what became of this woman, Lana the Younger?

She turned the page: more glossy pictures of herself, a new mother along with a young father and baby daughter. Mrs. Pringle swiped her fingers below one eye, smearing the wetness.

All I could ever ask for, it seemed it was here then—whatever *it* was. Promise, was that it? she asked herself. A bountiful hope? A wholly contented beginning to what would only get better? Or was I even thinking of the future at all, instead focusing only on my little Molly so in need of constant care and attention in those early years?

But that time, surely it wasn't wasted, Mrs. Pringle thought. *Was it?*

Years, years, years, years, years, amassed and piled high; finite living breathing things taken for granted as they occur, lived out in a blur and stockpiled for future reference, recorded on the walls of our souls. Collected, collected, collected. And captured here, reduced to this: she looked at the pictures of her past.

That was me.

She dragged a palm across the album's page, over the plastic covered photos protected from her surprisingly rainy sojourn, streaking the wetness. Mrs. Pringle closed the book, sealing the tears between the archived images belonging to lost and optimistic days.

Were they really so carefree and happy? she asked herself, placing the album on the bedside table.

She wasn't so sure. Not now. Perhaps she was just more accepting then. Or unthinking.

Lana Pringle admitted to herself that she was indeed confused. She also admitted that there was no turning away her new self that was fighting to emerge and dispense with the worn out stand-in. And she was tired of fighting with Ned as he wrestled to keep her enclosed and wrapped up tightly, fitting neatly and efficiently into that box of what used to be.

The dynamic has changed, hasn't it? Gone are youthful days of the sweet and the willing—the malleable young Lana, the small-town banker's wife. So, what happened? Exactly when did this change come about?

Mrs. Pringle realized she couldn't say. Perhaps it was just a slow erosion of the expected giving way to what was needed. But what she needed wasn't there for her; *Ned* wasn't there for her, and he had proved this time and again. Nothing here, nothing there, nothing now or then. It's all—well, in the end, it's all just nothing, isn't it? Everything is nothing.

Mrs. Pringle ran a hand through her dark brown hair.

You've got Molly, so pull up your socks, Lana. The thought sprang at her.

She stood. Crossing her arms before her, the woman gazed out the window to catch a portion of Whisper Creek, its swollen waters churning below the surface, rolling on to some unseen destination. Low in the autumn sky, the sun slanted the shadows of entangled trees across the turbid brown liquid.

Mrs. Pringle looked away and instinctively reached down to smooth out the disturbed bedspread.

What do I want? she asked herself. She turned again to the creek. Drawn closer to the window, her face now almost pressed against the glass, she peered into the void beneath the old wooden bridge. A change of life's clothes, that's what I want. A new *freshness,* a new rhythm, a new purpose. A new start.

The conclusive weight of the last three words unsettled her. She glanced at Ned's crumpled note on the dresser, and thought, Maybe you need a new start, too, because whatever you have to say, it's all too late. It's just too late. So grow.

Weary, tired of pleasing, tired of the tedious daily pantomime, tired of sheltering her daughter from a father's unreasonable doctrine, the woman opened the guestroom closet, searching for the beginnings of her new life. Finding a handle, she withdrew the rounded rectangular case and turned away from the confined space and the emptiness therein.

Having perused knickknacks on the shelves, decorative tiles, handmade jewelry, elegant vases and pots, the moon and butterfly girls walked out of the store, temporarily standing aside to let newcomers enter. They were thanked graciously, and the emblazoned door closed behind them, eliciting the ring of a tiny bell. The two set off to the next display window, just past a crowded florist shop.

Maneuvering past a group of costumed children, Heather and Molly briefly stepped into the street. Upon reclaiming the sidewalk, Molly was the first to spot the compelling Autumnslovian clothing. Hanging freely and on animated mannequins within the oddly shaped window, the unusual styles and colors appealed to her imaginative fashion sense.

"Heather, look. It's all so gorgeous, don't you think?"

But Heather wasn't looking in the window. Not a glance. She had caught sight of a familiar face, a face from a recent dream. With shopping bag in hand, the young woman was but a few steps in front of Heather, exiting from between buildings. Older now, her black hair was no longer braided in a lengthy plait but crudely cropped near the scalp, and she was dressed in featureless street clothes that hung loosely on her slender frame. In spite of the crowd, the woman noticed and appraised the costumed moon girl, and it brought to her stunning features a quick smile of appreciation. Heather smiled in return.

In that brief instant, Heather felt a great fascination, an incomprehensible pull towards the woman. Heather saw that her skin had lost its utter Maiden whiteness, having turned a radiant pink. Yet her lips still held their deep crimson and her eyes their extraordinary green. The woman's aura glowed in exuberant yellows and oranges, with occasional glimpses of passionate red.

The young woman turned away, heading up the street, and Heather noticed the elegant Maiden carriage with which she walked.

The moon girl reached out and grabbed her friend's arm. "Molly, come on."

"Why?" She asked, reluctant to turn her attention from the fanciful clothing. "Can't we go in here first? I'd like to look—hey!"

Heather was dragging Molly away from the window, pulling on her arm.

"Molly, come on," Heather said, her words adamant.

"Just where do you think you're going?" Fallasha asked. "Please remember our agreement."

Heather, now certain that her friend would follow, released her arm.

"Heather," Molly said, trying to keep pace, "where are we going?"

Tenaciously pursuing the Maiden before her, maneuvering in and out of the crowds, Heather said, "I don't know."

"Well, we should all turn back, then," said the brooch. "Look, let's not get too far away from the PortalDoor. It's dangerous to do so. Remember, you're in an unfamiliar world, a world that just happens to be entering an ominous transition."

The words finally sinking through her preoccupation, Heather asked, "What are you talking about, Fallasha?"

The brooch bit her lip. "Never mind."

Lagging, awaiting an opening between groups of parade-goers that were slowing the girls' progress, Heather accelerated into a sudden gap. Molly barely squeezed through afterward before the space closed again.

Heather craned her neck, having lost sight of the woman from her dream. "Darn," she muttered.

"Heather, what's up? What are you doing?"

"Molly, just follow me, okay?" There was no arguing with Heather's tone of voice. She shot a glance down at her brooch. "You, too."

"Like I have a choice." Fallasha glared into space. "Heather, I don't like this. Why the sudden departure from browsing shop windows?"

"I need to do this."

"What? Do what?" Fallasha asked. "Where are you going? What are you doing? What?"

Heather shook her head, earrings sweeping in a twist. Having reclaimed sight of the Maiden, she increased her pace. Molly struggled, but managed to keep at the moon girl's heels.

"This is *not* wise, and as your official tour guide, I must inform you of that fact," Fallasha said, irritation wringing her words. "I recommend that we return immediately."

Heather ignored her.

They continued to walk past the many creative window displays, between hanging baskets with lively flecks of colored bloom. Beneath their feet, the stone sidewalks gave way to a cobblestone street and then to grass, with the girls eventually stepping onto the planks of a footbridge that spanned the small river.

"Heather, look at the children playing in the water down there."

"Not now, Molly, not now."

As the arched bridge descended to reach the opposite bank, Heather sidestepped two RogueTags that pushed their way past, heading in the opposite direction. With leering provocation, their surly faces scanned the oncoming foot traffic. They looked a savage and intimidating force, strapping in their torn black shirts and purple armbands. Molly was quick in getting out of their path, but was knocked against the railing of the bridge nonetheless.

"Ow!"

The moon girl whirled, retracing her steps. "You okay?"

Molly grimaced while rubbing her upper arm.

Heather glared after the two RogueTags. They kept walking.

"Hurry up, you!" she heard one of the ruffians say as he shoved a costumed man, pushing him forward. When what little the diminutive man could do on a crowded bridge wasn't enough, the two RogueTags saw fit to manhandle, lift, and then dangle him over the side by his ankles. Laughing and taunting, enjoying his pleas, they eventually dropped him headfirst into the water.

Molly, looking for distance from the troublemakers, laid a hand on her friend's back, and said, "Let's hurry up." She glanced over her shoulder. Reluctantly, Heather moved on, again locating the Maiden.

"I'm advising you two—no, telling you two—that it is imperative that we return to the PortalDoor without delay," Fallasha said. "This is dangerous, just wandering off like you're doing. Incidents such as the one we just witnessed are not, I repeat, *not* on the schedule of Parade Day activities."

Heather said, with a brief glimpse at her brooch, "Don't you ever stop?"

Fallasha growled as the moon girl quickened her pace.

Molly ran to catch up with Heather. Feeling a safe distance from the ruffians, the butterfly girl had taken a moment to look upstream at the repetition of elegant footbridges that diminished with distance and the flow of brilliant costumes mirrored in muted reflection upon the water. Boats sailed in the background.

Rounding a corner, the Avenue became wider. Heather reduced her speed and Molly, in her haste, almost bumped into her. At that moment, Heather turned quickly to face the nearest window, her back to the intriguing Maiden. Molly pulled up alongside the moon girl, slightly winded and welcoming the opportunity to catch her breath.

"Watch yourself, Molly, we can't let her see us."

"Who, Heather?"

Heather glanced discreetly to her left.

"That woman behind me with the short black hair."

"Where?" the moon brooch asked. "Can you please turn so *I* can see her? After all, I *am* your tour guide. Come now. Have I no say in the matters at hand, being relegated to obscurity when bearing witness to the unfolding of current events? Is this what it now comes to, that my presence here is so little appreciated and undervalued?" When no response came, Fallasha snapped, "All right, then, be that way."

Molly cautiously peered past Heather and up the sidewalk.

"The one looking in the shop window? Why? Who is she?"

"Molly, you wouldn't believe me if I told you."

"Let me guess," Fallasha spoke up, within the tight huddle. "She was in one of your dreams."

"Yeah, she was. Only her hair was long and in a braid, and her skin was white." Heather didn't add the circumstances of the classroom and the teacher.

After a pause, Fallasha said, "I don't believe this."

"It's true! I'm not lying."

"No, I mean it makes sense," the moon brooch said. "I'm beginning to understand now."

"What makes sense?"

"Heather," Molly said, "there she goes. Your lady is walking away."

Heather and Molly turned from the window and continued their pursuit, lagging a bit at first before stepping up the pace. Crossing another street and rounding another turn, Heather found herself unexpectedly confronting an amazing monument, the Avenue dividing and going around it.

Enormous and glimmering like a mirage in sunlight, the mountainous creation sat on a sprawling island.

Heather stopped. Molly bumped into her.

"Ow!"

"Molly, look," Heather said. She stepped aside so her friend could see the vast structure.

The striking monument consisted of a great white temple crowning a steep rocky hill. Surrounding it, stone Maidens were positioned loosely in animated circles throughout a forest of silvery trees. Lost and found, a wide stairway spiraled up to the temple heights, while narrow paths ran throughout linking numerous sitting areas.

Like the real Maidens that had passed before the girls in the Parade, the stone versions were clothed in varying attire, walking or seated high upon Archmounts, in battle armor and without. Many were stationed about the grassy slope, alongside boulders or beneath trees, while others found place around the base and throughout the park-like setting. From fountains around the temple, waterfalls rained down and gathered in pools at the bottom of the hill. Surrounding the circular temple were columns carved in the likeness of Maidens, their faces stoic with features strong and proud, arms reaching up, entwined with the figures on either side in support of the domed and tiled roof. Above, positioned along the roofline, were the nine Ancient Ones, their hoods pulled down over bowed heads, their hands clasped before them. All walking in a circle, each led and at the same time followed.

Sporadically around the monument's base, the youngest of the stone Maidens, in groups or alone, picked up stone roses that had been cast about, placing them in their stone baskets. Sculpted representatives of the many tribes of Evermore, their costumes unique unto each, interacted with the Maidens throughout, conversing while walking, giving or receiving an offering, or locked in hands of accord. More Maidens were set in a variety of poses alongside the stairway balustrades that climbed down from each side of the temple to reach ground level. Looming over the girls and their brooch, the monument's effect was nothing short of reverential and awe inspiring.

"It's called the Ring of the Evermore Maidens," Fallasha informed the girls as they walked past the site. "It's a memorial created by Human-Kind sculptors gathered from throughout the four kingdoms. Long ago, it was presented to the Maidens following the TimeLight Battle of Orfandorr, to honor all they had accomplished in sacrifice for the Realm."

"Gosh," was all Molly could muster.

"Come on," Heather said, taking one last look at the spectacular tribute to Evermore MaidenHood. "We can spend more time looking at this later, but right now we've got to hurry. I don't want to lose that woman."

Before them, the Maiden had slowed when passing the stone figures.

Molly shook herself from viewing the monument to catch up to Heather. She could scarcely hear Fallasha's voice trailing her friend, spewing a continuous reprimand, "...by lodging an official verbal protest on behalf of myself, a kindhearted but wrongfully hijacked brooch. So, it is with the utmost urgency that I advise we return this very instant..."

The man in mud-caked shoes entered the house, closing the front door behind him, bolting it securely. On a whim, from his jacket pocket, he fished out a piece of jewelry, squeezing the locket and chain reassuringly in his hand, his undertaking a success. The man walked over to the fireplace and placed the gold sentimental keepsake in a small bowl on the mantle.

That old miner should never have let me get so close, he thought. Not for a moment. Though I must say, I did appreciate his kindness and was glad for his easy acceptance of my generosity. Admittedly, I was envious of him and his carefree lifestyle. Such an experienced hiker with widespread knowledge of the Stenmouth range, too—he definitely knew those caves.

"It was a shame he had to die," was said aloud, the words flat, without conviction.

On the hearth, the man set down the small bags he carried. One contained his gloves and the miner's worn and dirty shoes. He would burn them later.

From another bag he withdrew the book he had taken from the girl's backpack and slid it neatly onto the shelf alongside the volumes of hiking trails, almanacs, and yearbooks, not far from a small round LuminOrb. He, like young Heather, enjoyed the title, *Two Girls and a Mystery*. As well, he had noticed that it was a first edition in pristine condition.

A commendable souvenir, he thought with satisfaction. A piece of the child. His face dropped momentarily when he thought of her escape. I missed my opportunity, didn't I? The man said, resolutely, There will be others.

Crossing the room to the closet, he opened it, pulled out a hanger and hung up his jacket. He looked below to where the square-toed boots had been kept. In their place was a shiny new pair, purchased from a large department store in Thistlewhite, over three hours away. Like the previous set, they were to be kept clean and worn only on those very special occasions.

Closing the closet door, he leaned his back against it and then his head. In a rush, he felt youthful. He felt elated. He felt like everyday was fresh, a living dream—a new outlook on an ever-abbreviated stay.

Looking down, he traced the tracks of dried mud, in clumps and crumbs, to the bookcase. On the shelf, the new addition to his book collection stood out attractively, if only to him. He pictured the book jacket, an illustration of two girls entering an open door, on the cusp of electrifying discovery.

Yes, the two girls, the man thought. Sweet Heather Nighborne, such a lovely creature. I like when she's near to me. Even when she doesn't know I'm there. Molly Pringle, too. But being close to me can have such devastating consequences, can't it?

He laughed spasmodically, checked himself, and then headed for the cellar stairs.

Grandma Dawn awoke on the porch, at peace near the gentle sunlight that shone down to warm the fading life of the Bristol House garden. From her location, she looked at the remaining leaves that had managed to steadfastly cling to the trees.

Autumn and Autumnsloe, Grandma Dawn thought.

She started to rock, but not for long.

A thought jumped into her head: I hope Heather and Molly are having a wonderful time at the parade. It was followed shortly thereafter by yet another thought, one she would have chosen not to recognize, but instead quickly dismiss, just days ago: And I hope they've come to no harm.

Grandma Dawn watched as a calico cat walked soundlessly along the porch railing, balancing gracefully atop the narrow strip of wood. She was indeed a beautiful creature with her white, red, and black patched fur. Yet, most striking were her eyes of a light golden-green within a mask of black. The feline stopped and sized up Grandma Dawn. She gazed at the cat in return and then laughed at the staredown.

Seeing the stray again was no surprise, having observed the cat previously and knowing that on many occasions Heather had taken the time to feed her. She had even named the creature, calling her Miss Gypsy, the cat coming to trust the girl, and eventually allowing Heather to place on her a black-sequined collar. Then Grandma Dawn recognized the small tambourine that hung from it, in place of an identification tag, and she recalled that the sterling piece was a token from Heather's charm bracelet. Thinking it the perfect addition for Miss Gypsy's collar, Heather had asked her grandmother if she minded its removal and subsequent gifting. Not at all.

Heather was right, she thought. A perfect addition.

When the calico departed with a gallant leap from the railing, Grandma Dawn was yawning, stretching out her arms and legs. She looked at her wristwatch and then rose out of the wicker chair. As it temporarily rocked with its emptiness, the watcher in indigo attire, having returned, studied the familiar woman and setting, this time from behind the Victorian gazebo.

Grandma Dawn turned and made her way to the front door, her every movement closely observed. When the door closed behind her, the watcher continued to gaze silently upon the empty porch and its wicker furniture. Yet, curious and calculating behind the close fitting facial wrap, thoughts were streaming:

The time is near at hand. The Portent's child will soon be home from the Parade, and the Bristol House basement will play a key role. Therein lie the many Portals known only to the few. What has been foretold will take place soon and in accordance with the Portent. I can feel it. It's beginning. Undoubtedly.

⁓

Molly was the first to see the castle upon a distant hill, nestled among the trees. A single tower rose to the sky, supported by buildings of comparable design clustered below, banners flying high off their many spires. Its style was fluid and elegant like all the architecture she had observed in Autumnsloe.

"Heather, take a look at that castle. Wouldn't you just love to live there?"

Heather gave it momentary attention, before turning to her moving target once again.

"It's Castle Elderraine," Fallasha said, and when no one offered a response to her announcement, she added, "And it would be best for all if we simply abandon this most ill-advised journey and promptly return to the Bristol House Portal and home."

Heather's mask smiled.

The moon and butterfly girls stayed close to the Maiden, though not too close. Remaining lost among the vibrant sea of parade-day visitors, the girls left the street to file along the river, making certain to keep their distance from the occasional group of mischief-making RogueTags. It was here, near rows of houses, that the crowds thinned, but were still ample enough to provide concealment. Reaching a patch of open lawn, Heather and Molly followed the young woman, and others, as they made their way towards a dense group of buildings surrounded by an outer wall. Located within, soaring above chimney, vane, and rooftop, they saw four dominant bell towers. And as Heather's quarry headed for the walled entry gate, she felt it wise to slacken the pace.

"There you have Elderraine University," Fallasha pointed out. "One of the premiere institutions for higher learning here in Autumnsloe." When, once again, neither Heather nor Molly felt any inclination to comment on the information given, an exasperated Fallasha cried aloud, "Oh, what's the point?" After a quiet moment, she said, "Hey, you two, remember me? I'm your tour guide, that's *official* tour guide, in case you've forgotten." When still no one commented, she saw fit to add, "Having previously enlightened you with that most interesting detail of what lies across the grass and behind the wall before you, I must once again take this opportunity to object to this irrational behavior, this most irresponsible and reprehensible course of action. It is simply not prudent to follow after someone whom I find to be a complete and total stranger in an utterly strange land, gallivanting off like lost annendoles to only the Universe knows where…"

Mixing with others, the Maiden filed through the entry gate, two substantial wooden doors that stood at the open. At their approach, Heather and Molly could see the facades and domes of varying heights, their undulating and heavily patterned roofs lending a sense of fantasy to the setting. But the girls took little time to admire the spectacle of their surroundings, finding themselves too involved in the chase.

Students in costume made it easy for Heather and Molly to blend into the crowds that flowed and milled about the grounds, and obviously the young woman being tailed by the pair felt no particular need to look for stalkers. Yet, as a precaution, Heather—and thus Molly—slowed. They trailed her through one doorway and then another, into a large and beautifully furnished room displaying student-occupied chairs and desks. They exited at the opposite side of the lofty building, and then crossed areas of lawn circumscribed by flowing iron fences and laced with pebbled walks. Seemingly preoccupied and unaware, the lone girl continued her lively stroll with her pursuers discreetly at a distance.

When finally they saw the Maiden disappear through an immense gateway door, Heather cautioned Molly to slacken her pace. Here, the traffic had diminished, and the girls were more susceptible to being seen. Heather went first, cautiously opening the engraved door, only to see the young woman entering another building a short distance away. Eagerly, Heather waved Molly to follow, and after allowing three Parade Day partiers to exit, the two traversed another patch of grass. Having climbed a short flight of steps, they opened a handsome door bedecked with scrollwork. Solidly built, it swung easily.

The pair found themselves in a hushed reading room with gilded columns and large mosaics in subdued light. Across the floor, bypassing tables, lamps, and chairs, the shorthaired woman walked with purpose, displaying buoyancy in manner and stride. Heather saw that her aura bubbled a blushing scarlet in an amorous glow of pink.

The woman turned and disappeared into one of several doorways, with Heather and Molly following at a judicious distance. Of the many students that occupied this quiet and intimate setting, few if any paid attention to the three that had just passed.

Soon the girls were following the tall graceful figure down a spacious corridor, beneath a vaulted ceiling. They walked on floors of swirly blue tile, their boots and shoes clicking lightly with each step. The corridor darkened at the end, and the Maiden turned through another doorway. Heather increased her pace, and the girls passed an oncoming student bearing books and lacking costume.

With Molly dogging Heather's heels, the girls entered the doorway to find themselves in yet another corridor, this one of little light. They drew to a standstill. Before them, there was no sign of the young woman. Heather walked over to a lighted open doorway off the smaller passage. She looked in. Shortly afterward, Molly arrived to peer over her friend's shoulder.

The short narrow hallway opened upon a great room under a very high ceiling, lit from above. Just inside the door, on a wall of red wood, hung a man's cloak. Alongside was a pair of leather gloves with extended cuffs, crafted with dense tracery. Below, resting on a plush rug of stately design, was a pair of knee-high riding boots with similar markings. The room's yellowish lamps intensified the bright gold embellishments encircling the tops of the boots, and brought out the finery of the metalwork in places throughout the luxurious apartment. The overall effect was nothing short of regal.

At the hallway's end was a stairway that rolled down dramatically from an unseen location above. Her head turning, her gaze climbing, the Maiden slowly laid down her bag, her eyes never leaving the grand staircase. She watched as a lone person steadily descended, his large hand dragging atop the railing.

Profusely clad in varying shades of white, his costume was intricately layered, textured, and beaded. Blue jewels hung in elegant braid from the shoulders. His hat was large-brimmed and bounced slightly as he came down the stairs. The man in white swept grandly onto the carpeted floor.

Initially hesitant, the young woman rushed to embrace the extraordinary figure. As he stepped forward to meet her, his swirling cape seemed to overwhelm and devour the Maiden, now hugged in tight. In his white-gloved hand, he produced a red rose on an exceptionally long stem. This he presented to the radiant woman, wrapped within the folds of his mantle.

She didn't look at him, instead casting her gaze down before her. Yet her pink hand reached out against the white to accept the offered bloom. She looked at the crown of petaled red and then, softly expressionless, turned to peer into the eyes so charmingly lit behind the leaf-like slits of mask. Adulation enhancing her shine, she moved in tighter still, and he laughed, a deep rich laugh, a pleasant masculine sound that soared and fell away. Turning, oblivious of the two girls watching from the hallway's end, the couple ascended the stairs, one merging into the whiteness of the other, until they were lost in white altogether, and eventually lost from view.

Heather and Molly stood stationary, entranced.

"Gosh," was all Molly said.

Moments of silence passed, before Fallasha spoke to break the mood.

"Have you any idea who that was?" she asked.

Heather soberly shook her head.

"He was magnificent," Molly offered, with barely a breath.

"Come on," said Heather. "We better get back."

Standing there, a great wave of sadness had washed over the moon girl, and having coursed through her, drained her of all enthusiasm. At once the abandoned room seemed disturbed, emptied of some vital force by the two having departed. Something was missing; something essential had gone, leaving the tracings of loss to encumber the air. Heather closed her eyes, trying to dispel the grievous spirit that had arisen within her.

Molly looked at her oddly: "What, Heather?"

"I don't know. I just feel sad, that's all."

"Why?"

Her shoulders came up in a shrug. "All I know is I don't want to leave."

"But I don't understand."

"I don't either," Heather said, her voice low. "I feel like...like there's something here for me."

"Heather, I don't understand. Do you know that girl?" Molly asked. "I mean, other than from your dream?"

Broodingly quiet, Heather was at a loss.

Molly followed up, "Or that man?"

Almost imperceptibly, Heather shook her head.

Molly just stared with incomprehension at her friend's downturned moon mask, before Fallasha said, "Perhaps you do."

Mrs. Pringle hurried out to the car carrying the final two suitcases, both belonging to Molly. They were stuffed with only a fraction of her daughter's large collection of fashionable clothing and accessories, including four pairs of shoes. With mild grunts and exclamations, she managed to hoist the bags past the bumper and into the trunk, slamming the lid.

Lana Pringle was in a hurry. She was in a hurry to start her new life, to start up the car, to be out of the house before her husband arrived home from wherever he happened to be this day. He wasn't at work, she knew that much. Mrs. Pringle remembered she had left his note crumpled on the nightstand next to the bed.

Sliding into the driver's seat, the woman shut her door with a bang. She locked it and then fleetingly asked herself why. She felt tears start to well, fought the urge, and following a turn of the ignition key, listened as the engine roared to life without hesitation. The motor sounded good, good. Deep, rich, powerful. Good. She revved it again, and then shoved the gearshift into reverse. The car lurched.

Looking over her shoulder, Lana Pringle began to back down the wide driveway, navigating to the right, to the right, before she braked the car to a jerking halt. Motor running, pistons pumping, camshaft spinning, she listened, and heard herself breathing. Was her heart racing? Unsteadily, the woman turned her attention back to the Pringle house, the home in which she and her husband had lived for all of Molly's twelve years and longer. Hands lax, leaning too heavily on the steering wheel, Mrs. Pringle stared. Conventional, it struck her that the house no longer gave off the appearance of being sturdy or trustworthy. Rather, the structure seemed a ghost, fatigued and devoid of life.

Empty. The word plinged into her mind with a start.

Who chose the cold gray paint job with white trim? she asked herself. It had to have been her, she knew, because those decisions Ned let fall under her jurisdiction, barring his ultimate power of the veto. Mrs. Pringle tried to remember if at the time she thought that particular combination would look dignified. She couldn't recall, but one thing she knew for sure was that the worn-down house needed color, some bright, bright color.

Grandma Dawn heard the front door slam from where she stood in the kitchen. She stopped her preparations for dinner, and wiping her hands, called, "Who's there? Heather?"

When there was no answer, the woman marched to the kitchen door and leaned through the jamb.

She called out again, "Heather?"

Now looking down the lengthy hallway, Grandma Dawn could see that the front door was wide open.

What's this? But I just heard the front door slam.

Baffled, she began her long walk down the hall, still carrying the kitchen towel. Abruptly, Grandma Dawn stopped, concern knotting her brow as she watched the front door slowly close. Her head slightly askew, without hurry, she once again laid steps in the direction of the door.

Her gaze sweeping the family room as she walked by, she said, "Heather?"

Still no response.

Upon reaching the self-motivated door, Grandma Dawn opened it, and scanned the empty porch. Afterwards, she securely closed and locked the door, lingering for just a moment more, absorbed in thought.

An instant later, the woman set off towards the kitchen, stopping at the stairway. There, she craned her neck in the direction of the second floor.

"Heather?"

Again no response.

Not appearing overly concerned, she continued on her course. Had she only glanced towards the servants' entrance in the parlor, she would have noticed an indigo figure immobile at the wall, brushed by afternoon shadows. As it was, a pair of eyes studied Grandma Dawn's poised, familiar bearing in retreat, until her footfalls faded. Then, carefully opening the servant's door, the latest Bristol House visitor slipped inside to begin a soundless descent to the basement.

"It's really a phenomenal monument," Molly said, turning from the Ring of the Evermore Maidens. She and Fallasha had been admiring it as the girls continued their walk back towards the shops, and eventually the PortalDoor.

"The Maidens were extremely fierce in that conflict, overcoming heavy losses and afterwards turning the tide in the Great Battle for Azbethiem," Fallasha said. "Many generations later, it seems that HumanKind youth have forgotten the sacrifice of the Maidens, and that our Realm and way of life would be remarkably different if not for their contribution and ultimate victory."

Heather had been remote upon the return trip, and Molly simply let her be. She found no reason to call her out in conversation, no reason to break her moody silence. Yet, the butterfly girl stayed near at hand.

The girls passed an outdoor café, the lively occupants carrying on at the tables that encroached onto the sidewalk. Heather sighted another group of RogueTags, flashes of purple evident around their upper arms. The ruffians were loitering nearby at the corner and down a backstreet. Many glared as the girls walked by. Undaunted, the moon girl ignored them, but the butterfly girl pulled even closer to her companion.

"Those guys give me the creeps," Molly said, under her breath.

Heather concurred. "They're all over the place. I saw groups of them all along on our way to the university. Fallasha's right, they're trouble."

"Rather than scolding you, telling you that we shouldn't be here blindly roaming all over Autumnsloe in pursuit of someone you thought you saw in a dream, instead I'm going to say that I hope those RogueTags find little incentive to bother us," Fallasha said. "After all, aren't we just two young girls and a brooch walking down the street?"

At the brooch's bit of insight, Heather found little reason to comment and Molly relaxed a bit.

Walking slightly behind Heather, Molly studied her. The change in her friend was night and day, the moon girl having once again gone quiet, but this time with a dangerous edge. Was it in her walk, how she carried herself? Molly couldn't say. Maybe it was just that she knew Heather so well. But dangerous or not, Molly doubted that any RogueTags would find a twelve-year-old girl in a moon costume intimidating.

The girls crossed the bridge where Molly had earlier noticed children playing in the water. Soon they found themselves walking past the shops that had hanging baskets enhancing the storefront displays. Molly slowed to look, but Fallasha urged her on. Heather noticed more RogueTags milling about near a hot food stand, some leaning against a wall. Molly did, too, and again hurried to close the distance between her and the moon girl.

"Hey, it's the TimeLight travelers," one said.

"Is that right? TimeLight travelers, eh?" said another.

"This planet is for HumanKind only—*our* HumanKind."

Crossing the street, Heather and Molly walked faster. Heather looked straight ahead, but had surveyed the auras gathered behind her on the corner when she and Molly passed. Most were dark and murky, influenced with purples.

"I told you they were trouble," Fallasha said, her voice low.

Having gained the opposite side of the street, Molly looked at Heather. "How do they know we're TimeLight travelers?"

"Borray."

"Was he back there?"

"Yeah, he just wasn't in his costume. I saw his face at the Parade, when he lifted his mask."

"Now that you mention it, that voice back there did sound familiar."

"That's why I looked over, to see if it was him."

Rounding a corner, with relief Molly sighted the familiar stretches of grass, bridges, and shops in the distance. She noticed that Heather had increased her pace, passing a group of outrageously outfitted men and women, all hoops, flaps, and bold patterns, when they slowed to look into one of the stores. Almost at a run, Molly caught up to her friend.

"Hey, Heather, slow down. Look. There're the shops way over there. And close by is that statue in front of the courtyard. We're not far from the PortalDoor. There's no reason to hurry. We're almost home."

"Well, we're not safe yet."

Once again, Molly scampered to catch up to Heather's increased pace. "Heather," she said, breathless, "what's the rush?"

"Don't look behind you, Molly, but Borray and his RogueTag buddies are following us."

CHAPTER TWENTY-ONE

A Storm is Brewing

"I knew this was a bad idea," Fallasha said. "We never should have departed from the Parade Day Schedule of Events."

"Maybe not," was all Heather said.

With a quick glance over her shoulder, she noticed that the five Rogue-Tags were perhaps a half-block behind her and Molly, and closing.

"Fallasha, that alley up ahead. Where does it go?"

"I'm not sure. I'm well acquainted with the main streets and sights, but not certain of what lies down the smaller roads and alleyways. It could be a dead end."

"Some tour guide."

"Heather, couldn't we just run for the PortalDoor?" Molly asked.

"We'd never make it without these guys catching us. Come on, Molly." Heather accelerated and passed a few sidewalk strollers, including a short fat woman in a Maiden costume.

"But are you sure they're after *us*? And aren't there any policemen around?"

"Soldiers," Fallasha said. "There are no policemen. The soldiers insure that the Evermorian laws are enforced—along with the laws of whatever kingdom in the Realm they're assigned to, in this case Autumnsloe. Unfortunately, the Soldiers of the Crown can't be counted on to protect us."

"Why not?" Heather asked.

"Well, I'm not certain how much I'm at liberty to divulge—the purpose of our visit today was simply to familiarize you with Autumnsloe, Parade Day, its people, the Maidens, and some of its customs—a slice of Evermore, if you will—the Realm as we wish to remember it. Not this other part."

"What other part, Fallasha?" Heather said. "What do you mean?"

The brooch said, wryly, "It wasn't on my Parade Day Schedule of

Events to familiarize you with RogueTags and the more disreputable elements that seem to be fermenting these days."

"I still don't understand."

"Let's just say that at this time, Autumnsloe—or more aptly, the entire Evermorian Realm—is in a state of transition, and not for the better. A majority of the soldiers are secretly sympathetic with the RogueTags, believing in the rule of HumanKind by HumanKind."

"But aren't we HumanKind?" Heather asked, hastily passing more pedestrians. A large group loitered ahead, gathered in front of a sidewalk performer.

"Yes, but not *their* HumanKind," Fallasha resumed, once they were out of earshot. "They don't believe in outsiders, those who are different."

"And that means they're against the rule of the Maidens?" Molly said, trying to match Heather's pace.

Fallasha's face clouded over. "That's right. And the practice of ArcaniMagia in the land."

"ArcaniMagia? Is that the magic used by Maidens?" Heather asked.

"For the sake of all the Realm, yes, it's the predominate type. There are others."

"Boy, we could sure use some ArcaniMagia now. And a Maiden to go with it. So, Fallasha, as TimeLight visitors here in Evermore," Heather said, glancing over her shoulder, "this is not looking too good for us right now."

"No."

The moon girl passed the performer and his semicircle of spectators, and then after another glimpse behind her, ducked quickly into the alley.

"Come on, Molly!" she said. "Run!"

However clumsy, the two broke into a sprint in their bulky costumes. They ran beneath numerous overhead walkways, past shadowy doorways and barred and boarded windows. Molly had two hands holding her headpiece in place, Heather one, as their feet carried them over the bluish stones that paved the surface. Having descended slightly, the alley began to rise and curve quickly to the left.

The girls could hear numerous footfalls pounding behind them, reverberating through the confining tunnel walls that supported the walks above.

"They must've gone this way," said a RogueTag in pursuit. Both girls recognized the distinctive voice of Borray.

Heather had a lead of five or six paces over Molly. While running through a long unlit tunnel, Heather abruptly stopped and slipped into a shallow alcove to her right. In short order, she reached out to ungraciously snag and pull Molly in beside her.

"Agh—" Molly started, her breaths coming rapidly and in huffs.

In the dimness, Heather's finger went to the lips of her mask. "Shh-h-h-h."

Heather backed her friend behind her into a tight recess, just wide enough for one. If coming from the opposite direction, the moon girl would have been easily visible. As it was, the RogueTags, when passing, would have to look behind them to see the huddled girls.

The stampede of footfalls grew in volume. At the ready, Heather stayed relaxed but primed to defend Molly and herself in a flail of fists, if necessary. She held little if any optimism about their chances against the thugs.

The five were closer now, and they could be heard panting heavily. Moments later, they thundered past the girls' shallow hiding place. Hitting a hollow from a missing stone, one of the RogueTags lost his footing, and with a thud fell heavily to the ground just outside the tunnel, within sight of the secreted pair. Two others, sprinting close behind, tripped over the fallen bruiser, tumbling and skidding to a halt on the rough surface. Curses filled the air.

Backing, Heather squeezed Molly deeper into the cramped recess, though she, herself, still remained discernable in the shadows.

Still on their feet, Borray and another RogueTag continued past in pointless pursuit, hungry for a sighting. Heather could see them dwindling in size, running in and out of sunlight between overhead walks. She watched as they stopped, and after a brief conference split up, the gangly Borray sprinting down a different route, the other continuing forward on his current course.

The nastiest-looking RogueTag, the first to hit the ground, his pants and shirt torn, had slowly found his feet, and was adjusting his armband, pulling it higher. The other two were still down, though one had gotten to his knees and was taking inventory of his parts, currently inspecting a scraped elbow.

"Slatz, where did that 'Lick Borray go, heh?" asked the kneeling Rogue-Tag, Jartt, of the husky thug standing nearby. Pulling a hand dripping with red from his brow, he cursed his bloody forehead.

"He and Marscleff kept after them." Glowering down, the one named Slatz, his hair crewcut-short and bleached white, kicked at the other that was only now beginning to stir. "Spenghett. Spenghett, get up. Come on."

The short, chunky Spenghett groaned, and slowly rolled onto his back. His face was bloodied around the nose. "Slatz," he said, looking up through half-lids, "did we get the AlienDregs?" He brought up a leg, bending it at the knee where his pants sported a large tear. Another groan escaped his lips, this time at a lower volume.

"Not yet, probably not at all. Those two Rogues are useless Dweedles. And the 'Dregs probably got away." Slatz kicked Spenghett again, this time harder, and his meaty belly shook. "Now, get up."

Clumsily, Spenghett managed to stand, joining Slatz and Jartt. Slatz smacked him on the back of his head. Thick and springy, his pile of wild brown hair bounced in place.

"What'd you do that for?" Spenghett's face held a disagreeable twist. He rubbed his head. "You're the one who fell and made us trip over you."

"You deserved it for exactly that. You should have dodged me and caught those two 'Dregs. Now, it's up to Boring and Mushhead. And they're hopeless." Slatz cuffed Spenghett again. Then to the other, "What are you looking at?"

Jartt's ruggedly handsome face was screwed up, squinting into the shadows under the arch. "There," he said, "in the dark under the walk, hch. I thought I saw something move."

Slatz swung around. "Where?"

"There." The tall muscular Jartt pointed, and the trio started towards the niche in the wall where Heather and Molly had taken up hiding. Slatz broke into a run. The others followed.

Being a cold miserable day, it was going to be a stew night tonight, and Grandma Dawn had just finished cleaning the knife and cutting board. It would be awhile before it was time to add the vegetables and potatoes to the beef that was currently simmering in the pot. Pecan and apple pies had recently come out of the oven, and the aromas enticingly mingled to fill the kitchen air. With her yellow coffee press having yielded up a steaming cupful, Grandma Dawn sat down and opened her latest gardening magazine.

When a sudden gust of wind flung open the kitchen door, it startled the engrossed woman. Head darting with a swivel, she rose to close it, her thoughts awhirl.

Sitting down once more to her coffee and magazine, Grandma Dawn found the words of the article meaningless and the pictures of little interest. Her cogitations soon roamed to Heather and Molly, and again she made a wish for their safety. The trembling of the bare trees against the windows above further distracted her from reading, and Grandma Dawn made a mental note to remind Hank to prune the branches back. She sipped her coffee.

Continuous gusts and a low whistling whine brought forth more agitated taps, slaps, and scratches from the trees' limbs, wooden knuckles and bony fingers against the glass. The disturbance caused the woman to look up from the magazine's standoffish words and out at the cumbersome clouds that filled the sky beyond the starkness of trees.

A storm is brewing, Grandma Dawn thought. She felt her restlessness, a desire to confront it immediately, full force. In time, she concluded, all in its time.

When the kitchen door blew open a second time, it confirmed to her that the expected storm was imminent indeed.

"Aw, there's nothing here." It was Slatz.

All three RogueTags were examining the alcove, standing within the tunnel beneath the overpass, the railing above casting a shadow on the sunlit walk behind them. Slatz swung an arm into the empty recess. "If they were here, we'd have seen them. Besides, they couldn't both fit in here; there's not enough room."

"I saw something move," Jartt defended himself with a snarl.

"Spohr!" The blood-smeared Spenghett slapped at Jartt, and the latter responded with a crushing fist to the face, knocking Spenghett sprawling to the ground. Slatz laughed, as holding his broken nose, Spenghett writhed and balled up. "MaidenLick," he spit out at Jartt.

Jartt kicked Spenghett in the head, and he stopped his squirming altogether.

"Something did move, Slatz," the ruffian said, ignoring his unconscious peer. "Let's have another look at that hole in the wall, heh."

Driving in his pickup truck, Sheriff Dane replayed the vision of the dead man found by hikers: dirty, scraggly beard and hair, tattered shirt and pants, an old frayed jacket, and new, square-toed boots. He had been discovered lying on his back, his body suffering a great deal of internal damage after plummeting down the sheer face leading from the cave's mouth. It had been a lengthy drop.

Investigating around and within the partially concealed cave, Dane had found it to be the man's cavernous home, with its many natural tunnels veering off into the heart of the mountainside. Also, the sheriff ruminated over the discovery of the old man's mining implements, sleeping bag, and what was undoubtedly Heather Nighborne's backpack, containing a few books, magazines, and some personal odds and ends.

But the boots. Dane shook his head, pressing on the vehicle's accelerator. The boots.

Grandma Dawn pushed herself away from the table. With her tall gliding walk, she crossed the room to close the kitchen's dutch door that was banging against the wall. Finally able to catch hold of the knob, battling a ferocious blast of wind, with some effort the woman wrestled to close the breach. She was surprised when she heard a voice call, "Don't shut it yet," only to add, "please."

Grandma Dawn looked out to see Mrs. Pringle walking up the path, two suitcases in hand. The burdened woman stopped. The wind, in another prolonged gust, caused her clothes to cling to one side of her body and her hair to wave chaotically at air.

"Lana…?"

Talking over the wind, Mrs. Pringle said, "I know it's an odd question to ask of you, Dawn, but have you got a spare room in the Bristol House for a disillusioned spouse and her lovely young daughter?"

"Wow, Molly, it's a good thing you found that latch in the stone door behind you."

"It was disguised pretty well. I almost didn't. Luckily, I was able to feel it." Molly's mask smiled grimly. "Now what?"

The two were crouching within a small tunnel next to the water, having made their escape through a secretive door at the back of the alcove. It had led to a stairway that took them below street level, where the girls emerged from a discreetly hidden exit alongside a canal. In places, the narrow watercourse flowed against the continuous façades of buildings, their reflections rippling upon the agitated surface. Boats bobbed beneath the footbridges and alongside the landings.

"I think it's time to head back to the PortalDoor," Heather said.

Fallasha added, "Without being seen by Borray and his fellow Rogue-Tags."

"Good thinking," Heather said, the words coming out more sarcastically than intended.

Molly said, "Should we wait for dark?"

"Definitely not!" Fallasha said. "It's far more dangerous. Besides, I'm to have the two of you back to the Bristol House long before then."

Heather and Molly looked at each other.

"What now?" Molly asked.

"I don't know." Heather contemplated, before saying, "I wish we were wearing our clothes under these costumes. We could just leave them here."

Fallasha started to speak, but bit back on her words.

Politicians. Dane despised them as morally weak spotlight-seekers who always choose political expediency over doing what's best for those they serve—if ever they really serve anyone but themselves.

His pickup hit a pothole in the street. He bounced on the seat before beginning to brake.

He mulled over what a college instructor had once declared: Riding the winds of public opinion and special interests, politicians chart their course, aiming for a destination called reelection.

Even in Noble, he concluded. And what's worse, those politicians make my job difficult.

Stopped at the intersection, Sheriff Harland Dane thought about the mayor, thought about the upcoming election, about the mayor's chances for a second term.

Tight race, the sheriff considered. It makes political sense to publicize the discovery, but it creates an unwarranted sense of security among the citizens here in Noble.

Politicians, Dane repeated to himself. I tried to warn him. I sure hope that idiot knows what he's doing.

The traffic light changed to green. Easing into a left turn, Sheriff Dane took a last long drag from the cigarette he had been dangling out the open window. Afterwards, he flicked the remaining stub in an arc to the asphalt below. There it shone for a moment, skittered, restlessly rocked, only to have the roll of a heavy tire crush the light out.

"And so I think it's best that Ned and I separate. And frankly, Dawn, as much as I make it a point never to ask anyone for anything, I was wondering…" Hesitating, Mrs. Pringle searched for words, "…I was wondering if it would be a great inconvenience if I were to ask to stay for a while—Molly and me—until I've had a chance to get my life in order—you know, situate ourselves, sort all this out."

"Lana, you and Molly can stay for as long as you need."

"You don't mind?"

"Of course not."

For several moments, Lana Pringle didn't speak. Grandma Dawn could see her neighbor's façade start to crack, but she maintained her composure. Looking away, Mrs. Pringle reflected, before saying, "I have a feeling that the Bristol House will be a safe place to transition into my new life…"

"About Ned, I assume Molly doesn't know yet. How do you think she'll take it when you tell her?"

"I know that Molly will be shocked, though I'm also hoping she'll be relieved. Maybe she's seen it coming, maybe not. Either way, I think it's important that she stay close to her best friend. She's been through so much: her first dog Rufus, Stilped Roarhowser, the loss of Teacup, and now her parents' separation and probable divorce."

"Well, we'd love to have you stay with us, Lana. I've come to enjoy your company, and as you know, Heather just adores Molly. I'd have to think that she's her only true friend."

"I think they need each other, Dawn. A change has come over Molly just recently, and I've no doubt it's for the better. Spending time with Heather seems to have strengthened my daughter's spirit and lightened her mood. She came home so happy yesterday. I hadn't seen her that way in quite some time."

"I've noticed the change myself."

"As you know, I've been worried about my daughter for some time. Other than Heather and I—and her father—she really isn't close to anyone. And sadly, even though I know he loves Molly, Ned isn't much help to her emotionally, probably because he's so out of touch with his own feelings. Honestly, he just gets in the way."

Grandma Dawn took a sip of coffee, and then focused on her mug. Without looking up, she said, "Lana, I think there are some things you need to know before you decide that the Bristol House is where you'd like to stay."

Behind her cup of tea, Lana Pringle's eyes widened for an instant. She swallowed the sip of hot liquid. "Oh?"

Grandma Dawn considered her words very carefully before speaking: "You know how the Bristol House is somewhat out of the ordinary?" She paused.

Jumping to fill the conversational gap, Mrs. Pringle said, "Well, I'd have to say that I always thought the Bristol House was magical, if that's what you mean. It's beautiful—stunning, actually—to look at. And what you've done with the garden here is beyond description."

"Well, it is magical, in its way, to be sure. And there's so much I want to share with you, so much you should know…" Grandma Dawn exhaled on a gentle sigh. "I'm just not certain where to start—or where to end."

"Dawn, you're sounding *very* mysterious."

Grandma Dawn chuckled. "I'm sorry. Sounding mysterious or in any way dramatic is certainly not my intent. I just don't want to bury you with too much information at once. So, honestly, I'm trying to figure out how much to share with you right now."

"If you're wondering, well, we've got time. It's not like you have to explain everything to me today. Or ever, for that matter."

"It's just that—it's just that if you stay here, there are some things you're bound to find out, whether you want to or not."

"What are you trying to say? You don't practice odd rituals like black magic, things like that, do you?"

"Don't be silly. *Black* magic. Really."

Both ladies were smiling.

"Or harbor dangerous criminals?"

"Only assassins," Grandma Dawn said, lightly.

"Pretend to be someone other than who you are?"

"You'd be surprised."

"Would I?"

"Seriously?" Grandma Dawn looked into her mug. She tried again, "All joking aside, Lana, there's an element of danger when living here—"

"Look, if this is about Stilped, I appreciate your concern, but I believe it's okay now, that it's safe. Everyone in town seems to think the killer is probably long gone. I'm confident that we're just as safe here as we would be at home—more so, in fact, because I don't have Ned around secretly wanting to tie me up and stretch me out on the rack."

Grandma Dawn shared the laugh, grasping her neighbor's need for levity.

Mrs. Pringle continued, "In all seriousness—and I hope that I'm not being too forward—I know you could use the help around here, Dawn, and Molly and I would certainly love to pitch in. Even with Mr. Branson doing the gardening, this place is enormous. I've always wanted to ask how you manage to do it, the two of you in a big ol' house like this?"

"Well, actually, Lana, I've a lot of help here that you've never seen. Most times they're in and out so fast that *I* never see them. But they always seem to get the job done."

"Undoubtedly."

"But if there's ever a need, your help, and Molly's, would be most appreciated and welcome."

"So, it's settled?"

Grandma Dawn nodded. A mirthless smile came to her lips, and they soon parted to accommodate the tilt of her coffee mug. Sipping, she held the liquid behind a thoughtful pucker before swallowing. The sound of her mug coming to rest on the wooden table rang out in the still kitchen. Some branches scraped at the window. Grandma Dawn's gaze found her neighbor.

"What I'm trying to tell you, Lana," she finally said, "is that what's going on with the Bristol House right now might be dangerous. Heather could be in danger. It's a long story, and I'll fill you in with more detail later, but—"

"What do you mean, 'what's going on'? Is there a chance that my Molly could be in danger, too?"

"Quite possibly."

"Is she in danger now, *right now?* Where is she, by the way? I thought she and Heather were here."

"The girls went upstairs earlier. But to answer your question, is she in danger? No, not at the moment." Having said this, Grandma Dawn didn't know whether she truly believed her statement. "Molly is safe, or she wouldn't have been invited to—well, to spend time with Heather today." Grandma Dawn found herself nodding, reinforcing the words.

She saw Mrs. Pringle relax slightly.

"That's good to know."

"As a matter of fact," Grandma Dawn said, "I'd even venture to say that right about now, it wouldn't surprise me if those two girls were having the time of their lives."

"I think at some point we'll need to get out of these costumes and into some Autumnslovian clothes."

"Good idea," Molly said.

Fallasha remained silent.

Heather checked her pockets. She held out the remaining coins for her brooch to see. "Is there enough money to buy clothes for Molly and me in one of the shops?"

"No."

"For just Molly?"

"No."

The girls had crossed over the canal, the bridge connecting to a stone walk on the opposite side. They saw some people near the water on a boat ramp ahead of them, but could tell they weren't RogueTags. Of the four, two were holding hands, another stood idly by, while a fourth tied up a small boat to its moorage.

"We need to get back up to the street," the moon girl said.

"Look over there, Heather, some stairs."

"Great! Let's hurry, Molly. I don't want those RogueTags to find us. Besides, I told Grandma Dawn we'd be home in time for dinner. And I don't know about you, but I'm hungry."

Soon the girls were taking the steps at a brisk rate and had just reached a landing halfway to the street, when they heard someone yell, "There they are!"

Much to their horror, Molly and Heather looked down to see the three nasty RogueTags running over the bridge they themselves had recently crossed.

"Oh, no. They must have found the stone door," said Heather. "Run!"

Molly didn't need prompting as the two scurried up the remaining steps to find themselves on a narrow ramshackle promenade.

"This is not looking good, this is not looking good," Fallasha said.

"Which way?" Molly asked.

Heather glanced left-right.

"This way. Come on."

Molly followed on her friend's heels, clack, clack, clack, the two sprinting down a stretch of alleyway off the promenade before quickly ducking into another: a blur of yellow and green walls; a rhythmic jumbled bounce of door, window, window, door; passageway, passageway; archway, walkway; spattered footfalls; hollow echoes; shadow, light, shadow, light; sudden lefts, quick rights; and all the while the fierce panting of their hot breath sounding out in their ears.

"Are they coming?" Fallasha asked.

"I'm not...stopping...to find out," Heather said, charging into the next turn, through an archway off the current course. It climbed to the left, a series of long drawn out steps.

"It's a dead end," Fallasha said.

"Maybe," said Heather, her breath gasping out the word, before she saw an opening. She took it, and when she was sure Molly had not fallen too far behind, Heather increased her speed turning again left and then right.

Here the alley opened up substantially, gradually becoming a wide street. Buildings were clustered clumsily, some thrusting their facades out farther than others. Many of the structures' upper stories were suspended over the lower, creating a jumbled and claustrophobic feeling. Torn and faded awnings and crumbling overhangs concealed many of the cheerless windows and doorways. Nearby, washing that had been hung out to dry still looked dirty in the dingy light. Heather ran a short distance down the cluttered enclosure, before she unexpectedly reared to a halt. Avoiding some standing water, the girl retraced her steps. She slipped within the cover provided by a sheltered entryway.

Molly turned the corner and slowed when she couldn't see her friend. Heather reached out a hand and waved the butterfly girl to hurry her way. Breathing heavily, they soon huddled together, with Heather again positioning Molly behind her.

In gasps, Molly said, "This place looks, well, dilapidated, compared to what we've seen. It gives me the creeps."

Heather agreed.

"It seems we've found the underbelly of Autumnsloe," said Fallasha.

"Sh-h-h-h," the moon girl warned.

After a moment's silence, Molly said, "I don't hear them." Laced with huffing breath, her words seemed desperate, rather than optimistic. She swallowed and then continued her hardy intakes.

Fallasha said, "Hopefully, they gave up."

Her breathing still heavy, but calmer, Heather said, "Quiet now. Let's listen."

In the narrow confines, the costumed pair waited, endeavoring to silence their ravenous lungs. Momentarily, the girls jumped, when a lock clicked on the door behind them and a deadbolt slid noisily into place.

"Not very welcoming in this part of town," Molly said.

Waiting with ears attuned, the three heard nothing by way of a pursuer's footstep.

Relieved, the butterfly girl said, "I think we lost them."

Heather concurred, but her ears remained aware, awaiting sound.

Finally, she said, "No. They're coming. I can hear them."

Sure enough, it wasn't long before Molly heard the approach of the ruffians, their tread at a gallop.

"Molly," Heather whispered, removing her mask and headpiece, and setting them at her feet. She then shook out her hair and pulled it behind her. "I'm going to lure them away—"

"No!" Molly's voice was urgent, low. Then meekly, "Can't we just stay hidden?"

"No. There's a dead end not too far ahead that you can't see from here. I saw it from a little farther on. After they reach that part of the street and turn around, they'll probably find us on their way back. Right now, we can surprise them. If we wait, we won't have that chance."

Molly noticed the calm that had descended over Heather, the logical, emotionless way she went about talking, doing things, thinking situations through. She thought back to the incidents with Mrs. Peck in the classroom and Mr. Simpletripp down by the creek. Same coolheaded Heather.

"Is there any other way?" Molly asked. "Fallasha?"

"I don't—"

"Quiet, now, and listen," Heather broke in. "I'm going to lure them away, and Molly, you're going to make a rush for the alley, back the way we came."

Molly felt tears of fright begin to well. "No, Heather, I'll stay and fight the RogueTags with you."

"No," Heather said, reaching into her pocket. "You're going to do exactly as I say." The footfalls were closer. "Now, here's the PortalKey. When you see that their attention is totally on me, you run off the other way. Okay?" When the butterfly girl didn't answer, Heather again asked, "Okay?"

Molly looked at her friend. "Heather, aren't you afraid?"

"Doesn't matter."

By this time, the RogueTags had taken the corner and were headed towards the girls, their feet clattering on the stone floor.

"Okay?" Heather's voice was insistent.

Molly, tears rolling down the cheeks of her mask, said quietly, reluctantly, "Yes. All right."

Without delay, Heather peered quickly out of their hiding spot. And a moment later, she hurled herself across the path and below the knees of the first RogueTag that passed.

Molly's eyes widened. She couldn't believe this was happening, that Heather, without hesitation, had just taken on a man so much bigger than herself. He was a *man!* The RogueTags, they were *men*, and mean men at that! What was her friend thinking? Heather is just a girl—we're just girls. Overcome with fright, Molly found herself reluctant to leave the concealing refuge of the entryway. She pressed herself farther into the corner.

Tripping over Heather, Slatz had become airborne. After flipping in midair, he landed roughly on his head and shoulder, before slamming into the jutting facade of a building's brick wall with a conclusive "Ugh!" The big man lay still in a heap.

Heather scrambled to her feet, and backed away from where Molly was still holed up, moving towards a more spacious area within the widening triangular cul-de-sac.

"What the—?" Jartt pulled up, and shooting a look at the condition of his friend, his handsome features turned ugly. Wheeling on Heather, he snarled, "You little 'Dreg, I'm going to tear the limbs off that skinny body of yours, heh."

"Would you really hurt a girl?" Heather asked, backing farther away. She held out her hands. Plain as day, "Look. I'm just a girl."

From within her hiding place, upon hearing her friend's words, Molly marveled. Despite her fears, somehow Heather's voice gave her courage, hearing her friend speak with a RogueTag, trying to reason with him and make him aware of his shameful act of picking on a girl. It instilled in her a wary confidence: Maybe I *can* escape, she thought.

"Would you really hurt a child?" Heather asked again.

Jartt took a glimpse at his disabled companion. He smiled crookedly. "All I can say is, 'just watch.'"

Heather's gaze darted back towards the alley for an instant, but she couldn't see a third party.

Only the two, she thought.

Thriving on the rush of adrenaline coursing through her system, Heather continued to back up into the broader space, giving her friend more room to make a getaway.

And now Molly was cautiously inching out of the doorway shadows, stealing a glimpse at the downed RogueTag and at the broad back of Jartt sizing up the dwarfed Heather, before focusing in the direction of her escape route. Quietly, though not without harboring a sense of guilt at abandoning her friend, she followed Heather's instruction, returning the way they had come. And with each new step towards freedom, her pace increased.

The bulky Jartt approached, and Heather, with her girl hands relaxed and in front of her, hunkered down, expecting a rush from her combatant. Her green eyes never wavering from the man, Heather wanted to ask Fallasha how Molly was doing, but didn't dare. As the youngster slowly and steadily retreated, her brooch was able to track Molly's progress and remained optimistic, though mute.

A brawler, Jartt moved in closer, upright and cocky. "I don't know who you are or where you're from, TimeLight 'Dreg, but I doubt you're going home. I mean it, heh. Your friend, either, when we catch her."

Ignoring his words and just out of his reach, the girl steadily drew the RogueTag deeper into the cul-de-sac. If he charged, she didn't want to sidestep him, putting him in position to view Molly—if her friend was still visible at that point. But Heather also knew, if this brute tried to tackle her, she couldn't withstand the full impact of his large body and still have any chance of escaping.

Jartt spewed boasts, insults, and threats, before gesturing over his shoulder towards the recessed doorway. "Is she in there, too?"

"What?"

"Your friend. Is she there?" Menacingly, he crouched, ready to grapple.

"Where?" Heather asked, her gaze never leaving her attacker.

"Back there," and when Jartt turned to give a glance towards Heather and Molly's most recent hiding spot, Heather promptly stepped forward and threw a fist towards his eye. She connected.

Jartt recoiled, stood up straight, and then laughed, the girl retreating to reposition herself. "That's it? That's the best you can do?" He laughed again, though his eye was swelling, watering. Reluctant to admit it, the girl's punch had rocked him. She was strong. "'Dreg, I'm going to tear you up, heh, and when I'm done, I'm going to feast on your tender flesh."

Heather remained mute, still just beyond his reach. Behind Jartt, she noticed that the first RogueTag had started to stir, to slowly roll over, though he hadn't gotten up.

As Heather expected, Jartt finally charged. He lunged at her, intending to crush the girl within the clench of his muscular arms, but she quickly ducked, dropping to a knee. Heather seized the tall man's ankle, and though he reached down to grab hold of her, he was a second and a swipe too late. The girl had promptly yanked upward, lurching to her feet in the process, pulling Jartt off balance.

As the RogueTag fell backward and hit the ground, Heather tried to rush past him, but he was quick to trip her up with a foot. She cushioned her fall with her hands, but felt Jartt take hold of her shoe. He twisted, and Heather's mouth went open with the stab of pain, yet she rolled with the motion, using her momentum to pull herself free in the process. Planting her hands, the girl bucked and lashed out hard, managing to kick the RogueTag in the groin.

Jartt doubled up. Already on the ground, he rolled to his side, curling into a fetal position, his hands at his crotch.

In no time, Heather was on her feet and running after Molly.

"Great work!" Heather heard Fallasha say, not too loudly. "Wait! Don't forget your headpiece!"

The first RogueTag, Slatz, was still groggy, having crawled to his hands and knees. Giving him a wide berth in passing, Heather quickly dipped into the doorway for her headpiece and mask. She turned and took five rapid strides towards her escape, before coasting to a standstill.

"Going somewhere, 'Dreg?"

A crestfallen Heather said, "Oh, Molly..."

"Oh, no," Fallasha echoed in an undertone.

His nose crooked, his face still smeared with blood, the third Rogue-Tag, Spenghett, swaggered short and fat behind Molly. Her mask removed and in her hand, she was crying. He pushed her roughly, and she staggered forward, dropping her beautiful butterfly mask to the ground.

"You 'Licks, she almost got away," Spenghett called casually to his companions. When he noticed they were not only on the ground, but injured, he quickly wrapped his arm tightly around Molly. Hoisting her in front of him as if she were a shield, he backed up a defensive pace or two, asking, "Who else is here?" Frantically, he searched the doorways. He took another step backward and pointed at Heather with his free hand: "Stay right there!" Now scanning the windows, he noticed the frightened faces as they withdrew. "Tell me who else is here? Who did this?"

Heather remained stationary. And mute.

"Her arms are pretty thin," the RogueTag said, a little too loudly in case there was an unseen accomplice. Spenghett's plump hand gripped Molly's small wrist. "It's so easy to give it just a little twist." He started to put pressure on the forearm, turning it unnaturally away from the elbow. "See? So easy." Molly grimaced. The RogueTag leered at Heather. "Now, 'Dreg, who did this to my fellow Rogues?"

Heather looked over at Slatz, who had risen unsteadily to his feet. His pale head was hanging, his body supported by an arm against the wall.

"I did," said the slender moon girl in the bulky costume.

The Rogue scoffed. "Right." Putting more pressure on Molly's arm, her eyes squeezing shut and her mouth stretching open to cry out, Spenghett shifted his attention.

"Slatz, who did this?"

"I told you," Heather said, "I did—"

"Shut up, you! Slatz?"

Still propped against the wall, Slatz slowly turned his head towards his RogueTag companion.

"She did," he said, thrusting a chin at Heather. "The 'Dreg was hiding in the doorway there, and when I went running by, she jumped out and tripped me."

"Did she now?" Spenghett laughed at his friend, relaxing his grip on Molly. "I can understand. After all, a little girl like that can be a tough match for someone so much bigger than she is." He laughed again. "And Jartt, what happened to you?"

"Save the question and answer period, heh, 'Lick." Having stood, and now walking sluggishly and with a slight hitch towards Heather, the powerfully built Jartt said, "I think we have some business to attend to, don't we, 'Dreg?"

Heather was also aware of Slatz approaching from the rear, but she did nothing out of concern for Molly.

"I got her," Slatz said, brutally snatching Heather's arms and yanking them behind her. The girl stifled a grunt as her mask and headpiece tumbled out of her hands. Leaning over Heather's shoulder to look her in face, the RogueTag spoke through clenched teeth, "I could break you in half right now, do you know that? You're such a brittle little thing."

"Leave some for me," Jartt called, stopping to grimace and painfully adjust himself.

Heather noticed the continuous discoloration and swelling of his eye where she had punched him. Molly noticed, too.

"Sure," said Slatz. "Grab your knife, Rogue." Again speaking into Heather's face, he said, "I think we'll cut this one in teeny, tiny pieces."

Heather leaned her head away from his noxious breath.

From his belt, Jartt's knife flicked into being with a snap of the wrist, the steel blade catching a silvery glint. "Life isn't all fun and games, now is it, 'Lick?" he said, again approaching. "Business, heh. I love getting down to business."

Laughing and enjoying himself very much, his devilish face alight, Slatz spoke to Molly, "And now, introducing a different type of Autumnslovian magic: before your very eyes, we'll happily slice your friend to pieces." Fresh tears quietly trickled down Molly's cheeks. The RogueTag, Spenghett, sensing her hopeless submission, released his grip altogether; though he stood at the ready should the girl suddenly bolt. "And you can watch us do it, too. You don't even have to move a muscle." When Molly sobbed, the RogueTag asked, below a thick raised brow, "You *do* want to watch your friend be butchered to pieces, don't you?" Slatz roughly jerked Heather. "It makes for such fond travel memories."

Molly shook her head and spoke softly, wetly, "Please don't hurt her."

Slatz turned to share a greedy moment in connivance with the nearby

Jartt. "Please don't hurt her? *Please don't hurt her?*" He guffawed. "And why not? If you like, we'll even cut you a prime slice of moon-filet. You can take it home with you and share it among friends. But you mustn't forget to mention that it's a souvenir from the lovely Autumnsloe, from our welcoming TimeLight home to yours." Possessing a self-satisfied smile, Slatz ceremoniously bowed his white head of shortly cropped hair. Then he mischievously looked up and added, "With our blessings. Eh, boys?"

He turned to each, and they shared in a raucous laugh.

Yet for the jeering Slatz, if only he had kept his attention affixed to his captive's face rather than her friend's, he might have noticed the unusual change that took place. It was in Heather's eyes. They turned from light green to crystalline amber.

surprising Dispatches and a jelly Donut

Whack! Bounce, bounce, bounce, dribble, dribble, roll.

Suspicious, Slatz watched. Jartt stopped in his tracks and then began to warily backpedal. Spenghett took a single step backward. When her amber eyes momentarily caught Molly's attention, Aria smiled: private joke. Discreetly, she winked.

It was a brilliant ball that bounced among the five—not too small, not too large—a pattern of stars, suns, and moons: a spirited orb, circus colors. It landed loudly and echoed within the confines of the dead end street. Fascinated, everyone watched as the sphere, indifferently running its course with an occasional tiny hop, struck a stone post. At a loss for momentum, it caromed and puttered to a standstill.

The ball seemed to have come from nowhere.

Not sure what to make of it, Slatz pulled his captive with him to one side of the lane, while Jartt, knife in hand, withdrew to the opposite wall. Still standing at the street's center, Molly thought to take a sly deliberate step away from Spenghett, who remained behind her, nearest the alley entrance. The less than bright RogueTag paid little notice, nervously scanning the cluttered surroundings.

"Who threw that?" Jartt asked, his gaze cast to the rooftops. And then louder, "Who threw that, heh?"

No answer. The ruffians exchanged glances of bewilderment.

Another ball hurtled to the ground: bounce, bounce, bounce. And then another. More still. Soon, from out of the sky, balls rained down upon the street, vivid blurs hitting and slapping off the stone floor, off each other, and off the RogueTags, who ducked and shielded their heads. The deluge of balls became so concentrated that it was hard to see.

"Hey, what's going on here?" Slatz yelled, but his voice was lost to the bouncing and careening of balls. He had let go of Aria, the girl stepping away from him, head down. Not one ball touched her. Or Molly.

When the downpour finally subsided, the last few balls bounced innocently away and settled along the periphery of the lane.

"What was that all about, heh?" Jartt asked, scanning the sky, circling in place.

Slatz pointed. "Spenghett! Above you!"

Spenghett immediately threw up a chubby forearm and cowered behind it. Cautiously, he peered out. Hovering nearby was yet another brightly patterned ball, spinning slowly and with menace. In an instant, the orb flitted left and then feinted right. The next moment it slowed its spin, hanging back at a threatening distance.

"What the *sturk*?" Jartt said.

The ball took off toward the knife-wielding RogueTag, then abruptly stopped. Jartt flinched. The ball retreated.

"It's playing with you," Slatz said. He backed, his attention never leaving the sphere.

Spenghett straightened up and laughed, letting down his guard. "You 'Licks, it's only a ball. It can't hurt you. Someone around here is practicing their magic, that's all, trying to make us look like fools."

"You dumb Rogue, this isn't the work of a beginner," Slatz said. "Look around, look for the eyes."

"SearEye?" Spenghett asked, suddenly wary. "Here?"

When the shower of balls had first begun to pour down on the immediate surroundings of the neighborhood, a sprinkling of Autumnslovians had ventured out in curiosity, though they watched from the shadows, fearing RogueTag recognition and reprisal. Others continued to observe from the windows.

Rattled, the RogueTags scrutinized the onlookers, though Spenghett kept glancing back at the intimidating sphere.

"See anyone with the eyes?" Jartt asked, wiping the palm of his free hand across his chest.

"I don't," Spenghett said. "Slatz?"

"No." But the white-headed RogueTag continued to search. "This isn't an amateur production, Rogues. Watch out. I bet there's a Maiden around here somewhere."

In search of a shield, Slatz started forward to reapply a grip to his child-captive. With her face diverted, Aria thrust out her arm between them, creating a tension-filled distance. "Don't touch me." Her voice was firm, authoritative.

"You're joking, right?" the RogueTag sneered. "Get over here."

As he attempted to grab her, a circling pulse of bluish electricity rolled down Aria's arm, and then over her wrist, before it came to sizzle and arc at her fingertips. Slatz froze, and then retracted. Slowly, Aria raised her head and turned her eyes on the tough guy, glaring up at him.

His jaw sagged. "No… Wait…" The RogueTag gave a little laugh, and with trembling hands before him, he began to retreat. "The eyes. Right-so, I get it. It's you doing this…" He grinned to pacify. "Look. We were just having some fun…"

Her posture commanding, Aria stared, two points of neon-green ablaze. Wincing, Slatz threw an arm up before his ashen face and looked away. A quick read of Molly's eyes showed him no glow, no threat; then to the hovering sphere that, rotating slowly, seemed to be biding its time; and afterward, back to the girl with SearEye. The wide lane suddenly felt small, cramped.

The RogueTag's unusual behavior wasn't lost on Jartt and Spenghett.

"Slatz, what's going on, heh?" Confused, Jartt's instinct told him to stay put. He glanced at Aria, but from his angle was unable to completely see her face. "What's with the kid?"

"Yeah, what?" Spenghett pulled his gaze from the floating orb and focused on the shrinking Slatz. He saw the back of the blonde girl between the white-haired RogueTag and himself. "Afraid, 'Lick? Of what?" Reaffirming Molly's position nearby, he turned once again to the ominous globe. "What gives?"

Shying from Aria, Slatz continued to give ground, looking to bolt. "Look, it was all a joke," he mumbled, his desperate glances shooting the enclosure of street and cul-de-sac. "Honest." He laughed his little laugh again, this time at a higher pitch. "We really weren't going to hurt you."

The girl glaring SearEye turned from the retreating RogueTag, and strode confidently towards Molly, near the center of the wide street. Sensing a presence above, Aria's keen vision swept the sky and fixed on a large bird. Having previously circled and descended, it was beating its wings, landing on a rooftop's edge. Its feathers were a glistening blue, almost black, its beak sharply curved. On its upper chest, below a long gray and red vertically striped neck, was the feathered mark of the sorceress Mistraya: a purple flame.

I thought so, Aria said to herself.

"There, heh! SearEye!" Jartt pointed his knife in accusation. He began to draw back. "I thought that dweedle Borray said these 'Dregs were TimeLight travelers…"

Angling toward Molly on resolute steps, Aria asked, "Why is it that large strong men such as yourselves simply can't behave and have need to pick on innocent young girls? In case you haven't noticed, we're small and helpless—meek, in fact."

Realizing that Molly could be a strategic pawn in their current predicament, and if needed, could possibly lead to a safe release, Slatz said, "Quick, Spenghett! Grab the girl!"

Molly recoiled.

Aria tsked. "These boys, so rude."

As Spenghett made a rush to grab Molly, Aria reached a hand towards the floating orb, as if she were taking hold of the distant object. Without breaking stride, her lips at a murmur, lyricying, she cast her hand sharply downward, and the restless ball streaked towards Spenghett. The Rogue-Tag tried to duck in his defense, but was too late, the ball striking him flush in the forehead with a loud thwack. His head snapped backward and his body followed, sending his chubby form crashing to the ground. There he laid, spread out and broken, his features immobile, slack.

"Really," Aria said, now positioned alongside Molly. "Can't you three just play nicely? Pick up a good book? Take in an opera?"

Jartt looked at Slatz. "What's she talking about?"

After rocketing off Spenghett, the ball landed and bounced heavily on the street. The sound made by the unruly sphere on the flat stones was solid, as if made of wood or some other dense material. Its bright colors spinning cheerfully, the ball rolled to a benign stop.

With Aria positioned between the cul-de-sac entrance and himself, Slatz began to panic, desperate in his need for escape.

On the other side of the street, Jartt's attention was fixed on the young girl so easily showing them up. His features gripped in ugly contempt, he craved to bring her down.

Aria kept track of the RogueTags before and to each side of her, the downed Spenghett still splayed out cold. She gave Molly the offhand directive, "When you're standing this close, as with your sun, don't look directly at my eyes for any sustained interval."

Though she wanted to draw closer, Molly stayed in place nearby, leaving Aria sufficient room to maneuver.

Addressing the RogueTags, Aria said: "Perhaps we need to find a lockup for the three of you." Her luminescent eyes found Spenghett, "Or a hospital…"

"A lockup," said Jartt. "Oh, yeah, sure. If that's what you want, we'll happily oblige and turn ourselves in. Won't we, Slatz?" He laughed. "Slatz, come on, heh. Let's go surrender to some soldiers. We know a few, don't we? Friends of ours." He laughed again, though under the current circumstances, his companion was unable to share his humor.

"Spare us the jokes, Rogue. I don't think now is the time to push it."

Standing center stage, lyricying, Aria extended her arm, palm downward, and then slowly raised it.

Along the cul-de-sac's perimeter, one by one, as if filled with helium, the balls began to rise. They collected in large and small clusters and climbed steadily past the windows and eaves, to hover above the rooftops.

While directing this small bit of magic, Aria said to Jartt, "You know, I think there's still an offhand chance that a little man like you could learn some manners. What do you say? Tell me you'll behave yourself and mend your wicked ways." Aria was grinning. "I'm waiting. Promise me."

"Ugly Spohr. Like I care what you think, heh. I'm not scared of you, or any Maiden!" He stabbed the air.

Slatz said, "Rogue, shut up! Don't listen to her cobble-talk. I'm telling you, don't tease the flame."

"Yeah, yeah, yeah…" Jartt was quickly scanning side to side, checking out distances, plotting possibilities. Noting Molly's close proximity to Aria, the RogueTag prudently considered other options as he began to cautiously sidle back towards the alleyway entrance.

The heavy ball, which had incapacitated Spenghett, had again risen. Under the careful scrutiny of Slatz and an occasional glance from Jartt, it continued to buoyantly ascend to join the others that had amassed in bunches, like gigantic grapes. Still standing in safety near Aria, Molly watched, her head back, mouth partially open, as the colorful spheres set sail over the rooftops.

"Rogue, look around you," Slatz said.

In places throughout the cul-de-sac, Jartt saw more people beginning to collect. At his glare, some withdrew, while others, no longer afraid, continued to openly observe the event.

"It's a show, we're putting on a show," Slatz said, searching in vain for possible RogueTag sympathizers.

Aria chuckled. "And it's certainly not your best performance." She turned, calling out to the crowd, "If it's not too much trouble, would someone here kindly fetch a soldier, a superior preferably. These Rogue-Tags need a lockup, a place where they can reexamine their misspent youth."

Still inching towards a possible escape, Jartt paid no heed to the girl. Rather, sensing her distraction to be in his favor, he took to his heels, bolting for the exit.

The movement wasn't lost on Aria. Quickly, she waved an arm as more incantational words spilled from her lips.

In his seemingly uncontested escape, Jartt skidded to a halt with much of the street still before him.

"Run! Run! Get some help, Rogue! Run!" Slatz shouted. Then, his shoulders suddenly slack: "Why are you stopping, fool?"

"Listen!"

"What? I don't hear any—"

"Shut up and listen, heh, 'Lick! You'll hear it." Jartt hastily reversed course.

The sound. Everyone now heard it. At first almost imperceptible, it had grown steadily louder, a whooshing sound, continuous, rising and falling in volume.

"Slatz!" Jartt gestured with his knife. "Over there!"

Around the corner had come a figure in an ongoing somersault, head over heels, head over heels, whoosh, whoosh, whoosh, whoosh.

Its body an uninterrupted blur, it was hard to distinguish the features in motion. Hair flying, the acrobat was heading towards Jartt. In a flash, the tumbler came to a standstill, feet planted firmly on the ground. Hands on hips, blocking Jartt and his escape at the alley's mouth, stood acrobat-Aria. An excited buzz passed through the electrified crowd.

"You?" Jartt said. "But I thought you were over there." He pointed behind him, then turned, only to face the original Aria still standing where he had last seen her. SearEye. The RogueTag squinted.

Aria smiled and raised her hand, wiggling the fingers. They could have tinkled. Her words were bright: "Hello, there."

When Jartt returned his gaze to the second Aria, she leapt and threw herself into more somersaults, becoming a blur once again. As she bounded towards the thug, her flips grew in both height and distance. Blade at the ready, the RogueTag waited. Following the last bounce, the tumbler tucked and spun through the air—very high, very far. As the wheeling Aria descended towards his head, Jartt lashed out and up with his knife. Upon impact with the point: POP!, she burst like a bubble, rupturing into shreds. Those fragments soon enlarged and reshaped themselves into more tumblers yet—eight, ten, twelve!—bouncing around the befuddled Jartt.

"What the—?" Jartt looked at the tip of his blade, as if he didn't recognize it.

When passing, the Aria-like acrobats were lashing out at the knife-wielding RogueTag in an onslaught of slaps, kicks, and elbows. He side-stepped and squirmed evasively.

"Agh! Slatz! Help me!"

When the stationary Aria shot the white-haired Rogue a SearEyed warning, Slatz didn't dare move.

Jartt started to run, but the onslaught quickened. With one eye already puffy, his nose and mouth running red, he went on the offensive. The harassed RogueTag sliced the next tumbling-Aria that came his way, and the explosion of pieces transformed into a rabble of small red birds. Up to the rooftops they raced, setting into flight the larger, striped-neck observer that had perched there earlier. Molly watched the little birds dart and dive, their long narrow beaks scoring and harassing the less maneuverable scout, its wings ponderously beating a retreat.

"Wow," the butterfly girl said to Aria, "that was magnificent!"

"Thank you."

The spectators applauded. Aria bowed her head slightly, modestly.

Still attempting to evade the unrelenting assault of the tumblers, Jartt continued to dip, dodge, and hack.

Aria said, "Heather, think of something you really like."

Heather came to the fore, the searing green eyes fading in intensity. "What?"

"Quickly, now, Heather. Something you like."

"Right now?

"Yes."

"Why?"

"Heather! So many questions. Just think of something you like. Hurry!"

"Okay, I've got it."

"What did you choose?"

Heather told her.

Everyone watched as Jartt lashed out again, and this time the shards of bursting acrobat turned into a spray of syrupy rectangles and red sliced bobbles, splattering to the ground in clumsy chunks below his feet. The RogueTag found himself slipping about, his free hand plunging to the ground to maintain his balance. This time the ever-increasing crowd roared with laughter.

"Strawberry Waffles?" Molly giggled.

Aria laughed.

While his futile slashes raked the air, amid the tumblers' strikes and prods, Jartt covered and fought his way to more sound footing nearby.

"Your turn, Molly. Quickly now."

"Me?" She thought for a moment. "All right, I have it." She whispered in Aria's ear.

When Jartt struck with his knife yet again, and another acrobat was punctured, its remnants transformed into a swarm of fluttering butterflies of all varieties. They encircled the frustrated RogueTag in a dizzying funnel, his ineffectual weapon flailing out of the quavering cloud. The spectators clapped and cheered once more. A few cries of 'hurrah!' were heard. Rising above the spectators, the butterflies reshaped into autumnal leaves and scattered on the breeze.

Fallasha, caught up in the magic, couldn't help herself, saying, "Now *that* was a spectacular display, Molly."

A bit jealous, Heather rolled her eyes and muttered, "Predictable."

Aria laughed again.

Molly said, "This is fun."

As the Aria-acrobats continued to flip and bound in the vicinity of the confounded Jartt, his knife still stabbing and lashing, he glanced over at his useless companion.

"Help me, Slatz!"

"What? What do you want me to do, Rogue?"

"Allow me to suggest 'nothing,'" Aria said.

"I don't know!" Jartt continued. "But just don't leave me here like this, heh!" He swung his head to one side, but was unable to elude a smack to the cheek. His blade lashed out in vain. "Think of something! Hurry!"

Aria shrugged an 'I warned you.'

Slatz swung around, scrabbling to secure a weapon from among the clutter lining the wall behind him. Spotting a thick iron bar, he hurriedly bent to retrieve it. When he looked up, however, he didn't have time to protect himself with his newly acquired weapon. Descending towards him like a vicious buzz saw was an Aria-tumbler. At the last instant, her legs unfolded, and with feet forward, she smashed into the face of the astonished Slatz.

"Surprise!"

His weapon jarred loose, the RogueTag crashed into crates of discards and large barrels of refuse. The acrobat bounced up, and kicking off the wall, catapulted skyward in a great arc. Landing on her feet, the Aria-lookalike immediately transitioned into leaping somersaults, returning to join the attack on the hounded and battered Jartt. The feat elicited a great round of applause from the crowd clustered along the street's perimeter and bunched deeply at the far end of the cul-de-sac.

"Help!" Jartt yelled, fending off blows. "Someone here help me!"

Among the throng, the Rogue found few if any sympathizers—save one. Still in costume, his Mark of the Purple Flame hidden, he observed the events unamused.

"Your turn, Fallasha," Aria announced.

"Really? I get a turn? Oh, how utterly exciting." The moon brooch thought for an instant. "All right."

Aria leaned her head down, listened, and then nodded. "Here we go."

She sent another tumbler spinning in the direction of the flagging Jartt: whoosh, whoosh, whoosh, whoosh, whoosh. With a thrust, the knife hit home and the acrobat burst into a cloud of fine, fine shards that collected and reformed into more than a dozen huge sewing needles, each threaded with a tail of colored rope.

Drawing an imaginary loop above her head, Aria sent them, like missiles, circling and climbing upward before plunging at the whirling blurs of her likeness that were springing about. Pierced by the large needles, the acrobats burst into flurries of glossy ribbon, yellows, reds, greens, and blues. Easily adrift, they sailed into the eager hands and mouths of the nearby children. To their delight, when captured, the long pieces of confetti became chewy strips of gummy candy.

By now, all the spectators were riveted on the gigantic needles as they flew overhead in widening circles, before turning their needly points on the last of the three bullies.

"No!"

Frantic, Jartt ran in erratic starts and stops as the slivered projectiles, now flying low to the ground, honed in on him. Nearer they came, closing in from all sides, metal streaks in a targeted rush towards his body. He fell to his knees and covered up, quaking. Yet, directly before piercing the RogueTag's flesh, the needle noses pulled up as though steered by a crack team of acrobatic pilots. Swoosh! At once, the steel rails climbed, impressively soaring in tight formation. People cheered. Those spectators whose views were blocked by rooftops leaned out or ran to the street's center. There, they followed the paths of the silver streaks that ascended ever higher, their reflective bodies winking with sun. An instant later, the array of needles spread apart, pulling away from their collective center. Flaring across the vaulted backdrop of the heavens, some burst, crack! crack! crack!, into bright splashes of color, filling and tinting the once blue sky.

The stunt was greeted with resounding applause, wild screams, cheers, and whistles. Meanwhile, Jartt had risen to his feet, his pants soaked. He noticed that the onlookers were absorbed in the flight of the needles, and with all attention focused elsewhere, he decided the moment was ripe to steal away. However, upon taking his first step, a prolonged, ear-splitting screech could be heard, filling the air. Stopping in his tracks,

Jartt looked skyward to find that the remaining missiles were plummeting directly at him. He cried out and again threw himself to the ground, where he covered, the oversized needles screaming to earth in a circle around him. There, they shattered the stone surface, the ground shuddering with their rapid-fire impact. When Jartt looked up, he found himself caged, locked in on all sides behind the tall glistening shafts.

More applause and cheers erupted. Jartt seized and shook the bars that now trapped him. He howled in frustration.

"That was dazzling," Molly said to Aria.

"Truly an amazing display of iMagiNacia," Fallasha joined in. "I've heard so much about it, but never thought I'd come to witness its practice." Anticipating Molly's question, the brooch added, "iMagiNacia, a powerful specialized magic rarely performed anymore, where ordinary or playful objects are utilized as weapons—and at times, deadly weapons."

Briefly rising to take possession, Heather beamed proudly. "Wow! I didn't know you could do that, Aria. Sure beats pushing down teachers."

The crowd didn't stop cheering wildly until Aria gave a reluctant wave and followed that with another humble bow of the head.

To those assembled, when the applause had died somewhat, Aria asked, "By any chance, did anyone alert the authorities?" Her words rang out in the alley.

A voice replied, "Yes, but the soldiers will be slow in coming."

The girl wasn't surprised.

Briefly left to himself in the uproar and celebration, the encircled Jartt had managed to grab two ends of the colored rope that hung within reach. Pulling, he scrambled deftly up the needles and then vaulted over the top, landing catlike on his feet. Those around him began to scream. Flaunting his knife, the thug was on the move again, warding off the milling throng.

Aria had momentarily turned her attention away from the RogueTag. When she looked his way once more, the girl found the ruffian's cell empty. "You!" she called out, spying Jartt. "RogueTag!" At the girl's calling, the crowd quieted. "Enjoying your newfound freedom?"

Upon hearing Aria's words, and after some alert teens eluded him, Jartt latched onto a bystander, an unassuming and overweight middle-aged man. "Come here, you!" Muscling to perform a half-turn, a knife to his captive's throat, the RogueTag began to back down the street.

"Help! My TrueMate! Linnedin!" The woman's screams mixed with more screams, as confused, the crowd proceeded to make way for the ruffian.

"If anyone tries to stop me—including *her*—well, you know the story. See this man's neck, heh?" Jartt swiftly swiped the knife in front of the prisoner's soft pink throat for effect. "Wide open. I mean it."

Aria looked on as the RogueTag continued his cumbersome escape. Occasionally, he shot a glimpse over his shoulder, appraising the distance to the alley's entrance.

"And you," Jartt shouted, pointing threateningly with the shaft of his weapon, "I wouldn't think of following."

"Me?" Aria laughed. "I haven't the slightest inclination. However, chances are you won't get far."

The RogueTag's expression was smug, victorious. "Well, just you watch."

"It will be my pleasure."

The crowd was a jumble. Some observers, watching the RogueTag exit with his captive, were stunned into silence, while a handful, still unaware, were talking excitedly about what they had recently witnessed.

Jartt, dragging the frightened Linnedin, continued to backpedal and stepped around the stone-still Spenghett. Finding that lugging his hostage in retreat was unwieldy and irritating, the thug hoisted the man off the ground, a powerful arm strapped across the yielding belly.

Glancing before him and occasionally to the rear, Jartt didn't notice that large twisted vines were pushing up from beneath the flat stones that comprised the roadway's surface. Bunching and knotting only a short distance behind, they began to crawl in his direction. As the Rogue-Tag turned his head, a tendril entangled his heel, and with his prisoner pressed to his upper body, he toppled over backward.

The overweight man landed on Jartt's chest, knocking the wind out of the brawny youth, his knife rattling to the ground nearby. Now wrapping about his ankles, the vines began to entrap Jartt's lower legs. Dazed and gasping for air, the ruffian lay momentarily helpless as Linnedin rolled off him. The RogueTag tried in vain to maintain a grip on the hostage, but his arms held little strength. The man busted free and ran to his TrueMaite, the crowd separating and then closing ranks behind him. Room was made around the downed Jartt, the throng backing away.

Vision temporarily blurred, Jartt sat up, his large chest heaving. Taking deep breaths to recover, he noticed that the thickly rooted vines now entrapped his thighs. In an instant, the RogueTag had retrieved his weapon and was slicing at the greenery. When a coil of vine grabbed his wrist, the knife sprang free and skittered out of reach. Jartt rolled over, pulling the mass of entanglement with him, and fought to unsteadily gain his feet. Yet from all sides the vines kept reaching, adding to the restraints to further impede his movement. Soon he was immobile, enveloped to the neck.

At once, thrusting their way through the stone floor, a series of thick rigid stalks sprang up, large buds forming at the tips of each. Bulbous and swaying on end, they surrounded Jartt, leaning in lightly, tauntingly close to his face.

"Let me out of here!" Frantic, his large body heaved at the vines piled thickly around him. "Let me go, heh! You hear? Let me go!"

A few in the crowd cheered, while a spattering of others clapped. Most remained silent, however, watching with fascination.

The buds surrounding the RogueTag swelled and peeled, and large flowers bloomed, their petals frilly in white and pink. Emerging, rising at their centers, were elfin, dainty ballerinas, one to a flower. Slow to unfold, extending supple bit by supple bit, their heads poised, their proffered limbs weightless and fluid, they reached and arose to stand on tiptoe. With tiny steps they rotated, pitter-pat, their arms gracefully sweeping air, their lacy dresses of lithe petal swaying and bobbing. And when they had finished a complete revolution, they bent close to the head of the captured Jartt.

"Agh! What are you doing, heh? Get out of here, get out of my face!" The RogueTag snarled and snapped at those closest, but was unable to snatch them with his teeth. He spit. "Get out of here!"

Each bringing up their hands to form a cup, the pixielike creatures blew forcefully. A stream of minute blossoms left their upturned palms and swirled past Jartt's defiant features.

"Stop! Stop that!"

Dazzled, the dancers watched as their lively blooms, like dust, departed up the tormented man's nostrils, into his ears, and past his lips.

The RogueTag began to scream, his voice growing ever louder, until it tore the air in a prolonged, agonized wail. Abruptly, the howling ceased, and with his irises rolling back into his head, Jartt trembled, shaking the encompassing vines.

Dully, he refocused, and watching the smear of ballerinas that now flew before him on wings plucked from petals, he began to laugh, although his eyes remained overcast and somber. His laughter was wicked and inspired, prolonged and pitiable.

When the circling dancers dissolved and entered his pupils, Jartt threw back his head, wrenching it side-to-side. An instant later the RogueTag began to sob. His head tumbled, lolling ungracefully upon his neck. Tears flowed and words were muttered: "I promise, I promise, yes, I promise... I do, I do, I do..."

As his large arms and shoulders reared back, and his spine arched, snapping loose some of the vines that tethered him, he screamed out, *"I promise!"* And when a jarring spasm shook his body, Jartt's head slumped forward to a heavy end.

"There." Aria punctuated the word with a small but firm bounce of her chin. "I thought you would."

Around the motionless RogueTag, the flowers that had danced to and fro withered and receded to the earth.

While Aria pulled Molly closer and those assembled gave ground, large bulky vines continued to crawl along the street's surface, originating from a source near Jartt. The braided, ragged greenery twined around Slatz's wrists and upper arms, and pulled him noisily from the heap of refuse where he lay. Another vine found Spenghett and looped itself securely around his ankle. Both RogueTags were dragged towards Jartt, where a thickly bundled stalk had climbed up the back of his shirt, sending branches throughout the tangle of vines that encompassed him. Shooting up into the air, Jartt was hoisted high upon the tapering trunk. Slatz and Spenghett soon joined him, their prevailing vines winching up the two to dangle in unwieldy fashion beneath their fellow RogueTag, with Spenghett upside-down. Left this way, the defeated RogueTags would be on display for all to see until the soldiers arrived to cut them down, and then the street would heal itself.

Once again, those gathered broke into roaring applause, the sound thundering throughout the cul-de-sac. Molly turned to Aria, and wrapping her arms around her, hugged her fiercely. "Thank you. You saved us."

Politely, Aria dispassionately returned the hug, patting the girl's back. "Saved myself, too."

Molly just held on. Moments passed.

"You know, Molly, if we're ever going to get home, at some point you're going to have to let go."

Molly pulled back and looked her friend in the eyes. She smiled. "Heather." She threw herself back at the girl and hugged her tight again. This time Heather enthusiastically returned her hold.

"Hey, let's create some space here. You're squishing me!" It was Fallasha's muffled voice.

"Oh, sorry." Molly withdrew. "Heather, where's Aria?"

"Gone."

"Already?"

"Yep," said Heather. "She does that a lot."

The blonde broke away to retrieve the masks and headpieces, but two bystanders had already picked them up and returned them to her with an awed and awkward shyness, mistakenly thinking Heather the iMagiNator.

"Thank you," the moon girl said.

They simply gaped at her. On her way back to Molly, onlookers who had witnessed the events stared with reverence. Though they greeted the butterfly girl, too, most just wanted to get a glimpse of Heather.

The two helped one another on with their headpieces, and once in place looked each other over. They put on their masks.

"I think it's time we started for home, don't you?"

Molly smiled faintly and nodded her agreement.

"You okay?" Heather asked, over the circus-like atmosphere of the alley.

"I think so."

"Can we please hurry," Fallasha said, before self-consciously lowering her voice. "We're long overdue."

Heather turned to the three suspended RogueTags. Uncomfortably, Molly found herself looking, too.

"Are they dead?"

"I don't think so, Molly."

They continued to stare.

"I have to admit," Heather said, "*that* was amazing."

Fallasha said, "*That* was magic."

Molly agreed with a laugh, her tears welling up unexpectedly. "Scary at first."

Heather said, "It was like a weird sort of carnival going on all around me."

"iMagiNacia is like that," said a voice from behind them.

The two heads spun.

"I think you girls had better follow me. If I'm right, there will be more than just soldiers arriving here shortly."

"What do you mean?" Heather asked.

The stranger pointed upward, at the splashes of color that appeared to be dripping off the ceiling of the sky. "iMagiNacia performed like that won't be lost on the sorceress Mistraya. She'll want to know who did it. And word has probably reached her by now that it was the green-eyed Maiden of the Evermore Portent."

Mr. Simpletripp was struggling with the likeness of his latest bug-eyed creation, Heart Star Sally. Irritated, the dome-headed man sat back and listened while, outside, alarmed birds continued to bleat their shrill warning, a steady nagging that hammered the senses.

Again, that infernal cat!

Mr. Simpletripp slammed down his sculpting implements and squeezed the head of his current clay rendition until it oozed out the top of his fist. Then he smashed the statuette flat in disgust and afterward smeared his hand on his pants.

The piercing bird cries persisted.

From his chair, the pot-bellied man lumbered to his feet. He walked over to a rack on the wall, picked up a rifle, and cocking it, stomped up the steps leading out of the cellar studio.

Once in the yard, sighting the feline antagonist, Mr. Simpletripp raised his firearm and took aim, but was too late to squeeze off a round. The longhaired calico, Miss Gypsy, having spotted him, leapt over a bush to disappear within the dense shrubbery. Simpletripp lowered the rifle.

Hate that cat.

Spying a woodpecker, he shot it out of a tree in a cloud of feathers.

Deciding to bury the bird near the others, Mr. Simpletripp went to fetch a shovel.

Sheriff Dane hated donuts.

Parked in his pickup truck at Steadmans Landing, his was the only vehicle in the gray gravel lot. He was smoking another cigarette, his fourth today—third in the last half hour. And it smoldered at the end of his long fingers, below his rolled up khaki sleeve, held easily at arm's length out the window of the cab.

Returning the cigarette to his mouth, he took a long red-tipped drag, leaning to exhale in smoky dispersion to his left. The wind swept the cloud away in a rush.

I'm a secret smoker on a binge, he thought.

On another day, in a better mood, the thought might have seemed funny. Not today.

On the dashboard, close at hand, was a jelly-filled donut. The mayor's favorite. Centered on a light blue napkin, like a dullard, the puckered eye of burgundy stared glumly at the sheriff.

Another drag.

In Woody Stungrubben's office, there had been one donut left over from a meeting earlier that morning or perhaps directly after lunch, Dane didn't know. However, after leaving a hastily arranged meeting by Mayor Stungrubben, he had impulsively snatched it in passing. The sheriff wasn't even hungry, but like a spiteful child, he simply didn't want the mayor to have it. Looking over the puck of fried dough, he felt a creeping revulsion.

Mayor Woodrow Cortland Carver Stungrubben: Woody.

Where's the dignity in that? But what can you expect from a former car salesman turned mayor? Dane thought about the *huge* used car that Mayor Stungrubben was trying to sell the public right now. And he expected Dane's assistance in ensuring the sale.

Dane flicked loose the accumulated ash from the tip of his cigarette, before bringing it into the cab. He held the thinly rolled cylinder of tobacco vertically before his face, rotating it briefly, examining its smoking ashen tip, questioning his infrequent addiction. Turning to the dashboard, the sheriff reached and stabbed the cigarette tip-first through the soft exterior layer and into the heart of the donut. He twisted it for good measure, red jelly oozing out to greet his fingertips.

Stupid politician.

Dane slid down slightly in the seat of his truck, and looked out the window. Due to the sky's darkness, the hour seemed later than mid-afternoon. The wind still whipped, setting whitecaps loose on the gray, agitated waters of Faire Isle Lake. The sheriff shifted his attention as he followed the path of a plastic grocery bag that skittered by, catching on a nearby bush. Unable to free itself on subsequent gusts, it struggled in place.

Riveted, Dane watched.

The wind pressed its course, flattening the bag. The smoky blue of the black man's eyes focused on the limbs of bush that were pushing through, poking it from the opposite side, attempting, in the sheriff's view, to skewer it. The bag lengthened and flapped noisily, but couldn't break free.

Oh, man, oh, man. So, what do I do?

He glanced at his watch.

Pushing against a resistant wind, Dane opened the truck door. He climbed out and it slammed shut behind him.

Time for a walk, he thought, his mind churning, all whitecaps and waves. The sheriff hadn't bothered to don his hat. He took a few steps on the crunchy, forgiving gravel and stopped. For a few brief moments, Dane stood deliberating, motionless.

Setting course for the bush, the angular man walked over to the shopping bag like it was a small, trapped animal, and set it loose to hurtle away. Watching it slide and roll, Harland Dane knew it would only ensnare itself again, stuck in some newfound predicament. But isn't that the way? Passing near a brown trashcan, he started down the slope towards the lake.

Lana Pringle rushed out into the ragged gray of the blustery afternoon, struggling to grasp the elusive knob of the kitchen door. As she closed it behind her, the new Bristol House resident noticed that, within the diminishing sliver of light, a concerned Grandma Dawn watched her depart. When the heavy door clicked home in its jamb, Mrs. Pringle stepped away and strode for some distance before halting. There, she turned on her trailing husband.

"Ned, I don't think it's a good idea for you to come banging on the Bristol House door like that—as a matter of fact, please don't do it again."

"I knew you'd be here. I just knew it."

She brushed aside some freely blown hairs. "You found my note."

No response. Mrs. Pringle wheeled; her husband followed. In silence, the two walked through the vegetable garden. Drawing to a stop, Mrs. Pringle folded her arms before her, confronting yet another prolonged gust of wind. When it died, she said, "I'm not going far. I'm cold."

"Lana, of all places, did you have to end up here?"

"The Bristol House is beautiful."

"You know how I despise this place. It gives me the creeps."

"But, Ned, *I* like it here." Mrs. Pringle thought to add afterwards, in a much lower voice, "So does Molly."

After hitting her hard with his eyes, Mr. Pringle looked away. And though his distraught gaze climbed all over the waning greenery of a garden in seasonal decline, he didn't notice a thing. He said, "That girl's crazy, and you know it."

Mrs. Pringle knew he was referring to Heather. She kept her voice soft, barely above the wind's rush. "Please don't attempt to tell me what I know."

"I don't want my daughter around her, do you understand? I don't!"

Mrs. Pringle just nodded. Mr. Pringle waited, and when no response was offered, he spread his arms, palms up: "And?"

"I know you don't, Ned."

When no other words were forthcoming, Mr. Pringle asked, "Then why is Molly here?"

Quietly, calmly: "Because I'm here." After a pause: "And because Heather is Molly's best friend."

"But she's not well—she's sick! Do you realize that every time I see her, that girl is talking to herself? Why, you've seen her yourself. And remember what happened that day at school with the substitute teacher? I tell you, she's a whacked out kid! And I'm not the only parent in Noble who thinks so."

Mrs. Pringle continued to focus on a point far away.

"How do you know that at some time she won't hurt Molly?"

Her response came as barely a shrug. Mrs. Pringle turned her attention to the path at the edge of the vegetable garden, and she began to walk on the cobblestone. Her husband followed, flapping about her.

"Lana, you're subjecting my Molly to an undesirable influence. And this," Mr. Pringle looked up at the massive Bristol House, waving an arm, "this is an appalling place to live. It has to be so empty."

Mrs. Pringle laughed. It was lost on her husband.

Now, Mr. Pringle began to brandish his hands like signal flags, hoping to ensnare his distracted wife's attention, trying to emphasize the importance of his words. "So, in good conscience—I mean, if you *really* love your daughter—how can you bring her here to this, this dismal and deserted place?"

He waited. Mrs. Pringle didn't look up. With arms folded she continued to walk. After a time, she said, "But that's exactly why I *am* bringing her here."

Mr. Pringle's face held his confusion.

"Because I love her." For a short while, her pace quickened, and then she stopped on a decision. "Ned, I really am cold. I think I'm going back inside, if you don't mind."

"I do mind! I do! Think about it. What the hell are you doing? What are you doing to our lives, Lana—to your daughter, to me? After all this time invested, this is what I end up with, this is what I get: you're leaving?"

Mrs. Pringle turned and began to retrace her steps back to the Bristol House kitchen. The garden, agitated, swayed with the wind.

"Are you listening?"

Quietly: "I'm listening."

"*What?*"

Louder: "I'm listening."

"Don't do it, Lana. Don't! Your leaving has consequences that can't be undone. If you do this, things between us will be different—nothing will be the same. You can see that, can't you?"

Head down, Mrs. Pringle continued to walk, her husband hovering closely in pursuit. Finally, she stopped. They had reached the stepping-stones leading back through the vegetable garden.

"Lana, please. Please don't do something you'll regret."

The kitchen door in sight, she glanced at it before looking at her husband of fifteen years. "I've come to regret a lot lately, Ned."

Silence. The tireless wind refused to let it settle.

Mr. Pringle's gaze darted to the dutch door and back again. He lowered his voice, an attempt at reassurance: "Lana, you don't want to do this."

"I'm going inside now."

"Lana, don't!" For the first time in her life, Mrs. Pringle saw her husband start to cry, tears collecting behind his glasses before flowing down his cheeks. "Don't! Please don't do this to us, Lana, please. You'll destroy our lives. I know you're confused right now; I know you're unhappy. But it's a phase, I'm sure of it. It hasn't been easy for me, either, this-this difficult period in our relationship. But you'll see, in time everything will be back to normal—"

"You're not getting it."

"—and you'll be happy. Molly too. The three of us, we'll be one happy family again. Now stop this and come home. *Our* house is down the hill. Come home with me."

She started backing, a gust at her face. "I have to go. I'm sorry."

"Lana..."

"Read the note again, Ned. Read it. Understand the whys. Let the words sink in. And believe them. I need this separation, and I need to get out of that house." She shook the hair from her face. "I'll be in touch."

Lana Pringle was hugging herself, shivering, as she turned from him. With the wind sending his charcoal gray suit into a rippling frenzy, Ned Pringle watched her go. The woman's form was soon absorbed within the rectangle of the kitchen's golden light. The door slowly closed on the turbulent gloom of day. Click.

Heather and Molly were speechless.

"It's in the Portent Prophecies of MaidenLore."

"What is?" Heather asked.

"Your arrival here today."

"Is Molly in there, too?"

"Do you know who you are?" the man asked.

"Me? I'm Heather Nighborne." Heather stepped aside. "And this is my friend, Molly Pringle."

"Do you realize what you were doing out there?"

"Oh, that was—" Heather was about to mention that it was Aria who had worked the magic, but thought better of it. Instead, she dribbled off, "That was just something that happened, I guess."

"It was more than just something. iMagiNacia. The people in the crowd knew, too—they knew they were witnessing something special: a revelation come to life straight from the Portent Prophecies."

After a momentary look at Molly, Heather said, "I'm sorry if I don't understand. All we did was protect ourselves. We had to do what we did."

"Of course you did. It was written."

"Well, not at first. You see, we really tried to run from them, but they followed us."

"They had to."

Behind the mask, Heather tried to understand. "Why? They could have let us alone, right? We're girls, they're big."

"Really, they couldn't have. It was supposed to happen as it did."

"Because it was written," Heather chimed.

"Exactly that."

Exactly *what?* The moon girl hadn't a clue what the heck the man was talking about. Someone wrote that she and Molly were *supposed* to come here? Who told them? Fallasha? The Bristol House? And then to have to do that to the RogueTags, because the RogueTags were *supposed* to try to hurt them? And those guys had no choice? Hmmm. It's a question for Aria, to be sure. But later. First they needed to get home. And get away from this dead end street, the place where the sorceress was *supposed* to come looking for them. Heather wondered if that was written, too. The Portent Prophecies? Aria? Later.

But how do I know I can trust this man *now?* Heather asked herself.

The first thing she had noticed about him was the recessed eyes, so dark within their sockets. So very dark. They lent a sense of mystery to the person before her—unease, as well, reminding her of the sorceress. With a quick look, Heather saw Molly's frightened aura in blues and violets, but this didn't worry her, for she was able to make glad note of the man's, shining richly in brilliant orange and yellow. And though he was in costume, preventing the girls from seeing his true face—or any part of his body, for that matter—he momentarily struck Heather as safe, trustworthy.

A shy creature was hiding, standing on their new acquaintance's shoulder, peeking at the girls from behind the man's voluminous headpiece. The animal's long furry tail was visible behind the high collar. It unfurled and coiled, snaked and danced.

"Who are you?" Heather asked.

"Someone whose presence was requested."

"What do you mean?"

"I mean that someone was watching the events unfold here in the alley," said the mask of shadowed eyes. "And when it was clear that you were threatened by those three browgarths, I was summoned."

Molly pointed at the RogueTags. "Was *that* written?"

"Yes." The man cleared his throat. "But not in such detail."

"Are they dead?" Molly asked.

"Are they?" he asked Heather. When she didn't respond, he said, "Most probably not, but with iMagiNacia I wouldn't know. I'm no expert on rare forms of magic. If alive, it could be some time before they regain consciousness. By then they'll have been cut down by the soldiers or magically released by Mistraya, if she puts in an appearance personally." He looked at Heather. "But once again, I'm not the one to ask."

Although tall when crowned with the ample headpiece, the shadow-eyed man might have been of medium height when not wearing the costume of silver with shades of blue that hung loosely on his body. A diagonal line divided his mask. It started above the left brow and terminated on the opposite side, below the cheek. The upper part, with its deeply inset eyeholes, was blue with silver embellishments, the lower part simply white, with silver lips. Centered on the chin, secured in a cleft, was a narrow faceted jewel of blue that occasionally glimmered. His headpiece was puffy and embroidered, with much ornamentation and stitching, as was the rest of his outfit.

The little monkey-like creature, gaining courage, took this moment to reveal himself, climbing and sitting atop the fluffy headpiece. He wore a small costume in similar blues and silver. From within the perimeter of his fur-lined face, the quizzical eyes stared at Molly, his features hairless, human, and very much a child's. She beamed, and the creature, suddenly bashful, crawled back behind the headpiece. However, it wasn't long before he was again watching the girl from over the man's high collar.

Heather spoke: "I know it might seem rude, but it's getting late, and we have to get home."

"Maybe I can help you with that." The shadowed-eyed man regarded Heather. "Where do you two reside?"

"Um, the Milky Way," Heather said.

"The Milky Way, eh? Maybe I can't help you, after all."

Heather and Molly briefly exchanged a glance, the first girl taking a risk.

"Well, you see," Heather gave Molly another glimpse before continuing, "we're TimeLight travelers. We came all the way from the Milky Way to see your beautiful parade."

"That explains the Rogues picking on a pair of young girls."

"Yeah," said Heather, "I guess they didn't like us."

"They don't like much," said the shadow-eyed man. "I know you won't want to tell me the exact location of your Portal, but perhaps we can take you to its vicinity."

"We?" Molly asked. "You and your little friend there?"

For a moment, the mask was still, as was its voice within. "I was referring to the *we* as a group who works, shall we say, behind the scenes."

"Behind the scenes doing what?" It was an innocent question posed by Heather.

"Saving youngsters like you from certain disaster at the hands of a sorceress, for instance," the man said. He paused before adding, "And other things." The words didn't invite questions. The man's aura darkened.

Heather thought it better to change the subject. "We only need your help getting to street level and that should be enough."

"Are you sure? There are plenty of RogueTags still roaming the streets—and elsewhere. And there may be scouts, as well."

"Scouts?" Heather and Molly said simultaneously.

"Did you see that large bird perched on the edge of the roof, the one you chased off with those small red spinnerets?"

"Oh, yeah, that."

"That was a scout. When the balls fell from the sky and into the street, iMagiNacia was detected, and powerful iMagiNacia at that. In all likelihood, Mistraya sent out the scout to report firsthand what had happened. But then you scared it off."

"Did the bird get back to Mistraya?" Molly asked.

"Did it?" The man looked at Heather.

"Doesn't it say in the Portent Prophecies?" the moon girl answered, coolly.

The man threw his head back and laughed. "You're quite amusing."

Heather didn't know how to respond. "Thank you," finally escaped.

The mask turned to Molly. "To answer your question, the sorceress seems to be long in arriving. Chances are, the bird never returned to tell her what it had witnessed here." The recessed eyes again appraised Heather. "Now, if you would, please follow me." Then he stopped and readdressed the girls. "Are you sure you only want to go to street level?"

"We're sure," Heather said.

Molly wasn't so certain. The man behind the mask perceived her doubt.

"You have reservation?" he asked the butterfly girl.

"Well, I—" Molly glanced at Heather. "Well, maybe we can go to street level, look around, and decide from there whether or not we want your assistance to go any farther."

"Perhaps. Heather Nighborne?"

"Molly has a good idea." The moon girl shifted her attention. "If it looks like trouble, maybe you can take us closer to the PortalDoor."

The stranger was pleased at the reconsideration, relishing what he saw as their growing trust. He looked the girls over. His creature let out a squeal.

"Well, then," said the mask's silver lips, the shaded eyes taking a last look at the sky, "let's hurry."

CHAPTER TWENTY-THREE

Revelations and Words of Wisdom

"What are you doing?" The words were whispered.

Heather looked ahead to be certain that the shadow-eyed man would be unable to overhear. Slowing to create distance and reassurance, she tucked her chin to look at her moon brooch. "What?"

More whispers:

"What are you doing?"

"We're following this man, and he's taking us to street-level. From there, we go home."

Fallasha gave a sharp exhale of disapproval. "How do you know you can trust him?"

Following a narrow course between the jumble of alleyway houses, Heather looked at the man's back, his cape obscuring most his torso. Atop his puffy headpiece rode the small, child-faced creature, with all fours clinging onto fabric. Generally facing forward, his gaze occasionally followed overhead the passing of a recessed window, or glanced behind at the moon and butterfly girls. Heather watched the animal's tail dance in balance to each bounce. She turned back to Fallasha.

"Honestly, I don't know if we can trust him," Heather continued at an undertone, stepping to avoid some refuse. "But after Aria's show back there, if Mistraya or her scouts are looking for us, I'm not sure we have a choice."

"Where's he taking us?"

"I told you: street-level."

"But *where* at street-level?"

Heather's gaze returned to the shadow-eyed man leading them down an unknown path, the walls high on either side, the rooftops blocking the light with their jutting, irregular overhangs. Following the movements of his undulating, slightly billowing cape, the moon girl said, "I don't know."

She studied the man's shine, currently benign in subdued clouded colors. They didn't bounce or radiate with any great energy, rather they remained calm, composed. Or cloaked. She glanced at Molly. The girl behind the butterfly mask was fascinated, focusing beyond Heather at the creature bobbing like a jockey upon his mount. A moment later, Molly was navigating the littered floor as the three continued to sidestep the intermittent debris: large ceramic receptacles, barrels, crates, swollen bags, stacks of papers, and piles of clothing. Molly's gaze caught Heather's. The butterfly girl put up her hands and shook her head, as if to say, *What are we doing; where are we going?*

Heather walked backwards for a few steps, long enough to shrug an *I don't know.* When she turned back around, she saw that the shadow-eyed man had stopped ahead and was waiting, watching. His small companion squealed, and the man set off once again.

The girls were led on an uneven route, around projecting and angled walls, past barred and boarded windows, beneath arched overhangs, and beyond the occasional fork that led elsewhere between reticent stone facades. Heather found little of interest in the infrequent design work carved above windows and bordering doors and arches—overall, the route upon which they were being guided seemed grim and uninviting—forbidding.

"Are we almost there?" Heather asked, though knowing they had yet to climb to street-level.

"Almost," was said with a slight spin, revealing a side of the mask's nose and cheek. But it was only a glimpse, and soon the two were tagging along behind the man once more.

"We're following you," Heather called, feeling more and more ill at ease, "but we don't even know your name or who you are."

The man didn't look back. They passed under an arch and then another, and found themselves in a dimly lit enclosure lined with trash, surrounded by boarded windows and a beat-up door of peeling paint. The narrow alley rambled onward, but their mysterious guide rapped on the splintery door with the back of his gloved hand: a cadence of muffled taps. A small hinged panel, located at head-height, opened a leery crack amid the door's planks.

Heather barely heard the words proposed, "For the Four."

"For Evermore," returned the masked man, his words not quite a whisper.

The square panel snapped shut, and with the sliding of two dead bolts, the entry door opened.

"Quickly now," said the man, following a pivot. His headpiece barely clearing the lintel, he maneuvered through the door's narrowly accommodating gap, the creature having climbed down to perch behind his high collar. Reluctant to follow, Heather watched the floating end of his cape trail and disappear within. She glanced briefly at Molly, her aura glowing in agitated and apprehensive purples and blues.

Fallasha whispered, "I thought we were going to street-level."

"Maybe this is the way."

"I have my doubts. Speaking as your much-denigrated tour guide, I must, however humbly and quietly, voice my objection and say that it is clearly not in your best interests to venture beyond that cheerless and rotted door before you."

Heather hesitated. Decisions. She looked at the narrow walk ahead of her before turning and directing her gaze past the approaching Molly, back the way they had come. She avoided her friend's inquiring stare, looking instead at the sky above. There, Heather caught sight of a distant bird, dark with a large wingspan, gliding before a backdrop of wispy-clouded blue.

One of Mistraya's scouts? She wondered.

Following her gaze, Molly also looked up. Sighting the bird, her agitated aura grew brighter, and she hurried the few remaining steps to the moon girl's side.

Feeling it their safest option, Heather whirled and stepped over the threshold and into the darkened quarters.

Fallasha let loose a wearisome sigh.

Once indoors and unable to see, Heather felt herself hastily pulled aside where large hands patted her down, searching for concealed weapons in the voluminous folds of costume fabric.

"Hey, what are you doing?" she asked, to no response. When she heard Fallasha gasp following a tug, the moon girl spoke out, "That's my brooch."

"Don't speak unless spoken to," came the gruff reply. The intrusive hands continued.

Molly had been yanked inside and the door quickly closed behind her. Heather could hear hands brushing through the folds of her friend's costume and Molly's brief but mild protest. When it was over, a meager light slowly went up on an oil lamp in the far corner. The two girls found themselves standing across the room from it.

The shadow-eyed man spoke: "Heather Nighborne and Molly Pringle, though you are here as our guests, we ask that you refrain from quick movements of any kind. As well, Heather Nighborne, we will strike out at the first sign of an incantation uttered under your breath, or otherwise."

Feeling betrayed and hemmed in, Heather's impatience surfaced, rough and bristly. "You said you were taking us to street-level."

"In due time. However, I thought it important that first you meet some acquaintances of mine. Now, I must ask you to kindly remove your masks, and Heather Nighborne, your headpiece as well."

Heather's vision was adjusting to the lack of light, revealing a windowless chamber painted with long strokes of shadow amid vague silhouettes. Yet, because of the emanation of auras, she knew the room in which she and Molly stood held many people. Most of the auras shed strong but subdued reds and blues, their anticipatory pulses excited yet constrained. She heard rustling as Molly grappled to pull off her mask. Heather realized she had little choice and did likewise, quickly brushing aside the hair from her face, setting the mask and headpiece on the floor beside her. She wanted her hands free.

In the dimness, Heather sensed a multitude of eyes upon her exposed features. She felt vulnerable, naked, her own face catching light, while those before her remained backlit, their features indistinguishable. Tense moments passed.

"So, you're the answer to the Portent, eh?" It was a woman's voice, snapping out cold and sharp from the center of the room. Molly flinched. The woman sounded old. Unlike the others, Heather noticed her aura shone in hardened blues and garish, unmoderated yellow-greens.

Assuming the question was meant for her, Heather said, "That's what he," the girl pointed at the nebulous form of the shadow-eyed man, "told me."

His creature squeaked, and the man turned to it in soothing whispers. "You don't know?"

"If what he told me is the truth, I guess I know now." The words were innocent.

Molly let out a tiny, nervous giggle.

"If without question you are the answer to the Portent, do you understand that you must protect yourself?

"Well, how am I supposed to do that?"

The room broke out in laughter.

"I assume much as you did earlier today off the alley, in the old Weavers Quarters, utilizing the power that you displayed there. From what I understand, you had quite a way about you." The woman's shine burst with an amused brilliance, before receding to resume its low uncompassionate glow. "Your enemies will want to find you, child, and they will surely try to kill you."

The girl blinked a number of times in rapid succession, as she digested the words, a slow absorption of comprehension. There followed a thick moment of silence, before Heather asked, "Why?"

A lone guffaw broke out before being strangled with a snort. Unable to be contained, it split the air again. Another joined in. Soon, there were laughs all around. Heather could now make out more figures in the murk, some on the floor and against walls, more still in chairs and occupying random benches.

Heather added, "Who are my enemies? I mean, I didn't do anything to anyone. I've never even been here before." The girl's gaze drifted throughout the room, searched the perimeter, landed on Molly nearby, and then returned to the bold blunt aura of the woman. "Besides," she said, her voice losing volume, "how do I know that *you're* not my enemy?"

"You don't," the incisive voice spit. "However, I am getting the distinct impression that you really *don't* know, do you?"

"Know what? I-I'm sorry. I don't understand."

"In time she will come," the woman started, before others joined her, "With magic appear, to waylay three powers, in green of the Sear. She'll cast them aside, and draw them upright, displaying her powers, the light within Light. Having done this, she'll journey away, to return once again, at a much later day. With darkness so rife, spread o'er the land, uniting the four, from under the hand."

One voice continued the verse, but trailed off noticing the others had stopped.

"In your poem, the 'she' is me?" It was Heather.

"It is."

The girl turned briefly to Molly. "I guess you're not in there."

Molly giggled, others laughed.

Heather shrugged. "I don't know what to say. Are you *sure* it's me?"

"Did you perform iMagiNacia today?"

"Kind of."

More laughter.

"You're modest, child, unless there's something you're not telling us."

"I'm not sure what you want me to say."

"The truth: were you assisted out there as the iMagiNator?"

"Yes."

The room seemed to draw back, at a loss for air.

"Who aided you, child?" It was another voice, deeper, a man's. "And from where?"

The girl shifted her weight, fully intending to guard her secret of Aria from these strangers. "Well, Molly, here, helped." Heather gestured in the vagueness. "You see, if she wasn't there, all three would have ganged up on me. So Molly helped to spread those guys out. They were easier to deal with that way."

There was a murmuring, a release of tension within the room.

"But there was no one else aiding you?"

"There was no one else, Matron." Heather and Molly recognized the voice of their mysterious guide. "I saw her performance. She had the green SearEye. Beyond a doubt, Heather Nighborne was the iMagiNa-tor behind the defeat of the three RogueTags."

"Is that so?" It was the woman's voice again, crackling, prickly, and penetrating.

"Yes," said the shadow-eyed man. "And there are others here in this room who witnessed today's display of iMagiNacia. As well, outside these walls, word of her amazing performance is quickly spreading among us, initiated by those who observed the events firsthand."

Heather was thankful that the shadow-eyed man had spoken up and redirected the attention away from her, for she didn't want to lie. Ever. Instinct told her that it was necessary to withhold the secret of Aria, al-though she couldn't pinpoint why. And having done so thus far, Heather was breathing easier for it. She was uncertain what these people would do if they knew of her other half, but she didn't want to find out. Aria was hers to protect.

"Then, indeed, it looks as though you may very well be our answer to the Evermore Portent, child. And as such, you, at some future date when magic has been expelled from the land, will return to assist us. You've come early and placed this first visit today to give us hope in the future, when the Realm will be impoverished in spirit, encumbered with sor-row, and much blood will have been spilt. And so it is written."

"And so it is written," the others murmured.

Before them, Heather remained stationary and on display, gazing in return at their formless faces. All the while she was absorbing, absorbing, filtering—processing perceptions; the slightest of sounds and vaguest of sights were committed for logging, filing, and future reference. Such was the operation of the moon girl's mind.

Standing nearby, Molly was feeling lightheaded. Sparks swam. Like fireworks, tiny explosions of thought were bombarding her gentle con-sciousness: Heather? Are they sure? Her Heather? *That* Heather? The one standing there? The solution to this world's problems at some future time? Can it possibly be true?

Incredibly, Molly found herself wanting to laugh, although she didn't know why. Perhaps it was fueled by a stealthy and creeping sense of awe? Of pride? Of the obvious? The reasons mattered little, because her thoughts had streamed on, returning to the question of Heather's true identity.

Within herself, Molly was sifting for the truth, struggling to lay claim to the incontrovertible, the dawning reality: knowing her friend as she did, somehow the possibility of Heather being the answer to the Portent didn't really strike her as all that farfetched, no more than the enchanted rooms of the Bristol House, or the girls traveling to Parade Day. After all, it helped to explain the presence of Aria and what took place today near that alley. How else could Heather possess any knowledge of iMagi-Nacia? And then there's Heather's fearlessness, and her fascination with Maidens, and her strange dreams, and the book of Autumnsloe, and Mrs. Peck, and Fallasha, and her SearEye, and just all of it. And splash: *why else would they even be in Evermore?*

Was Heather truly the green-eyed Maiden of the Evermore Portent? Molly had no doubt. She looked over at her friend. Heather's posture didn't show her to be overly excited at the prospect as she stood subdued, intent.

The Matron continued, "But I must warn you, there are no guaran-tees for your safety or return. For though you might appear to be the answer to the Portent, you may still be only a possibility on an abbrevi-ated stay. There have been others before you."

Heather was lost. She knew she was supposed to be or do something special, but wasn't sure exactly what. And once more, she realized that she needed to speak with Aria for clarification. What was this all about, anyway? And why her? The room felt hot and suddenly, so did the girl.

"Where have you *disciplined* to perfect your iMagiNacia? Surely, it wasn't the MaidenHall Academy."

"Of the ShadowSlip Wood in Autumnsloe," Heather recited. "I've heard of it—and I even went there once—well, twice, really—"

"Did you?"

"Yeah—um, yes, but it was only in a dream." Heather heard mutter-ings. "I-I've never studied magic, there or anywhere. Everything you saw today, everything that happened in the alley, well, you might say that it just comes from somewhere inside of me."

More murmurs.

"Once again, you didn't have to discipline and perfect your magical weaponry?" The woman's voice was razor-edged, icy. Her aura glared in similar fashion.

"No, it must be built-in—I think I kinda came ready-to-use." Heather laughed stiltedly. "You know, like when you get a new toy, open the box, and it's already assembled and ready to go, and it even has batteries and everything? It lets you do things right away, without having to read the directions. Know what I mean?" When no one responded, Heather added for further clarification, "I think the best way I can explain it is, I feel—" and here the girl pondered, "I feel like there's another part of me that's been here before—to your world—but that part of me comes and goes." More low rumblings from those gathered. "And so I guess I'm surprised at what I came up with today."

"That's quite remarkable. You're merely a child, and yet from what I hear—I didn't see your work firsthand, mind you, but *felt it*—your practice of iMagiNacia is advanced far beyond your years. Very polished for one your age who has never studied our LightCraft. How do you account for this?"

"I can't, I guess. I only came here with my friend, Molly, to see your parade. I didn't plan on being mixed up with those RogueTags, even though I know now that I was supposed to all along." She pointed. "He told me that."

"Yes."

Murmured assents.

The woman continued her interrogation, "How many times have you been called upon to use your iMagiNacia?"

"How many—?" Heather let loose a small shy laugh. "Well, not much, really."

"How many times?"

"Well, if you need to know exactly, this here, today, was the very first time."

The room burst out in animated conversation.

"Hush!" cried the woman, and the voices died. "The first time, eh?"

"Yeah—I mean, yes—yes, Matron, ma'am."

"You may not realize this, but your feat today was more astounding than you know."

"Really?"

"Yes."

"Probably because I had to do all that stuff, you know, because it was written." Heather scratched an itchy shoulder through layers of fabric.

"Without a doubt." The woman laughed, gentle where Heather expected a cackle. "You are Evermorian?"

"I always thought I was born in my home in—" she found Molly's obscure form for an instant, "—in the Milky Way. But I'm adopted, and," the child's voice lowered, "I've never met my mother."

"I see."

"Or my father."

"Come here, child."

"There?"

"Yes. You see where I am, do you not? Here, kneel here." The woman's movement of hand suggested the space in front of her. The boy who had been sitting there, his legs folded beneath him, rose and made room. Heather hesitated, and then edged forward, picking her way through the tightly packed gathering, the swish of her costume stirring the silence of the room. She knelt before the woman's large chair. A slight spicy scent wafted to greet her, subtle in its flavoring. Pleasing.

Someone coughed.

Facing the Matron, Heather saw more of her features, though still indistinctly. She was indeed old. Many wrinkles mapped her face and her mouth was recessed and drawn in an uneven line. A shawl wrapped her head and flowed around her neck.

"Lean closer," she said to a cautious Heather, then, "Come, closer, child. Closer, now. There."

Heather watched as two veined and misshapen hands, shakily produced, sought out her face. Upon contact, they were cold, and Heather momentarily withdrew. But then the girl felt her skin warm to the woman's touch, her searching, probing caress. Heather's face began to heat up as if the hands were drawing energy to it, and to them, as they sought the pointy protrusion of her nose, the smooth and tender roundness of her nostrils, her chin and cheeks, her lids and lashes, and eventually her brow.

With the woman's head slightly inclined and slowly nodding, trance-like, Heather noticed her wrinkled mouth pulling up ever so slightly at the corners. "So, that's what you look like. I wondered..." The smile grew. "Such a soft, youthful face with pleasing features. Yes, you're love-ly. I like that, pretty child." Beneath the aged palms, Heather found her own grin starting to grow. She couldn't help herself. "Ah, and she bears a bountiful smile. Yes. I like that, also."

Heather pulled slightly away. "I'm really ticklish," she thought to admit, though didn't know why. Eyes closed, the girl didn't notice the toothless mouth agape in a lopsided grin.

"Are you, now?" The palms reseated themselves on either side of the girl's face. The fingers rolled over her cheeks and back towards her ears. Heather felt them probing deeper, when suddenly she went limp, her head falling forward into the supportive hands that deftly caught her.

Disregarding the laws of physics, they easily propped her up.

Molly gasped. "Heather—!"

Immediately, an arm of restraint fell before the butterfly girl. Afraid for her friend, Molly fought to push it aside and rush to her aid, but was easily held in check.

"Stop that! What are you doing? You stop—!"

"Silence that girl!" blared out—a man's voice—and a hand rapidly covered Molly's mouth. She struggled, kicking and squirming. Only when she had finally calmed was the girl lowered to the ground, the hold on her relaxed, and her mouth freed up. Crying stinging tears of exasperation, of helplessness, Molly could only watch her friend's inert body succumb to the touch of the elderly stranger.

With Heather's face in her hands, the Matron's fingers delved past layered and instinctive barriers, parted emotional curtains, and drew aside psychological partitions: they sought the child's sheltered and sequestered soul. Unable to free herself, Heather drifted in a paralyzed state, while the inquisitive hands were free to explore and draw from the fortified ramparts, guarded recesses, and secluded passageways of the young girl's mind, including those regions where darkness dwelled and light was but a stranger. The bony hands felt for potential, felt for inequity, felt for the mantle of evil and its prospects therein before they began to withdraw.

"Ah, but what is this?" cried the woman, and her hands returned to their press. Her chin went up, her mouth hung open, a saggy withered circle, and her wispy eyebrows climbed rapturously upon her forehead. Her shriveled face began to roll in slight circles as she ferreted further. Helpless, Heather could feel the probe of the LayerTrace prodding and boring in its drive to infiltrate and unveil on behalf of the Matron. Only, the girl's mind continued to circumvent its challenges, setting entrenchments and impediments, and rebuffing the encroachment at every turn—and this without Heather's active intervention.

The old woman finally lowered her hands. She shook her head, still in a half-conscious state. "You've an area within that's inaccessible to me, child."

Dazed and fatigued, Heather opened her eyes. Standing nearby, the boy's supportive hands found and steadied her shoulders in the insufficient light, as she sought to remain upright while kneeling.

Forced to maintain her distance, Molly saw her friend come around. Relieved, she took in a deep breath before exhaling in a quiet release. Her tears wiped away, she sniffed.

The woman continued: "I'm unable to see that particular part of you, feel what it is in you that resides there. Beyond that mental wall could dwell an enlightened heart, or one that is charred and wretched in its blackness and bears a purpose that is less than well intentioned.

"But of that which I was able to examine, I must say that your Light is extremely brilliant—stronger than any I've ever encountered, including Starbrill's, here," she bowed her head in the direction of the boy, "and your character I find virtuous."

"What would you have done if you found that I wasn't so virtuous?" Heather asked.

"'Evil,' you mean?"

"I guess so."

"Humph. Yes. While your power is still underdeveloped and before it has had a chance to fully mature," the woman smacked her lips and considered her words, "we would have set you aside and dealt with you properly." The Matron looked up and in the direction of Molly. "Your friend, too."

Arms tightening at her sides, Molly squeezed off a shudder, her uneasy gaze spilling elsewhere.

"But since your virtue is not at issue at present, we need not worry ourselves about such follies of the soul." She inhaled wheezily. "Need we?"

Heather nodded, and then quickly shook her head to the contrary. A little, "No," escaped.

"Nonetheless," the Matron continued, "I must ask that in the future you be vigilant knowing that we all carry inside us the seed of evil and its possible proliferation. As you possess a great capacity for Light, you've also a great potential for its counterpart. If left unmonitored this could result in the emergence and eventual domination of the shadowy forces of your nature. This will not bode well for HumanKind, having one as strong as yourself in possession of a power such as yours. While an odious transition continues to take a firmer hold here in Evermore, there are and will be many more souls bound to its blackness, and they will never find reclamation and redemption—they will never find peace. It is my hope that you be mindful, then, and not allow yourself to be drawn towards their path, away from the Light. Use your power for good, child, but only for good. And do not permit your resolve to weaken in the face of what may appear to be stronger forces in the difficult times to come. Prevail, child, prevail for all of us. This is why I requested that you be brought before me today; this is what I ask of you."

Still weak, Heather said, "I'm sorry, but I'm not sure what you mean."

"You will come to understand in time. As a potential fulfiller of the

Portent Prophecies, as our Astille Lia Staleen DiYoh, you will face difficult tasks ahead—the utmost being that you must try to remain alive, and as I've said, there will be powerful forces at work to insure that you do not."

The woman bowed her head, placing a gentle hand on Heather's shoulder. "And if this weren't enough, I find it necessary to burden you further. I'm aware of a perilous forbodement, both here and at your hearth. I see watchers in the sky…stealthy figures in the gloom… a lapse at the doorway… excavations and hollows."

"Is it Mr. Simpletripp?" Heather's stomach gave a turn. "Is he going to hurt Grandma Dawn?"

"I cannot see faces. I perceive only danger and the possibility of your ruin. I am able to see, however, that your grandmother is one who is strong at the source. So I should not squander your time worrying on her account, child."

Heather relaxed a bit at hearing these words. The Matron's hands sought out her face again, and in passing briefly touched Heather's brooch. The woman recoiled. "Ah! There's unexpected life there."

"It's Fallasha, my brooch."

The elderly woman's hand returned to Fallasha's face. Amused, she said, "You, too, are lovely, small brooch."

"Thank you," came the partially smothered response from beneath a small, crooked finger.

"Little crescent moon, you mustn't fall to another, you realize that."

"Yes," said the brooch.

"Good. It won't do."

Heather asked Fallasha, "What does she mean?" Then to the Matron, "What do you mean?"

"*She* knows, and that's enough, child. And you'll learn, if necessary. You've so much to hold dear, now is not the time."

Again the shaking elderly hands were placed before the face of the moon girl, and Heather leaned into them, now seeking their warmth, their comforting press.

"There, there, child. Do not worry, not yet. All is well… But I do see a storm, so you must go to its gathering. Yes… Yes, you must go."

Heather wanted only to keep her face in the Matron's palms, feeling their protection, their sanctuary. The touch filled voids inside of her, somehow making her stronger in the whole. But then the hands withdrew.

"Enough, now. You must go."

Heather immediately felt their loss, a breeze cold upon her soul. She blinked in the gloom. Unsteadily, the girl climbed to her feet aided by the young Starbrill. "Before we go, can I ask a question?"

"You may."

"Well, actually, I have two questions. Since you know my grandmother, do you know my mother?" Heather then thought to add, "Or my father?"

"No, I only know of your grandmother through that which you have shown me."

The girl looked down. "Oh."

With Heather's disappointment evident to the Matron, the woman said, her voice gentle with the girl, "I'm sorry." Her knobby hand reached and finding the girl's face, guided it up towards her own. "You had a second question for me?"

Heather nodded. She leaned against the palm that still rested aside her cheek.

The crumpled mouth relaxed and spread benevolently. "Yes?"

Heather pulled her face away from the hand. Collecting herself, she stared directly at the matriarch. "Well, this might sound rude, and I hope it doesn't, but who are all of *you?*"

"A fair question."

There was a spattering of laughter.

"Let's just say that we are the children of the ClearWeave: that which you cannot see, but is wholeheartedly entwined in the fabric of Evermore's existence, and undoubtedly its fate. According to the Portent Prophecies, at some point along your journey we *will* meet again."

"The ClearWeave? Meet where? Here? But I'm not sure I'll be able to find it."

Laughter again.

The icy voice by now had completely thawed, and the woman's words were laced with warmth. "Yes, child. Here in the Realm of Evermore. And you will be much needed then—though there will be others that strongly disagree, I should think. Now go. We will take you to street-level, where you can find your way home. Heed my words and be wary. There are dangers always, in the skies as well as on the lands. And though I am very old, I do hope that we, you and I, will meet again." She turned to Molly. "And you, my other child, may also very well prove to be a factor in all of this, though I cannot see that being so at this moment in time. But admittedly, my vision is limited and incapable of seeing all."

"But if we do meet again," Heather asked, "as the Portent says, how will I know you? I can't see your faces."

"Don't worry, child. The ClearWeave is all around. What matters most is that we'll know you."

Heather understood. "Well, goodbye, then."

The woman raised her hand, and Heather bent slightly to meet it. She touched the moon girl's forehead lightly with her fingertips.

"I fear so, child, until your return." Her lips gave way to a fleeting smile, drawn in melancholy. The Matron's aura radiated its sadness in waves of somber blue. "The knowledge that I've given you here today is so much, perhaps too much, child, for one so young."

Molly couldn't help but agree, and wondered how her friend was able to cope with all that had been revealed and placed upon her. No longer held captive by constraining arms, from her position near the wall, the girl continued to observe and marvel at Heather's stoicism. Molly knew that she, herself, would have wanted to push it all away long ago.

"But to not consider your safety," the Matron continued, "in light of who you may rightfully be, I feel that would be a mistake of greater degree. May you leave well armed with this realization and not handicapped or crippled with its onerous implications and consequences. It is my hope that your well-versed iMagiNacia will make all the difference when the wisdom of your tender age has all but failed you."

Heather had only a vague notion of what the woman's words meant. Her head continued to pound. It felt clogged. "Thank you," she said, though born only of politeness. The Matron's fingers slid from the moon girl's brow and, searching, took hold of her gloved hand. When the woman's head rotated slightly, Heather noticed the spotted reflection of the yellow oil lamp in the glassiness of her eyes.

"May the Universe guide and protect you, child."

Heather slowly backed away. She released the Matron's hand, her lips mouthing the words: thank you. Feeling a bit sheepish, the moon girl found her way over to retrieve and replace her headpiece and mask. She felt the eyes of the room still upon her, as she fumbled in the dimness. Molly, having already donned her butterfly mask, was allowed to offer assistance. As a last touch, at arms length, she straightened the moon girl's mask.

Heather didn't seem quite herself.

"Are you all right?"

Remote and abstracted, Heather made only the slightest inclination to the affirmative.

Molly wouldn't let her go, and gave her another attentive once-over.

Heather managed a smile. "I'm okay, Molly." Her words were quiet and hardly reassuring. "Honest." She turned to the shadow-eyed man.

"Are you still going to lead us to street-level?"

"Yes. Are you ready, Heather Nighborne, Molly Pringle?"
The two masks nodded.
"Then follow me."

Surprisingly, his walk beneath a stormy sky and near an agitated lake was calming to the sheriff.

Dane asked himself the question once again, So, if it wasn't the old miner, then who could be the killer?

And once again he concluded with the same answer: Almost anyone.

With the placement of the boots on the old miner's feet and the girl's backpack in the cave, Dane now knew the killer wasn't a drifter, come and gone—and it certainly wasn't the old miner. Too pat—forget the inconclusive forensics. Simpletripp? Quite possibly, despite the loyal wife's alibi and no known motive other than the appeasement of his own sinister character. The sheriff felt strongly that it had to be someone in the area of Noble, and most probably from town. But Noble was just big enough to make their ongoing search not so simple and yet small enough to make it not quite impossible. But where to pick up the thread?

He hated to admit it, but without a break, the investigation would in all likelihood remain stalled and unsolved—unless of course, you happened to be Mayor Woodrow Stungrubben of the Royal Order of the Jelly-Filled Donut. Then you create an unsubstantiated truth, and allow the town of Noble to think that it's in safe hands under his guidance, and that no crime will go unsolved and no murderer unpunished.

Fraud.

Dane squinted into the wind, the tiny airborne particles stinging his eyes. The wheat-like grasses around the lake were sweeping in waves, at the mercy of capricious winds. As a gust raged, the sheriff stopped and screwed up his face, turning his head. He felt the blast wane, and then rage some more, before it finally slacked off, continuing its forcefulness at a lower intensity. To his left, the lake thrashed and surged, full of the day, full of its confused self, brooding and gray.

I should be getting back, Dane thought.

Continuing his walk against the wind, the sheriff noticed the treetops bending under the hand of the unseen force.

Stand your ground, he thought. Stand your ground.

Dane still had an unannounced trip to make, dropping in on some Noble residents, and he needed to determine his intentions, formulate a strategy.

He knew it was bad politics to let on that he disagreed with the town's mayor on whether or not the killer had been captured—or in this case, found dead. And yet the sheriff knew that more lives in Noble would be at risk if he simply went along with the Mayor's wishes and spouted the agreed upon line.

Sign off? Not a chance. Dane knew himself, knew he couldn't get on board and make the announcement without being dead certain. He also knew that should the killer strike again, even if it happened to be years from now, he would feel responsible both professionally and morally. He knew better than to put his head in that ever-dangling noose.

So, what to do? Well, whatever he did, it was important that he act promptly, because later this afternoon, Mayor Woody Stungrubben was holding a press conference to announce to the world his town's prowess in the apprehension of the Stilped Roarhowser murderer. And Dane was expected to be present, standing behind the good mayor at his podium.

He cleared his throat and spit to the right, the wind whipping the gob behind him.

The sheriff's mind shifted gears and began to travel old ground, searching for any road that may have eluded him: Is there even the remotest chance that the old miner could have been the murderer? Conceivably. After all, he was found wearing the boots from the scene of the crime. And then there were the photographs of the Roarhowser kid up in the cave, found in the vicinity of Heather Nighborne's backpack. Which means there's a possibility that Woody Stungrubben could be correct in his assumption. But not likely. As a matter of fact, it's highly unlikely. There's a better chance that the world is flat and that this dim bulb of a mayor will be reelected.

Dane could feel the strength of the wind, now at his back, pushing him along. He could feel the give of the graveled path beneath his boots and hear its crunching stones. With the parking lot still some distance away, there was enough time to plot a course of action—if only he could determine what it should be. He knew, too, that internal politics could make his life more than difficult in an understatement, more than miserable as a matter of fact, and that the wrong words getting back to the wrong ears at city hall could be devastating to his career. He had to be careful. More than careful.

Before him, Sheriff Dane watched scraps, pamphlets, and papers carry and tumble on the gusts. Here in the open, the wind was merciless in its erratic thrusts. He knew that at some point every single piece of this windborne rubbish would hit upon its own personal snag, finding its own frustrating dead end. Unless of course circumstance happened upon the scene to provide that much needed break.

Grandma Dawn approached with the kettle.

"Sorry, Dawn, I guess I haven't said much, have I, since I came in?"

"Perfectly fine with me. How are you feeling?"

"Honestly, I'm not sure." Mrs. Pringle momentarily sat back and withdrew her hands from around her cup for access. Grandma Dawn poured. "I guess there wasn't a whole lot to talk about out there. Ned's prepackaged dreams got away, mine got lost—or buried."

Grandma Dawn hesitated for an instant on her way to returning the kettle to the stovetop, but said nothing. The branches continued their stiff raking and prodding at the windows above. The wind cut loose in a long shrill wail.

"Dawn, when you were a little girl, remember your coloring books—?"

"Lana, I wouldn't—"

"And how the lines were so clearly defined and you wanted to color and stay within them, and create what you thought to be the perfect picture? Remember?"

"Yes, Heather and I often colored together…" Having seated herself, Grandma Dawn scooted in and her chair yelped at the flooring.

"I think the older we get, the more those lines become blurred, and all the colors that seemed so right then, so appropriate, now only seem vaguely familiar and so utterly banal. It's funny. Way back, in the beginning, what seemed so fresh and bright, so optimistic, well, all of that faded with age to become old, worn, and just…" Mrs. Pringle hunted for her word in the windows above, "…lackluster." She brought her attention back to the table, with nodding confirmation: "Lackluster." The woman searched for her spoon. "But along the way, somehow, it didn't matter anymore what color anything was, or whether you were mindful of the lines that were drawn for you, because at some point you realized that you had lost sight of the picture." Mrs. Pringle slowly shook her head, tiny, almost imperceptible movements, her smile wan. "The color, the lines, the book, the time spent, the reason you chose that picture in the first place… *everything*…" Mrs. Pringle dreamily stirred her tea, "…they became so…" her spoon clinked upon the saucer, "…irrelevant."

Grandma Dawn's coffee cup, long since empty, had been pushed away, and was now situated alongside the yellow coffee press. She took a mo-

ment, surveying her hands, calm and at rest upon the tabletop, the varia-
tions in the wood grain nearby. Finally, the older woman spoke. "Lana,
have you ever considered that right now, in that book of yours, maybe it's
less about the coloring and more about simply turning the page?"

She looked up and met the gaze of her neighbor.

In a far corner, opposite the solitary lamp casting forth its frugal light,
the shadow-eyed man waited for the approaching girls. Having navigated their way through many people, Heather stopped and turned towards
the center of the room. Even in the ill-defined light, she could tell all the
heads had followed her, a last look at a future hope. Heather felt their
pull, grabbing and catching at handles somewhere within her.

She said the word softly: "Bye." She waved, calmly left-right.

The moon girl saw hands go up in the room, whispers of movement
in the dimness.

The shadow-eyed man opened a door that led to a narrow flight of
steps, rickety and scarcely lit. With a sweep of cape, he exited smoothly
before the two girls, with Molly close behind.

Heather began to follow on the heels of the butterfly girl, when she
stopped.

"Molly, wait." Then louder: "Wait!"

Molly and the man stopped their ascent, and looked down on Heather.

"Please come back for a minute," she said. "I'm sorry you guys, but
there's something I need to say."

The moon girl fidgeted and removed her mask, where it hung at an
angle to one side of her headpiece, the other side unattached. Her face
bared, she looked at those assembled before her, still outlined in light
from the corner lamp beyond. She felt Molly and the shadow-eyed man's
presence behind her.

"Everyone, I feel I have to say this, and I don't think it would be right
if I didn't."

Heather looked at the Matron, unable to see her face. Her aura shone
at a low and patient ebb. "Continue."

"Well, you see, I think that it-it's very nice of you to think of me like
you do," Heather started, "but I really don't want to do this—I-I can't
do this."

"Do what?" the aged prophetess spoke for all.

"Save your world. I'm sorry—everyone, I'm sorry—but I've given it some real quick thought, when I was walking over to this side of the room from over there, and I really don't want to do it."

The Matron laughed. "Child, I'm not sure you have a choice."

"I don't mean to be rude, but I think I do have a choice, and I don't want this, to be the green-eyed Maiden of the Evermore Portent, your Astille Lia person. So, I think it's probably best that you take me off your list. What happened here today outside in that alley to those three RogueTags, that might never happen again. Do you realize how lucky I was? Really! I was just lucky with all that magic and stuff: balls falling out of the sky, acrobats bouncing all over the place, needles flying around like space ships, and all the rest. Why, you said so yourself, Matron, that it was remarkable that I had all this ability, when I've never practiced—*disciplined*—in your LightCraft. What I mean is, the part of me that comes and goes, what if the next time it doesn't show up, and those guys hurt me—or Molly, or *you*, if I'm supposed to be protecting you? You have to forgive me, Matron, ma'am, but I don't think doing this thing for Evermore is a good idea. Like you said, there have been many before me. What if I tried to help you guys and couldn't, and then I let down all of these worlds and a Realm, and all sorts of people were hurt because I couldn't save them, you know, when I was supposed to and you thought I would? I don't want that-that responsibility. That's a lot. It's not like I'm trying to save a bird with a busted wing or something. We're talking about a *Realm* here. Do you realize that sometimes I forget to make my bed and-and brush my teeth? And if I can't remember to do those things, how the heck am I supposed to save the entire Realm of Evermore? Whew! No thanks! And I-I mean that in a nice way."

Heather looked out at those gathered in the room. They were stone silent. She could see their auras atrophying, becoming smaller and disappointedly anemic.

Heather continued. "I'm sorry if I'm letting you all down. But I think it's better that I let you down now, instead of having you see me get beat up or killed the next time I'm trapped by a bunch of RogueTags in an alley. I really didn't want to fight them out there. Molly either. We ran from them. Did you know that? *We ran from them.* That doesn't sound like a thing your green-eyed Maiden would do. It sounds more like what young girls running from big guys would do. And that's because that's what we are, we're just young girls."

She felt Molly's hand on her back in support.

"I-I know that when your Realm of Evermore becomes all those things that the Matron said would happen to it, that you will be looking for someone special to help you, someone from the Portent. But that's not me. I'm only Heather Nighborne from a little town somewhere on a little planet far off in your sky. Geez, you guys, at night I don't even know if you can see our planet twinkle from here. Anyway, all this that happened today was just an accident, I'm sure. And I know that the man who brought us here to this room said I have SearEye and all that, and even though that *was* me, I'm not really her. Know what I mean? I'm not the girl you think I am.

"The girl in the Portent doesn't have a treehouse, or a Grandma Dawn, or live in a wonderful big house with magical rooms and a beautiful garden. Or have a great friend like Molly Pringle. I do. And I know my grandmother would miss me terribly if anything happened to me. She wouldn't understand my disappearing to become the girl in your Portent. She just wouldn't. And-and I know she loves me very much, because she's taken care of me ever since I was a little baby, when my mother and father couldn't. So, I could never just leave her and come here and do what this girl is supposed to do for you.

"You guys, I can't save your world. Me? I couldn't even save our friend, Stilped, who was horribly murdered and buried on our property, not far from our house."

Molly dropped her hand, letting it fall to her side.

"So, you see, I really appreciate that you want me to be this special girl of yours—and I almost *was* a minute or two ago—and it was really exciting to think that I could be this awesome green-eyed Maiden of the Evermore Portent, but I'm not. Really. I'm not her. Just me. And believe me when I tell you that I would *love* to be her and save your world. It would be, well, really great and-and splendidly stellar and all that. But I can't, because I'm just a twelve-year-old girl who came to Autumnsloe today to see your parade. So, I'm really, really sorry everyone. Very sorry."

"Wait!" a young boy's voice rang out. Heather looked to see Starbrill standing next to the Matron. "How do you know you're not the answer to the Portent? Just because you suddenly feel that you might not be able to do something, it doesn't mean you're not the person whose job it is to do it."

Uncomprehendingly, Heather just stared at him. "What?" finally popped loose like a cockeyed spring.

The Matron said in a gentle voice, "Starbrill, sit." She placed a hand on his upper arm. "Sit. It's all right."

"No. No it's not, Matron. I'm sorry, but Heather Nighborne doesn't know if she is or isn't the green-eyed Maiden mentioned in the Portent. I felt something in her when I touched her just now, when I helped to hold her up. Something deeper than most. I say she *is* our Astille Lia."

"Your vision is keen, young man, but you, too, are still a child. And this child, Heather Nighborne, has every right to feel that she's not the answer to the Portent. Every right indeed. Now kindly stand down, Starbrill, that's a good lad. It's all right. Do go and sit and bother yourself no further with this. When it acts, the great and formidable hand of destiny won't consider any of our feelings. It never has. Heather, you are always encouraged to do as you must."

"Thank you, Matron."

The woman nodded, her aura alight in ruby reds and sequined golds.

Heather's eyes swept the room. "So, I guess, *finally*, goodbye, everyone—and I think this time I really mean it—unless you guys want me to keep talking. Then I'll say it again in a couple of hours." Heather laughed, giddy with relief. "And thank you so much for being so nice to Molly and me, and-and for not finding me evil and then killing us. And I hope that you do find your Portent girl and that she saves this beautiful place of yours like she's supposed to, and that you're all happy again after being so sad when your Realm will become so, well, so impoverished, and-and encumbered with sorrow, and, uh, everything else that's supposed to happen to you guys.

"And I know that when I'm up in my treehouse at night, and I see a twinkling star up there in the sky, I'll think of Autumnsloe and what a great and, um, *unusual* time I had here today. And it really was super special, but now I have to get home, so Grandma Dawn doesn't worry about me and I'm not late for dinner." Heather lifted an arm and bent her head near the pit for a sniff. Her face contorted. "Whew! And I guess I'll be taking a bath, too." She laughed easily. "We really had a pretty good workout today."

Molly giggled.

"So, please excuse us." Heather turned behind her. "Ready?"

Molly nodded.

"Okay." Heather turned to the people in the room. "Thank you, you guys. I'll never forget this place, I promise."

"Of that," said the Matron, "I am certain."

CHAPTER TWENTY-FOUR

In Exploration of the New and Unexpected

Following the daylight arrival in the garden and subsequent stealthy descent into the basement, the indigo stranger passed through the Entry Room before settling in a light-deprived recess belonging to one of the initial storage rooms.

To a modest degree, the visitor's blue eyes had adjusted to the overall gloominess. Despite the meager contribution of cloud-diffused light from the small windows perched high along one wall, darkness held fast to the corners and confined aisles, its reign supreme over the room's draped and naked contents scattered and stacked throughout.

The visitor reached into a sleek charcoal rucksack and withdrew a small apparatus, not overly bulky in design, but not totally flat either. It took just a moment to quietly don and adjust the Moonlight°Prisms, magical eyewear used to detect the presence of PortalDoors.

PortalDoors were most easily recognized when bathed in moonglow. The filtered beams of bluish-green would illuminate the magical residue shed by a PortalDoor and its accompanying Corridor along the expanse of the TimeLight Bridge. When worn and activated, Moonlight°Prisms added to the viewed environment the cooler, more muted colors of the lunar light spectrum, while blocking a percentage of daylight and the artificial light of indoors. This made the goggles a powerful asset for use in Portal detection.

The stranger had donned the only known pair, developed in the LightCraft function houses of the Vigen°Darr, the crafting smiths who dwelled along the shores of the Tabeer River, near the River Weep.

Aided by the enhanced eyewear, the visitor moved with a covert yet elegant glide, vigilantly scanning the packed room of antique furniture and old trunks resting right side up and on their sides, open-mouthed and closed, emptied and spilling forth in a jumble their most varied and treasured belongings. Nothing glowed, nothing glinted, nothing stirred—the Moonlight°Prisms detected no sign of a PortalDoor.

If covered, there stood a chance that any Portal could avoid detection, so the figure took time to silently lift and sift through any potential stifling piece of material. To be thorough without sound was proving to be difficult, but the visitor performed the task with a quiet diligence and steady proficiency. It was only part of the mission assigned, after detecting an accelerated use of magic in and around Noble, and this following Heather Nighborne's alarming encounter with the WhisperEye Mirror. The unusual activities brought attention to bear on the porous Bristol House, lending credence to the perception that it could possibly be the home of the green-eyed Maiden of the Evermore Portent.

The shadow-eyed man ascended the precarious steps, his long cape billowing behind him. The boy-like creature, bouncing with every footfall, was hanging off the back of his headpiece, occasionally turning to look down at the girls. Silently observant, he trailed a costume-covered arm. The light was still weak on the derelict staircase, and Heather, following Molly, kept trying to peer above them, but even with her acute night vision, she was unable to pierce the gloom. Soon, however, they reached a creaky, loose-planked landing, revealing a door to one side. The man stepped back a pace.

"We're almost at CityCentral, the uppermost level of Elderraine, which you may have determined to be situated on top of a large hill, above the water. Outside this door is your route to street-level, and as such, it is here we will part ways. I must once again ask, are you certain you don't require guides of the ClearWeave to take you any closer to your Portal?"

"Where will we end up at street-level?" Heather asked, much to the satisfaction of Fallasha.

"When you surface, you will not be far from the Ring of the Evermore Maidens monument."

Molly looked at Heather. "Isn't that where this entire situation with the RogueTags began? Remember? We were walking back from following—?"

"So, what do you think?" Heather saw fit to interrupt.

Molly said, "I think we'll need to get around those RogueTags that were hanging out by the café and near that corner without them seeing us."

"I'm not sure we'll be able to do that, Molly. We don't know any of these back streets."

"The ClearWeave will see to it that your passage north and west of here shall prove to be uncomplicated and without interruption."

"How are you going to do that?" Heather asked. She saw the grim man's shine enliven with mild amusement, subdued yellows and oranges, tinged with green.

"I know the café of which you speak, and I know the corner. Allow me to put this delicately and say that we have ways of becoming involved in various organizations and functions here in Evermore." The hues of his aura became brighter. "And also allow me to say that under certain circumstances, this can help to sway particular events to our advantage."

The shadow-eyed man was bending slightly, his hands together. The creature's head was positioned next to his own, alongside the fabric that covered his ear. The Evermorian animal was gazing at the two girls, its two small hands hanging onto the large collar that had been flattened beneath its torso.

"What's your pet's name?" Molly asked.

The question took the man by surprise. He stood up straight, reaching a hand towards the creature.

"My pet?" He laughed. "This is Pallár Tøtsin—you may just call him Pallár. And he happens to be a geetalvasse."

"A geetalvasse?" Molly asked.

"Yes. Their home can be found in the Ancient Rain Forests of Tabeer, in the Kingdom of Springshoot Green."

"But why does he have a little boy's face?" Heather felt compelled to ask.

"Why do you possess a young girl's?"

The moon girl shrugged. "I don't know. I guess I kinda just came that way."

The man said, "Pallár Tøtsin came his."

Heather harbored more thoughts and questions on the subject, but determined it wise to let the topic drop.

The butterfly girl asked, "May I pet him?"

"If he allows it. It is his choice, Molly Pringle." He turned to the creature and spoke in a very strange tongue, consisting of chirps, whistles, and clicks. Pallár Tøtsin listened before responding in kind.

The creature looked at Molly, and unexpectedly, he sprang towards her. The butterfly girl gasped and shrank, but upon landing the creature grabbed onto her headpiece, stabilizing himself atop it.

"Hold up your arm, Molly Pringle," said the shadow-eyed man.

Molly offered it, and Pallár grabbed onto her wrist like it would a pole, swinging around and coming to rest on her upper arm and shoulder with a whistle and click, its tail wrapping the girl's forearm. The creature stared at her mask and then began to carefully finger the butterfly wings and their delicate connecting chains.

"I think he likes you, Molly," said Heather. "Well, your mask, anyway."

"Pallár, you are adorable." Molly brought up a hand, and Pallár raised and positioned his chin so that the butterfly girl, scratching gently, could work her fingers along his downy jaw line. She stroked his soft fleshy cheek and scrubbed his furry collar. Pallár inclined his head her way until Molly finished and withdrew her hand, regarding him fondly. "I wish I had a friend just like you."

"You do," said Heather, "only I'm a lot bigger and not as hairy. And don't even think about petting me."

Molly giggled, never diverting her attention from the geetalvasse. "So long as you don't try to sit on my shoulder."

The two girls laughed while the man's demeanor remained subdued. The Evermorian creature returned to find continual interest in Molly's mask, inspecting various parts of the intricate, colorful wings.

"Should Molly and I wait here until you tell us the RogueTags are gone and the way is clear?"

"No, you have a tunnel's distance to travel yet. Word will get out, and by the time you've reached the area, it will be empty of RogueTags. But I must warn you to still be on your guard. With the RogueTags gone, it does not mean there won't be other dangers."

"Thank you. I understand—I think we both do." Heather turned to her friend. "Ready?"

Molly nodded and turned to Pallár. Her mask put on a sad face. "You have to go back to your owner now."

The shadow-eyed man laughed. "I am not his owner and he is not my pet, Molly Pringle. We are friends, Pallár Tøtsin and I. He is welcome to come and go as he pleases. It has been said we have a relationship that is mutually beneficial to one another."

"Oh!" cried Molly, as the geetalvasse jumped from her arm and back onto the shoulder of the shadow-eyed man, departing as unexpectedly as he had arrived.

"Can I ask, what's *your* name?" said Heather.

The mysterious man shook his head. "I can tell you Pallár Tøtsin's name, but alas, Heather Nighborne, I cannot tell you my own. Perhaps someday you will come to know it."

I don't see how, thought Heather, but instead said, "Who knows? Maybe I will." She shot a look at Molly. "Are you ready?"

"I'm ready when you are."

Heather brightened, as did the features on her mask. "I say let's go home."

"As I said, there will be a tunnel," said the man, "a long tunnel. Upon entering, just beyond this door, you will climb some stairs and turn immediately to your right and walk for some distance guided by a pale light, but there should be no one to delay your progress. Stay on the wider main route, and do not venture from it. Once you reach the street, however, make certain that there are no souls present, and only then make your exit from the tunnel."

The girls consented.

"And now, your LuminOrb." The shadow-eyed man produced what appeared to be a small ball in his upturned palm. Placing his hand over the shiny marble, he mumbled an incantation, removed his hand, and the globe began to grow. Once it had reached the size of a baseball, it grew an inscribed conical hat. Heather thought it looked like an upside-down ice cream cone with only one scoop (fleetingly, it made her wonder if strawberry ice cream existed in Autumnsloe). With his free hand, the man took hold of the tapering handle to turn the 'Orb upright, and following an unhurried hand-pass over the top, the sphere ignited with an internal burst of light. The LuminOrb began to glow.

"Wow!" said Heather. "You know magic?"

"Nothing to rival yours, Heather Nighborne. Nothing close. Many here in Evermore know small bits of magic, little things, as it is part of our Waizai culture, but these insignificant acts certainly do not qualify as disciplined magic, a magic such as iMagiNacia." He offered the 'Orb. "Here. Careful."

"So, this is just plain old magic?" Heather succeeded in grasping the conical handle. With a curious finger, she touched the cool sphere to determine its temperature.

"Just plain old magic. MagiCommon." The shadow-eyed man laughed. "You seem impressed."

"Well, you know..."

"Heather Nighborne, though I know you can produce a much brighter 'Orb, it is both a courtesy and an honor to provide this to you to guide you on your way. It's light is not overly bright—which speaks of the unremarkable strength of my magical power—but it will serve its purpose. As well, be aware that should you use your great power at any time, this could possibly draw the magical eyes of Mistraya to you—and us—and it is crucial that we avoid that at all costs. So please, I must ask that you refrain from performing any of your astounding feats of iMagi-Nacia here in the tunnel or near its exit.

"You should also know that once daylight touches its surface, the LuminOrb will dim and extinguish, and afterwards shrink in size. Simply exit the tunnel, and discard of the smaller globe somewhere along your route, but not near the tunnel's entrance."

"Okay. Sure. Can I ask why?"

"Magical residue, Heather Nighborne. The scouts may pick it up, if they happen to be flying overhead—and make no mistake, they will be looking for you. Some animals and people can read the residue until it eventually fades, so again, be discreet.

"Won't there be magical residue on my hands?"

"No. Only the magical object used will bear any residue of its act. So, in this case, you needn't worry. But do not be caught with that LuminOrb in your possession, for questions will be asked, and it could very well put you at a disadvantage if your intent is to arrive at your Portal-Door safely." The departing guide bowed slightly, Pallár balancing on his shoulder. "Heather Nighborne, Molly Pringle, it has been my pleasure to be of assistance today."

"It has been our pleasure to have had you provide it," said Molly.

Heather was impressed. "Wow, Molly! I like the way you said that."

Molly giggled. Her mask reddened. "Thanks."

Having said their farewells, with Molly giving the geetalvasse just a bit more welcome attention, the two girls opened the door and climbed a short flight of steps leading into the bowels of the tunnel. Behind them, they heard the door close. And there the girls stood, lost to the darkness, save for the 'Orb and its almost adequate light.

With an eerie wail, a banshee wind raced headlong through the trembling entanglement of leaf and limb, warning of the approaching storm. Listening beneath the high windows overhead that showered her in a gray light, Grandma Dawn was chopping the rosemary leaves in preparation for dinner, a solitary figure at the kitchen counter.

Still seated, leaning forward, Mrs. Pringle watched the stately woman, though not really. She was propped and anchored from head to table via chin, hand, forearm, and elbow. Roaming at their leisure, her eyes were in no particular hurry to go anywhere and yet had no interest in finding rest.

Occasionally, with a spoon, Mrs. Pringle pushed at the teabag that hunched glumly on the saucer. There was something about the small sodden bag of Humpty Dumpty that annoyed her. With a few gentle shoves of the spoon's tip, the roly-poly sack scooted its way to the edge before a final push sent it toppling to the tabletop. Pluh. Not much of a fall. Not much of an impact. No scream, no splat, no shards. Still, Lana Pringle watched as a liquid umber gathered around the base of the little leaper, signifying an internal bleeding, satisfying a barbed compulsion.

Much better, she thought.

Sitting up, she continued to prod the teabag with her spoon, pushing it to seek shelter under the brim of saucer, all the while resisting the temptation to squish it flat till it burst. "When are the children coming down, Dawn?"

Grandma Dawn's knife stopped its rat-a-tat on the chopping block countertop. She looked up. "Pardon?" Head poised, eyebrows raised, distant air. "The children? Anytime now, I suspect."

"Maybe I'll go up and look in on them, see how they're doing."

"Well, you can, but—"

"I think it would do me good to walk around up there, become acquainted with the layout of the place." Mrs. Pringle shrugged.

Grandma Dawn laughed, albeit a bit nervously. She returned to her chopping, setting upon the remainder of rosemary with a blistering blur of the knife.

"What? What's so funny?"

Grandma Dawn felt herself teeter on the brink of a giggling fit. She stayed the impulse. "You're more than welcome to go upstairs to the third floor and look for the children, but you may have a difficult time finding them with all those rooms." Her face broke into a great grin.

"What, Dawn?" Mrs. Pringle felt compelled to chortle. "What are you finding so humorous?"

"Nothing. I don't know. I…" Grandma Dawn brought her knife hand up to her mouth and pressed the backside against her lips, the steely implement angling lazily, its tip pointing towards the floor. Her eyes shone with glee. "You're right, though, Lana," the words were coming from behind her hand, "perhaps it *is* time that you learned about the layout of the Bristol House."

Directing her attention back to the countertop, Grandma Dawn took her triangular blade and pushed the fine bits of rosemary into a pile, saying, "But the third floor can be quite confusing in its arrangement. You may find yourself wandering for awhile—for a long, *long* while." Head down, Grandma Dawn's face again held a wide grin. The knife continued to scrape inattentively at the pile of green.

Leaning back in her chair, Mrs. Pringle folded her arms across her chest, amused. Thoughtfully nodding, she said, "You're really enjoying this."

Grandma Dawn giggled, fought it, and brought a sleeve up to dab her eyes. "I'm sorry. I don't know what's come over me. Really… I guess I've a lot on my mind at the moment…" Bits of laughter galloped, as she continued to blot her eyes. Collecting herself with a sniff, Grandma Dawn said, "Let's do this. If you go up there, and then the children come down alone, I'll have them return leading a search and rescue team." She burst into laughter.

Mrs. Pringle contemplated the self-entertained Dawn Thibble. "Dawn, you're enjoying this *way* too much." Grandma Dawn set the knife on the counter and tilting her head back slightly, brought a finger up to place at the end of each damp eye, attempting to stem the flow of tears. Mrs. Pringle continued, "Molly's told me about the Bristol House library, and how she and Heather can get lost it has so many rooms."

"And trust me, that's just the library. So, you can go on up, but honestly, you may end up drifting from room to room—" and here she talked through a laugh, "but one thing I know for sure is that, without a doubt, you'll be anything but bored."

Her hip finding rest at the counter's edge, and following more facial dabs with a nearby hand towel, Grandma Dawn said, "Seriously, Lana, if you wouldn't mind waiting, I'd be happy to take you for a tour after dinner. We can roam at will. And I think you'll be amazed at what's up there."

"Sure. I can wait. It's just that I didn't want to sit here and sadistically punish my poor tea bag for the next hour or two for no apparent reason."

Grandma Dawn glanced at her neighbor's suitcases that stood by idly, patiently, two strangers awaiting a bus. "Lana, how about this? Let's wait until Molly returns, and then she can take you on a personal tour of the third floor. She's somewhat familiar with it. Also, it would give the two of you some time alone should either of you need to talk. Right now, if you'd like, I'd be more than happy to show you your rooms, let you unpack and get situated before dinnertime."

"Great idea. And if you don't mind, I think I'd like to lie down for a bit, too, though I can't say I'll be able to nap."

"Yes, by all means do. Poor thing, you must be drained."

Lana Pringle pinched hold of the tea bag gingerly, dragging it from under the refuge of her saucer. As if dangling a repugnant mouse by the tail, she dropped it into the remaining liquid at the bottom of her cup. It hit with a tiny, sodden splash. After wiping a hand through the small spots of tea that now sprinkled the tabletop, Mrs. Pringle gathered her cup, spoon, and saucer and walked them to the sink before returning to fetch the suitcases. Stepping between them, she hoisted both.

"Here, let me take one of those, Lana. They look heavy," the older woman said, her wet hands moiling within the loose folds of the hand towel. She pitched it sprawling to the counter, a slipshod parachute.

"That's kind of you, Dawn, but not necessary. I'm afraid they're mine to drag around."

"You sure?"

"Uh-huh."

"Okay, then, Lana Pringle, allow me show you to your new Bristol House quarters."

From what the girls could determine, the tunnel looked as if it had been carved out of raw earth and reinforced with thick curving beams that curled down from a central spine overhead, fortifying the moderately craggy walls.

Molly marveled. "I bet this is what it looks like if you were swallowed by a huge sea serpent."

"Could be. Let's hope we never find out for sure," said Heather, inspecting what looked like ribs, repetitious supports that wound into the murkiness.

"I wonder how they stay up there? Heather, can you hold the 'Orb higher?" The butterfly girl's mask was tilted up to the ceiling, examining the ribs. One hand held her headpiece in place. "They almost seem to be floating under the rock, not against it. And look, along the walls, those supports don't actually come down to touch the ground, either. I guess everything just floats. You know, they're not at all like those photos you see of wooden beams taken in a mineshaft."

"You mean like those photos *you* see of wooden beams taken in a mineshaft," said Heather. "I haven't seen any lately." She laughed. "Anyway, I think these curved beams are holding up the walls by magic."

"Yes, I would have to say that's an *excellent* guess, Heather," said Fallasha.

Heather began walking and Molly followed, as the two embarked down the long corridor on their way to street-level.

"But you heard what 'Mr. No Name' said back there at the door," said Molly. Heather laughed at Molly's name for the man who wouldn't give it. "If strong magic or iMagiNacia is used, Mistraya will know and find out about these tunnels. So, if magic *is* holding up the ceiling and walls, how come Mistraya doesn't know about this place?"

"Excellent question. I would have to think that it's because this is a constant low-grade magic, Molly," Fallasha said, "much like what holds up the buildings above ground that are so integrated with the Autumnslovian landscape. I would even hazard a guess and say this low-grade magic probably registers as nothing more than a constant magical buzz with the sorceress. However, anything stronger, like an intense burst of iMagiNacia on an Autumnslovian street, for instance, would no doubt jolt her magical receptors. And *that* is when Mistraya, or one of the Influenced, would begin to hunt down the source."

"The 'Influenced'?" asked Molly.

"Yes, one under the spell of Mistraya—no pun intended."

"Are the RogueTags, well, Influenced?" asked Heather, constantly scanning ahead while they walked. She passed the 'Orb to her alternate hand.

"Currently, to a great degree," said Fallasha.

The moon girl asked, "How do you know all this, Fallasha?"

"All what?"

"About Mistraya, the Influenced, low grade magic—all that?"

Hurt fleetingly passed over Fallasha's small features. "Well! Have you forgotten? Why, I'm your tour guide! I have to know and keep apprised of all things Evermorian."

"But who told you?"

"My dear Heather, suffice it to say that I have my reliable sources concerning the sorceress Mistraya and the Influenced—what she does, how she does it, who is hurt, captured, tortured, maimed, and killed by this evil woman and her conspirators." Fallasha smiled when she noticed Molly raise a grave hand to her chest. The moon brooch continued, "Mistraya has a bloodlust, to be sure, and she doesn't hesitate to make use of it as she vies for power, always prowling...prowling, until the opportune moment arrives...and then..." the brooch lowered her voice to a dramatic undertone, "...then, she moves in closer...she bides her time...quietly...hiding stealthily in the shadows...and then...then when her victims least expect it... *she pounces on her prey!*"

Molly jumped; Heather rolled her eyes. The three went quiet, the girls' hollow footfalls echoing in the blind hallway, the scant light supplied by the 'Orb suddenly seeming even less than inadequate.

"Well," said Molly, with a glance over her shoulder, "I don't know about you two, but I say enough about Mistraya and the Influenced."

Heather laughed. In the dimness, Fallasha wore her smile smugly.

The three continued on, led by the moon girl's subdued light that she held steadily aloft. Ahead, the cast shadows that stretched before them shrank at the approach of Heather's LuminOrb. Occasionally, exposed boulders on either side protruded out into the path, along its uneven borders, their shadows dancing and bobbing with the passing of the girls. They found the temperature in the passageway cool, but not uncomfortably cold.

As the shadow-eyed man had requested, the two visitors stuck to the main walk, bypassing the much darker recesses that appeared frequently and obscurely. Along the meandering route, Heather and Molly were aware of many gradual dips and rises before the tunnel ran level for some distance.

"How far does this thing go?" Heather asked. "I think we're hiking across the entire city."

"A long way, that's for sure. Or maybe it just seems that way, because we're walking in the dark."

"Far too far, if you ask me," said Fallasha. "We really are running much too late, girls. None of this was on our Parade Day schedule. You do realize that I could be the recipient of a severe reprimand and possible suspension for allowing your behavior today to upend and supersede the Bristol House Parade Day Schedule of Events?"

"But Fallasha," Heather said, "we *had* to do all this stuff. Don't you remember? It was written."

"Not funny." Fallasha pouted, before joining the girls in a laugh. "Oh, you two... I give up."

"Fallasha," Heather said, "I think that's a *great* idea."

"Rude!"

"No, I mean it—"

"Rude!"

"—but in a nice way."

"Oh, *really?*"

"Will you please listen? If you'd just, well, relax, and come along with Molly and me, then you'd see, you'd have a really good time."

"Humph!"

"Really, Fallasha. And," Heather lowered her voice and added lightly, "it sure wouldn't hurt if you could stop being so bossy."

"Rude!"

"I didn't mean it to be rude. I meant it so—"

"Rude!"

"I meant it so you could, well, get along and just have fun with us, that's all."

"Oh, of course. 'Fun.' Glad you brought the word to my attention. Yes, we certainly had a lot of *fun* fighting those RogueTags back there near that alley."

"We did, didn't we?" The features on the moon girl's mask were alight.

"Heather," Molly said, "I don't think Fallasha means it that way."

"Really? What kind of fun does she mean?"

A slight groan escaped the moon brooch.

The girls had been walking for some time. Recurrently, they passed more of the darker passages, but continued their course upon the main path.

Finally, Heather stopped in front of one. She tried to peer in, taking a step farther into the void, her torch extended out before her.

"I believe I know what you have in mind, Heather, and it is my advice as your completely disregarded and totally abused tour guide, that you stick to the greater path as suggested and promised."

"I'm not going anywhere, Fallasha. Molly?"

Molly drew alongside. "What's wrong?"

"Nothing. At least I don't think so. For a second, though, I thought I saw a light."

"Down this tunnel?"

"Yeah."

"Don't do it," Fallasha warned again. "I know what you're thinking, young Heather, but my unsolicited advice is that you refrain and do not follow your impulse. Besides, we've been rambling all over who-knows-where and Autumnsloe today. And we are running much too late. Might we simply go home now? Please?"

The two girls stood side-by-side, trying to see what lay ahead in the lightless passage.

"You know what I think, Molly? I think that the ClearWeave have a bunch of tunnels that run beneath—Fallasha, what's the name of this city again?"

"Elderraine." The knowledge was passed on icily.

"Elderraine."

"Like a network?" Molly asked.

"Like a web."

"Geez, Heather, that's pretty impressive, don't you think?"

"Yeah, I'll say. *Very* impressive." Heather waved the torch before her, trying to pick up something that would pique her interest. "I bet this tunnel goes on for a long way, like the wider one we're in. And I'm sure that there are even more tunnels that connect with it."

"Do you think we're being watched?" Molly asked.

"Yeah. I was just thinking that same thing. The ClearWeave probably wouldn't just trust us to follow the tunnel without making sure that we stayed on the course like we're supposed to."

Fallasha added, "Especially if they're familiar with your tendency for taking the occasional detour and costing us hours on end of time spent in complete disregard of the Parade Day schedule."

"Fallasha is right, though, Heather. We really shouldn't go any farther in that direction. We promised Mr. No Name that we'd stay in the main tunnel."

"And we will. But I just think it's pretty amazing, don't you, that by coming through these tunnels the ClearWeave can get around Elderraine without anyone seeing them?"

"Yes."

"Heather, please," said Fallasha. "Let's simply proceed to street level, shall we?"

"Okay, okay. Come on then, Molly. Let's get to the street. I don't want to get home late. Besides, if we take too long, Fallasha, here, might get canned."

"Rude!"

"It wasn't rude. I was just looking out for you, not wanting you to get dumped, that's all."

"Rude!"

"I mean, if you get dumped from the Bristol House job, there aren't a lot of people who will want to hire a nagging moon brooch with a mouth that doesn't have an 'off' switch."

"Rude!"

"You two, really," Molly interjected. "Let's not start this again—"

"Apologize."

"I'm sorry?"

"I can only hope my next job has me pinned to the dress of an Evermorian ball gown," said Fallasha, "instead of being stuck to the costume of some ungracious moon girl who is afraid of being the green-eyed Maiden of the Evermore Portent."

"Rude! And I am *not* afraid!"

"You certainly are. I heard you back there." Fallasha's voice became high-pitched, *"I don't want this, to be the green-eyed Maiden of the Ever-*

more Portent."

"I am *not* afraid."

"Are too."

"Please, you two—"

"Not."

"To."

"Nagger."

"Baby."

"Hey, you two, what's that?"

"What?" asked Heather, head spinning, 'Orb reaching.

"Over here." Molly gestured to the wall opposite the smaller tunnel's opening. "I thought I saw something glitter."

Heather brought the torch over near the far wall. "I don't see anything."

Fallasha said, "Move closer," before adding in a much lower voice, "Sissy."

Annoyed, Heather shook her head and moved closer to the wall with the light, muttering, "…and I guess it's also written that my moon costume has to come equipped with the rudest piece of jewelry in the entire universe…"

"Ru—! There!" Fallasha said. "Wait! Go back… There!"

On the wall before them, the light of the torch illuminated several square images, each slightly larger than the size of a waffle. They appeared to be glowing on a smoother surface of the tunnel's wall.

Molly placed her hands on her hips. "Well, I'll be darned…"

"What?" said Heather.

"Well," Molly giggled, "if you must know, I was really only trying to quiet the two of you and distract you from arguing for the rest of the afternoon."

Heather said, "You mean you really didn't see anything?"

"Honestly?" Embarrassed, Molly tucked her head and hunched her shoulders. "No."

"Look. That's a castle image," said Fallasha.

"Castle Elderraine," said Molly.

"And the arrow points up," said Heather, "which means that the tunnel behind us must lead to the castle."

"And that looks like a symbol for the Ring of the Evermore Maidens," said Molly, "and it's pointing the way we're headed, so at least we know we're going in the right direction."

"What's the image below it?" the moon brooch asked.

"Looks like the symbol for an Autumnslovian restroom," said Heather. "Hard to tell."

"Disgusting," Fallasha mumbled. "Such poor taste…"

"It's probably a symbol," Heather continued, reveling in her brooch's revulsion, "for something that we don't know anything about, is my guess. Any ideas, Molly?"

"No."

"What about these others?"

"Sorry, Heather," Molly said, shaking her head, "I'm afraid they don't mean anything to me."

"How about to our 'completely disregarded and totally abused' tour guide?" said the moon girl. "Do they mean anything to you? After all, you *are* up-to-date on all things Evermorian, right?"

Fallasha stewed for a moment. "All right, Heather. I understand and accept your need to abuse me, because I've read many a knowledgeable book on the topic of how people come to despise those in rank above them—especially when, like yours truly, they happen to be more diminutive in size, more strikingly beautiful," Fallasha wiggled her eyebrows, "and without a doubt, more stunningly intelligent—"

"You forgot to mention 'more totally in love'—" said Heather, "—with yourself."

"In my quest for a greater good, for the sake of decency, peace, harmony, and in search of a better world, I shall choose to ignore that last comment in our incessantly strained discourse," said the moon brooch, nose up. "But I do have a proposal for you."

"What's that?"

"What do you say we declare a truce?"

"Yes! Please!" said Molly. "Oh, thank you!"

Heather said, "Yeah, right. Whatever. So, Fallasha, what about these symbols? Do you know what they mean?"

"No, I haven't the slightest clue, but since they point in the opposite direction, I suspect they're of little consequence on our current heading."

"You know, I bet that all along there were images at the end of every one of these smaller tunnels," said Heather. "Only, we weren't close enough with this torch to make them light up."

"Like a map," said Molly, "or a directory to guide someone traveling down here. Of course you'd have to be carrying a torch and then these images would light up as you went by."

"Unless," said Heather, raising a gloved index finger, "unless you were new here and didn't know you had to be close to them—"

"Or no one told you that you had to be close to them."

"Yeah," Heather chuckled, "or no one told you. Or suppose you weren't supposed to be down here in the first place! Then after you snuck in, you wouldn't know about these directions or where you were going, and then these tunnels would turn into a very crazy maze."

"Yes, and you'd probably be left wandering around down here, lost for a very long time."

"Yeah, and then you'd just walk through these tunnels, like a zombie," Heather put out her hands and began to walk stiff-legged, torch jerking, illumination bouncing, "going round and round, and after awhile you'd become weaker and weaker, and before long you'd just drop. Then you'd start crawling around on all fours, until you couldn't go any farther. And then, because you didn't know any better and there wasn't anyone around to tell you, you wouldn't find the directory on the wall with a symbol pointing to a restaurant or an all-night drugstore, and finally you'd end up too weak to do anything but think about how you're just sitting here starving to death, wishing you had a strawberry milkshake. But then you'd have to die first from being so stupid, because you didn't bring any food in your backpack, just a camera and an extra pair of socks."

Molly was laughing heartily. She managed, "Wouldn't be surprised."

"Oh, *please*," said the brooch. "Don't you think that the ClearWeave keep watch on these tunnels? Don't you think that they're listening to all your senseless prattle right now?

"Didn't think about that," said Heather, "but I did figure they were watching from a distance. You really think they're listening?"

"They're listening."

Heather looked up, saying into the blackness, "Hey, you guys, want to hear a *joke?*"

"All right," said the moon brooch, not bothering to hide her irritation, "now that we've stumbled onto and established the existence of these wall images and determined that they are here for direction, but only if you happen to be in possession of one of these torches, may I suggest we make haste for that distant and all too elusive exit at street level?"

The pair recommended walking. For some time, no one spoke. They passed a few more openings off the main corridor, with Heather waving the torch in their direction, wondering if they were all tunnels or short stairways that led to doors, like the one where they had left the shadow-eyed man and his furry companion. They saw nothing.

"Fallasha," Heather said, breaking the silence, "have you ever noticed that it takes you ten times as many words to say something as it does any normal person?"

Fallasha gasped.

"Heather!" Molly shushed, but couldn't refrain from giggling.

"I thought we had a truce," Fallasha said, apparently hurt.

"We do. I didn't mean it to be mean," Heather said. "I really was just wondering, you know, after hearing you talk like you do and everything."

There existed a moment's silence, before Fallasha said, "Define 'everything.'"

"Well, you know, *everything.*"

The brooch waited. "And?"

"And..." Heather shrugged, *"...everything."*

Molly shook her head in exasperation. The girls continued their walk down the lengthy corridor, with Heather and her brooch at a constant bicker.

"So, what if you really *are* the green-eyed Maiden? Then what? Are you simply going to desert this Realm and its needful inhabitants?"

"But I told you, Fallasha, I'm not. I'm no more the green-eyed Maiden of the Evermore Portent, than you're the real nice moon brooch that's so much fun to be around."

"Rude! You're right. There's no way you can be the green-eyed Maiden," Fallasha shot, hotly. "Why, the green-eyed Maiden of the Evermore Portent would be kind and generous, considerate and compassionate. You're more like the moldy moon head in the outrageously fluffy costume."

"And any second here you're going to be the nagging little moon brooch who got left in a tunnel—"

"Hey, look!" Molly said. "What's that?"

"Nice try, Molly," said Heather, "but you've already used that one."

"No, up ahead. See it?"

The moon girl stopped. In front of them, the many-ribbed tunnel gradually curved to the left. At its end, straining down from above was a funnel of cool, gray daylight. Heather immediately broke into a jog.

"And there's a circular staircase directly beneath it," said the moon brooch.

"I see it, Fallasha. And I bet it goes up to street-level."

when two moons collide

Having parked the car nearby, oblivious of the wind, Mr. Simpletripp walked behind the worn squarish building and towards the back of the lot, along the dirty white cinderblock wall. There was a forced casualness to his step as he discreetly scanned the area, checking to see if anyone might be watching.

Hanging from his slimy right hand was a bag of medium size and weight—nondescript. It was full of moist slippery bones, bones with stringy tendons and the jelly-like cartilage still attached, bones with the richness of watery red around the pliant rubbery joints. Earlier, Mr. Simpletripp had taken his time, relishing the way the skin worked easily and loosely over the flesh, savoring how it peeled up cleanly with a simple slice of his sharp blade, and then how efficiently the glistening steel severed the limbs. Often, he had cut to the bone and sometimes through it, as was his need, so achingly eager in the carving.

The man didn't know why, didn't question the small thrill he received in disposing of the remains as he did, tossing the bag towards the rear of the open dumpster, where it settled out of sight, among the disorderly contents. Mr. Simpletripp just knew that now his hands felt uncomfortably sticky with soppy residue from his earlier act. Not too far away, he caught sight of and headed for the men's restroom.

a lo

Harland Dane turned his pickup truck into Glen Denny's Pump and Serve, bouncing up the entry curb with a bump and a lurch. He coasted and then pulled alongside the old style yellow and red pump, braking to a halt. Glen's youngest son, Tommy, at the driver's side window of a customer's car, looked up briefly in acknowledgement, before refocusing to conclude his conversation. With a pat on the roof, he stepped away, talking loudly over a sudden squall.

"Hi, Sheriff. Fill 'er up?" The wind flattened the stiff locks of black hair to his head, revealing a pale part, crookedly severe in contrast.

"Yeah, Tommy, thanks," Sheriff Dane said through the partially opened window. He began to roll it up and stopped. He lifted his mouth to the remaining crack and said, "Can you check the air in the rear right tire, too, while you're at it? I think I've got a slow leak."

"I'm on it."

The next aisle over, following a pop and release of the emergency brake, an older style Centurion slowly accelerated with a bub-bub-bub and pulled away. Sun-scorched and faded blue, it crept towards the street, riding low on weary shocks, bumper stickers shouting biases from the rusted chrome bumper. A sleek black luxury Translandia sedan glided in to fill the vacancy with a lively ring of an overhead bell. The cheery sound seemed incongruous in contrast to the somber gray of day.

Tommy looked up and waved. "Be right with you, Mrs. Jorgenson!"

The middle-aged woman mouthed an 'okay' through the partially tinted window, her freshly coifed hair safe within the sealed confines of the automobile. After flashing her teeth's broad hi-beams at the boy, she turned back to the car's controls, bringing the engine's purr to a quiet standstill.

Dane stepped out of the truck's cab, easing the door shut behind him.

"Where's Pop?"

The kid stood toward the back of the pickup, unscrewing the gas cap. He gestured with a poke of his head. "Over in the garage doing a tune-up for old man Simpson." He plugged in the pump's nozzle. It slid roughly and lodged into place with a jarring metallic grunt. "Windows?"

Tommy saw Dane nod. He couldn't hear his uttered, "Yeah."

Hit by a bluster of air, both the lanky teen and sheriff squinted, the latter bringing a hand up to screen the side of his face. Tommy pulled the wipers away from the windshield.

The sheriff spoke loudly, "A tune-up? On that beat up old scrap heap of his? I don't think he even drives it. Why bother?"

Tommy called, "Dad tried to talk him out of it," before turning from the latest gust. He lifted the waterlogged squeegee from its sudsy bin with a casual shake and returned to the pickup's windshield, dripping a trail that spattered the light cement with a series of water blots. "But Mr. Simpson didn't wanna listen." With a laugh, the kid continued, sluicing the window with the spongy side of the squeegee. "Said it's time, that

'Old Bessie' needs a 'seein' to.'" Eliciting the occasional squeak, Tommy was pulling the squeegee's rubbery blade across the glass. Concluding at the windshield's edge, he wiped the watery excess on a rag he pulled from his pocket. "And old man Simpson wants her innards cleaned up every five years, whether she needs it or not."

A rueful smile posted itself to Dane's lips, albeit only briefly, and the sheriff walked away, leaving Tommy to his duties. Turning his head from a fierce rush of air, he rounded the side of the old gas station that still provided service—the only one in town—and moved towards the restrooms, lost in thought. Coming mostly from the west, the wind was shoving at him, pushing, pushing, and then subsiding, before pushing some more. Stopping, he stood stiffly in defiance.

Don't you ever let up?

Dane shifted his weight. Rather than continuing to hold firm against the wind-bursts while they rushed over and around him, the sheriff finally allowed himself to sway with the buffeting. Admittedly, he was beginning to like the feel, the relenting give of it all.

His mood markedly dour, the mustachioed sheriff inspected the nimbus clouds as they piled high against each other, coalescing, forming a dense knot of rain-laden blue over the dull hills. Some lighter strips momentarily appeared, breaks in the curdling of cloud cover, but no sunlight sifted through the packed sky.

They can't even get out of their own way, he thought.

Sheriff Dane checked his watch and knew that the mayor, in time for the evening news, would soon be holding his press conference, and that he, Dane, had better hurry with his intended visits. He found himself eager to get on with it, get it behind him. Now, if he could only get the ladies alone.

Reflexively, the sheriff rummaged into his breast pocket and pulled out his pack of smokes. He wasn't going to light up. The man just wanted a pacifier, that's all. Is that too much to ask? Besides, he'd already had his quota for the day—more than his quota.

The wind took the opportunity to climb all over his pants and shirt in agitated ripples, folds, and flaps.

After a tussle with the unseen force, the sheriff was finally able to get a cigarette to his mouth. He began to walk away from the station and toward the street, his head down and to the side, a protective shoulder up, the cigarette being manhandled by a shifting gust. Coming to a standstill in the vicinity of a large blue dumpster, near stacks of used tires, Dane stabbed two long fingers into his breast pocket. With a squeeze, he withdrew his matchbook, freeing up the folded cardboard from within the cellophane wrapping of the cigarette pack.

Why not? Hadn't he earned it? It wasn't his original intention, but things happen, you know. The muse of addiction overwhelms the steadfast soldier of resolve. And you want a cigarette ever so badly—taste it before lighting up, feel the expansion of its glowing super power in your lungs. Then, after the first thirsty drag, you hate yourself.

Around a mocking flash of toothy white, his mouth continued to embrace the tobacco stick.

The sheriff's mind wandered back to his days of heavy smoking: the college parties, the after meal cigarette, smoking with a morning cup of coffee, lighting up over texts and class notes before finals, and throughout the poker parties with the fellas, talking and laughing, the tobacco baton bobbing in accompaniment to the lip music. Then there was the engraved lighter—a gift from Dominique. Both long gone. But that was before he met the wife and quit the filthy habit.

Behind him, Sheriff Dane heard the metallic slamming of the restroom door. He turned. Mr. Simpletripp was walking towards him, an oily grin stretched across his counterfeit face. The two glared, one with contemptuous cruelty, the other with a shrewd cold scrutiny. Neither released their laser grip that held and traveled the shrinking distance between them.

"Sheriff Dane," the tall, big-bellied man finally said in greeting. His tattered red shirt, sleeves ripped off at the shoulders, was embellished in front with a large peace sign, its sincerity as faded as its presence on the fabric.

The black man gave a nod. Only one, ever so slight, slightly just courteous.

"Smoking these days, Sheriff?"

He's getting off on this, Dane thought. Something's up.

Simpletripp seemed smug, as if he were laughingly aware of that all too obvious detail that eluded the sheriff. The big guy's manner was brazen, declaring, Catch me if you can.

Is there *something* here, evident in front of me?

Intuition told Dane that he should go and check the restroom, and yet that same intuition told him not to bother, that he wouldn't find anything of interest. And if there had been, the time for discovery had passed. Simpletripp was now only steps away. Overtly, Dane visually frisked the man down. The sheriff was looking for the slightest hook to latch onto, that barely perceivable unknown. As Simpletripp brushed by on his way to the car, Dane pivoted and watched him in retreat.

Hey, ugly man. Did you kill Stilped Roarhowser?

Climbing into his old dented vehicle parked a short distance away, Mr. Simpletripp slammed the driver's side door. Dane stood his ground, as the car's starter motor rasped loudly before catching, turning the engine over with a roar. Obscured behind tinted glass, Mr. Simpletripp gunned the motor, spilling forth voluminous clouds of smoke. Putting the battered car in gear, he inched it forward, ever so slowly, its engine throbbing, fan belt squealing—reminding Dane of the lethargic advance of a dangerous shark. The dome-headed man cruised around him in a tedious half-circle, as the sheriff, never turning, watched from the periphery of his left eye before picking him up on his return with the right. The car accelerated in a cumbersome prowl towards the exit, allowing Dane time to read the bumper stickers *We Are One* and *Coexist*. The junker dumped itself sloppily onto the side street.

Tracking Mr. Simpletripp's vehicle until it was out of sight, the sheriff felt a shift take place. Embracing a renewed sense of justification, he bent slightly at the waist, his back a crawling windbreak to the air's lashing current. Dane cupped his large, sheltering hands around the delicately slender cigarette and the freshly sparked match. The sudden flare of fired-up hope hissed, only to blow out in smoking disappointment. Whiff. Dane straightened up, pulled loose another match, and huddled once more. Same result. The man began to walk, taking long strides, the cigarette and matches annoyingly arrested in his curled hand.

Hate these things.

At that instant, the sheriff wondered what he detested more: the cigarettes and their manufacturers or his intermittent craving for them. But with little reflection, the answer was obvious: Harland Dane detested his weakness.

Approaching the dumpster, the sheriff mused, A good place to dispose of bad habits and evidence of personal struggles. At a wane in the wind, he tossed them in.

Should've kept that lighter, he thought.

The circular staircase that led up to street-level had a look reminiscent of the most elegant of Autumnslovian design. The handrails wove in and around the balusters, looping and graceful, flourishes embodying the stalks of plants, their leaves interweaving and supplying sturdiness to the cylindrical structure.

Moving nearer the stairway, Heather waved a slower Molly onward from deeper within the tunnel, but placed a cautionary finger to the lips of her mask. She pointed upwards, to the top of the stairs, to be certain that the butterfly girl had understood her message. Molly had, slowing to a walk and waving, before she resumed her lively gait.

Heather recalled the words of the shadow-eyed man, that once the LuminOrb was touched by daylight, it would go out. As a result, before she encountered the filtered light from overhead, she stopped and placed the torch on the tunnel floor. From there it cast its tepid light in all directions, except where obstructed by its conical base.

Just in case we have to come back, the moon girl thought. Rising, Heather was startled when she caught sight of her image nearby, a reflection on a mirror-like wall.

Backing, Heather said in an undertone, "Come on, Fallasha," before she turned and continued toward the cool light. "Let's have a look up those stairs."

"You're not going to leave the LuminOrb on the floor of the tunnel?"

Heather stopped and looked back at the abandoned torch. "Why not?"

"The man with no name said to take it with you and dispose of it far from the entrance."

"But it goes out at the first sign of daylight."

"So?"

"So, I don't want it going out. What if we have to come back down here for some reason?" When the brooch didn't answer, Heather continued, "If we do need to come back down the ladder, and the light has gone out, we won't be able to find our way around in the dark. Not only that, but the LuminOrb is what lights up the wall signs."

Fallasha continued her silence.

"What's wrong?"

"Nothing."

"Fallasha, before we leave, we can come back and get the light. It'll go out, and then we'll get rid of it, just like we were asked to do."

"What if, for some unknown reason, we're unable to come back down here to reclaim the 'Orb? Then what?"

Heather resumed walking towards the stairs. "Someone will pick it up. You said yourself that the ClearWeave is watching us. Remember? I wouldn't be surprised if they're listening right now and thinking about what a stupid argument we're having."

"That is so rude!"

The moon girl shut down with a sigh. Upon reaching the stairs, she grasped the handrail and stopped. "Fallasha, what's gotten into you?

Why are you so mad?"

"Nothing and I'm not," the moon brooch fired back, haughtily. "I have no idea what you're going on about. There's absolutely nothing wrong."

"Sure seems like something to me." With an irritated shake of the head, Heather began her ascent, the light spilling down and illuminating the top of her headpiece and shoulders.

"Quiet, now," the moon girl said, tilting her head back, her hand pulling at the rail, taking the stairs slowly, alertly. She circled once and then again.

"Heather." Molly's soft voice floated up from below.

Having almost reached the source of light near the top, Heather looked down over the fancy handrail, her costume awash in street-level grays. With a quick gesture, Heather beckoned her to follow.

"It would not have harmed you in the least to have waited for her," Fallasha whispered. "She is, after all, your loyal companion."

Distracted, Heather murmured, "Go away." Her neck was craned, her attention focused, as little by little, she pushed her extensive headpiece up through the hole in the tunnel ceiling. Instantly, she retracted and backed down a few steps.

"What's wrong?"

"I've got to take off this headpiece," the moon girl said, continuing to whisper, beginning to unfasten her mask. "I'm not sure what's up there, I don't want this bulky hat being the first thing poking up."

Heather removed her mask and then her headpiece, handing them both to Molly, who was now directly below her on the stairs. Once more, the moon girl put a finger to her lips. "From here on out, we'll have to keep our voices down, okay?"

Molly quietly assented, and so whispers were to follow.

"Can you see up there?" Heather said, her thumb a pointing piston. "Weird, huh?"

Squinting, Molly looked past her friend.

Above, light was entering the translucent walls of a tall rectangular compartment that sat directly over the exit hole. Through its tinted sides, from their vantage point below ground, the girls could see the leafy boughs overhead, and beyond that, bits of blue sky. Also visible, extending directly upward from the top of the handsome booth was a tapering metal pole that held aloft six graceful arms. Positioned at the end of each was a cluster of light globes.

"Molly. It's a lamppost. We're coming up to street-level in the bottom part of a huge lamppost. I'm going up."

Fallasha said, "Be very careful."

The moon girl paused in her ascent. "I will." She started to inch her way upward.

"You realize that you haven't the vaguest notion of what it is you may encounter up there, outside the base of that lamppost."

Heather froze. "I know."

"Could be most anything."

Heather exhaled, perhaps a bit too loudly. "Right."

"I think that it's vitally important that you keep the level of noise to a minimum, also," her brooch continued. "There exists the undeniable possibility that whomever is up there may possess the capacity to not only see you, but to hear you. It may be that the structure above is simply not soundproof."

"Got it. Already thought of that." Heather started to raise her head up into the enclosed space.

"Oh, and one other thing."

A halt. Heather lowered herself again, a turtle back into its shell. *"What?"*

"Do not hesitate to enter that cubicle slowly. And once there, I would hasten to advise that you refrain from convulsive or rash movements of any kind. Those are the ones that will be noticed and will undoubtedly draw attention to yourself."

"Fallasha, are you done?" Not waiting for an answer, Heather replied, "Good."

"Rude!" shot the heated whisper.

Heather's eyes slowly broke the plane of street-level. She ducked back quickly when she saw someone hustle by on her left.

"What's up there?" Fallasha asked.

"Can you hold on a second, please? I really haven't had a chance to look."

"Yes. By all means. May I urge you, once again, to practice caution when undertaking your ascent?"

"I got it, got it, got it. Now, can you please just take a break or something?"

"You're asking me to relax, is that it?"

"Yeah, relax. Just relax. That'd be great."

"You want me to simply stop advising as if I'm not here?"

"…might not be a bad idea…"

"So, you want me to act as though I'm no longer your official tour guide, giving time-honored direction and exceptional advice. Am I hearing you correctly? Is that how you would like me to act?"

"Fallasha, act like you would if someone were about to break off your little moon nose in a very kind and un-rude way."

"Well, if that isn't offensive…"

Heather scowled. Yet again, she raised the top of her head above ground. When the girl felt it safe, she rose up farther, extending her upper body partially into the cubicle. She found that the lamppost was situated in a long narrow courtyard, hidden among a maze of walkways that ran between bountiful trees and large planter boxes overflowing with a variety of greenery. In smaller planters scattered throughout, individual young trees had taken root, and at the base of each sprouted a myriad of blooms.

On either side, rising above tall concealing hedges, Heather could make out the facades of shops, their canvas awnings overhanging wide walkways. From her low vantage point, scarcely recognizable through the foliage, she could see only a few of the storefronts' higher windows. However, the moon girl realized this was a good thing, for that meant the windows couldn't see her, insuring an obscured departure for her and Molly from the confines of the lamppost.

Nearby, Heather watched as a man walked a small creature at the end of a leash. She supposed it was an Autumnslovian version of the dog, though the combined features of the four-legged animal were like none she had ever seen—it looked like it had a large furry snakehead. Heather also observed that there was activity on the opposite side of the hedge, on the wide walk to her left, though she was unable to determine exactly what the partial glimpses could be. Shoppers? On the far side of the planters, two people in their Parade Day outfits strolled past unoccupied benches.

Heather started when, close to the lamppost, a cluster of teens suddenly appeared. They were engaged in spirited conversation, some leaning on others, with a few sporting masks atop outlandish frill and fluff. Yet, while sticking head and shoulders above ground, Heather realized that not a soul had noticed her. As well, it occurred to the girl that she couldn't hear any exterior sound: no conversations, no footfalls, no street noise or commotion of any kind. She watched as, without a sound, the animated teens moved on.

Heather lowered herself back into the hole. She squatted on the stairs and looked down at Molly, her voice now at a normal volume, "Hey, you guys, I can't hear a thing outside, so I'm thinking that the lamppost is soundproof."

Fallasha spoke up, "Are you certain?"

Heather ignored her. "Not only that, they can't see me, either. It's like a one-way mirror up there, the kind they use in police stations when they're interrogating someone in one of those little dirty rooms, you know, the ones with peeling walls that always seem to be painted green."

"I don't know how you can be so certain, Heather," said the brooch. "I'm not convinced your head was all that visible, being that it was barely protruding into the cubicle. Furthermore, the people that happened by were no doubt in a hurry, self-involved, and not paying any particular attention to an ordinary lamppost that was unobtrusively standing nearby."

"Fallasha, look up there. Go on, look. See? There's a big hole in the ground right above me. You think they'd notice it—or maybe a blonde girl's head and shoulders sticking out of it, if they could see inside that lamppost?"

"Not if a passerby happened to be preoccupied or distracted by planter boxes, leaves, branches, and such—and in all probability by each other. If that were the case, they assuredly wouldn't be looking down. That's why people have the unfortunate experience of stepping on broken glass, gum, and a variety of other objects that lay scattered about at their feet. To be certain beyond all reasonable doubt that they're unable to see you, perhaps you should do something that would instantly garner their attention."

"Like what? Landing a jet plane inside that cubicle up there?"

"I meant something small. Like waving your hand at one of them."

"Fallasha, I'm trying to tell you. They can't see through those walls."

"All right. Have it your way. I just happen to think that if Autumnslovians can't see or hear inside the base of that lamppost, how come Mr. No Name didn't make mention of that fact?"

"How should I know? Maybe he forgot? Or have you ever figured that maybe he figured that I would just figure it out?" Heather comically cocked her head and raised an eyebrow. "Go figure."

Fallasha sighed. "Do as you must and ignore my sophisticated and unparalleled advice. However, I think that you're exposing us to the possibility of even more danger."

"Fallasha, I don't understand why you're arguing. What's the big deal? It's simple: we just leave the lamppost when no one is around to see us."

"Well, whatever you decide to do, we very much need to hurry," the brooch said, snippily. "Time is of the essence, as they say, and we really do need to get home. All this running around, getting waylaid following people, alley running, RogueTag encounters, meetings with the ClearWeave, long tunnels—all taking valuable time—really, may we please simply hurry and get home?" The brooch again sighed deeply.

"Time spent in distraction and not pertaining to schedule is causing me unthinkable distress and I'm finding it very irritating, I'll have you know, very irritating indeed. I shall have no choice but to admit to my superiors that this entire endeavor has amounted to little more than an unbearable waste of time, like a larkish flit into the countryside, dreadfully regrettable, while being so annoyingly unpalatable and traumatically demoralizing. Why I even bothered to agree to come along I shall never know. I should have simply stayed home mending socks in the sewing room. It would have been time better spent, I should think."

For a moment, Heather didn't move. Then she stood. "Excuse me, Molly. I need to get by."

"What are you doing?" Fallasha protested, as Molly pressed to the rail to let Heather pass.

"Please keep your voice down."

"Why? What does it matter? According to your test results, not a soul can hear us. Look, we need to get home," Fallasha went on shrilly. "Can't you see? Tick, tick, tick, the clock is counting out the precious time spent on such trivialities as frivolous backtracking, when what we really need to be doing is proceeding forward. Do you not agree? We should be forging ahead, aggressively moving out through the base of that light post above and making our way towards the PortalDoor and home."

Heather reached the floor of the passage, and proceeded to walk into the blackness, toward the light of her LuminOrb that still sat on the tunnel floor.

"Heather Nighborne, I feel obliged to protest. You must turn around immediately. We are wasting valuable time." Then Fallasha brightened. "Or perhaps you've come down to recover the LuminOrb. If that's the case, you should have simply said so and spared me the momentary, and might I add, unprecedented grief. Why anyone would wish to treat a lovely brooch, such as yours truly, with such harsh disrespect, I can only wonder."

The moon girl drew to a halt before the reflective wall. Mirrored, she could see that when shining up from the floor, the 'Orb's light gave her face a devilish look, illuminating the undersides of her nose, lips, mouth, and chin, as well as the area below her brow. She turned a cold eye on the reflection of the little moon brooch.

"Fallasha, don't you ever stop?"

"Wha—?"

"Don't you ever stop?"

"What exactly are you implying?"

"Well, that you never turn off your mouth."

"Agh! That is so *rude!*"

"That is so *true*. All I keep hearing you say, over and over, is how we need to get back, how we can't be late, how you could be canned, how I shouldn't do this, how it's important we do that… Don't you ever stop?"

"Well, that's my job! That's what I was sent here to do! I'm your tour guide, remember, looking out for your safety."

"But can't you ever have fun? Just have fun!"

"Just have fun? What? What are you saying? Do you realize that if Aria hadn't come upon the scene and intervened at a most opportune time, those RogueTags might have killed you and Molly—*and me?* Or taken us in bonds to Mistraya? Do you? Might I remind you, this is not a game? It's not a joy ride to the zoo or a visit to your favorite theme park. You're in Autumnsloe, and this is real life, Heather!"

"Yeah, Fallasha, but don't you ever have any fun trying things, doing things? You always make sure that we *don't* do things. Boy, you shouldn't have been a brooch, you should have been a *stop*watch. You're so, so, so… argh! You just make me so mad, that's all. You're always asking a bunch of annoying questions and making all these ridiculous suggestions, like you're the one in charge, or something. *We* were the ones invited by the Bristol House, not you. You're Fallasha. You're a moon brooch. That's it. You're only a brooch. Can't you just come along, because you have to, because I wear you, because you don't have a choice?"

"*I*, Heather Nighborne, am a brooch who happens to have your best interests at heart. Do you think that I wanted to accompany you and your friend, here, on this trip?" Fallasha's voice was getting louder. "Do you? Let me tell you something, young lady, there are a lot more important and interesting assignments that I could have been involved with— and have been involved with—that didn't and don't require babysitting two pre-adolescents, who, for some inexplicable reason, happen to be under the impression that they're in some kind of wholesome fairyland and are here simply to have fun. Do you think that's why the Bristol House sent you here? Do you?

"So, this is my assignment, and I've accepted it. I was told by my superiors that I was to accompany the two of you to the parade and afterwards, to see you home safely. And look what has happened! Just look! We've gotten completely off course and here we are, hours later, across town in a tunnel!"

"I don't agree with you, Fallasha. Molly and I, we've had such a great time, even if we had to lug you around with us to do it. And boy, if you weren't forever getting in the way—and all the time you just kept that little moon mouth of yours going, like, like the keys were locked in the car, but your motor was left running and you couldn't shut it off: blah, blah, blah, blah, blah. I just kept hoping you'd finally run out of gas!

"Yeah, we're across town! Yeah, we're in a tunnel! But we fought RogueTags and beat them! There was awesome iMagiNacia! We got to see what it's like in those crummy Autumnsloe alleys and streets, not just on the beautiful Autumnsloe avenues on Parade Day. And we were even able to find out about the ClearWeave and meet the Matron! Isn't that so much more exciting than just going to the parade?"

"Not when your life's at stake, young lady! Think, Heather Nighborne! Think! What if you and Molly had been killed back there, or if it hadn't been an agent of the ClearWeave that we followed, but instead some kidnapper who was one of the Influenced, what would you, your guardians, or I have done then? Huh? What?"

"What if, what if, what if! Those things didn't happen, did they? We weren't killed and we weren't kidnapped. What if you just let us be, just let us go on having fun and seeing things that Molly and I want to see? Why do you have to be so serious all the time? Why do you want to make *us* so serious? Join in, Fallasha, join in with us; just have fun!"

"Fun? *Fun?* Is that all you think about? How about trying responsibility? What about consequences? These are things that, if you do happen to be Evermore's green-eyed Maiden, you'll need to consider. You're going to have to grow up, young lady, and *fast!* So, let's get our roles straight here, shall we? Yes, I am, as you say, 'just a brooch.' But as your brooch, I am also your guide, and I have been assigned the unfortunate task of looking after you. And when you choose not to be responsible and go gallivanting off to only distant suns know where, I still have to be the one to rein you in, to make certain that you two girls are safe, and that you become acquainted with this new land you may soon be seriously enmeshed with—even if you 'just want to have *fun.*' Furthermore, I need to get you back to the Bristol House not only on time, but also in one piece! Do you understand? Can't you see that I have been unpleasantly encumbered with the utterly thankless job of looking out for a little self-centered, entirely unmanageable, and wholly spoiled *brat!*

"You are not my mother!" Heather's eyes were burning wet, her voice trembling, her gaze hotly on Fallasha's reflection before her. "You are not! I don't have one, remember? But maybe it's a good thing that I don't. Because if she was anything like you, believe me, I'd run away from home. Do you understand, Fallasha? You—are—not—my—moth-er. You are only a little moon brooch attached to my costume. Nothing else."

"Well! If I *was* your mother—and thankfully I'm not—and if you *did* run away from home, I certainly wouldn't bother wasting my precious time looking for you!"

"And I would be better off for that, I'm sure! And one more thing! I am *not* the green-eyed Maiden, theirs or anyone's. The green-eyed Maiden is responsible, and brave, and-and strong, and smart, and-and-and she's able to save people when they're in trouble and need help, because they're about to die.

"Do you know where I was when my friend Stilped died? Do you? Well, let me tell you! I was right there that night. That's right. I was right there, close by when he was killed so horribly, and I wasn't smart, and I wasn't strong, and I didn't act responsibly, and even though I should have gotten to him, I couldn't. I couldn't. And if you don't think I know about consequences, you're so *wrong!* In my mind I've seen Stilped's dead face dressed up so creepy and ugly and sticking out of the ground so many times now, so many times—and not only during the day, but after dark, too, when I dreamed about him night after night after night. And for a boy who never did anything to anyone, his consequences were that he died in such an awful, awful way, because I couldn't be there for him. Poor Stilped. Poor quiet Stilped.

"But the green-eyed Maiden, she would have been there for him. She would have come to the rescue and fought off his killer and saved Stilped! So, don't you see? *I* didn't! And *I* couldn't, because I'm not *her!* I'm not that Maiden-person. I never will be! And you won't see me going around saving people in Autumnsloe or in Evermore or anywhere *ever,* because I can't! That job belongs to someone else. So, you *stop!* Just stop all this nonsense about me being some green-eyed Maiden of the Evermore Portent and stop wanting me to be something that I'm not! You leave me alone, Fallasha! You got that? *Just leave me alone!"*

The tunnel seemed to have grown monstrously large and gaping, its swollen blackness overpowering, swallowing the little light that lay ineptly at Heather's feet.

She hadn't noticed that a distressed Molly had walked up to stand nearby, slackly holding Heather's headpiece and mask, taking the scene in. Her aura was a sorrowful and heartbroken blue with little emanation. Heather quickly looked away, before crouching to retrieve the LuminOrb.

"Come on, Molly," she said, moving toward the stairway, her pace increasing with every step, aware of their shadows large and wavering on the wall. "Let's get going. We need to get home."

Several steps later, the light from the LuminOrb dimmed and expired.

"And this will be your room, Lana."

Mrs. Pringle lowered her suitcase onto the elegant carpet, having left Molly's in the girl's new room. "Dawn, it's nothing short of lovely: the canopy bed, the beautiful antique furniture, the gorgeous wallpaper, the chandeliers, wall sconces, oh, and that lamp and chair—everything. Gosh, though I don't know what my plans are at this point, looking around, I think I'd like to enter the raffle."

"Pardon? I'm not sure what you mean. The raffle?"

"You know the one. It's the raffle where the person whose name is drawn gets to live in this Bristol House Shangri-La for the rest of their life."

Grandma Dawn chuckled. "Ah, *that* raffle."

"All joking aside, I'd like to start paying you some rent for our room and board as long as Molly and I continue to stay here with you. And then, as soon as I'm able—most probably after Ned and I sort our-selves out—I'll begin looking for a more permanent place in town to call home. Meanwhile, one of my first priorities will be to find a job and begin generating some income."

"You know there's no hurry, Lana. You and Molly can stay as long as you like."

"I know… and I appreciate that. Dawn, you've really been so kind to me. And Heather's presence is helping my daughter pull through such an extraordinarily rough time with the loss of her friend and dog. You've both been so invaluable to us. As overused as the line may be, I'm not sure I can ever really repay you for your generosity."

"We never know what tomorrow brings."

"That's for sure. I certainly didn't think I'd end up here at the Bristol House." Mrs. Pringle suddenly eyed her neighbor. "What? What's the joke? There you go again with that secret smile of yours." As Mrs. Pringle laughed, she caught sight of a piece of furniture. "Oh-h-h-h-h, and I love the little secretary desk near the window. It's perfect, just perfect."

"Is it?"

"Yes, and it's exactly what I need. It's like this house of yours read my mind. Over the next few days, if I seem scarce, it's because I really need to do some writing. In my journal. And don't be surprised if you find me glued to that chair doing it."

Grandma Dawn, her laugh pleasant, easy, said, "Feel free."

Mrs. Pringle radiated her happiness, or perhaps it was gratitude, through the layers of fatigue and stress that subtly draped her countenance.

"Okay, then," Grandma Dawn said, lightly clapping her hands together. "Lana, let me leave you to your unpacking."

"Sounds good. At some point here, I'll retrieve the other two suitcases still in the car. And no, no help is necessary, thank you."

"All right. You know where the bathroom is, and if there's anything else you need, I'll be downstairs in the kitchen."

"Thank you, Dawn. Thank you, again. And I know Molly is really going to love her new room, too."

"She should. It's right across from Heather's."

"Molly, I can probably do it, but it would be a really tight fit for me to stand up in here. And I'm not sure how we're supposed to get out."

Heather was standing on the top step of the circular ladder, bent slightly at the knees. Rotating her body, her hands searched, pressing and feeling their way around the glass-like walls that enclosed her on all sides.

"You'd think that Mr. No Name would have told us how to get out," said Molly, her voice drifting up to Heather from a lower step.

Heather instinctively froze when a couple appeared from behind a planter box. Sauntering away from the festivities in pointy ears and puggish snouts, they seemed to be dressed as some kind of Evermorian animals. As the pair outside carried on in what appeared to be casual conversation, Heather resumed her search, convinced they couldn't see her. Her hands crawled along the uppermost corners, pushing at and brushing over the various areas, only to come away disappointed. It didn't help that her recent argument with Fallasha was weighing on her. The two continued to occupy the same costume in a cold, mute standoff. Heather had noticed tiny glints on the cheeks of her little brooch.

"I can't find anything anywhere on any of the sides, Molly. I don't even see a handle or a knob."

"What about under the ground, right around the hole, before you even go up into that room? Did you look there?"

"Yeah. Nothing. I checked before coming up." Heather turned her face skyward and ran her gloved hand near the base of the post, above her head. A pattern appeared, lit on the ceiling of the cubicle, only to fade when her hand moved away. A soft electrical drone emanated from the image at the hand's passing.

"Molly, I think I found it! I found something, anyway. Might just be the light switch for all those globes out there." Absorbed, Heather held her palm out above her, and slowly approached the small square of ceiling once again. When she was only inches from where she had first seen the pattern, it materialized again, as did the low electrical hum.

"What's that noise I keep hearing?" Molly asked.

"Whenever I put my hand near the ceiling, it lights up with an image and makes that sound."

"What does it look like?"

"The image? It looks like one we saw back there in the tunnel. Remember the symbol of the two lines of connected V's, and how the pointy parts overlapped in the center?"

"Yes."

"I think if I touch it, this lamppost will open somewhere, probably on one of the sides."

"Before you do," said Molly, "don't forget to make sure that no one's around, especially if we don't know how the lamppost is going to open."

"Yeah. If it grows like that Portal clock did in the sewing room, I think there's a good chance people might notice." Heather scanned the area throughout the courtyard. She didn't see a soul on her side of the two shielding hedges. "Here goes."

She touched the lighted image and, following a deeper electrical thrum, there was a slight click. Noise from the outside was suddenly evident within the chamber: birds, distant conversation, the jingle of trolley bells, and the expansive breadth of city activities.

Molly asked, her voice once again at a whisper, "What just happened?"

Heather was miffed. "I don't know. Maybe nothing. Just a bunch of noise." Rotating in a circle, she examined all sides of the lamppost base. Gently, she reached out and prodded them, hoping something would give. And it did. The side to her right, like a door, had sprung open just a crack.

"I found it," Heather said, her words softly spoken.

Her gloved hand held the door slightly ajar, while through the translucent sides of the base the moon girl scanned the area again. No one. She cast a brief glance at the stairway below her feet.

"Come on, Molly. Here. Hand me my mask and headpiece. Let's get home."

CHAPTER TWENTY-SIX

Questions, configurations, and perhaps a plan or two

Mrs. Pringle approached the pale gray light.

Why do I keep finding myself at windows? she asked herself, feeling as if for years she had continually viewed the world from within the confines of an aquarium. But positioned before the glass as she was this day, the view seemed different, roomy, and at odds with her past.

She looked out over the grounds of the Bristol House, which were currently heaving and swaying in a furious gust. Down the hill, she found Afterglow Drive, running east-west. Beyond, the landscape spread south under the somber sky, roads slicing up the open land that swelled and waned over hillock and hollow, the greater heights cresting with sweeps of trees among craggy shelves of rock. At the horizon, the mountains were painted in a gash of purplish-blue.

What a revealing view! A person really can see a lot from these Bristol House windows, she thought. Sure is a long way down to the street, too. The words popped into her head: *a queen's view from a magical mountain.*

And so it seemed.

Mrs. Pringle spotted the Whisper Creek Bridge, the waters below muddied, with a broken bough wallowing slowly downstream. She watched, as briefly, its limbs became entangled with the hefty girth of Lower Bridge. But the force of the current working and churning with untold strength below the surface, pulled the bough under and then free from the oak in a slow twist, allowing the broken branch to continue on its water-swept journey.

Wandering across the creek, Mrs. Pringle's gaze found the entangled rise of the gigantic Oak Triplets, their bare upper arms cast triumphantly skyward, their spindly fingers gathered in bunches at the furthermost tips. Far below, nearer the base of the trees, a few of the sheltered leaves still clung, but with little hope and not for long.

Where is that hideaway treehouse that the girls love so much, the one Dawn told me about? she asked herself. Isn't it up there somewhere among those branches?

Mrs. Pringle craned her neck first here, then there, trying to get a better angle for a possible sighting. However, the Bristol House denied any view of the structure perched precariously high within the trees, shielded by a multitude of overlapping boughs.

The woman marveled at the mighty oaks nonetheless, before shifting her focus to a much closer sight, almost directly below her window, at the base of the steep hill: the Pringle house. It was a view that she had purposely been avoiding.

Mrs. Pringle brought her hand up to rest her fingers delicately on one of the window's horizontal muntins. She wondered at the sight below, the tiny gray boxes with white trim clustered alongside the creek. It looked familiar, but from this vantage point seemed miles and miles away. Nonthreatening. Out of reach. And there in the drive was the lifeless rectangle of Ned's car, the front wheels cranked hard right.

Did I really live there all these years? Or was it someone else? Or both?

The woman grimaced, feeling the throbbing of a headache coming on.

Best lay down, she thought. The unpacking can wait.

She blinked several times before daring herself to once again look down the hill at the Pringle residence.

What a perspective, she thought. From here, it looks like an entirely unfamiliar house, like it belongs to someone completely different. In a slide to the bottom of her emptiness, Mrs. Pringle concluded: I suppose it does.

"You'll be pleased to know," said the shadow-eyed man, "that the implant of the MindKey was successful."

The Matron's voice crackled to life. "And when have I ever failed to achieve such a purpose? How would the girl and her companion ever hope to find their leave otherwise?" The old soothsayer repositioned herself, sitting more erect in the chair. "I assume that by now they've reached the tunnel's end, discovered the stairway, and made a successful departure?"

"Yes, Matron," the man said. "But word has it not without an argument."

The woman was taken aback. "I'm surprised. The two girls fought?"

"No. The Maiden Portent and her brooch."

"I see. How serious was this altercation?"

"I'm not sure of its implications, Matron, lasting or otherwise. I was told it was quite a flare-up. The two became excessively heated and loud, so much so, that at one point we were almost pressed into action and forced to reveal our discreet positions in order to calm the girl and her brooch."

"Mmm." The clairvoyant bunched her soft cracked line of lip, before continuing. "It is my belief that the brooch has had quite an interesting past. Having had only brief contact, I was able to determine that that small piece of jewelry, albeit trustworthy, could become a detriment; that if captured and pressured for information, she would easily succumb to divulgence.

"With regard to the Intended's friend, Molly Pringle, unfortunately I was unable to orchestrate a SayerTrace to determine her strengths and weaknesses. As an unknown quantity, we must keep an eye on this one and prevent her from capture. And it would surprise me little to learn that Heather Nighborne draws particular strength in the bond of friendship with the child. A good reason to see to it that Molly Pringle stays alive, wouldn't you agree?"

"I will make the others aware."

"Yes, do."

"Despite our inconspicuous tracking, the Maiden Portent and her friend, Molly Pringle, seemed aware we were witnessing their passage to street-level, nonetheless."

"Oh?"

"Yes." The shadow-eyed man was unable to contain his mirth. "The Maiden Portent, she asked aloud of the darkness if we would like to hear a joke."

Starbrill broke into laughter.

The Matron turned on the boy. "You find that amusing, do you?"

Shutting down, he withdrew, grateful to be swallowed by the shadows.

The room in which they stood had long since emptied, with many of the ClearWeave having departed to resume their everyday roles among the citizenry of Evermore's four kingdoms, discreetly spreading word of the meeting and the possibility of the Intended. Shedding light for two, but never of any use to the Matron, a flame still flickered on the wick of the oil lamp in the corner. With it, three swollen shapes danced upon the walls.

"Everyone gathered here seemed to agree that this Heather Nighborne may very well be the Intended. Are you of like mind?" she asked.

"Let's say I'm of a strong inclination, stronger than with any of the others. Her display of iMagiNacia was beyond compare, I must admit, though others have shown glimpses—"

"Bah! All merely MaidenHood possibilities—nothing more!" the Matron said, with a disgusted wave of her hand. "And as a result they have not lasted, lingering for only a brief flash before they were located and smote out. Yes, there have been glimpses of enhanced performance, to be sure, but they've all amounted to little, as we know. I sense strongly that this one is different. It is obvious, is it not? She has a development that the others have not possessed. None before Heather Nighborne have been endowed with the green SearEye, nor have they had to prove themselves in quite the same manner with a confrontation reliant on the advanced use of iMagiNacia." The Matron cackled.

"This is true."

"iMagiNacia," the elderly prophetess added. "Who would have thought?" Following a moment of silence, she said, "And though the child succeeded admirably, still, I bear strong reservation."

"If I may, why so?" asked the shadow-eyed man, his small furry friend asleep atop his headpiece.

"The area within that I could not penetrate with the SayerTrace…" She raised her bony hands and clasped them above her chest; there they wrestled. "It worries me, for I am uncertain what potential lays hidden there and how well grounded her foundation in Light. She could harbor evil sure enough, and of grave concern is her potential to turn. If the sprouting seed of evil exists already, cloaked within that inaccessible part of the child, then eventually the Dark will no doubt fully claim her. The staggering consequences of such a shift could be that if we have nurtured and entrusted her with our widespread ClearWeave configuration and activities, then armed with that knowledge she would have the potential to reveal and destroy us—wipe us out, generations of infiltration and positioning. Everything."

"But Matron, did you not say so yourself, that we all possess the darkness and the possibility of turning?"

"So true, Starbrill. But most of us are in possession of the inner strength to fight off such inclinations and temptations. Others have the predisposition to more easily stray. Also, as we know, there are some that simply never regard the Light within, betraying true glory while tamping out the slightest glimmer.

"And then there is Astille Lia Staleen DiYoh, the Intended, our green-eyed Maiden of the Evermore Portent. The young Heather Nighborne, she is unique. Due to her predestination and all that it engenders, she will be faced with an even greater pressure to turn, far greater than that which any mere HumanKinder will have to endure ever."

"So," said the shadow-eyed man, "how are we to behave in regard to the girl?"

"She must be looked after, for certain, but at the same time, she must be held suspect. For now, reveal only what is necessary. Remember, the Portent Prophecies tell of another's diabolical rise."

"I understand," said the man. "But is it not unclear just who the wicked one prophesied will be and when that soul will be revealed?"

"Yes. And that's why we must keep this child safe but at arm's length until we are certain that she can be trusted completely—or until we have no other choice but to take her into our confidence. Unbeknownst to her, she is in possession of the MindKey; unwittingly, she has made use of it once to exit the tunnel. She may have need of it again, as it could save her life."

"But is that not an argument to reveal its implantation to her?" asked the man.

"No."

At the sharpness of the spoken word, the geetalvasse stirred with a slight squeak, but continued to cling and breathe deeply upon its cushiony bed above the shadow-eyed mask.

The Matron continued, "Remember: For the Four, For Evermore. All else is meaningless. We can help her to survive, and yet, she must also make use of her own skills—her own daring, cunning, and intellect—to prosper. It is not our role to babysit the child, but to encourage, assist, and intercede when necessary—but only when necessary. It is a difficult line we toe, and because we know what will be in store for us—for the entire Realm—in the Dark Spell to come, her survival and ultimate return to Evermore is undoubtedly in our best interest, if she is truly the Intended."

The man and boy agreed.

"And she is so very young, so inexperienced to have to go up against the forces of the Dahklarr Herth that are now alarmingly stirring and unifying within the Realm. Soon—" The Matron stopped and felt the colossal wave of chaos, panic, oppression, battle, suffering, and loss infiltrate her senses. She fought to hold at bay the low rumble of that which was yet to come, and then cleared her throat. When she began again, her voice was subdued, grave. "Soon…" Her chin came up, her head rolling, her mind now alive, overrun with the rumbling. Nevertheless, she persevered, "Soon…" but all words died. The woman choked up, and with a deep breath sank into her chair, into herself. Tightly shutting her eyes didn't help to dissipate the stampeding, battering, turbulent vision that besieged her. It thundered through her open senses, her mouth slack, chin heavy upon her chest. All was so burdensome, so very, very burdensome. So much devastation. So much death. She didn't want to see any more. Stop the vision, oh, stop the vision! Undeterred, it surged on. Saliva found its way over her gums and lower lip in a trickle. She began to tremble.

The room had gone quiet, each to their own, as the two watched the Matron endure her trance, her frail body shaking. Finally, the tremors subsided and the woman looked up, uncertain of where she was, her expression clouded. Sitting back, her quick shallow breaths rasping, the old seer collected herself, and having recovered sufficiently, her voice snapped in question, "Are we positioned for the girls' return to their Portal?"

"Yes, Matron, along all possible routes. As I have reported, they have left the tunnel and we are strategically stationed, prepared to follow them."

In an effort to further disperse the vivid manifestations that so gripped her, the Matron tilted her head to the ceiling and shook it, her brow pinched at its center. She straightened, and as if nothing had happened, said, "Splendid, splendid. Let's keep watch over both children and attempt to discreetly insure their safety, although as you know our priority must invariably rest with the Intended." The woman drew a long breath and exhaled noisily. "Heather Nighborne, she's a smart girl, is she not? And sweet." The Matron turned in the direction of the boy. "Don't you agree, Starbrill?" She chuckled softly.

Starbrill blushed. It was almost impossible to hide anything from the Matron. He knew that she was historically among the ClearWeave's most powerfully perceptive, with a strong ancestral bloodline harkening back to the Mystics of the Ancient Archannites.

"You performed the SayerTrace when touching the girl's face. Could you have not—?"

"Yes, my young Starbrill. To answer your impending question, my intentions in doing so were threefold. Firstly, since commonplace sight was never intended to be mine, I wanted to feel and acquire an impression of our Intended's facial characteristics—or as you might say, 'what she looks like,' and this you may have perceived at the time. Secondly, to touch a glove or sleeve could have given me contaminated information concerning the girl, perhaps confusing Heather Nighborne's details with those of a tailor, seamstress, or even laborer who spooled the costume's thread. And finally, of course, it was essential to come in contact with Heather Nighborne's costumeless head to insure the proper implant of the MindKey."

"But may I ask why—?"

"Starbrill," the Matron interrupted the boy again, "the implantation of the Mindkey was necessary, as I said."

"But couldn't we have waited until her return," the boy argued, "as the Prophecies predict? Then we could be more certain as to whether or not she really is the Intended."

"An excellent question. A better question might be, Why make her aware of the ClearWeave's presence to begin with? According to the Portent Prophecies, when she does return—assuming she is the green-eyed Maiden mentioned—I believe we'll want her to be aware of our presence, because the ClearWeave, and thus Evermore, may be in dire need of her assistance at the time—and she may have need of ours. So, with our disclosure, she's come to know and trust that we are on an identical side fighting for the future of Evermore."

The shadow-eyed man spoke up. "But what if she or her companions are captured and reveal to others our existence?"

"Their assertion would be nothing more than words on the wind. How would they prove our existence? We can quickly seal the door at the lamppost. And anywhere else, for that matter. Haven't we done it before?"

A grunt of approval escaped the man's lips. "Often enough."

"But concerning Heather Nighborne and the implant of the Mindkey: when and where in Evermore will she return? We don't know. And would we have the good fortune to arrange another meeting as we did today, that would allow access to her for the SayerTrace and implant? Will I be on hand upon her return to do so? Will Starbrill? And would she knowingly allow it? There even stands the possibility that time and aging pass at a rate of speed in her world that is distinctly different from that of our own. So, in what year will she return to us and at what age? Far too much to ask of happenstance and fortuitous opportunity. I felt it wise to insure the implant for her sake and survival—and ultimately ours.

"Furthermore, I feel it is wise to let her determine this small intrusion for herself, stumble upon its presence and power blindly, if at all. This will protect us, and as well, tell us more about her intelligence and power of analysis. For now, she has utilized the MindKey's possession to make leave of the tunnel, but she knows not how to reenter this concealed dominion over which we hold claim. In time," she said, rocking her head, "all in good time. And with the implantation, should she live long enough, she may well discover her power over our MindLocks, and utilize the full potential of the hand-activated symbol—our symbol, the sign of the ClearWeave—to enter the secretive doors that lead to our many passages and sanctuaries. It is good, as I said.

"But I must reemphasize that we need be wary—perhaps only at first, perhaps always—for should she possess a malignant evil, then we must see to it that our Realm is protected. For that reason, the threat must and will be eliminated at any cost and by any means—in other words, if necessary, we will kill the girl."

Starbrill looked away.

"Dare I add," said the woman, "even if it involves temporarily aligning our agents in joint effort with the forces of the Influenced, thus risking discovery of our organization and its duplicity, albeit for the greater good."

Over the boy's smooth-skinned hand, the Matron placed her shriveled own. Years of experience, of life and living, rode patiently upon her gentle countenance. "Do not worry yourself with this." She pressed his hand, her gaze perpetually far off. "Perhaps she is our Astille Lia, the Intended, and if she is strong within, you need never be anxious for her.

"You, young man, you who must one day take this tired old woman's place in the hierarchy as the omnipresent eyes of the ClearWeave, must not be swayed by your emotion for the girl. You must see and see clearly, without bias of any kind. From clouded sight springs misperception and faulty reasoning, followed by disastrous recommendation," she smiled wryly, "thus resulting in ruinous action. It is difficult enough with lucid vision to make well-founded choices and from them to administer sage advice."

Ever obedient, the boy seer whispered, "Yes, Matron."

"Now," said the prophetess in the direction of the shadow-eyed man, "let us obtain information on the progress of our girls, shall we, and then report to me your findings."

"Having left the tunnel, my last report had them on their way to the Avenue, not far from the monument, Matron. I will bring word as it becomes available."

"Do. Starbrill?"

The boy lowered his head towards her. "Yes, Matron."

"You see this child as exceptional and unimpeachable?"

"I believe I felt something strong and virtuous inside of her, yes."

"And as for her being the answer to the Portent?"

"She is our Astille Lia. Of that I have no doubt."

"Well, let's see if you are correct and not distracted in your Sightfulness, influenced by HumanKind's proclivity for infatuation. As of now, I see our Intended as being unable to reach her PortalDoor without incident. Do you still feel her, my young Starbrill? And if so, can you not also sense this?"

"Yes, I can still feel her, Matron."

"And?"

"And, yes, I see impending complications."

"Thanks, Tommy." Dane's hand held the open truck door.

"You got it, Sheriff. I'll tell Dad you stopped by." The kid agreeably slapped the truck's left front fender.

With a push off the running board, Dane climbed into his truck and wind-aided, let the door slam behind him. He started the engine and slowly crawled out of the stall. However, instead of moving towards the street, he pulled to the side of the station. There he sat in the confines of his truck while it idled humbly around him.

The sheriff's blue eyes slid along the cinderblock wall, over the stacks of tires and then past the dumpster, before coming to rest on the men's restroom. He studied the stark white icon depicting a man within a circle of blue. His gaze followed the wall again, this time in reverse, coming to rest on where Simpletripp had parked his car.

Hey, sleazy man. Sleazy, sleazy man. Fess up. If you killed the boy, what was your motivation, huh? Why the gruesome display of carnage? Are you really twisted that way, or are you only slinking around for the show, for the thrill of it?

And the boots. Those older style boots were purchased years ago, and before the old miner got ahold of them, I bet they were worn only a few times—the night of the murder being one of them. And they were just your size. Fit for a scumball.

So, sleazy man, what's the scoop on those boots, huh? Why were they worn so infrequently? Were they special in some way? And how did an old man in rags come to be in possession of boots that were almost new? And the wrong size? I wonder, sleazy man, after the miner put them on, if it was you who gave him the big heave-ho down the cliff? Or do you just like running around playing Mr. Sinister, getting off on the nega-tive, bad boy attention, while the actual perp runs loose? So, what is it, sleazy man? Are you the real thing, or just a Mommy's boy with his girdle pinched three sizes too tight?

Dane's fingertips tapped the steering wheel thoughtfully. After a final look at the icon of the man on the restroom door, he gunned the engine and made for the street.

The expansive room was scarcely lit, columns and alcoves and arch-ways and vaults, the murkiness clinging and slinking and lurking with-in—so much a wanton sanctuary, a luscious womb for cultivating the pervasive entity known in Evermore as the Dahklarr Herth—the Dark. Almost tangible, almost living and breathing, the Dahklarr was the emptiness of the Universe just short of life, perpetually gestating, await-ing yet another birth and opportunity for domination.

Although the floating globes that drifted throughout the room shed little light with their puny and pitiful flames, their spheroid shapes shone in sharp-edged mirrors that lined every wall between pillar and doorway. Yet, as one walked through this chamber of multiple reflections, the orbs of varying size followed silently, sliding to reposition themselves, their clustered movements repeated vaguely in mirrors once and again and again and again.

At the head of the room, within a perimeter defined by statues of nocturnal beasts, rested Mistraya's throne. It stood steps above a slick floor that in spots glistened with a feeble light reflecting off its surface, a surface that, in all other instances, held the night.

To the rear of the throne, situated before the lengthy fall of curtain bearing the Mark of the Purple Flame, rose a towering pedestal upon which rested an immense golden bowl. Covering its surface were scenes depicting a whirl of HumanKind drowning in a sea of roiling serpents. Soaring up from this vessel was a great blaze, alive with the leaping tongues of purple flame. The blaze, though of considerable proportion, gave off not a modicum of heat and shed not a modicum of light, lend-ing itself perfectly to the cheerless ambiance of the room.

"So, Soldier One, you witnessed this deed firsthand, did you?" Mistraya's voice was soft, tranquilizing.

"Yes, My Mistress, as did many others," said the gray-masked man, having recently changed out of his Parade Day garb. He was antsy, scanning the glassy floor for movement. Concealed beneath his gray uniform, the Mark of the Purple Flame that was etched into the skin over his heart glowed and burned with a prickling of pain, causing him immense satisfaction. "By the time the entire display of iMagiNacia had finished, quite a crowd had gathered."

"I see."

"Also, they cheered the girl's performance."

"Did they?"

"Talk is that she is the green-eyed Maiden mentioned in the Portent Prophecies, having come to Evermore for the first time. Her strong display of magic, the likes of which I've never seen, made many believers among those assembled."

"Oh?"

"Yes. And I think the girl used more magic than was necessary to subdue the three RogueTags."

"Do you? And why would she do that?"

"To make a powerful impression so word would spread of her visit."

Mistraya rose from her high-backed throne, the drapery of her gown coalescing, lost to the background. Striding away, she trailed a very long train that was magically elevated a finger's width above the floor. The only indication of its presence was when it smothered the reflections of glowing yellow as it swept over them.

Against the inky chamber, the woman's very white skin shone out a ghostly purple, culminating in soft yellowish highlights at the tip of her nose and along her lower lip, while her violet-black eyes retreated, veiled beneath her handsomely arched brows. And there they smoldered, stoked by the embers of suppressed rage. In contrast, the sorceress had a way of chilling her words as they calmly escaped her lips.

"I knew it. I should have visited the scene myself, when I felt the child's strong magical presence disturb my system. Instead I sent you and a bungling scout who never returned."

"The bird, we found it, My Mistress. The small red spinnerets conjured up by the girl had overtaken and killed it. It is my belief that she recognized the scout for what it was."

"Undoubtedly."

The graceful sorceress began to pace, the pale fingers of her right hand rising up to cup her chin, her long nails frosty blue. Abruptly, she pulled her hand away, and turning, asked, "Where are the two girls now?"

"Rumor has it they were escorted away, though I cannot confirm the report. The crowd closed in around them, and by the time I was able to make my way to the site, the girls had disappeared."

"The ClearWeave?"

"If there is such a thing—"

"What do you mean *if?*" The softly spoken words were barbed.

Suddenly afraid, the commander answered, careful to tiptoe verbally: "I've been told the notion of the ClearWeave is only mere rumor and speculation, made up by those—"

"They're *real!*"

"Yes, My Mis—"

"And though we've been unable to secure evidence to confirm their existence, rest assured they are living among us."

"Yes, My Mistress." He felt the burn of the tattooed Flame disappointingly dwindle. He clasped his quivering hands behind him.

"The ClearWeave is real," she said in a softer tone, to herself, as she continued to walk the room.

Her flare-up of anger subsiding, the pain over Soldier One's heart increased in intensity. He closed his eyes, blissfully languishing in the pleasure received.

"Have you notified the Rogues?" Mistraya asked, turning from him.

"Yes, but some we've not been able to locate, so it has been difficult to cover all possible routes. We've no idea where the girls are headed—or where they're from, for that matter. For all we know, at this very moment, they could be sequestered right next door."

"Or making their way through the crowded streets of Autumnsloe," countered Mistraya. "Perhaps they're TimeLight travelers destined to destroy my vision for the Realm."

Soldier One jumped slightly when he found the sorceress's seemingly disembodied face glaring at him from a mirror. Her arms were crossed before her, displaying just a hint of flesh, the long cuffs plunging into obscurity. "We've our scouts covering the main avenues?"

"Throughout the skies of Elderraine."

"Have some Rogues on foot below."

"As you wish."

"And you've passed on the descriptions of the girls—with and without their masks—to the Influenced?"

"Yes, My Mistress." Discreetly, he resumed his anxious surveillance of the floor.

"Good. Then we will spot them soon enough." In the meantime, thought Mistraya, I'll do some SightSharing with a few of our winged brethren. Perhaps through their eyes I may see something they're overlooking. My intuition tells me in all likelihood those girls are still in CityCentral.

The thought brought a rush of excitement, a pulsing of her purplish blood.

Not far from the sorceress, barely distinguishable in the lesser light, an intelligent pair of eyes focused keenly on the proceedings. Round and amber, they gazed out from within a black hood belonging to a large, horned bird of the night, its feathers layered in muted greens and blues. Its movements restricted, the creature was fastened to its perch by a crystalline anklet that was ever so thin but magically unbreakable. Concerned for the well being of Heather Nighborne and Molly Pringle, the creature monitored the conversation, on the hunt for any tidbit that could possibly be of assistance to the pair.

At the base of the far wall, beneath the mirrors, the bird spied two deadly pinpoints of red as they slowly and silently advanced in the direction of Mistraya's throne. The bird knew them to be eyes belonging to either Maif or Raif, the two great winged lizards that patrolled the premises, making meals of vermin-type undesirables, snatching up most anything that moved. At the most inopportune of times, in an attempt to sate their enormous appetites, one or both of the unpredictable beasts would surprisingly burst from the room's drear and snatch a mouthful of one of Mistraya's many guests, seized as if by the Dahklarr itself. And following one or two crunching adjustments of the lizard's ferocious bite, the visitor would be dragged away screaming until the screams were no more, to be devoured at leisure in some inky-black recession within the walls of the Castle Allurid. Mistraya found the disturbance of the screams and pleas annoying and was delighted when the cries were cut off abruptly, mid-utterance.

Craning its head, the bird listened as the uniformed man asked, "And what would you suggest I do upon receiving word of their sighting, My Mistress, knowing this girl to be different and more advanced in her abilities than the others? Shall we capture the child and bring her to you for purposes of interrogation?"

"Interrogation?" she asked, her voice creamy smooth. "How sweet. You do mean torture, don't you?" The sorceress smiled thinly. "I would think the answer obvious, my devious fellow. She's too dangerous. Like all others that have come before, kill her immediately and without compunction. Her friend, too."

"Yes, My Mistress."

"Remember, it's crucial that this girl not leave Evermore to return in accordance with the Prophecies."

"I understand."

The silence hung heavy, waiting, waiting, lingering.

Finally: "Soldier One?"

"My Mistress?"

"If you ever do cross paths with this *child,* and should you square off against her, face-to-face, would you please remember this one choice morsel of information? I think you will find it of immense value."

"And that is what?"

"*That* is this: the child will kill you."

The softly spoken words carried certain power, a lack of doubt, as if the mere assertion made it undeniably so. In the silence, Soldier One swallowed despite himself. "I understand, My Mistress."

"Do you?" Her words were silky.

"Yes." Another swallow. "I believe what you are saying is that if I should ever have to face off against her, the battle is already lost, and that it best I approach any encounter with this possible answer to Evermore's Portent dishonorably, underhandedly, and without warning."

"A fine triumvirate, would you not agree?" Mistraya said, letting loose a magical flow that rewarded her top commander.

Soldier One closed his eyes gratefully as the thrill caused by an even greater pain coursed through his system, emanating from its source: the Mark of the Purple Flame.

Emerging from the sheltering trees of the courtyard and onto the spacious Avenue, Heather said, "Over there's the Ring of the Evermore Maidens." With a glance skyward, she said, "Here, come on." She gestured for Molly to follow beneath a sequestering overhang. The two slipped in, out of the sunlight. "We want to go in the opposite direction, though," the moon girl pointed, "away from the monument and back towards the PortalDoor."

Around them, the sidewalks and barricaded streets were still teeming with Parade Day visitors, the usual traffic held at bay. While Molly casually peered through the glass door into a shop behind them, Heather leaned out from below the visor of canopy, scrutinizing the skies. She could see ominous birds gliding above, before diving toward lower ground. There she lost sight of them, blocked by the rise of buildings or the foliaged girth of trees. It wasn't long, however, before she would see them reappear—or some very much like them—once again ascending, their large wingspans rocking with the air's currents. The moon girl observed that, with the exception of one, perhaps two, the auras of the birds were hostile with reds and malignant grays and greens.

Not good, Heather thought. Not good, not good, not good.

Wondering whether or not to tell Molly about the scouts for fear of her reaction, Heather dismissed the thought—for the moment.

Ding, ding! Ding, ding!

"Molly, look! That's the ringing we've been hearing. They're Autumnsloe trolleys. They must be running now that the parade is over."

The two watched the trolley car as it made its genial approach, swinging wide along the circumference of the immense monument.

The streetcar's exterior was reddish-bronze in color with a yellow roof. Long and narrow, sporting flanks of windows on both sides, its overall design incorporated a smooth flow of curl. A third of the trolley car was open to the elements, and it was here that the passengers hung off the posts that rose at intervals floor to ceiling. Some riders waved. Others hopped aboard, catching the slow-moving trolley in transit. One passenger, a woman, had disembarked after looking their way. She walked towards the girls.

Ding, ding!

"It reminds me of a beautiful jewelry box," Molly said, as the hovering trolley moved on.

"Yeah, with a heck of a lot of space for all your watches and bracelets."

"I wonder what's making the trolley go? I don't see any animals pulling it, and I don't think it has an engine—at least I don't hear the sound of one."

"We're in Autumnsloe, Molly," said the moon girl. "How else would they run and float off the ground like that?"

Molly stated her conclusion in verbal collaboration with Heather: "Magic!"

With a discreet glance at the sky's winged inhabitants, Heather asked, "Fallasha, are we right? Are the trolleys in Autumnsloe run by magic?" When her brooch didn't respond, the girl asked, "Fallasha?"

Heather looked at the brooch, as did Molly. Her little moon face set, the tiny eyes just blinked, staring straight ahead.

"I think Fallasha is mad at me, Molly, and so I guess she's not talking."

Molly looked hurtfully at the moon brooch. "Fallasha, are you really not going to talk to us?"

Still the little brooch refused to speak.

"We can get by without her." Heather angled her head towards Fallasha. "I don't see why I shouldn't just tear you off and leave you here."

Eliciting a small gasp, Molly brought her gloved hand up to the lips of her mask. She said, "Would you really do that, Heather?"

"Why not?" Heather said, bluffing. "What good is she anyway?"

"Look," Fallasha huffed, finally breaking her silence, "first of all, don't ask me questions. I'm simply a brooch on your costume—nothing more—going where you would like to go, doing what you would like to do. After all, wasn't that your wish? So, girls, when you find yourself in a bit of a fix between here and the PortalDoor, you'll simply have to figure out that particular situation for yourself. And this should make you extremely happy, not having to be saddled with the responsible experience of my presence, my infallible direction, and my ever wise and always prudent advice. So, why be serious? After all, there's no need to worry. Go on. Just have fun."

The moon brooch retreated into her silent pout, as the sidewalk became more congested with shoppers and bystanders.

As the moon and butterfly girls made room by moving towards the street, three people in wide-brimmed party hats exited the soap and candle shop. Small bells tinkled on the door while pleasing fragrances made their escape. While the ladies huddled near the girls, pointing and deciding where to go next, the woman from the trolley walked up. She sported a headpiece that had lofty feathers of red with spotted tips. Following the twitter of recognition by all parties, she joined the group in animated conversation.

Heather pulled Molly back under the shelter of the awning, still unsure about making her aware of the dangerous birds overhead. Instead, she engaged her in conversation about the unique Autumnslovian candles and holders that were on display in the store's window, while she decided on an overall course of action.

One of the women close by, her party hat overflowing with orange tissue, waved and detached from the group. She headed toward the secluded courtyard where Heather and Molly had recently emerged from the lamppost. The woman was soon lost from sight.

Meanwhile, Fallasha had a recommendation. Having recently become aware of the many scouts, she thought it would be a great idea if Heather and Molly hopped aboard a trolley and rode it in seclusion to the PortalDoor. However, the vain brooch, still feeling the sting following her argument with Heather, struggled with sharing her thoughts, feeling that the girls could use a good lesson in appreciating their amazing tour guide. Yet, with danger lurking in the sky, Fallasha knew she needed to swallow her pride, wanting no harm to befall the girls. Glancing at the people still chattering within earshot, the brooch decided it was best to wait until they departed before speaking out with her idea. But the group lingered. After watching another trolley go by, irritated, she glared at the bystanders, wishing they would hurry and go away.

Unnoticed by the girls, in the nearby courtyard, the woman in the headpiece of orange tissue waved enthusiastically to an approaching friend, and ran the last few steps to join him. They chatted for a moment, until a gang of RogueTags shoved their way by. Words were exchanged, and the Rogues, making an about-face, returned to confront the couple. Taunting them, the ruffians drew their blades. In an instant, people sprang from the nearby hedges and doorways, ambushing the toughs. Following a brief skirmish that revealed glints of additional weaponry, the RogueTags were soundlessly and efficiently overwhelmed, their bodies dragged off. A moment later, the courtyard was calm once again. The woman in orange, along with her companion, strolled arm in arm back to the Avenue, looking to blend in with its ocean of Parade Day occupants.

Back under the overhang, Heather said, "Hey, Molly." She began to turn and guide the butterfly girl away from the women in party hats, keeping her voice low. "Let's get going towards the PortalDoor. At least we know that the ClearWeave has gotten rid of the RogueTags. Look over there. Remember that café where they were all hanging out? They're gone now."

But Molly hesitated and then stopped. "Heather, there sure are a lot of scouts up there. What if they recognize our costumes?"

Heather said, "I was hoping you wouldn't notice until we crossed the street. I didn't want you to worry." With a subdued smile on her beautiful butterfly mask, Molly placed a gloved hand on her friend's arm in appreciation. "Anyway, if we're spotted, that's a question we don't need Fallasha to answer," the moon girl said, with a glance at her still silent brooch. "They'll probably fly off and we'll be reported to Mistraya."

"Then what?"

"Chances are she'll come after us, or she'll send some of the Influenced."

"Either way, it's scary."

"Yeah," said Heather, glancing askance at her brooch, "it wouldn't be much *fun.* "

Fallasha, however, paid no heed. Impatiently, she continued to wait for the three women to go away, so she could share her idea and get back in the good graces of the girls. But they kept chatting, laughing, and occasionally gesticulating. She looked up at the moon girl's mask.

"Heather," she whispered. She dared not raise her voice louder, afraid of being overheard and noticed. She tried again: "Heather." But in the bustle and noise of the passersby, the moon girl didn't hear her, and instead turned to her friend.

"Molly, see those striped awnings across the street, hanging above the smaller shops? Let's get over there and walk underneath them for a while. They'll help us to stay hidden from the scouts while we travel up the street for a block or two. Molly?"

Molly didn't say anything as, captivated by the visual, she looked at all the people dressed in fancy and intricate costume, walking and milling about on the cobblestone streets, passing through the shadows cast by the phenomenal architecture and autumnal trees. She could see that the easygoing breeze was causing the leaves to whiffle, the flags to flutter, and the store signs to swing slightly, occasionally emitting a creak or two. The day was pleasantly warm, and within her costume, so was the girl. Finally, Molly spoke. "Autumnsloe sure is beautiful."

Heather grabbed her sleeve and turned her smoothly but forcefully. "Molly, look down."

"What?"

"Quick. Look down."

Molly did. She glanced peripherally to see that Heather was doing the same, their faces turned from the street, staring at their shoe tops. "Why? What's going on?"

Glancing over her shoulder, Heather saw a scout fly past at a distance not too far away. Beating the air for momentum, and then gliding on its generous wingspan, it raked low over the moiling crowd. Its dark wings and body glistening blue, its striped neck easily discernable, the bird carefully scanned the people that flashed by below.

"Scout."

"Did it see us?"

Her attention never leaving the bird, Heather said, "I don't think so."

"We're wearing masks, though, Heather. Why did you want us to look down? What difference does it make?"

"Well, don't forget, they've had a look at our faces, our masks, *and* our costumes. So, I thought if we looked down, our large headpieces might help to hide our costumes when the scouts looked at us from above." Heather continued to watch the receding bird as it climbed and hovered on the breezes, its keen eyesight inspecting all that lay below.

Molly followed her friend's line of sight. Seeing Mistraya's scout, she said, "That was close, wasn't it?"

"Yeah. And you're right, Molly. Autumnsloe sure *is* beautiful. Dangerous, too." Heather grabbed her friend's fluffy sleeve again, this time in a gentler fashion, and began to lead her. The moon girl looked quickly at the deceptively tranquil sky, with its hovering pinpricks spotting the lighter blue. "Come on. Let's get out of here."

In the serenity of her Bristol House room, Mrs. Pringle was lying on the thick coverlet of her draped canopy bed. Despite being enamored of her comfortable surroundings, the woman was unable to nap. Her thoughts, like viscous liquid, pumped morosely through her head, spinning monotonous wheels of past, present, and future. Painfully, her head throbbed. She finally sat up and rubbed her temples, dully looking out the window at the sky. Upon doing so, Mrs. Pringle found herself slowly dropping her arms and rising to her feet, spellbound.

Still moody and windblown, the clouds looked unusual, oppressive, their undersides no longer loosely hanging down in a ragged softness. Instead they appeared tightly stretched, like they were being sucked into the vast heights of the earth's atmosphere. Mrs. Pringle couldn't recall having seen anything like it before. Within her, its strangeness provoked an agitation, disturbing what little harmony she had achieved.

The room seemed overly warm and her skin felt clammy.

Maybe what I need is a relaxing bath, she thought.

Lana Pringle looked down, drawn to the movement in the Pringle driveway below, as a small blue sports car zoomed up and braked to a halt behind Ned's sedan. Opening the door and getting out was a young woman, her shoulder length russet hair blowing slightly in the diminishing wind. She moved briskly, the car's door slamming behind her on a sudden gust.

Though the individual was dressed casually in a loose fitting sweatshirt and jeans, Mrs. Pringle thought she recognized her from the bank where her husband worked. The small blue convertible confirmed it.

"Clarissa? What's she doing—?" She watched as in the distance the woman rang the bell and knocked on the door.

As revelation readdressed the persistent questions posed only fleetingly and just long enough to dismiss as irrational, Mrs. Pringle nodded gently, once or twice, her words a faraway murmur. "Oh. Okay."

Again rubbing her temples, she turned away from the breathtaking view.

Having advanced cautiously amid the bustle, from awning to awning, the moon and butterfly girls had gone as far as they could under the cover of canvas. Reaching the last of the colorful rectangles, they stopped.

"What now?" Molly asked. She positioned herself to discreetly watch the many birds that hung airborne, some circling in lazy loops. "Maybe they're not all scouts, Heather."

"Maybe, but we can't take that chance." Heather leaned out and was able to observe that most the auras emanating overhead were still of questionable character.

The brooch followed the back end of yet another trolley as it receded, easing its way through the dense foot traffic, its bell clanging. Despite the Parade Day goers crowded around them, Fallasha thought it high time she made her thoughts known about hiding under the protective awning before hopping aboard the next trolley. As the little brooch began to do so, she was drowned out by Molly's words.

"Maybe we should have taken Mr. No Name up on his offer to take us closer to the Portal."

"Maybe," said Heather, leaning near, having to talk above the din of the Avenue and those conversing in close proximity. "But Molly, I didn't know Fallasha would stop talking to us and I didn't want the Clear-Weave to figure out where our PortalDoor was."

"That was good thinking, Heather." Molly looked at the moon brooch. "Fallasha, are you really not going to help us? We sure could use your advice."

Before Fallasha could answer, Heather said, "You heard what she said back there. She's angry, Molly. Just forget about her. She's made up her little moon mind not to talk to us."

Fallasha started to speak up, wanting to say that wasn't so—not any more—and she had a plan, but was jostled by someone's arm in passing. Moments later, a cluster of performers, several who were very tall and all wearing overelaborate headpieces that made them all the taller, strode in front of the moon and butterfly girls. They stopped, continuing their lively conversations about what they had just purchased and where to eat. Pinned behind them with their backs to the wall, the girls couldn't see the street. Heather looked at Molly.

"I think we're stuck for the moment."

The butterfly girl giggled and said, "Seems that way."

Fallasha was still trying to talk to Heather, but her words were lost in the many furry protrusions of the sleeve in front of her. Trapped as they were, not one of the three noticed Mistraya's scout, drifting close and low, peering in beneath the awning. Coming up empty, it banked to the opposite side of the street to inspect the shoppers beneath the coverings there.

The performers moved on.

"Finally, some air!" Heather said, exasperated, rolling her eyes. When they refocused, it happened to be on a large shop down and across the wide Avenue. The moon girl shot a circumspect glance at the blue above.

Attempting to speak out again, Fallasha began to convey her idea in a voice too low and too late, as Heather said, "Come on, Molly. Follow me and keep your head looking down. I've got an idea."

She stepped out into the noisy crush of foot traffic, Molly right behind her. Both girls kept their heads inclined toward the street. Meanwhile, whenever possible, Fallasha kept an anxious eye on the perilous heavens.

Ned Pringle was lying on the couch, one shoe off, his tie loosened, and the uppermost button on his shirt undone. While someone pounded at the front door, the banker remained unaware, oblivious as the television blared out its narration. He repositioned his forearm, propping up his head, his heavy glasses askew.

"Shudd I haff anuthuh ja-rink?" he wondered, looking at the lonely glass of ice on the coffee table in front of him. It was sweating, producing yet another fluid ring of remiss on the shiny wood finish. Just then, the cubes repositioned themselves with a fairy-like tinkle. At the sound, the banker smiled with a sudden childlike beaming—and just as suddenly, his face went vacant as the smile faded, though not completely. It lingered numbly as barely a hint on the lips. Being only a social drinker, Mr. Pringle's eyelids felt heavy and his mouth dry after this, his fifth glassful. Or was it his sixth? Seventh? Obviously, the man loved good scotch.

He took off his glasses and with a flip, tossed them near what remained of his drink. They careened across the slick tabletop like a small plane in a belly landing, sliding past the cylindrical, ice-filled conning tower. Mr. Pringle watched them disappear off the far side of the flight deck. In a blur of near-sightedness, he sought out the phone across the room, atop the narrow accent table. He recalled how earlier, sitting upright in its base, the handset's keypad had lit up, ringing tenaciously at frequent intervals. But the phone had gone silent, its display dormant and tiny numbered face asleep.

Wouldn't have been Lana. Probably Clarissa. Don't feel much like talking right now, Mr. Pringle thought, falling back onto the pillow. With a foggy half-laugh he added, Couldn't if I wanted to. But Clarissa doesn't matter, doesn't matter. The other woman, how important is she when your family is falling apart? The heck with Lana, anyway. Caused us to fail, that's what she did. If she hadn't been so cold, hadn't started crossing me, I would have never gone looking. Never… Never.

He threw a forearm across his face, his rolled sleeve creeping higher. The beating at the door continued, as the television still trumpeted its deep-voiced commentary. The occasional words "Ned?" and "Ned, it's me, Clarissa. Honey, are you all right? Open up, okay?" were lost, drowned out.

Was that laughter and merriment, the clinking of glasses that he heard? Dinner? Were they all at dinner? He lifted his elbow; one eye revealed. It popped open. And then squinted. Something fuzzy, furry, was happening on that big screen of his. What was it? Mr. Pringle's mouth hung cockeyed, a rubbery pit, and out of it inched the head of a languid eel. Suddenly withdrawing his tongue, he made several smacking sounds.

They are. They're at dinner, all of them, the entire family, he thought. I can see them. They're beautiful, beautiful people. They're having a great time, too. Just look at them. We need more sound. Someone please turn up the sound, will you? It's hard to hear, hard to understand. Where's that remote?

Mr. Pringle started shifting on the couch, hoping the remote would surface within reach. Then he stopped short, feeling his head swim as though the couch were a rowboat dipping and lurching between waves. With his arms tensed, his fingers bit into the cushions to steady himself, and Mr. Pringle's head surged up from his neck like a bloated sun.

"I'll be dawghed! Thay argh!" He started to chortle, slapping his thigh, bawling grandly, "Luk ah 'um, wihl you! Juss luk ah 'um! Thassuh famlee! An juss lissen tuh 'em laff. Juss lissen! Aw, thuh're soo-o-o-o happ-ee-e…" Mr. Pringle's arm was dangling at a loose, sloppy angle over the side of the couch, his hand now within inches of the remote control. The man guffawed through his tears. "Yessir! Now, *thass* suh famlee." His head sank back into the folds of his neck. He mumbled, "Yessir, thassuh…famlee…"

Across the room, pictured on the television screen, spotted hyenas had gathered around a downed Cape buffalo in the fading twilight. Closest to the prey, those of higher rank had torn loose their first pulpy mouthfuls of red. Others waited to get theirs.

"Yessir, thassuh…famlee…"

⁂

Sheriff Harland Dane was making his way across town, his truck bouncing on the unevenness of the dirt road, kicking up a rooster tail of embroiled dust behind him. The man preferred the dirt shortcut rather than facing the snarl of cross-town traffic. Besides, he was in a hurry. Too much time spent ruminating, a habit that drives the wife crazy. Calls it dawdling. But he knew she was wrong. Men don't dawdle.

With the dense cloud cover still heavy over the land, he rolled down the window. Soon Dane was hanging his arm down against the truck's exterior door, his hand and metal watchband striking it with each jolting bounce. Strange. He felt hot. Oddly enough, so did the air of late afternoon. It had begun to feel sticky, oppressive.

Looking in the rearview mirror, he saw that small beads of perspiration had formed on his brow. He brought his arm inside the cab and brushed a sleeve across his forehead.

What's with the sweat?

Heads still lowered, Heather and Molly worked their way across the congested thoroughfare, sometimes bumping into strangers, at other times navigating around clumps of merrymakers. Some were inebriated on assilloberry extract, a traditional Autumnslovian concoction. When the girls heard another trolley coming up the street, its bell cheerily ringing out, they avoided its path by hurrying through the less traveled center of the Avenue. Fallasha had finally found the opening she desired, and the timing couldn't have been better.

"Heather, if we could only—"

"Not now, Fallasha, okay? I need to concentrate on getting to the other side of the street."

"But—"

"Not now."

Fallasha wanted to scream in frustration. She realized her behavior had isolated her from the girls, hindering her Bristol House mission. Recognizing that she had put the girls at even greater risk by letting them think her unavailable, a sinking feeling weighed on the moon brooch, dragging her fiery spirit down.

I know, I know. It's my pride, she reasoned. Again my injudicious, spiteful pride. Am I never to learn?

Downhearted, Fallasha realized what she really wanted was to cry.

Instead, the small brooch attempted to focus on what was transpiring around her. She struggled to keep alert, to stake a wary eye out for danger on the ground and in the air. The moon brooch felt she had relinquished control of their situation by retreating from the girls, and that without her exceptional guidance surely nothing short of unmitigated catastrophe was close at hand. It didn't help that, positioned as she was on Heather's upper body, she found her scope of vision was at best severely limited.

As Heather and Molly arrived on the opposite half of Parade Day Avenue, the foot traffic seemed to clot, denying them access to the concealment of the wooden overhang that covered the elevated sidewalk. Concerned with their glaring exposure on the street, the moon girl couldn't resist a glance aloft.

"Scout," she said, and the girls looked down at the ground as they walked around the stalled bodies. After a moment, and then only stealthily, Heather looked up at the passing creature. The bird, having flown by, pumped its wings, before it drifted over the Avenue, trolling left and then right. In a banking reveal of its tremendous wingspan, the scout turned the corner in search of its prey down the adjoining street.

"We've got to get onto that covered walkway," the moon girl said.

"Heather, what do we do then?" Molly asked.

"You'll see. We don't have much farther to go. Only up to the corner. But we're bound to be spotted if we stay here in the street."

"It looks pretty jammed up everywhere," said Molly.

"I know." Heather saw a sudden gap between revelers. "Come on."

Through it, she and Molly made headway but stalled shortly thereafter. The butterfly girl cast a worried look above the bystanders.

"Heather, trapped like this, if a scout attacked us, we won't even be able to run."

The moon girl had no answers. In the dense traffic, Fallasha was at a loss, as well, able only to see the costume currently pressed into her face in a close-up of shifting, scratchy material.

As Mistraya's StealthSlayer weaved slowly through the crowd behind them, Heather and Molly didn't see him in white and red. His costume was simple and not at all voluminous, thus allowing him easy maneuverability. His masked face was red, a ribbon of black covering his eyes above lips of white. He felt for his SlipProng, a metal skewer with a handle. Concealed within a secretive pocket at the hip, it was easily within reach—just a simple slide of the hand.

While on the elevated walk, he had recognized the girls from the description provided indirectly by Soldier One, and in unhurried fashion through the crowded Avenue, he made his way in their direction. The red-faced man felt that if he could simply maneuver behind them, he could take out both with two skillful, well-placed thrusts—the girl in the moon costume to be the initial recipient of his narrow spike. They would continue to stand limply, most likely without notice, in the crush of bodies, and after a moment's pause, he would simply retreat, losing himself in the crowd. As a trained StealthSlayer, he'd never failed. And he must not now, if he was to be praised by his Mistress.

Seeing the girls stalled in the glut of Parade Day revelers, he realized that, trapped as they were, this was a gift indeed. He felt that the Dahklarr Herth was somewhere, smiling his way. And as he stalked his prey, he found himself smiling, too. But inconspicuously and only for an instant.

Easy kill, he thought, drawing ever closer to his targets, who stood anchored to their spots. Over his heart, The Mark of the Purple Flame burned with sweet agony.

Far too far behind the assassin, rising tall out of the crowd walked the woman who had disembarked earlier from the trolley, her red plumage bobbing with each step. Realizing she could never catch him in the congestion on the street, she reached into her pocket and removed a bright orange handkerchief, flashing it briefly in the air—as if to unfurl it—before wiping the corners of her glittering lips. She returned it to her pocket.

Above, through an open second story window, an old man set down his pipe, blowing one last smoke ring, and quickly retreated into the room's lowlight interior. There he opened one of many cages along the wall and placed a gloved hand before a small, poisonous bird. His index finger extended, on it was a modest offering, a bit of the gelatinous residue of Autumnsloe's own bread worm. After sipping the portion up through its straw-like beak, the bird zipped out through the large door of the cage, whereupon it perched on the window's sill. Smiling like an affable Santa Claus, the old man reached for his pipe and took a long drag. In a series of quick, well-measured increments, he set to blowing smoke into the air before him. It coalesced, forming a depiction of the red-faced man, with his pointy headpiece easily recognizable. A moment later the bird had gone, its miniature wings a blur. Having briefly admired his work, the old man dispersed the smoky image with a wave of his hand.

Back on the street, Heather was frustrated. She said loudly, over her shoulder, "Molly, can you back up at all? Let's try and return to the center of the street, and then maybe we'll be able to get around all these people. It looks like the only way. These guys in front of me won't budge, because I heard them say they're waiting for some 'Ghost Dancers' to perform."

"I can't back up, Heather. There're too many people bunched up behind me. It looks like we're stuck here for awhile."

Heather gave the sky a quick once over.

"Molly, if we stay here too long, I'm afraid the scouts will see us. We really need to get under that cover as soon as we can."

Festive music was on the air and the gathering was boisterous all around. Having patiently angled his way through the crowd, the red-faced StealthSlayer was now positioned behind the girls, separated by only a woman and child. Weary from standing, the child drew towards the mother, wrapping decorated sleeves round her baggy, costumed legs. Efficiently, the assassin slipped into the newly created opening to stand at Heather's back. Composed, tattoo ablaze with aching pleasure, his gloved hand stealthily slid to wrap around the haft of the SlipProng, removing it ever so slowly.

Not far above, the small bird hovered, its tiny wings keeping it afloat in indistinct fans of glistening feathers. Sighting on its target below, the bird pushed a poison-infused mucous ball into its barrel-like beak, and spit it sharply toward the mark.

His shoulders jumping and mouth contorting, the StealthSlayer refrained from slapping at his exposed neck. However, an instant later, his body seized up and the assassin fell forward, slumping against the spectator standing to Heather's left.

Instinctively, Heather stepped towards the butterfly girl.

"What's happened?" Molly asked.

"I don't know. He just fell over. Maybe he's sick."

"That's strange." Molly said, as she and Heather looked on in curiosity.

"Hey, what are you doing? Get off of me!" said the moon girl's neighbor, jerking his shoulders, while clumsily turning. When the spectator pushed backwards a step, creating a slice of room, the dead StealthSlayer toppled face first at his feet, the SlipProng trapped under him. His eyes fixed in a lifeless stare, his mouth was still set in the white-lipped grimace of moments passed. The pain that had once seared his chest with caustic pleasure had all but ceased.

"Hey, give him room!" the spectator shouted, and those around him withdrew, creating a slight parting leading toward the raised walkway and its desirous cover.

"What's happened?" Heather heard a person ask over the clamor and music.

Someone else bellowed, "Looks like somebody couldn't hold his extract." Others laughed.

Two men hastily appeared to attend the downed man.

Upon inspection, the bald, heavyset one said, "He's all right. Just needs a little rest and a bit of air, that's all. He'll be fine."

"Yes, indeed," said the skinny one with the loose fitting shirt. "Better than ever."

When they hoisted him between them, there was no sign of the weapon that had previously rested between his abdomen and the ground. His pointy headpiece had been removed and his face covered with a cloth. The word *dehydration* was heard mentioned and oft repeated afterward.

With little delay, Heather grabbed Molly's arm and made for the opening in the throng. The partying around them still loud and raucous, Molly trailed her friend, the two moving closer to the short flight of stairs ascending to the sidewalk and its abutting boutiques. It wasn't long, however, before their progress was stalled once again, the girls finding little wiggle room in the squeeze of bodies.

When the crowd finally began to advance, Heather shouted, "Molly!" over her shoulder, but before the moon girl could press into the immediate space created to her left, it sealed up tight. Heather scowled. "Excuse me!" she said, loudly. "Excuse me! I need to get through!"

A woman managed a half-turn.

"Where would you like us to go? We're packed in like canned spillion."

Seeing it was of no use, Heather yelled to Molly, "I think we're stuck again."

"Scout!" was her friend's response, and the girls turned to face the ground, the tops of their headpieces brushing against those in front of them.

Heather waited before looking up. She heard Molly say, "It's clear." Together, they watched the back end of the bird as it sailed off.

"We've got to get out of here. We just have to, Molly. It's only a matter of time before we're seen."

"I know, Heather. But how?"

Heather looked around, her movements limited. She felt pressure from behind. "I don't know."

"Scout!" Molly said again, and both heads dipped, ducks on a pond.

"Let me through! Let me through!" shouted an approaching man. Quickly, Heather and Molly turned to see, head and shoulders above the others, a broad-shouldered man in yellow suspenders and a torn blue shirt pushing his way rudely through the masses and toward the raised walkway. The moon girl saw his aura to be a determined, muddled brown, but of harmless intent.

Cries of "Hey, watch it!" and "Look out!" and "How rude!" rode over the Parade Day cacophony, but no one dared stop the burly man. His brown hat pushed back off his forehead, he continued to bully his way through the throng, cutting a swath directly in front of the moon and butterfly girls. After he passed, Heather took Molly's upper arm once more.

"Come on! He's going our way!"

And the pair moved in behind him.

Above Parade Day Avenue, observing the festivities from a broad, vine wrapped balcony, a tastefully attired woman turned to the finely tailored man on her right.

"Seems Halster's bold maneuver has freed them up, and the girls are again on their way. Brilliant stroke, my love."

The gentleman pulled his attention from the activities to look at her, a slight turn of the head. "That may get them to the sidewalk, but they're not home free. Not yet."

"Oh, dear me. Do you see something I don't, darling?" She sipped her frosted beverage of fermented EverRipe.

"Perhaps. See the two dressed as jesters in the large diamonds of yellow and white? The one in front, he's carrying a staff in his right hand. I think they're StealthSlayers. They've been tailing the girls for some time, since we had Borsten's group of tall performers squeeze in front of them at the corner, concealing the young pair from the scout."

"Where, darling? I don't see them."

"There, across the street and two blocks back, climbing the stairs to the sidewalk. The woman jester, she's the easiest to spot, wearing that headpiece that looks like a half-shell, with sequined balls all along the edges. See her? She's holding a large fan with those same yellow balls."

"I do! Yes! Dare I mention I like her hat? Heavenly."

"Remind me, dear, to purchase one for you."

"I will."

She nipped his face with a kiss. "You've the eyes of an eckrill, darling." Then: "Oh, dear." Playfully, she reached for the handkerchief in his breast pocket. Chin-up in concentration, she dabbed at the bright red lipstick spotting his cheek. "There. Can't have you going around looking debauched, now, can we?"

He pulled away slightly. "I hope Haslow's kept a watch on that deadly pair from his window. If he hasn't, there's no way we can warn his people and have them placed in time from the inn."

"The girls are two blocks ahead of their pursuers, darling. There's no need to worry." She sipped her drink from an exceptionally tall-stemmed glass. "Dear, your EverRipe. It's turning. If you don't hurry and drink it, it'll grow dreadfully bland."

The man looked behind him, towards the door. "Waldaar? Have Jereen dispatch Welsling and Jortess."

"Right away, Sir." With a dignified bow, the butler withdrew.

The woman asked, "But darling, if there's trouble, can Jereen and Welsling reach the girls in time?"

The man took up his frosted glass and sipped. "Mmm. No." He swallowed the sweet, intoxicating liquid. "There exists a sole purpose for their dispatch, my dear."

"Oh, and what's that, darling?"

"Yes. It's for the discreet cleanup of the girls' corpses should they be overtaken."

ℓ

Finally climbing the steps to the sidewalk, Heather and Molly followed in the wake of the large man until he clumped into a delicatessen, his boots heavy on the wood flooring. At that point, avoiding the shoppers pausing at the boutique doors, surprisingly, the girls slipped into a steady current that moved them smoothly under cover. Swept along, Molly followed in step behind her friend.

"Heather?"

"What, Molly?"

"Can we stop for a minute?"

"Why? We're moving pretty good."

"I know. But look over there. See? The Ghost Dancers that you were talking about are beginning their performance. Can we? Please. Just for a second or two? I think we're safe under this overhang."

Overhearing, in disbelief, Fallasha scoffed. Her voice was lost to the crowd, when she said, "I advise you not to stop, girls. This is not wise. I repeat, not wise. Please, let us make haste and simply scurry along to the PortalDoor."

Molly continued, "And look, over there in the street. See where all those people are standing? What are those small men doing?"

"I see them," said Heather. "Wow. It looks like their hands are on fire. And that one—"

"They're making glass vases and bowls, Heather. That's what they're doing. See? That one man has hot, hot glass in his hands, and it's soft and he's able to shape it…"

"Wow. Has to hurt."

Molly giggled. "They probably have really thick skin."

Watching the glass molders, Heather slowed, pulling Molly out of the flow of traffic, toward the edge of the elevated sidewalk. Standing among the other spectators, she glanced above her, making certain that they were safely under cover. The moon girl was barely able to hear Fallasha's protest, a sulky, half-hearted appeal from below. Unable to determine what she was saying, Heather didn't ask for clarification.

Still some distance behind Heather and Molly, the pair of jesters moved steadily among the pedestrians on the sidewalk. From their exclusive upper story balcony, the dapper man and his TrueMate could only watch in fascinated horror, as the two assassins of the Influenced continued to close in on the stationary girls.

"Those girls had better not linger long."

"Here, darling," said the woman, taking up his empty glass, "Let me fix you another EverRipe. You're looking overwrought."

"Wow, Molly, it's no wonder we weren't able to make any progress. Look at all these people waiting to see the street shows."

"The Ghost Dancers, Heather. Look!"

The girls watched from the walkway, while on a stage toward their side of the street, a host of Ghost Dancers started the routine, moving slowly, while their counterparts merged in, materializing out of nowhere. Encircling a portion of the stage, the Autumnslovian Parade Day Orchestra began to play under the direction of a diminutive conductor on a lone, upraised stand. Strangely melodic, the music swelled, created on peculiar instruments in a bizarre production. The pulse increased.

The dancers now began to step quick and lively with the music. Dressed head to toe in fragmented pieces of the rainbow, large and small, the performers strutted, their movement divinely rhythmic. Threading in and around, they began to pace faster and faster. Bodies nimble, erect, and expressive; leaps and landings, legs thrusting, sweeping, entwining; music pounding, cadence resounding; prancing, lifting, spinning in choreographed progression did the Ghost Dancers dance.

Joining in with the orchestra, a large choir began to sing and chant to an increasing tempo.

The moon girl couldn't hear Molly when she said, "Heather, look! They're fading, like ghosts!"

On stage, the dancers were becoming translucent, appearing lit from within, so that against the conical white background, the colors flowed and flickered, whirling before and behind each other, intermingling to create new tones in a tumultuous display of dazzling flash. As if on unseen cables, some dancers ascended above the others, and some above those, and then all began rising and falling, wave upon wave of alternating hues, a phenomenal heaving kaleidoscope that climbed toward the heavens.

"The girls are doomed." From aloft, on their tastefully furnished balcony across the Avenue, the man said in an undertone, "It's too late. Even if the youngsters started on their way again, they'd never escape them now."

"Oh, why did they have to stop for the dancers?" said the woman.

"And here they come, here come the StealthSlayers. We can only hope that Haslow has been attentive and has his people in place."

The woman turned away from the scene, and clutching her True-Mate's upper arm with both hands, inclined her head against it. "I can't bear to watch."

Down on Parade Day Avenue, the pulsing roar of music drowned out all other sound, utterly. Briefly distracted, Molly glimpsed right, only to return her attention to the dancers. A moment later, however, the butterfly girl refocused on the walkway, on the two figures in jester costumes that approached. Something about them made her skin crawl. It was the way they fiercely glared at her, exuding malicious intent.

Molly impatiently pushed on Heather's arm. No response. She pushed again. Still nothing. Finally, she grabbed and shook it, rocking the moon girl. Tearing her attention away from the dancers, Heather leaned in.

"Behind me!" Molly shouted over the uproar.

The moon girl shook her head. "I can't hear you," was lost.

"Behind me! Look behind me!"

Heather shook her head again. In exasperation, Molly stepped back a pace, the moon girl now able to see past her and down the length of sidewalk. With the jesters' murderous auras pulsing loudly like the music, their insidiousness obvious in a glimpse, Heather pulled at Molly and they started to run. However, they didn't get far before they had to slow, impeded by the casual pace of others on the sidewalk. The girls threw glances over their shoulders. The pursuers increased their pace. Trapped behind an old, slow-moving woman, the jester in the lead audaciously bumped her off the walk and sent her sprawling onto those gathered in the street below.

Following another glimpse behind her, Heather said to no one, "We're trapped."

On the street side of the walkway, people were standing three and four deep, blocking any hopeful escape as they watched the riveting performance of the Ghost Dancers. Coming up the rear, the two predators moved intently. A large group of young men had filed out of a game store, bags in hand, but were too slow and too late to halt the quick approach of the Influenced, though the lingering bunch was substantial enough to block any pedestrians that followed.

There's still a chance we can make it to that market door up ahead, Heather thought, even as the progress in front of the girls diminished to a crawl.

Just then, a small man with a big hat, riding on the back of a tame aspergothe, decided to mount the market stairs from the street. The charming beast's long neck, craning across the path of the onlookers and into the market's open door, caused happy confusion among those in the vicinity, and all movement in front of Heather and Molly came to an abrupt standstill.

Heather turned around to face the deadly jesters in yellow and white. Pulling Molly behind her, the moon girl walked toward the pair and stopped. To her right was the display window of the market, its bright colors beaming with wares. To the moon girl's left stood rows of spectators, but none turned around, their attention fixed outwardly on the dancers in the street. Behind her, foot traffic was snarled due to the diminutive man and the people fawning over his beast. And now nothing stood between Heather and the oncoming assassins of the Influenced, one only steps behind the other.

Heather stared. The music still blasted in her ears. She couldn't hear Fallasha barking orders and recriminations, or Molly shrieking for help, or herself, as she screamed out for Aria. No other sound but the overwhelming flood of Autumnslovian music. The deadly duo drew closer, yards away. The one in the lead lowered his staff, and Heather detected the dart-like protrusion that pointed her way. Save for Molly and Fallasha, she noticed that everyone around her seemed oblivious to her plight. And still, the killers advanced, now mere body lengths away, appearing dreamlike to Heather, the balls and plumes and diamonds of their costumes flowing in detailed slow motion. Then for her, all music ceased to exist, and there was no sound in Heather's world, only the pounding of her heart that hammered on at an exhaustive roll. Feeling her body instinctively relax, the moon girl made ready to grab the barbed staff and lash out with her foot.

Then it happened. Like that. A wooden rectangle below the StealthSlayers fell in, and they dropped from view. And like that again, the sidewalk was back in place, looking as it had before. And in a moment, the stretch of walkway refilled with pedestrians, and Parade Day activity recommenced. Heather blinked. She let down her guard and stood upright, and she turned to Molly, who was crying and jumping and hugging her, and the music burst in and was screaming all around, and Molly just persisted in holding her tight, and Heather's adrenaline was still pumping, and with her arms dangling loosely at her sides, she simply watched as everyone began walking by as normal is and does.

Heather blinked again. "What happened?"

CHAPTER TWENTY-SEVEN

Fractures and Friendships

"Dear, you can look up now."

"The children. Did they survive?" asked the fashionable woman, her words spoken in a breathless manner.

"Yes," said the well-dressed man. "Seems Haslow spotted and tracked the StealthSlayers after all, and was able to have his people in place and at the ready. Quite a clever plan, too. Well coordinated."

"And the children are unhurt?"

"Completely, dear."

"Not a mark?"

"Not a mark." Pulling himself from the balcony of the stylish upper story dwelling above Parade Day Avenue, he entered the spacious living room and seated himself in the leather armchair, the light from a nearby window reflected in his glossy black hair. "It looks like they're traveling north, on their way home, bringing them under Syden's watch."

"So, that's it, Halstehn? Isn't there something more we can do for the children?"

"No. We wait, watch, and assist, if necessary. In the meantime, you and I, we can relax. For now, at least." He chuckled.

"Nothing more?"

"No, Charessa, dear, I shouldn't think so—oh! But wait. There is one thing, now that you mention it."

"And what is that, darling?"

The distinguished gentleman beamed at his elegant lady, holding up his long-stemmed glass. "Why, an EverRipe refill, if you would, please."

"Molly, come on," Heather said, though her friend didn't seem to hear above the roar of music. "Come on, we've got to get moving."

The moon girl backed away, releasing herself from the twining of Molly's arms. She took her hand and pulled the butterfly girl into the flow of pedestrians upon the walkway. As quickly as they had come, the man and his aspergothe had gone, having backed out of the market door before turning and parting the crowds. Plodding up the busy Avenue, the rider and his beast soon joined other unusual animal traffic that was becoming more prevalent now that the Parade Day barricades were being removed.

Caught up in the smooth stream of sidewalk traffic once again, the girls traveled under cover. Soon, the blare of music began to fade and the spectators lining the elevated sidewalk began to diminish in number, though many still sat facing the street, their feet dangling over the edge. As they proceeded, the moon girl was on high alert, checking all around for threatening auras.

"Heather, what happened back there?" Still shaken, Molly had pulled alongside her friend.

"I can't say for sure, but those guys were definitely coming after us."

Molly faded a step or two behind her friend, before speeding up to ask, "How did they disappear like that?"

"The ClearWeave."

"What do you mean?"

"The ClearWeave, they're on our side, trying to protect us, and I think they dropped those two creepy clowns into a tunnel where they had people waiting to jump on them." Heather knew it would relieve Molly somewhat to know that they were being looked after. She added, "I'm going to be extra careful from now on, just the same. But I'm glad you noticed those two. I should have been paying more attention."

"Heather, the Influenced, the people who want to get you, they know where you are now. The Matron warned us."

The moon girl felt slightly irritated that her friend also seemed to think she was the Maiden mentioned in the Portent Prophesies. "Molly, try not to worry, okay? I have a plan to keep us safe until we reach the PortalDoor."

"What is it?" Fallasha had been ready to ask the same question, but Molly beat her to it.

"You'll see. Just follow me."

Molly fell into step behind her friend. Constantly vigilant, the two continued along the elevated sidewalk. Approaching the corner, Heather said, "There it is."

Fallasha's face flashed its concern and eventual dismay.

Across the street, at an angle to the corner, was a theatrically conceived storefront, splashing with all the style of an Autumnslovian stage presentation. Columns depicting swirls of drapery were placed intermittently along the building's exterior and were mimicked in smaller columns that surrounded the upper story windows. Dancing over the surface of the façade were many giant masks at dissimilar angles, each unique in appearance and expression. Miniature masks encircled the larger columns, emerging in relief above the sculpted folds. The store's main entrance reminded Heather of the stage in the Bristol House Ballroom in the way that the carved replicas of curtains hung above it and flanked its two sides. The smaller entrances, hugging each corner of the storefront, had a similar appearance.

Molly read the sign above the main doors. *"The Crown & Scepter"*—then in smaller letters beneath—*"Royal Costume Emporium of Evermore."* Written below that, in even smaller letters, she mouthed the words: *"Regally Sanctioned."*

"Come on," Heather said to Molly. "If we're ever going to make it to the PortalDoor, we need to get out of these costumes."

Fallasha gasped.

Following yet another meticulous scanning of the skies down both avenues, when Heather felt certain it was safe, she led Molly out from under the overhang and across the bustling avenue in a swarm of Parade Day partiers. They climbed the curb, passed over the sidewalk, and scooted along the red-and-white tiled entryway. Crossing the broad door's threshold, neither of the girls nor their small companion noticed the large bird with the striped neck hidden amid the boughs of a nearby tree. Yet, Mistraya's scout spotted them, and following the spread of its great dark wings, the creature reared up and took to the sky.

"So, what do you think happened to Slatz and the others?" Borray asked Marscleff. He watched as a scout approached and passed close overhead. He felt the bird's eyes on him, but declined to acknowledge his winged brethren.

The two RogueTags were traveling down a smaller street that paralleled Parade Day Avenue. Long shadows were thrown at angles across the cobblestone surface. Borray's posture was hangdog. His fellow Rogue wasn't looking too cheerful, either.

"I don't know," Marscleff responded, kicking at a rock and missing. "But maybe we shouldn't have kept going like we did, when the other Rogues tripped."

"Well, we couldn't just stop and wait for them, now could we?" said Borray. "We were chasing after the AlienDregs."

They meandered into the street, giving wide berth to someone's horned ossendorf that must have gotten loose. The stench-spitting animal was off leash, sniffing near a corner, before heading down an alley.

"Slatz, Jartt, Spenghett… They're all going to be mad, that's for sure. I mean, since we didn't catch the 'Dregs—"

"Who cares about Spenghett? He's just a lousy droorp." Borray sulked. "But Slatz, sure, he's not going to be too thrilled with us, coming back like this without them…"

Marscleff asked, "You think maybe they caught the 'Dregs?"

The young RogueTags wandered back onto the sidewalk.

"Doubt it. They tripped and fell, remember? They were out of the hunt."

"Maybe Slatz and Jartt didn't catch them, but they might have put the word on the street. I bet that, right now, those two AlienDregs are running for their little lives." Marscleff snickered.

The thought, however entertaining, wasn't enough to pull Borray from his funk, from a feeling of having fallen short of accomplishment. It was yet another addition to a pile of frustrations, his heap of inadequacy. He watched the birds circling overhead, and then turned to his scrawny and hollow-cheeked friend. "So, what? We're still coming back empty handed. We probably should have never stopped at your brother's house for a bowl of snackpuggle."

"Oh, yay, but it was all right to stop and play some ClakkerSlam at the arcade."

"Right, and I noticed how bored *you* looked doing it, too, 'Lick. Weren't you the one who wanted to play the best of three?"

"One game apiece hardly decides the winner, now, does it? And you're just mad that I beat you again."

The gawky pair walked in silence before Borray said, "Come on, Marscleff. You and I both know we shouldn't have stopped for anything. We should've kept on looking for those girls."

"Yay, and let's face it, unless we catch the 'Dregs ourselves, Slatz or Jartt will be sure to slap us around pretty good." Marscleff noticed Borray was no longer walking beside him. He stopped and turned, asking, "Hey, what are you doing? Come on, I've got to get home. I'm supposed to be watching my younger brother, helping the little dordlescutt with his homework."

Borray was standing taller, though still stooped, vulture-like. He was gazing down an adjoining street that connected to Parade Day Avenue. "Hey, Rogue, I've got an idea."

"What's that?" Marscleff made ready to leave.

"What if those sprees haven't been caught?" Borray began.

"So? Even worse. That means they're probably long gone by now."

"But suppose they're not? Suppose we aren't the only ones looking for the girls?" When Borray's attention climbed to the sky, so did his companion's. "And what if the AlienDregs knew this and went into hiding until they thought it was safe to come out and head back to their PortalDoor?"

"Look," said Marscleff, "I know what you're getting at, but Mistraya's scouts could be patrolling the skies for a lot of different reasons. It's not like they haven't done it before."

"Never mind that. If those 'Dregs thought they were in danger, and figured that we were still looking for them, where would they go?"

"How would I know?" Marscleff responded. "They could be anywhere, including your mom's house. You wouldn't dare touch those girls if she were close by. She would paddle your—"

"Shut your flapping maw and listen, 'Lick! Where would those sprees go if they knew we were looking for two girls, one in a moon mask and the other in a butterfly mask?"

Marscleff stared at the long-necked, hawk-nosed Borray. Finally, he shook his head, at a loss. "I don't know. Your sister's house maybe?"

Borray slapped at Marscleff's head, the latter ducking.

"Hey, what'd you do that for?"

The lanky RogueTag grabbed at Marscleff, and the smaller youth cringed, expecting another blow. Instead, taking hold of his comrade's shoulders, Borray roughly turned him to face down the sidewalk toward the large Avenue.

"What, Rogue?" His shoulders were up and his head tucked defensively. "What? I don't know what you're—" It was then that Marscleff noticed the large store on the corner, scouts perched along the building's roofline. He relaxed, rising out of his self-protective crouch. "The Crown & Scepter."

"Finally." Borray punched him on the shoulder playfully.

"Ow!" Looking down at his arm and then at his friend, Marscleff backed off a pace. He rubbed his shoulder, grumbling, "Hate when you do that."

"Now, here's what we'll do. You'll wait and watch the side door on this smaller street here, and I'll watch the one on the Avenue. We can both monitor the main door between us, the one that faces the corner. If we see the 'Dregs go in or come out, we'll nab them. Wouldn't that be tasteful?"

"But I have to get home, Borray. My brother Zinnitt…"

The RogueTag rested a hand on Marscleff's shoulder, and due to his poor posture, Borray naturally leaned in close. "Remember that time Slatz knocked your front teeth out?" A slightly pained expression registered on Marscleff's face, and he tightened his lips protectively. Detecting his fear, Borray added, "Marscleff, if we don't come up with those two 'Dregs, it could happen again."

Through the clutter of the Bristol House basement, the indigo visitor moved noiselessly and with grace, a breeze of a shadow's advance. Behind the Moonlight°Prisms, the mysterious caller inspected the jam-packed walls and the few pieces of wonky furniture that lay scattered throughout the immense room, surrounding the plump, weighty plop of beanbag chairs. Long sturdy fingers reached up to adjust one of the many dials on the goggles, calibrating for the lack of light. The massive collection of playthings in the toy room now became easily discernable to the viewer, without the usual adjustment to the basement lighting provided judiciously by the Bristol House.

Relegated to a specific area near a playful grandfather clock were heaps of cars, buses, boats, tractors, and trucks. Some vehicles were dented and beaten, others looked to be unscathed.

Departing from a station close by and traveling throughout the room was a model train. With an occasional whistle, the engine and its cars could be heard running over bridges and through long tunnels somewhere out of sight, chugging past robots and roller skates, board games and wagons, playful pianos and xylophones, model planes and building blocks.

The goggled seeker noticed innumerable stuffed animals, piled high. Small to great, there were dogs, cats, turtles, and giraffes, and many, many more, all cute and cuddly. While countless were worn and lacked eyes, noses, or limbs, others were completely intact, appearing new and untouched.

Stacked on shelves along one wall were dolls, most still in their boxes. They came in all shapes and sizes and in all styles of dress, some inelegant and others refined, dolls from film, television, and storybook, realistic and cartoony, antique and contemporary, from Asia, England, and the European continent; from Africa, South and Central America; from Russia, Scandinavia, and North America—from all over the globe. And then the stealthy seeker recognized those dolls that were familiar, the ones mixed in with the dolls of planet Earth: the dolls of Evermore. There were Maidens on Archmounts, Ancient Ones, and soldiers of the Crown's four kingdoms; there was Emperor Kratkuffe, and characters dressed in the tribal, high desert garb of SummersBreath Still, while others were bundled to withstand the frigid climes of Winterspire.

Through the Moonlight°Prisms, the visitor continued to survey the Bristol House's room of neglected and rescued toys, past the aisles of bicycles, skateboards, and balls of all sports.

And there! A glint of yellowish light shone out. A small TimeLight Portal.

Goggles surveying all, the seeker crossed among the room's contents to stand before a playhouse, its design well known to her. The size of a small shed, the replica, replete with integrated trunks and boughs, resembled a house that one would find high within the towering trees of the tropical kingdom of SpringShoot Green. Through the bluish-green illumination of the Moonlight°Prisms, streaks of cool yellow light, leaking from around and under the perimeter of the closed playhouse door, revealed the Portal.

Soundlessly, the indigo figure reached into her rucksack and removed a hand-sized metallic object. In its center was a large faceted jewel. She slid her fingers through the holes along one side, thus allowing the bulk of the PortalSealer to rest in the center of her thin-gloved palm. Holding the device toward the playhouse, the visitor murmured in Lyrica, the Lyric of Activation, and then reached to open the miniature door. Inside, visible for an instant was the sizable room belonging to an actual TreeDwelling in SpringShoot Green. And beyond its many windows lay the heavily forested landscape, with hanging bridges and distant treetop structures. A moment later there was a brilliant glare of light, emanating from the jewel at the center of the PortalSealer. It locked onto the perimeter of the playhouse door, its radiance discernable only with the goggles. The image of the SpringShootorian household, seen through the door, flickered once and then again with an electrical crackle and hum, before it dissolved completely. What remained was simply the interior of a child's playhouse. The keyless Portal door had been sealed.

Upstairs, alone in the kitchen, concocting dinner for four, Grandma Dawn suddenly stood bolt upright, having felt the sensory bump.

Standing still as stone, her hands now stationary on either side of the rolling pin, she waited. Moments later, she resumed her preparations, a little too aggressive in the smoothing and spreading of the dough.

Back down in the basement, hidden in a room separate from that of the toys, the intruder in black continued to await the fall of night. Yet, he should never have fallen asleep. For having done so, and unlike Grandma Dawn, he was unable to perceive the potent use of magic in such close proximity, the sealing of a PortalDoor in a room close by. However, skilled as this executioner was, it would be difficult to find fault with his dereliction of duty, for he was unaware of the greater spell cast over him. The enchantment had made him drift off into a heavy slumber. It came compliments of the Bristol House.

Mistraya scrutinized the crowded street below her as it raced smoothly by, a blur of vivid shapes, snatches of texture, and flashing of masks. Seeing through the eyes of one of her scouts, the sorceress was oblivious of all that transpired back in the grim chamber of her castle. While entranced, it was there that her body sat slumped upon the throne. Knowing the act of SightSharing made her vulnerable, Mistraya made an effort to surface periodically from the half-conscious state. However, it was not at all unusual for her to continue uninterrupted for hours at a time, in this case obsessively focused on the bird-eyed vision spread below. And of course, when magical contact was made, any and all scouts would willingly share sight with their Mistress.

Like a changing of channels, the sorceress would fly with a particular scout for a time, only to move on and share sight with another, and another afterward, and so on. This made her mindful of where her scouts were positioned and what was transpiring in the streets of Elderraine.

Exultantly the sorceress watched, as the Parade Day spectators looked up discreetly to see the birds, having noticed the passing of their shadows, and having heard the forceful whoohp, whoohp of their heavy wings as they pounded the air. Mistraya gloated over the frightened expressions that registered on the faces of the people that filled the streets, picnic greens, and walkways. Of those aware of the scout's presence, most were fearful of eye contact, fearful of reprisal, as if making themselves noticeable would draw ire and punishment. Sometimes it did.

Yes, be afraid, Mistraya thought. Be very afraid. And to think, the worst is yet to come.

Shackled to its perch alongside the throne, the great bird of the night observed Mistraya and the superior sneer that twisted her preoccupied features. Never knowing when the sorceress would reestablish her presence in the castle's mirrored chamber, the creature decided it best to bide its time before acting. Like Mistraya, it was always at risk when focused elsewhere in a trancelike state.

Its wings temporarily tucked for clearance, a scout entered the small half-opened window high above, to the rear of the room. It drifted, circling the vast chamber once and again, before approaching an empty perch near the throne. Passing over the hooded bird of the night, its extended talons raked across the back of the manacled creature. The night bird screeched, despite its desire not to do so, as more of its feathers drifted lazily to the shiny floor.

But Mistraya didn't stir from her trance. Not for the moment.

Readjusting its position on the perch, the scout patiently awaited her Mistress's attention. From the opposite side of the throne, the hooded bird of the night glared at the feathered informant, loathing the Mark of the Purple Flame visible upon its chest. The night bird would have loved to tear open that part of the scout with a single swipe of its razor-sharp talons, but under the circumstances, it seemed highly unlikely that any such event would occur. Bound and vulnerable as it was, the hooded bird seemed much more likely to be the recipient of such an action.

Mistraya stirred. Disoriented, she slowly pushed herself to sit upright. "Well. What have we here?" she said in her customary manner, her words tinged with frost. "A visitor. And you have some information for me, do you?" She stood up unsteadily, facing the scout, her shapely contour blending with the lightless beyond. "Let's see, shall we, what it is you have to share."

The deep-set eyes of the sorceress fastened on the scout. The bird went stiff, before rearing its hideous head upward, the neck and chest rising in tandem. With the iron grasp of its talons keeping the bird firmly in place upon the perch, the wings went limp, hanging loosely astride its body, as the hooked beak, pointing upward, opened wide.

What followed always fascinated the night bird, when words were gurgled forth, called up and out of the gaping beak.

The words were wobbly, mechanical: "I-I-I-h-h-h-have-e-s-s-s-spotted-d-t-t-t-the-g-g-g-g-girls-s-s. T-T-T-They-v-v-ve-g-g-g-gone-e-i-i-i-into-o-o-t-t-the-C-C-C-Crown-n-n-a-a-a-and-S-S-S-S-Scepter-r-r-r."

"Ah. Have they now?"

"Y-Y-Y-Y-Yes-s-s-s."

"Have we any Rogues in the vicinity?"

"I-I-I-I-s-s-s-saw-w-w-w-o-o-o-only-y-y-B-B-B-Borray-y-y-a-a-a-and-d-d-M-M-M-Marscleff-f-f-f."

"None bigger, rougher?"

"N-N-N-N-No-o-o-o."

Mistraya sighed. "Those two. They're such…boys."

The bird was silent, remaining stiff on its perch, head back, beak open.

"All right. I will contact them personally. Are they *back-Avenue?*"

"A-A-A-At-t-t-t-the-e-e-e-m-m-m-moment-t-t-t-y-y-y-yes-s-s-s," gurgled up. "N-n-n-near-r-r-r-t-t-t-the-e-e-emporium-m-m."

"How convenient. Excellent. You've done your duty." Mistraya held out her hand, and the bird's head went even higher with the sudden flow of wondrous pain. And then the winged informant relaxed and sighed, enraptured in a rush of prickled pleasure. "Now, go. Follow the girls from above until we're able to seize them on the ground. If there are complications, leastwise, find out where those two are bound. I'll send others to assist you."

"Y-Y-Y-Y-Yes-s-s-M-M-My-y-y-M-M-M-Mistress-s-s-s."

The painful flow ebbed and the bird, having sufficiently recovered, pushed off the perch. After circling thrice, it exited the window high above, but not without a glancing bounce off the jamb.

The Crown & Scepter Costume Emporium was an enormous store, with high decorative ceilings supported by draped pillars that were spaced throughout the interior, each enhanced with sculpted masks spiraling their way to the top. Against the walls on each side were wide, carpeted stairways sweeping up to a spacious mezzanine that overlooked the lower floor. Located on both levels, rising above racks and stacks of clothing, were mannequins, posed and dressed in costumes ranging from refined and extraordinary to whacky and farcical. No two were alike.

The shop's walls, divided at intervals by shallow columns in the mask and drape motif, were filled with huge colorful murals depicting festive scenes from Evermore's Parade Day. Up front, masks entirely covered the walls surrounding the three entrances. Attendants pulled them down for patrons with the aid of telescoping poles, and carefully hung replacements shortly thereafter to fill any vacancies. Mirrors were everywhere, mounted in dressing rooms, at the end of aisles, and encircling the base of every pillar. Finally and above all, adding to the festive atmosphere, exotic draperies, splashed with dazzling color, were looped across the ceiling in rows of billowing arcs.

In a steady stream through the entrances, Parade Day patrons flowed in and out, browsing and conversing, all eventually assisted by the many cheerful attendants on duty. Following three children and their mother, the girls threaded their way up the stairs.

"So, I must speak up and let you know that I find it mildly amusing, to say the least, that you thought to come here, of all places."

"What?" said a surprised Heather. "Are you talking again, Fallasha?"

After a quiet moment, the moon brooch replied in a contrite tone of voice, "I find I must set aside our petty grievances and furnish you with up-to-date information on the great Crown and Scepter, Royal Costume Emporium of Evermore. After all, that is what I was sent here to accomplish today. I *am*, in fact, your tour guide."

"Off and on."

"Fair enough, Heather. So, may I inquire why you think that you're in sudden need of a change in costume?" the brooch asked.

Heather stepped to one side of the mezzanine landing, temporarily isolated near an aisle. "Well, I kinda figure it's obvious that we have to," said Heather. "I don't really want to. I love these outfits. But if we don't, we could be easily recognized by the scouts—or people like those creepy clowns—and then we might never make it back to the PortalDoor."

Standing nearby, Molly was lending half an ear, trying to keep her mind occupied by looking through the depleted racks of costumes, marveling at the unusual designs. Her hands at work separating the outfits on the rack, she glanced over, relieved to see Fallasha breaking her silence. When the brooch started to speak about the costume store, Molly tuned in completely:

"Because a great number of Evermorians make their own costumes, every year many are donated, or exchanged, after the parade. As one of the official costume emporiums of Evermore, The Crown & Scepter adds additional costumes to the mix as well, contributing their own original designs produced by an enormous staff working in all four kingdoms throughout the year. Due to the fact that not all Evermorians are capable or have the means to make their own costumes, they are made available at no cost whatsoever, in this particular case, considering its location, to mostly Autumnslovians," Fallasha then added at a whisper, "Not to mention a few TimeLight travelers that I know." The brooch cleared her throat, continuing at a slightly louder volume, "Along with your trade-ins, all costumes will be scrutinized, repaired if necessary, cleaned and pressed, and afterward made available to the public for the following year's parade."

Heather couldn't help but notice that Fallasha no longer spouted her information with relish, as she once had. She interrupted.

"Fallasha, do your batteries need replacing or something?"

"What? Why do you say that?"

"Because you're acting like—is there something bugging you?"

The moon brooch said, a little too lightly, "No. Nothing."

"Oh-oh. When you use only two words, I know something isn't right. Okay, come on. Tell me what's bugging you."

"Well," she said, with a huff, "if you really must know, I understand your need to change costumes, but…"

"Fallasha, but *what?*"

"Well, Heather, you might say I'm very attached to the current costume you're wearing. Very attached. There is none more beautiful, except perhaps for Molly's, but of course, hers doesn't have an absolutely amazing brooch attached, and as a result, falls far short of being on a par with your own. However, getting back to the moon costume itself, it's a remarkable work in its design, mood, color, stitchery, and combination of fabrics—as of course is Molly's," and here Fallasha sped up her words, when adding under her breath, "but as previously mentioned, it lacks that certain something very charmingly brooch-like." She sniffed and cleared her throat. "And the Bristol House worked very diligently on these costumes, putting in long hours—eagerly and happily, mind you—getting them ready for you and your Parade Day visit here today."

"Fallasha, I hope you believe me when I say that I really love this costume, and I'm sure Molly loves hers, too, but if we don't get new ones, we could be spotted and captured by Mistraya or the Influenced."

"I know, but—"

"May I help you?" An attendant had walked up behind Heather. Instinctively, the surprised moon girl took a step forward and wheeled sharply, her fists balled by her sides. The woman stepped back a pace, her aura still beaming in warm hues, though interspersed with startled orange surprise and light green puzzlement.

Heather's mask blushed red. "Oh, I-I'm sorry. You scared me."

"Apparently." The woman, efficient but breezy, was middle-aged, slim and of medium height, with hair that was shoulder length and streaked with brown and gray. She wore her wine-colored glasses on top of her head. "My name is LaoReena. Is there anything I can help you to find?"

"We're kinda looking," said Heather.

"For other costumes? Oh, but yours are so splendid. Here, let me have a look at you. Now turn for me. And I love your brooch. You didn't get that here, did you?"

"No. Actually, we got our costumes," she turned to Molly, "some-where else."

Following Heather's gaze, the saleswoman looked with greater atten-tion at the butterfly girl. "Oh, and look at you! Don't you look lovely. You both do. Brilliant, just brilliant."

Heather said, "Thank you. We—my friend and me," the moon girl's finger wagged back and forth between herself and Molly, "are tired of our costumes, I think, and so we thought about maybe getting new ones. And since we're visiting from out of town, we'd like to exchange them."

"By all means. And of course, The Crown & Scepter Costume Em-porium will be happy to assist you. However, you do understand that you must leave your beautiful costumes behind in the exchange. And though we have others that will fit you, in all likelihood the most unique costumes have been taken. Assuredly what's left won't compare to the beauty of these, I'm afraid." Standing back and admiring the moon and butterfly girls, she added, "I must say, next year some lucky parade-goers will have access to two very amazing outfits. And one lovely brooch."

"Oh, well," said Heather, "I'm not sure we can do that. I mean, I'd like to take my brooch with me, if you don't mind. It's special." Heather looked down at the little moon. "Really special."

Below, Fallasha's eyes became moist.

"Here, let me see…" said LaoReena. She tilted her head back, and examined the moon girl's brooch through her glasses, turning it this way and that, attempting to peer behind it. She didn't notice Fallasha grit-ting her teeth during the undignified process. "Young lady, I'm afraid that your brooch is permanently affixed to your costume."

"Oh."

"Interesting though… I wonder how it was done?" LaoReena had lowered her head to get a look at an irritated Fallasha from the side.

"Oh, you know, probably magic." Heather exchanged a glance with Molly once again. "Well, maybe I'd better keep my costume, but my friend, here, I think she'd still like to exchange hers."

"No," said Molly. "Really. If you're keeping yours, I'm going to keep mine."

"Are you sure?" asked the moon girl. "I mean—"

"Yes."

Heather was mildly surprised. "Oh, all right. I suppose it's settled, then. I'm sorry to have bothered you. I guess my friend and I, we-we've decided to keep our costumes after all."

"No bother in the least," beamed the jovial woman. "And I certainly can't blame you for doing so." The woman glanced up at the many shoppers that were now hovering nearby. "Girls, if you'll excuse me. It looks like the store is beginning to fill again in preparation of this evening's events. Parade Day."

"Sure..." said Heather, watching the back of the attendant as she walked away.

"What now, Heather?"

"I don't know, Molly." Heather was absently tapping a finger against the lips of her mask. "I guess we'll have to make a dash to the PortalDoor and hope we're not seen on the way."

Fallasha spoke up. "I'm sorry, Heather. I tried to tell you that I was attached to this costume..."

Heather looked over her cheek. "That's okay. You're right, anyway. These are beautiful costumes, Fallasha, and I never really wanted to give mine up in the first place."

At her words, Fallasha glowed.

"Heather..." It was Molly, letting the moon girl know there was someone browsing nearby.

"Okay, come on, Molly. It's time to take a chance and do something crazy—live dangerously."

The butterfly girl didn't laugh. The two made their way past the many shoppers crowding the aisle and then down the stairs. Heather was constantly checking out auras, on alert for anything suspicious or malevolent. Molly followed close behind. As the girls approached the side door leading to Parade Day Avenue, Molly pulled Heather aside.

"What's up? I don't see anything unusual around us." The moon girl was still searching.

"It's not 'around us' that I'm worried about, Heather. Look Outside." Exercising caution, Molly gently pulled Heather away from the window. "There's a RogueTag out there."

Heather stared. "Hey, that's Borray."

"No way. Are you certain?"

"Yeah. What do you suppose he's doing here?"

"You don't think Borray is still looking for us, do you?"

"Doubt it, but it looks like he's waiting for someone." Heather craned her neck. "I don't see any other RogueTags, though."

"So, what now?" asked Molly.

"Easy. We'll just go out the other door, the one farthest away, and then take our chances on the backstreets for a while. Come on."

But when the girls neared the opposite door, it was Heather's turn to halt their progress.

"Molly, we can't go out this door either."

"I see him, Heather. It's that other RogueTag." The girls loitered, Molly's masked face near Heather's, the two staring at the lackadaisical Marscleff through the window. He wasn't paying too much attention to the exit, but enough that he might notice the pair if they left. "So, what do we do now? We'll never get out any of these doors without either one of them spotting us." Molly added, "There's a good chance they'll see us even if we try to sneak through the main door between them."

"I agree. I'm thinking that maybe there's a back entrance, you know, where they drop off big shipments of clothes and stuff."

"Heather, wait." The voice belonged to Fallasha. It was low, but firm.

"Wait? Wait for what?"

"It's too dangerous."

"It's not dangerous, Fallasha. We can just go to the back   "

"No, I mean it's too dangerous for you and Molly to continue wearing these outfits. I realize that—"

"Forget it, Fallasha. We've already decided we're not exchanging them."

"Heather, I'm afraid you're going to have to. Even if there's a back entrance, and we're able get out safely, in your current costumes, we're certain to be seen and eventually seized."

"You don't know that for sure."

Molly said, "I think Fallasha's right, Heather."

"What? Now you, too?"

"I'm sorry, but yes." Noticing what the moon brooch had apparently sighted, her voice marked by resignation, Molly said, "Look up in the sky."

The moon girl did. Outside the large windows of the storefront, circling overhead at various elevations, were many more scouts.

Heather said, "Molly, I have a feeling that Mistraya knows we're here."

Borray, still positioned outside The Crown & Scepter, watched as foot traffic passed before him on the sidewalk, intermittently obstructing his vision. Blink, blink, blink, like the strobe down at the Jott House Dancehall, where he would go and watch the couples StrummStep and SidleGlide. However, he wasn't too concerned with crowd interference when watching for the girls. As a matter of fact, leaning against a lamppost, Borray didn't even bother concealing himself, for in his heart he really wasn't convinced that the 'Dregs would be appearing anytime soon.

Yet, to Borray, the surveillance of the shop wasn't about finding the girls—well, not completely. It was about hope and purpose—he needed both—and about giving Marscleff reason to stick around and keep a fellow Rogue company.

And it was also about avoiding going home. Such a miserable place for a Rogue. With his two sisters away at university, he'd been left alone with Mother and Dad. And neither approved of the direction he was bent on taking with his life. He had grown tired of their continuous carping, saying that if he wasn't working towards a university degree like his sisters, he should redirect his misguided energies toward trade school—or going out to land a job. So what if that's what they did at his age? That was *their* dream, not his.

At the time, he tried to tell them he had a job, and that as a RogueTag he was working on his future, elevating HumanKind to the status it deserved within the Realm. That for far too long Maidens have been controlling the kingdoms, and who are they anyway? They're immortal, so how can they have empathy for HumanKind and comprehend our needs? And how can they be qualified to govern us? *We* are the ones who should choose our leaders. *We* are the ones who should determine which laws best suit us. *We* are the ones who are mortal, and as mortals, we know what it means to age and die. They don't.

And aren't the Maidens the cause of all the unrest throughout the Realm? If they would just stop minding our business, shaping policies between kingdoms, and allowing the Ancient Ones to have judgment over all, Evermore would be the better for it. HumanKind knows what's best for HumanKind. No one else. Let's let the Maidens be the figureheads, and make Emperor Kratkuffe our supreme leader, the HumanKind leader of all HumanKind, of all Evermore.

Borray glanced down at the wide central door situated between Marscleff and himself. Nothing. No sign of the AlienDregs.

A sudden thought occurred to Borray. What would he do if he or Marscleff actually spotted the girls? It was a notion that was fun to think about, fun to entertain. Can you imagine how impressed Slatz would be if he and Marscleff captured and marched those two 'Dregs into the café on the corner—perhaps even after a bit of cuffing around to find out exactly where they're from and the location of their PortalDoor? Those other Rogues would be in awe. They would. Maybe he and Marscleff could first have the girls take them to their PortalDoor, and then go through it as TimeLight travelers, to find out what their world was like before turning the 'Dregs over to Slatz. Then everyone would gather around and listen, while he, Borray, told them about life on an unfamiliar planet, stories of its people, their kingdoms and customs, how they dress, what they eat, what some of their animals looked like, and how evolved they were magically.

Borray's mind seized up. He realized his fellow RogueTags would frown on his TimeLight travel, as they frowned on the travelers who visit Evermore. Yet the young man admitted he would want to journey to the girls' world anyway. He would just have to have Marscleff commit to secrecy.

Borray looked at the sky, at the concentration of birds circling the store and those at rest on surrounding buildings and in the trees. Maybe Mistraya really did send her scouts after the girls, wanting them for some reason. He had to admit, the notion gave him a bit of a head rush. Of course, Borray worked hard to dismiss the nagging question of why Mistraya would even bother to concern herself with a couple of alien girls. Nonetheless, he was enjoying his fanciful notions and his glorious ascension in the esteem of his peers.

Borray imagined himself and his partner turning the AlienDregs over to the RogueTags of higher ranking, who would then hand them off to the sorceress. Eventually, Mistraya would find out it was Borray and Marscleff who had captured them, none other, working from his— Borray's—plan of keeping the costume emporium under surveillance. Thereafter the dark enchantress would think differently of him. Maybe then he'd get his tattoo.

As it was, the one time Borray had met Mistraya was when she had unexpectedly turned up at a small RogueTag rally. When introduced afterward, the charismatic sorceress had hardly given him a glance. And though he couldn't say for sure, she had seemed offended when Borray asked to receive the Mark of the Purple Flame. At the time, he didn't know that not even Slatz had a PassionFlame. Borray remembered with hot embarrassment how Mistraya had declined with a patronizing smile, as if talking to a child, saying that he wasn't ready to draw on its power. *Yet.* He remembered she had added the word 'yet.' That was important. To this day their interaction played like a movie sequence running through his mind: Yet. A little word with such big promise, a word that meant 'maybe in the future.' Wouldn't it be great if the future were here? Now? In front of these doors?

The young Rogue studied his reflection in the glass. He wasn't bad looking, he thought, though he certainly didn't exude the toughness of a Slatz or Jartt. Borray adjusted his purple armband, pulling it higher on his bony arm, and afterward reevaluated the improved reflection. Right-so. Not bad. He watched himself shrug. He may be short on muscle, but he had what those other two Rogues lacked, didn't he? He had brains.

With another glance at himself in the glass doors, at the slouching neck and skinny frame, Borray felt a sadness begin to creep through him like a morose fog, settling over the grander vision of himself, obscuring any hope for something more. What caused that feeling? He could never say, could never pinpoint its source. It was just sadness, that's all. Just sadness. But there were times when it burned inside, ferociously hollowing him out, and there was nothing to quell that fire in the hole, and make the pain, so wholly debilitating, just drain away. He was sure, though, that he wouldn't have thoughts like this, wouldn't feel this way about himself, if only HumanKind were in power. And he knew that being unable to personally aid his fellow HumanKinder made him feel helpless and inferior, made him feel little. Like a tiny teese in a land of preying felynxxes. It was that simple.

Borray?

The young Rogue jumped. His head flashed left, right, and then up at the compact ball of purple flame that blazed not far from his face.

"Wha—?"

Atop his long neck, Borray's head reared back. He shook it and stood up straight, no longer leaning on the lamppost. Remaining at eye level, the flame rose with him. Mistraya's translucent face could be seen in the midst of the purple apparition.

Borray, I am in need of your services.

His eyes slid left and right. He wanted to see if anyone passing had noticed the hovering flame. No one seemed to.

Borray, look at me. You know who I am, do you not? It is Mistraya, and I'm talking to you. This is real. No one else can see me. Only you. I am talking only to you.

The Rogue piped up, his voice initially high-pitched. "I-I'm here. Is that really you, Mistraya? Or-or am I really at home dreaming?"

Borray. It's probably best you lower your voice. Talk gently, and I will hear you. And you are to address me as My Mistress, never informally by name. Now, we are wasting time. I'm interested in finding two young girls in costume—

"I've seen them!"

Have you now?

"Yes! Dressed like a butterfly and a moon."

Well, it seems you may have, at that.

Borray was nodding his head vigorously. "I have. Yes. That's why I'm waiting here with my fellow RogueTag, Marscleff. He's at the other door. You see, it was my plan all along, and I told him about how the Alien-Dregs—girls—would probably be trying to get back to their world—"

They're TimeLight travelers?

"They are."

You're certain?

"Yes. One of the girls, the one with the butterfly mask, I think, said that they were only here for the parade." The young man was antsy on his feet, unable to keep himself still. "My Mistress."

Their PortalDoor is where?

"I don't know. They said they're from the Milky Way. I just met them this morning. At the parade. We were on a big rock off the Avenue—"

That explains why I was drawn in that direction. I felt her strength.

"What?"

Nothing. Borray?

"Yes. My Mistress."

Stop bouncing.

"Oh, am I bouncing? I didn't know." Borray laughed, nervously. "All right. My Mistress. Right-so. I don't know if you can see my feet from where you are in that little flame of yours, but right now they're acting pretty still." He laughed again. "Not moving." Nodding. "*Very* still."

Borray, the girls...

"Yes. Slatz, Jartt, and Spenghett went looking for the girls, too—

Those Rogues, they're with you?

"No, we—"

Didn't think so.

"We were running after the girls, when those three tripped and-and I don't know what happened to them."

I believe I do.

"But Marscleff and I, we're the ones who followed the girls here."

Did you?

"Yes."

Constantly? Like two shadows?

"Well, actually, after a brief detour. You see, we were waylaid for a bit." Borray gulped, his protrusion of Adam's apple prominent on his skinny neck. "You know how those things are. They have a way of catching up with you. My Mistress."

They do, don't they?

"Yes. But-but now we're here just waiting for the girls to come out, because I had a feeling they—"

Mmm-hmmm.

"—might be in there. Yes." His head bounced, small eager nods.

A feeling? Only a feeling? So, you're not positive they're in The Crown & Scepter?

Blank-faced, the young RogueTag stared at the flame. Feeling cornered, Borray finally shook his head. "No."

In other words, you lost them.

"Yes, well, we were waylaid, like I said…" A sense of doom was descending over the young man. What was once an advantageous situation seemed to have deteriorated. Quickly.

I see. Perhaps you'll be astonished to know that they **are** *in there.*

"Really? Well, I knew that, Mis—My Mistress. I did. Call it a hunch, a great, great hunch. And I put it into play. Killer instinct. And here we are." Borray was bouncing again. "Yes. My friend and I. We are right *here*. Waiting." He skittered a laugh. "Ready."

Mistraya let him finish, before her cool voice patiently carried on.

Good. And now I want you to go in and get them for me.

Nonchalantly, Borray swung his arms before him and hit the end of his fist with an open palm. Thwok. "Go in there."

Yes.

"Sure. Easy pickings." Thwok.

Now, be aware. Your fellow RogueTags, Slatz, Jartt, and Spenghett?

"Yes?"

All three were almost killed by one of those girls, the one in the moon costume.

Borray stopped dancing foot-to-foot. His face dropped and his head stooped toward the flame. "What?"

Mistraya ignored his impertinence.

Yes. The moon girl. She is said to be the green-eyed Maiden of the Evermore Portent."

"The green-eyed Maiden—?"

"What I need is for you to carefully slip into the emporium and surprise her and her friend, the girl in the butterfly mask. If you are unable to kill the pair, I at least want you to disable and capture them.

Me? The single word arced and flamed out like a comet in the night sky. "Disable and capture. Sure." Through his pants, Borray's hand felt for the small weapon in his left pocket. His fingers squeezed the folded pocketknife, nervously spinning it widthwise.

My preference is that you kill them. I don't particularly care how.

"Yes. Kill them." He looked stunned. "Yes. Yes, I will."

Do you know what they look like without their masks?

"No. My Mistress."

Mistraya faded, and Heather's head soon materialized, turning slowly before him within the ball of flame, Molly's afterward.

These images were MindDredged from a witness who was at the scene

*earlier today in the old Weavers Quarters, where your three RogueTag com-
panions met with their unexpected humiliation. Memorize the faces.*

Borray committed the faces to memory as best he could. "I think I
can spot them."

Think?

"Oh, no. Know—I mean, I *know* I can spot them."

Good.

The image of Molly dissolved and the RogueTag could again see
Mistraya's face centered within the flame.

"Maybe I should wait before I go in," Borray said, "just in case they're
expecting us? It might be better—"

Now. You will go now.

"All right." His voice was high-pitched, airy.

Borray?

"Yes, My Mistress."

*The girls are in The Crown & Scepter for a reason. We know what their
costumes look like presently. We do not know what new costumes they'll
choose, if given the opportunity. We must hurry and find the girls before their
costume-change or identify them if the change has taken place. I want them
stopped from reaching their PortalDoor. Do you understand?*

"Yes, My Mistress."

*Good. There are others on their way to assist you, but until they arrive I
want you to waylay those girls. I will be arriving shortly, as well.*

"You? My Mistress? Here?"

*Yes. Once again, you're to ambush and disable those girls at the very least,
kill them if possible. Those are your orders. Your friend, Marscleff, I'll inform
him of the girls' presence and send him in after you.*

Borray had sobered up. "Yes, My Mistress."

I'll look in on you shortly.

The Crown & Scepter was full of life, the aisles brimming with activity. The busyness taking place, in front of the dressing rooms that lined
the back walls on both floors, was plentiful and constant. Emporium
attendants monitored the traffic as shoppers, waiting to try on costumes,
stood in animated bunches outside the louvered doors or occupied the
chairs and couches nearby.

Over the railing of the mezzanine, Heather kept a keen lookout on
the level below, her gaze constantly roving, evaluating auras, while peri-

odically scanning each of the three entrances. Under LaoReena's knowledgeable direction, Molly was the first to choose a new costume. Hurriedly, the butterfly girl selected an ensemble that was simpler and far less impressive than her current outfit, but also less cumbersome and conspicuous. It consisted of a wide blue hat, its brim folded up at the front, revealing just a glimpse of hair. Clustered behind the brim were four furry balls. A broad circular collar of stiff ruffles covered the shoulders. The costume body was loose, but not overly bulky like its predecessor, gathered at the waist with a shiny belt. Embroidered pinwheels appeared to dance over the surface in subdued tones. There were no gloves, and unlike her butterfly boots, the shoes covered only her feet.

LaoReena then turned her attention to Heather, pulling the girl away from her lookout's post atop the stairs. Meanwhile, a young male attendant drifted over, and after complimenting Molly on her butterfly costume, led her to a corner dressing room. Knocking first to make certain it was unoccupied, the youth then stepped aside, and Molly entered, dragging her new garments past him. She closed the door securely behind her.

It was at that moment Borray cautiously entered The Crown & Scepter, attempting to blend in on the crowded floor. He edged left through traffic, keeping the wall behind him. Locating himself within range of the center door, Borray hid behind a nearby mannequin. Shortly thereafter, Marscleff, having entered the emporium through the opposite door, scanned the many patrons before spotting his companion's crouching reflection in a mirror. Marscleff angled his way through the congested store, past people perusing, carrying costumes, and trying on distinctive masks. Most shoppers were in pursuit of party attire to wear to the ongoing Parade Day festivities, many of which would carry on throughout the night and into the wee hours of the following morn.

Borray was trying to keep his case of the jitters in check while peering around a mannequin's leg, searching for the girls among the busy patrons. Having nonchalantly walked up from behind, Marscleff tapped him on the shoulder. Borray jumped and let out a yelp.

"Don't do that!" he said, twisting and punching air. "I'm trying to concentrate."

After noticing how pale his friend was, and how easily he cringed, Borray regretted his outburst. Marscleff was obviously frightened. Borray assumed that Mistraya had informed his Rogue companion that the moon girl was possibly the Maiden Portent mentioned in the Prophecies, and of the damage the girl had inflicted on the three tougher Rogues. Fidgeting, Marscleff stood near, too near, maneuvering behind his friend in an attempt to place Borray between the potential threat and himself. He felt that at any moment a jagged bolt of lightning was going to shoot out from behind a clothes rack, arcing across the room in their direction. When Borray tried to speak to his Rogue companion, first looking over his right shoulder and then his left, Marscleff evaded him, ducking in opposite directions. Finally Borray spun and stood looking down on the cowering Rogue, hands on hips.

"Will you stop that?"

"What?"

"Acting so foolish. We've got to find those girls for Mistraya."

"All right." Nervously licking his lips, slightly crouched, Marscleff peered over Borray's shoulder. "You start walking, Rogue. I'm right behind you."

Borray faced into the heart of the teeming store, his companion squarely behind him. He began to walk out from behind the mannequin, cautiously scanning the room. A moment later, he felt Marscleff's hands lightly on his back, as if he, Borray, were his human shield. Irritated, he shrugged him off and whirled.

"Stop that! And keep your hands off me! What's wrong with you?"

"What makes you think there's something wrong—?"

"Being scared isn't going to make this any easier, you know."

"I'm not scared," Marscleff responded, his eyes never resting.

"Right. Now, I'm thinking we need an organized plan of attack, so here's what we're going to do: before we check upstairs, you're going to cover that side of the floor, over there," he pointed, "working your way down those aisles. I'm going to do the same, covering the aisles on this half of the store, and then we'll meet up on the mezzanine. Make sure you don't let them slip past you. That means that once we've passed the stairs, we're also going to have to look over everyone that comes down afterward. We can't let the girls get behind us and out those front doors. Now, we need to hurry, because there's still the chance that we can spot them before they change into new costumes. Got it?"

"Yay."

"Good. Any questions?"

"Yay."

"What?"

"This place is really big and there are a lot of people in here."

"I know. Anything else?"

"It makes our job difficult."

"Marscleff, we need to get going here. Anything else?"

"What do I do if I see them?"

"Come get me. Or if I'm lost in the crowd, and you think the 'Dregs won't notice, just RogueWhistle."

"Then what?"

"Then I'll come."

"Yay, I know that. But then what will we do?"

Borray looked around, and felt it best he whisper. "We kill them."

"Kill them." Marscleff's head bounced like a bobble-head doll. "How?"

"I have a pocketknife."

"Oooh. A pocketknife."

"Right. A pocketknife. So?"

"That's it? A pocketknife? You might as well go after them spitting seeds of laskis out of a straw or-or throwing feathers. Do you—? How—? Did Mistraya tell you who that girl in the moon costume is, and that she thrashed the others?"

"Yes, she did."

"Then why are we doing this—other than we're attempting to die before either of us ever gets a GirlMate?"

"For two reasons, 'Lick. First, if we don't kill or capture those two girls, we'll probably be punished, maybe even tortured or killed by Mistraya. Second, don't you see that this is our big opportunity?"

"To do what? To see if there really *is* life after death?"

"No, you perf. This is a chance to earn our PassionFlame. Not even Slatz or Jartt have one. And like all those others, that girl in the moon outfit might not be the Maiden Portent. It's happened before, remember?

"Yay, but Slatz and Jartt aren't Rogues anyone gets the best of easily. Especially a spree."

"But did Mistraya tell you exactly what took place?"

Marscleff shook his head.

"So, we don't know if the girl had help or what happened. Look, you heard Slatz say there have been plenty of phony Maidens, and we know they've all been killed. So, if we can kill this girl and her friend, everyone will know who we are. We'll be respected and looked up to. Don't you see? This is the chance of a lifetime. Those two girls didn't come our way by accident. The Universe chose us to do this. Us! You and me! It put us here in front of this store, hanging at the ready, and now Mistraya is requesting our service in duty to the Realm. That just doesn't happen by accident, you know. There's destiny at work here. We'll be able to do what Slatz, Jartt, and Spenghett couldn't. And Mistraya will reward us handsomely, and bestow on you and me what everyone else would die to have, Rogue, the Mark of the Purple Flame."

"Yay…" Dreamy, Marscleff seemed to be coming around, eagerness finding his face.

"*And* you know what's so beautiful about this entire thing, don't you, so beautiful indeed?"

Marscleff was grinning conspiratorially. "What?"

"Those 'Dregs haven't a clue that we're in the building; no clue that we're here to get them. That means the advantage is ours."

"Yay…Yay…" Marscleff's interest was ever increasing as he looked past his companion, searching the aisles enthusiastically. "Let's go. I'm ready. This, my friend, is going to be good."

"Believe it. Come on then." The taller RogueTag turned to begin his search for the girls.

"Borray?"

He turned. "What now? Hurry!"

"I've got to ask."

Borray glared at him impatiently.

Marscleff swallowed. "Have you ever killed anyone?"

"No, but if you don't shut your gob and get moving, you might just be my first."

With LaoReena having temporarily stepped away to lend advice to another browser, Heather was left to sift through the costumes on her own. Fallasha had grown uncharacteristically quiet, and the moon girl felt her brooch to be a hefty weight upon her costumed chest. Ever mindful of Fallasha's presence, Heather continued to pull aside each new outfit on the rack, and after a perfunctory once over, she was on to the next. The moon girl knew she had to hurry and find an ensemble. Yet, while doing so, she was also trying to keep an eye on the dressing room door, on Molly, making certain that no one slipped past to harm her friend.

All the costumes appeared to be well made, with some more striking than others, but to the moon girl, every single one was lacking. Soon Heather was not just casually sliding each costume aside to inspect the next, she was slinging them, one after the other, shoving them away, yanking and yanking, her mouth bunched, her features set.

Rejecting yet another costume with an impetuous slide and swish on the rack, Heather exhaled sharply and whirled to look at Molly's dressing room, the door still closed. The girl then turned her attention to the stairways on each side of the mezzanine, inspecting them for RogueTags or threatening auras. Something in her was wanting, yearning to tear into anything for any reason, hungering for a clash.

When her hostile gaze searched the aisles in an aura scan, Heather noticed her likeness in a mirror, one of many encircling the base of a nearby column. Staring, she was suddenly struck by the hardness in her face and anger in her stance. The moon girl softened and for a moment looked away. Now tentatively approaching her reflection full on, Heather regarded herself wearing the extraordinary costume that gave her such pleasure. What she saw was the essence of the moon, full and mysterious, shining out in blue-green splendor. She thought of the treehouse at night, enclosed high within the branches of the Oak Triplets, with the many, many stars watching silently from above—the glistening eyes of the kindred, looking out for her, the moon girl.

"I love the night and stars," she said, admiring the jeweled accents that sparkled on her costume. Pensive, she studied her face. "I love the moon."

Her words gentle, Fallasha said, "You are the moon."

Heather looked down at the reflection of her lovely little brooch for an instant, maybe longer, before turning away.

I hate all these other costumes, thought Heather.

It was then that she caught sight of an outfit she thought perfect.

Alone in the high-ceilinged dressing room, its wallpaper red with vertical stripes, Molly had unfastened her mask and headpiece, slipped out of her cuffed boots, and proceeded to remove the remainder of her outfit. Surprised to find that tears were sliding down her cheeks, she continued to work as quickly as possible, aware of the need to hurry. Having taken off her stunning butterfly costume, Molly laid it down on the long cushiony bench and folded it as best she could. It was a bulky thing. She placed her mask and headpiece neatly on top of the lumpy mound before putting her boots directly below on the carpet, perfectly side-by-side.

Beneath the soft glow of recessed lighting, she climbed into the new costume. Her vision distorted by wetness, the girl's hands worked quickly though clumsily, fastening the large number of buttons. She pulled back her brunette hair, placed the silly blue hat on top of her head, and then wiped her eyes with an embroidered cuff. Having slipped into her shoes, Molly donned the outfit's mask. She took a moment to inspect the ensemble. Lit by a series of small round bulbs that ran the perimeter of the mirror, Molly refrained from bursting into tears at the sight of her new costume.

Gone were the beautifully intricate butterfly mask, the lavishly decorated suit and headpiece, and the stylish boots and gloves. In their place was a modest outfit of unsophisticated design: a simple eyemask, its swooping flame-like extensions covering her brow and cheeks, with a large yellow jewel centered just above the brows. Visible below this swirl of blue and red was her lower face, her mouth finding little reason to smile. Molly continued to gaze, before tearing herself away from the inadequate reflection. At a rush, pushing through the dressing room's louvered door, she spilled out into the room, looking for Heather and LaoReena amid the aisles of costumes and customers that covered the mezzanine.

LaoReena had been quite surprised when Heather told her that she wanted to try on a boy's costume. It consisted of a black velvet jacket patterned with small glass stones—black on black—bordered with dull gold curls; a matching gilded stripe lined both sides of the velvet pants. Protruding from the open jacket was a white ruffled shirt. The costume had a mask that was wide enough to wrap most of Heather's head. It was a combination of three faces: the two outer expressions, one happy and the other sad, each shared an eye belonging to the angry face in the center. The area across the eyes was painted with black and gold curls above golden lips. The outfit was topped with a black bowler hat.

Upon seeing Molly burst from the dressing room, and after a final, cautious scan around her, Heather grabbed up her new costume and its accessories. She glanced at Molly as they passed; her look wasn't returned. Not knowing what to say, Heather had remained mute. No longer the butterfly girl, Molly's new outfit was hardly interesting by comparison. Heather could see her friend's weakly pulsating aura and feel her wretchedness, and it added tension to the somber air that already surrounded the moon girl. She quickened her stride.

Waiting until Molly had taken up her position as lookout, it was with great sorrow that Heather entered their dressing room. She found herself unable to look at Fallasha when closing the door behind her. She swiftly peeled off her mask and headpiece, and after placing them near Molly's, sat on the bench to slide off her ankle boots. Off came her pants and shirt, encumbered with its many layers of material. Crudely folding her costume, Heather propped the upper half against the wall, keeping Fallasha visible. As quickly as possible, she began to dress in her new outfit.

Fallasha finally broke the silence. "I think I much prefer your Bristol House costume."

Heather nodded, head down, concentrating on the buttons. In her haste, she threw the ruffled shirt over her head, having declined to unbutton it completely when first removing it from the hanger.

The moon brooch said, "By changing costumes, you're doing exactly what the moment dictates is necessary."

"Am I?" Heather pulled and brushed the tiered ruffles into place.

"Heather, I must admit that what happened back there in the tunnel—"

"Fallasha, don't—"

"Please. I need to say this."

"Don't. Let's not."

"What?"

"Apologize. If you start apologizing, then I'll have to, too. I should never have led you and Molly off like that. It's all my fault. All of it."

"You're wrong, Heather. What happened in the tunnel leaves me undoubtedly, and to the greater extent, at fault."

"At fault about what?"

"Your current situation—Molly and yours. And mine."

"Forget it. You had nothing to do with this situation." Heather had punched her feet into the black, shiny shoes before dropping to a knee to tie the laces. Her movements were exaggerated, forceful.

"As your beloved brooch, occasionally respected tour guide, and astonishing repository of boundless information, I should never have ceased speaking to you—to either of you. And for that I feel myself to be undeniably humbled and deeply remorseful. And I fear that because of my irresponsible action, you and Molly have come to find yourselves in this problematic situation, with most of it due to my stubborn pride. Had I been doing my job properly and in the spirit for which I was appointed, I would have forthwith told you and Molly to hop aboard a trolley and have it deliver you safely to the PortalDoor. Then all would have been different, with the three of us safely returned to the secure confines of the Bristol House sewing room, and not trapped within this building, as for all intents and purposes, we appear to be."

Heather looked up. "The trolley." She tapped the palm of her open hand against her forehead several times. "I should have thought of that." She deliberated a moment. "Well, we probably wouldn't have had enough Autumnslovian money to ride it anyway."

"Heather, the magical trolleys are free for all to ride, paid for by tax feallans. My plan was a good one. I was simply never able to get it across to you, because, and rightfully so, you had stopped listening to me."

"Fallasha," Heather stood, "this jam we're in can't be your fault, okay? I've been pretty selfish, just taking off like I did, making you and Molly follow me through the streets of some strange place I'd never been before, not knowing where I was going. So, you can blame me. I should be the one apologizing to you." She stopped dressing and looked solemnly at the moon brooch. "I'm sorry, Fallasha, for everything I did that was disrespectful. And I'm sorry that Molly and I have to leave you here in Autumnsloe. I'm tempted to tear you off that costume right now and take you with me."

"I wish you could, but unfortunately I'm magically attached."

"Are you sure?"

"Positive. As a matter of fact, before you leave me, I need to ask a very important favor of you."

"Just name it. Anything." While looking at the brooch, Heather put on her coat, shoving her arms forcefully through the sleeves. She whisked up her hat. "I'm sorry, I have to hurry." Planting it on her head, she briefly looked at herself in the mirror, and disliked her costume immensely. Again Heather took to adjusting the cockeyed ruffles of her shirt. "Hate these things. They look so stupid—"

"I need you to fracture me."

Heather froze. "What?"

"Break me. I want you to fracture me."

"You mean break you, as in 'in half,' break you?"

"That's what I mean."

"Are you serious? Why would I do that? If anything, I'd rather save you, tear you off and take you out of here."

"I've already told you that that's not feasible. And you can't take this costume in its entirety with me on it. They'll check."

"The Crown & Scepter?"

"Yes."

"Well, I'm not breaking—fracturing—you, that's for sure."

"But you have to, *I* need you to."

Heather crossed her arms before her, looking down on her brooch. She shook her head.

"Heather, you don't understand. If you leave me unbroken, I'll be found here and undoubtedly fall into Mistraya's hands, and I assure you, that would be a fate worse than my fracturing. They'll detect life in me. Hurt me. So, go on. It's truly all right. As a matter of fact, I must insist."

"One word: No." Heather picked up her mask.

"But you must. Remember what the Matron said? I mustn't fall. Heather, it's all right and for the best. I promise. Besides, don't you remember? I'm just a brooch."

"No, you're—!" Heather lowered her voice, "No, you're not. I just said what I said, well, because I was angry, that's all. I promise, Fallasha, I didn't mean what I said back there—well, all except that Maiden thing, you know, about not being her."

"Want to know a secret, Heather?"

"What?"

"I truly admire you." Her eyes looked at Heather adoringly.

"Don't. Fallasha, please… I mean, how could you? For what? I was so cruel to you. I treated you so mean—"

"Enough. You were right, you know. I do talk too much. I've always been unable to hold my tongue—or keep a secret just that. I've never told you this, and it really should remain a secret—see what I mean?" Fallasha gave a short, sardonic laugh, "—but I used to be a spy once, and I did go on special assignments."

"Wow, you didn't tell—"

"I was demoted. That's nothing to brag about. It seems that I couldn't keep, as you once said, my big moon mouth shut. And so I was posted to the Bristol House, and I've never been happier. And when I was given my assignment to be your tour guide, and met you, I knew I was meeting someone special. You are special, Heather—Molly, too, although for reasons all her own."

Heather jumped at a sudden pounding on the locked door.

Molly's voice was excited. "Heather! Come on! We need to hurry. The RogueTags. They're in the store downstairs looking for us. They've probably been here a while, under the mezzanine where we couldn't see them, and they're about to come up the stairs. Hurry!"

Pound! Pound! Pound!

"Heather?"

"I'm coming, Molly."

Fallasha whispered, "Heather, do it."

The blonde girl shook her head. "I can't."

"You have to. Hurry. If you don't, I'll be captured and forced to talk. The pain will not only be prolonged and intense in its agony, but Mistraya will find out about you, Molly, Aria, Grandma Dawn, and the Bristol House. The consequences could be rather frightening for all parties involved."

"Well, then, come on. Right now! Let's go! We'll fight those Rogue-Tags."

Pound! Pound! Pound!

The brooch's gaze shifted quickly to the door and back. "We're not fighting anyone," said Fallasha. "Not yet, anyway."

"Well, I'm not fracturing you, that's for sure."

"Heather, let's not argue. There's no time. You have to fracture me. Really. It's far more important that you and Molly arrive home safely. If you engage in a fight of any kind, we don't know what might happen. Mistraya's scouts are stationed outside The Crown & Scepter as we speak, which surely means that she knows you're here. The sorceress is probably on her way this very moment. So hurry! Do what you must; do your duty. Fracture me."

The moon girl was shaking her head. "I wish…"

"You wish…?"

"I wish I *were* the green-eyed Maiden of the Evermore Portent. Then I'd be able to save you."

Fallasha laughed lightly. "Heather…"

"What?"

"Nothing." The moon brooch smiled. "Now hurry. You've not much time."

Pound! Pound! Pound!

Pound! Pound! Pound!

"Heather?"

"One second, Molly." The costumed girl got down on her knees and leaned towards her brooch. "I can't. Don't you see, Fallasha? You're asking me to kill you…"

"I'm asking you to save me. Now hurry."

"Uh-uh. No way. Now I have to go. You heard Molly. Those Rogue-Tags are in the costume shop and they're coming up here."

Pound! Pound! Pound!

Heather shot a look at the door. She turned back to Fallasha. The brooch's eyes implored her. Heather just shook her head slowly, her voice low, hoarse. "Don't ask me."

"But I must. This one last favor."

Pound! Pound! Pound!

uprising at the crown & scepter

Coming out of her trance, Mistraya was startled when she saw the peculiar child standing before her. Dominating the girl's face were widely spaced eyes, large and liquid—and they stared, two sentries guarding infinite secrets. Of average height for a twelve year old, she was thin, almost frail, and wore a white pinafore over a dress of maroon with black hose. Parted in the middle, her oily brown hair stopped just below the shoulders, and when pushed behind the ears, the locks refused to stay. Her hands were clasped out of sight, her voice small.

She said, "You've been SightSharing."

As always, Mistraya's voice was cool. "Bayliss, I don't like you standing there when I return from…wherever it is I go. I believe I've told you that before."

Registering no emotion, Bayliss continued to regard the woman, no sound parting her blood-red lips.

Standing, the sorceress said, "Why don't you locate the saddle-chair and Mastery Harness for Maif or Raif. It looks like this afternoon will find me on the town."

The girl gazed at Mistraya for several moments, before she turned and walked away, absorbed by the shadows. When she could no longer be seen, Mistraya and the night bird could hear her shoes clicking on the glassy floor. Finally, the taps faded out altogether.

The sorceress thought, I wish one of my great lizards would make a meal of that child.

Heather closed the dressing room door quietly yet firmly behind her. The mask that wrapped her face, displaying three emotions, obscured the confusion that had been aroused in the girl's mind. Heather didn't attempt to identify any of the feelings that churned within her—she wouldn't think to—though subconsciously she embraced one, allowing bridled fury to drive her. And though the face that was centermost on her mask conveyed it, somehow she kept this emotion hidden—even from herself—within a shell of pragmatic calm, as she contemplated their survival.

In search of her companion, Heather hurried past the many patrons that spilled out from aisles and bunched in front of the long line of dressing rooms, weaving towards the nearest stairway. It was there that she sighted Molly through the traffic, her shine pulsing at a low boggy ebb. The girl, in her new clown outfit was standing back from the balcony railing, the crowd briskly moving around her, though Molly was still able to keep a close watch on the stairways while overlooking the floor below. Heather drew to a standstill beside her.

"Where are they?" she asked.

Molly moved forward, approaching the rail. Heather followed. The clown girl didn't point.

"Borray is down there. See him? He's in the third aisle from the front of the store."

"Yeah, I see him. I think he's coming towards this stairway. Where's the other RogueTag?"

"Over there, on the other side. He's about halfway up those stairs, below the dancer in blue on the mural."

Heather looked over Molly's shoulder to the opposite side of the store, where Marscleff was caught up in the flow of traffic ascending the stairway. Conspicuously, he inspected those on their way down.

"Okay. Yeah. What have they been doing all this time?"

"It looks like they're checking people out, looking for something."

"Think they're looking for us?"

"I'm not sure. Maybe. But would they even know we're here?"

The blonde considered this, before saying, "Come on, Molly. The stairs on this side are clear. There's still a chance—" Heather was aware of Molly staring at her empty lapel, "—there's still a chance we can make it down before Borray reaches them." Heather kept talking, though she noticed Molly's tears. The girl that now wore the angry face became irritated, though she didn't know why. "I bet we'd be able to get past those two RogueTags in our new costumes without being noticed, but I can't be sure." A part of her hoped they'd be discovered so would have no recourse but to take on one or both. "I don't think either of those guys know what we look like in our new costumes."

The clown girl dismally bobbed her head, looking downward.

Heather asked, "Are you okay?"

Molly nodded again, before saying, "I guess you couldn't figure out a way to bring Fallasha."

"No."

Uncomfortable, thrusting her hands deep into her pants pockets, the three-faced girl looked away. In her left pocket, Heather felt the jumble of a few loose feallans, in her right the shrunken LuminOrb with its incriminating magical residue. Luckily, she had remembered to transfer the items from the pockets of her moon costume when changing. Heather squeezed the marble-sized ball tightly, again reminding herself that she was not to be caught with the LuminOrb in her possession and, at the first opportunity, needed to dispose of it. It was an incriminating link to the ClearWeave. If captured, she knew questions would be asked and damaging information, perhaps, disclosed.

Heather said, "Come on. We have to get out of here while the way is clear. Borray still hasn't reached the end of the aisle."

The pair maneuvered around a group of young shoppers that stood excitedly chatting, all appearing to be of similar age to the TimeLight travelers. Having descended partway down the stairs, Molly grabbed Heather's arm.

"Heather, the PortalDoor!"

"What about it?"

"The key!"

The girl in the boy's outfit instinctively patted her pockets. "I don't have it."

"I do—or did! Remember you gave it to me when you were going to fight those RogueTags in the alley? I left it in my butterfly outfit. It's back in the dressing room."

"Molly, we need that PortalKey, or we can't get home. You'll have to go get it. Hurry, okay? I'll stay here and keep a lookout."

"Heather, I'm so sorry—"

"Molly, it's all right. Just hurry, okay?"

Heather noticed that Molly's glance again swept across her jacket's empty lapel. Then she watched as her friend turned and jogged up the stairs on her way to the dressing room at the back of the mezzanine.

Quickly, the three-faced girl located Borray below, who was now inspecting the customers in the aisle nearest the main door. She saw that Marscleff, across the room, was nearing the top of the stairs.

Heather was relieved at not having to go back into the dressing room. She'd rather remain a lookout near the top of the stairs, preoccupied with tracking the two RogueTags. Wanting a better view, while keeping an eye on the busy floor below, the girl in the boy's costume started backing up the stairway, forcing those descending to maneuver around her.

"Young man!"

Realizing the words were directed at her, Heather half-turned only to run into a bulging sea of blue, a jeweled and sequined dress. The girl bounced back a step.

"Young man! Please!" The titled woman's voice was shrill. "You *will* move out of my way! Immediately! Now scoot!"

Unruffled, Heather looked the pasty woman over. She stood wrinkled and rouge-cheeked, a domineering presence. The lady wore a massive belled dress with wide conical sleeves housing gloves that flaunted many rings, and an ample three-coned hat wrapped with gauze and netting. Reddish-orange accents spotted her costume and saturated her lips. Small ringlets lined her forehead. Before her face, on a tapering stick, she held an elaborate eyemask encrusted with jewels. Behind her followed an entourage of eight young women, all dressed in similar costume.

Heather tried to step aside to allow for the group's passage, but there was no place to go. All movement had ceased due to congestion at the top and bottom of the staircase. She noticed Borray arguing with a couple of young girls, apparently wanting them to take off their masks. Frightened, they refused the skinny Rogue and were calling out for an attendant's assistance.

Oh, no, thought Heather. Those guys, they *are* searching for us. And they must know what we look like. Not good. Not good, not good, not good.

Heather was glad that she had chosen to wear a boy's costume, her hair tucked up securely under the crown of her hat, making her less likely to be identified.

In response to the pushy woman, Heather said nothing, not wanting the lady to discover that she was a girl in a boy's outfit. Instead, she stood her ground and pointed, indicating her desire to pass.

Her eyes now an animated part of the partial mask held up to her face, haughtily, the woman said, "Out of my way, young man. We're late for my party and must make haste. Now, if you would, kindly move aside."

Heather pointed again, wanting to slide past, but the woman's rotund dress and her refusal to give ground made it impossible.

"Come, come. Can you not speak? What is wrong with you? I'm

asking that you move out of my way, immediately, so that my girls and I may proceed down this stairway. Can you not comprehend that we are in a hurry? See there? My coach awaits us directly outside those very doors, so scoot, scoot." The velvety-gloved fingers dismissively brushed the air.

But with Heather unable to give ground and the woman unwilling to do so, there was no way for either to proceed. The girl had a sudden urge to drop on all fours and crawl under the rude lady's circus tent of a skirt, past her legs, until she reached the other side, while the snob helplessly flounced and squealed about. If Heather wasn't feeling shards of surliness, she might have been amused by her little fantasy. As it was, she looked away, and became exasperated, realizing she had lost track of Marscleff, who must have reached the top of the far stairway. That meant the RogueTag could be anywhere on the upper floor—even near Molly. The girl inside the boy costume fought to remain calm, focusing only on locating Marscleff as quickly as possible.

Heather was suddenly aware of loud voices rising up from the floor below. Heads turned throughout the shop—hers included—and those on the stairs craned their necks, while some pushed to the rail for a better view. Below, Borray was madly shouting at the attendant, pointing and waving his skinny arm. He was telling her to go ahead and call some soldiers and that, regardless, he, Borray, was going to have a look at the faces of those two girls in masks. Standing behind the attendant, the young pair feared to reveal their faces to any RogueTag, and so steadfastly refused. The attendant remained calm, while more people and employees gathered around, encircling the Rogue. She told Borray that he was to move along, letting the girls alone, and to go cause trouble elsewhere.

Heather continued to watch as a rugged man, apparently the girls' father, came sprinting across the floor, halfway in and out of a costume, trailing bits of his street clothes. He pressed past the attendant, and was soon yelling at Borray, his threatening finger in the RogueTag's face. The young man began to retreat.

Heather was relieved when she noticed that Marscleff had returned to the railing of the mezzanine, looking down on the action from the top of the opposite staircase. Although the traffic had come to a halt on that stairway as well, it wasn't nearly as crowded, and had Marscleff wanted, he could have hustled down to assist his fellow RogueTag. But he remained where he was.

Since many shoppers had crowded the rail, Heather was able to hike up the remaining stairs and past the insolent woman in the prominent dress. In turn, the lady stepped down to fill Heather's vacancy, and happily discovered she had acquired an unimpeded view of the action below. Her glittering mask pressed to her face, she fervently leaned in closer. All atwitter, her entourage gleefully surged to the rail, a succession of frilly, conical hats.

Seeing this gave Heather an idea. She maneuvered to get an unobstructed view of the insolent woman's hat, standing slightly above and behind her. Reaching into her pocket, the girl removed the LuminOrb, positioning it within her loosely curled fingers, directly on top of her thumbnail. Keeping her hand low, Heather discreetly flicked the small glass sphere as if it were a marble, and after arcing in trajectory—bullseye!—it landed in the woman's multi-peaked hat, nestling securely among the layers of gauze and netting with little sound.

Heather waited. No one seemed to have noticed her exploit, or said nothing if they did.

Looking down at the lower floor, she watched while Borray made a humiliating retreat, leaving the girls with their protective father, masks intact. Having dispensed with the LuminOrb, Heather turned, seeking to locate Marscleff, who was no longer visible at the railing of the mezzanine.

At the dressing room door, breathless, Molly gave the knob a twist, but the door was locked.

"Hello?" Molly said, jiggling the knob. "Anyone in there? I left something in my costume pocket. Can you please open the door? I'm in a hurry." She waited, before shaking the door again and knocking. "Hello? Anyone in there?"

Molly thought she heard shuffling inside, but no one answered. She hurried to the nearest attendant, who was assisting some shoppers.

"Excuse me," the girl in the clown outfit said, "I left something in the dressing room, in a pocket of my old costume. The door is locked and it sounds like there might be someone in there, but no one is answering. Can you please help me?" Molly thought to add, "I'm really sorry to bother you, but I'm in a hurry."

"Glad to help." Displaying a cheerful, round face, the attendant slid past Molly and spoke over her shoulder as she strode, "Let's see what we can do for you. I didn't let anyone go in after your friend came out. I thought you girls might be using the dressing room again, since I didn't see you carry out your street clothes or previous costumes. But that doesn't mean someone didn't get by me and go in, because as you can see," the woman held up her hands, "the store is packed this afternoon with people getting ready to go out for this evening's events. And there are many more shoppers arriving as we speak."

Following the attendant, it struck Molly that the woman was everything short. She was short in height with short blond hair, racing along on short energetic steps. Probably had short feet, too, but Molly didn't dare attempt a peek.

The woman arrived at the door, and then turned to the trailing Molly, a curious look on her face. "Did you say the door was locked?"

"Yes."

"Well, it's unlocked now." She drew back, and Molly saw the door was slightly ajar.

"Oh!" The girl in the clown outfit didn't know what to say. "Well, it wasn't—" she looked up, but the attendant had already walked away with the same energetic traipse toward another shopper, "—a moment ago…"

She pulled open the louvered door.

"That's strange."

Inside, the lights were off. A feeling of dread tugged at her. The girl was reluctant to enter, but knew she had to hurry. She knocked on the door's jamb, leaning her head in.

"Anyone in here?"

No response. Unable to see, Molly remembered how the dressing room was generous in size, big enough to fit three to five people changing at one time.

"Fallasha?" She waited. "Fallasha? Are you here?"

No answer from the brooch.

"So strange…" the girl whispered.

Molly vaguely saw the bench as it ran along the back wall, disappearing from the light. The costumes were at the far end, the girl knew, to her right—in the dark—at least that's where she had piled hers.

"Fallasha?" Where could she be, if no one's been in here?

Molly took another small step and squinted into the shadows at one end and then the other. The clown girl gasped when she saw a face to her left peering at her from out of the darkness. An instant later, Molly recognized her own reflection and giggled nervously.

I wish this dressing room wasn't so large, she told herself, though she remembered having liked the roominess.

Since the lights had been on when she changed out of the butterfly outfit, Molly had no idea where to begin her hunt for the switch—if there was a switch. If one existed, she couldn't recall having seen it. Uneasy, she withdrew from the dressing room to seek assistance.

With a glance above, Molly realized why it was so dark in this corner of the mezzanine. Overhead, a large piece of cloth, one of many that draped The Crown & Scepter's ceiling, held back and diffused the light. There was also an oversized mannequin that stood outside the dressing room door, its large shadow pressing in. And maybe she hadn't noticed the corner's dimness before, because the light had been on inside the dressing room. Or maybe her mind had been preoccupied with other things…

Concerned about the time it was taking to retrieve the PortalKey, she frantically looked around. The girl spotted the short attendant assisting customers three aisles away. When she realized there were more people in queue, Molly looked for a different attendant. Although she noticed many, all were engaged helping others. It looked like someone was inside the dressing room next to hers—at least the door was closed—and she felt that the numerous shoppers were far too busy to be bothered with her silly questions, as they chatted and laughed among themselves, sorting through the racks or trying on various masks. Feeling shy and not wanting to be intrusive, Molly turned back to the dim corner and louvered door. The girl felt she was being foolish, childish, not wanting to go into a darkened dressing room with so many people hovering right outside. For heavens sake, she wasn't six years old anymore and afraid of the dark!

Placing her left hand tentatively on the doorframe, Molly entered the room, if barely. Feeling for the switch, she began to lightly slap along the wall to her left, just inside the door. The girl was sure that by this time Heather would be impatiently waiting, wondering what was taking so long. As she continued to probe in the blackness, Molly thought she could hear her heart thumping out the words: Hurr-REE, hurr-REE, hurr-REE, hurr-REE.

Unable to find a light switch on either side, Molly began ducking and weaving, allowing the muted light from outside to illuminate the uppermost sections of the opposite wall. Again she was unable to detect a switch.

What now? she wondered, though the answer was frighteningly obvious.

Molly took a deep breath, and drumming up her courage, finally stepped fully into the room, turning to her right. Once inside, the shadows stole over her like a sly, sooty blanket. With her back to the mirror, walking away from the door, she began to drag her hands along the wall. The girl intermittently felt the soft, embossed sections of wallpaper as they slid beneath her fingers, brush, slide, brush, slide, brush. Having stepped four or five paces into the room, she didn't notice that behind her the broad rectangle of light that sliced through the doorway had started to narrow, the louvered door outside swinging around on silent hinges. By the time Molly became aware of the diminishing light, it was too late, the door shutting quietly. Frantic, the girl gasped and wheeled.

It was so dark! Were her eyes open or closed? She couldn't tell, and so squeezed.

Pressing herself to the wall, Molly shrank from the crush of blackness.

Bayliss, where are you?
The cheerless girl didn't flinch as she looked at the face that had materialized in a ball of purple flame before her. No emotion touched the girl's features. She stared blankly.

Bayliss?
"I'm looking for the Mastery°Harness." Her words were little, robotic.

You've not found it yet?
A pause.
Finally, "No."

Back in the throne room, Mistraya gazed into the purple flame that floated slightly above her raised palm. She arose from her throne.

"Where are you, Bayliss?"
"In the room where we keep the harnesses."

Though the words she spoke remained cool, the child sensed Mistraya's irritation: *I'll be right there.*

Eyes scrunched tight in the dressing room, terror gripped Molly as she trembled in the blackness. With a scream stuck in her throat, she feared to breathe, expecting to be mauled by an unseen force. Paralyzed, Molly dared herself to look, willed herself not to be afraid.

Act like Heather! she told herself. Be brave!

Molly opened her eyes. They went wide, her jaw dropping. With wonder, she watched as the lights in the room gradually became brighter. Stepping away from the wall, she looked around. The room was perfectly empty. Gone were the costumes and hangers, any sign that the girls had ever been there. To her right, on the wall above the bench, Molly noticed that a crude circle had been drawn in red, an arrow pointing to it. Within, hanging on a straight pin that had been pushed deep into the wall, Molly recognized the PortalKey.

She started to walk toward it when she was drawn to the mirror fringed in lights. She stopped in her tracks.

"How peculiar is that?"

In the upper right corner of the mirror, Molly saw another red circle and arrow. But unlike the one that held the PortalKey, there was nothing inside this one, just the room pictured in reverse. She quickly strode over to the glass, and looked at the mirrored possibilities. At different angles, she saw various parts of the ceiling and room in reflection, but nothing struck her as significant.

Could there have been something there at one time? She wondered. But what could have been stuck to the glass? And who took it? She looked around, mildly indignant. And where's Fallasha?

Suddenly aware of the time, Molly grabbed the PortalKey, and placing it in her pocket, she bolted for the door, but then abruptly stopped and turned. The girl recognized that the red scribble that had surrounded the key was slowly fading, becoming invisible. She turned towards the mirror, to look at the other circle and arrow. It too was paling. Molly shivered and hurried toward the door.

"How utterly bizarre."

Shoulders rounded, head hanging and bouncing sulkily with each step, Borray headed toward the staircase, which, unbeknownst to him, was the one nearest Heather. After his encounter with the father of the two girls, he felt at a loss. The scene hadn't gone as planned. Why was that? It should have. After all, Mistraya had presented herself, came to them in a ball of celestial flame, choosing both him and Marscleff personally. This was a Universal event unfolding, wasn't it? A shifting of cosmic wheels, large and opportunistic. It was a life-altering incident, he told himself. No, bigger than life. It, it was huge! No! No, wait: Enormous! Right? *Enormous! Yes!* Nothing less.

So, then, what happened back there?

He looked over his shoulder for the man who had embarrassed him, who had stopped him from unmasking the girls, but he, along with his two daughters, had vanished.

The RogueTag asked himself, Why didn't those girls just cooperate? All they had to do was lift their masks and expose their faces. That's all I wanted. Just a peek under those masks. It would only have taken a second. Then I would have left them alone. Dumb sprees. Wasn't it Jartt who said, 'Never trust a spree?'

Up till then, all the girls that I confronted took off their masks, didn't they? And from what I saw, Marscleff also stopped maybe half as many sprees without a problem—well, maybe a third. Everything was going so smoothly, too. I mean, sure all those girls were scared. They were supposed to be. After all, I'm a RogueTag, aren't I? People are scared of us Rogues, and they do what we want them to. They'd better. We're intimidating. A force of importance, commanding respect and instilling fear, *that's* who we are.

Borray stood near several shoppers lumped at the bottom of the stairs, waiting for traffic to begin flowing again, waiting to go up. The RogueTag tried to catch and make sense of the conversations he heard around him.

I bet they're talking about me, he thought. Are they laughing? Are they? They'd better not be.

Making his face as nasty as possible, Borray looked around him. Not a soul looked back, talking quietly with one another or just focused elsewhere.

He noticed when he first walked up that some bystanders had tactfully moved farther away from him, giving him a wide berth. As much as he liked that—that they were terrified or put off by a RogueTag such as himself—a part of him was disappointed that they found him loathsome in some way. Was he really that unlikeable?

Borray thought, As a Rogue, don't these people realize that I'm fighting for their cause, *our* cause? That I'm trying to elevate the status of HumanKind in the Realm, risking my life, opposing the rule of Maidens? Ignorant fools. All of them.

He supposed that he couldn't expect the average Evermorian citizen to find a RogueTag admirable. After all, those who did, didn't they join and become RogueTags themselves?

Borray crossed his lean arms in front of him, chewing on his recent humiliation. The RogueTag blinked away tears.

If those little iggets had just lifted their masks, he said to himself again, everything would have been great!

But they didn't. And maybe he should have let it go, just moved on before their father arrived. Until then, how could he have known they weren't the 'Dregs? How? But what if they really were the pair Mistraya is looking for? The age and height were about right, weren't they? So, he *had* to check them out, didn't he? *Yes!* After all, Mistraya was the one who sent him in here. He was under her orders. And didn't Emperor Kratkuffe personally appoint her Sorceress to the Court? So, that made him, Borray, official. This was his opportunity to shine. Remember? It was, after all, meant to be.

The young man hooked his thumbs in his pockets, thrusting out his chin.

So, if that's the case, why did he almost get pounded to a pulp by some big 'Lick? And why does the Universe always find satisfaction when working against him, insuring his failure? It gets old.

Can't I win, even sometimes? he thought.

Borray stared at the floor, at the space between himself and the person who stood several steps in front of him. Blinking several times, the RogueTag felt that familiar fog beginning to crawl, seeping in with its isolating presence, edging forward, casting a pall over his sense of well-being, and covering his newfound exultation in a bitter shroud of disappointment. And just when it looked like something good had come his way, that something was finally going right. This always happens. Always!

Borray wanted to stomp his foot hard. He felt his lips quivering and pressed them together. Harder.

Snap out of it! he scolded himself.

What if Mistraya suddenly popped up again in that ball of flame and saw him blubbering this way? She wouldn't take him seriously as a RogueTag, now would she? He couldn't let *that* happen. No. Being a RogueTag was who Borray was, what he saw himself as, for the sake of HumanKind everywhere.

Borray looked for Marscleff but was unable to spot him. Probably searching the mezzanine, Borray reasoned. The RogueTag then turned his attention to the windows, expecting to see Mistraya arriving outside. In his head, he could see her walking through those doors, sucking the energy out of the room with her presence like she does, drawing it all to her, as if the sorceress were the center of the universe and everything revolved around her.

But Borray didn't see Mistraya in front of The Crown & Scepter, just the many birds that had collected on the buildings, in the trees, and on the lampposts.

With all those scouts out there, the people in the store must be aware that something is going on, he thought. I mean, all they need to do is look out the windows, for Evermore's sake, and see all those big disgusting birds hanging around, looking like they're about to kill something.

It was then that Borray was struck with a flash of insight.

What if the two AlienDregs saw those birds from inside the store and knew they were Mistraya's scouts? What would they do then?

Well, what *would* they do? the RogueTag asked himself. They wouldn't go out the front or side doors, that's for sure. Not with all those birds out there. They'd suspect something was up.

Borray glanced towards the back of the store.

No, I have a hunch, he thought. Call it instinct. They're still in here. They are. I can feel it.

As Borray surveyed the spacious costume emporium, a question sprang to mind: How can Mistraya really expect just two people to cover The Crown & Scepter thoroughly? And where was the help she had promised him? Where was *she?* He dismissed the thoughts, telling himself the sorceress knew what she was doing.

Maybe the 'Dregs were in a dressing room down here and we overlooked them...

He and Marscleff hadn't checked behind any of the doors. How could they? It would have been indecent. People might have been naked in there! That means by now the girls could be out on the floor, wearing their new costumes. Better hurry. If they're up on the mezzanine, Marscleff will probably find them. And if he RogueWhistles for me, I'll hear him. I just need to let him know where I'm going to be. Besides, if the 'Dregs get past him, they'll eventually be heading my way, anyhow, coming down the stairs. Yessir, call it intuition, that old killer instinct.

The stagnant queue before him began to move and mount the steps, but Borray didn't continue up to join forces with his companion as planned, in a search of the mezzanine. Instead, he stood still and let the crowd circulate around him, like a rock in a smooth flowing stream. However, it wasn't long before Borray was on the move, slicing through the crush, trying to hurry, advancing toward the cargo and delivery door at the back of the store.

I think that's where those girls will be headed, he said to himself, nudging past more shoppers. No, I *know* that's where those 'Dregs will be headed. Easy pickings. And my PassionFlame? Coming soon.

Borray patted his pants pocket, feeling the slight bulge of the small knife.

How can I go wrong?

Over and around the racks of clothing, past the mannequins and masks on display, Heather watched Marscleff. He was still in the vicinity of the far staircase, close to where she saw him last. Heather followed the young man, making certain that she kept her distance, pretending to be browsing, keeping obstacles and people between the RogueTag and herself. Periodically she would look out for Molly. She was surprised that Marscleff wasn't checking the dressing rooms, though he did seem intent on bullying any girls he encountered that matched Heather and Molly's general descriptions, demanding that they remove their masks. Cowed, most girls did. Although once, when an attendant objected, Marscleff slinked away, back towards the stairs.

Heather watched for a while, but finally thought better of it, seeing that the RogueTag wasn't going far. She presumed he was waiting for Borray. Returning to her post at the stairway landing and looking down on the lower floor, she saw that the snobby woman with her spiky hat and trailing entourage were now exiting the emporium's central doors, customers parting before them. Through the windows, Heather could see the woman's coach parked alongside the curb with unfamiliar beasts harnessed to pull it.

Where's Borray? the girl asked herself, scanning the long strands of people mounting and descending the stairs.

Moments later she spotted him. The RogueTag was no longer in the aisle near the stairway, but had stopped in the center of the floor. There he stood signaling to Marscleff above him, pointing to an area beneath the mezzanine.

What's that about?

When Borray had finished, Heather saw Marscleff disappear into the aisles of costumes directly behind him.

He's going to search this entire floor for us, she thought, temporarily attracted by the boisterous teens gathered at the top of the stairs. The girl behind the angry mask wished that she and Molly could join them and be part of their lightheartedness, rather than facing their current difficulties. Heather brought a hand up to her empty lapel, and then quickly diverted her thoughts to devising a plan for escape that seemed ever so obvious.

Heather thought, With Borray and Marscleff each looking like they're headed to the back of the costume store, Molly and I can easily make it down the stairs and out the front door. In our new costumes, the scouts will never recognize us. Now we'll be safe getting to the PortalDoor! I hate to say it, but if those two RogueTags are trying to catch us, they're really not very bright. Heather became suddenly wary, thinking, Unless there are more RogueTags waiting for us outside, in front of the store.

Heather heard the teenagers screeching playfully and giggling. Again, she cast an envious glance in their direction, but was soon drawn to the floor below. Instinctively, Heather took a step back from the railing.

"Oh, no," she muttered, throwing a glimpse over her shoulder. Where's Molly? And what's taking her so long?

She refocused on the lower floor. Heather began to count.

Not good, not good, not good.

The three-faced girl worried that Molly would have a panic meltdown if she knew that over forty creepy people in gray clothing were pouring into the store below, their auras smoky black and deadly. In uniform, with their faces hidden behind grim gray masks, they quickly fanned out, threading their way among the shoppers. Only a few noticed.

Their masked leader, indiscriminately wielding a RazorSlicer, was now butchering his way to the top of the stairs nearest to Heather, eight assassins close behind him, stepping over the bodies. People were screaming and cowering, diving out of his way. Horrified, Heather quickly moved towards the center of the mezzanine railing, where she counted another eight killers on the far staircase. She watched as they stopped halfway up.

The girl could see that traffic was being halted on both staircases, as the GraySuits scrutinized those who were trapped on the stairs, the younger females being forced to remove their masks for inspection. Some shoppers at the top and bottom hastily retreated, while others, midway on the stairs, were being hailed and compelled to undergo inspection.

Molly. Heather had to locate her, and they needed to find a way out of this mess. On the lower floor, the girl in the boy's outfit saw that the GraySuits had neatly spread out and now held positions in front of the aisles, with two remaining at each of the three entry doors, temporarily sealing off all traffic in and out of the store.

Standing within the crowd of shocked onlookers, Heather didn't recognize the man who had just reached the top of the stairs, holstering his RazorSlicer at the hip. However, if she were unmasked, Soldier One would have easily recognized her. With a wave of his hand, he set Mistraya's assassins in motion below. Hypnotized, the girl watched as they began to move down the aisles, thuggishly pushing their way through the crowds of Parade Day shoppers, stopping people in their tracks and harassing them. They began to isolate and roughly pull the masks off of suspect girls. Angry shouts, screams, and sobs were filling the air, and Heather looked on as attendants and shoppers were interrogated and needlessly dragged aside. If they put up any resistance whatsoever, they were severely beaten with SlugClubs and SawTooth Knuckles.

Realizing she and Molly were trapped, Heather pulled away from the railing, zigzagging down the corridors of costumes to eventually emerge not far behind the commanding figure of Soldier One. An eye on the apparent leader before her, hidden by a gauze-draped mannequin, she stationed herself with a clear view of the corner dressing room. The girl still hadn't sighted Molly, but thought she could easily be intercepted when returning to the stairs with the PortalKey. Concerned, Heather had no idea what could be taking her so long.

At hearing the shouts and screams from below, people had stampeded out of the aisles and dressing rooms to the mezzanine's railing to see what was taking place, and soon their own shrieks of horror and voices of outrage joined with the clamor below. Patrons who tried to push to the stairs were prevented from doing so, due to the GraySuits on either side who had strong-armed their way to the top. There, they backed the crowds off, and the many who put up a fight, or happened to be unfortunate bystanders near the melee, were left broken and bleeding, writhing in agony or simply not moving at all. Heather heard the cries that followed the heavy smacks of 'Clubs as they met flesh and bone, and her rage surfaced.

Where are the soldiers? she wondered. Aren't they supposed to protect these people?

Seeing that the proceedings on the ground floor were going as planned, Soldier One turned his attention to the mezzanine, to the flock of teens that, only a short time ago, Heather had envied. At his approach, with their backs to the rail, they began to cower, whimper, and shriek.

"Remove your masks! Now!"

"You leave them alone!" shouted a boy roughly seven years of age, bravely stepping forward in the constricted space. "They didn't do anything, so don't you touch them!" Like a small dog, he barked out the phrases, "You're ugly! You're an ugly man!"

"Jessen, don't!" a woman's voice sounded from well within the crowd, far too late to silence her son and far too distant to restrain him.

Heather thought she heard Soldier One's throaty laugh amid the chaos. The GraySuits in the vicinity found the scene amusing, the boy harmless, their concentration on the greater threat posed by the adults.

His PassionFlame circulating its divine anguish, the commander stepped towards the boy and, with a large muscular grip, seized him, a handful of fabric at the chest.

"Ow! Stop that! You leave me alone!"

"Don't! Don't hurt him!" The mother was hemmed in, attempting to push her way through the bystanders. "That's my son. He's a child. He doesn't know any better."

Hoisting him easily above with one arm, Soldier One reached up and slapped the boy before ripping off his mask. The mother screamed. The commander tossed the mask casually aside, his savage eyes never leaving the child. Still held aloft, the boy erupted with a defiant swinging of fists, the arcs falling short of their mark. But an unexpected kick caught Soldier One squarely on the jaw. For a moment, the man stood stunned.

"How dare you, you impudent little churse." The voice was guttural, deep, disturbing.

"Put me down, you hear me! Put me down!"

"I'll put you down, all right."

"Stop!" the mother screamed. "Don't hurt him! Please! Let me through! Let…me…through!"

Jessen continued to kick and holler at the brawny man who held him aloft. Heather could hear Soldier One's laughter, his large shoulders shaking. He turned and carried the boy, kicking and punching, toward the rail, while the GraySuit troopers kept the restless crowd at bay.

"You put my son down! Put him down!" A tawny-haired woman in a dancer's outfit had finally broken free of the throng, past a surprised GraySuit. She dashed out and grabbed the boy's legs, preventing Soldier One from throwing him over the balustrade into the pandemonium below. A well-intentioned man joined in her effort, lunging at Soldier One, but a sharp kick of the commander's heavy boot to his midsection left him doubled up. A knee to the face finished him. And still, the muscular man held Jessen out before him, the mother on her knees desperately hugging her child's thin lower limbs.

"Let go of his legs," commanded Soldier One, now using both hands to hold the boy.

The woman refused, making her body a sack of dead weight, dragging Jessen down, pulling the man off-balance.

"Lady, let go of his legs," Soldier One said, his words a warning.

Still the woman refused.

Bringing one hand to the rail for support, straining to keep the boy aloft, Soldier One started kicking the lady. Her body absorbing the brutal blows, one after the next, the mother clung tight. Above, tears flowing, the boy was screaming, hammering on the man's muscular forearm, his blows ineffectual.

The bystanders that packed Heather's side of the mezzanine remained transfixed by the events and intimidated by the GraySuits that stood watch, their bloody SlugClubs at the ready and in need of only the smallest excuse. And so the mother continued to receive thumping blow after blow, her trunk jerking with each.

"Please. Don't...hurt him." Balled around the boy's legs, her body starting to loosen and go slack from the pounding, the woman said, "He's just a boy."

And though the mother's words were muffled, Heather heard them. That's when the girl, unable to contain her rage, sprang out from behind the mannequin and ran top speed at Soldier One. How could she have known that her strength was beyond human, never having had to use it before in such a manner?

The thickset man, his concentration focused on the mother, never saw the girl racing toward him until the last instant. His foot was reared back when Heather slammed full force into Soldier One with her shoulder lowered and head tucked, a battering ram of compact sinew that snapped his masked face forward. As she drove through him, lifting him off the ground, her wiry body propelled the bulk of Soldier One's torso rearward. The shock of the collision coupled with the need to maintain balance caused the man to release his grip on the boy. His arms spread wide, flailing at air, he tumbled backward over the railing. Soldier One's scream was short-lived as he fell from the height of the mezzanine, but it resonated throughout the openness of The Crown & Scepter.

Heather heard the shattering crash of his impact, but never saw the vertical support bar of the clothing rack that impaled Mistraya's lead warrior, or the fragmented mirror that cleanly beheaded him. She only heard the abrupt silence, followed shortly thereafter by the screams.

Heather was fluid, still in motion. Seeing that she had helped to release the boy from the man's hold, her mask precariously askew, she quickly skipped back a few paces. The girl caught sight of her bowler hat that had popped off upon impact, as it lay partially crushed on the floor. Blond hair bouncing at her shoulders, Heather bent to retrieve it with a rapid sweep of her arm. That was when her mask tumbled loose and fell to the floor. The girl hastened a glance at the stupefied crowd, but didn't see the GraySuit who yelled, "It's her! The green-eyed Maiden!"

"The green-eyed Maiden?" said one bystander.

Another: "It's the green-eyed Maiden!"

The inspirational words were taken up and spread quickly through the store.

Now aware of the presence of their heroine from the Portent, and energized by her audacious act, the shoppers emerged from their stupor and turned on the GraySuits. Though suffering a great many casualties, young and old, the patrons rallied and by sheer numbers overpowered the deadly troopers on the mezzanine and eventually throughout the store. Yet their victory was only temporary. It wouldn't be long before Mistraya's Purple Flame reinforcements battered their way into The Crown & Scepter to subdue the rebellious Autumnslovian citizens.

Meanwhile, Heather had quickly snapped up her mask, and having turned, without so much as a glance behind her, she bolted into the corridors of clothing, on her way to the dressing room and Molly.

conflict and the conflicted

Darting around a mannequin's pedestal, Heather almost smacked head-on into Molly. The blonde leaped sideways, managing to avoid a collision. However, when Heather landed, her ankle turned and she tumbled to the floor, her mask and hat flying out of her hand.

In an instant, Heather was up again, placing weight gingerly on her foot.

"Ow!" She bared her teeth, sucking air.

"Heather, are you all right?" Molly was next to her, handing the girl her errant mask and hat.

"Come on, Molly, we have to hurry." Heather started limping, as she skip-hobbled down the high-partitioned aisle.

"What's going on? I heard all the noise, and thought it would be safer to come this way—"

"Molly, we need to get back to the dressing room."

"Why? What's happening—?"

The girl in the clown outfit didn't have time to finish her sentence, as Heather, favoring her left ankle, half ran, half-limped toward their dressing room, a quiet sanctuary in the back corner of the mezzanine. She needed more time to think, to plan.

With Heather's ankle impairment slowing her progress, Molly easily caught up to her.

"What is it, Heather? What's going on?"

"Now? What's going on *now*, at this very minute?" Heather said. "I'm not sure. All I know is this costume store is no place for visitors from the Milky Way."

Feeling vulnerable and afraid, Marscleff had concealed himself, his body enveloped within a rack of hanging costumes. Something horrific was happening up front on the mezzanine of The Crown & Scepter. There were screams and shouts amid sounds of conflict.

Hail the green-eyed Maiden! Hail the green-eyed Maiden! Astille Lia! The words rang out again and again. Upon hearing them, Marscleff had dared to peek his head out to look around. And now he was watching the two girls, one in particular who had tripped and fallen not far from where he lay hidden. The RogueTag was quick to recognize her as the one Mistraya wanted them to kill, the one considered to be the Portent girl.

Marscleff thought, *The green-eyed Maiden of the Evermore Portent!!!* Holy Borridor and the Sacred Universe!

Immediately, the young man felt his knees begin to shake. He resisted the urge to dive to the floor between racks.

I shouldn't have let Borray talk me into this, thought Marscleff. I should be home right now watching my baby brother, reading the latest *MindSqualor* comic.

He watched as the two girls talked briefly, the Portent girl gingerly putting weight on her foot, testing it.

She's hurt! Even so, he thought, do I really want to do this, to try and kill these girls? And how? I don't even have a knife or SlamRod. But if Mistraya turns up in a ball of purple flame and sees me hiding here in the clothes rack, she'll kill me where I stand, I'm sure of it.

Marscleff realized he was sweating profusely, pulling his boney arms in tight, close to his body.

Yay, I know. I can at least follow these sprees, he thought, and later tell Borray where they are. Then *he* can kill them. Not me.

Marscleff was now positive that he didn't want anything to do with this entire costume store mess, the fighting and the capturing or killing of the girls. Truth be known, if he hadn't been given the assignment by Mistraya, and if Borray wasn't around, chances are Marscleff would have summoned the courage to ask the Maiden girl for her autograph. And the RogueTag realized that he didn't care whether or not he had a PassionFlame. The young man just wished he were home.

At times, Marscleff questioned whether or not he really wanted to be a RogueTag, whether he had the resolve. And now those strong doubts resurfaced. Maybe he should have gone to the conservatory, concentrating his musical efforts on the three-tiered castathrollian, like his father, a renowned conductor, had wanted. However, despite the fact that Marscleff was highly accomplished on the instrument he had played since age three, his father never failed to remind him that he was inferior to his older brother, a well-known virtuoso. So, finally, and much to the consternation of his parents, Marscleff had walked away from his music. Just gave it up cold. It wasn't long before he started hanging out with Borray. And shortly thereafter, Marscleff took to wearing his purple armband.

Only wimpy thrigs play the castathrollian.

Instantly, the RogueTag felt empowered at the thought. Watching as the girls scrambled away—one awkwardly—Marscleff noisily disentangled himself from the clothing, having first made certain the scene was clear of possible threats. He stepped out into the aisle and, crouching, hastily slinked after the pair, keeping what the RogueTag felt to be a safe and reasonable distance. Marscleff could still hear the sounds of confrontation taking place on the mezzanine as he reached the end of the aisle. There, the young man watched, his head jutting out from around the end of a clothes rack, as the girls hurried past the oversized mannequin and discreetly entered a dressing room in the dimly lit corner. Once inside, the blonde pulled closed the louvered door behind them, though not completely.

Should I sneak up on the AlienDregs? he wondered. Then what? That's the green-eyed Maiden in there! Maybe I just need to get close, watch them and make sure they don't leave until Borray comes to find me. Then I'll point their room out. Or if Mistraya comes in another ball of fire, I can tell her where the girls are holed up. She'll understand my not wanting to approach the 'Dregs without a weapon, especially after what happened to the other three Rogues.

With a glance behind him down the aisle, Marscleff saw a GraySuit fall to the ground, having been attacked by two Autumnslovian men. They were grappling, the fists finding flesh in dull thuds, a knee to the throat, a SlugClub knocked away. Sickened, he didn't wait to see the outcome of the struggle, quickly turning the corner. Now deliberately creeping closer to Heather and Molly's dressing room, slipping around the ends of the clothing aisles one and the next and the next, the RogueTag came to rest behind another large mannequin that towered over him.

Marscleff had settled in, his attention focused on the dressing room beyond, when behind him, racks of clothing overturned in a sprawling smash and clatter. Wrestling within the garments spilt in disarray were two figures, fists and elbows flying. More patrons jumped into the fray, including two women and a boy, joining forces against the elite soldier. Marscleff watched with astonishment, as the child jumped up and brought both knees crashing down on the gray mask of the pinned opponent. When the GraySuit screamed out in pain, the boy climbed to his feet and repeated the action. All the while, a pounding was being delivered to the soldier's squirming, struggling body. Two comrades in gray joined the combat, swinging their SlugClubs and ThunderHackers.

Panicked, and wanting to escape the violence, the RogueTag bolted from behind the mannequin. Feeling immediately vulnerable in the open, Marscleff glanced indecisively about before racing to the nearest place offering safe quarter, the dressing room next to Heather and Molly's. Sweeping the area with a final, horrified glance, he backed through the partially open doorway, glass from the room's shattered lights crunching underfoot. Grateful to be ensconced in the darkness, the RogueTag immediately crouched and pulled the door closed behind him, leaving only a crack. His eye affixed to the narrow opening, Marscleff waited, attempting another vigil in the direction of the girls' dressing room. Unable to see much, he pushed the door open wider. Observing the shuttered backside of their partially open door, he heard the fighting on the floor spread as more racks of clothing were overturned, while people outside his scope of vision scuffled, grunted, cried out, and died.

When the large mannequin near his door toppled to the ground, the RogueTag felt the walls shake and the floor bounce beneath him. He quailed and drew back from the door. Sweat trickling from his brow, aware of his breathing, Marscleff waited. Close by, he heard a barrage of footfalls, men charging from the scene, running back toward what the RogueTag determined to be more fighting at the front of the mezzanine. Unfortunately for Marscleff, he didn't hear the two men who sneaked up in the darkness behind him, from the back of the dressing room.

He only heard the words, "Filthy RogueTag."

By then it was too late.

Mistraya waited for a particular face to appear in the midst of the purple flame. None did. Sweeping out of the cavernous Gilded Room, her fingers squeezed to smother the ball of fire. When dropping her hand, the sorceress kept it tightly fisted, the long nails biting into her palm.

Mistraya was frustrated, yet one would never guess it. Outwardly, the sorceress appeared calm, despite the fact that she was unable to contact Soldier One at The Crown & Scepter via TeleFlame.

Now gliding down Castle Allurid's Great Hallway, a repetition of towering gothic arches beneath clerestory windows, Mistraya was on her way to the Harness Room and stables. The figure of the sorceress was repeatedly lost and found in the filtered light, dwarfed by mammoth pillars that she passed on either side, their filmy shadows crisscrossing the glossy floor before her.

Turning sharply, she strode confidently into the Picture Gallery. In the gloom, Mistraya could hear one of the two winged lizards crawling toward her, its belly skimming across the floor.

"Maif. Follow me." It was an assured command crisply delivered.

Mistraya cast her hand before her, as if scattering seeds. Small sparkles burst to life and illuminated the room's spaciousness, the paintings remaining shaded and secretive. The woman strode through the trickle of twinkling mizzle that gently drifted to the floor, some briefly settling on her head and shoulders like confetti before dimming and going out altogether.

Again Mistraya held her hand before her and called up the purple flame. In it, she could see the image of Borray's terrified face.

The lanky RogueTag was cowering behind the open door of one of the lower floor's rearmost dressing rooms, stupefied by the fighting and chaos that surrounded him. Borray had witnessed several bodies that fell or were thrown from the mezzanine—some were women and children.

What is happening here? he asked himself.

Observing the actions of the GraySuit Troopers, he was terrified by their outright savagery, though he knew they were fighting for the betterment of HumanKind.

Noticing the TeleFlame that bloomed before him, Borray stared into it, shell-shocked.

"My Mistress."

Borray, where are you? The voice of the sorceress was icy smooth, calm, and struck him as out of place.

"I-I'm at The Crown & Scepter."

I assumed as much. And your friend?

"Marscleff is upstairs. We're looking for the 'Dregs. I'm just finishing here on the lower floor. Right now, I'm searching the dressing rooms, being certain that the girls aren't hiding—"

*Being certain **they're** not hiding…?*

Borray swallowed. "Yes. My Mistress. Then when I'm done here, I'll be joining Marscleff—"

Suddenly a loud scream pierced the air. Borray looked away from the flame and saw a GraySuit falling from the Mezzanine. He hit with a loud crash.

Borray, what just happened?

"There's all sorts of fighting going on, My Mistress, and I've seen some people get thrown from the balcony. And-and I'm checking on a hunch to make sure that the 'Dregs don't get out the door in back—"

Have you seen Soldier One?

"Is he here?" Borray remembered the hefty man previously from two or three of the larger RogueTag rallies. "If he is, he might be—" Borray ducked reflexively and glanced sideways at a sudden crash. He continued to look in that direction, speaking distractedly, "I've heard all sorts of screaming, My Mistress. There's a lot going on. A bunch of GraySuits rushed up the stairs not too long ago. They had weapons—their Slug-Clubs and Sawtooth Knuckles. And-and some even had RazorSlicers. They were beating and hurting people. I didn't see them come into the store, but suddenly this place exploded—"

You don't say?

"Yes. The GraySuits, they're looking for the girls, too, aren't they? They seemed to be—"

Borray. Soldier One.

The RogueTag continued to gaze anxiously toward the front of the shop. "No, I'm sorry, I haven't—" Borray gasped and shrank when a spiked projectile slammed against the door, while Mistraya heard crashes in the background. Three people went rushing by, pursued by a trooper. Carefully, the Rogue peeked back out.

What is it?

"Someone up on the mezzanine—" More shattering smashes could be heard amid the clamor, the RogueTag flinching, his face grim.

Borray?

"Someone up on the mezzanine must be practicing Incendiary Magic! Maybe it's the green-eyed Maiden!"

Explain yourself.

"GraySuits, three of them, they just fell from the balcony. They... they were on fire." Borray gasped again, his face stricken. "The costumes, everything, it's all catching fire. My Mistress—?"

Turning back to the purple flame, he found it had vanished.

In the interior of the broad, lavish coach, Lady Mellich sat staunchly facing forward near the carriage door window. Across from her sat six of her girls, with two more far to her right, at the window opposite.

Bump.

The coach lurched. Murmurs and annoyed glances were exchanged among the woman's entourage. Another lurch.

"Oh, come now, really…" said the Lady Mellich, to herself. Extending the stick of her eyemask, she tapped on a small glass partition between her and the driver. "Darsgood? Darsgood, can you please be more accommodating when attempting to maneuver this carriage? For that, I'll thank you in advance."

Another unexpected pitch took place followed by angry mutterings and miffed expressions.

The woman's stick again went to the partition. Tap, tap! "Darsgood, please!"

The glass finally slid open, the driver struggling to navigate the road while periodically glancing through the opening. "Milady, you have my humblest apologies. However, a swarm of these large birds insists on attacking the beasts, causing us to swerve severely. Elbrost has fallen from the back of the coach, Milady. But we daren't stop to retrieve the poor man."

"Oh, dear. I'll thank you to carry on with due haste then, Darsgood. Send someone for Elbrost later."

"Yes, Milady."

The window shot back into place.

"How dreadfully annoying," puffed Lady Mellich. "Birds? Wait till the game warden hears about this."

Up on the mezzanine, in the thick of the fight, a middle-aged man, practiced in the Art of Incendiary Magic, had set some of the GraySuits ablaze, causing them to blindly fall or be thrown from the balcony. It wasn't long, however, before the magician was wounded, brought to his knees by a well-pitched RazorSlicer embedded in his back. He attempted to regain his footing, but was stomped face first to the ground where he lost consciousness, the life slowly bleeding out of him.

Meanwhile, Mistraya's elite, at one time on the defensive, had rallied to turn the battle in their favor. Their focus now was on subduing what remained of the uprising and then turning their efforts to locating the Maiden Portent. As the wounded and dying were carried down from the mezzanine, they passed through inspection points at the base of the stairways. There, fearing a costume change, the gray troopers were thorough in their examination of all young girls approximately Heather and Molly's age.

On the lower floor of the emporium, the fire continued to slowly spread, smoke billowing up to the ceiling, where it floated to the rear of the mezzanine. Some of the employees, assisted by patrons, were desperately pulling hoses loose from under the staircases and pouring water on the heated blaze, inhibiting its advance. Having panicked, shoppers had stampeded the front doors, temporarily overwhelming the GraySuits stationed there. A few were able to get out and sound the alarm—though no Autumnslovian soldiers or firefighters would ever arrive. Medical assistance did, however, as Mistraya's elite force permitted doctors to enter and take away the injured and dead civilians piled near the front doors. Despite the fierce and continuous fighting, a thorough inspection of the lower floor had been accomplished, and with his forces in control of the battle there, Soldier Two was able to redirect a great many of his troopers. After all, the GraySuits assumed they knew where the real prize was. She was awaiting them upstairs, hidden somewhere on the mezzanine.

Borray watched as the battle for The Crown & Scepter progressed. Bursting from behind the dressing room door, running an aisle over and tumbling into a rack of clothes, crouching behind a display of masks, the RogueTag gradually navigated toward the back of the store.

While the fire seemed to be under control and almost out, racks of charred costumes were left smoldering and sodden. Smoke lingered beneath the mezzanine, clouding the vision of the GraySuits still occupying the lower floor. Borray found this fortunate haze working to his advantage, helping to obscure his rearward advance, while he negotiated over and around the prostrate bodies of troopers, customers, and store attendants.

Borray tried not to think of the civilian casualties as dead. Instead, he thought of them as *removed for a reason*. This is the way it had to be if HumanKind was going to displace the Maidenhood, he figured. Those loyal to the Maidens and the Archannitian Decree must be put to rest, set aside, creating room for those who think anew and embrace the awakening. Everyone must realize that the future is for the rule of HumanKind. Not Maidens.

Speaking of which, thought the RogueTag, the Maiden Portent must be found. And eliminated, removed for a reason. And I know just where she's going to be. Instinct.

Amid the chaos and fighting, Borray had forgotten to take out his knife. He didn't really know why. The thought just hadn't occurred to him. But now, after dragging aside the dead GraySuits that had apparently been guarding the entrance to the storage and delivery room, and once inside having closed the heavy double doors behind him, he pulled the weapon from his pocket. He felt the shape so foreign in his hand, felt its light but deadly weight. However, he didn't want to open it, release the blade from its secure housing and bring it into plain view. Not yet.

I'm sure it's sharp, he thought, even though I've never used it. When I see the Maiden, though, *that's* when I'll open it. And that's when I'll kill her and her friend. AlienDregs.

Whomp!

Borray recoiled when someone slammed forcefully into the opposite side of the doors behind him. He dove to his belly, the small pocketknife spinning loose across the slick floor. All arms and legs, the RogueTag awkwardly scrambled to retrieve his weapon. Upon seizing it, he swiftly pried out the blade and then climbed to his feet. There Borray stood, gawkily leveling the undersized blade before him, a tiny protrusion poking out from the ball of his large hand. Carefully, haltingly, he approached the double doors. When Borray drew close he lunged, shoving his shoulder against the metal and hurriedly locking the knob. There.

Borray slumped against the door, breathing heavily, his face sweaty. He thought he could hear the combatants still fighting on the other side, but it mattered little. He was safe now. No one was going to get to him through these sturdy doors.

Soon, I'll unlock it, he told himself. But first: the RogueTag swiped the knife before him, slicing air. He jabbed and parried.

I can do it. I can. Bring on that skurd of a Maiden. And watch me kill that little 'Dreg for the good of all HumanKind.

Peering around the dressing room door, through a haze that hugged the ceiling high overhead, Heather noticed that most people had swarmed toward the front of the mezzanine, engaging Mistraya's troopers, leaving behind few stragglers. The girl grimly observed the fighting as it fiercely continued, with Autumnslovians making use of weapons taken from dead or wounded troopers. At the moment, there wasn't a soul in the vicinity of their dim corner, by the mannequin that had toppled to the floor. Whiffing the air, she looked up at the ceiling.

What's with the smoke? Is the building on fire? Oh, yeah, great. What next? A meteor through the roof? Heather coughed and waved a hand in front of her face. We really do have to get out of here. But how? Where can we go?

Heather withdrew.

Her mask and hat on the bench, Heather remained next to the dressing room door, where she could cautiously look out on occasion and take stock of all that was occurring nearby. Thinking that she and Molly were safe for the time being, Heather kneeled to inspect her painful, swollen ankle. At the gentle prod of her finger, she winced. Not good.

Neither of the girls had spoken since racing to sequester themselves in the dressing room. Rather, for the longest time, they simply stood and listened, Heather lost in thought. When glancing at the place where she had piled her old costume, she frowned, but a sudden racket close at hand kept her attention fixed on the door, holding her question for Molly in check.

The pair could hear the fighting as it raged, ebbing and flowing towards them with periodic entanglements between adversaries. Once, when the conflict had become ferocious directly outside, someone had slammed into one of the nearby dressing rooms with a bang. The walls around them shuddered. They listened to the struggle, the grunts and anguished cries. Heather felt it necessary to square up to the closed door, preparing for an intruder. When they heard someone race away, against Molly's wishes, Heather slid her head out to assess the danger. What she saw was a dead GraySuit on her back, the woman's mask ripped from her face, her throat slit. Lying motionless over the body was a young girl, not much older than Heather or Molly, a RazorSlicer buried to the hilt at the base of her skull. Tempted to retrieve the weapon, Heather decided against it, worried about its gruesome impact on Molly. She pulled the door closer, narrowing the view out the opening.

Looking through the haze, Heather was aware the smoke had thickened.

Withdrawing, she told Molly that everything was still kinda safe, and that it looked like most of the fighting had moved away for now and toward the front of the store. A short time later, when there was more tussling directly outside, the clown girl moved closer to her friend, with Heather positioning herself between Molly and the door. Still, no one bothered the girls.

"Molly, we—"

"Heather," Molly interrupted in an undertone, holding up her hand, "what happened out there? All those people yelling 'Hail the green-eyed Maiden.' What did you do?"

"Are you sure you want to know?"

Molly nodded.

Heather bitterly half-laughed. "Sure?"

"Is it funny?"

"No."

"I heard people screaming."

"They were. Molly, we have to find a way out of here." Heather went quiet as someone ran by yelling in rage. The cry faded, and was followed by a distant thud and crash. The girl continued: "We do, we need to get back home."

"Heather, you're changing the subject—"

"Did you get the PortalKey?"

"Yes, it was right there—" Handing the key to Heather with one hand, Molly pointed to the papered wall, where the brighter red markings were no longer visible, "—hanging on a pin. Fallasha, the costumes, hangers—everything else—they were gone."

Heather was concerned. "I was wondering about that. Who do you think took Fallasha?"

"I don't know."

"Did you ask if an attendant—?"

"Heather, no one came in here after you left. Not a soul. The attendant said so—at least she didn't see anyone."

"Molly, someone must have come in here. Fallasha didn't just walk off…"

Molly saw sadness fill her friend's face.

"I meant to say, 'Fallasha and the costumes just didn't walk off by themselves.'"

"It was too weird, Heather. When I got here, the door was locked. I'm sure of it. So, I went to fetch an attendant, and when we got back, the door was *un*locked. I didn't go far to get her, so if anyone had gone in or come out I would have noticed them."

Heather opened the door a crack and took a careful look outside, before withdrawing. "Really?"

"Yes, but the door wasn't only unlocked, it was ajar, like someone was waiting for me to return. When I came in here, Heather, the lights were out completely. I couldn't find a switch." Molly briefly scanned the walls around her and still didn't see one. "And then someone shut the door behind me and left me totally in the dark."

"Wow."

"Well, that's not all. Then the lights came on and slowly got brighter."

"No way."

"Way. And the PortalKey? It was on the wall there, like I said, but it had been circled in red with an arrow pointing to it."

"No way."

"Way."

"So, where is it?"

"The PortalKey? I just gave—"

"No, the circle and arrow."

Molly shrugged. "I guess it finally disappeared. It started to fade right before I left to come find you."

"Wow."

"Yes. And when I went to leave, the door had been locked from the outside—it has a keyhole, in case you hadn't noticed—I checked. Anyway, I had to pound on the door until an attendant finally heard me, and then he used his key to let me out. And that's one reason I took so long—."

Heather held up her hand, placing a cautionary finger to her lips. Her ear to the louvers, she waited, then cracked the door and poked her head out. This time, it was a while before she retreated, quietly closing the door.

"Molly, listen... Do you hear that?"

Molly started to shake her head no, but then froze. She whispered, "Yes. Yes, I do." The girl swallowed. "It's gone quiet, is that what you mean?"

"Yeah."

Heather stuck her head out again and moments later pulled it back inside.

"Molly, we have to think up a plan to get out of here, as quick as we can."

"Heather, will you please tell me what's going on out there?"

"Okay." Pause. "Molly, we might be trapped in here—in this dressing room. Now, are you sure you want to know what's been going on?"

Unsure, Molly nodded.

"Remember those two creepy clown people that were after us, the ones that fell through that trap door?"

"Yes."

"While you were back here in the dressing room, I counted—well, let's just say I counted a *lot* of those same kinds of people—it was their shines—coming into The Crown & Scepter. They were all wearing gray masks and uniforms. Some blocked off the stairs and wouldn't let anyone up or down. Then they started stopping all the girls our age and making them take off their masks. And on the floor below us, the same thing happened. There were creeps everywhere, pushing everyone around, beating people up, and tearing off girls' masks, too."

"So, Mistraya is looking for us, for sure? No doubt about it?"

"Yeah," said Heather, "no doubt about it. So now it looks like there are creepy people on both stairways, on the floor below, and at the three front doors."

"So, what's happening up here on the mezzanine?"

"I just checked. There aren't any shoppers and there aren't any of the store's helpers."

Molly brightened. "So there's no one up here?"

"Oh, there're people up here, Molly."

"Who?"

"A bunch of creepy people."

⁓

"Milady, we can't keep this up much longer," Darsgood said through the open pane. "The orranteens are getting spooked."

The highborn Lady Mellich felt the coach swerve unsteadily before righting itself. "What *is* going on here?" She pulled back the drapes and looked out the side of the coach. The woman was surprised to see large black birds overhead, circling the carriage and flying sporadically alongside. She tapped again on the glass with her stick. "Are these the same birds that we saw outside The Crown & Scepter?"

"I believe they are, yes. In lower social circles, Milady, they're well-known as Mistraya's scouts."

"Are they? Well, humph. And what do Mistraya's scouts want with us? Should they not be pestering the little people?" The woman took to straightening out the folds of the puffy dress that crossed her lap. When the coach suddenly reeled, the girls in the entourage screamed. Darsgood was temporarily lost at the partition glass, trying to control the orranteens that pulled the carriage. Then he was back.

"I'm sorry, Milady. The beasts are running into each other in confusion when the birds dive at their heads."

The scouts were now plunging at the windows, scraping at them with their claws. The girls were again panicked, screaming.

"Ladies," said the woman to the eight girls, "stop that screeching this *instant!* It's most unbecoming, not to mention undignified." She exhaled sharply. "Darsgood. What *shall* we do?" The woman's lips met heavily, her jowls wobbling.

"I'm not sure, Milady. It could be dangerous if we were to stop."

Suddenly the carriage was up on its three left wheels. An instant later it came down heavily with a jolt, pitching to and fro before finally smoothing out its ride.

Amid the cries of the girls, Lady Mellich shouted, "Pull over!"

"No! No!" shrieked the young ladies, as yet another scout showed its underbelly to the window in a fly-by, its shadow briefly darkening the compartment.

"Hush!" Lady Mellich said, closing the drape. "Darsgood, pull this coach over. Immediately."

"But Milady, I don't think it's safe!"

"Well, it's certainly not safe to continue, now is it? Pull over. Go on. Do as I say."

The coach began to slow before finally drawing to the side of the road.

At the right side window, one of the girls began to part the drapes.

"Don't!" exclaimed another, and so the first promptly pulled her hands away, as if the curtains were electrified.

"What are the birds doing now?" inquired the woman of the small sliding partition in front of her.

"They've backed off and are circling, Milady."

"Are they bothering you or the beasts?"

"No, Ma'am."

"Good. Then we'll wait here until they tire and fly off."

Lying on his side, the practitioner of the Incendiary Magic opened his clouded eyes slowly, if but a little. As they focused somewhat, Raestoff LarTarstil remembered that he was up on the mezzanine, and that he had been wounded in the uprising. The pain Raestoff felt was immense. Feigning death, the magician watched through nearly closed lids as assassins hauled out the dead and wounded. The men, women, and children were thrown over their shoulders or dragged by an ankle or wrist. Masks had been torn off the girls, their faces unmoving, lifeless—smooth-skinned, innocent of years.

He thought, By now, the mezzanine must have been cleared of captured Autumnslovians—if the GraySuits left any alive. Hopefully, the fire and smoke have allowed the young Maiden, and others, to escape the building unharmed. At the very least, it may have afforded some the opportunity.

Raestoff knew when he began the diversion that the fire from the flaming troopers would quickly be brought under control by his people. Members of the ClearWeave had a way of knowing such things—and a lot more. He also knew that it wouldn't be long until Mistraya's troopers found him to be alive. When that happened, they would undoubtedly administer to him, if only for purposes of interrogation. Incendiary Magic had been banned in Evermore and only a few were still knowledgeable and practiced in the ancient art form. Mistraya's people would want to learn the secretive whereabouts of the Scribal Parchments of InferNotions. Raestoff couldn't let that happen. The magician knew he was too weak to fight, but he needed to make certain that they killed him before any interrogation could begin.

But how?

Pain racking him, the man fought to retain consciousness.

The uprising has been lost, he assumed. And the young Maiden? Has she yet to escape the premises?

Raestoff LarTarstil recalled the sight of the valiant girl, their Astille Lia Staleen DiYoh, and how she had come racing out of nowhere to deliver a telling blow that sent the GraySuit leader hurtling to his death—and a gruesome one at that.

She's the Maiden of the Portent, no doubt, thought Raestoff, and the hope of all Evermore. And certainly the girl is worth the life of this ClearWeave member and magician. And so now I must die. In the process, how do I take some of Mistraya's elite force with me?

Seeing two troopers top the stairs nearby, the magician began to lyricy, softly speaking words of incantation.

He felt a heavy kick to his thigh, but didn't allow it to interrupt his phrasing.

"I think this one's alive," said the voice from above. "He's mumbling."

"What's he saying? Anything we need to know?"

The trooper squatted and angled his head near. "Might be information on the Maiden. Hard to tell."

Raestoff saw the gray mask spattered with red blood that hovered before his partially closed lids. Still he muttered softly. He told himself to hurry and finish the spell, that he hadn't much time. Almost finished, almost there. Just a moment longer.

The GraySuit leaning in close screamed, "Incantation!" At the same time, he plunged his RazorSlicer deep into the magician's throat. But he was too late, as the final words had found air.

Instantly, fire erupted over the GraySuit's body before leaping onto the plush carpet and attacking his comrade. Then the flames surged along a fiery route, slicing jaggedly towards both stairways. For the time being, the magical blaze kept a distance from the racks of costumes on the mezzanine, but seemed to seek out targets. Amid shouts, fire sprang onto troopers topping the mezzanine landing and those beginning their descent. Ablaze, the GraySuits fell and rolled, but could not quell the flames that consumed them. Their measures only caused the carpets to ignite and sent two or three burning bodies tumbling down the stairs, their shrieks piercing the air.

Of the two GraySuits who had been standing near the magician, the first—a reeling torch—went screaming along the edge of the loft. On the lower level, Mistraya's troopers looked up to see their brilliantly lit comrade attempt to leap from the balcony. He slammed into the railing, and, rebounding, staggered blindly before crumpling to the floor in a flaming heap. The second GraySuit, in an effort to smother his own flames, dropped to the floor. There he rolled and rolled, but only till he rolled no longer, the fire feasting on his inert body.

But such was not the case with the practitioner of Incendiary Magic. Although confining itself to the front part of the mezzanine, the blaze didn't touch the body of Raestoff LarTarstil, its dead creator. Rather, crackling and hissing around the perimeter of the prone figure, it chose to keep a reverent distance, as if protecting its master. As for spreading to the rest of The Crown & Scepter, the fire bided its time.

"And you've checked everywhere?" Mistraya asked.

Bayliss didn't respond immediately, as if the question had to penetrate many layers of consciousness before it reached her answer center. The girl finally said, "No. I don't suppose I've checked *everywhere*."

The sorceress smiled, a patient patronizing smile. "Everywhere here in the Harness Room?"

The girl's attention was diverted to the great lizard, Maif, who was entering the castle's stable.

"Bayliss, I'm speaking to you."

The impassive youngster turned back to Mistraya.

Her composure intact, the sorceress said, "Bayliss, where haven't you checked in the Harness Room?"

A long pause. Finally, "I don't know."

Mistraya held out her hand, palm up. To the purple flame that materialized, she said, "Joffin?"

The StableMaster's face appeared. "My Mistress?"

"Gather six StableHires and bring them to the Harness Room immediately."

"Is there something wrong, My Mistress?"

"Yes. Something has gone missing," and here Mistraya turned to the girl, "and something has yet to."

Painstakingly slow at pulling it closed, Heather stepped back from the slatted door, her words low, "They're searching all the dressing rooms, Molly, coming our way."

Heather stood with her weight on her right leg, favoring the turned ankle of her left.

All at once, cries filled the air, the troopers having discovered several patrons hiding inside a nearby dressing room.

Molly trembled. "What do you think they're doing to them, to the people they find hiding?"

Heather looked at her gravely. "Hurting them."

Molly waited for more.

Heather thought of the girl with the RazorSlicer buried in her neck. "That's all you need to know."

The two stood idly, intermittently making eye contact, listening to moans of agony and terrorized voices that pled for their lives or those of their loved ones. Moments later, the voices ceased.

"They're getting close, aren't they?"

Heather nodded. "Here's what we're going to do. Molly, as soon as one of those creeps tries to open that door, I'm going to shove it back at them as hard as I can. And then I'm going to run past—I might have to jump on them first, I'm not sure. If they think I'm their green-eyed Maiden, they're going to chase after me."

"But Heather, your ankle. You're hurt."

She waved Molly off. "I'm going to distract them from you, whatever way I think is best."

"But Heather—"

"*That's,*" the blond girl said, overriding her friend's protest, "when you're going to go run and hide in the clothes racks—no matter what you see out there, Molly, just keep running—just run and hide somewhere until you have a chance to make it down the stairs. Anyway, once you're outside, get on a trolley."

"Are you sure, Heather?"

"Yeah. There's no other way. I couldn't get a good look, but there must be a fire somewhere, because smoke is starting to fill the mezzanine up here. That'll help you make it outside without getting noticed. But we need to hurry."

"I'll fight with you, all right? Let me fight. You're my friend, remember? We'll fight together."

"Molly, you're not going to fight. You're going to get home safely. Here. Here's the PortalKey."

Molly reached out her accepting hand, her voice softly breaking, "Do I have to?"

Outside and closer yet, more shouts and cries could be heard.

"Yeah."

Tears forming, Molly said, "First Fallasha, now you. I wish I knew what had been in that other red circle with the arrow. It might have been something that could have helped us."

"What other circle? You didn't tell me there was another circle."

Lady Mellich stared straight ahead. The stalled coach was getting hot, and with the curtains drawn the girls became restless and started to squirm. Many were feverishly waving handkerchiefs, fanning themselves, and daubing their faces. Once again, the woman reached with her eyemask.

Tap, tap, tap! The coachman opened the window.

"Milady?"

"Darsgood, have the birds started to disperse yet?"

"No, Milady. I'm sorry to have to inform you that the opposite has occurred—more have arrived. They're circling above, going way up, and some just continue to fly by, like they're inspecting us. When they get close, if I can, I slap them away. My guess is that they're looking for something."

"Well, what can they possibly want with us, anyway?"

"I'm sorry, Milady, but I simply haven't a clue as to why they're behaving as they are."

"Well, I'm starting to bloom in here and I've half a notion to part these drapes and open this window!"

"It may not be safe, Milady. Currently, the birds don't seem to be bothering us. However, should we get underway again, I can't promise that will be the case."

"So for how long do you expect us to remain pulled over to the side of the road this way? We've a party to host, you know. A great many people are going to be in attendance this afternoon, and our presence is expected."

"I understand, Milady, and would love to get the orranteens moving again to accommodate your need for haste. However, should we attempt such a thing, we risk not only the welfare of the beasts at the hands of Mistraya's birds, but our own, as well. So it may behoove us to simply wait here for the moment."

"For how long, Darsgood, and for what? We have no idea why these birds of the sorceress insist on attacking the orranteens?"

"No, Milady, I'm sorry, I don't believe we do."

"Well, I'm not happy having to sit here in a hot coach with the windows and curtains closed, Darsgood, when our Parade Day Party is going to be taking place without us."

"Rest assured, I understand Milady's irritation."

"Rest assured, Darsgood, if we don't start for home soon, you will *more* than understand it."

Towards the rear of the mezzanine, the trooper coughed amid the smoke. She stood over the three people she had dragged from a dressing room. Assisted by her comrade, they had beaten and then sliced them to death—deservedly so, she felt. The enemy. At the thought, her PassionFlame glowed and released a toxin of glorious pain.

As the rush subsided, the female behind the gray mask noticed a trail of smeared blood leading from a dressing room and into the racks of clothing across the aisle.

"Who crawled out of here?" she wondered aloud. The Maiden? Her accomplice?

She unhinged the RazorSlicer from her belt, its curved, pronged blade springing to the ready, locking into place. On her guard, she followed the blood-soaked route. Nearing the rack, she reached out her free hand and began to carefully part the hangers of clothing that obstructed her view. Below, on the floor, she caught sight of a pair of ankles fitting into blood-smeared shoes.

That's no child. The enemy?

Still cautious, she peeled aside the clothing, until she revealed the recumbent body of Marscleff, badly beaten.

A RogueTag? she thought, taking note of his purple armband. A comrade in the fight. The woman looked him over and thought, With such a puny build, if he's fought, you can rest assured he hasn't done a lot of damage.

"Rogue." She kicked him lightly, one hand still holding the costumes aside. "Hey, Rogue." Hurriedly, she cleared away the garments that sequestered the young man, casting them to the floor. "A medic will be with you shortly." The GraySuit glanced away from the racks, hoping to spot the doctor through the thickening haze. She coughed again and turned to the motionless youth. "Do you hear me?" The woman prodded him.

Marscleff tried to speak through swollen lips of red ooze. Following a brief scan of the area, the trooper lowered herself to a knee. "What's that you're saying?"

Incoherently, the RogueTag burbled.

The woman said, "I can't understand you." She coughed once more.

Again scrutinizing her surroundings for possible ambush, she leaned her head closer.

"The last dressing room…" Marscleff managed.

The woman's gaze wandered to the dim corner. "What about it?"

"The green-eyed Maiden…"

The GraySuit took another look that way. She stood and with a gesture, attracted the attention of six nearby comrades. When Mistraya's trooper was sure they were watching, she pointed toward the closed louvered door of the corner dressing room. With smoke now heavier on the mezzanine and starting to settle, the seven warily moved in that direction. Other GraySuits, alerted with hand signals and now apprised of what was occurring, were soundlessly hustling over to take up key positions along the aisles, sealing off possible escape routes.

Meanwhile, curled up nearby, among the clothing scattered on the floor, Marscleff died a RogueTag.

Molly was walking towards the mirror, pointing. "I didn't think it was worth mentioning, Heather, because there was nothing inside of it. It was there, right in that corner."

"Here?" Heather asked. Leaning, she pressed against the glass with one hand for support while she reached above her with the other. As her open hand approached the mirror's corner, both she and Molly heard the thrum. Oddly, Heather felt the sensation of its presence, its nearness, in her mind. The symbol of the ClearWeave lit up on the reflective surface.

"The ClearWeave!" Heather whispered. "I think it's a ClearWeave door. I can't reach high enough, though, so I can't get my hand over that symbol to open it."

"That's it, Heather! A door!"

"Sh-h-h."

"Sorry." Molly gave a worried look toward the dressing room door. She noticed a smoky haze was filtering through the louvers, and joined Heather in lowering her voice to a conspiratorial whisper. "It must be, Heather, because that explains how our clothes disappeared and why Fallasha wasn't here when I came looking for the key. Geez. That's a relief."

"What's that?"

"Fallasha. She's safe. The ClearWeave have her."

"No. I mean what's that noise?" Heather was staring at the louvered door. "I thought I heard someone cough."

"I didn't hear anything…"

Without another word, her movements rushed, Heather returned her attention to the uppermost corner of the mirror. Extending herself again, she stood on her very tiptoes, her face in pain. She lifted her nagging left foot, balancing on the right. Again, the image above her hummed and the icon lit up, but the girl fell short of reaching it. Bending at the knees, Heather tried to jump, but with her injured ankle, she found it difficult to get far off the ground. Upon landing, she grimaced.

"Molly, I can't reach it." She turned to face her friend helplessly.

"Can I?"

"No, Molly, probably not. I'm taller and can jump higher, even with my bad ankle."

"So, what now?"

Heather stood looking at the louvered door. Molly followed her gaze. "What, Heather?"

From outside came another smoke-induced cough, its sound partially suppressed by a sleeve.

"Quick!" Heather whispered. "Get down."

"What?"

Heather pushed Molly to the floor.

A moment later, the knob on the door began to turn ever so slowly, ever so quietly.

As the search for the Maiden pressed on throughout the mezzanine, the GraySuits had sprayed torrents of water onto Raestoff's magically ignited blaze that now stretched the length of the balcony and spilled onto the stairways. And though they hadn't been able to douse it, surprisingly, the fire refrained from spreading, as if it had a mind not to do so.

Heated smoke continued to rise up and press itself against the ceiling, until at last it condensed in a huge violet cloud that emitted minute orange sparks. From the periphery of the blaze, pencil-thin rivulets of flame sped off, snaking along the carpeted floor toward the back of the building. Dividing and intersecting to create more rivulets, they quickly sliced down aisles, pivoted sharply between racks, flowed into dressing rooms, and angled around mannequins. With a mind of their own, the flaming veins hastened their way throughout the mezzanine in strips of molten, yellow-orange, much to the fright and amazement of the GraySuits. Helplessly they watched as the hot streaks zipped around and between their legs and shot up the walls to ignite the ceiling.

Outside of Heather and Molly's dressing room, the eyes of the six GraySuits burned and watered with the accumulation of smoke. Dizzy and wanting to hack, yet fearing that another cough could alert the Maiden to their presence, one GraySuit silently backpedaled, his nose and mouth buried in the crook of his arm. Although unsure of what wizardry to expect, Mistraya's remaining troopers stood armed and eager to charge, while the female GraySuit continued to slowly turn the knob of the door. When it rotated no more, she looked back at her companions. All ready. With a pull, the woman burst through the door, followed closely by the others.

The dressing room was empty.

"Stupid Rogue!" she said with a growl.

"Wait!" said a second GraySuit. "There. On the bench. It's the Maiden's mask and hat."

The woman looked around the room. "Well, then, where did they go? I don't think—what's that?"

All five watched as, curiously, thin trails of fire slipped through the doorway, running rapidly along the floor. Without hesitation, they divided into many more streams and quickly climbed the walls.

"What the—?"

"Run!"

At the fear-inspired word, flames leaped from the floor, ceiling, and walls, their ragged arms of scorching heat gathering Mistraya's elite in an everlasting embrace.

"I'm sorry, My Mistress," said the StableMaster. "I don't know how the Mastery°Harness could have been misplaced like that."

Mistraya's attention wandered to Bayliss, standing next to him. The girl looked back unflinchingly.

Joffin continued, "You know I always put it in its proper location when it's not being used."

"I don't care whose fault it is. See to it that it doesn't happen again. It could cost you more than your job. I don't just conjure up Vigen°Darr °Harnesses out of thin air."

"Yes, My Mistress," the man said with a penitent bow.

Mistraya said, "I'm ready."

The StableMaster turned. "The doors!" He joined Bayliss who had stepped away.

Four StableHires pushed open the wide doors. At the intrusion of daylight, the many night creatures pushed farther into their stalls.

When the sorceress climbed onto her seat within the pilot compartment atop the great lizard, the beast unfurled its considerable wings, and with the first thrust propelled itself airborne, while the third took it out of the doors, and by the seventh it had soared over the Great Fanged Cliffs, gaining altitude.

Steering via the magical harness from within the tall vertical quarters, Mistraya guided the winged lizard towards Elderraine and The Crown & Scepter Costume Emporium.

Heather and Molly were running down a meagerly lit corridor, with just enough illumination to reveal their way. Molly kept pace right behind her hobbling friend. Through the wall, they could hear the crackling and popping of the fire that rampaged through the mezzanine.

Heather slowed and Molly followed suit. They stopped beneath one of the sconces, a haze of smoke visible in the scant light. There, Heather looked her friend over. The sounds of LampOrbs bursting and a mirror shattering caused the girls to look at the pokerfaced wall, wondering what scenes were playing out on the other side. The temperature in the hall was rising.

Heather turned back to her friend. "Molly, are you okay?"

Out on the mezzanine floor, more 'Orbs could be heard popping along with the crashing of debris that was falling from the ceiling.

When Molly didn't respond, Heather grasped her friend firmly but gently by the shoulders, saying earnestly, her voice low, "It's going to be all right. Okay? We're going to get home safely." When Molly simply continued to stare, Heather added, "We were able to get out of the dressing room just now, weren't we?"

Molly nodded.

"Now there's only a little way left to go. We can do it."

Molly nodded again. She managed a frail smile, keeping her tears in check. "I know."

"Good." Heather, calling up a small smile of her own, squeezed once reassuringly and then dropped her hands. "Now come on, we need to get out of this building."

"Heather, your mask and hat…"

"Yeah, I know. I didn't have time to grab them when I heard those creeps outside the door."

"But you'll be easier to spot without them."

"I know. Doesn't matter. We'll just have to keep going, Molly. We don't have a choice."

Molly went quiet for a moment. Expectantly, Heather waited.

"You know—"

Behind the wall, startled cries were heard as timbers cracked and fell.

"What?"

"That was quick thinking—"

Screams.

Heather shook her head uncomprehendingly, while wishing Molly would hurry.

"—back there in the dressing room, having me get on my hands and knees like a stepping stool."

"Yeah, well, I wasn't close enough to the bench to stand on it and touch the mirror. And being the tallest, I thought it was probably best that I was the one to reach up. I hope you don't mind."

"I don't mind." Molly shot a worried look over her shoulder, at the corridor behind them. "I just hope they don't find that mirror-door."

"They won't find the door unless they're ClearWeave. And the Clear-Weave is on our side."

"Where do you think this hallway is going to lead?"

"We'll know soon enough. It looks like those stairs up ahead will take us down somewhere to the back of The Crown & Scepter." After hearing more screams amid the fire's crackle, Heather added at a rush, "Now, let's get out of here."

I wonder how Marscleff is doing?

Borray's thoughts skipped like stones before sinking, one after the next. Feeling alone, isolated, he tried to stay emotionally afloat, latching onto any positive spark, if only for an instant. If the content or direction of the thought started to bring him down, he quickly sought a fresh one. But all of them, they just kept sinking. Down.

Is he still up on the mezzanine? Or was that him pounding on the doors? He pushed the thought of Marscleff away. There were just too many possibilities, and few of them good.

Dejected, head hanging, the RogueTag was standing in the storage and delivery bay. Earlier, thinking it easier and safer to hide in the dark, he had located the NonCraft Control to extinguish the overhead lights, leaving only a few along the wall to burn with a stingy glow. He never did return to unlock the wide metal doors. The reason? Because when people inside the store found that the doors wouldn't open, after a time they began to beat on them. Frantically. It frightened the RogueTag. He turned and looked at the doors now. They stood starkly quiet, cold and secure, two solemn barriers between the RogueTag and the unspeakable things on the other side, some of which he wished he hadn't seen.

Were the people pounding and kicking on other side running from something, trying to escape? Mistraya's GraySuits? The Maiden girl? Who was on the other side of that door? And what happened to them?

Borray didn't know and didn't want to find out. He looked down at the small knife clutched in his hand, the hard metal sliding in the moistness of his palm.

He wondered, Would I really be able to kill the girl? If she were standing right here, right in front of me, would I stick this knife in her heart?

Isolated in the gloom, the longer he waited for the Maiden, the more Borray had his doubts. He shook himself.

What has gotten into me? he asked, suddenly bringing himself to stand at his full height. What am I doing? Look at me! I'm becoming a three-sided morkel! Come on! I can do this! I can. I'll kill her, I'll kill the green-eyed Maiden of the Evermore Portent. And I'll do it for all HumanKind!

The RogueTag ferociously swiped the air. Then he settled and considered the blade he held in his hand, twisting it this way and that.

Across the room, a knob rattled somewhere in the shadows. Borray heard a door open.

The fabric that draped the ceiling of The Crown & Scepter had long since burst into flame, and with fires burning and blocking the stairwells, dozens of GraySuits on the mezzanine were trapped. Some began frantically knotting costumes together into ropes to drop from the balcony railing—if they could ever get near it—while others continued to man the mezzanine hoses until they began to stumble and drop, rendered unconscious from the smoke. Still others toward the back of the mezzanine were burned alive, the smoke and heat pressing down from above, searing their lungs and charring their skin. When the thin lines of flame that had previously run routes throughout the upper floor spontaneously erupted, the once patient fire grew defiantly out of control.

From the mezzanine, the fire had spread blazing lines down to the lower floor, bursting into widespread flame before the three front doors, preventing exit. From there a multitude of glowing rivulets sped toward the back of the emporium at an alarming rate. The remaining troopers were caught off guard and surrounded by a fire out of nowhere. It wasn't long before the entire Crown and Scepter erupted into a ravenous inferno, feasting on its contents, while gnawing through the supporting beams of the ceiling and the bowstring roof.

Upon hearing the door open, Borray had slinked farther into the darkness, near a line of sewing machines. He hid behind some racks of costumes that extended along one wall in rows three deep. More clothes were folded and piled on shelves behind him, while masks were propped, stacked, and strewn everywhere.

The RogueTag gripped his knife. How small it felt in his hand! He hunkered down and waited.

Somewhere before him, he heard steps, a quiet shuffling within the quiet room. Borray watched as the massive delivery door slid open along its smooth track, and he squinted at the sudden sliver of light. In it, two youthful silhouettes squeezed through, their slender bodies framed against the final hours of daylight.

CHAPTER THIRTY

Borray Makes a New Friend

"**S**unshine!" Molly whispered, as soon as the girls reached the Avenue sidewalk, out of range of the large delivery door. They walked quickly past the spectators that gathered to watch the fire at The Crown & Scepter, heavy smoke pouring from the windows.

"Yeah, it's good to see, but look how late it is, Molly. Grandma Dawn—and your mother, too—are going to be worried. *And* probably mad. I'm sure they're wondering what's happened to us."

Heather, feeling exposed and thus likely to be recognized without her mask, was checking out auras of those in the vicinity. She also checked the sky in a quick onceover. Satisfied that she and Molly were safe for the time being, the girl turned her attention to the stretch of Parade Day Avenue. It was still bustling in the late afternoon, people perusing the shops, watching performances along the route, all slipping in and out of the long shadows that stretched across the worn cobblestones. Many gawkers had stopped, drawn to the blaze at the costume shop. Others proceeded past the growing knots of onlookers, while avoiding the occasional coach or beast.

"Not good."

"What, Heather?"

"I don't see any trolleys." The girl scanned the area to their left, a strip of green that was situated behind the sidewalk and between buildings. "Come on. We can hide in that small park over there until we see one coming. There're bushes and trees, and it's right on the big Avenue."

The pair picked up their pace, Heather favoring her hurt ankle if only slightly, not troubling to turn when they heard the crashing of timbers from within the costume emporium.

"You know, Heather, I just thought of something."

"What's that, Molly?"

"It's getting late. What if the trolleys are no longer running here in Autumnsloe?"

"It *is* the 'Dregs, and they're heading towards that little park. I knew it! I did! And look, the supposed Maiden, she's not even wearing a mask."

Borray retreated from the slice of rectangle that comprised the door's opening. He had an idea. Running over to the racks of clothing, he started swiping through the costumes, looking for one that might loosely fit him. Swish, swish, swish. Borray halted. He disentangled a hanger, pulling a costume free from the rack. Briefly, he held it up. Wrinkled, it possessed a slight odor from having been worn and returned.

It'll do.

Around him, the RogueTag smelled smoke and heard the muted impact of falling wreckage, but in his haste paid little heed. He thought he heard a weak pounding at the double doors leading to the main floor. No time. Grabbing the trousers, he quickly threaded his legs through the waist and out the ankles. Borray pulled on the baggy shirt and then buttoned the cloak around his neck. Since there wasn't a mask attached to the hanger, he snatched one off a shelf in the dark and put it on. Like the used outfit he now wore, it too smelled, but covered the RogueTag's face sufficiently and comfortably.

Borray raced back over to the delivery door for another look.

No! It can't be! The 'Dregs have disappeared!

The RogueTag was crestfallen. Then he spied the pair rushing for a trolley.

With a push and slide of the heavy door to better accommodate his exit, the young man hurriedly pressed through the opening. The people on the sidewalk stared as he passed, but Borray's focus was on the girls. He couldn't lose them. He just couldn't. He knew that the Universe was providing him with yet another opportunity to earn his PassionFlame.

Ding! Ding!

With Heather limping in the lead, she and Molly raced to catch up to the trolley that was slowly advancing up the Avenue. Upon reaching the sleekly designed coach, the girls couldn't find an open spot between pas-

sengers that were hanging from the sides and stuffed tight in the doorways leading to a crammed inner compartment. Searching for a vacancy,
Heather lamely raced to the other side of the car, uncomfortably aware
that her face was visible for all to see. Much to her disappointment, she
found there were no places available.

"It's full, Molly," Heather said, returning to her friend.

"What now? Can we please just get home?"

"Come on, let's walk."

Seeing that Molly was upset, Heather took her elbow to offer reassurance, briefly walking beside her. Meanwhile she scanned the skies. "It's
weird, isn't it? Have you noticed how there're no scouts, Molly? Boy,
remember how they were flying all over the place before we went into
The Crown & Scepter?"

A series of prolonged, high-pitched sounds resonated in the distance.
Heather peered, a lingering look over her shoulder. "I wonder if those
are sirens."

"Do you think they have fire trucks here in Autumnsloe?"

"Could be. If they do, they're probably headed to The Crown &
Scepter."

Molly turned toward the smoking building, then quickly looked
away. She said nothing. The two walked on, gradually angling back toward the curb. No longer were there canvas overhangs to hide the pair.

"I think you're right," Molly said. She paused before adding, "Maybe
they're only in the front of the shop."

"The fire trucks?"

"The scouts. Maybe they're only watching the three front doors."

"Maybe—" said Heather, speeding up to pass a tethered beast burdened with wares. She waited while the animal-intrigued Molly hurried to her side before continuing, "—but that doesn't seem right. Why
wouldn't they be circling and watching all the doors if they thought we
were inside?"

"I don't know," said Molly. "Maybe they thought the creepy people
had us trapped upstairs. Anyway, I'm just glad they're gone."

"Well, since you're in the mask, Molly, how about if you keep a lookout for the scouts in the sky? I'm going to keep my head down, just in
case they fly over and know what I look like."

"Heather, the way those people were shouting about the green-eyed
Maiden in The Crown & Scepter, probably everyone in *Evermore* knows
what you look like by now."

Flattered, Molly's words brought a smile to Heather's lips. "I sure
hope you're wrong."

Following the girls, Borray was thrilled when they were unable to find a place on the trolley. It made his task easier. Although the two maintained a good pace, the RogueTag's was better, his strides lengthier and coming more swiftly. With his attention solely on the girls, he was only a short distance away and closing.

Ding! Ding!

"Heather, a trolley! Another trolley is coming! Get ready. It looks like there's room on this one."

The blond girl, her thick hair swinging at the shoulders, turned to see that Molly's observation was correct. Relief rushed through her as they broke into a half-run towards the middle of the street, Heather ignoring the pain in her ankle.

"You know, Molly, we don't have that far to go to reach the Portal-Door," the girl said at a breathy gallop.

"Heather, look! There's a group of RogueTags running towards the costume shop. Wait! On second thought, don't look! Keep your head down!"

"Molly, they're not going to recognize me from a block away, silly. Wow! Will you look at the smoke pouring out of The Crown & Scepter now?"

The girls slowed at the trolley's approach.

"Heather, why do you think it's taking so long for people to come and put out the fire?"

"Maybe Mistraya controls them like she controls the Autumnslovian soldiers and doesn't want them to come. Maybe..."

"What? Maybe, *what?*"

Heather shot Molly a look. "Maybe she figures we're still inside, and she doesn't want us to get out."

"You mean she doesn't want the green-eyed Maiden to get out."

Heather cringed at the reference. "Yeah."

"But if the firemen don't hurry and get there, the entire costume shop and everything in it are going to burn to the ground."

"Looks like it'll probably do that whether they get there or not."

Ding! Ding!

Sitting bolt upright inside the boxlike cockpit of flapping fabric, the wind having little impact on her hard-set features, Mistraya was gently rising and falling with the great lizard on which she rode. Maif's wings were outstretched, muscular and veiny, with only the occasional beating of the ends needed to remain aloft. The clumsy creature on land now majestically airborne, the reptile glided towards its destination.

There!

The sorceress saw the city of Elderreine in the distance, an array of geometric shapes spread over an expansive hill, alongside the immense Arrenian LakeSea. Mistraya squinted into the late afternoon light that glared off the water. Nearby, she saw the long plume of smoke that was drifting, dissipating above the city.

What is happening at The Crown & Scepter? fretted the sorceress, as troubled images and possibilities flashed through her mind. *I've not been able to contact Soldier One, any of his lieutenants, or even those of lesser rank. What has happened to my elite squad, my small private army? Are they alive?*

The Maiden child, could she be that powerful? Could she have annihilated my troopers, my army of formidable GraySuits that took so long to secretly amass and train?

Her blood boiled at the thought.

With an irritated pull on the magical harness, the sorceress corrected for a truer flight path to her destination. Urgently, she spurred on her lizard.

I need to find out what's happened.

Tap, tap, tap. "Darsgood?"

Fed up with the heat in the stifling coach, the Lady Mellich dabbed her brow with a frilly handkerchief, as the pane slid open across from her.

"Milady?"

"Darsgood, let us proceed on home, shall we? It's uncomfortably hot in here, and I fear that at any moment the girls are going to swoon."

"But surely, Milady—"

"See here, Darsgood. I will have no further discussion on the subject. Stir the beasts. There's a good man."

"But Milady, what if the birds should begin to attack?"

"Why, by all means keep on going, Darsgood. We must. We've a party awaiting."

At the rear of the trolley, Heather spotted two vacant poles alongside one another. Latching onto the one nearer the front of the vehicle, she pulled herself up and onto the running board, Molly doing likewise directly beside her. Heather then took another step up to stand on the edge of the trolley's floor, before an empty spot on the bench facing her. She received a curious glance for doing so from a passenger nearby, but Heather hoped that others might fill in behind, further preventing her from being spotted.

Feeling self-conscious without a mask, she looked away from the street, towards the trolley's sparsely occupied interior. While Heather was facing inward, looking through the open vehicle for suspicious auras on the street, Molly continued to be on the lookout for the presence of scouts overhead. Had the girl been able to identify advancing predators wearing costumes, she might have noticed the RogueTag now only steps away.

Having selected his mask in the dark, Borray didn't realize he had donned an Evermorian Funeral Mask, a glossy black facade barren of any decoration save one white teardrop below the left eye. By custom, ceremonial masks such as his were worn only on the sacred funeral grounds, never elsewhere, and were made available to all citizens at costume emporiums throughout the Realm, costume emporiums such as The Crown & Scepter.

Approaching the slow moving trolley, Borray increased his pace, the knife open and discreetly concealed in hand. Aboard the streetcar, the two girls hung as meaty targets for the determined RogueTag, their bodies easily available to a swipe or thrust, although Heather was situated higher off the street.

They're right there, thought an excited Borray, his pulse quickening, the tempo of his step increasing. *Right there.* Those sprees are *history!* Now I mustn't fail. Let's see, should I kill the Maiden first and then her friend? Yes, yes, that's what I'll do. But I must be quick. And I cannot miss. I don't dare. If I miss, and she really is the Maiden promised, then the 'Dreg'll kill me. Can't allow that to happen, now, can we?

Borray was excited. Within his mask, the RogueTag felt a grin coming on.

Oh, how happy am I? he thought. How happy! The young man couldn't remember the last time he had smiled and meant it. It had been so long! But I'm smiling now, he thought, placing the knife so that only its point was visible, though he still tried to conceal it.

Borray found it curious that the one who was supposed to be the Maiden Portent seemed reluctant to look around or behind her, apparently attracted to something inside the open interior of the trolley.

Perfect.

And her friend kept looking up toward the sky and at the rooftops that lined the Avenue.

Doubly perfect. The cosmic wheels are aligned and on my side. It's all going my way! This is it! The Universe wants me to succeed! It wants me to earn my PassionFlame! Finally! And why? Because It agrees with me that Evermore should be ruled by HumanKind!

Borray's face broke into a wide grin. Immediately, he fought to lose it, concentrating on the task at hand.

The RogueTag hurried to position himself alongside the trolley—it was moving at a leisurely glide now—as he walked below and behind the girls. Borray slid in closer, trying to appear nonchalant, his gaze darting nervously over the throng that milled on the Avenue around him.

Why are these people glaring at me? Can they tell I'm about to kill someone? Am I that obvious? I should be difficult to spot, blending into the crowd. So, why the looks?

Stop. Get ahold of yourself, an inner voice hissed.

Borray bit his lip.

Those people, they're not staring at me; they're afraid of me, that's what it is. Why? Because I'm a RogueTag, and I'm dangerous. They sense it. And I'm about to kill the green-eyed Maiden.

Gripping the knife tighter, he imagined himself suddenly turning, jumping, and stabbing upward at the girl.

Right-so, that's how I'll do it, he reckoned. I'll turn and jump. And then I'll stab her—agh! agh! agh! Three times—twice while she's falling off the trolley. Then when her girlfriend tries to run, I'll take care of her, too, and quick. Agh! Like that. Afterwards, I'll just walk away. No one would dare come after me, either. Why? The RogueTag smiled inwardly. Because I'm a killer.

Borray walked a little prouder—and faster, as he continued to keep pace with the trolley.

That's right. I'm a killer.

Borray suppressed an all out grin of satisfaction. Killers were humorless people, he surmised. So, they act serious, especially before the taking of a life. Or two.

Right-so, then. Be serious, he told himself. Here we go. Concentrate. Easy. Get ahold of yourself. Breathe.

Not daring to look fully in the Maiden's direction for fear of giving himself away, he saw the soft blur of her back and lower legs out of the corner of his eye. Borray took a deep breath. He squeezed the handle of his weapon. It seemed to swim loosely in his squishy fist. He closed his eyes, then opened them. They were clouded. The RogueTag blinked and blinked again. His vision still seemed blurry. More blinks.

This mask is hot, he thought. It was then that a voice from within hissed heatedly: *Will you just do it? Just do it! Do it now!*

No.

What?

No. I can't, Borray told himself. I'm-I'm way too low. I can't do much damage from here on the street with her standing above the running board like that. What's she doing way up there anyway? The girl should be lower, standing next to her friend. Stupid spree! Besides, with the trolley moving along like it is, I might miss. I'll need a much better angle.

A better angle?

Yes, a better angle, if I'm going to be sure and kill these two.

Borray thought he heard the voice inside of him sigh.

The trolley continued to roll, gaining more speed, the RogueTag quickening his pace to keep up.

Situated above Borray and the street, Heather's attention was fixed upon an Autumnslovian pickpocket working the Parade Day crowds, his aura aglow in unscrupulous blues and devious browns. As he hung off the post directly across from her, on the other side of the trolley, the girl was trying to determine what the man was doing, and if he posed any threat to her and Molly.

Borray took hold of a vacant pole and pulled himself up adjacent to Heather, his wet palm sliding on the slick metal. He couldn't believe his luck! He was standing right next to her, the Maiden Portent! And she seemed totally unaware of his presence, staring off in front of her. Blind man's plunder!

So, now what? the RogueTag asked, excitedly looking away.

Now what? came the whispered hiss. *You kill her, that's what! Just kill her!*

Again, he evaluated the feel of the knife in his hand. Borray squeezed it tight, feeling the hardness of its handle within his palm, its undeniable, no-nonsense weight. Firm-mouthed, he was breathing quickly through flared nostrils, unable to bring himself to look at the girl.

Has she noticed me? Is she looking at me, waiting for me to look at her? Is that it? Is the Maiden waiting for me to look at her, so she can kill me? She is, isn't she? The Maiden wants to look me in the eye when she kills me. I bet Maidens do that. They do. I just know it. Oh, Sacred Universe! What am I doing?

Stop! said the voice inside. *Just stop! You're almost hysterical.*

Am I? Borray looked down at his shaking hand and inconspicuous knife. I am. You're right.

So, stab her already. If you get any closer, she'll be wearing you.

Borray felt hot, his face moist. He was aware of sweat trickling down his shirt. He swallowed.

Right-so, here goes.

Another gulp.

Slowly, Borray's head pivoted toward the blonde girl beside him.

There she is! Great Gal*loops!*

The RogueTag looked away. Gathering himself, again he dared to slowly turn and face the profile of the Maiden. He continued to stare. The girl, she's so pretty, so young!

Borray looked down and away.

I can't do it.

What!

I can't. She's just a girl. What am I doing?

What are *you doing? Kill her!!! That's what you're doing!*

I can't.

I don't believe this.

Borray leaped off the trolley, his feet striking on cobblestone. He started to walk away, his head low. Inside, the young man felt the all too familiar fog descend once more, the cold yet burning ache of failure settling in to chafe away at his core.

What are you doing? he scolded himself. *What are you doing? Get back there! You can't just walk away like that.*

I can't?

No.

Why?

Because you're a RogueTag, that's why! You're a killer, remember? You've a job to do. Now, get back there. You must to keep your honor intact. You have honor, don't you?

I suppose.

You sup——? The voice inside groaned. *Then go back. Go after her. You have to kill that girl.*

But I can't. I just can't. She's not going to hurt anyone. She's only a girl. A girl, for Evermore's sake!

Yes, but that girl soundly defeated your three RogueTag companions.

Borray stopped. He brought a hand to his face and stood stationary for a moment. Then he wheeled.

You're right.

Of course, I'm right! Now go and kill her!

The RogueTag began to run, and when he was close enough to the trolley, he slowed to a brisk walk. Soon, Borray was once again behind the Maiden, knife at the ready. The young man edged closer and increased his stride.

As he reached for the vacant pole next to Heather, Borray's sweaty hand slipped and he let go. He stumbled and was thrown off stride. Detecting movement, Heather briefly looked to her left, only to find no one there. She turned away and continued her conversation with Molly. The two girls were discussing what Molly thought were scouts above the rooftops. Agreeing that the birds were too small and with Heather noting their nonthreatening auras, the conversation concluded, with Molly turning her attention to the sky once again.

Almost dropping the knife, as he sought to regain his balance, Borray found himself paces behind the trolley. Noting the approach of likely passengers, the young man accelerated in an effort to grab the desired pole, but was too late. An interloper took hold of it, swinging up easily as the car passed.

Raging at the Universe, Borray's brain screamed out, *Don't you do this to me! Not again! Don't you dare ruin my big chance! This is my moment! Do you hear? My moment! You owe it to me! It's mine!* Tears blurred his vision. *So, give me another chance. Please! And I won't fail. I promise.*

Borray was surprised when in front of him someone unexpectedly disembarked from the trolley.

The RogueTag glanced skyward. Thank you! he said to the Universe. You're still on my side, the side of HumanKind. And this time I won't fail you. I won't. *I can't!*

He hurried to close ground and make certain that no one else got to the unoccupied trolley post before he did. It stood there awaiting him, right next to Molly.

When Heather noticed a couple of people seated inside the trolley discreetly pointing and gesturing, at first she thought they had recognized her as the green-eyed Maiden. Yet, catching the words 'funeral mask,' and then realizing that they were looking beyond her, she couldn't resist the temptation to turn her head for a glimpse. In doing so, she noticed a threatening blue-violet aura interspersed with filthy grays. A creepy person? Heather watched as the stranger in a glossy black mask reached for a post and hauled himself up on the other side of her friend.

Quickly the RogueTag's knife came up from below at a backhand, headed for Molly's throat.

"Molly, look out!" Her shout lost to the cacophony of street noise, Heather's free hand shot forward and grabbed hold of Borray's wrist, stopping the knife mid-trajectory. As the RogueTag pushed, Heather shoved back with surprising strength, reaching down and across at an off-balance angle, the knife's blade inching towards Molly's throat, shaking along with the struggling RogueTag's hand. Swiftly, Molly reared back, leaning towards the street.

"Molly, jump off…I can't keep this knife…away from you…much longer…"

For a moment, Molly stood paralyzed, staring at the weapon held in trembling stalemate directly before her face. Suddenly, the girl threw her weight forward, and with her left hand, she seized Borray's wrist, and assisted Heather in pulling and wrapping his knife arm around her pole, the one she was holding. Then she hugged the upright tight, trapping the RogueTag's arm in place.

"Ow! You stupid little 'Dreg! That hurts. Let go of me!"

Now the RogueTag was struggling, attempting to wrest his arm loose from the girls' grip. That was when Molly, sensing Borray's arm slipping from their grasp, speared out with a finger and poked him as hard as she could in the eye. Recoiling in pain, Borray was finally able to yank his arm and knife free.

"Ow-w-w-w-w-w!"

Kill her!

But my eye.

Kill her!

I can't see!

Dazed, Borray was hanging back on the post, his eye burning and tearing.

The few people nearest on the trolley shied away in confusion.

"Molly, duck!"

The girl turned questioningly toward Heather.

Now calmly, with raised brows, "Molly. Duck."

Molly slid down, still gripping the pole.

The way is clear! Go after the Maiden! Borray's assertive inner voice suddenly commanded. *Go now!*

Following several blinks, Borray leaned aggressively forward, intending to grasp the now vacant space on Molly's upright.

Waiting for the attacker's advance, Heather held her pole firmly with both hands and, pivoting, swung her legs forward. With her knees initially drawn up, she kicked out viciously, over Molly's head, at the black mask. Crack! Her feet slammed into his face, throwing him backwards, the mask flying free. Heather's ankle screamed with the impact. So did the RogueTag.

"Hey, what's going on over there?" someone yelled across the interior of the trolley.

Heather looked up, smiling.

"Nothing."

Falling backward, Borray's shoulder hit hard, his head immediately thereafter. Slapping onto the cobblestone street, the RogueTag rolled, finally coming to rest on his face and stomach. There he lay unmoving.

Get up!

I can't.

Again the inner hiss: *Get up!*

I told you, I can't.

You have to.

Groggily, Borray was finally able to raise himself up onto his hands and knees, the land whirling in a sickening, off-kilter spin.

Your knife, the voice said. *Where's your knife?*

He searched the swaying cobblestone street until he spotted it within reach.

A bystander came running over. "Are you all right?" he asked. The man thought the RogueTag had accidentally fallen from the trolley.

A small crowd began to gather. Holding his shoulder, Borray blundered to his feet, while others came running to assist, the frills and extensions on their costumes jiggling and bouncing with each footfall. Words of concern filled the air.

"Let go of me!" The RogueTag said, and tore himself away. He momentarily stumbled while he craned his neck. Borray watched as the trolley diminished in size, his fantasies of grandeur diminishing with it. The blonde girl, clearly visible, was hanging off the upright and looking his way.

"I'll get you!" The young man screamed as he pointed, temporarily forgetting his fear of the Maiden. "Do you hear?" He forcefully jabbed the air. "I'll get you!"

Borray glared as the despised Maiden brought her free hand into view. With it, she gestured goodbye with a small, sprightly wave.

Calmly, Mistraya steered her winged lizard, Maif, over the buildings of Elderraine, her mind a boiling cauldron of hate, revenge, and seething determination. Reaching the lengthy stretch of Parade Day Avenue, the sorceress pulled at the reins and the beast banked and headed north, toward The Crown & Scepter, a dense trail of smoke marking its location.

"They're attacking again, Milady!"

The coach veered sharply before righting itself.

"Keep on, Darsgood, for you must."

Unable to stand it any longer, Lady Mellich turned to the girl at the far window.

"Open it."

"Pardon me, Milady?"

"Go on," she said, her sweeping fingers encouraging. "Open the window."

Gasps and cries to the contrary filled the air.

"But the birds are out there…" said one of the entourage.

The woman huffed. "Well, crack it a bit, then. This is ridiculous. It's far too hot in here. As for me…"

Lady Mellich parted the curtains and lowered the coach door window. The girls were frightened, though not a word dared to escape their lips.

The cool refreshing breeze rushed in, sweeping hair and garb about.

Lady Mellich inhaled deeply through her nose. "Heavenly."

"Marlerray," coaxed one of the girls. "Go on, open *your* window."

"It is open, Arlisk."

Arlisk frowned and tried again. "You know what I mean. Put it *all* the way down. Go on, the breeze feels good."

Marlerray still hesitated.

Arlisk leaned in closer, across the aisle. "Do it, you silly thing. Milady has. What can possibly happen?"

Stupefied, Borray was holding his head as he reeled toward the sidewalk. Inspecting his hands, he saw blood. When he noticed a band of RogueTags crossing the Avenue, he turned away, hoping they wouldn't recognize him. When they were distant enough, Borray stopped and leaned against a tree. He brought a hand up to his painful eye.

You should have killed her when you had the chance. You waited.

"What?"

The Maiden, hissed Borray's now familiar inner whisper. *You should have killed her.*

"Yes. I know, I know." The RogueTag began to cry. "I'm so useless."

Stop your bawling. You look pathetic.

Borray sniffed in a loose, fluid intake. Head down, he hugged himself.

Stand up, you hear! And knock off your blubbering! Be a RogueTag, for Evermore's sake!

"You're right. I'm a three-sided morkel or worse. I've failed." Sniff. "I should have killed her. She wasn't even looking. I missed my chance." Borray paused, and suddenly suspicious, asked, "Who *are* you?"

I'm you.

"What?"

I'm the other side of you, the side you continue to disregard, the side you refuse to heed. But you should, Borray. You really should.

"Why haven't you talked to me before?"

I have been talking. A lot.

"You have?"

Yes.

"Then why haven't I heard you?"

Easy answer, Rogue. You haven't been listening.

"I haven't? Well, maybe I should have been." The RogueTag wiped his nose on his sleeve. "All right, from now on I will." Borray snuffled, holding his tears in check, though his words were soft and soggy. "I promise."

You had better. Or trust me, you'll never kill anything.

As the trolley neared their destination, Heather searched the crowd, looking for menacing auras. Molly, while standing beside her friend, had returned to scanning the skies, buildings, and trees for scouts.

"Molly, there it is, up ahead of us."

"Oh, I see it! The footbridge. It's so, so...*gorgeous!*"

For the first time in a long time, the girls laughed.

"Come on. Let's get home."

The two disembarked, and after allowing the trolley to pass in front of them, they hurried toward the green lawns and the familiar footbridge that spanned the river.

Still harassed, the luxurious Mellich coach hastened down the wide street in the direction of the expansive estates of Elderraine, their mansions secluded behind enormous gates and walls. Intermittently it swerved and jerked, with Darsgood whipping the orranteens to a thunderous clatter.

Scouts continued to dive at the beasts, but were ineffective in slowing them down, causing only the occasional stumble. The orranteens, going on the offensive, were able to snatch and sink their teeth into some of the pesky birds, while downing a few to be trampled under hairy hooves. Every so often, the scouts would take aim at the driver, but with a swing of his forearm Darsgood sent them screeching away.

Inside the coach, Lady Mellich and her entourage were enjoying the fresh breeze that ruffled the curtains, although the girls exchanged worried glances with every lurch and jolt.

Unexpectedly, a bullet of a blur shot through the open coach window. Upon landing on the seat next to Milady, Mistraya's scout transformed into a tuxedoed gentleman. Amid screams from the girls and a flinch of astonishment from the woman, the man took a perfectly comfortable sitting position, unperturbed. The carriage interior went quiet.

Calmly looking over the lady, suavely, the gentleman said, "I was wondering when you were going to open that window."

The man was ugly, with a great hooked nose and vertically striped neck of gray-and-red that wrinkled and sagged in places. His irises were hard red, like a scout's, his hair a muted purple, and his tuxedo blue-black. He spoke through bloodless lips.

"Just *what* are you doing here, young man, frightening us this way. How *dare* you!"

The scout-turned-man ignored Lady Mellich, scrutinizing the girls, one to the next. "You!" he said to the girl second from the window. "Yes, you. Look at me. Let me see your eyes." Reluctantly, she looked at him, and he lingered before moving on. Having viewed all the girls, the grotesque intruder inspected the compartment. Seeing there was nowhere to hide, he turned his attention back to Lady Mellich, who had contracted to her corner. "I'm looking for a particular girl, a blonde girl with green eyes."

"Well, at the moment, I'm unable to recall the eye color of any of my girls—"

"She's not here," the man interrupted.

Lady Mellich said, not indignantly, "Well, I should hope not. Why would any of my girls—?"

"These girls are older than the one for whom I am searching."

The woman cleared her throat, summoning up her best false courage. "And just what makes you think that we had something to do with this particular green-eyed blonde?"

"What, indeed," said Marresh, reaching up into the netting of the woman's hat, where he casually retrieved the LuminOrb. He studied it, rolling it with the fingers of his left hand. His black nails were long, curved, and pointed, his hands a dull, yellowed leather.

"What have you there?" said the lady, distrustfully, still leaning away.

"Honestly, I'm not sure." Holding the small crystalline ball between his thumb and forefinger, he eyed the woman. "Where, may I ask, did you get this?"

"Why, I've never seen it before."

"Really."

"Yes. What is so special about that small glass sphere?"

"That small glass sphere that I found in *your* hat?" The man smiled to himself, while contemplating the orb. "Magical residue."

"*Magical residue?* Surely, you're joking. What would *I* be doing with anything that has magical residue, now, I ask you?"

"What indeed? So, I ask *you.*"

"How *impertinent* of you, young man. I don't know, quite frankly, what that small ball is and how it got there, and as I've said, I've never seen it before. Why, we only ever use NonCraft Controlled implements at the estate. Now, will you please go and leave us in peace?"

After a moment or two of rolling the 'Orb in his hand, Marresh rose and gave a baleful last look to all the ladies. Trembling, they cowered. Instantly, in a blur of transformation, the scout leader became a bird in flight headed out the window, the LuminOrb clutched firmly in one claw. Once out of the coach, the man-turned-bird circled above, and then headed back to The Crown & Scepter, a cloud of scouts in tow.

Borray traversed a small street that ran perpendicular to the Avenue. Ahead was The Crown & Scepter, where he now saw that the spectators had grown substantially. Smoke was pouring out of a hole in the roof, flames leaping up amid black clouds. Still shaken, Borray looked around at the faces.

I'm glad Marscleff isn't in there, he thought, hopefully.

A small bloom of purple fire grew in front of him: Mistraya!

Borray, I see you are outside. Where?

"Near The Crown & Scepter, My Mistress. The g—"

And the girls?

"I'm afraid that the girls are on a trolley, My Mistress, headed up Parade Day Avenue."

And why are you not in pursuit?

"I was, chasing after them. I-I lost them. I couldn't keep up, I'm afraid. They were able to get on a trolley, leaving me behind—"

On their way, no doubt, to their PortalDoor. By the way, that trolley you mentioned, the one the girls were able to board, leaving you behind? If memory serves me correctly, all trolleys within the city of Elderraine are slow moving, are they not? Mistraya emphasized the words 'slow-moving.'

The RogueTag's face dropped. He stared dumbly.

I thought so. Borray, is our Maiden child responsible for that bloody head and red eye of yours?

Borray was suddenly aware that his eye, head, and shoulder still smarted. His face reddened.

Borray?

"Yes. Yes, she is, My Mistress, indirectly, I suppose." Borray refrained from mentioning that it wasn't the Maiden who was responsible for his injured eye, but, more embarrassingly, her friend.

Unexpectedly, the sorceress smiled wickedly. *You're lucky she didn't kill you.*

But I could have stabbed her! thought the RogueTag. I could have killed *her.* He looked away, before turning back. "Yes. My Mistress."

Are they traveling north on their route from the shop?

"Yes. I'm not sure exactly where they are, right now, but they haven't been out of my sight for long."

Good. Then I'm on my way.

Borray looked up. High overhead through the lingering smoke, he could see the great winged lizard bearing Mistraya's canopied cockpit. Descending on a slow angle, it whizzed by, headed up the Avenue.

The sorceress looked down on the burning costume emporium, internal flames eating at her own placid exterior. With just a glance, she knew her elite force had been obliterated.

"Yes," she vowed for all and none to hear, "I *will* kill the Maiden Portent."

Having crossed the small street, the girls approached the crowded courtyard, recognizing the tarnished statue of an eminent man rising high upon its pedestal.

"Heather," Molly whispered. "We're almost there."

Heather looked around her, checking the auras. "No RogueTags, no creeps or scouts, just people walking by, some playing games on the grass, and some shoppers over by the stores. Everything looks great, Molly."

"Heather, the porch with the PortalDoor, I can see it. Look. There it is!"

"Finally."

"Let's hurry."

The two broke into a run. Just past the statue, Heather drew up and stopped. "Molly."

Her friend skidded and turned, walking back several paces. "What?"

Heather stood rigidly.

"Heather, what?"

"I'm…" The girl was still, trancelike. "I'm feeling…"

"Heather, what's wrong? What are you feeling? Come on, the Portal door is just across the courtyard. We can't stop now. We're almost there. Please, let's go."

Mouth dropping, Heather whirled and looked to the sky.

"Ah, there you are my little Maiden child," muttered Mistraya from her windblown compartment. "And her friend, too. How accommodating. Standing still in the open like that makes you wonderfully easy targets. But how would you know? Alas, I fear I must say goodbye to such a sweet and pretty pair. So endearing. And now, my young duo, it's time for this chapter featuring the latest rendition of the *Green-eyed Maiden* to close. Unfortunately, 'happily ever after' will not take place at its conclusion. But rest assured, 'The End' *will* be your final sentence. And gleefully enough, I'm just the one to impose it."

Descending above the grassy area, approaching the courtyard, Mistraya began her incantation, dennunciating quietly.

The oddly shaped object, airborne above the river, caught Heather's attention, its aura widespread in lifeless emanation, sucking energy like a black hole. Approaching rapidly, a sudden flash sparked from the rectangular structure atop the winged creature.

"Molly, run!"

The girls broke into a sprint, as an arc of charged magic hurtled from the sky like lightning. Fortunately for Heather and Molly, the bolt hit the statue that marked the entrance to the busy courtyard. Its marble legs shattering directly above the girls, the prominently posed figure toppled over, crashing headlong into the earth. Its impact caused the ground to tremble, sending those in the vicinity sprawling to the courtyard floor. A thin cloud of dust filled the air. Promptly, Heather was on her feet assisting Molly.

"Come on! Get up."

"Heather, what is happening?"

"Run and hide! Quick. Over there."

Heather could see Mistraya and the beast, having passed overhead, preparing to turn for another strafing of the courtyard.

"Why? The PortalDoor is over on the other side—"

"Molly, just run for the closest cover!" Heather gave her friend a slight push in a direction opposite from the stairs and the PortalDoor, into the interior of the quadrangle. Having done so, she took to her heels, and even with a noticeable limp, quickly overtook Molly.

"Come on! Farther!" Heather led Molly away from the courtyard entrance, to where there were many more sheltering objects to conceal them: trees, planters, and a series of smaller statues surrounded by hedges, to name a few. Her painful ankle slowing her, the girl finally dived for shelter, and then came up looking to spot Molly. Crying and shouting, people were still scattering, running frantically about. Heather hoped that she and Molly might have become lost amid the fleeing courtyard inhabitants.

Borray stood among the spectators gathered around the backside of the Crown & Scepter. They watched as, with an enormous crash, the structure's roof collapsed, fireballs broiling up and out of the hole, accompanied by an immense roar. The next instant, the fire seemed to swell, feasting on the newfound oxygen, flames and smoke surging into the sky.

Behind him, the RogueTag could hear a NewsBarker, standing on the corner, singing out in rhyme all he knew about The Crown & Scepter, from its glorious past to its present condition. However, no mention was made of the GraySuits, the green-eyed Maiden, or the insurrection. No cause was given for the fire's beginning, either, the 'Barker vocalizing only that the fire had 'mysteriously started.'

But the RogueTag's mind was occupied, feeding on itself, attempting to digest its own spate of current events.

I should have killed her! Borray thought. I should have killed the Maiden Portent. Why didn't I? I was right there. *She* was right there. All I had to do was stab the little 'Dreg. Just *thrust!*

Borray stomped his foot. Bystanders looked at him, but he didn't care.

I could have done it. I fell apart when I had my chance. And I missed my calling. The RogueTag stomped his foot again. Right there! She was right there. I can't believe it, can't believe it.

Borray rotated in a pent-up, frustrated circle, those near him stepping away, giving him distance, thinking the young man peculiar. Stopping, he clenched his fists.

And where is Marscleff? Borray skimmed over the faces in the crowd. Maybe I should go looking for the Rogue. After all, I'm the one who asked him to stay and look for the 'Dregs.

But a persistent feeling told him that the hunt would be in vain, and that his RogueTag friend was still inside The Crown & Scepter. The thought crystallized and struck his consciousness with the force of a sledgehammer: Marscleff was no longer alive.

That can't be!

Desperately, with manic glances, Borray continued to search among those standing nearby.

He has to be here! He has to!

At the sounds of more devastation from within the collapsing building, Borray refocused on the fire. He stared, the flaming vision searing to memory a lasting imprint.

Can it be? Is he still in there, burning with The Crown & Scepter?

Borray struggled, unable to keep at bay the brutal reality.

Marscleff is dead.

Tears finally broke free, running down his face, where they hung briefly in droplets at the jaw line.

Could that have been Marscleff pounding on the double doors? Was that him?

He moaned.

I should have let him go home to his brother. I just wanted the Rogue to keep me company, that's all. I never thought all this would happen.

Borray broke down, convulsing.

"You stop that!" he snapped in a hiss, straightening.

People stared.

"It's you, isn't it? You're back."

I am, continued the hiss, now in the voice that only Borray could hear. *And I have some questions.*

"What?"

Are you a RogueTag?

"Yes. Yes, I think so."

You think—?

"I am."

Are you sure? It's what you want to do, isn't it?

"Yes."

So, no doubts about it, then, you're a RogueTag?

"Yes. I'm a RogueTag. Definitely. It's who I am and who we are."

We are?

"Yes, we are. We're tough and we're intimidating, and we die for our cause."

He shot glares around him. Those Borray caught gawking looked away. Bothered, some drifted off to stand elsewhere.

We are, the young man thought. We're intimidating.

He squeezed his concealed knife.

And we can kill.

And we kill.

The RogueTag's head slowly bobbed in comprehension. We can, he thought. We can kill.

Yes, we can.

I can kill. And the next time I see that Maiden, I *will* kill her. And the next time I'm supposed to kill someone, I *will* kill them.

You can. You're a killer.

I'm a killer.

Borray took stock of the knife he still gripped in his hand. He watched while two girls the age of Heather and Molly approached, both dressed in lovely costume. Squeezing and releasing, squeezing and releasing, Borray felt as if the knife that he clutched in his hand was starting to come alive, starting to breathe, its steely heart starting to beat. Squeeze and release, squeeze and release. He knew it was so.

You're a killer.

That's right, everyone. I'm a killer.

He clutched the knife harder, sliding his fingers forward to meet the blade, where he felt its honed edge slice his flesh. A sweet release of wetness, a sharp, welcoming pain filled him, pinching, instantly electric, glorifying; it felt to Borray as if he were suddenly growing inside himself, filling out into every recess of his shell. He swelled, expanding his chest.

He heard the two girls giggle, their laughter light, their banter lively. The children had passed the RogueTag and were walking towards the park. Looking over his shoulder, Borray could see them cutting across the green.

I'm a killer now, the RogueTag thought.

You are, said the hiss.

And from here on out, I will never fail.

You will never fail. Ever.

Not ever.

Pulling away from the crowd that stood watching the flaming demise of The Crown & Scepter, Borray followed after the two frolicsome girls. He claimed them. They were his.

Flying low through the sunless courtyard, the mottled gray lizard passed close to Heather, displaying an armored belly. Its body was thick and powerful, its wings were pushing off air. Peering from behind a bushy hedge, the blonde girl glimpsed the raven-haired sorceress sitting stiffly upright within the canopy. Unconsciously drawn, Mistraya turned in Heather's direction, but too late to spot the youngster.

Heather glanced right and saw that Molly was close by, concealed beneath the wide overhanging lip of a large planter, near a bench. She noticed, too, that as the great lizard flew in their direction, bystanders were scattering in panic, running into buildings, frantically diving for concealment, and racing from the courtyard. Heather couldn't tell what was occurring on the lawns near the river, but she had no doubt that the picnickers were fleeing as well. Looking across the vast courtyard, try as she might, Heather couldn't see the PortalDoor that would take them home to the Bristol House. Atop the lengthy stairway, the door was hidden, lost to the rear of the porch.

"Heather!" The girl barely heard Molly's voice. "What now?"

"Stay down," Heather said, keeping her voice low. "We don't want Mistraya discovering where we want to go. If she knows where the Portal-Door is, one of two things will probably happen." Heather scanned the skies.

"What's that?"

"She could destroy the stairs." The girl turned her attention back to Molly. "If she does that, then we won't be able to climb them and reach the door."

Molly nodded her understanding. "What's the other thing?"

"Well, the second thing is way worse. She could leave the stairs alone and destroy the PortalDoor instead." Heather thought, If she does that, chances are we won't be able to get home to Grandma Dawn and the Bristol House ever again.

The sun, sinking lower in the sky, was casting its golden glow on all it touched, including the sorceress and her great winged lizard. Circling in a wide loop not too far above the courtyard, Mistraya's awareness was drawn to the depths of the basin and its buildings that were awash in late afternoon blue.

I sense your power, Maiden child, thought Mistraya, aiming to detect the smallest of movements. Your capabilities are strong. Dangerously strong. So, perchance you are the Maiden Portent after all, and if so, I daren't risk another pass through the courtyard. Perhaps it would be best if I were to lure you out and kill you as soon as you show yourself. Nothing personal. You see, I need to accomplish this small task before your power grows to a size rivaling my own. As well, you must not reach that PortalDoor.

The sorceress glared down upon the quiet of the motionless courtyard, feeling its tension, its constriction in fear. There, people were hiding, one of which held for her a particular interest, an excessive fascination.

Opening the door, Mistraya stepped out of the cockpit and balanced herself skillfully on the bumpy back of Maif, at the base of the neck.

She called out, her voice becoming magically magnified, "Young Maiden, my name is Mistraya. Here in Evermore, I am the sorceress appointed to the court by none other than our good Emperor Kratkuffe, himself. I know that you're down there and will soon leave our beautiful land of Evermore." Her alluring voice, icy calm, continued in creamy smooth delivery: "I just want you to know how very sorry I am that my firebolt may have frightened you. I assure you it was for the best and that I meant no harm."

Truth be known, thought the sorceress, I'm only sorry I missed.

"Please allow me to explain. There was an appropriate reason for my use of firepower and it was this: word has reached me through my various channels that there were assassins awaiting your arrival here in the vicinity of your PortalDoor, assassins who wished to do you harm. Sadly, they belong to the same uncontrollable underground group that caused so much trouble at The Crown & Scepter Costume Emporium earlier today. But we, the forces that rule here in Evermore, have cracked down and taken steps to insure that those responsible for such reprehensible actions have been dealt with in an appropriate manner. In short, those forces that have so boldly disrupted Evermore's Parade Day activities have been dealt a severe blow this day. I am here to inform you that we have nearly wiped them out and that only a few remain. But as they see their numbers shrink, they have become a desperate group. The good news is that we, the virtuous forces of the Crown, have them on the run."

When Mistraya paused for effect, Molly looked over at Heather questioningly, a strange, distant cast to her eyes.

"How does she know we're in the area of the PortalDoor?"

"Easy," replied Heather. "She guessed."

"Are you sure, Heather? Maybe we've got it all wrong. Maybe the ClearWeave are the ones trying to kill us. Have you ever thought of that? I have. Think about it. It was right after the tunnel, when we were on our way here, that the ClearWeave could have sent those two creepy people after us. And then, when they didn't succeed, maybe the Clear-

Weave sent a bunch more to The Crown & Scepter."

Heather felt herself wanting to believe the words she heard from both Molly and Mistraya. However, recalling her experience with the WhisperEye mirror, she fought the inclination and said, "I don't think so, Molly. It doesn't make sense."

"Well, maybe not everyone in the ClearWeave is against us, just a few. And maybe those are the ones who are part of that underground group that Mistraya is talking about. It's possible, you know. Did you ever think that after they met you and thought you were the true Maiden of the Portent, they might have put the word out to have you killed? The Matron warned us things like that could happen, remember?"

"Oh, I don't know, Molly—"

"Heather, maybe Mistraya *is* on our side and maybe she really *was* sent by Emperor Kratkuffe to see us off and make sure we reach the PortalDoor safely—especially after what happened at The Crown & Scepter. You know, with all that the Bristol House has done for us magically, would it surprise you to learn it made sure we were protected by Mistraya and the Realm of Evermore during our visit?"

Still circling on Maif above, the sorceress began again to project the manipulative Voice, "Now, I want you to know that when this dreadful, worrisome information reached my ear, that there are assassins intending to do you harm, I was nothing less than extremely upset and beside myself with worry—utterly so, I should add. Immediately, I mounted Maif, whom you now see below me, and as swiftly as possible I rushed to your aid, and that of your companion, to prevent what we would regard as a very unfortunate incident, very unfortunate indeed. I thought it to be of the utmost importance that I personally arrive on the scene and attend to your wellbeing, insuring that, as honored visitors to our delightful world, you are protected by any and every means available. And much to my great relief, I see that I've reached you just in time. It was my intention, when shooting that magical bolt down into the area, to send a message to the assassins, scaring them off and letting the group know that you are protected by nothing less than the Crown and its royal legions."

In the courtyard below, still in hiding, Molly said to Heather, "It could be true, you know. She could be telling the truth."

"Yeah, you're right. She could. But then again, she could also be lying." Heather looked at her friend quizzically. To her, Molly seemed remote, not real, like she had faded within herself, and that something about her manner just wasn't normal.

"You feeling okay, Molly?"

"Sure. I'm feeling really great right now. Why?"

"Because we're kind of in a lot of trouble."

Now, here comes my big reward, thought Mistraya. Let us see, shall we, if I'm able to VoiceSway you out to where I can see you.

"So, I'd like to apologize for the rude reception that you might have thought you were being given in Evermore, both here in this courtyard and earlier at the costume emporium. I'm sure these incidents struck you as unfriendly and inhospitable, especially to TimeLight travelers such as yourselves visiting a foreign land.

"But that was then, and I say let's put these unfortunate incidents behind us, shall we? And in the name of positive interplanetary relations coupled with exemplary Evermorian graces, I'd like nothing more than the honor of accompanying you and your companion to your Portal-Door with Royal protection, seeing to it personally that no other may do you harm along your route. And once there, to send you safely off, bidding you a fond farewell and pleasant journey on behalf of Emperor Kratkuffe and the lovely Realm of Evermore. For what you've endured, it's the least I can do, to end your visit on such an memorable note."

"Heather, isn't she brilliant?" Molly said, still shielded by the planter.

"No."

"I think she is. Should we let her show us to the PortalDoor?"

"No."

"But it's so sweet of her to offer, don't you think?"

"Molly, when that explosion hit the statue just now, and we fell?"

"Yes?"

"By any chance did you land on your head?"

Mistraya was surprised by her lack of success when attempting to lure the girls out of hiding.

Am I losing my touch? she wondered. Determined, the sorceress continued, "Once again, I'm sorry, truly, *truly* sorry about the inconvenience of the very necessary but unfortunate matter that required my attention just moments ago. If you only knew me, you'd understand what a HeartTrue friend I can be, and that I certainly meant no harm to either of you. Rather, I wished only to frighten off those who intend to inflict grave injury.

"Perhaps if you were to step out into the open and introduce yourself, I could apologize directly for my inappropriateness. If you would kindly oblige me, you can rest assured that no further harm will come to you or your companion from any quarter." The sorceress smirked. "Of that, you have Mistraya's word."

Below, Molly asked, "Should we introduce ourselves, Heather? It sounds like Mistraya's sincere. Maybe she really wants to see that we get home safely."

"Maybe. But I doubt it."

"Why, Heather? How can you be so sure?"

"Because, Molly, that woman has the darkest shine I have ever seen."

When the courtyard didn't stir, following a frustrated exhalation, Mistraya rushed to add, "So, feel free to step forward and allow me to bestow upon you a royal apology from none other than Emperor Kratkuffe, himself."

Still, nothing moved.

Come on and bite! Mistraya thought, her eyebrows plummeting in a stern V over her nose, her mouth a sneering smear. I'm speaking directly to the two of you—targeting you. Why am I unable to lure you out of hiding? All right, one last time, girls, and then it becomes a nasty scene.

She tried again, her delivery smoothly convincing as it carried down into the courtyard: "Young Maiden, please, as an esteemed representative of his royal majesty, Emperor Kratkuffe, I'm asking that you and your companion reveal yourselves so that we can meet. Must I return to tell the good Emperor that, due to circumstances surrounding your unfortunate reception, you were unable to grant me an interview? We must not have that. Dare I reveal, it would positively crush our great leader's regal pride? So, I must implore that you show Evermore the greatest consideration and present yourselves. Let's get acquainted, shall we? Let's be friends. Surely, you can trust me, wondrous being that I am, adored by Evermorians everywhere. For, if you cannot trust the good sorceress, Mistraya, royal appointee, than who can you trust, I ask you?"

"Heather, are you sure it's her shine you're seeing that's so dark, and not the dragon's?"

"Molly, let me put it this way. If we go out there and introduce ourselves to that flying windbag, we'll never see home again."

"How can you be so sure?"

"Molly, what's gotten into you? You seem really, *really* weird. Have you forgotten? That's Mistraya up there. She's not handing out free toys and cookies."

"But all the nice sorceress wants to do is introduce herself to us and take us to the PortalDoor. What's so bad about that?"

Heather shook her head disbelievingly. "Molly, if we step out there right now, right this second, and say hello, you know what Mistraya is going to do?"

"Say hello in return and then show us to the PortalDoor?"

"No. She'll kill us and feed us to that big lizard of hers."

"Heather, I don't know why you're saying those mean things about Mistraya, but I think I'm going to go and say hello to the Royal Sorceress of the Crown. She seems like such a nice lady."

"Molly, if you try to do that, I'm going to have to tackle and gag you."

Molly looked at Heather with that same distant expression. "You're my friend. You wouldn't do that."

"Molly, I *am* your friend. That's why I would."

The hush from below continued.

All right, I see that the Maiden child is not a naïf, thought Mistraya. It's obvious that using the Voice is not going to work.

The sorceress brought up her hands and began to examine her blue nails.

Let's see what happens when I employ a little magical violence. She smiled her malevolent smile. It so goes against my grain.

Her feet spread and firmly planted, Mistraya stood a commanding presence just forward of the beast's wings, as it circled its large, lazy loop. Dropping her hands, she looked down into the courtyard.

The smile still stretched on her face soon gave way to a frown, however, as the sorceress thought, How I hate to practice restraint. I just hate it. Yet, with The Crown & Scepter burning today, unfortunately, I see I'm going to have to limit my wanton destruction. It's such an utter bore, but imperative all the same. It creates so much political trouble for the poor Emperor when I destroy things. The hapless man simply has no sense of humor about it, none at all. And I certainly hope I don't hurt anyone in the process of ferreting out those girls—but if I do, oh, well. Can't say that I didn't try to apply that *light touch* to my destructive inclinations.

Mistraya's gaze on the courtyard turned ugly.

"Very well, my young Maiden, since you so rudely declined to introduce yourself to me, allow me, if you would, to introduce myself to you."

Dennunciating, drawing on the dark power of the Dahklarr Herth, the sorceress let loose with a volley of blinding white FireBolts from the ends of her arms that hit throughout the courtyard, shaking structures, collapsing stairways, and dispersing tiles. Windows shattered, and a great deal of debris fell noisily to the courtyard floor. Screams could be heard, as huge, yellow and magenta clouds of smoke from the magical strikes burgeoned skyward.

Above, an impatient Mistraya waited for the smoke to clear, the clouds rising up to engulf her.

"Pooh," she said, waving a hand before her face. I so dislike a dusty mess. And disturbances such as these I find so terribly annoying. Really. Must an act of simple destruction be so untidy?

Mistraya peered below. Though she was unable to see as the dust continued to rise, the sorceress asked, Are you still alive, Maiden child? I can't tell with my own enchantments having disrupted my MagicAwareness. However, at the moment, if I can't feel you, there's a very good chance that you're not alive. And wouldn't that be a shame? It would be. Because, if you must know, it simply breaks my heart to think—and here Mistraya smiled—to think that maybe, just maybe, you're dead.

CHAPTER THIRTY-ONE

Faceoff at the PortalDoor

Molly huddled in the smoky chaos, her head covered, her eyes shut tight, the devastating explosions having broken the spell that the Voice had cast over her. She was coughing from all the dust and debris that made visibility in the courtyard scarce. Squinting, she rose and frantically looked around her.

"Heather!" she screamed among screams. "Heather, where are you?"

Molly waited and then yelled again. "Heather!"

"She's not here."

The words came from Molly's left, the smoke gradually clearing.

"What? Heather?"

"I'm not Heather," said a commanding voice. "I'm sorry, but I'm afraid that your friend is no longer with us."

"What?" said Molly, her word weak.

A lump in her throat, the girl could barely make out the person walking toward her, a hazy shape slowly revealing itself.

"However, young lady, I advise that until Heather returns, you stay hidden where you are."

"Aria!" Molly wanted to leap to her feet and hug her.

"Quiet, now. And please stay down for the moment, in case Mistraya resorts to more of her bomb blasts. Before we attempt our advance toward the PortalDoor, I've a little something to attend to."

From her hiding place, Molly watched as Aria turned her back and began working her hands in fluid movement above her, weaving what the girl in the soiled clown outfit thought could only be an incantation. Molly looked up. The tall buildings all round made her feel like a fish looking out of its bowl. Vaguely, through the declining smoke, she could see the underbelly of the great lizard as it circled overhead, Mistraya standing imposingly on its shoulders.

All around Molly and Aria, the courtyard was emptying out, with people frantically racing for the streets and the entrances to the surrounding buildings. Few, however, ran for what remained of the external stairways, leading to the floors above. When the haze dispersed, no one wanted to chance being caught on the steps in mid-flight, trapped in the open and thus at the mercy of the deadly sorceress.

Helping Molly up, Aria said, "Follow me. There's not much time. Let's try to get a little closer to the PortalDoor while there's still a bit of smoky cover to hide us, assisted by a spell I lyrisied only moments ago to distract our sorceress."

"Can't we just run all the way to the 'Door?" asked Molly, the stairway intact and visible in the dusty confines.

"Mistraya is dangerously unpredictable and deadly. It's probably best if we make our way by degrees."

"Will we be able to do that with Mistraya watching from above like she is?"

"Honestly? I'm not sure. A better question might be, 'Do we have a choice?'"

ﻉﻞ

As the dust thinned below, Mistraya's attention, oddly enough, was drawn elsewhere, towards the horizon. A multitude of tiny specks were approaching rapidly, growing larger.

Ah, well, she thought, it's high time my scouts returned to find me. How pleasing, too. It's so heartwarming to know you're loved. Instantly, the brow of the sorceress darkened. According to Marresh, she thought, it seems that pursuing the Mellich coach turned out to be a chase for naught, now, didn't it? Mistraya refocused on the dusty basin beneath her. You did that, didn't you, Maiden child? You distracted my scouts and sent them elsewhere, while you and your friend escaped from the royal costume emporium. Brilliant maneuver, I must say. When I was first informed of the fire, I ordered my GraySuits to simply let The Crown & Scepter burn to the ground, hoping that you'd still be inside. But instead, they were the ones who were trapped. So unfortunate. Such a terrible waste of a good costume emporium, too.

So, I'm waiting. Where are you, Maiden child?

The sorceress crossed her arms before her and began to tap her foot.

Are you still down there? Still alive? I find myself unable to feel your presence. But then, as I said, when my magical ability to perceive is disrupted, I feel so little. I do. It's a shame, really. At times, it can be so *empty* being a dark sorceress. The woman smirked. And I promise to tell you all about it when I see you—if you're still in any condition to listen.

As she probed the courtyard, searching for the girl among the wreckage, the sorceress thought, Seems I underestimated my own strength with those FireBolts. And I made such a mess, too, in the process. Mistraya brushed at her shoulders. But then potential Portent Maidens have a tendency to bring out the worst in me.

The sorceress closed her eyes, utilizing her MagicAwareness, trying to feel a draw to the Maiden's power. They immediately popped open.

"She's stronger. How can that be? The Maiden child is stronger?"

Mistraya had only just uttered these words, when she looked up to find herself surrounded by a great many distorting bodies. Slowly, fluidly did they slide and slip around the befuddled sorceress, all the while their mutterings reached her as a babble of sound.

"What's this?" Mistraya seethed at a whisper. "iMagiNacia from below? So, those flecks on the horizon were not my scouts, after all, but this conjuration of the Maiden's? How dreadfully, dreadfully *tedious!*" This last word the sorceress snapped off.

On their sides, backs, and bellies, the life-sized replicas of the girl Bayliss swam around Mistraya. Watching, the sorceress fumed as they filled the sky, blocking out the late afternoon light at times, somberly swarming about with the sensuality of a writhing school of eels.

Mistraya dared not touch the elongated bodies. They held for her a particular repugnance, a secret pushed aside, a disturbing truth that she could not dispel.

When one of the contorted bodies floated by very close to Mistraya's ear, Bayliss's small, detached voice asked, "Why did you kill my parents?"

Another Bayliss, "Yes, why?"

"Why did you kill my parents?"

"… kill my parents?"

"Yes, why did you…?"

"…kill my parents?"

"Why…?"

The voices joined together in an endless unnerving chant.

How do you know, Maiden child? she questioned. *How could you know?!*

Angry, Mistraya looked earthward. Yet she was only able to see the unrelenting progression of maroon-clad bodies in white pinafores and black hose, the uninterrupted swirling of disjointed, undulating girls.

"Why did you kill my parents?"

"Yes, why…?"

Mistraya threw her arms out, her head back. "Disperse!" But the many slithery Baylisses just continued to weave about her. "Disperse, I say!"

Much to her surprise, Mistraya realized that the Bayliss replicas were indeed dispersing, but in an unhurried, methodical way, and not as she wished. They were swimming the air currents, rising above her and eventually flattening out, interlocking neatly like puzzle pieces comprising a giant Escher-like tapestry. The enormous rectangle of fabric began to swell downward, growing menacingly bulbous. It floated above the sorceress, who stood defiantly atop her beast, the pair still circling over the courtyard. Warily, she kept her attention fixed aloft on the hovering, distended piece of fabric, while down below, citizens in hiding witnessed the ongoing spectacle with heightened curiosity. One person stood alone, her green SearEye visible to Mistraya, if only the enchantress had thought to look.

Yet, above her the Bayliss-patterned fabric continued to bulge, growing fatter by the moment. Finally, unable to bear it any longer, and wanting to destroy the manifestation of iMagiNacia before it could destroy her, the sorceress shot bolt after bolt of magic into the heart of the burgeoning textile.

KA-BOOM!

The tapestry exploded, releasing an abundance of tiny feathers. They swayed on the breeze, floating down around the statuesque sorceress as she stood with clenched teeth. She heard cries of joy and applause from those hidden below.

As the feathers passed before her, Mistraya began to laugh.

What's this? Is this the best you have to offer?

But then the sorceress realized that she was unable to see the courtyard below.

"Ah, so you think you can escape behind a veil of feathers to your PortalDoor? It *is* here, isn't it, in the courtyard? It seems I was right, after all. Is it a regular doorway or something unusual, like a tree or statue? It seems to me we'll simply have to solve this irritating mystery."

Black hair flowing behind her, the sinking sun's orange light coloring her features, Mistraya threw up her hands.

"Let us trade spells, then, shall we, child? Allow me to show an inferior what a great enchantress can do."

She began to dennunciate, casting a rhythmic dark charm.

Soon, the feathers all around turned to rain, a sparse, quiet sprinkling of translucent mist. Though she steadily became wetter, the sorceress didn't seem to notice, concentrating instead on the courtyard below.

"Where are you?" she called down, her voice cool. "It's time to step forward and show yourself in the mizzle. By transforming the feathers and turning them to mist, I'll be able to see you now—but only if you show yourself. Come. Come to where I can see the green-eyed Maiden of the Evermore Portent. Introduce yourself to a powerful enchantress, you cowardly little Maiden child."

Ah, but you're very quick to amend a spell, thought Aria. The girl didn't dare look up. If she still retained the glow of SearEye, even in a diminished state, she was sure that Mistraya would detect her immediately. From their new vantage point beneath the partially collapsed canopy of a recently abandoned fruit stand, Aria regarded the stairway to the PortalDoor, and then looked through the drizzle at the rubble strewn before her and Molly, impeding their progress. She sized up the distances, calculated the stops, and wondered if they could cover the remaining stretch of courtyard without being spotted and possibly killed by Mistraya.

Yet, standing confidently in the shadows, Aria smiled.

"What's so funny?" Heather asked, taking possession. "I think we're in a lot of trouble here."

Hearing Heather's voice, Molly looked over.

"I was thinking," Aria said, "that Mistraya must be wary—or afraid—for she's made no effort to land her beast and confront me directly. This is good. Let her stay away, and let's see if I can't conjure up something else to shelter us, as we attempt another small advance toward the Portal-Door."

"Aria, can't you just, you know, blast her out of the sky or something?"

"I'm able, but the sorceress and I share a history."

"What do you mean?"

"I mean I intend to do things as I see fit."

Heather was momentarily taken aback by Aria's curtness.

With her hand moving in an exact arc above her head, Aria lyrisied the words that altered the mizzle. Soon, their tempo increasing, the clear drops of mist became opaque and multicolored, while the awnings, rooftops, and courtyard tiles began to tip-tap in continuous rhythm. Molly saw that the rainfall, alive in a blur of colors, had become denser, limiting her vision. Throughout the courtyard, she could hear the whoops and cheers of spectators. The girl held out her hand, palm up, feeling the harmless peppering of the speckles, and collected the tiny offerings from the sky.

Molly couldn't believe her eyes. "It's candy! They're sprinkles, the kind you put on cupcakes."

"Follow me!" Aria said, grabbing Molly's arm.

The girl let the captured sprinkles fall from her hand. She followed Aria, squinting into the thickening downpour all around her.

Having traveled a third of the way to the stairs, Aria said, above the restless slush and patter, "Down, get down there! Quickly!"

Breathing heavily, Molly crouched behind the wide base of a lamp-post, and watched as the other girl sought concealment behind a large shrub not too far away.

Aria said, "All right, so now it looks as if the most difficult part awaits us, navigating across that remaining stretch of courtyard without Mistraya seeing us."

"There aren't a lot of things to hide behind on the way, are there?"

"Unfortunately not. But for now, Molly, let's stay under cover where we are."

Feeling the breeze start to blow with greater intensity, the blonde girl thought, I'm glad, for the moment, that we're staying put. Apparently, Mistraya has altered my spell and conjured forth something new.

Aria was correct. The sorceress had.

⁓

Still standing near the neck of the great lizard, candied sprinkles lodged in her hair and covering her robe, Mistraya had finished dennunciating another spell. Now she moved her hands in practiced fashion, as if drawing something to her. And that something was the wind.

In the courtyard below, with sprinkles still raining down, Aria and Molly felt the breezes turn to forceful gusts. Soon, the blasts of wind began to blow the candies aside, where they no longer reached the court-yard floor. Instead, the tiny colored bits were blown off course, coming to ground in other parts of the city.

Glancing aloft, through amber eyes, Aria could see a distant Mistra-ya, head bent, hands on hips. The sorceress was trying to spot the green laser lights of SearEye.

Now comes the difficult part, thought the magical girl. Mistraya's blown away our cover, and we need concealment that will allow us to make it over to the base of our stairway. Aria grimaced, flexing her lower leg, taking stock of her aching ankle.

What did Heather do to us, anyway?

Hidden by the shrub, Aria spread her legs and arms and began a new Lyrica cadence. With blonde hair blowing forcefully behind her, her neon green eyes pitched down and away from the sky and wind, Aria worked her iMagiNacia.

From behind the lamppost, Molly watched as the now infrequent sprinkles, no longer windblown, began to turn brown. Falling heavier, they grew larger in size, like hail, and more concentrated, making visibility difficult once again.

Molly could discern the spectators' cheers and applause for Aria's feat of iMagiNacia. She saw that, around her shoes, the brown morsels were quickly accumulating.

She looked appreciatively at Aria.

"Chocolate chips."

Quickly, Molly cupped her palm, collected a few, and then popped them into her mouth.

Still gliding in circles, the sorceress didn't wait to witness the full effect of Aria's iMagiNacia, the veiling of the courtyard to provide cover for the girls' escape. Rather, she promptly initiated a response in her own MalevaMagic.

Irritably brushing away the chocolate, she thought, By rapidly working this modest little magical feat, I can isolate the Maiden Portent and her companion in the open.

The wind that had all but subsided began to roar and a swell of imposing clouds swept up to rapidly assemble above the courtyard.

"Now," said the enchantress, smoothly, "Let's see if I can catch you unaware, running for your PortalDoor."

With just the slightest movement of Mistraya's hand, accompanied by the concluding words of her spell, the clouds parted, resulting in magical sunrays lighting and heating the chocolate downpour that assailed the courtyard floor.

"Now, where shall I find you?" asked Mistraya, peering down into the slow dissipation. "Know, when I do spot you, Maiden child, with but a few words, your reign as the Maiden Portent will end swiftly in a flash of light."

"Molly, quickly now. Follow me!" Aria said, racing by.

Heads down, pelted by chocolate chips, the girls started their dash across the open stretch, dodging small bits of rubble and occasionally slipping on the chocolate and soggy sprinkles. Unexpectedly, Aria seized Molly and dragged her to a sliding halt.

"Aria, why are you—?"

"Molly," she yelled over the downpour, "we have to go back!"

"Back?"

"Yes! Back as quickly as we can. Now, come!"

The two reversed course and sprinted as fast as possible to their previous shelters, Aria ending with a dive and roll. She was having trouble running, finding her painful ankle irksome.

"Aria," asked Heather, breathing heavily, as she momentarily seized possession, "how come you stopped?"

"Feel how warm it's getting? I'm afraid Mistraya is one step ahead of us and will be destroying our cover. Had Molly and I continued on our course, we would have been revealed, the sorceress sighting us in the open."

"Really? Are you sure? That brown stuff is really falling out there; it looks pretty thick. I'm sure you could have made it across easily."

"Watch."

With the weakening downpour of chocolate still able to impede her view, the sorceress waited for the full reveal of the courtyard, the brown chips continuing to melt and vaporize in air. Now under the intense rays, the chips piled on the ground softened and coalesced, and after turning to chocolate syrup, the liquid began to magically evaporate. Mistraya felt the fireballs impatiently housed at her fingertips, awaiting her command. She peered through what remained of the downpour, looking for two specific targets at which to hurl them.

With their cover burning away, Aria realized her impending vulnerability, that she could soon be detected in the retreating shadows of the large shrub. Seeing Molly was safe behind the lamppost, the girl rushed for a more secluded hiding place, throwing herself beneath a large tree close by. Swiftly, she was on her feet, standing alongside the trunk. Having felt somewhat constrained in her movements, Aria thought it a good time to slip out of her black costume jacket, and so draped it over a limb. She rolled up the long, white sleeves of her ruffled shirt.

"Boy, were you ever right, Aria. I'm glad you decided to turn back from the stairs."

"It would have been trouble, Heather, no doubt. One or both of us might have been hurt, or even killed. But let's try again, shall we? We need to hurry, too. If Mistraya's scouts arrive, I'm certain she will send them down to find us. Unless, of course, we can think of something that will prevent such an occurrence…

"All right, then, time for another spell." Aria clapped her hands lightly together. "Let's hope this one succeeds in getting us across that open area and to some shelter near the stairs. I need this iMagiNacia to be grand in scale, and unfortunately for me, that means it will be power draining."

Aria slid her hand past her face, fingers outspread, and began to lyricy, green eyes aglow.

So, thought Mistraya, I've magically outmaneuvered the Maiden child and her companion, and yet they're nowhere to be found? How can that be?

The young Maiden saw it coming, didn't she? Felt the sunrays' heat and anticipated my next move. And now the girls remain in hiding.

Mistraya looked up, the surliness that inhabited her striking features lifting slightly. "Ah, my scouts! Finally! This will definitely put an end to the game of 'Find the Hidden Maiden.'"

AmalgaMinding with Marresh, the lead scout, the sorceress ordered him to direct his flock of birds into the courtyard to seek out the Maiden and her friend. Dissolving the mental link she initiated and utilized with servile animals of the Purple Flame, the sorceress watched as Marresh led the throng between buildings and down into the expansive quadrangle.

Meanwhile, with LaserDarts tingling in readiness at her fingertips, Mistraya played the patient, merciless game of flush, reveal, and destroy—a game that, in the past, she had played victoriously.

Finishing her incantation—her Lyrica, Aria's eyes dimmed to amber. She looked up to see the swarming scouts descending upon the courtyard from the opposite end.

The blonde girl laughed. "Timing is everything." She looked over at Molly. "Ready to head for the PortalDoor?" When Molly assented, Aria turned her attention back to the scouts, and waited. She waited some more. When she felt the moment was right, she waved her hands before her face. That's when the quiet Autumnslovian courtyard seemed to explode.

On the uppermost stories of the high graceful buildings, windows blew out, and from them, in torrents, coconut shreds, cinnamon, and brown sugar sprayed forth in a blizzard that engulfed and blinded the descending scouts. Below, from the lowermost floors, masses of melting ice cream in assorted flavors and textures surged through curved windows and sculpted doorways, rushing to bury the tiled basin of the courtyard in waist-high goop. Fired from elegant balconies and verandas, mammoth raspberries and pieces of peach the size of overstuffed chairs, along with banana slices as big as tabletops, clobbered the birds, followed by rounds of colossal cherries and enormous chunks of apple and pear. Massive candy disks cleaved the air and toffee chips whizzed like ax wedges to mortally wound Mistraya's winged servants. Assorted nuts the size of cannon balls shot over the heads of Aria and Molly, pounding the swarming birds, knocking them out of the sky to the sludgy landscape below.

Injured and disoriented, the remaining scouts struggled to stay airborne, slamming into each other, into trees, walls, statuary, and stairways, before plunging to the dessert-covered terrain. There, they became mired and then buried under an avalanche of advancing ice cream toppings: butterscotch, caramel, and hot fudge that, overflowing the gutters, streaming from downspouts, and pouring out of drainpipes, drowned the once-intimidating birds, one particular scout still clutching a LuminOrb in his talons.

All the while, below the impenetrable confection-filled sky, two gingerbread men in white overalls, yellow boots, and red scarves shoveled clear a path for Aria and Molly. Untouched in the pandemonium, the girls trudged close behind, across the treacherous stretch of courtyard.

"Hey, Aria!" said Heather, over the raging storm. "By any chance are you hungry?"

"Famished!"

"Thought so."

Aria looked around at her handiwork, breaking into the engaging grin that she shared with Heather. "I suppose I could have conjured up honey-baked hams, mashed potatoes, and roasted turkeys, but where's the fun?"

"And what is this?"

Spiraling above the fracas, Mistraya squinted into the blustery disturbance. She could see nothing through the turbulence. Licking her lips, she tasted the brown sugar and cinnamon that filled the air.

"What happened to my birds in that maelstrom of iMagiNacia?" she asked, coolly. "I'm expecting a report. Why are they silent?"

The sorceress tried to connect via AmalgaMind with Marresh and others, but was unable to do so. She then attempted to SightShare, to no avail.

In that mess below has the Maiden taken the lives of my scouts, as well? Has she? Rage gripped her.

The sorceress couldn't help but be impressed with the strength of the girl's magical prowess. For one her age, her abilities were *way* beyond that of the average Maiden child—way beyond the advanced adult. And grudgingly, Mistraya admitted that she, herself, was magically tiring; she didn't know how many more times she would be able to trade spells with the young Maiden and hope to come out on top.

Youth has endurance, she thought, age wily experience. However, without assistance from my scouts that would allow me to kill the girl from afar, it looks like I'll have to find her myself and confront her face-to-face. But first, I'll need a conjuration to weaken the girl.

Mistraya looked down on the confusion below, thinking, And at the same time, I need to clear up this magical mess in a hurry. If I don't, she'll undoubtedly reach her PortalDoor. Hopefully, she hasn't done so already.

Speaking rapidly in Dennuncia, the language of the Dahklarr, she pushed her hands up and then brought them crashing down.

Like a dam bursting at the far entrance of the courtyard, a huge wave of water plowed forward, churning up and clearing away the ice cream landscape and its medley of toppings. As the swell continued its impressive sweep, it rushed high past the lower windows, washing toward the opposite end, toward Aria and Molly who had now reached the stairs to their Portal home.

Above, Mistraya smiled smugly. "That ought to start events going our way."

The sorceress hurried into the cockpit, where she sat and seized the magic reins. She gave them a flick.

"Maif! Down! Down, now! Into the courtyard and quickly!"

"The Portal stairs!" cried Molly. "We're here! Aria, you're a genius."

"Not so quick, Molly," said the young blonde, dismissing the gingerbread men with a wave of her hand. "We mustn't get overconfident—"

Hurriedly, Aria looked around. Something was amiss. The windstorm of blown toppings was unexpectedly quelling, and she could see spectators in the windows of the buildings, the structures returning to their pre-tempest state. The ground trembled. Aria's mouth dropped when she saw the wall of water headed their way.

"Up the stairs, Molly! Hurry, hurry, hurry!"

The girls mounted the stairs at a gallop, Molly in the lead. Aria, her bad ankle slowing her, was falling behind.

Throwing terrified glances toward the monstrous wave, Molly wondered if she would be able to outpace it in her haste to reach the porch. Aria, on the other hand, had slowed considerably. She looked at the approaching wave and realized that she would be unable to avoid it. The girl also saw Mistraya in her lizard-mounted cockpit flying just behind the water's swell.

Reaching the porch, Molly whirled around, holding up the key.

"We made it! Aria...?" Molly looked down the stairs, where her companion was hopping on one foot, taking the steps one-by-one. "Aria! Hurry!"

"Molly, I'm not going to make it. Go without me. Go!"

"Create a spell, Aria! Use your iMagiNacia!"

"There's no time. Go home without me!"

Dumbstruck, the girl simply stood, staring at Aria.

"Molly, *go!*"

Awakening from her stupor, Molly ran to the PortalDoor at the back of the porch, just as a firebolt hit where she had been standing, breaking the stairway loose. At the same time, the crest of the huge wave crashed through the stair railings, taking Aria and Heather with it, washing them away.

"The accomplice was able to get away, but I have the Maiden." Mistraya raised her fist triumphantly. "Oh, I have the Maiden! She's mine! She's mine, mine, mine! *And* I know the location of their Portal-Door. I can hardly wait to see what kind of havoc I can unleash upon their world. But first to matters of immediate import: Let me drain the courtyard and land Maif."

Spiraling down, the sorceress kept a wary eye out for the Maiden Portent, LaserDarts at the ready in case of a ruse. But as the water subsided, Mistraya caught sight of the young girl. She lay unmoving, entangled low in the railing of the stairway that had swung free, held aloft amid the mangled framework that remained attached at its base.

Water slapped off the walls and slowly drained out the ends of the courtyard, while the sorceress circled again. In passing, she studied the Maiden aspirant: her long wiry body, soggy hair over a hanging head, and strewn, motionless limbs.

I'm surprised! Despite all the recent magical interference, I can sense the Maiden child. There's barely any life in her, thought the sorceress. The woman no longer felt exultant. Rather Mistraya was subdued.

It's the end of a worthy adversary, the most impressive green-eyed Maiden yet to come my way.

"But you're mine!" she suddenly screamed, raising her arms in triumph, the looping end of the Mastery°Harness squeezed tightly in one hand. "You thought you had eluded me, *but you're mine!*"

The sorceress laughed, now turning her attention to landing Maif in the waist-deep water.

Caught up in her euphoria, Mistraya didn't sense the life that flowed back into the limp Heather, as Aria surged to the fore, reclaiming the girl's body. But instead of taking overt action, she remained motionless save for one simple thing: Aria opened her mouth ever so slightly, and from the tip of her tongue, she let loose a delicate, crystalline snowflake that floated downward towards the courtyard floor. When it touched the surface of the water, from that point and emanating out, the liquid solidified to become a bed of ice.

Only moments before, as the sorceress landed her winged creature, Maif's feet had touched down, barreling through the water in a trail of splashes. But when the liquid froze, the great lizard's forward progress stopped abruptly. Its short legs, instantly frozen within the thick ice, snapped and tore loose, causing the lizard to screech in agony, sliding on its bloody stumps. Losing her grip on the reins, Mistraya was flung loose and sent hurtling from her compartment. She hit the ice with a grunt, skidding and spinning across the glassy surface. While desperately attempting to latch onto any object in passing, the sorceress was dennunciating a magical spell to save herself. But time ran out, and the woman slammed into the wall of a nearby building, full force. Following the loud thump of her impact, Mistraya lay still.

Delicately, Aria disentangled herself from the railing. She clambered down what remained of the stairway and its railing and onto the courtyard's frozen, slippery surface.

"Are you all right, Heather?" she asked, brushing herself off, looking herself over.

"Yeah. I'm okay, I guess. Looks like we're a little sore." The girl gave thought before asking, "Aria, how come you gave up possession after making that bubble to protect us, when we were about to be hit by the wave?"

"I knew that Mistraya would notice the drop off in power and think you—we—were close to dead."

"So, that's when you decided to make the bubble disappear and have us get all tangled up in the railing?"

"That's right, right before the water subsided, and then, after conjuring my magical snowflake, I temporarily turned possession over to you. Earlier, with the wave coming, I knew that if I kept pace with Molly on the stairs, Mistraya would have a chance to destroy either one or both of us, or the PortalDoor before we reached it—she's a very powerful sorceress, you know—and so I dropped behind and feigned greater injury."

Heather was rubbing the knot on her head. "Boy, you didn't have to hit our head so hard on that stone step, you know, before hanging us all goofy-like in the railing."

"Actually, I did. As well as sensing our power, I knew Mistraya would also tap into the Maiden's pain, our pain. It helped to convince her of our deteriorating condition when she approached. We'll have a slight headache—and it does hurt—but I think, if I remember correctly from a certain incident with a shovel in the Bristol House garden, that you're used to such clobberings."

Heather laughed, still rubbing her head. "Yeah, I guess I am." She paused before adding, "You must be, too."

The two looked over at the downed sorceress. Lying on her side, Mistraya's back was to the girls.

"She's not dead, Aria. I can still feel her."

"Yes, I know. I feel her, too. It's her power. She's not conscious, though, Heather, and there's something I need to do."

Aria initiated the walk toward the unmoving sorceress.

"Aria, are you sure you want to do this? Go closer, I mean. This reminds me of the time I slapped a wasp. Nailed it right before I was almost stung. After I hit it, when it was lying there on the ground, I wanted to get a good look at it. But I didn't know whether it was a good idea to pick it up or not. Know what I mean? If it was only stunned, it could still sting me."

"Yes. And this wasp, here, has quite the stinger. What did you do?"

Heather smiled wryly. "What do you think I did?"

"You picked it up."

Heather said, "Yeah," before mumbling, "Got stung, too."

Aria looked the sorceress over.

Heather said, "I'm not feeling too good about this. That's Mistraya right there. A little while ago she was trying to kill us."

"I understand, Heather." Aria knelt and gently but heedfully rolled Mistraya onto her back. Afterward, she stood and stepped back a pace. Eyes briefly aglow, Aria spoke softly in Lyrica, and brought her hands up, enfolding them over her chest.

Below, needles shot out of the ice on both sides of the sorceress, trailing a thick mesh of magical twine. They landed and buried themselves on the opposite sides of her body, plunging through holes belonging to pink buttons that had magically appeared affixed to the surface of the ice. The needles resurfaced to leap and dive through the remaining buttonholes before disappearing altogether. On her back, Mistraya lay laced to the ice.

"Better?" Aria asked.

"Yeah. Better. But I still don't trust her."

The young girl again approached the downed sorceress. Kneeling closely by her side, Aria remained quiet for some time, contemplating Mistraya's inanimate face.

Finally, she spoke, her voice low. "So peaceful in your damaged sleep, aren't you? I should kill you, if only I could. Part of a prophecy to come, you and I, we will be pitted against one another in due course, with the fate of Evermore in the balance."

Aria looked up to see spectators gathering, approaching haltingly in bunches from the ends of the ice-filled courtyard. She turned her attention back to Mistraya.

"Enjoy the time which follows, wretched sorceress. For you and your kind it will be the first of many prosperous years, since they will all be dark in your vein. But do remember:

'When Sun and Moon their days gone past,
Allow the two to merge at last,
Deposing reigns of ill long worn,
For Evermore, Arise Reborn!'

"We mustn't forget the Portent, my elder sister. For though I see you everyday, you cannot see me, and think I'm dead. But I am in hiding. I am. Right in the midst of your darkly clouded vision."

Aria leaned over and lightly kissed the brow of Mistraya.

"Until when and then, Lussitaria. As I remember you."

Unexpectedly, the hand of the sorceress shot out to seize Aria's wrist. Around her, some of the onlookers gasped. Yet, the girl didn't flinch. Tenderly she peeled away the firm, long-fingered grasp, setting the hand of the unconscious sorceress gently down on the ice. Then Aria uttered a spell that drew the cords more tightly around the recumbent Mistraya.

Still showing SearEye, Aria arose and, with words and a wave, called for snowflakes. They began to lightly fall to the Autumnslovian earth. People had begun to stray from their buildings, but upon seeing the beast flapping its wings in a dying gesture on the bloodied ice, most kept their distance.

Aria stood before the damaged steps. Looking up at the balcony and the PortalDoor, she raised her arms and lyrisied. Immediately, a wide stretch of water poured from the front of the porch, materializing where the stairs had torn free. Hitting the frozen surface below, in front of the girl, the waterfall crystallized, and in doing so formed a new stairway. Aria put her hand on the icy railing and began to climb. Behind her, a lone soul started to clap, but no one else joined in, and so the sound trailed off.

"The sorceress, that's your sister?" Heather asked, coming to the fore.

Aria nodded.

"What happened? How did she get to be so, well, so Mistraya?"

"You'll have to forgive me, Heather, but at the moment, I'm hardly in the mood for a very long story."

But Heather persisted. "So, if Mistraya is your sister, and you're part of me, that means that—"

"That she's your sister, too?"

"Yeah."

"Yes, but not quite. Not yet."

Aria turned on the stairs, looking at her sister laid out below. Her amber eyes again displaying SearEye, the Maiden lyrisied and waved her arm in a precise arc above her. What had once been snowflakes falling soon became pieces of fruit clopping down onto the courtyard floor.

"Aria, what did you do?" Heather asked.

"Snowflakes were for a sister that once was. The falling fruit is for what she's become."

"Hey!" Heather ducked and threw a protective arm over her head. She rushed up the remainder of the stairs. "They look like apples, Aria. Ew, and they're rotten," Heather said, picking one up off the top stair, kicking away the brown mushy others that had gathered on the landing. "They don't really hurt when they hit you, silly things." She cast the fruit aside.

"Hey, Aria, I've got to ask you a question. Are you and I—or just *you*—the green-eyed Maiden of the Evermore Portent? Or neither of us?" Heather waited. "Aria?" She waited a bit longer. "Are you there?" Heather sighed. The girl walked to the PortalDoor and tried the knob. Locked, it didn't move. "So now how am I supposed to get home?"

"The PortalKey?"

Heather jumped at the unexpected voice. She looked over and saw Molly waiting at the far end of the porch, against the wall. She was holding up the key. The girls didn't move toward one another.

"Aria's gone?"

"Yeah, Molly. She's gone." Heather stood silently.

Molly approached, key in hand. The girls looked at one other before they fell into an easy hug. Entwined, they just hung, each as if propping up the other. Neither spoke.

Finally, Molly said, "We made it."

"Yeah." Heather regarded the PortalDoor. "Almost." When they separated, she said, "You didn't go through. How come?"

Molly shrugged. "I don't know. It didn't seem right. Instead I watched and waited."

"Aria told you to go. You should have gone."

"I suppose I should have." Molly went quiet before adding, "I almost did when I thought that you and Aria…you and Aria were dead."

Heather turned away and walked back to the edge of the balcony, Molly drawing up alongside her.

"You know," said the blonde girl, "it's weird."

"What's weird?"

"Aria. I felt her sadness, Molly. I've never felt any of Aria's feelings before."

The two gazed silently down on the courtyard, each mulling over their thoughts. They didn't notice that the buttons alongside Mistraya were unhurriedly popping loose from the ice, one here, one there.

Dully, Heather was taking note of the many scouts she could see dead and frozen within the ice, when Molly said, "You know, there were times when I wasn't sure we'd ever make it back, Heather. Did you ever feel that way?"

Heather took a long moment before she gave a brief chuckle. "Honestly, I guess I never really thought about it. Maybe, I think, once."

When Molly noticed the singed landing where Mistraya's bolt had just missed her, she moved closer to her friend. The two watched the fruit drop against the beautiful backdrop of Autumnslovian architecture and trees. Clop. Clop, clop. Clop. Clop, clop, clop. It began to pile up at various places within the courtyard, most notably over and around Mistraya, where another button that bound her had just popped free. Not too far away, the great lizard, Maif, had settled, its mouth contorted, its wings awkwardly bent. Attached to the creature's back, Mistraya's cockpit canopy was tilted, angled in cockeyed fashion. The crowds were larger now, clustered around the perimeter of the courtyard. Most just stared at the girls, Heather in particular. In the sky, all remnants of the Bayliss tapestry, along with Mistraya's conjured clouds and sunrays, had long since disappeared, yet the rotted fruit continued to materialize, dropping out of nowhere.

Beside the sorceress, another button broke loose with an indistinct pop, causing her bindings to slacken further.

Finally, Heather said, "Here, let's have the PortalKey."

Again, the girl produced the strange, white-faced key and handed it over.

"Come on, Molly. Let's get inside. I don't know about you, but I'm hungry and tired." Heather looked up at the fading twilight sky. "And I suppose we've got some explaining to do."

closing the Door on Evermore

Standing on the porch before the flowing motif of the PortalDoor, Heather was admiring its artistic handiwork. She ran her slender fingers across the intricate design.

"When we walked through here and came to Autumnsloe," she said, "I didn't notice how really great the PortalDoor looked from the outside."

"I did," said Molly, "but only because I had to go back and get the PortalKey."

Although emotionally exhausted, the girls began to feel a restrained sense of excitement, a sense of accomplishment, a fantastic journey completed.

Key poised, Heather asked, "Ready to go home and see the Bristol House again?"

Molly nodded. "Geez, am I ever."

Neither of the girls laughed.

As she lowered the key to the lock, Heather stopped. She could hear a voice—or voices—behind the door. The girls exchanged quizzical glances.

"Who can that be in the Bristol House sewing room?"

Smiling, Molly had perked up. "Hmmm. I wonder."

Turning her attention back to the elegant brown knob, Heather attempted to insert the key into the jagged hole at its center. Moving it this way and that, the PortalKey refused to go into the lock.

She looked at Molly. "Okay, so what do we do now? Knock?"

Mistraya groaned. She brought a hand up to her head.

How I hate a headache, the sorceress thought. So untimely. Really.

She sat up on the ice, easily pulling loose the Lilliputian cords that once held her, the pink buttons clinging to the magical twine before dropping free and rolling away. People in the crowd around her gasped and withdrew, fearing the unpredictable sorceress; some hurried away. But Mistraya ignored them as she gained her feet. Tidying up with little hurry, the weary sorceress brushed herself off, and then shook her head, gathering and setting loose her long black hair behind her.

Mistraya took a short restorative breath, and exhaling sharply, set off in the direction of Maif. Fascinated by the sorceress, some of the spectators followed, cautiously keeping their distance. Others watched through windows overlooking the courtyard. A cloaked charismatic figure isolated upon the ice, Mistraya grew despondent as she approached the winged lizard. Looking at the massive twisted body, lifeless in a pool of its own blood, a great rage welled up in her.

The sorceress snarled at a whisper, "Although I'm far more powerful, far more accomplished, and far superior in every way, Maiden child, somehow you've managed to outwit me. And in the end, you have taken everything: a majority, if not all, of my GraySuits and scouts, and now one of my treasured great lizards." Nastily, Mistraya looked up toward the recessed PortalDoor and thought, But I know where you live. Perhaps I need to pay you a surprise visit. Don't worry, though, I'm never one to overstay my welcome.

"It doesn't go in there."

"What do you mean, Molly?"

"The key doesn't go there. It goes in below the knob, in that smaller, old-fashioned keyhole. See it?"

"Sure," said Heather. "But then why the other one?"

"Beats me."

Heather inserted the key in the hole and gave it a turn. The tumblers spun smoothly, terminating with a decisive click. When she grasped the doorknob, the girl hesitated a second before attempting to twist it.

"Please open," came her quiet request.

Gratefully, the knob turned and Heather pushed. As the door swung inward, the familiar, magical interior of the Bristol House sewing room was revealed to the girls.

Whispers rose among the crowd, as the now composed sorceress started for the waterfall stairs. She stopped. Those who followed halted a short distance behind. When Mistraya turned to face them, some recoiled. She observed them sedately, some shifting uncomfortably. No one looked directly at her.

Let them follow, she thought. Like so many annendoles, so easily guided. Besides, the Maiden child has bested me today—thus far. And the story will spread by word of mouth, telling of her victory. But if I alter the ending, killing the girl, then let that be what is passed between the tongues and ears of the citizenry and from the exploitive mouths of our NewsBarkers.

She turned and began her ascent up the frozen staircase. Trailing a short distance behind, the hangers-on followed.

Mistraya thought contemptuously, I don't know what it is about the Evermorian minions. They simply can't resist a show—or better yet, a showdown.

Stepping over the threshold, the girls passed through the Portal, traveling along the infinite expanse of the TimeLight Bridge. Arriving instantaneously, they seamlessly entered the sewing room, walking between the two bronze Maidens in armor and beneath the third Maiden that resembled Heather, only without hair. Entering behind her friend, a distracted Molly stopped, and with a mixture of emotions, took a lasting look out on the fantastic, foreign world of Evermore. Reluctantly and gratefully, she closed the PortalDoor behind her.

With a slight hobble, Heather took her time as she drifted to the center of the small room, near the two mannequins on which hung the girls' street clothes. Her gaze feasted on everything around her.

"Here we are," said Molly, mustering a bit of enthusiasm, "finally safe and sound."

"We're back," said Heather, turning to look up into the face of the bald likeness of herself that, lying on her belly, gazed down playfully from atop the PortalDoor, her cheek still in hand. The blonde girl walked a few steps closer. "Did you miss us?" Heather thought she saw the girl's smile increase in size. Heather explained, "We look a little different than when we left, I know, but that's because we had to leave our Bristol House costumes back in Autumnsloe. I even had to leave—" Heather watched as the smile faded from the face of the bronze representation of herself, "—my second mask there..." Looking away, she quickly changed the subject, "Boy, sure is hot in here."

"It is, isn't it?" Molly said. "I wonder why?" She looked around thoughtfully, before asking, "Heather, who do you think we heard just now talking on the other side of the PortalDoor?"

"I don't know. But since we came inside, I don't hear those voices any more."

Heather walked over to the open top half of the pointed dutch door that led into the larger sewing room. She stuck her head and upper body through, teetering on her belly. "Well, whoever it was," she said, her voice spilling into the other room, "they're not in here, either. Unless it was the mannequins. Hey, maybe they were having a costume party."

Molly didn't laugh. "That's strange," she replied. "I know we heard voices. I thought it might be..."

Heather looked over. "You thought it might be...?"

"Never mind." The clown girl peeled off her hat and eyemask and laid them on a chair near her mannequin. Molly could feel Heather watching her all the while. She looked up to find her friend still awaiting an explanation.

"You thought it might be...?"

Molly haltingly continued, "I was hoping it was...I mean, I was hoping that...that there was someone..." Molly's voice hurriedly trailed off with: "...someone waiting for us, that's all."

"Someone? Molly, I don't understand. Your mother? Grandma Dawn? The nightman on the stairs? Who? Someone I know?"

"Yes." She struggled to meet Heather's eyes. "Someone we both know." Molly continued in an undertone, "Someone who came with us to Parade Day."

Instantly, Heather bowed her head, looking at the floor. With clumsy hands trying to find shelter in her pockets, the girl faced her friend. "I— there's something I need to tell you."

Molly was concentrating on prying off her left shoe with the toe of her right. It was being stubborn. The girl didn't look up. Her voice suddenly shaky, she asked, "It's about Fallasha, isn't it?"

Immobilized, Heather blinked once and again. Then she nodded.

Carefully, Mistraya had mounted the waterfall stairs leading to the porch. Upon reaching the landing, she gazed across at the ornate door.

"Ah, and so the Maiden child's PortalDoor. Must be. It's the only one here on the porch. Can it be unlocked? Is that possible? Let us see, then, shall we, just how lucky a Sorceress of the Dahklarr Herth can be?"

Molly was staring at Heather, fighting off a sense of foreboding. "You did leave Fallasha in the dressing room with your moon costume, didn't you?"

Heather nodded, her lips tight, her voice low. "Yeah."

"Well, then, there's no need to worry, right?" Molly's eyes were pleading. "When the ClearWeave took our costumes, they also took Fallasha. So she's safe, right?" Her friend didn't speak. "Right?" Molly waited.

Heather was struggling with words, loose threads of multiple beginnings dangling freely in her mind. She was at a loss, wondering exactly which one to choose, wondering how to start to explain what happened there in the dressing room at The Crown & Scepter.

The blonde girl pictured Fallasha, the moon brooch with whom she had argued so frequently, but in the end had come to hold dear. She remembered how the brooch had asked Heather to save her, to fracture her and by doing so take the life out of the small moon. That way, Mistraya wouldn't get her hands on the talking brooch to find out her secrets before killing her. Heather had to do it. There really wasn't a choice. There wasn't.

The girl remembered, too, how, while on her knees, she had carefully held the brooch and how Fallasha looked up calmly, encouraging Heather to fracture her. With each hand gripping an end of the crescent that was Fallasha, and feeling the ever increasing tension as she slowly tightened her hold, Heather had found herself hesitating. She tried to look away, but couldn't, all the while focusing on the face of her friend.

Finally, Fallasha had whispered, "Do it *now.*"

And Heather did. But she had had to close her eyes—only for a moment, only until the deed was done. Heather recalled how the brooch had felt in her hands prior—warm to the touch—and then when the little moon snapped, the abrupt and freeing split-second jerk, and afterward how she had held the separated halves of Fallasha that were broken across the face, just under the nose. Heather remembered the eyes of the brooch, no longer animated and full of life but dull and dead like small stones. The girl had stared at the lifeless lips, too—still fleshy—that hung slightly parted. She so craved to hear them speaking. And with her hands trembling, Heather had laid Fallasha down, her tiny body still clinging to the costume's fabric.

I should have said so many things, Heather thought. I should have told her how great it was to meet her. And how nice she was. And smart. And I didn't. I didn't tell her anything.

Her face stricken, Heather fought back tears, determined not to cry.

"Heather," Molly said, walking over to her friend. "What are you trying to tell me?"

"Molly, I killed Fallasha."

The small group of onlookers clustered behind her on the porch, Mistraya stood before the PortalDoor. Putting her ear up to it, she heard voices. The sorceress turned the knob silently and without hindrance.

Ah, it *is* unlocked. I thought so. Poor, forgetful girls.

Pulling her head away from the door, Mistraya turned to the gathering behind her, and brought a finger to her lips.

Very slowly, she began to push the door inward.

Tears were streaming down Molly's face. "Fallasha was right, Heather. You had to fracture her. If you didn't, Mistraya might have gotten ahold of her."

"Fallasha said that the sorceress would magically torture her to get information and then kill her."

"Whoever Fallasha is, she was probably right," said Mistraya's cool voice from the doorway. "Especially the part about killing. I'm very good at that. Want to see?"

Molly cried out in horror. Heather shoved her friend aside, into an upholstered armchair, before hurriedly pivoting to charge at Mistraya. Immediately slipping on the area rug, the girl toppled to her side where she rolled. Scrambling to her feet, only to slip again on the tricky carpet, Heather would never arrive in time to engage the sorceress. Mistraya stood with her hands raised, rapidly dennunciating. As the sorceress stepped forward into the small sewing room to shoot the deadly AccuBarbs from beneath her fingernails, she didn't see the young man in a hooded shirt who had broken free from the small group. A disciple of the ClearWeave, he made a rush for Mistraya, and grabbing her cloak at the neck, pulled her off balance back onto the porch. The hardy man caused the sorceress, her long hair in a sweep, to spin and fall on top of him. There they wrestled, as the powerful Mistraya tried to raise a hand to fire a volley through the doorway at Heather, the young man snatching at her wrists and knocking down her hands.

"Who are you?" Mistraya sneered, inches from his face. "How *dare* you assail me."

The ClearWeave disciple didn't answer, but instead bucked and writhed, attempting to slip from under the sorceress and gain the advantage. He snatched at her face and came up empty.

Some in the small gathering cried out and began a hasty retreat down the stairs. Others gawked, too stunned to move, surprised that anyone would ever attack Mistraya.

"This…just doesn't…seem to be…my day," said the grappling sorceress. "Nor yours either," she concluded, managing to twist her hand until it was pointed in his direction, though he still had hold of it. Following a quick recitation, Mistraya shot a pulse of blue radiation into his head. The disciple jerked rigid before going limp.

Meanwhile, Heather reached the heavy PortalDoor, hurriedly pushing it closed. This caused Mistraya to lunge toward the entryway from her knees. Slamming her shoulder against the door, she was able to prevent it from shutting completely.

"Molly! The PortalKey!" Heather shouted over her shoulder.

"I don't remember where I put it." Up from the chair, Molly began to frantically look around. "Is it there in the keyhole?"

"I don't see it," grunted Heather, her full weight propped against the door. "Let's hope it's not outside, still in the lock."

The girl rotated so that her back was pressed to the PortalDoor, her arms slapping down against it, her feet spread wide in strong-legged resistance. However, soon her shoes began to lose traction, skidding on the smooth wooden flooring, while, outside, Mistraya clambered to her feet, applying more force against the door.

"Did you bring the key on your way in?"

Molly's gaze was darting over the furniture around her. "Yes, I did. I remember now. I just can't remember where I put it."

Heather's feet continued to slide.

"Hurry, Molly, check your costume. I can't hold the door much longer."

"I am..." Molly was furiously patting herself before plunging her hands into her pockets.

"It's here! I found it!"

Immediately, she ran to Heather and added her weight to the blockade with an "Umph!" The door closed a bit, but with the sorceress now on her feet with better leverage, the gap soon widened, and continued to slowly increase in width.

Heather said, "Molly, the PortalKey. Can you give it to me?"

Upper arm and shoulder to the door, Molly handed the key to her companion. Maintaining her resistance, Heather blindly poked around with the key before finding the hole of the lock. Pushing with her palm, the PortalKey rattled and sank into place.

"Okay, when I say 'go,' shove with all your might... Give it everything."

Molly nodded.

Outside, with her hands pressed to the PortalDoor, Mistraya wedged her boot between the door and the threshold, preventing it from closing completely. The sorceress then began to dennunciate a spell that would blast the heavy door inward, causing it to land on top of the girls.

Inside, Heather yelled, "Go!" and the girls threw a burst of energy into closing the door. Grunting, Heather's feet worked for traction on the glossy floor, while Molly's pumped and slid in vain.

"Agh!" said the sorceress. Feeling the surge of the door, she broke off her spell. Mistraya's well-wedged boot held firm, however, and she said over her shoulder, "Anyone willing to assist a sorceress in need?"

No one in the crowd stepped forward. However, most turned and fled down the stairs.

"Didn't think so," grumbled Mistraya, glimpsing the dead man at her feet.

Under the hectic circumstances, unable to smoothly make use of the Voice to coerce assistance, the sorceress returned to weaving her spell. Meanwhile, with the girls tiring, the door began to give more ground.

"Molly, push!" yelled Heather.

"I *am* pushing!"

The slice of open door was at its widest point yet and still increasing.

"Molly, I'm afraid we can't hold the door by ourselves," said Heather, seeing the long fingers of Mistraya's hand reaching in to wrap and grip the edge. "We..." The girl grunted, feeling her shoes slip all the more. "We need help!"

At the sound of those three words, the bronze Maidens in armor on each side of the PortalDoor sprang into action. The two statues turned and threw themselves against the door, and together with the girls, they popped Mistraya's boot free from obstructing its closure.

"Ay-e-e-e-e-e!!!" screamed the sorceress, releasing her grip while being thrown backward. As the door slammed shut, she stumbled over the body of the dead disciple, but managed to keep her balance.

Molly yelled, "Quick, Heather, turn the key!" but her friend had already done so. A loud click was heard.

As Heather and Molly slumped against the sealed PortalDoor, breathing heavily, the Maidens promptly returned to their previously held positions as armored sentinels. From there, they began another transition in form, a result of the key having been turned in the lock.

Heather pulled Molly away from the door. The pair watched as it went through a series of transformations before finally settling to become a large bronze sculpture. On top of a metallic rock face stood the bald Maiden, once again bound in bronze fabric pulled to either side by the two taller Maidens. Now in robes, their attitudes were exuberant, their thick braids falling behind them. The clock above the door grew in size and reestablished itself in the center of the rock face, the PortalKey protruding from the keyhole to its right.

Molly and Heather stood back from the sculpture.

"That was close," said Molly, still somewhat breathless.

"I don't think Mistraya's done yet," said Heather, retrieving the 'Key. "Come on. Hurry."

"What do you mean she's not done?"

"I mean that she might just come blasting through that wall, shooting stuff around like she did in the courtyard."

"Really? But I thought the PortalDoor was sealed."

"It might be, but since there's no one to ask how PortalDoors work, we can't be sure."

She led Molly into the larger sewing room, shutting the lower half of the dutch door. Behind it, Heather dropped to a knee and hid herself. She looked up. "Molly, go downstairs and wait for me."

The girl crouched down beside Heather. "No way."

The pair locked eyes, Molly's determined.

A slow smile grew on Heather's face. "Okay."

Molly followed her friend's lead, and they cautiously reared their heads up, peering over the lower half of the door, waiting for something to happen.

"If I tell you to run, Molly, you have to do it, okay? Will you promise?"

Molly looked at Heather, whose focus on the sculptural PortalDoor never wavered. Without turning her way, Heather said, "Molly?"

"All right, I promise," said her friend after a pause. "But only if you run, too."

On the porch, Mistraya stepped back, after having attempted to turn the doorknob without success. Again she could hear the muffled voices on the other side. The sorceress looked behind her. Only a handful of people remained.

"Seems I've lost my audience," mused the sorceress. Looking down on the inanimate person in the hood, she added disdainfully, "In more ways than one."

Mistraya gathered herself.

"I've never attempted to blast through a PortalDoor before," she said. "This should prove interesting."

"Nothing is happening, Heather," whispered Molly, while she and Heather continued to keep watch in the direction of the bronze sculpture, the clocks in both rooms continuing to count out the wait.

"Let's give it more time. It still might."

"If Mistraya blasts through that wall, what do we do then?"

"Hope that the Bristol House hasn't mixed up the rooms too much on the third floor, so that we can get downstairs real fast and warn Grandma Dawn."

Mistraya cast her spell perfectly and watched as the PortalDoor exploded inward in a burst of smoke and debris.

BOOM!

The sorceress waited several moments before cautiously moving forward through the impacted doorway, AccuBarbs at the ready.

As the smoke cleared, she was able to discern some overturned chairs, a large table on its side, and a room in disarray.

Hiding behind the tabletop were two elderly women covered with debris, one with her head down and hands to her face, the other coughing from the settling of dust. A third woman was peeking out from an adjoining room, her glasses hanging crookedly on her nose, while a fourth peered around a corner. All were fear struck. Scattered across the floor was a board game, its playing cards and holographic pieces strewn everywhere.

"I'm sorry for intruding," said Mistraya, as another large ceiling tile fell to the floor. She smiled wanly. "Yours is not the interior I had anticipated. Am I still in Autumnsloe? I am. Seems I have the wrong address, then. By the way, allow me to inform you that your door is shared by others, though, I assure you, they're hardly worth mentioning." She spotted the popular Evermorian board game, its lights arcing and sizzling in malfunction near her feet.

"Oh, and look. I see you're playing *Portals and Planets*. How fun. Well, don't let me interrupt. Please. Carry on, as if I never disturbed you."

With that, the sorceress turned on her heel. Stunned, the elderly ladies watched as the woman departed. Upon her exit, sporadic clapping could be heard outside.

CHAPTER THIRTY-THREE

At Rest Between Worlds

"**I** think we're safe now."

Molly's head rose up over the bottom half of the Dutch door, alongside Heather's.

"Are you sure?"

"No. But if Mistraya was going to blast through that wall, I think she would have done it by now."

They stood, opened the lower part of the Dutch door, and let themselves back into the smaller sewing room.

"Let's get out of these costumes, Molly, and get downstairs. Grandma Dawn and your mother are probably really worried. I'm sure we're late—real late—getting back from the parade."

The girls strode over to the mannequins to retrieve their street clothes, all the while uneasily aware of the PortalDoor—now a bronze clock—and the alcove wall behind it. When the clocks in the large sewing room and its smaller adjunct chimed out in a melodic tone signaling the half hour, Heather looked outright at the sculptural timepiece.

"Hey, Molly," she said. "Notice anything funny about the clock?"

Molly turned from her mannequin. "What about it?"

"Look at the time."

Fascinated, the brunette took a step closer. "How strange is that?"

One shoe off and exhibiting a slight limp, Heather ran momentarily into the bigger sewing room before returning. "It's the same time on the red grandfather clock in the other room."

"Maybe someone forgot to wind them."

"No one winds the Bristol House clocks, Molly. And they're never wrong."

"You know, now that you mention it, I've never seen you or your grandmother do it."

"Yeah, we never have to. They run on magic, I guess, and rewind themselves. Molly, that means it's only three-thirty here in Noble."

"Maybe it's three-thirty in the morning. Did you ever think of that?"

"Yep. But there's daylight in the room next door, so that means it's only three-thirty in the afternoon."

"Oh, that's right. But on what day?" When Heather rolled her eyes, Molly giggled and said, "So, we're not late getting home after all?"

"Seems that way. I guess the Bristol House makes sure we're never away longer than we should be."

"Whew!" Molly plopped herself on a chair. "That's a relief. It feels like we've been gone for a week."

"Yeah, it sure does."

Heather began to take off her costume, eager to get into her everyday clothes. Seeing that Molly was taking her time about it, and knowing they were no longer in a hurry, she slowed and then stopped altogether. Heather found the chair near Molly's.

"I wonder why it's so hot in here, Heather."

"Yeah. What's with that? No matter what the season is, the Bristol House is always the perfect temperature." The blonde girl briefly scanned the room, but lost interest when she didn't spot anything unusual. Her mind wandered.

The pair didn't talk for a while. Molly looked over at Heather, her friend still lost in thought. She noticed that Heather's mood had changed, and watched as the girl got to her feet and returned to peeling off her costume. As if someone had thrown a switch, Heather had taken to brooding, and Molly suspected she knew why.

"You all right?"

Slipping out of her black pants, Heather nodded.

"So, what are you thinking about?" Molly asked, with a forced lightness.

"Oh, I don't know…" The girl reached up and retrieved her pants that were hanging over the mannequin. "Everything, I guess."

"Feel like talking?"

When Heather looked up, Molly saw the sadness that had overtaken her. Heather shrugged.

Molly waited before saying, "Everything? That's sure a lot of stuff to think about."

A slight smile found Heather's face, but it didn't brighten. "I was just thinking about Evermore, the Maidens, Mistraya, Aria, Fallasha, The Crown & Scepter, Mr. No Name, the Matron… Lots of stuff."

"But we made it, Heather. We made it to Evermore and back again. Isn't that great?"

"Yeah." Heather glanced at the PortalDoor clock. "And we were able to leave Mistraya in Autumnsloe. I hope." Having pulled her blouse on over her head, the girl dropped to the floor to put on her socks.

Molly asked, "Do you think there are more magical people like her in the other three kingdoms?"

"Evil like her, you mean? Who knows? Probably. You know, I still don't know who was in the WhisperEye mirror yesterday. That awful woman said she was my mother, but now I don't think so. Anyway, for all I know, *she* could have been contacting me from one of the other kingdoms. So, I guess that means Evermore is full of magical people, both good and evil. Full of magic, too."

Molly chuckled. "It is, isn't it?" After a time, she added, "Remember what the Matron said, that Evermore is going to have the Dark Spell, where everything becomes…"

Molly was searching for a word, when Heather said, "Dark?"

She giggled. "Yes, dark. But that's when the green-eyed Maiden is supposed to appear, at least according to the Evermore Portent. She's…" Molly observed her friend carefully, "…she's supposed to save them."

Heather was putting on her red shoes, one of them with a grimace. As she did so, the girls again slid into silence, each to their own.

"The green-eyed Maiden," Heather finally said. "The ClearWeave, the people in The Crown & Scepter, they all think I'm her…" The statement trailed off, but not her moody introspection. "And *I'm* supposed to save Evermore. Sheesh. Like I told the Matron, I couldn't even save Stilped. Or Fallasha. How in the world am I ever going to save a super-gigantic Realm? And who am I supposed to save them from? Or what? That's four different kingdoms, Molly, and they're not even on the same planet. To do that, I would have to be strong and smart. And brave. I'm not any of those things—"

"I think you are."

Heather drew a pensive smile. "Well, thanks, but nowhere near what the green-eyed Maiden is going to have to be. I'm not her, Molly. I'm not. It was Aria who did all those things, not me. The people in Evermore just don't know it."

The two drifted into their quiet worlds once again. Having tied her shoes so that now she was completely dressed, Heather sighed. Rising, she found the leather armchair once more, where she leaned back with a flop.

"Molly, you're super smart. What do you think?"

"About everyone believing that you're the Maiden?"

"Yeah."

The girl pondered Heather's question.

"Molly—?"

"I'm thinking, Heather." Eventually, Molly let loose with a gentle laugh. "You know what I think?"

"What?"

"I don't think it's important what everyone believes. What's most important is that you really did some very special, green-eyed Maiden things on your own, like when you saved Stilped."

"But I didn't—"

"You did, too, Heather. Only it was in the classroom at school with Mrs. Peck. Aria would never have come around if you hadn't stood up for him. And you saved me from Borray on the trolley, and Aria was nowhere in sight."

"But don't forget, I couldn't save Fallasha, Molly. In the end, just like Stilped, I let her down."

"No you didn't, Heather. Are you listening?" Molly became slightly nettled. "You really did save Stilped. And Fallasha? I think you saved her, too. Because if you hadn't fractured her, like she said, the RogueTags or those creepy people would have taken her to Mistraya. And then the sorceress would have tortured her in some magical way until she told secrets about herself, and then Mistraya would have found out more about you and me, the Bristol House, Aria—all those things and more, because I think Fallasha knew a lot—"

"Fallasha told me she used to be a spy."

Molly absorbed the information before continuing, "And if Mistraya had been able to find out all Fallasha knew, your little brooch might have made it easy for the Influenced to come looking for you here. You stopped all that from happening, Heather, because you *are* brave."

"You really think so, Molly?"

"Yes."

"But if it really was the ClearWeave that took Fallasha from the dressing room, then—well, then I killed her for no reason." Heather looked away.

"But you didn't know, Heather. How could you? Fallasha didn't know, either, that the ClearWeave was going to take her out of the dressing room, or she never would have asked you to fracture her. Right?"

"Molly, I don't know. I mean..."

"Heather, come on. You're a hero. You are!" But when the girl refused to be cheered, Molly persisted. "I know you cared about Fallasha. I did, too. But she asked you to do something that was really difficult, and you did it. That was very, very brave." When Heather still seemed unconvinced, Molly leaned forward and added in a gentle voice, "It can't be easy to hurt your friend, even when you know what you're doing is best for her."

Despite herself, tears began to roll down Heather's cheeks. She hurriedly got up and walked to the dutch door, apparently to reacquaint herself with all that occupied the larger room. From behind, Molly thought she detected her friend's shoulders shaking. She watched as Heather's arm came up in a swipe across her face. The girl remained at the open upper door.

Molly, meanwhile, returned to her own thoughts, about her friend, Evermore, and the day's events. The room's heat made her feel clammy, uncomfortable. She repositioned herself in the chair. When the girl heard Heather approach, she looked up. "Heather, is it true? Was Fallasha really a spy?"

"Yeah." Sitting, Heather's mood seemed to have brightened a bit, though her eyes were ringed in red. "That's what she told me. But then I guess Fallasha got canned, because she talked way too much."

The girls laughed, Heather more than Molly.

Molly rose and began to undress, still reflective. She said, "I've been thinking."

"About what?"

The girl hesitated. "Stilped."

Heather just stared, her newfound spark dimming. Molly noticed.

"I think it's important, Heather. With Stilped, there's one thing you may not have thought about."

"What's that?"

"That maybe it was already too late. Did you ever think about that? Maybe you couldn't have saved him even if you did everything right and you hadn't been hit over the head. Maybe…"

"Maybe? Maybe what?"

"Just maybe Stilped had already been killed by the time you and Aria arrived. And…" here Molly chose her words carefully before finishing, her voice low and hurried, "…and no matter what you may think, it's not your fault that Stilped is dead."

Heather remained stationary.

"It can't be your fault."

Suddenly alert, Heather turned to Molly. "How do you know?"

Her hands crumpling and pressing a portion of her costume's fabric to her chest, Molly faced her friend. Her mind was racing. "I…I just know, that's all."

Heather looked at her curiously, perhaps even skeptically. Noticing

her friend's struggling aura in uncertain greens and embarrassed oranges, the girl didn't pursue the subject.

However, Molly wanted to keep on talking in the worst way, wanting
to reveal to Heather the entire story of how she had invited Stilped to the
treehouse the night of his murder. But the girl couldn't bring herself to
revisit that painful event and its secrets—and she knew to do so might
only invite probing, mortifying questions from Heather. Molly returned
to undressing, lost to herself, willing the wheels of her thoughts to disengage. The brunette girl stripped off the remaining parts of her costume,
hanging them as best she could on the mannequin. When Molly noticed
that the white ruffled shirt belonging to Heather's black suit had fallen to
the floor, she distractedly picked it up and draped it on the jointed model.

"I suppose what I'd really like to know is," said Heather, finally breaking the silence, "are all those people right? Am I really the green-eyed
Maiden? Is Aria? Are we both her? *Or* I was thinking that maybe Aria
and I, together, are a sorceress, like Mistraya."

Molly shot Heather a look. "What gives you that idea?"

"I didn't tell you this—haven't had time, really—but Mistraya is
Aria's sister."

"What? Really? How do you know this, Heather?"

"Aria said so, down on the ice when Mistraya was unconscious.
Mistraya's real name is Lussitaria."

"So, does that make you Mistraya's sister, too?"

"I don't know. I'm not sure what it makes me. I asked Aria, and she
said that I wasn't *yet*—whatever that means."

Contemplating her friend, Heather debated whether to ask the question that was on her mind.

"Hey, Molly…?"

"Hmm?"

Heather deliberated a moment longer and then shook her head.
"Never mind."

The young brunette was tightening her belt, slipping its leather
tongue into a pant loop. She looked up. "What? Do *I* think you're the
green-eyed Maiden?"

Heather nodded.

Molly flashed a half-smile, grabbing her shoes and walking over to the
chair. "It really doesn't matter to me whether you are or not, Heather."

"What do you mean?"

"Because all I care about is that you're my friend, that you're Heather
Nighborne, and I think you're pretty special." Molly grunted, now pulling on a tight shoe. "I think all of us are—can be—a lot of things, and

that we're all able to do more things than we believe we can. And I'm sure that a lot of times the only people stopping us are ourselves."

"Why?"

Molly shrugged. "Maybe because we're afraid. I know that for me, being afraid almost stopped me from doing things I was able to do when I finally got the nerve and tried."

"Yeah, I know. I saw you." Heather was wearing a crooked grin. It faded. "Do you think I'm afraid?"

"Not you, Heather; not in a million years." Molly couldn't help but laugh as she stood up and found an agreeable spot on the floor. She lowered herself. "You, you're never afraid—not for yourself, anyway. I think if you really were the green-eyed Maiden, you'd only worry that you wouldn't be able to save people when they needed you."

"So, what happens if I'm her?"

"What do you mean?"

"I mean, what do I do?"

Molly frowned as she laid back. She talked at the ceiling, musing. "If you *are* that special Maiden, Heather," Molly fiddled with the uppermost button on her blouse, "it's my opinion that you shouldn't think too much about it."

"Really? How come?"

Molly's hand went still. "Simple. If you are her, I think you'll just become her."

"Why?"

"Because with all those things written, like the Portent Prophecies, I don't think you'll have a choice." Molly was examining the sewing room ceiling, following a wooden beam that went over and behind her. Her brows went up, her head tilting back. "So, why worry about it?" Bright-eyed, she popped up and looked at her friend. "It's simple. You, Heather Nighborne, are already great. If you're also the Maiden of the Portent, you'll just become greater."

Suddenly shy, Heather smiled her generous smile. It broke onto her face like a sunrise, chasing the remnants of night that so infused her features. She found herself blushing.

"But Heather?"

"What?"

"If it turns out that you really *are* the green-eyed Maiden, will you invite me to Parade Day, so I can see you riding on one of those Arch-mounts?"

Heather laughed. "Molly, if I really *am* the green-eyed Maiden of the Evermore Portent, I'll want you riding next to me."

something not quite Right

Mrs. Pringle again rubbed her aching temples, the headache persisting. She walked into the washroom that had been designated hers, located down the hall from the one now shared by Heather and Molly.

The unseasonal sticky heat, warming the rooms of the house, did little to improve Mrs. Pringle's disposition. She recalled having opened her bedroom window earlier, only to find it was stiflingly warm and humid outside, as well.

Such unusual weather for Noble late in the year, she thought. And to think just earlier today, it was cold and blustery—miserable. What *is* happening around here?

The bathroom was long and spaciously wide with enough room for a standing mirror, chair, chaise lounge, candle stands, and plants—not to mention tub and toilet. How the greenery could grow in a room with no outside light remained a mystery to Mrs. Pringle. She hung her towels on a rack before leaning over the antique propeller fixtures of the bathtub faucet.

I've never taken a bath in a clawfoot tub before, she thought. Her head pounding, Mrs. Pringle adjusted the hot and cold taps until she felt water rushing over her fingers at the desired temperature.

Irritation momentarily gripped her when she realized that the hairdryer and makeup bag were in her other suitcase. Leaving the water to run at a very slow rate, she hurried to retrieve the remaining two suit cases that were still in the car.

Prowling the Bristol House basement's varying degrees of darkness, the woman in indigo again modified the settings of the Moonlight°Prisms. She now clearly saw, lined wide and deep along the glossy tiled floor, a succession of vintage automobiles, their circular headlights staring bug-eyed from above shiny bumpers. Beyond the ever-changing data displayed upon the °Prism glass, the visitor could distinguish reflective surfaces of hood, fender, and chrome stripping that, for her, gleamed blue-green within the blanket of dimness.

After walking the many rows of vehicles without spotting any Portals, the stealthy figure looked up at the series of arches that rose above a balcony, against the far wall. Recognizing a Portal, its yellow-green light glimmering between columns, the woman quietly headed for the stairs.

Mrs. Pringle closed the trunk of the car, having removed the two suitcases. Her headache drumming worse than ever, she cast an annoyed glance up at the restless cloud cover, the sky's oppressive grays coming to settle like a weight upon her brow. Hoisting the suitcases, one to a side, Mrs. Pringle set off across the drive, through the vegetable garden and towards the kitchen, the humidity and heat further draining her already depleted spirits.

"Heather, are you sure this is the way downstairs?"

"Molly, on the third floor of the Bristol House, can you ever be sure of anything?"

The two were walking through a room of hats. Heather loved this room with its uniquely hatted busts along one counter, floor-to-ceiling poles ringed with hanging hats, and shelf upon shelf displaying the head coverings individually, never stacked. All unique. All inspired. All voguish. But most of all, Heather loved the fact that in one corner, the room provided materials to make one's own hat, and over time she had made several, all very Heather.

Though she was tired, Molly stopped and slowly scanned the room. "Heather, do you think we can come back here sometime and try on hats?"

Heather had reached the door on the opposite end of the room, holding it partially open. "Sure. But only if we can stop in at the soda fountain first."

Molly lit up. "A soda fountain? Where?"

"Through this door."

Aloft on the balcony and facing the arcade, her back to the vintage cars below, the indigo seeker removed from her functional rucksack the PortalSealer. She slid her gloved fingers through the holes and held out her palm, the large jewel pointed in the direction of the columned archway and the fragmentary image of the PortalDoor.

Abruptly, the visitor stepped one way and then inched back the other, at first seeing only the glass display cases beyond the arch, against the recessed wall.

There!

Hovering between the columns, a different scene had flashed before her—sometimes Portals were like that, an evasive slice of another world emanating from the TimeLight Bridge. The woman slid her goggled head slowly and carefully to the left.

Exactly there. That's it.

Through the Moonlight°Prisms, she was able to gaze upon the snowy landscape of Winterspire, its clustered buildings and peaked towers visible just over a rise and through gently falling snowflakes. Orange lights marked the windows within the frigid blue atmosphere. After reciting the Lyric of Activation, a brilliant beam shot forth from the jewel of the PortalSealer, defining the perimeter of the archway. A moment later, with a brief buzz, the wintry landscape flickered and dissolved.

In a dimly lit basement room not so far from the indigo clad woman on the balcony, the figure in black stirred. Roused by the use of magic in the vicinity, the TimeLight Assassin opened his eyes, uncertain of what had awakened him. As a precautionary measure, his rigorous training had taught him to remain motionless until he identified his environment and was assured of his safety, and so the infiltrator refrained from lifting his masked head. Instead he gazed upon that which lay before him, soaking up essential data, making note of the muggy warmth of his surroundings. Temporarily at a loss as to where he was, he remained calm. It took several moments, but then it registered: The Bristol House.

Groggy, fighting the desire for further sleep, the assassin asked himself, What came over me? How could I have fallen asleep while on assignment?

Conscious of the shame that assailed his senses, he deflected the emotion and focused elsewhere. Eager to recognize and classify the slightest sound, he waited, remaining patient while continuing to inspect the territory within his field of vision. Aware now only of his breathing, and having heard no other sound, he edged his head up to further inspect the gloom. As with many of the basement's perimeter rooms, little illumination filtered through small ground-story windows along the top of one wall.

Still daylight, but not for long, he thought, dismissing the relief he felt at not having overslept his intended time for action, while observing the early dusk that had settled outside. Shortly, it will be time to find my way upstairs to seek out the Maiden Portent, preferably while she and her grandmother are asleep.

At that moment, the assassin found himself awash in the tingle of an indescribable sensation, so light and fleeting in its passing, but recognizable in the innermost reaches of his awareness: Magic. Gently, it shook him with its radiance.

Someone is *performing*, the assassin thought. And in an interconnecting room. Can it be the young Maiden recklessly practicing her hand? And here in the basement? What can the purpose of this magical exercise be? No matter. This calls for a change of plan. The executioner allowed himself to be pleased, thinking, There's no need to risk going upstairs to search for her, when it looks as if she's come to me, and hopefully alone.

Soundlessly, in mindful increments, the TimeLight Assassin progressed to his feet. Once there, he set off, beginning his vigilant search for the marked Maiden and the magical power source, his vague shape a mingling stalking shadow intent on annihilation.

In his pickup truck, Sheriff Dane turned off Lone Oak Avenue and onto Afterglow Drive, his vehicle's yellowish headlights dispelling the gloom within their conical reach. Crossing over the Whisper Creek Bridge, the sheriff pressed his lips firmly around the unlit cigarette that only moments ago had angled impotently, pointing to the dusty floor.

Dane checked his watch. He shouldn't have stopped for the new pack of smokes. And he was irritated that he had spent so much time at the house of the dead boy's aunt. Of course, he hadn't planned on staying long, but Mrs. Stendant insisted. She wanted to thank Sheriff Dane for finding Stilped's murderer and expressed her appreciation by cutting him a large wedge of homemade chocolate cake, but only after she cried.

It's nearing four, he thought. Almost time for the mayor's press conference.

With a bounce and a succession of lesser squeaky aftershocks, he swung the truck up the driveway. Sheriff Dane accelerated, directing the vehicle to follow the pebbled drive lined with trees and hedges, winding up Thimble Hill to the Bristol House garage.

⚓

Lightly setting down the suitcases and closing the kitchen door behind her, Lana Pringle waited for Grandma Dawn to look up from the counter. But the woman seemed preoccupied, her knife stationary, her hands at rest.

"Dawn?"

"Oh!" Startled, Grandma Dawn turned surprisingly quickly.

"I'm sorry—"

"No, please. My mind is just…elsewhere. I'm sorry, Lana. Is there something I can help you with?"

"Dawn, you wouldn't happen to have a couple of aspirin, would you? I didn't bother to bring any with me, and it seems I've acquired quite a headache in this heat."

But Grandma Dawn's attention again had wandered, her head at a subtle tilt. "I'm sorry, Lana," she said, refocusing. "You wanted—?"

"Aspirin?"

"Oh." She broke into a brief smile. "Upstairs, in your bathroom. The medicine cabinet above the sink, bottom shelf."

"Great. By the way, I'm running a bath right now—shouldn't be at it too long. Sure you don't need any help preparing dinner? You'll be having two more at the table than usual, you know, and—"

"No, I'm fine, really. Thank you, Lana. As a matter of fact, take your time. Dinner won't be served until six, so there's no hurry. I've a large salad in the fridge, a loaf of bread about ready to go into the oven, and…" Grandma Dawn broke off her sentence, a curious look upon her face.

Following her neighbor's gaze, Mrs. Pringle turned and watched with wonder. Without any wind to assist it, the door behind her had opened, swinging and gliding to a stop.

"Oh, and here I thought I had shut it."

As Mrs. Pringle moved to close the door, Sheriff Dane popped his head through the opening, simultaneously knocking on the jamb with his large hand.

"Anyone home?" he asked, opening the door wider.

"Oh, Sheriff Dane," said Grandma Dawn. "Please, please come in."

"It's so weird. Every room that we've been through is hot," said Heather. "It's never been like this since I can remember."

Having entered a side door situated at the lowest part of the intimate Art Deco theatre, the two girls were walking up the carpeted center aisle, rows of plush seats laid out six wide on either side. The smell of freshly popped popcorn filled the air.

Molly's stomach was growling. Heather overheard.

"That popcorn smells good, huh, Molly?"

"*Really* good." The brunette began to look around, taking in the blue-green décor of the theatre, the scenic tapestries, their wide multi-patterned borders, and the geometric pillars of Art Deco design. Opposite the screen, behind the glass snack counter, was the popcorn machine, both girls intending to pay it a visit.

"This place is so elegant and beautiful, Heather," Molly said. "Even though you've told me about the Bristol House theatre, I never imagined it to be so...so *resplendent*. I just love it." Stopping and turning behind her to face the draped screen, she asked, "How often do you come up here and watch movies?"

Heather shrugged. "Whenever I can."

"What do you usually see?"

"Whatever is playing." Tired, Heather forced a smile. "The movies the Bristol House chooses are always great. And the part I like best is that the movie never starts without me." The girl pointed to the small curved balcony at the back corner. "Grandma Dawn and I usually sit up there when we're together. If I'm by myself, I usually get real close, so the people on the screen are really, really huge."

Heather had started up the aisle again, toward the snack counter, but then stopped. Following close behind, Molly bumped into her.

"Oh! Sorry," said Molly. "I was looking around and didn't see you stop." She peered at Heather oddly. "What's wrong?"

"I don't know. I just had this funny feeling inside."

"Is it Mistraya?" Panicked, Molly swiftly turned and looked at the door through which they had just entered. "She's not coming, is she?"

"No. No, it's nothing like that. It's just this weird, tingly feeling. I can't really explain it, but I felt it earlier, too, just a little while ago."

The blonde stood poised, as if she were listening for a particular sound. However, in this instance, she was simply awaiting a sensation.

"I don't feel anything, Heather."

"Come on, Molly. Let's get downstairs. Something is going on."

"Please, Sheriff Dane, won't you sit down?" asked Grandma Dawn.

He declined. Somewhat awkwardly, the three stood immediately inside the entrance to the kitchen.

"Then can I at least offer you something to drink, Sheriff?"

Removing his hat, Sheriff Dane rotated it, running his hands habitually along the brim. "Thank you, Dawn, but no. I won't be long. I just wanted to drop by and share some good news. As a matter of fact," Dane said, turning to Mrs. Pringle, "I'm glad I caught the both of you here. It saves me a trip."

"Well, actually, it's good that you stopped here first, then, Sheriff. It looks like Lana and Molly are going to be staying with us at the Bristol House for awhile."

Dane's brows went up, but he said nothing. He looked at Mrs. Pringle, who contrived a plaster smile.

"Yes," continued Grandma Dawn. "And although I've yet to see how she feels about it, I've decided the time might be right for me to take a much needed vacation."

Surprised, Mrs. Pringle regarded her with curiosity.

"I know I haven't told you, Lana, but please, not to worry. Should it come about, we'll work out the particulars. But in the meantime I'd like some coffee." Grandma Dawn made her way to the stovetop. "Tea, Lana?"

"Oh! *Liquid!* That reminds me. Excuse me, you two," said Mrs. Pringle, "but I've got the bathwater running upstairs."

"This will just take a second, Mrs. Pringle. Have either of you heard about the mayor's press conference this afternoon?"

The women looked at each other.

Grandma Dawn said, "Lana and I have been quite preoccupied today, so—"

"It's starting right about now," Dane said, looking at his watch. "In a nutshell, we have reason to believe that we've found the murderer of Stilped Roarhowser." Both women gushed with relief, as the sheriff continued, "It turns out the killer is an old miner who lived in a series of interconnected caves on the outskirts of town."

"What's his name? Anyone we know?" asked Mrs. Pringle.

"Doubt it. Seems the murderer lived a secluded life in the hills for years and rarely, if ever, came into town. But we're still in the process of wrapping up the investigation, so at this point, I don't have a lot to share. I just wanted to tell the two of you before you heard it elsewhere, since the murder took place here on the Bristol House property and your girls were probably Stilped Roarhowser's only friends."

Grandma Dawn asked, "How did this miner meet the boy?"

"At this point, we don't know and may never find out."

"What do you mean?" asked Mrs. Pringle.

"It seems the perp was found dead by a couple of hikers after a tumble down the steep slope of a mountain there in the Stenmouths, near the old mining camps above Watershed Lake. I—"

"The bath!" Mrs. Pringle burst in. She placed a hand on Dane's forearm. "Excuse me, Sheriff, but I've got to run." The woman began to back towards the hall and stairs. "Can you fill Dawn in on the details, and I'll get them from her later?"

"Sure."

"Oh, it *is* good news. Thank you, Sheriff Dane," said Mrs. Pringle, as she turned and headed quickly for the hall. Dane and Grandma Dawn stood listening to her footsteps thumping on the stairs, fading in intensity.

It was Sheriff Dane who spoke first. "She forgot her suitcases."

"I'll take them up to her shortly. Lana is a bit distracted these days."

"She looks exhausted. Is she going to be all right?"

Grandma Dawn continued to look in the direction of the stairs. "In time, Sheriff." Taking a deep breath, she exhaled slowly. "Everything in time."

The most distinguishing characteristics of the televised speaker were his bow tie and the close-set eyes punched into his big, blubbery dish of a face.

"...and as a result of excellent detective work and with the help of the alert Noble citizenry, we are pleased to announce to everyone today that the killer of the boy, Stilped Roarhowser, has been found."

The man cleared his throat, his pate shining through the thinness of his dome-wrapped hair.

"From the outset, it was a horrific, perplexing case, surely among the most gruesome in Noble's long and respected history..."

The television continued to blast forth the voice of the honorable mayor, Woodrow C. C. Stungrubben. Dominating the screen, his gray-headed, wobbling, two-chinned face was splashed with the rapid, irregular bursts of flashbulbs. He blinked a lot.

"...a drifter, now identified as Clarence Taylor Tipton, seventy two years of age, who had taken up residence in the old, abandoned mines..."

Across the room, his breath raspy, Ned Pringle lay in a contorted position, passed out on the couch. His head was thrown back at a disagreeable angle, his mouth wide open, limbs cast awry.

"I'd personally like to thank Sheriff Harland Dane, who unfortunately couldn't be here with us this afternoon, his deputies, and all the law enforcement officials who diligently worked to bring this horrifying and baffling case to its conclusion..."

On the coffee table close at hand, the ice in Mr. Pringle's glass had mostly melted, and the ringing of the telephone was lost as was a confused Clarissa on the other end of the line.

"Thank you. And now I'll take your questions..."

Tick, tock, tick, tock. The wonky clock continued to mark time, right on Bristol House schedule. Under the bright light of day, the grandfather clock would have been awash in playful colors over its slender, curvilinear body, a body that widened at some points and thinned in others. At the top, on a zany face ringed with frolicsome numbers, cartoonish hands pointed out the late afternoon hour. But in the darkness of the toy room, the jocular clock stood partially hidden, obscured behind rows of dolls and racks of bicycles and skateboards, its brilliant surface subdued. Tick, tock, tick, tock.

Near the clock something moved. Or did it? Hardly noticeable, the TimeLight Assassin moved slowly, cautiously toward his destination—his prey—drawn by another's use of magic.

Now momentarily at rest, the man barely breathed, still fighting off what remained of the Bristol House-administered sleeping spell. And although the assassin's power to terminate the life of another had been slightly diminished, the ability to still do so effortlessly remained. And thus the deadly intruder paused, while once again feeling the magical power radiating from another basement room, reaffirming his earlier assumption.

It had to be the young Maiden Portent, he thought, the one he had been sent to destroy.

Located within one of these many basement rooms, he simply needed to get closer and perform an accurate reading to pinpoint her location.

"Molly, this can't be the way downstairs."

"How do you know?"

"Because look at the end of the hall. There're the stairs to the attic again. This is the second time we've been this way." Heather began to pace, limping slightly, her irritation apparent.

Molly stared blankly at her friend, traces of fatigue from a long day noticeable on both their faces.

Heather talked aloud, as if nearby there was a third party to overhear, "We're supposed to be going downstairs. Why is the Bristol House doing this to us?" The girl fumed. "Before the theatre and those library rooms, we went through the hat shop, the soda fountain, and then there was that park with the big, gushing fountain, the arcade, the ice rink, and just now, the room of shoes—oh, and I almost forgot, the hall of flowers. I don't understand it."

Molly tried to stifle a yawn. "I have to admit, when we went through that bedroom with the large feather bed, I was tempted to lie down for awhile."

"Oh, yeah, that's right. I forgot the bedroom…"

Heather took to striding up and down the hall, still displaying her slight limp, as she walked off her frustration. Calming herself, she became thoughtful, and was soon looking up at the ceiling. "I don't know why the Bristol House doesn't want us to go downstairs, Molly, but I have this, this *feeling*. I have a feeling that something's not right, and I think the Bristol House knows it. And maybe it's trying to protect us and wants us to stay up here until that something wrong is fixed."

"Protect us? Protect us from what, Heather? Mr. Simpletripp?"

"I don't know. Maybe."

"Heather, if there is trouble downstairs, you don't think that the Bristol House would expect us to go back through that PortalDoor where Mistraya could be waiting, do you?"

"No. I don't think the Bristol House would ever send us someplace dangerous on purpose. Remember all those keys? I bet there are other PortalDoors, and that the Bristol House would have us go somewhere else in Evermore through one of them. But I also think the Bristol House can understand that we need to get downstairs right now, so you can go home to your Mom and Dad and I can see Grandma Dawn before she gets worried. Besides, I want to make sure that she's okay—that everything's okay." Heather returned to addressing the lofty hallway ceiling and its Victorian wallpaper. "So, I'm surprised, Molly, that the Bristol House would keep us up here like this."

"Maybe it's not going to, after all, Heather."

"What do you mean?"

"Maybe you talked the Bristol House out of it. Look," Molly said, pointing to the end of the hall. "Where the attic stairs were just a moment ago, now there's a door."

Grandma Dawn was walking the sheriff to his car. Still clutching his hat, Dane swiped a sleeve over his brow.

"Oh, by the way," he said, "I'll need Heather to come down to the station and identify her backpack and the contents." Seeing the immediate look of concern on Grandma Dawn's face, the sheriff said, "It's my guess the killer found it on the grounds the night of the murder."

"I remember Heather saying it had gone missing."

"We discovered it in the cave. I just want to make certain that everything is accounted for, that it's all there."

"I expect the girls back at any moment, Sheriff, if you'd like to wait."

"No. It's not necessary." They reached the edge of the vegetable garden. Below, the land viewed from atop Thimble Hill was no longer touched by sunlight, the dusky sky waning. "There's one other thing, Dawn." Dane hesitated as he regarded the woman. Momentarily looking away, he scratched the crown of his head. The sheriff cleared his throat, and began by mumbling, as he again turned his hat in his hands, "Dawn, in law enforcement, sometimes intuition plays a key role in investigations, going on a hunch." Dane contemplated the walkway at his feet, as he sought a path to continue. "Now, the miner, our suspected killer, was found wearing a ragtag collection of clothing. But his boots were like new."

Grandma Dawn waited, and when no words were forthcoming from the sheriff, she filled the unexpected lapse by saying, "Mmm-hmm." When the silence continued to drag, she added, "You're saying the boots the miner wore matched the prints made here on the grounds, at the scene of the crime?"

"Right. And the boots were the wrong size, much too large for a short, older, and probably underweight man. Now, one could ask, If a man is in need of shoes, is it so far-fetched that he would be found wearing newer boots, even if they were the wrong size? And the answer is no. Yet, there wasn't any additional padding stuffed inside them, no extra pairs of socks, and no blisters or irritation on the man's feet. But maybe he had just recently found the boots, you see."

Grandma Dawn continued to wait on Dane, wondering where he was headed.

"And the miner didn't have a car or horse, so he probably didn't get them in town, because if he walked, the boots in question would have been scuffed, and dirty, and his feet sore. And there were no tire tracks near the cave and no other shoes found in the miner's possession. Which leads me to believe that someone could have given them to him. But why would someone walk into the hills with a new pair of boots just to hand them over to the miner? Then again, maybe the old man stole them from a camper somewhere nearby. However, there weren't any recent campfires in the immediate area and why would a camper be wearing new, clean boots—or even have them in his possession? And the hikers that pass through, they're *wearing* their boots—and the type of boots the miner had on weren't hiking boots. Now understand, this is all conjecture."

Not sure how to respond, Grandma Dawn crossed her arms in front of her.

"And make no mistake, there was other evidence found in the cave that points to this man as the killer of Stilped Roarhowser, including Heather's backpack."

"So, what are you trying to say, Sheriff Dane? Are you telling me that the murderer could still be at large?"

The sheriff smiled wryly. "Oh, no, Dawn, I would never say that. You see, the mayor is convinced that the murderer has been caught."

"I see. Well, then what—?"

"No, I would never say that, could never tell you that, because if I did say anything that disagreed with my superiors here in Noble, well, then, let's just say I've got a family to feed—and in a small town like ours, word has a way of getting around and reaching even the darnedest people." Dane was pulling at his chin, squeezing it. "So, I would never say that. No. Uh-uh."

Grandma Dawn looked warily at the sheriff, almost a sidelong glance.

He continued, "And far be it from me to offer *any* information to the contrary—to anyone, including you. So you mustn't misconstrue my thinking out loud, here, my sharing these facts that have yet to be released to the public, if ever they are."

Now looking directly at him, Grandma Dawn's face didn't change expression. "I know you never would do that, Sheriff Dane, would never say that there may still be a murderer on the loose, when in fact our mayor is confident that the killer has been found. You would never say such a thing to me."

"Or to Mrs. Pringle."

"Or to Lana."

"Right. Never any information for just the two of you."

"Never."

The sheriff put on his hat. "But I wanted to tell you the good news in person, on behalf of our esteemed mayor, that the killer has been identified and there is no longer any reason to be worried, and that the town is safe once more."

"I'll make sure that Lana knows, Sheriff Dane. Thank you very much for your visit."

"My pleasure." Dane turned to leave but checked himself. "Speaking of visits, don't be surprised if my men and I happen to find ourselves visiting the neighborhood at odd hours and for no apparent reason. Just know, it's not that we're checking up on you, making sure that everything's safe. After all, there's no longer any reason to do that. But if you do see us *visiting*, feel free to wave." The sheriff dipped his chin. "Have a nice evening." Disengaging, he ambled down the path toward the drive.

Standing among the remnants of the year's vegetables, Grandma Dawn watched the sheriff departing against the violet-blues of impending night. When Dane reached the drive, she heard him clear his throat and spit.

The assassin in black blended with the nighttime scenario of the desolate basement room filled with graves, headstones, and sarcophagi. The air was cold, and a mist hugged the uneven dips and rises of ground, which served to slow his progress considerably. Nevertheless, the infiltrator advanced patiently, the soundless placement of each footfall ever so deliberate. His muscles rippling beneath the fabric of his skintight suit, he stole among the random clutter of tombstones that rose and leaned at varying angles out of the shrouded earth, past bulky gnarled trees, heading for a ghostly green light shining from within the stately tomb ahead.

With his next mist-covered step, his boot departed from the soft give of moist earth and he felt a stone stair firm beneath his sole, and so mounted the obscured few steps without falter. Slipping past a succession of stone mermaids posed atop their wave-like bases, the man approached the deteriorating mausoleum, sliding behind a column located to one side of the doorless entrance. There he pressed against the marble, the cold rough stone at his back merely an irrelevant detail, his Adaption°Suit temporarily taking on the pattern of the wall itself. Finally peering around the crumbling jamb, the intruder scrutinized the scene inside the mausoleum. The interior, carved thoroughly out of stone, resembled an old style captain's quarters. At the rear were four great angled windows, and books partially lined one wall near a table and chest. Opposite, resembling a canopy bed, the assassin could see a tomb on which lay the carving of a man on his back, his hands at rest below the tricorn hat on his chest. Not far away, seated at the fancy table, was Heather's nightman on the stairs, bathed in the soft greenish light of his lantern. The wall behind was visible through his weak image, the burly watchman browsing through a thick tome, the captain's nautical logbook.

A ghost? Can it be? Here in the Bristol House? Without moving his head whatsoever, the deadly stranger went to his Cache°Belt, pulling loose the lone module of Slumber°Netting. The unusual weapon was first developed after the supernatural encounters experienced by Time-Light Assassins on Quariel Lumis, the ghost planet. Since then, there had been little reason for him to use the weighty weapon, because quick extermination of a combatant was preferred over merely putting one to sleep. But as many a TimeLight Assassin had discovered when attempting to complete their mission on Quariel Lumis: ghosts were hard to kill, especially since they were already dead.

The thought brought only the vaguest hint of amusement to the masked face of the assassin. Then it disappeared, lost to his impassive features.

Slumber°Netting in hand, his movements quick and agile as a cat's, the man crossed the door's threshold and cast forth the weapon. Without conscious thought, he had calculated the distance between himself and the apparition, and sent the compact wad high in his direction.

But glimpsing the motion, the nightman was surprisingly fast to his feet, his hand flashing to seize the hilt of his sword nearby. Nevertheless, he was overcome by the swiftly expanding web, the envelopment of the ghost almost instantaneous.

The nightman struggled, his sword soundlessly falling to the mausoleum floor. Shortly thereafter, the ghost fell also, still squirming in the °Netting's Ecto°Cocoon, his oversized hands tearing in vain at the bindings.

In an instant, the TimeLight Assassin was next to him, leaning close.

He whispered, "Quickly, the Maiden Portent, she is here. Where?"

Angrily, his arms now pinned to his body within the constricting Slumber°Netting, the helpless nightman glared at the intruder.

"Sleep will overcome you momentarily. You've only a short time to tell me what I want to know, if you wish to awaken released of the °Netting. I ask again, Where is the young Maiden, in which room? It is her, is it not, performing here in the basement? Answer me quickly."

Sleep was in fact beginning to overtake the ghost, though he fought to stay awake. Numbness was settling over his body.

"Tell me what I need to know. Again, the whereabouts of the Maiden Portent?"

His eyelids ever so heavy, frustration and disappointment evident upon his features, Heather's nightman on the stairs' last look was in the direction of the tomb, where rested the remains of his former sea captain, Scarbones Bristol. He cried out gutturally, a small entreaty begging forgiveness. Then he slept.

In the tub, Lana Pringle was pulling herself to her feet, the water draining off her body with a rush. Her head felt no better, its pain still pulsing with a steady stab, the aspirin ineffective.

She looked at the array of floor candlesticks, and thought, Sometime I'll have to try soaking with just the candles lighting this room. This bathroom is so cozy, just like I need it to be right now: a sanctuary. Better yet, a womb. A womb with plants.

Mrs. Pringle wanted to nap, but her mind remained far too active. While at rest in the tub, she had been preparing what to say to Molly when the girl eventually came downstairs.

And that could be any moment! She needed to hurry.

Pulling a towel off the rack, Mrs. Pringle wrapped it around her body. The woman didn't care that her hair had become wet, didn't care about the remains of her makeup. She just wanted her world to stop pitching in upheaval, but knew that what she had set in motion was only beginning: the depth of the valley awaited her before the revitalizing rise to the other side.

How do I tell Molly that our family as she's known it will be no more? So many ways to do it; so many things to say—and then, again, so many things to avoid saying to such a sensitive child.

My Molly.

With thoughts churning in her head amid the heavy pounding, Mrs. Pringle began to dress.

With night having set in, the man emerged from under the Whisper Creek Bridge, a large-brimmed hat helping to conceal his features. Once inside the Bristol House gates, he shied away from the main walkways while climbing Thimble Hill.

Finally, finding a spot to his liking—one that fit the partial description in his possession—and hidden by foliage, he set down his shovel, lantern, and leather bag, the latter containing his ceremonial boots worn on only those special occasions.

From the bag he removed his gloves, and slipping them on, rechecked the distance and alignment before starting to dig. He knew he was taking a chance working this close to the house, but he was feeling desperate these days. He needed to find something soon, something that assured him he was at least on the right property when looking for the treasure.

Admittedly, he was beginning to lose hope, to doubt. And that wasn't good, knowing that with every passing day, his life was that much shorter.

Cautiously descending the back stairs, the girls treaded lightly, the wall sconces illuminating their way. Molly pulled at Heather's shoulder, stopping the girl.

She whispered, "Heather, who turned on these lights?"

The blonde leaned in close. "The same people who wind the clocks."

"Oh."

Heather resumed her descent, but then halted when Molly stumbled noisily on a stair. Turning around, she whispered, "From here on out, we need to be extra careful, in case there really is something going on in the Bristol House, okay?"

Embarrassed at her clumsiness, Molly soundlessly agreed.

Reaching the second floor landing, Heather looked down the hallway. All seemed normal from where she stood. If anything was going on, it would be on the lower floors, she theorized.

When aromas of food from the kitchen drifted up the stairs to reach their noses, Molly whispered to Heather, "If there *is* something going on, it sure smells good."

"Yeah, well, maybe that something going on is 'cooking.'"

"And that usually means 'eating.'"

The girls turned on the landing and continued down the stairs. Behind them, crossing the hall, they didn't see that Mrs. Pringle had just come out of the bathroom and was heading towards her room. She didn't see them, either, their heads and backs quietly disappearing from view.

When the pair finally reached the bottom of the stairs, right outside the kitchen door, the smell of food was nothing short of heavenly. Heather put out her arm and held Molly back, while she noiselessly crept forward. Peering slowly around the jamb, she saw her grandmother, checking on something in the oven, her mitted hand at rest on the metal door's handle.

Heather didn't enter right away, but looked the kitchen over. Everything seemed to be in order: the cozy golden light, the great cooking smells, and her grandmother preparing dinner as usual. She watched as Grandma Dawn headed for the sink. Normal.

So, thought Heather, why do things just not feel right?

Having rinsed a small pot and set it along the sink to dry, Grandma Dawn walked over to the counter. Sensing a presence, she glanced up to see Heather standing in the doorway. She immediately brightened.

"Well, welcome back, young lady. You don't have to stand there, you know. You can come in. After all, you live here."

Despite her wariness—and weariness—Heather couldn't help but flash a grin. Seeing Grandma Dawn brought forth a desire to be held and made the girl want to run to her. Suddenly, Heather felt shy.

"Where's Molly?"

Heather half-turned. "She's right here." An instant later, Molly was following her friend into the room. Both girls headed for chairs at the table, Heather doing her best to disguise any indication of an injured ankle, not wishing to worry her grandmother and open herself up to unpleasant questioning. Molly, looking up through the kitchen windows, noticed the cloud-burdened sky now drained of its light, and so stopped beside her chair.

"I think I'd better be getting home, Heather," she said. "I don't want my parents to worry."

"Molly?"

The girl looked over at Grandma Dawn.

"You're mother is upstairs. She's been waiting for you to get back. She wants to have a word with you."

"She's here?"

"You'll probably find her in the room just past Heather's."

With a look that said, That's strange, Molly exchanged glances with Heather before turning and exiting toward the stairs.

When Molly had left the room, Heather asked, "What's Mrs. Pringle doing upstairs?"

Setting a cup and her yellow coffee press on the table, Grandma Dawn slid out a chair and sat down. She poured. "Mrs. Pringle and Molly are going to be living with us at the Bristol House for a while."

"Really?" The girl wasn't sure how to respond.

Having taken a sip, Grandma Dawn set down her mug.

"Yes, and the timing couldn't be better."

The woman in indigo entered a basement room of garden embellishments through a decaying wooden door. In the gloom, overgrown brick pathways ran between rolling mounds of dirt and dried grass, with dim blue lights placed throughout in an inadequate attempt to guide the walker. But squinting through the °Prisms into the unexpected and heightened brightness of blue, the woman was unable to see with clarity. She quickly crouched behind the toppled statue of an oversized garden gnome, its face planted firmly in the dirt. Silently, the secretive caller made agitated adjustments to the sensitive Moonlight°Prisms that allowed her to see in spite of the intense glare. Finally confident that the blue illumination would no longer trouble her, she rose just enough to scan the room from her hiding place.

The goggled visitor felt the gentle wind suddenly gust at her back. At the current's change in direction, she heard the squeaking response of rusted weather vanes as they turned, including the one that topped the dilapidated barn in the distance. But the seeker found no PortalDoor, as she covertly passed an assortment of pink flamingoes, birdbaths, and trickling fountains.

Closing in on the barn, the slinking figure noticed her reflection slide by on metallic gazing balls, and scrutinized the many lawn ornaments, scarecrows, and statuary that lay strewn about in the enormous but cluttered room.

As she crouched near a precariously balanced chimenea, its stack angled up into the gloom, the woman thought she detected the sheen of a PortalDoor on the surface of a nearby fountain. Moving closer, with a slight adjustment of the goggles to peer beneath its rippling waters, she was able to perceive lowland dunes, dry riverbeds, and empty gulches belonging to the desert kingdom of SummersBreath Still.

Producing the PortalSealer and wiggling her gloved fingers into place, the indigo clad woman thought it mildly ironic that, to journey from this particular Portal to that hot, dry desert world, a traveler would begin with a cool submersion in water.

"So I expect that Molly is going to need your support, as she goes through this difficult time," Grandma Dawn concluded. She was at the kitchen counter, filling a tall glass with lemonade for Heather, the ice cubes stressing and cracking.

Hoping for a glimpse of the moon, the girl looked up through the windows, past the trees, at the overcast backdrop of nightfall. Uncomfortably hot, Heather shifted in her chair.

Immediately, she sat up a little straighter as the sensation of magic unexpectedly fluttered within. At that same instant, turning from the countertop with lemonade in hand, Grandma Dawn lost her grip on the wet glass. It fell, shattering on the kitchen tiles.

"Oh, my! Silly me. Here, let me clean this up and get you another."

Instantly, the TimeLight Assassin stopped all movement. He closed his eyes, his head moving back slightly—almost imperceptibly.

There it is again.

As the words floated through his mind, the reception of magic set his core to lightly pulsating, creating a pleasing, rippling effect. But the sensation was not at all relished and was dismissed only as an *occurrence,* while the assassin calculated the distance between himself and the dispersion of magic based on the strength of the charge received.

Calculating, calculating, done. He reopened his eyes to the dimness.

Not much farther, he thought.

The man was breathing heavily. He felt the heat that gathered under his hat, sweat dripping down the back of his shirt. Leaving yet another deep hole uncovered, dirt piled in mounds around it, he leaned on his shovel and blinked away the sweat that burned his eyes. Afterwards, he plugged one nostril while snorting to clear the other.

No luck, he thought. Again. But surely this is *that* Bristol House, is it not, the one he'd heard rumors about as a youth before undertaking his life-changing journey? Hadn't he scoured the Academy Archives and investigated all accounts and clues concerning Scarbones Bristol and his massive fortune? And before the pirate's so-called 'glorified recovery,' hadn't Terentius found the true meaning of this miserable existence on Earth? Sure, the pirate changed hats and came clean, but only after amassing a fortune, and a special fortune at that.

The man thought, So, then, where is it? I want it; I want that treasure, the gold, the booty, and the long privileged life of abundance that goes with it. I want everything. Isn't it a fair exchange for my sacrifice? It is, surely.

Another shovelful and nothing.

He slammed the blade of the shovel into the earth where it stuck like a hatchet.

"I want it!" he snarled, his teeth clenched. "And I want my youth! Give it back!"

He kicked the lantern and it toppled, extinguishing the light.

"Mom?" Molly said the word softly, as she timidly entered the unfamiliar bedroom. Though unable to put it into words, the room felt swollen in its luxuriousness, in its mystery and welcome snugness.

A single light burned on the open secretary desk, near the windows. Stretched out on the coverlet and traced by a strip of lamplight, Mrs. Pringle lay asleep with her back to the door. As quietly as possible, Molly walked around the wide, decorative footboard. Noticing the suitcases set against the wall, near the closet, she came to a brief standstill, before continuing to the bed's unoccupied side. Once there, she gazed at her mother's careworn face, on the beads of sweat that pimpled her skin.

The girl looked up at the four cloth-covered posts that rose in elegant curves to meet overhead, and then around the room at the new surroundings, the hall light spilling in through the open doorway and across the area rug. Slipping off her shoes, Molly climbed carefully onto the bed, the mattress spongily giving way under each knee. Nestling alongside her mother, then gently readjusting, the girl pulled up her knees a little more. She settled.

Molly listened to her mother's rhythmic breathing, elevating strands of the girl's hair in exhale. Rushing over her exposed flesh, she felt waves of air from the old-fashioned upright fan that futilely swept at the heat with a murmured whir.

For some time Molly lay facing the windows, blankly looking out at the cover of night, when she heard her mother stir. Feeling the shifting of weight on the bed, Molly knew Mrs. Pringle had lifted her head momentarily. The girl didn't jump when she felt her mother's hand come to rest on her side.

Her voice little in the room, Molly asked, "Mom, does Dad know we're here?"

Her mother's response was heavy with sleep, distant: "Yes."

"Are we going to be staying?"

"Mmm. For awhile, honey."

Molly felt her mother's sleepy hand start to slide off of her and onto the coverlet. Keeping her awake, near, she said, "Mom?"

"Hmm."

"Are you all right?"

Mrs. Pringle didn't answer right away.

"Oh...I'm fine, I suppose."

Moments passed.

"Is Dad?"

More moments, ticks from the clock.

"He will be, honey. We'll both be. It'll take some time, though. Some readjustment for all of us. Talk soon, okay?" The words had been half-mumbled, absorbed into the pillow.

The silence that ensued gave weight to the encompassing darkness and the seconds tapping out. With a whir, the wall clock's bells chimed three-quarters of the hour.

"Molly?"

"Yes?"

"Are *you* all right?"

Molly reached back and took her mother's hand and, despite the heat, pulled it over her, encircling herself with the woman's arm.

Mrs. Pringle waited for her daughter's response, but soon they were both asleep.

"So, you enjoyed the parade today?"

"Yeah," said Heather. "Autumnsloe is really a special place. I loved the buildings and the town of Elderraine. Molly did, too. You should have seen it, Grandma Dawn. The trees grow out of the buildings, or the buildings are built into the trees. I'm not really sure which." Heather covered her mouth and yawned. "There was the river with all the boats, the beautiful bridges, and the people in costumes playing games and having picnics in the parks. Molly and I, we looked through some of the shops, too. Oh! And in the parade you should have seen the Maidens on Archmounts! I just love the Maidens!"

"They're really something, are they?"

"Grandma Dawn, *I* want to be a Maiden and ride an Archmount."

"You do?" Heather's grandmother was chuckling, recalling scenes from her own childhood, fending off a sudden wash of melancholia. And a temptation to share. Tonight, she thought. Later tonight. The girl is tired after her TimeLight adventure.

"Yeah. Me and Molly, on Archmounts." Heather brought her arm up and yawned into its crook. "We had great costumes, too. Molly was in a beautiful outfit with a huge butterfly mask. Mine was a moon mask with a little talking…"

Grandma Dawn looked up from her coffee. "With a little talking *what?*"

"Well, it was a mask that, when you put it on, it becomes your face. So, that way when you talk, the mask's lips actually move, just like you weren't wearing one. You know what I mean, don't you? You put it on, and it's your face, but it's not really your face, because it has all sorts of decoration and stuff…because, you know, it's a mask."

Heather was flagging, and her grandmother knew it. She asked one more question.

"Anything remarkable happen?"

"Everything! We had Autumnslovian treats in the park that we bought with the feallans that the Bristol House gave us. Molly got to pet a Geetalvasse, and it jumped on her shoulder. She wasn't scared, though. We saw the ghost dancers, too. But the Maidens, they were the best!"

Heather was tempted to get up and walk tall and graceful—Maiden-like—for her grandmother, but found herself too tired to bother. Grandma Dawn noticed that the girl was now struggling to keep her eyes open.

"Feel like a nap before dinner?" she asked.

"I am pretty tired. And I'm really, *really* hungry."

"You had an apple to hold you up—make that an apple and a peanut bar, as a matter of fact." Grandma Dawn noted the empty wrapper near Heather's glass. "What do you say you take a nap for a bit? I'll call you right before dinner is ready—you won't even have to set the table.

"I suspect that Molly may want to nap, as well, though I know her mother plans on talking to her," the woman continued, "to let her know that they'll be staying here for a time. Then, if Molly isn't as tired as you are—which I doubt—Lana would like a tour of the third floor."

For a moment, Heather looked concerned. "What if they can't find their way back?"

"Why wouldn't they? The Bristol House would make certain they did."

"Yeah, but what if it decided not to let them come down the steps?"

Grandma Dawn was looking at Heather thoughtfully. "Why would it decide not to let them come back down?"

Heather thought before replying. "I really don't know." But her grandmother wouldn't be deterred.

"Did the Bristol House almost decide not to let you and Molly come downstairs?"

"Yeah. It kept taking us everywhere but down. I finally asked it to let me and Molly go where we were supposed to—and for some reason it did."

Grandma Dawn said only, "Well, I'm not exactly sure what that's about. But what do you say we get you a nap?"

"Something's not right."

"Oh?"

"Yeah. The Bristol House isn't behaving like it should. Have you noticed all the rooms are really warm, like the Bristol House is sick and running a temperature? And-and I keep feeling some kind of weird, well, feeling in my stomach."

Scooting out her chair, Grandma Dawn stood up. "Come on, young lady. I've got a bit more to do before dinner."

"You don't believe me?"

Heather's grandmother walked over and, standing behind the girl, placed her hands on her shoulders. She leaned slightly forward, Heather looking back and up. "I do believe you. About everything. And I want to hear more about Autumnsloe and the parade today, okay? You and I, we've a lot to talk about this evening, a lot of sharing to do. But first I want you to go and get some rest before dinner. Go on. I'll come and wake you when it's time."

Heather rose and, as was her custom, leaned into her Grandmother. She found herself wanting to stay at her side.

"Do I have to take a nap?"

"Come on, now, off with you, young lady."

"You sure I have to?"

"Yes. You've had a long day. I bet I could put you to bed right now and you'd sleep through the night." She kissed Heather on the forehead. "Now, go!" The woman swatted Heather lightly on her bottom, sending her in the direction of the kitchen door.

Heather briefly squirmed and arched her back in an effort to avoid her grandmother's hand, before she broke away in a fit of laughter. Once in the hallway, however, she stopped after a few steps and returned, secretly looking in on Grandma Dawn, watching as the woman resumed her preparations. Heather thought she looked as if her mind was on something other than cooking. The girl retreated from the door and began to mount the stairs to her room. But after the first few steps, she thought better of it and headed for the couch in the living room. She loved that couch—and room!—finding both really comfortable. And they were closer to her grandmother.

CHAPTER THIRTY-FIVE

Rogue Dreams

Heather kicked off her shoes and slid onto the living room couch, enfolding her arms around the fluffy end pillow, pulling it close. Facing the room, her gaze wandered, lightly touching on the antique furniture and accessories before finally coming to rest on the large painting of Scarbones Bristol centered over the mantle. There she lingered, waiting for him to wink, blink, or smile, as he'd done so many times in the past, but nothing typically extraordinary occurred. And so Heather turned her attention to the fireplace, staring into the recessed rectangle that had hosted many a cozy blaze for generations of Bristol House residents and guests. At the moment, no fire flared from its grate to warm the room. Actually, Heather felt this room, like the others, was far too hot already.

So weird, she thought, asserting once again, Things are just not right.

The girl tucked her forearm beneath her cheek, repositioned it, and then bit down on a yawn. Closing her heavy lids, she started to sink into sleep, agreeably surrendering to the luscious undertow. With her consciousness virtually suspended, peaceably, easily—gratefully—Heather rode the blissful currents that encompassed her.

"So, did it finally come t'rest with ya, child, tha' truly yahr the green-eyed Maiden?"

Heather's eyes shot open at hearing the peculiar voice. It was deep and rough, yet the delivery was not unpleasant. She sat up and quickly scanned the room, before she focused on the painting.

"Oh, no. Not you, too?"

"Wha'?"

"Calling me that name."

"Well, lass, yahr her."

Annoyed, Heather changed the subject. "I know who you are."

"Do ya, now?"

"Yeah. You're the pirate, Terentius "Scarbones" Bristol."

"Aye, that I am, that I am. And I know who you be, lass."

"Well, whoever you think I am, I'm *not* that Maiden."

"Oh, yahr not, eh?"

"No. Or at least, at least I don't think I am. My friend, Aria, she might be the green-eyed Maiden, but not me."

"Eh? And pray tell, who be this Aria? Another lass like yerself?"

"She's someone who—well, you may not believe this—she's someone who lives inside of me."

"Does she now?" The pirate was amused. "Inside o' ya, eh, missy?"

"Yeah."

"But this Aria is not you?"

"No."

"Do *ya* live inside o' you?"

"Of course. What a silly thing to ask."

"And ahr ya *you?*"

Heather looked over the man.

"I belie'e I asked ya a question, lassie." His voice was teasing, playful. "Ahr ya you?"

"Yeah—yes, I'm me."

"Then that leads me t'belie'e tha' this Aria, she be you, too."

"But she's not, Mr. Bristol."

"Scarbones, lass."

"Scarbones."

"Heather Nighborne." The pirate reached up and tipped his tricorn. "Pleased t'make yer acquaintance."

"Hey," the girl said, "how do you know my name?"

"Why, that's easy, missy." The pirate laughed. "Many a day and e'enin', I'e stood 'ere jus' listenin', ne'er blinkin' me eyes." He leaned forward in the painting, saying in a confidential manner, "Also, Me happen tah ha'e heard a rumor o' two concernin' ya…"

"Well, if you must know, Aria visits, but she's not here all the time. Just every now and then. Besides, I was born here, here on Earth. Aria wasn't. She was born in Evermore—at least it seems like Aria was born there. I mean, she knows about iMagiNacia and everything."

"Argh, iMagiNacia, ya say?"

"Yeah, it's a special type of magic."

"I may ha'e caught wind o' it…"

"And her sister is Mistraya. Maybe you've heard of her, wherever you are, there in that painting. She's an evil sorceress in Autumnsloe."

"Aye, I'e heard o' her, miss. And I'm pleased t'announce that I'e ne'er directly had the pleasure o' mixin' words with yer sorceress. Ne'er trust the like. I'd gut her as look at her, I would."

"Well, anyway, Aria could be the Maiden in the Portent, I suppose. But really, I don't think I am."

"Can't ha'e one without the other, lassie."

"What do you mean?"

"I mean either ya both ahr or ya both ahrn't. Get me drift? And if yahr, it sure will ha'e made me stayin' 'ere worth the effort —ya know, ha'in' me attendin' tah me duty, seein' tah the buildin' o' the Bristol House and all."

"What? I mean, what do you mean? I mean, you're not making a lot of sense, you know."

"I'm tryin' t'say that if ya truly ahr the Maiden prophesied, then me life will ha'e been more worthwhile than e'er imagined, when I was 'ere last, doing me duty fer E'ermore."

"You? You're from Evermore? But I thought you were a pirate captain."

"Oh, I was. Indeed I was. And a good one, too. Cap'n o' the *Ill Wind*, lass. Had t'get that de'ilish part o' me out o' me system, ya know, attracted tah the pirate life as I was. Comin' tah this 'ere planet twasn't easy, and took a wee bit o' adjustment. Oh, I was high-spirited then, all right, an advent'rous youth runnin' round on the high seas, not havin' tah think o' worry 'bout fulfillin' me appointed duties."

"But if you're from the Realm of Evermore, how come you talk like one of *our* pirates?"

The man's voice suddenly lost its pirate-speak. "One might say that, over the years, I acquired it on the job. How could I not? Can you imagine me not talking like a pirate while dressed this way? Preposterous! And the crew, they might have thought I was from some strange far-off land, to boot! I couldn't have them thinking *that*, now could I?" He winked. "But as I was sayin', Me came t'right meself o'er time, and married a stout wench, I did, and built this 'ere Bristol House. It took a couple o' hundred years, and lo and behold, wouldn't ya know it, now we'e taken ya in. And look a'cha." Scarbones Bristol was beaming down on Heather. "Imagine. The green-eyed Maiden o' the E'ermore Portent living 'ere in me own Bristol House."

"Will you please stop saying that?"

Scarbones laughed heartily, caught himself, looked around culpably, and then lowered his voice to an amused undertone.

"All right, then, ha'e it yer way. Fer now."

The captain looked distracted for a moment, as he placed a hand over his stomach. "Thar's somethin' goin' on way down in me guts, there is. And tis givin' me a bellyache and causin' me t'worry." Yet, it wasn't but a moment later that Scarbones' impish look returned.

"Then, about t'day's little odyssey t'Autumnsloe, missy: what do ya think the powers that be had in mind, then, eh? Ya almost got killed, ya know—or so, that's the rumor."

"It's true. I did. Molly, too."

"But when twas all finished and done, ya didn't get killed, now, didja?"

"No." Heather gave herself a brief onceover. "Because here I am."

"So, s'posin' I tol' ya twas a test? A Prophesy e'aluation, if ya like? And ya had t'remain ali'e tah prove that yahr the Maiden o' the Portent?"

"If you're making a joke, I don't think it's funny."

"Wha'?"

"Going to Evermore and having it turn out to be some kind of a test of some silly Portent—and I don't even know what a Portent is. No, I don't think that's funny, and I'm not sure that I ever want to go again. Oh, it was really beautiful and all that. Molly and I had a great time at the parade."

"Then why ye be gripin', missy?"

"Because, like you said, I almost got killed. And so did Molly. And, and I have a hard time thinking of that as fun. Or funny." Tired, Heather's short-fused anger quickly rose to the surface, as she indignantly stared back at the pirate—albeit with little effect. As a matter of fact, the girl noticed that her anger rather tickled him, and that angered her all the more. "I don't know if you know this, but in Autumnsloe, we fought some RogueTags, were chased by Mistraya's scouts, and had a bunch of creepy people try to kill us. I saw people get beat up and murdered, and watched a costume shop burn down—almost with us in it. A guy named Borray attacked us, Mistraya nearly killed us, and we almost didn't make it home. And all because of this Portent thing of yours. So, no thanks! I've decided, you can keep your Evermore."

The pirate became mockingly pouty. "Without a doubt, tis got yer sails all aflutter, I can see tha'."

"Yeah, well, it would have gotten yours aflutter, too, if you had to ki—fracture—your friend to save her from Mistraya." The girl sighed, suddenly deflating. "So, I don't mean to be mean, but I've had enough of this green-eyed Maiden nonsense. For a little while, I was okay with it when I was talking to Molly, but not anymore. And I think it's more important to you than it is to me—that I'm her, I mean. I just want to be Heather Nighborne from Noble, okay? Now, I'm tired, Mr. Scarbones, and if you don't mind, I'd like to get back to dreaming a different dream."

"All right, then, ha'e it yer way. But before I go—and actually, twas my main reason for turnin' up t'day before I recei'ed word ya needed some convincin'—is not to persuade ya, but tah thank ye and tell ya that yah'e done me right, lass. Aye, ya ha'e, yah'e done me right and proper. Tis good fer a seafarin' fellow that came to be an esteemed diplomat t'know. I'm proud, I am. Right proud."

"Of what?"

"O' you, o' course, bein'—ya know, bein' that person who yahrn't— and li'in' 'ere in me Bristol House."

Heather rolled her eyes in exasperation.

The pirate in the painting suddenly lost his jocularity and became thoughtful. "Be ya sure that, like a younger Scarbones in his day, yahr not afraid o' who ya truly might be and whatcha must do? Because try as ya might, lassie, it has a way o' sneakin' up on yer rudder, ya know."

"What does?"

"Why, yer destiny. Took me a long time t'embrace me purpose fer comin' 'ere, a long time indeed. Lucky fer me, I was given a chance t'do what I was meant t'do right along. And I made the way possible fer ya. Tis no coincidence that ya ended up at the Bristol House, missy."

"What do you mean, it's no coincidence, Mr. Scar—".

"Bah," the captain admonished. "Tis modestly Scarbones, lassie, Scarbones indeed and only. Kin welcomes the pri'ilege o' familiarity, so thar's no title needed. And as yer the—well, ya know—that makes ya kin."

Heather just sighed, mouthing the words: I'm not her.

The pirate maintained his rascally look, as he lowered his voice. "All right, if ya must insist, I will in good faith, then, accept yer silent plea." The captain brought a large masculine hand to his chest and roared with mirth. Moments later, he caught himself, again cutting his laughter short. He looked around, expecting someone to walk into the room after overhearing him.

Heather said, "Please, can't you and everyone just leave me alone?"

"Please yerself, and refuse t'belie'e what e'eryone else sees clear as day. But I respect and maintain that the Portent will find ya against yer wishes—as a matter o' fact, lassie, it already has."

"You're making fun of me. And you're a dream. You're not real. You're not!"

"That's right. I'm not real." The captain pointed. "And yahr not— well, yahr not *ya know who!*" Again, he roared, before catching himself. With one hand atop the hilt of his sword, the other reached to the right, somewhere off frame, and returned with a tankard of ale.

Heather said, "This is a dream. And now I'm going back to sleep."

Promptly lying on her back with a flop and a rustle, she closed her eyes. The girl could hear the pirate still chuckling. She crossed her arms.

"It takes awhile t'settle in and do what's respectable," he said. "'Tis a selfless act, ya know."

Heather's brow bunched thoughtfully at the pirate's words. She rolled onto her side and looked at him, propping her head. "What is?"

The captain was taking a swill. He wiped his mouth on his sleeve. "Why, 'tis a selfless act, givin' yer life fer E'ermore, fer the greater good. Maidens do that, as do the occasional Maliden."

"Maliden?"

"Male Maiden, missy. Yahr lookin' at one."

"What I'm looking at is a bad dream. And now, if you don't mind, I'm going back to sleep, so I can wake up."

Heather reclined and, feigning sleep, could still hear the pirate laughing softly to himself. Truly, Heather wished she were a Maiden—on an Archmount—but not the one responsible for saving a Realm. Yet, she wasn't going to tell the captain that. Heather felt that he would only continue to poke fun.

Here I am asleep, she told herself. I'm in the living room of the Bristol House, on a couch, just sleeping away. Yes I am. And now I'm going to wake up. I'm going to wake up, and Scarbones Bristol is going to only be a painting.

When she could no longer hear the pirate, her right eye searchingly popped open, only to find the captain awaiting her. And when Scarbones noticed her peeking, he guffawed once more.

"Gi'e in and gi'e yerself t'E'ermore, Lassie. Yahr ahr green-eyed Maiden, t'be sure."

"I told you, I'm just plain old Heather Nighborne from planet earth." Heather positioned herself for sleep once again. "And when I wake up, I'm going to talk to Grandma Dawn. She'll know..."

The pirates voice was fading. "Aye, Dawn Thibble. That she will, lassie. That she will... Dawn Thibble, she be one who knows..."

Adrift in sleep, Heather found herself wandering, patches of light appearing and passing, soft-edged and indistinct. When the girl was finally able to focus, the patches turned into sky between the boughs of trees. Approaching the fringe of the heavily forested area, Heather stopped and peered out from behind a tree, her senses keenly aware. Cautiously emerging from her shelter, she hurried across the sloping meadow towards a shaded, boulder-strewn creek. To her chest, Heather carried a snugly wrapped bundle secure in a sling that crossed her back and shoulder, a bundle that, she was aware, needed her protection. Seeing no one, she stole vigilantly through the foliage along the water's edge, seeking available cover whenever possible.

The stream, it's murmur quiet and comforting, meandered lazily over pebbles, around boulders, and near ancient trees with their undergrowth. Overhead the wind whispered on the bough, causing the treetops to sway, their woodland colors rocking against the purest backdrop of deep blue. The three moons of Autumnsloe were still visible in the early morning light: a large circle of turbulent violets, a middle-sized dusty green, and a slightly smaller penetrating red. Their recent alignment of only days ago was no longer discernable.

At the creek, Heather removed her bundle from the sling and placed it gently on the ground. Then she froze. At what sounded like another's approach, she hastened a look upstream, while instinctively grabbing up the swaddled roll. Yet, Heather could see nothing out of the ordinary that might cause her or her baby harm. Calming, she set the sleeping child down again, carefully, delicately.

Heather, in her dream a young woman, was crouching over the creek concealed in a cloak of blanched olive green, its cowl and sleeves encircled in the gold ringlet design of the MaidenHood. After another heedful glance upstream and then down, she splashed water onto her face, and then paused before splashing some more. Dipping with cupped hands, she brought water to her thirsting lips, locks of crudely cut hair falling free along her pale cheeks.

Heather rose with the newborn, still sleeping snugly in its sling. Judiciously, she made her way downstream, staggering at times due to weariness.

Rounding an embankment, the woman was breathing laboriously, trudging toward the greater envelopment of greenwood, with its labyrinth of trees and trails. Slogging to a spot just inside the first sheltering boughs, she rested, propping herself against a trunk for support. Her head swam, but she fought off the need to lie down, knowing that sleep would too easily find her—and undoubtedly for far too long an interval.

Now was not the time. Later. Later.

When Heather had regained sufficient strength, she pushed off and toiled forth on a path both foreign and familiar. The wooded environs seemed to embrace her within its shaded, cloistered tranquility, as the young woman traversed the forest floor, over gullies, ruts, and fallen logs, between mossy rocks, and past copious shrubbery. Often, to avoid detection, she veered off discreetly marked paths, sensing her way.

"I mustn't lose strength," Heather heard herself say. Or courage.

Burdened with the knowledge of impending loss, the hooded figure trudged onward, recognizing the vaulted alignment of trees that led to a glade. She could hear the surging waters of Gibbous Falls in the distance, and glimpsed an extraordinary rock formation rising up within the clearing. Instinctively, Heather knew this to be her intended destination. Partway along the tree-lined corridor, she again paused in brief respite and then prodded herself onward.

Almost there. Almost.

Approaching the small clearing, Heather slowed. While still safely hidden in wooded seclusion, she stopped and leaned against a large rock, checking once again on her sleeping baby.

Before long, however, she began to impatiently look around, thinking, Where can that woman be?

Heather started to fret. Having recently communicated via Whisper-Eye Mirror, the woman in question had agreed to meet her here, near the CrescentRock Portal, on this day and time.

I mustn't stay away long, the young mother kept thinking. No one must know of my visit here. No one. And, she added sadly and shamefully, no one must know of my beautiful child.

Heather removed the slumbering baby from the sling and held the newborn in her arms, where it stirred. She let the baby's tiny, intricate digits wrap her index finger, alongside the white ring of the Evermore Maidens. Attempting to memorize the beloved features, an image the young mother wished to capture for a lifetime, she gazed upon the infant's face, the infant she would surely never see again. Pulling back her hood, she leaned down to kiss her baby goodbye, before pressing her near.

At the sound of footsteps shushing through the grass, Heather looked up. Before her, the sun had crested the treetops, fanning out across the glade. Approaching out of that light, from the direction of the rock Portal, came the graceful, long-limbed person with whom she had communicated. Lifting the tiny, green-eyed baby, Heather stepped forward and placed her tenderly into the awaiting arms of the woman she recognized as a vigorous, more youthful Grandma Dawn.

CHAPTER THIRTY-SIX

In search of a feeling

Heather awakened. She lay motionless for a moment, staring with slow focus at the chandeliers above, letting her sleepiness subside.

What a strange dream—what strange dreams.

With her head feeling thick and the world around her remote, Heather yawned, wiping her eyes with her palm. They were wet, as if she had been crying.

Weird.

Sitting upright on the couch, Heather noticed that the living room was even hotter than when she had first laid down to sleep. Beneath her clothing, the girl was swimming in sweat.

This isn't right. There's just way too much un-Bristol House-like stuff going on.

Reluctantly, Heather stood, feeling grumpy, both her ankle and the small bump beneath her hair throbbing. She stared rudely at the painting of Scarbones Bristol, welcoming a confrontation. But the man didn't move, holding his familiar pose, the gleam lively in his eyes. The next instant, Heather was no longer paying attention to the pirate.

What *is* that?

There it was again, the sensation that came alive somewhere inside, causing a thrill, like a euphoric shiver of her senses.

What's causing that feeling? Is it coming from somewhere in the Bristol House?

With sleep still clouding her features, the girl walked into the foyer and stopped.

Funny. Across the parlor, the door to the basement stood open.

Heather tensed and straightened, as the tingling sensation again rode through her.

That feels so bi-zarre... Can it be coming from downstairs?

Her intuition was pulling, drawing her toward the doorway, coaxing her inside, where the blackness seemed palpable and restless.

But from where downstairs? she wondered. *Servant's quarters or basement?*

Heather stood stationary, uncertain, her senses still muffled and infused with sleep. However, the mystery was too great, and so, intrigued, she allowed herself to be drawn across the parlor and through the open door. Quietly, Heather descended the steps and in little time found herself stopping before the large double doors leading to the basement.

It's coming from in there, she thought. *I can feel it.*

The girl pushed and pulled at the ringed handles, but the substantial doors refused to give, barring her entry.

Wow. That's never happened before.

Heather wandered along the sconce-lit passageway toward the servant's quarters, halting before a stark black-windowed door.

This is just way too weird. I don't remember a door being here.

It gave grudgingly, opening into darkness. She entered, and the door swung silently closed behind her.

Where is this? I've never seen this basement room before.

Far above Heather, beyond the beams of a trestle that cut diagonally overhead, burned a lone, distant light. It shone large and round like the moon through the skeletal remains of a nearby tree. To one side, a towering, pointy-roofed structure climbed into the boundless heights of the room. It appeared decrepit.

In front of her, beyond patches of dry grass, long lines of railroad cars stretched into the distance. The hulking shapes blended vaguely into one another, and their rows of shattered and missing windows stared, caching their secrets in reclusive compartments behind them.

Where am I?

Having shaken the numbing aftereffects of her nap, Heather walked with an occasional hobble between the rows, glimpsing parallel trains on parallel tracks through gaps and open boxcars. Maneuvering past pieces of steel track haphazardly piled, she stopped and tensed.

There it was again! That feeling. Could it be caused by something inside that railcar close by?

She looked over the exterior, steel-slabbed and riveted, and then stared into its empty windows.

Did something move? The girl thought she saw a flicker of motion, while hearing a jostle.

As quietly as she could, Heather approached the rear entry of the car and hoisted herself up, mounting the stairs to stand within a small outer compartment. A tall opening to her left revealed the detached car behind, and allowed a thin shaft of pale light to enter. To her right, past a door with a busted window, was the silent interior of the carriage.

Could whatever is causing that feeling be in here?

Heather peered inside.

What am I looking for, anyway?

With difficulty, the girl attempted to make sense of the interior shapes, but even with the weak light angling hazily through some of the windows, she was unable to do so. Heather pushed the door inward, listening to the groan of the rusted hinges and feeling the brittle paint snap free beneath her palm and fingers. Inside, nothing moved. Her eyes adjusting to the dimmer light, she stepped farther into the gloom, trying to absorb the slightest sensation.

Hearing a rustling before her, Heather glanced to her left in time to see a large shape coming at her, its aura a brusque, raging crimson. Quickly, she dropped to a crouch as the bird brushed overhead, departing through the open doorway. It cleared the roof of the adjacent car, and with a beating of its powerful wings, the owl flew off into the night-like atmosphere.

Heather rose to her feet, riding the rush of adrenaline while ignoring the throb of her ankle. She turned her attention back to the jumbled interior of the carriage and tried once again to distinguish the forms. Noticing that a majority of windows were hidden behind roll-down shades that blotted out the exterior light, Heather carefully maneuvered down a perceived center aisle. Stumbling over a cushion and then the dilapidated framework of what were once seats, she reached out and pulled aside some of the shades, bunching them in crumply disorder. With the additional light, she could now see that the seats were mostly missing and debris was strewn everywhere.

She thought, Nothing in here—unless that funny feeling I had was coming from the bird, but I doubt it.

Reversing course, Heather climbed out of the car and lowered herself to the ground. She looked around and became inexplicably attracted to a group of featureless buildings rising boldly above the trains. Heather angled toward them, zigzagging through the shorter lines of boxcars, while scrambling over their linkage. Beneath her feet, the brush of grass had become sporadic. Ankle smarting, Heather continued over stony ground, enticed by a muted light in one of the ground level windows, visible between the rusted husks of the remaining cars.

Shovel lying at his side, the digger was sitting by his leather bag, despondent.

All this is so futile, so desperate, he thought. And time is ticking away, along with this puny HumanKind lifespan of mine. I should never have agreed—never!—but I was a young man then, I was loyal. How was I to know my Earthly posting as settler and observer was going to become irrelevant, a waste of my life? To be the 'Ears and Eyes of Evermore while Elsewhere?'

The man scoffed.

What for? The news has it the Maidens are disbanded now and that Evermore, as I once knew it, has been in complete disarray since the Bloodlet Overthrow. I hear the Maidens have even abandoned their rightful place alongside the great Knowledge Stone and the Pool of Reason. No point in going back, even if I could. The damage is done. These days, no one gets near those waters. And no one comes out.

He leaned forward and rested his forearms on his knees. He thought of Stilped, the boy he had killed.

Of all the towns in the entire world, that child's Aunt had to live here in Noble—the same place where a 'Bristol House' is located. But then, how would I have stumbled onto it if not while visiting my wife's sister?

"My luck." He set the lantern upright and chuckled, adding, "Certainly not Stilped's. Although, after spotting him in the Park, I did attempt to avoid the boy. I had worked far too hard establishing a new identity in a new town to have him expose me."

But Stilped had to be down by Whisper Creek that night didn't he, had to notice me? There I was walking with my shovel, off road in the wooded area, on my way to do some fortune hunting. And of all people, I run into my son, Stilped, sneaking out after dark to meet his friends.

The man laughed scornfully, attempting to relight the lantern, the flame of the match wavering weakly.

The chance encounter, the meeting between father and son, had taken place on the night of the quiet boy's death. Fleeing from the commotion caused by Ms. Gardner's barking dogs, Stilped was hiding in the oaks, awaiting Molly and Heather. When he heard someone coming, he garnered his courage and shined his flashlight in the face of the approaching individual. Quick to raise an arm to the harsh beacon, the man in the hat shied away.

"Who goes there?" the meek voice said, quavering.

"If you'd be so kind as to lower your light," the man responded, good-naturedly, "I'd be happy to tell you."

At first, Stilped was frightened. The voice sounded so familiar. With the beam no longer in his face, the man lowered his arm. In the indirect light, one can only imagine the boy's shock upon recognizing his clean-shaven father. Conflicted and overwhelmed, Stilped stood planted, unmoving. When father recognized son, both the Roarhowsers became momentarily speechless.

"Dad?" The boy finally offered, confused. "Dad, is that really you?"

The father let loose a little laugh, thinking of a thousand stories to tell his son, a thousand lies. But he concluded in the eternity that seemed to define the awkward moment that he would kill his son in a manner reminiscent of the town's Pet Stalker, the Pet Stalker gone too far.

He finally spoke, feigning excitement, "Can it be? Stilped? It is! It's you! Oh, I don't believe this. Finally! What a relief! Why, son, I've been searching all over for you."

Seeing Stilped was dumbstruck, the father kept talking, working to engage the boy and win him over.

"As you can well imagine, surviving that cave-in was quite an ordeal—ah, but it's a long story…" the man laughed nervously. "We've a lot to catch up on, you and I. And, as you can see," he laughed again, "I'm definitely not dead. Nowhere near such a state."

Still the boy didn't move or speak.

"So here I am. I've come for you, and thank heavens I found you!"

Stilped finally seemed to come around, instantly flooded with emotion and the realization that his father wasn't dead after all.

The man recognized this, and threw aside his shovel. "Stilped!" He opened his arms encouragingly, and the boy rushed into them.

"Oh, Dad… You're alive." Stilped was crying, and through his joyful tears added, "I missed you so much." The youth held fast, and his father held Stilped in turn, looking down on him, wondering where to dispose of the body.

After bringing Stilped home with him, the father encouraged another hug from his trusting son, who then became easy prey for a kitchen knife thrust under the ribs.

Idiotic boy, the man had thought after Stilped went limp in his arms. Always so stupidly naïve and trusting—just like his mother. "So, for your trouble," he said, holding the sagging boy at arms length, "and for dirtying my floor, I think I'll disembowel you like an Autumnslovian tarskendale, and then adorn you with some pets for good measure, establishing my *own* Pet Stalker routine.

Letting the dead boy drop to the floor in a graceless pile, the man laughed, proclaiming, "Stilped Roarhowser, the King of Gullibility!"

Then he reflected: The Pet Stalker. Wish I'd thought of it. The role certainly suits me more so than the real culprit, Simpletripp. He's inventive, though, I'll give him that. Secretly, I've watched him take his pleasure with the slow dissection and shocking presentation of his victims. Yes, he's creative, all right. But I'm better. Much, much better.

Stilped's father turned his attention to the green iguana, a souvenir from Central America—a souvenir commemorating his fortuitous freedom. At the time, he had loved the way the lizard could survive in two different worlds, in treetops and under water. But now, viewing the scaly thing behind the glass of its cage, the man realized he had lost his fascination with the confined reptile, regretting the spontaneity of his purchase and the responsibility that ownership entailed.

"Pets. Hate the creatures. Their dependency and loyalty disgusts me."

When shrill barking and whining sounded from a nearby room, suddenly inspired, he thought, Ah, I hear another volunteer, and so to the mix I'll just add that little stray Pringle dog Stilped insisted I pick up on the way here, and crown the child's head. Nothing like—dare I say it?— a copy*cat* Pet Stalker. Why, I think I've found a new hobby. And now, speaking of a cat, I believe I must also catch one. It won't take much effort on my part, however. To do so, I need only put out a fresh bowl of milk. See? So easy. I'm going to like being a Pet Stalker, I can tell.

Weston Stilped Roarhowser III—as he was once known on this planet—nonchalantly threw the bloody knife in the sink and rinsed his hands before wiping them on a dishtowel. Retrieving a cold slice of pizza from the refrigerator, he bit off a hunk, and chewed while observing the boy, saying, "Believe me, Son…" The man took a moment to swallow, gesturing with the pizza, "…if I hadn't done you in, someone eventually would have. It was bound to happen, you know. Survival of the fittest, as they say, and it's true." He tore off another mouthful, adding as he chomped, "On any planet."

He returned to the refrigerator, and opening it, pulled out a can. Popping the pull-tab one-handed, he looked down on Stilped.

"Beer?"

Afterward, having considered the possibilities, the murderer thought it a brilliant ploy to bury Stilped's body on the Bristol House grounds. It was a risky move, and one that would curtail his treasure hunting excavations for a while.

Such a loss of time and purpose.

But he was certain that news of an ugly murder would scare off those other diggers, the diggers who for years had been searching for the riches with hopeful holes of their own.

"That treasure, it's mine!" the man had growled sharply, and afterwards threatened softly, "Stay away."

Once or twice he had come upon the sight of Mr. Simpletripp attempting to find Scarbone's plunder with the use of a metal detector. He spied to make certain the slovenly man was unsuccessful. And then later, not to be outdone, the digger had purchased a detector himself, employing it periodically while dressed in the manner of Mr. Simpletripp.

Two years ago in Central America, following the earthquake and subsequent cave-in, Stilped's father knew he had been given a gift for which he had long wished: the ideal opportunity to achieve his freedom. Afterwards, he had set it up so perfectly, pretending to have been killed, buried alive, and then cutting loose his ties to family and Evermore in the process.

Burdened with a wife and son, he felt, restricted his earthly experiences while preventing the chance for more wondrous adventures. Shortly after his wedding, the man had come to regret the decision to marry Ellen Avondale, feeling trapped in a farcical union imposed upon him by the MaidenHood mandate to live a common family life on another planet. But back then, he had been a loyal Maliden assigned to Earth, just like the legendary Terentius 'Scarbones' Bristol, himself.

And now here I am, the digger thought, striking another match in the night, and producing another weak hesitant flame.

Life on Earth: what a waste of my immortality, he thought. What a waste!

With shaking hand, Stilped's murderer was finally able to light the lantern, and it hissed, rising to a steady glow. He checked his watch in the light, noting that the night was that much older.

He thought, I should have stopped aging after twenty-eight years, like all Evermorian bound Malidens and Maidens.

For the Four, Oh, Never More. You owe me, you fetid Realm! You hear! *You owe me!*

Angrily, he arose, and snatching up his shovel, went back to work.

Through her Moonlight°Prisms, the woman in indigo looked over thick, sturdy tabletops toward the potter's wheels that were staggered throughout the room. Shelves of hand-thrown ceramics lined two of the walls. On the tables, partially completed vases, mugs, and other oddly shaped, coiled entities were surrounded by blocky bags of clay. Against the back wall, past the dull gleam of metallic sinks, rested two brick kilns. One stood open, radiating the luminous yellow-green of a Portal and the TimeLight Bridge.

Quietly, the visitor glided between tables to stand before the kiln. She raised her hand with the attached PortalSealer, thinking, The Bristol House is astoundingly porous, and probably impossible to effectively safeguard. It will take months, if not years, to seal its many Portals. And even then, when the new rooms arrive, there's no guarantee they'll be Portal-free.

So near, so very near, thought the TimeLight Assassin. Powerful magic. The Maiden Portent, it must be her, performing in one of the adjoining rooms. He gave a quick scan to his surroundings. But through which door?

Not inclined to await another emanation, he decided to choose.

Feeling the tingle that again coursed through her, Grandma Dawn trembled with the pleasant sensation. She then covered the beef stew, turning down the heat. She knew that closing the Bristol House Portals was for the better, yet she couldn't help but wonder if the use of such potent, attention-drawing ArcaniMagia was worth the risk of discovery.

ArcaniMagia, she thought. The ancient magic that I learned and practiced in my youth. I was very good at it, too. But then that was so long ago, another lifetime away. Who knows what I would do if I ever needed to make use of it again?

Removing the oven mitts, the efficient woman glanced at the clock, and then hurried into the small dining room to finish setting the table.

Heather was walking through a small dressing room that appeared to be in complete disarray. Dangling on cords, a few bare bulbs lit the space, with moths dancing and flitting about the pale yellow globes.

So weird, she thought. Who would ever think that a door from the railyard would lead into this goofy room?

In what seemed to be part of a Big Top circus tent, there were curtained walls and drapery doors, lopsided cupboards and chests with overflowing drawers. Stuffed in an open armoire labeled WARDROBE was a lively assortment of shiny shirts, pants, and misshapen shoes of humongous size.

Beneath a fanciful mirror, fringed in pink, was a wide vanity. On it were littered boxes and jars and combs and canisters; there were wigs and tissues and bowties and books. Farfetched hats, miniature and oversized, were scattered throughout, among fake noses, big ears, and bold frizzy wigs.

On each side of an empty, crooked coat rack hung a series of framed photographs, each featuring clowns, clowns, clowns, and clowns. Below the pictures, in a heap of flashy colors, discarded garments had accumulated beside a big base drum. On the cluttered vanity, in an oversized ashtray, a lone cigar burned.

Making a face at its pungent smell, Heather hurried past, brushing aside the curtain that hung in place of a door.

Letting the drapery fall into place behind her, Heather stepped into the afterhours of an amusement park. Throughout, its frozen rides and hooded booths were sporadically lit by kerosene lanterns, their exhalations hissing throatily at the night. And though the place seemed deserted, Heather half-expected someone to appear out of nowhere.

Nearby, angling skyward, umbrellaed cars were hoisted on metal arms, and just beyond sat the empty half-shells of a static Tilt-a-Whirl. Other rides appeared lifeless and forgotten, dried spiders balled up in clusters of posts and spindles. It seemed to Heather that the park lay sleeping, waiting for a bunch of people to arrive and wake it all up: the lights, the sounds, and the motion—*the fun*.

Brushing hair from her damp forehead, she began walking down a wide, dirt lane, passing connected booths where the unlit signs could still be read: *Freaks of Nature* and *Dog with Human Face* and *World's Ugliest Man* and—Heather's favorite—*Giant Bearded Praying Mantis from another Planet*. Yet, the shut up booths didn't make the girl feel uncomfortable, however the thought of seeing any person or creature in the aforementioned conditions did. Drifting past an isolated ticket booth, she felt a hot breeze that rippled through the canvas structures, dispersing some wrappers at her feet.

Heather passed the Cotton Candy Factory and after that, Hot Dog on a Stick. Hungry, she sure wished they were open. She could just make out the announcements that in daylight would burst forth with Sno

Cones, Hot Buttered Popcorn, and Candied Apples.

Instinct told Heather to turn down an aisle of game booths, and so she did. Though lightless, these weren't closed up, their display of toys and other prizes hanging loosely, rocked by the wind. Withdrawn in the cavernous booths, a multitude of stuffed animals looked out on the passing Heather, but the girl, unable to see them clearly, remained impervious to their button-eyed, take-me-home stares.

Striding by the elaborate merry-go-round, Heather peered at what she could see of the stationary mounts speared by their spiraling metal posts. To her, in this light, the painted horses appeared to be staring in open-mouthed terror, unable to break loose and gallop away. Turning, she looked instead at the immense spoke and girdered ferris wheel that soared above her into a breathless beyond, a few of its angled seats rocking, prompted by the wind. She followed the curving trajectory of the great ellipse as it gradually disappeared, absorbed within the vast expanse of darkness.

I don't like these rooms, thought Heather. It was then she felt that sudden, internal, light-dancing sensation.

Heather stopped in her tracks. Finding herself in front of the House of Mirrors, she gazed at the black curtained doorways of the entrance and exit. A sense of foreboding gripped her. Knowing there was but one way to the bottom of the mystery of what was causing her innards to quiver, the girl set off up the ramp leading to the interior halls of reflective gloom.

Pulling aside the entry curtain, Heather thought, Should've kept that LuminOrb.

The TimeLight Assassin edged through the partially open door, his body clearing its knob and jamb by mere fractions. Sidling against a wall, he lingered just long enough to collect and register information on his newfound surroundings, anticipating the next vibration of magic that would allow him to pinpoint direction and distance. Smoothly skimming past the room's contents, the deadly intruder came to an abrupt and unexpected standstill.

Entering yet another basement room, the woman in indigo attire was instantly mesmerized by the sight before her. The murky room was full of people frozen in a multitude of positions. The goggled Bristol House visitor relaxed when she realized they were wax representations from many places and walks of life. Closest to her were movie stars and magicians; circus performers, opera singers, and belly dancers; sports figures of various eras; classical and jazz musicians—rock and rap stars, too, all poised, looking very much alive.

Occupying a majority of the immense room, she noted legions and battalions, formations of soldiers from many places and times. On foot or atop animals, they carried weapons and banners. Some appeared purposeful and dour, while others were laughing, teeth parted, mouths open in stone cold merriment.

Around the periphery of the humid room stood cavemen and astronauts; lords, gentries, slaves, and serfs; courtesans and odalisques, along with detectives, arch villains, and comic book heroes. Off in one corner, a group of merrymakers were locked in positions as if conversing and mingling at a party. These fashionable characters were clothed in the latest dresses, suits, and casual attire.

Moonlight°Prisms in place, the seeker wandered the floor among the vast array of individuals, looking for the yellow-green luminescence of a Portal. Unable to discover one, she paused as, again on the °Prism lenses, notes of the Portal-less room were logged and the location coordinates committed to apparatus memory. Moving down an aisle near the wall, she cautiously slipped through a door leading into the adjoining, high-ceilinged room. Gazing about, the environs struck her as familiar, with its high row of arched windows and stacks of draped furniture. The woman realized she was again in the first basement room she had passed through after descending from the garden.

Originally, she had chosen not to delay in an Entry Room that might be heavily trafficked, preferring instead to ensconce herself deeper within the basement. Upon her second visit, however, not having encountered a soul, she decided now was an appropriate time to search the room for Portals. What the Maiden hadn't realized was that, from somewhere among the wax figures in the room behind her, the TimeLight Assassin had soundlessly detached. Lifeless heads turned and observed the deadly stalker as he crept after the woman.

Heather was lost in the House of Mirrors, roaming down the many lowlight passageways. Confounded by the multiple images of herself, she simply closed her eyes and reached before her or to the side, feeling for an opening, hoping to encounter another corridor in the complex maze of mirrored walls.

After groping her way up two flights of stairs, and now wandering on the third floor, Heather was ruminating on pesky questions: What the heck am I supposed to be looking for? Could these strange feelings inside of me really be caused by something in the Bristol House basement? Why is it so hot? And why has the Bristol House brought me to the House of Mirrors? I mean, couldn't it have let me through the large basement doors at the bottom of the stairs like it normally does? Why all *this?*

That's when Heather felt the electrical pulse of magic dazzle her innards once again.

It's here! Close by, too! But where?

Turning a corner, she encountered a longer stretch of corridor. Oddly, on one side, the wall wasn't mirrored. Instead of her reflection, she found herself looking down through a window into an expansive high-ceilinged room. The darkened space was stacked with what looked like furniture, mostly covered with blankets. On the wall directly opposite were a series of familiar arched windows, each full of the night. Through them, Heather witnessed the evening's first flashes of lightning, followed shortly thereafter by the grumblings of thunder.

Heather redirected her gaze into the space below and recognized it as the Entry Room behind the large basement doors, the room the Bristol House had refused her access to only a short while ago.

Much to Heather's surprise, a person walking in the gloom drew her attention, an aura shining out. At first glance, the girl had a fleeting impression that it might be Grandma Dawn, due to the height of the woman and her elegant carriage. And though Heather couldn't make out her features, nor had witnessed the magical effect of the Maiden's handheld device that had recently sealed the Portal beneath the baby grand piano, she came to the conclusion that the mysterious visitor couldn't possibly be her grandmother. It was that certain *something* that intuitively told her so.

As she more closely examined the woman's aura radiating calmly in curious oranges and dutiful yellows, Heather thought, Sure looks like a Maiden, but then what would a Maiden from Evermore be doing in the Bristol House, anyway? Hey, what's that?

In another aisle, close to one of many doors, Heather spied the movement of another aura, subdued in cunning grays. It struck her that the shine belonged to a man.

Boy, that person sure seems to be taking their sweet time, she said to herself, watching as he slinked closer to the Maiden-like visitor.

Heather's mouth dropped when his shine suddenly turned smoky black and deadly—like those creepy people from Autumnsloe.

The girl thought, That woman has no idea that the guy with the ugly shine is sneaking up on her—and he's definitely not her friend.

Heather began to pound on the glass with her fist, but neither of them paid heed to the ruckus. The girl pounded some more, but was unable to get the attention of the Maiden-type.

She can't hear me, Heather thought. And I bet that guy is going to hurt her unless I hurry and warn her!

The girl raced down the corridor and turned a corner, hoping to find a stairway to the lower floor, but was unable to see one, only the endless echoes of her image. And in the maze, Heather couldn't recall where she had come up or her route through the confusion of hallways, so couldn't retrace her steps.

Stairs! Stairs! Stairs! her brain screamed as she hobble-ran down the mirrored passageways. Once, when encountering a dead end, the girl slammed into a reflective wall. Momentarily dazed, Heather looked skyward, toward the small pin lights that burned weakly from the ceiling.

"You stop this! You hear me?" she said, scolding the Bristol House. "I need to help that Maiden-person and you're stopping me. So let me help her, okay?" Heather's face looked its nastiest. "You let me!"

Backtracking, the girl whipped around a corner and through an opening to encounter a heavily reinforced steel door. Opening it, she stepped through and into the Bristol House Armory, whereupon Heather noiselessly descended the stairs.

The dinner table having been set, Grandma Dawn was treading softly down the second floor hallway. Her mind was absorbed with the current basement activity and the day's events centering on her granddaughter. Passing Heather's closed bedroom door, the woman assumed the girl to be asleep and so decided not to wake her—not just yet. A bit farther on, she paused and momentarily looked in on Mrs. Pringle through the open bedroom door, and saw that Molly had curled up beside her mother on the bed. Both seemed to be asleep in the sweltering heat.

Let them all sleep, she thought. Lana and the girls are exhausted—*I'm* exhausted. Dinner can always wait and be reheated.

Entering her own bedroom, Grandma Dawn closed the door and then locked it. Crossing the room, she slid aside a concealed panel on the wall and removed her Evermorian Box of Safekeeping, a square container with carved and gilded sides. Slabs of precious Evermorian stone in glistening, striated green-blue covered the top and bottom faces. Upon lifting the lid, Grandma Dawn could hear the restless, gurgling waters of the Pool of Reason that floated up to her from within the empty, silk-lined box. She leaned close and whispered her TrueName and the waters materialized, swirling within the enclosed space, and they rushed and whispered in return, asking for her request. The Maiden-in-exile revealed to the magical box what she wanted to retrieve, and then reached inside. Dipping her hand into the whirlpool of water, she withdrew a white PortalRing, completely dry to the touch. After closing up the box and returning it to its hiding place, the woman slid the ring onto her right index finger. Once in place, the loose ring resized itself, shrinking to a snug fit, its opaque green stone turning a translucent blood red against the surface of lustrous white.

Grandma Dawn gazed at the piece of jewelry, feeling the pulse of the ring throbbing to match her own heartbeat, tightening and loosening ever so slightly in correlative rhythm, the stone slightly fading and brightening with each pulsation.

"It's been a long time since I've worn you. But with events happening so quickly here at the Bristol House, I fear I'll be needing you sooner than later."

Again making use of the Moonlight°Prisms, the multi-dialed apparatus all the while logging coordinates and information, the Maiden spotted another Portal shining forth from beneath the fringes of a blanket, its seeping, yellow-green glow unmistakable in the gloom. Walking over to the draped piece of furniture near the corner wall, noiselessly, methodically, she started to peel off its shroud, revealing the sturdy proportions of an antique cylinder desk.

Now motionless, the TimeLight Assassin observed the woman from a cautious distance, his acute vision discerning the movements of her vague form, as she made ready to seal another Bristol House Portal. Though limited to those aspects of MagiCommon useful to a Time-Light Assassin, in the activation of weapons per se, the man had been briefed on the procedure of Portal closure and thus recognized its implementation.

So that's who has been performing, creating the magical vibrations. A Maiden—and not the child I was expecting. Apparently, she's attempting to make the Bristol House impermeable to TimeLight Travelers by closing a majority of its Portals. If she's successful, the Maidens will effectively limit those who arrive and depart through the known Portals that remain active, thus insuring the safety of particular individuals—or perhaps just one. The Maiden Portent? Undoubtedly.

When I reveal to my superior how invaluable the Bristol House can be in enabling our TimeLight infiltrations and operations between worlds, I've no doubt he will want to take possession of this property with its useful Portals intact. Therefore, I believe it essential that I stop the Maiden from sealing these Portals.

With that in mind, the assassin reached into his Cache°Belt for one of his deadly, soundless weapons of the Vigen°Darr, the magical Tendril°Blade.

Though the roll top of the cylinder desk had been left open, revealing tiny, dust-filled compartments and marble-faced drawers, the Maiden ignored them, concentrating instead on the light she saw below. Visible within the desk's ample kneehole was the Portal, radiating with its alluring promise of elsewhere.

With the PortalSealer in place on her palm and fingers, the Maiden raised her hand. At that moment, from over her shoulder, she detected movement, and instantly dropped, her left forearm shooting up in defense. Whirling toward her, gaining in circumference and speed was the metal disk of the Tendril°Blade, its poison-tipped wires extending in a blur from the toothy rim. Honing in, the hurled device made necessary adjustments to the Maiden's evasive maneuver. Impulsively, to save her life, the woman lashed out with a one-word command, sending a split-second ScorchPulse at the deadly weapon. When the disk exploded close by in what appeared to the Maiden to be the detonation of a thousand suns, her world burnt white with blindness, the brilliance of magnified light through the Moonlight°Prisms too much for her eyes to endure.

Nevertheless, the trained warrior dove and tumbled to where she remembered crates and cabinets to be, and in the process recited a spell that sent a volley of foundation-shaking StingBolts in the direction of her attacker. She heard the explosive aftermath followed by electrical buzzing as upstairs the Bristol House lights stuttered and shut down. Uncertain whether or not her attacker had been eliminated, the Maiden scrabbled her way around the covered furnishings, and ended by huddling next to a stacked china hutch, beside a tall curio cabinet, the wall and Armory room door a few aisles behind her. There she waited.

Calming her breathing, her ears attuned to even the slightest sound, running through the Maiden's mind was the thought, In battle I am mortal. Today may be the day I die for Evermore.

With only moments having passed since the floor and walls had pitched and suits of armor had rattled and toppled, Heather stumbled through the now disorderly confines of the Armory, knowing that a fight must be taking place between the two people in the adjoining room.

I'm too late! she thought, still intending to assist the woman if she could.

Hastening toward the door and battle, a winking of green lights drew Heather's attention to a curved dagger embellished with small jewels. She noticed the weapon was attached to a suit of armor similar to that worn by the bronze Maidens who had helped drive back Mistraya at the PortalDoor: Maiden Armor. Skidding to a stop with an ankle-smarting wince, the girl didn't hesitate to slide the gold-bladed weapon from its jeweled scabbard, precious gems along the hilt blinking as one. Not wasting another valuable second, Heather turned and raced to the door, the Bristol House shaking with another round of explosions.

Dashing out of her bedroom on the way to get Heather, the Bristol House lights no longer operable, Grandma Dawn almost collided with a startled Mrs. Pringle and Molly in the dark hallway. Both mother and daughter were sweaty, disheveled.

"What's going on?" Mrs. Pringle asked, panicked. "Where's Heather? And what's happened to the lights?"

"I'm on my way to wake her. I've got to hurry—"

"What's causing the house to shake this way?"

Grandma Dawn was briskly backpedaling towards Heather's room, Mrs. Pringle and Molly following. "It's coming from the basement. I'm going down there now, as soon as I wake Heather."

"Dawn, you're not—!"

"It's best you and Molly get outside, away from the house, until we find out what's happening. Now. Please hurry." Grandma Dawn turned and hastened toward her granddaughter's room, pausing before the door. "I'll send Heather down to you."

Mrs. Pringle turned to Molly, "Let's go," and then to Grandma Dawn, "Should I phone the police or fire department?"

"The lines are dead, Lana, and you can see the lights aren't working. Now go on. Get yourselves outside. Quickly. I'll join you as soon as I can."

Grandma Dawn pushed the door open and rushed into Heather's night-filled room. Lightning speared the sky outside, flashing to illuminate the girl's tidy, empty bed. Seconds later, another bolt flickered to expose the grim expression that passed over the woman's features. She retreated while the atmosphere rumbled.

Pausing at the top of the stairs, Molly turned and watched as Grandma Dawn sped out of Heather's room, down the hall towards the front stairs and the basement door. The girl was surprised at the older woman's athleticism.

Where's Heather? she wondered.

"Molly! Come on!" said Mrs. Pringle, hurrying back up the stairs to retrieve her daughter. She pulled at her wrist. "We need to get out of here!"

When the house shook again, Mrs. Pringle grabbed onto the banister, and then grabbed ahold of Molly as the girl tripped and stumbled past.

CHAPTER THIRTY-SEVEN

Heather, the Maiden, and a Friend

"**H**ey," Heather whispered from the shadows, in the heavy heat of the basement, "you okay?"

Instantly, the Maiden thrust her hand in the youngster's direction, ready to blast the source of the words, but caught herself when it registered that the voice belonged to a girl. She lowered her arm.

"You move quietly. I didn't hear you."

"I'm Heather Nighborne," the youngster said in an undertone, lying on the floor behind a stack of boxes, close to the Maiden in indigo. "I live here."

"Stay low and don't move, or you won't for much longer."

When it dawned on the woman that Heather was probably the one that her sealing of Portals was meant to protect, she added, "You need to get out of here, out of this room and probably out of this house to somewhere that's safe—if there exists such a place for one of your stature."

The Maiden and Heather ducked reflexively when a spray of darts slugged into the wall and wood around them.

"Cluster°Darts," she whispered aloud.

Heather said, "But if I try to get back into the Armory, he might see me this time. I'm pretty sure he didn't notice just now when I crawled through the door. Besides, I came down here to help you."

"I'm not sure that was a wise thing to do. You don't know this, and neither does our friend, here, but I'm definitely operating at a disadvantage right now."

Another °Dart stabbed the wall: *thwack!*

Lyricying, the Maiden leaned around the side of the hutch and shot a series of StingBolts helter-skelter into the room that shook with the small-scale explosions. After a short wait, the response was another group of deadly °Darts splintering the furnishings around the two.

Through the basement windows, lightning flashed, followed shortly thereafter by a thunderous roll.

The Maiden's masked cheek stayed close to the protective piece of furniture, her lips barely moving as she spoke. "He? You said, 'he.'"

"Yeah, I guess I did. When I first saw him, I thought the creepy guy was a 'he,' like I thought you were a 'she.' I saw both of you from the House of Mir—from a window way high on the wall. He was sneaking up on you, while you were doing something over there somewhere." The girl didn't dare point. "I pounded on the window, trying to warn you, but you didn't hear me."

"At the moment, hearing isn't necessarily my gravest concern."

The woman leaned out and shot another StingBolt. The basement rocked with the blast.

Heather said, "You know, you're sure wrecking a lot of stuff."

From somewhere above, lightning strobed through the greenery. The sky roared and the ground shook, but it didn't deter the digger from his obsession.

This has to be the place; it has to be.

He looked at his shovel filled only with dirt.

So, then, why nothing? Again? He growled out the HumanKind saying on Evermore, "Time is forever and forever running out."

Starting before the oddly bent tree, he rechecked the distance, pacing it off once again.

The man had been gouging out another deep hole in the Bristol House garden, and so far, it had revealed nothing of the treasure.

It has to be here.

Maybe I should try using my magic. But then again, maybe not. Like a unique HumanKind fingerprint, they would know I was the one practicing, wouldn't they. Too risky. I'm dead, aren't I—dead to Earth and dead to Evermore. I'm my own man, with an unflagging allegiance to just me.

Besides, Scarbones Bristol made finding his fortune impervious to magical assistance, didn't he? I read his book, the one with half a poem, and thus half a clue to the treasure's location. Damn the man!

Pondering, he momentarily leaned away from the shovel, one hand holding it upright. He removed his hat and rubbed his brow harshly on his sleeve.

This has to be *that* house, that garden. The Bristol House, there's no other like it. I'm an archeologist; I studied the books, pored over the clues.

Unexpectedly, unaccompanied by any flash or roar, the ground shook. The lantern tipped off the mound of dirt, and when tumbling into the hole, the light went out. Retrieving it, the digger took time to relight it, time he saw as wasted.

Shovel at the ready to resume his digging, the man froze as the ground beneath him quaked again. Concerned, he looked up and a moment later slipped into the open where tree and bush no longer concealed him. Across the sloping garden, he saw flashes in the Bristol House basement windows, and again felt the ground shudder under his feet.

The thought sprang on him: That shaking isn't due to the thunder.

The man withdrew into the greenery and leaned his shovel against a tree.

Having quickly descended the stairs and exited the kitchen, Molly and Mrs. Pringle were moving through the muggy air of the vegetable garden.

"Molly, wait for me by the driveway. As soon as Heather comes out, I'm taking the two of you to the police station and—Molly?" Mrs. Pringle looked around. She caught sight of her daughter hurrying back towards the house. The girl started to run. "Molly! Come back here! Now!"

"Mom, I think Heather is in the basement." Posed at the Dutch door, Molly's features were fleetingly defined by a strobe of lightning. "I'm going down there."

Another thunderous rumble shook the house as the girl ran back through the kitchen, pots, pans, and cutlery clanging and clashing, dishes and tableware smashing, falling to the floor.

"Molly!"

The TimeLight Assassin was checking the arsenal in his Cache°Belt. He had plenty of weaponry left, and those most recently developed would be a surprise to the Maiden. He had pulled loose some Cluster°Dart spores and began counting them.

What's that?

Balling his fist, spores safely tucked inside, he slipped smoothly between two chests and stood stock-still, listening. Somewhere behind him, he could hear pounding on the heavy entrance doors. Instinctively, he cringed slightly as a StingBolt shot past and blew two candelabras off a high shelf against the back wall.

That Maiden is shooting as if blind. Either she's an extremely bad shot, he thought, or she's hoping one of her errant 'Bolts will hit me.

The doors continued to shake and thump as someone persevered in their effort to gain entry to the basement. The magically-linked energy spheres of a RumbleBall, cast by the Maiden, skidded to his right, breaking to bits a pile of wooden boxes, while in back of him, the deadly intruder now heard louder, more substantial blows on the doors, as if someone were attempting to kick them in.

The TimeLight Assassin reached into his Cache°Belt and returned the spores to their proper compartment before removing a small object from another. Following a slight twist of its capsule-shaped form, it elongated and sprang tail feathers. A faint red light at its tip began to blink at regular intervals, before glowing steadily. At the sound of someone's final, futile kick at the stubborn doors, he released the tiny Projection°Probe with a flick of the wrist, sending it in the direction of Heather and the Maiden.

"I'm not certain," whispered the indigo woman, "but it sounded like someone was trying to get in the double doors across the room, those that lead upstairs."

"Yeah, I heard it." Heather was wondering if it could have been Grandma Dawn.

A flash lit the row of windows: lightning. Thunder bellowed.

"What do you think he's doing now?" asked the girl in an undertone, wiping the sweat from her brow. It had been dripping into her eyes.

"Our *friend?*

"Yeah, our friend."

'I think he's waiting to see what I do next. I've no idea where he is, and so to keep him at bay, I've been shooting StingBolts and RumbleBalls in his direction, hoping to achieve a lucky strike. I'm thinking that now he's laying low, waiting for me to expose myself, hoping he can get a clear shot."

Noticing the large holes in the furniture behind her, Heather gripped her dagger tighter.

"He made those big holes?" she asked, still at a whisper.

"Yes, with his weapons of destruction. He has a variety of them, all silent. This is why you must keep low. And as still as possible. The weapons are magical; once on course, some not only increase in size, but are attracted to sudden movement."

After a pause, during which the two listened intently, Heather asked, "Are you a Maiden?"

"Are you?"

Just then a projectile fractured the wood slightly above Heather's head. It hissed after impact.

"Acid°Cutter," the woman said. "For your own sake, be certain you're not bobbing your head when you speak."

"I'm coming closer," said the girl in response, and shielded by the low stack of boxes, Heather crawled cautiously towards the additional protection provided by the taller china hutch and buffet, passing behind the Maiden.

"You're really taking a chance, Heather Nighborne, moving like that."

"What's your name?"

"Call me Avella."

Now beside her new ally, Heather climbed to her knees before standing, dagger in hand, and tried to peer between the furnishings.

Avella said, "You need to know I can't see."

"Me, either. These pieces of furniture are way too close together. And it doesn't help that it's so dark in here."

Along the wall, another flash filled the windows.

"No, I really can't see."

"Well, maybe it's your glasses," Heather offered. "Even though they're really great looking and everything, with all those dials and stuff, you might just need a new prescription—"

"I have white-blindness." The Maiden slowly reached up and removed the Moonlight°Prisms. "I can't see due to an explosion while wearing these. Our enemy doesn't know that, so he's being extremely cautious in how he attacks us."

Heather bit her lip, looking into the woman's eyes in the dimness, and aided by a flash from the windows, glimpsed her dilated pupils, milky white and clouded. "Well, maybe I can spot him for you." Thunder having roared, in the stillness that followed, the girl surreptitiously leaned out and scanned her surroundings, thinking, I'm not sure I like it when it's quiet like this. It creeps me out.

If only she had looked up, Heather would have noticed the tiny red dot on the small pointy shape that silently circled above.

The TimeLight Assassin had maneuvered closer to the pair, and was now positioned behind several old television consoles. He waited, and it wasn't long before the man sighted the Projection°Probe as it circled, having reappeared from behind a large grouping of furniture. Stopping above a clear area in front of the assassin, it beamed down a recorded three-dimensional image of the huddled Avella and Heather for all to see.

Who is the accomplice alongside the Maiden? the killer wondered. Ah. The young Maiden Portent.

"How weird is that?"

"What?"

"Avella, I hate to tell you this, but I think our creepy friend knows exactly where we are," said Heather. "And I mean *exactly*. And he also knows I'm here with you."

Heather watched the woman's aura dim in disappointment and then re-illuminate and swell in fierceness, in defiance and anger.

"How do you know this?"

"Well, it might be hard to believe, but right now, on the other side of all this furniture we're hiding behind, there's this kind of realistic image of you and me that's being projected." Heather was again peeking out the far side of the china cabinet.

"It sounds as if he sent out a °Probe," said Avella, "and of course I couldn't see to knock it out of the air. Even though the image will fade shortly—if it hasn't already—you've been revealed, and more than ever it's imperative we get you out of here. Let's start moving toward the Portal that's under the desk. It's probably our only chance."

Whizzing on either side of the pair were three more projectiles, hitting low and towards the ground, one after the other: *Thwack! Thwack! Clink!* An Acid°Cutter skidded and sparked on the ground only inches from the Maiden. Wobbling, it shimmied to a standstill. Afterwards, it hissed menacingly, releasing a toxin that ate into the floor.

"He's an assassin."

"What?"

A flicker of lightning.

"Our friendly assailant. He's a TimeLight Assassin. From Evermore."

A boom of thunder.

A TimeLight Assassin from Evermore? Heather's mind flashed on the Matron's words of warning: *...you must try to remain alive, and as I've said, there will be powerful forces at work to insure that you do not.*

"Really? How do you know that?"

"I saw the weapon that he hurled at me earlier, before I caused it to explode and lost my vision in the process. Also, I asked you if the person you saw was a he or a she. Depending on the gender, it tells me the Evermorian clan."

The two continued to whisper in the dimness.

"Clan?"

"Yes, clan. And purpose. If it's a female, chances are she came to the Bristol House to kill *me*, perhaps having learned of my reason for coming."

Avella didn't mention that the clan—the secret society of the She-Cloister—another infiltrator of the WhisperEye Network, was the sworn enemy of the MaidenHood, and had avowed to wipe them out.

If indeed SheCloister, and possibly armed with information gleaned from the active Network, could the attacker also be here to kill Heather? The Maiden wondered.

Heather asked, "What if it's a male?"

"Don't ask. But I will tell you they're mercenaries and a soulless lot. Now, since I can't see, we're going to have to work together. I need you to do something for me."

"But wait," said Heather. "Why are you here? I mean—"

"What color are your eyes?"

"What?"

"Your eyes. What color are they?"

"That's kind of a silly question to ask, don't you think, with a Time-Light Assassin out there and everything...?"

Another piece of metal whizzed by and struck wood, imbedding itself with a *thwack!*

"Are they green?"

Heather remained mute. She wiped her face.

"Here. These are primarily used for Portal detection." Moving slowly, the Maiden offered the goggles. "They'll aid you when looking for the assassin in the dark. Hold these °Prisms up to your eyes, but only for a moment. I don't want you looking through them for long, in case I have to send out a StingBolt or two."

"Or in case there's lightning in the basement windows."

"Right. Or if there's lightning. If either happens, and you have the Moonlight°Prisms on, we'll both be left blind. You're to use these to find out where the assassin is in this room. But you'll need to do so carefully—and I mean carefully—or he could end up with a clear shot at you. And if he has that, then surely he will kill you."

Thwack! Thwack! A pair of Cluster°Darts hit on the opposite side of Heather's hutch. She stood rigid, unmoving, as they penetrated the cabinet's backside and interior before smashing through the glass door close to her face, embedding themselves somewhere behind her.

"I don't need them."

"What? You don't need the °Prisms? You can see in the dark?"

Heather was looking through the broken glass and the large holes in the hutch. "There he is. I can see him—well, not *him*, but his shine. He's there, all right, behind the tallest row of covered things. But between that guy and us are all sorts of aisles and stacks and stuff."

"Point my arm."

"What?"

"Point my arm in his direction."

"Really?"

As thunder shook the heated land and sky, the TimeLight Assassin took from his °Belt a cylinder no longer than his gloved index finger. He cast the object above him, and it immediately unfolded and expanded into a transparent rectangular deflector, floating in air.

Now, thought the assassin, with the Mirror°Shield in effect, I intend to draw the Maiden's fire, and when I do and she's on target, it will repel the salvos back in her direction. If she and the young Maiden are not killed with the return fire, she'll think I'm holed up here, when all the while I'll be closing in on her and the child.

An instant later the Heather-aimed volley of StingBolts shot his way. Upon impact with the Mirror°Shield, they immediately bounced back in the direction of their origin.

"Get down!" Heather pushed the Maiden backwards, and the pair tumbled to the ground. There they covered up, Avella rolling to protect Heather with her body as explosions ripped the air, destroying the furniture that had shielded them. While the floor rocked and debris showered to the ground, a massive container tipped over, and upon impact, its upper corner fractured the Maiden's lower leg. She cried out and furiously tried to pry off the heavy receptacle. Quick to respond, while on her back, Heather used the strength of her legs to raise the container, pushing it up and onto a toppled end table. Avella, her face contorted, slid her calf free and then held it in both hands. Breathing deeply and slowly, she felt for damage, and then gasped while pushing the bone back beneath the skin. In agony, she turned to Heather.

"The Portal," she said. "Guide me to the Portal."

"I don't know where it is."

"It's behind you, inside the kneehole of the desk."

Did the Mirror°Shield reflection kill the girl and the Maiden? I can't see them.

The TimeLight Assassin was now closer to his prey, having swiftly slipped between the room's stacks and rows. Though no fire had broken out, embers from the destroyed furniture were visible in the dark, glowing red among the charred remains.

Are they dead? Is this battle already over? A feeling that could only be described as disappointment began to emerge. He stuffed it.

Abandoning his current shelter of crated articles, the killer stole ever closer, settling unnoticed beside an empty bookcase. He quickly inspected his surroundings, before casting up a Hover°Flare.

"What's that?" Heather squinted up at the light that exposed both herself and the Maiden, illuminating their corner of the room. "Quick, over here."

She helped the wounded woman to move within the refuge of a collection of draped nightstands, dressers, armoires, and steamer trunks. Breathing heavily and losing blood, Avella was sitting up against some furniture blankets, head back.

"What's wrong?" the Maiden asked.

"The TimeLight Assassin has thrown a light up above us. There's brightness all around."

Peering into the surreal glare of cool light and the resulting jumble of stark shadows, Heather took stock of their surroundings. She saw the cylinder desk, the drapery that once covered it folded back neatly, sagging slightly over its opened, roll-top compartment.

Avella asked, "How far away is the desk and Portal?"

"Right across the aisle. Not far. But the room's all lit up, and I think he'll see us if we try and make it over there."

"Just looking around you, do you see his shine?"

Heather scanned, her field of vision limited. "No. Should I stand and look?"

"Will you be exposed in this light?"

"Yeah, *really* exposed."

"Then don't. Foremost, we mustn't let anything happen to you. And furthermore, if we're to remain alive—" Avella winced when a stab of pain racked her, "—we need your eyes—I need your eyes. So, be aware and keep searching for him. In all probability, he's watching and waiting, but there's always the chance he could be advancing."

The woman pulled back the thin tight hood that covered her head. In a swift reveal, she began removing the deep blue wrapping that masked her sweaty face. This in turn disclosed a band of sheer fabric that firmly held in place a thick braid of hair crossing over her head.

"That's unusual," Avella said. "Must be new."

"What?"

"What he's using, it must be a new weapon, similar to my own Sting-Bolts."

Her face displaying grave discomfort, by feel, the Maiden loosely wrapped her lower leg with the lengthy blue cloth to stem the flow of blood. When done, the magically imbued fabric melded the narrow strips into one and tightened to just the right degree.

Up close, even under the circumstances, Heather couldn't help but marvel at the Maiden's striking appearance: her china-white skin with hints of scarlet at the cheeks, glimpses of auburn hair with the color repeated in the delicately arched brows, and, below an elegant nose, the woman's tangerine lips. Her sightless, crystal blue eyes looked at nothing external.

The girl pulled her gaze from the Maiden. She noticed the smear of blood on the floor leading directly to them, disclosing the route they had taken should the assassin notice it. In the stillness, the youngster wondered if he was near.

Still on the lookout for auras, Heather whispered, "Does it spook you when it's quiet like this? I think I'd rather have a bunch of stuff exploding."

Directly outside, immediately following a flash, and thunderclap shook the Bristol House.

"Like that?"

"Kinda."

Having placed the jeweled PortalSealer in her small charcoal rucksack, the Maiden peeled off her bloodied gloves. Revealed were her porcelain hands, and on her index finger a white PortalRing, the jewel blinking steadily but faintly. She set the gloves on the floor next to her rucksack. Avella drew a deep breath, before turning to Heather.

"Now, I don't have much energy left. So, I'm going to shoot out that Hover°Flare—you're going to point my arm—and then we'll have to hope we can make it to the Portal undetected. I'll need to go in front of you, to expand the doorway. Once this is done, you'll quickly have to help me inside."

"Where are we going?"

"Anywhere. Anywhere but here."

Molly and Mrs. Pringle were rushing through small living quarters, the girl opening doors, looking for a room with Heather and Grandma Dawn in it.

"Molly, where are we?"

"By the looks of it, I think these are the servant's quarters."

"Mol—?"

The daughter raced out of the room with her mother in pursuit.

"Molly, where are we going?"

Breathless, the girl looked over her shoulder, "I don't know."

Heather steadied the Maiden's arm, looking down its length, aiming it at the floating light.

"Fire."

Upon hearing Avella finish her Lyrica, Heather felt the subtle recoil as a StingBolt shot from the Maiden's fist. In a burst, the Hover°Flare briefly intensified and then died out.

"Go."

As quietly as possible, amid subdued grunts and gasps, Heather helped Avella cross the aisle to the cylinder desk, pulling and sliding in a strange swim across the floor.

"It's here," Heather whispered. "Right in front of us. Do you have a PortalKey?"

The Maiden reached out with her PortalRing, blindly waving it in front of her. "In the kneehole."

Heather grasped the white wrist and guided it into the rectangular cavity. Speaking her own TrueName, the Maiden's body tensed slightly as the Portal enlarged, the desk growing in size until it towered above the pair in the shape of a deeply recessed doorway. Within the short hall, muted scenes faded one to the next.

"Quickly. Help me inside," said Avella. "We must hurry." Her voice was calm.

Heather, her ankle ablaze with pain, held the Maiden under the arms and pulled, while Avella propelled herself onward with her good leg. "My feet. Help me get my feet inside."

A lightning burst filled the windows. In a double take, Heather glimpsed the assassin as he reared up above the trunks, his arm swinging forward with the pitch of a weapon.

"Look out!" Heather yelled over a crash of thunder, pushing the Maiden aside. But Avella wasn't the intended target of the Toxin°Saucer, the deadly weapon heading instead for her young companion. In a sudden, protective move, the Maiden grabbed Heather's arm. Yanking the girl behind her, deeper inside the hallway, she simultaneously swung her right arm in an exaggerated arc. Attracted to the nearest movement, the expanding circular blade instantly shifted direction and embedded itself thickly below Avella's elbow.

The Maiden screamed, but her piercing howl died abruptly as she collapsed to the floor in gurgled convulsions, her fitful upper torso remaining outside the confines of the Portal. Not wanting to be trapped inside the doorway, Heather instinctively dove over Avella, and while tumbling into nearby shadows, removed the dagger from her belt. In one fluid motion, when coming up onto her knees, the girl flung her knife with stunning accuracy at the assassin's swirling aura.

Ready to pitch another deadly weapon, the killer quickly retracted at the sight of Heather's vague and hurried movements. Unfortunately for the man in black, the blade of the dagger buried itself in his upper chest, at the shoulder. He stifled a cry and jumped down behind the tower of trunks on which he'd been standing.

Heather ducked behind the back of an overstuffed chair, her mind racing.

What to do, what to do?

She shot a look at the Maiden, now lying deathlike on the floor to her right. When violent convulsions began a second time, the girl made up her mind and rushed to her companion, though when she reached her, the woman had once again gone motionless. Not knowing whether she was still alive, Heather seized Avella's shoulders in an attempt to drag her completely inside the Portal.

"You won't make it." The assassin's voice came from somewhere nearby, but briefly looking up, Heather couldn't detect an aura.

Standing just inside the PortalDoor, ankle screaming, the girl kept at it, trying to slide the Maiden's head and upper shoulders awkwardly around the jamb.

Twack! The Fester°Dart flashed by Heather's face and stuck in the jamb of the Portal, its deadly poison injecting wood.

"I said, You'll never make it. A TimeLight Assassin is trained to throw with lethal accuracy using either arm."

Another Hover°Flare went up, and a moment later the executioner revealed himself, confidently stepping out from behind a lofty, expansive stack of books.

He said, "You can come out of that Portal doorway now, or I can kill you where you stand."

"Molly, where are you taking me?"

"Mom, I told you, I really don't know. I'm looking for Heather, that's all. And Mrs. Thibble."

The pair listened to a distant peal of thunder.

Mrs. Pringle said, "I'm not sure whether the thunder is coming from inside the house or out."

"Or both."

"Molly, do you realize that we're returning the way we came?"

"Are you sure, Mom? How can that be? We just went through all those small rooms in the servant's quarters. It's surprising that they'd lead us back to the stairs. I thought we were headed in a different direction."

"Aren't those the basement doors up ahead on the right, the ones we were pounding on until you started kicking them?"

"Heather wouldn't have minded, Mom—or Mrs. Thibble, either—

if they knew we were trying to reach them in an emergency. And we haven't seen any other doors along this corridor that would let us inside. So what was I supposed to do?"

"Those doors seem pretty thick. I doubt you'd have been able to kick them in."

The girl flashed with irritation. "Mom, I wasn't trying to kick them in. I only wanted the doors to unlock or have someone hear me and open them. The Bristol House sometimes has a way of doing things—" Molly stopped in her tracks. "Geez, one of the doors is ajar." The girl started to run. "See what I mean?"

"Molly, can you slow down? I'm not sure going in there is a good—" Picking up the pace, Mrs. Pringle watched Molly disappear through the tall, planked door. "...Idea."

The woman broke into a sprint.

Under the eerie light, Heather studied the TimeLight Assassin as he walked toward her, his sinewy body clad firmly in black—cat-like. His Adaption Suit, adjusting to the newfound illumination, began to lighten. His face was masked, his aura polluted and grim. She watched as a gloved hand reached up, and displaying little emotion, yanked her dagger out of his right shoulder. Below, his arm hung uselessly.

Much like a Parade Day costume, the sheer mask had become his face, the lips moving. "I believe this belongs to you." He tossed the bloody dagger to the floor, not far from Heather's feet. "Don't attempt to pick it up."

"Is she dead?" Heather asked, standing, having let Avella slump back to her lifeless position.

"She soon will be." The killer's voice was dull, having little inflection. Life was a fact. "And so will you."

He struck Heather as a ghost of a man, there but gone.

The TimeLight Assassin considered, saying, "Emotion captures my interest, and so I told myself if I ever encountered a Maiden Portent— you see, you are the ultimate prize—I wanted her to watch me as I killed her up close and in the light. I hope you don't mind. You see, I'm a NonBeliever."

Unenthusiastically, the girl asked, "In what?"

"In you. In the Evermore Portent and the Prophecies. I was sent to find and eliminate you. But you see, like all the Maiden Portents before you who have perished under our hand, you really are just a little girl. And if you're not, and truly are the Appointed One, I'd like to see you save yourself. So, go ahead. Save yourself. I'm waiting." Through a brief silence, the two looked fixedly at one another, the man calm, only steps away and closing. "But really, you can't, can you? And so you won't." His chin lowered slightly. "What's it like, knowing I'm going to kill you?"

Heather stared, the distant lightning at the windows not registering, the subsequent roll weak, protracted. The TimeLight Assassin now stood before the girl.

"You're not afraid?"

In a sudden movement, Heather kicked for his crotch. But nonchalantly, his gaze never leaving her face, the executioner caught the sole of her shoe in his left hand. Heather tried to pull her foot away, and the man easily held it. He started to apply pressure, pushing and forcing her toes upward, towards her shin. On her weakened ankle, Heather began to collapse.

"Does this hurt?"

The pain increasing, Heather bit her lower lip. As he held her shoe, unexpectedly she jumped off her standing leg and kicked out, her aim directed again at the man's groin. But with the grace of a dancer, he stepped aside, and while raising her foot higher, let the girl fall. Heather put her hands below her, but it did little to cushion the blow when her upper back and head hit the ground, arms splayed. The man in black released his grip, dropping her foot.

"So, you're supposed to be *the* green-eyed Maiden." His voice was heavy, cold. "Really? You're the One? Or should I say *just another One?* And to think this is the best that Evermore's latest Maiden Portent can do, flopping to the ground next to a paralyzed, dying Maiden?"

Heather's voice was equally cold. "I did get you with my dagger."

The gray, putty eyes looked vacantly at the girl, but Heather sensed a shift behind them: her barb, like the thrown knife, had stuck. She knew, too, that her dagger was now only inches from her hand. She sensed its magical pull, like a magnet.

"What's it like being a TimeLight Assassin?" Heather asked, buying time, her hand beginning a furtive slide toward the jeweled hilt.

Unresponsive, he continued to stare.

"I mean, do you like hurting people while asking them what it feels like? I'm just wondering, because I bet to be a TimeLight Assassin and do all those nasty things like you do, you never really want to know what you're *honestly* doing. I mean, I don't mean to barge in on your thoughts and stuff, but you kind of got me thinking, wondering what it's like." As her hand continued to creep, her gaze stayed locked to the killer's.

Heather forced a breathy laugh. "You know what I'm thinking? I'm thinking it's like you're a house, but there's never any lights on inside, just a bunch of cobwebs. And you never get any sunshine in the windows and stuff, because they're all boarded up. And you wouldn't get any visitors, either, no way, because it's like there's never anybody home, with weeds and stuff growing all over the place. I bet," Heather brightened, "I bet you're like a Mr. Simpletripp house with that big, ugly scorpion bolted on the wall…" The man continued to stare stonily, the girl rambling, "I wonder if you'd like Mr. Simpletripp? Oh, wait. I forgot. You can't like."

Menacingly, he took a step toward Heather, her hand still inching its way.

"When you were a boy, did you ever have parents?" Heather didn't wait for a reply. "I didn't either. But I had Grandma Dawn. She really loves me, you know. And I love her, too. She's really great. Too bad you couldn't like her, even a little. Everyone should have a Grandma Dawn." Heather could now feel the hilt of her dagger brushing up against her fingers. Stepping forward, the TimeLight Assassin stood over the girl. "Boy, that's got to be so horrible—I mean, never having parents to love you. Or *anyone.*"

As Heather uttered the last word, her hand made a play for the dagger, but as quick as she was, the girl was too slow to surprise the assassin. In a flash, he stepped lightly on her wrist, pinning it, the dagger resting loosely within her open, upturned palm.

Heather continued to look up at the menacing man, feeling the weight from his boot increase, the pain to her wrist intensifying.

"Did you ever have a pet?" she continued. "Or a wife maybe? Or even a girlfriend?" *Umph.* "Do you have puppies in Evermore? I was just wondering… Ow!" Heather held a plastic smile and gave a breathless chuckle. "That hurts." She was tearing up, despite her want to the contrary. "Did I make you mad? I'm just—" *Umph.* "—wondering, but in a nice way." Heather briefly closed her eyes. She laughed in a painful, distracted way. "If you want to know, right now you're hurting me. Yeah, you're hurting me pretty good." She looked back at the man, the pain rising to greater intensity with his increased weight. *Umph.* "You're really hurting me now. Really. A lot." *Umph.* "A lot. Can you…stop, please?"

"I'm going to kill you." He increased the weight on her wrist.

A strange squeal came out of Heather's throat.

"What does it feel like?"

Umph. "It feels like it hurts. I mean, like a lot. It really, *really* hurts.

So, can you stop?"

"Tears are coming out of your eyes. Is it a result of the pain you're feeling?"

"No, it's because…" *Umph.* "…you never had… anyone to love you." She skittered a teary laugh. *Umph.*

Heather, despite herself, was breaking down, starting to cry.

"I want to know…" he said, applying even greater pressure to her wrist. "Are you afraid of dying?"

"You stop it! Stop it now!" With surprising force, the girl swung a fist at the side of his knee, and it staggered him, but he didn't buckle.

Heather's eyes were rolling back with the intense pain, and she was writhing on the floor below the towering man. With her free hand the girl made another grab for the dagger, but by the time her arm crossed her body, he had swiftly kicked it away.

"I'm going to kill you now."

Heather started hammering on the muscular leg that pinned her wrist, but the assassin seemed to be enjoying the pain, absorbing the blows. He lifted his other boot and balanced for an instant, the sole casting a shadow over the girl's face. When he brought his boot down, he stomped it next to Heather's head with a loud smack.

"I'm going to kill you, green-eyed Maiden. And the next time my foot comes down, I'm going to bust your skull open and step on your brains. Do you understand? You will die. Again, let me ask you, how does it feel?"

Far-off thunder rolled, as Heather continued to hammer on his leg, her extraordinary strength inflicting pain that would cause another to crumple, but the man seemed impervious. Up came his knee-high boot, and with tremendous force, it slammed down—again next to Heather's head. For a moment, she stopped hitting the man, and when he laughed, the girl resumed throwing blow after blow, but her assailant refused to fall.

"Goodbye, green-eyed Maiden. I promise, this will be the final blow. I've enjoyed our time together and now I must truly take your life."

Again, the man raised his foot, but it never came down. From somewhere out of the darkness, a fork of violet lightning crackled through the heated basement air, striking the TimeLight Assassin and throwing him across the aisle and the remaining expanse of floor. His body tumbling, he hit with a tremendous smack against the stone foundation wall.

Heather was up on her feet and rushing toward Grandma Dawn, the GuardianMaiden appearing from the shadows, her face alight with blue SearEye. The girl buried herself in her grandmother's clothing, hugging her fiercely. Her grandmother returned the hug.

"Are you all right?" she finally said, her SearEye losing intensity.

But Heather wouldn't let go, wouldn't look up.

"Heather," Grandma Dawn's voice was gentle. "I need to know how you are. Did that man hurt you?"

Still the girl held her grandmother. She shook her head.

"How's your wrist? Can you hold up just the wrist for me to see, please?"

Heather held it up. It was red, beginning to swell. Grandma Dawn inspected it.

"Rotate it."

She did.

"Move your fingers."

The girl wiggled her fingers, her body shaking with her tears.

"You're bruised, but you're going to be all right. Everything is all right now."

Heather remained buried in her grandmother's arms.

"Now that we know you're all right, I need to attend to the Maiden."

Pulling her head away, the girl made her voice heard. "Avella." Dropping her arms, she gazed up at her grandmother. "Grandma Dawn, you're a Maiden? I never knew you were a Maiden. You never told me."

"I intended to. We've lots to talk about, you and I, but later."

With a glance at the motionless assassin, Grandma Dawn hurried to Avella's side.

Heather said, "She saved my life."

"Did she? Maidens do that."

"But Avella went blind. She said it was because of the bright light in her °Prisms."

Grandma Dawn carefully turned Avella onto her back, and following a glance at her wrapped leg, began inspecting the damaged arm, pulling at the sleeve, ripping and exposing the disk-embedded gash. Below the entry wound, the forearm had turned completely black—charred—a grayness creeping upward. Avella opened her eyes, though barely.

She murmured, "Shalessa Ny-Estille Les Senflorienne?" Grandma Dawn's TrueName.

"Yes, I am here, Avella An-Anille Lan Wyncormerethe," said Grandma Dawn, her hands busy, as she pulled away what remained of the Maiden's sleeve. "I thought they might send you."

"I asked to come." The response was weak.

Heather's grandmother paused, momentarily regarding the distressed features of her childhood friend in a face so much younger than her own. "You've quite a wound, and I need to attend to it."

Grandma Dawn rose, looking around. Referring to the disk that was stuck in the Maiden's arm, she said to Heather, "Don't touch the blade."

The woman started to tear the blanket that had covered the cylinder desk.

Heather grabbed up her jeweled dagger, handing it to her grandmother. "Here, use this."

"Where did you find this?" She didn't pause for an answer, wiping the blade and cutting out some swatches of cloth, as well as several strips.

"In the Armory. It was gleaming at me when I went through."

"It's a Maiden dagger." She handed it back to Heather without looking at her.

"I know."

"You know, then, that you're qualified to have it."

When Heather didn't respond, the woman looked briefly at the child, then back at her work.

Heather let go a hoarse, contemplative, "I know." She added, "Grandma Dawn, a little while ago I threw it for the first time, but it was like I had been doing it my whole life. I mean, I didn't have to think about it, I just did it. And I threw it at the assassin, trying to hurt him."

Using a piece of cut cloth as a buffer, Grandma Dawn freed the poisonous disk before placing a tourniquet around the arm above. She tightened it with a grunt.

"Did you? Then you had to."

Grandma Dawn wrapped the disk securely in the larger piece of cloth and rose. She began pulling open the drawers now on either side of the desk-turned-Portal until she found an old wooden ruler.

"Yeah, the dagger went into his shoulder."

Grandma Dawn didn't look up this time, but merely smiled, her motions never slowing. Making use of the fabric strips, she wrapped the measuring stick alongside the Maiden's leg, stabilizing the fractured bone.

"This will have to do for now."

"Grandma Dawn, how come her arm isn't bleeding around the wound?"

"Because the arm is dead."

"Is the assassin?"

"Yes."

Heather gave him a look. Lying against the base of the wall, he resembled a broken marionette.

Unnoticed, peering through one of the basement windows, Stilped's murderer had been watching with fascination. To him, the otherworldly events he had witnessed were not unfamiliar.

Dawn Thibble a Maiden?

Gleefully, the man pulled away. He had seen enough, sufficient confirmation that the Bristol House was indeed *the* place, the place that would eventually bring him untold riches.

I am the Count, he thought, referring to a book he had read once upon a time, and this my little island. It is here, somewhere, that my treasure lies hidden, awaiting me, so my life can begin anew in glorified fashion. I shall return to collect that which is due me.

A thought occurred to him: Perhaps the treasure is inside and lies with the lady and her granddaughter? Do they even know of it? If not, at the very least, maybe they know the whereabouts of the missing piece of the poem? Hmm. I see I'll have to investigate further.

The man laughed aloud.

But Dawn Thibble a Maiden? A *Guardian*Maiden at that? It makes perfect sense. I should have seen it sooner——it was her aging that threw me.

So then, who and what does that make her granddaughter? A Maiden, too? A Nearling Maiden, perhaps? A *Portent* Maiden? I believe so. I believe, too, that such information is valuable, and must be worth something to interested parties in Evermore.

The man felt he was walking on air. He wanted to whistle a tune, but refrained.

I saw what occurred just now in the basement. And *that* was quite a show, yes, indeed. A TimeLight Assassin, a wounded Maiden, and a Portal to boot. *And* a victorious Dawn Thibble, Maiden extraordinaire, practicing ArcaniMagia in the new world.

He laughed again.

There's a lot going on at the home of Terentius Scarbones Bristol here in the quaint little town of Noble. A lot. And I'm going to find out more. Oh, yes, I'm going to find out much, much more. There's a fortune to be tapped here, a fortune indeed. And one doesn't necessarily have to dig with a shovel to find it, either.

Oh, the future looks bright; the future looks so very, *very* bright.

Jubilation filling him, the man buoyantly retreated into the foliage to reclaim his shovel, bag, and lantern.

Down past the garden, towards the creek, two cats could be heard fighting, their raucous wails, like disturbing sirens, carrying into the night.

Pets?

He headed their way.

"Give me your dagger."

"My dagger?" Heather handed it to her.

"Now look the other way."

"Why?"

Grandma Dawn stopped. "I'm going to have to perform some gruesome surgery here, and I'm not sure you'll want to see it—"

"Dawn, lookout!" Mrs. Pringle's voice rang out from behind them as Molly screamed.

Shoving Heather aside, Grandma Dawn was quickly on her feet, lyricing as she dropped the dagger. A DeflectionRay sliced from her fingertips, causing the advancing disk to veer and explode near her side. Gasping, the woman reeled, falling to the ground, her waist-length hair tumbling loose. Rolling to her side while reciting quick words of Lyrica, she struck out with a green SuspensionBeam. The TimeLight Assassin, having thrown the Tendril Blade, was up and leaping for the darker aisles. But in midair, the beam caught him and held him stationary. Helplessly suspended, the man watched as Grandma Dawn climbed to her feet and calmly walked toward him, her face glaring SearEye. When she was a short distance away, she said, coolly, "You should have died the first time. My apologies. I'm getting old." The woman then lowered her voice. "When I found the basement door to be locked, I began running through many rooms to get here. While doing so, the Bristol House broadcast your voice, as if you were beside me the entire time. And I heard every word you said to my granddaughter. Every word.

"And now," she said, her voice a harsh whisper, her look baleful, "I'm going to kill you. However, before I do I must ask you, knowing this, how does it feel that moments from now, you'll be dead and no more?"

From within the beam, the killer glowered defiantly. At one point, the woman thought she detected his fear, but only for a moment.

Grandma Dawn said over her shoulder, "Heather. Lana. Molly. I'm going to ask that you turn your heads, please." Grandma Dawn didn't look to see whether or not they had, her attention focused on the suspended figure. The woman waited briefly. Then she raised her right arm, and the assassin rose with it, hovering over her head.

"Good-bye."

When she brought her arm and the SuspensionBeam down, the TimeLight Assassin slammed viciously into the stone wall, his head hitting with a dull thud. Again she raised her arm and followed through for a second time, and he hit with a thick slap. As she began to elevate him for a third time, the woman stopped herself. Holding him poised momentarily within the beam before releasing him, Grandma Dawn watched unflinchingly as the assassin slid to the floor, a trail of blood marking his course down over the stone.

Absolutely riveted, never turning away like the others, Heather realized she was witnessing a side of her grandmother she had never known. This was not the woman that helped her with homework, made her favorite breakfast of strawberry waffles, or drank mugfuls from a yellow coffee press. Rather, this was the woman Heather remembered as heartlessly crushing a snail alongside the petunia bed, its shell left in pieces, clinging to a squishy ooze.

Turning from the TimeLight Assassin, Grandma Dawn said, "He's dead now," and then collapsed.

Heather and the Pringles ran to her, but by then she was pulling herself to her feet.

Mrs. Pringle said, "Dawn—?"

"I'm fine, everyone. Really. I'm sorry if I worried you just now."

But Heather noted her grandmother's ashen face and the blood that had soaked through her blouse. Her features drawn, Grandma Dawn, perhaps for the first time to the child, looked old and vulnerable, while ironically enough, never more formidable.

The stoic woman returned to Avella and the Portal, the others at her heels.

Where her grandmother's sleeve was in tatters and hanging loose from the wrist and shoulder, Heather noticed swirling elegant tattoos that extended down the left arm, a revelation.

"Grandma Dawn," Heather said, her words hushed. "You're bleeding."

Glimpsing her shredded clothing, the woman was surprised. "I am."

"You're not going to die, are you?"

"No, Heather," she said, giving another glance to her wounds, thinking, This changes things, I'm afraid. She added, "But I am going to need some medical attention."

"Dawn," said Mrs. Pringle, "I can take you to the hospital."

Grandma Dawn smiled wistfully, fleetingly. "I wish it were so simple. Seems I need a special kind of hospital and doctor." Grandma Dawn returned to business. "Come on, Heather, help me."

With controlled haste, they carefully set Avella against the front corner of the PortalDoor, within the short hallway.

"Heather, I'll also need your help with the TimeLight Assassin. We need to hurry."

Dazed, Molly and Mrs. Pringle watched as if in a dream, while Heather and her grandmother half-carried, half-dragged the dead assassin to the front of the TimeLight Portal.

"Just let go of him here, Heather."

The two released the Bristol House infiltrator, and he dropped heavily to the ground. Heather was tempted to remove his black mask—to see what he actually looked like—but the moment passed, replaced by a sudden, strong revulsion—she really just wanted him gone. Her hand went to the naked dagger, now in her belt. She stared.

Seemingly tireless, Grandma Dawn was inside the PortalDoor, making adjustments to the wounded Maiden, repositioning her legs and arms, propping her just so. Without warning, Grandma Dawn sank to her knees. Nauseous, she sat back on her haunches, lowering her head. It was evident that the persevering Maiden was becoming increasingly unwell.

"Grandma Dawn?" Heather rushed to her side.

"Dawn?"

Her hand seeking and finding Heather's, she looked up at Mrs. Pringle, Molly next to her.

"Lana, I'm going to need your help, and I have a huge, huge request that asks far too much of you."

"Just ask. Please."

Unsteady, the woman began to sway and caught herself. "Remember when I told you I was planning on taking a much needed vacation?"

Lana Pringle nodded.

"I never imagined it would happen so soon, but I'm afraid the time has come. The request I ask is for you to take care of my granddaughter here at the Bristol House until my return."

Heather started to protest, but with a look, Grandma Dawn quieted the girl. Utilizing her good arm, she seized the assassin's shirt and in a display of exceptional strength pulled him partially inside the Portal-Door with a heave, Heather stepping aside, backing away.

"But Dawn, is it safe, not only for Heather, but for Molly and me? There's a whole lot going on here that I don't understand. The things that I've witnessed this evening, well, I—I've a feeling I'm not in Noble anymore, if you know what I mean."

"There's no place safer, I assure you. Not for Heather. Not now. As you become familiar with the Bristol House, you will see that it has a mind, will, and heart of its own. It heals the human spirit, and it heals itself. Don't ever discount the Bristol House, Lana. By morning, this room will have been cleaned up and there will be no sign of this evening's struggle. Please rest assured that while away I will do everything

I can to see that this house becomes a completely safe haven once again and remains that way."

"I don't mean to argue, but can you guarantee that? There's a lot at risk here." Mrs. Pringle's hand sought the nearness of her daughter.

Grandma Dawn shook her head.

"But Dawn, surely you can't expect me to keep Molly and Heather here if there's danger. What if something were to happen again like what transpired tonight?"

The weary Maiden hadn't any words to offer in response.

In sharp exhale, Mrs. Pringle paused and then reluctantly consigned herself to the task.

"How will I contact you if I need your advice or assistance?"

"You can't, Lana. But I'll be in touch as soon as I possibly can. First, I need to rid myself of these poisonous slivers, and I must do so as quickly as possible. But the healing process may take some time. And Evermore needs my help as well. Heather and Molly will explain what they know. I only hope you'll understand and come to embrace with discreetness that which you're being exposed to."

"Dawn, I just watched you kill someone. I'm having a hard time—"

"Mom, she had to."

"Molly's right, Lana. A TimeLight Assassin, he would have killed us—all of us. This man is not of this world, and every world is governed by its own laws."

Obviously still conflicted, Mrs. Pringle watched as Grandma Dawn backed into the Portal. She pulled and positioned the black-clad corpse behind her, but not without steadying herself at one point to remain upright.

"Heather, you mind Mrs. Pringle."

"But where are you going, Grandma?"

"First of all, we're going to have to dispose of this assassin at a Portal somewhere far from here, along the TimeLight Bridge. And haste is essential. Others will have sensed the magic used here tonight, and we'll need to lure them away, making them think this basement battle occurred elsewhere. When that's done, I've relatives I haven't seen in some time. I—Avella and I—certainly need their help. And this being the period of the Dark Spell, they may just need mine. For Evermore. For you. Come here, Heather. Quickly."

From her knees, with one arm, Grandma Dawn hugged her grandchild. To Heather, she felt extremely cold. "You take care of yourself until I'm able to return."

"When will that be?"

"I don't know. Lana—Mrs. Pringle—will take care of you and Molly until that time."

Heather nodded, trying not to cry. "Can't I come with you?"

Grandma Dawn's gaze soaked up her grandchild, a long and silent draw, before she said, "No. Wait for me. I'll be back."

"But I'm a Maiden, remember? I'm the green-eyed Maiden. They want me in Evermore. I-I can go there with you."

"No. No, you can't, I'm afraid. Now is not the time. There are things I must do, things you must do."

"How do you know?"

"The Prophecies."

Glancing down at the two beside her, satisfied with their placement inside the Portal doorway, the woman turned to Mrs. Pringle. "Thank you, Lana, for looking after my grandchild."

A million questions poised at the tip of her tongue, a million doubts cast in the face of reason, Mrs. Pringle nodded again, her hands gentle on Molly's shoulders.

But to the young blonde, her world inconceivably amiss, something terrible was going on here, far worse than the invasion of a TimeLight Assassin into the bowels of the Bristol House, much more challenging than battling Mistraya at the PortalDoor, much more devastating than anything she could ever begin to imagine. The girl's words that followed meant so much, but reaching out with little hope, they barely escaped her lips: "Please don't leave me."

With a final look at Heather, her gaze never wavering, Grandma Dawn pressed the white jeweled ring to her heart, once, twice, and in a flickering hum the three figures disappeared.

Heather blurted, "Wait!" Solemnly, she watched as the Portal climbed down in stages and reshaped itself into a desk.

With the Hover°Flare overhead losing brilliance, the room was beginning to fall again to the shadows. Molly reached up and gently removed her mother's hands to go to her friend, but the girl found the gesture in vain. Heather had bolted towards the basement door and the stairs.

CHAPTER THIRTY-EIGHT

A Girl's Lunar Oath

reaking out, shedding the frosty luminescence of cloud cover, the circular moon cast its blue-green light over the impassive face of the Bristol House. Near the weighty presence of the dwelling, Heather stood in the garden, feeling at one with the moon and its aloneness, finding its soft glow comforting, the wicked twist of trees attractive, and the impenetrable shadows inviting. The air had cooled, and despite the parting of clouds, a light sprinkle had begun to fall.

So much to think about.

Heather wiped away her tears, tears born of jumbled feelings she couldn't identify or comprehend, from an inflamed wound that would likely never heal. She kept telling herself that her grandmother really did love her and in time would return, and yet illogically, the girl struggled to believe it.

Grandma Dawn will come back, Heather insisted. She said she would.

But what if she can't? What if Grandma Dawn wants to and then something unexpected stops her, and she isn't able to return and tell me. What then? A lot can happen in Evermore. I know.

"I'll go find her," she told the moon. "That's what I'll do."

At that moment, looking skyward, Heather made a pledge to the ancient celestial sphere that she would journey to Evermore and join her grandmother. Instantly, the girl felt better, buoyed by the notion.

Besides, she thought, I belong there. Grandma Dawn has gone off to Evermore. My mother and father are probably in Evermore. And I'm from Evermore.

"I *am* the green-eyed Maiden," Heather proclaimed to the night. Then she whispered, "I am."

Down near a bed of hollyhocks, in fine web-like strands of yellow-green, the garden Portal once utilized by Avella revealed itself beneath the shifting light provided by the moon and runaway clouds. As Heather watched, the PortalDoor dissolved, sealed by an unidentifiable source within the TimeLight Bridge.

It was raining harder now. Behind her, she heard a mechanical stammer and turned to see the Bristol House lights flutter to life, the vigilant eyes of a revived sentinel overseeing the darkness. Soon afterward, Heather could hear Molly approaching, calling out, her shoes crunching and scraping on the pebbled walk. Her voice grew louder as she neared.

"Heather? Heather, where are you?"

Yet, taking another moment for herself on this drizzly night, Heather gave a last look at the now shrouded moon, reaffirming her promise, and finding courage and solace in having done so. Only then did she turn to the path, climbing the hill.

"I'm over here, Molly."

Some Things Never Die

Ragged fingers of cloud slid before the moon, casting the rough outlying acreage of the Bristol House grounds again into blackness. Little could be seen under the selfish sky, but in the stillness a lot could be heard, especially the scraping of a shovel as it chewed into the soil, pulling up mouthfuls of dirt, creating a hole large enough for the skinned calico cat.

The new pair of ceremonial boots—the left one bearing a gold locket on a chain—walked over to pick up and deposit the remains of the feline. Having positioned the body as needed, the clouds parted, revealing the postman Wilson Talbott as he again put his shovel to work. Carefully filling the hole, Stilped's father buried the small unfortunate creature, save for her furless head that stuck out of the ground at an unsightly angle. Around her neck, left to hang from its sequined collar, a silver tambourine charm glinted blue, reflecting the drifting light of a seemingly indifferent moon.

It is my belief that, as adults, we react to incidents unwittingly layered into the foundation of our being at childhood, and that most of us go through our days never realizing the existence of these hidden layers and the momentous impact they can have upon our lives. They can be debilitating, causing a downward spiral of self-destruction, or they can motivate us to higher levels of achievement and, at times, destroy us in the process. For this reason, I've chosen to write about children and have fashioned my characters with the notion of early conditioning in mind.

ACKNOWLEDGEMENTS

Above all, I would like to thank my first reader/editor/True-Sister Leila Joslyn for her invaluable, creative, and detail-oriented mind; her finely tuned intuitive judgment and timely suggestions; her ability to lend herself to my elaborate vision; and her prowess and patience when enduring this obstinate author determined to breath life into his unconventional two-and-a-half year old child—and for her amazing ability to love this unruly creation from the outset and in every awkward stage of its growth.

I would also like to thank my patient, discriminating, and encouraging first and final draft readers and listeners: Rowena Craighead, Cathleen Cherry, Regina Younger, Susan Anderson, Patricia Jackson, Shannon Jackson, Lindsey Thurston, Joan Petty, Briana Blanos, Joanna Hawthorne, Judah Hawthorne, Mercie Hawthorne, Micah Hawthorne, Valerie Wiesner, Hanna Wiesner, Sonora Wiesner, Shary Feldmeier, Joan Fleming, Greg Kopta, and Louise Murphey, as well as my models who posed for the many illustrations to come.

And I must not forget to acknowledge Betsy Pringle for her initial inspiration and suggestion of a child's name, for without her, my Heather would not have her Molly.

As well, when doing research for my novel, I am ever indebted to the knowledgeable Detective Ryan Hobbs and Officer Robert Ziegler of the Prescott Police Department for their time and advice; to the informed Glendale Fire Department retiree Rollin Garard for his firsthand experience with fires and burning buildings; and, finally, Robert Upchurch MD for his understanding of head wounds and other assorted ailments and afflictions.

Too, I would be remiss if not mentioning Mr. Mo, Moses Glidden, who from the outset willed me to words.

And deepest gratitude to all those unmentioned who inspired and encouraged me in some form along the way.

Born in Burlingame, California, David Saccheri spent the majority of his life in the San Francisco Bay Area, where he worked as an illustrator and conceptual artist in the computer gaming and film industries. He has illustrated books and websites, and has taught digital and fine art both privately and at the college level. After moving to Arizona, David turned his creative energy towards writing and began to put into words the story that had been evolving for more than a decade: that of Heather, the Maidens, and Evermore. These days David writes, paints, teaches, surrounds himself with those he loves, and grows roses at his storybook house in Arizona, longing for a more enlightened world and ruing the demise of civility, integrity, and kick the can.

39089013R00355

Made in the USA
San Bernardino, CA
17 June 2019